I0708359

Life Amongst the Giants

Reuler Press
Home of otherworldly stories.

LIFE AMONGST THE GIANTS

Copyright © 2023 Rene Reul

All rights reserved. No part of this book may be reproduced or used in any manner without the prior written permission of the copyright owner, except for the use of brief quotations in a book review. It is illegal to copy this book, post it to a website, or distribute it by any other means without permission.

To request permissions, contact the publisher at reulerverse@gmail.com.

The story, all names, characters, and incidents portrayed in this production are fictitious. No identification with actual persons (living or deceased), places, buildings, and products is intended or should be inferred.

Cover art and Illustrations by Rene Reul
Instagram.com/Reulerverse

Edited by Sabrina Zanello Jackson
SabrinaZanelloJackson.art

Published by Reuler Press
Reulerverse.com

Paperback ISBN: 979-8-9892851-0-5

This edition first printed December 2023

To Anna, Frankie, Diego, and all who supported me. Without you, this world wouldn't exist.

Table of Contents

Back Matter

Preface

Tell me, what does the giant look like in fiction today? I'm guessing your answer is a hulking brute with a cloth around his waist and a club over his shoulder. That's from *Jack the Giant Killer*, which was inspired by *Jack and the Beanstalk*. Both were written around two centuries ago. Somehow, in this world filled with innovative storytelling, *that's* still our impression of a giant. I couldn't believe it! I looked long and hard for works that didn't portray giants as blockheaded brutes, but they were few and far between. The manga and subsequent anime series *Attack on Titan* has giants in a quasi-modern, post-apocalyptic setting, but even it suffers from most of them being "mindless," and in the end, it is a human conflict that drives the plot, not a giant one.

In every piece of media I found, giants were either hardly present or a joke—a threat only because of their size. This made me wonder, why them? Why, in this postmodern world where they say everything's been done before, has no one tried to modernize giants? Wizards and fairies have been modernized. Vampires and werewolves too. It seems every mythical creature under the sun has been explored in contemporary fantasy, but there is a gap for giants. I searched and waited for the book, movie, or TV show that would correct this, but none ever came.

So, I wrote it myself.

Life Amongst the Giants started as a series of short stories I told a childhood friend during our sleepovers. The stories explored a society never seen in our media. In them, intelligent giants ruled the world, and humans were pets. At first, I thought they were "too weird to write." However, my friend loved them and encouraged me to make them into a book series. I didn't want to write about a world where people were pets, though. There was something specific I wished to convey with this unique story; I just didn't know what it was yet. I brainstormed, journaled, and imagined giant stories every night before I went to bed, but no matter what idea I came up with, it didn't feel right.

Then, when I was fourteen years old, I watched the Studio Ghibli film, *The Secret World of Arrietty*. That night, the answer came to me in a dream.

I drifted off that night thinking of giant story ideas as usual, and in my sleep, I was transported to another world. I was a tiny human on a planet that had not only giant people but animals and plants as well. Unlike on Earth, where humans dominate, those here were helpless. I was constantly running for my life, dodging giant people and monsters alike, until finally, I came across a massive forest. Even though it too was filled with monsters, it was a perfect place to hide. I recall ducking under the sprawling roots of a redwood tree to hide from a gargantuan threat *boom*ing in the distance. When I woke up, my heart was pounding, and I was overwhelmed with the desire to write.

The first version of *Life Amongst the Giants* was written in a green journal made of recycled paper. The pages were loosely woven together and difficult to write on, but I adored the forest smell they carried. It was the perfect tool to start building this expansive world. When I started my notes on Planet Copius, I was a freshman in high school and an extremely inexperienced writer. Not only that, but I had few references for how to write a story with giants, let alone modernize them. I was on my own, creating a world solely from my imagination. Still, I had a burning desire to show the untapped potential of giants to the world. No matter how many versions it took, I would tell this story.

It took ten years to build the world and write the first book, but it's finally here: a world dominated by giants, where humans are at the bottom of the food chain. Both an ode to survival and an allegory for oppression, the harrowing tale this book became is much bigger than I'd dreamed. In reading it, I hope you'll come to love it as deeply as I do.

Without further delay, I, Rene Reul, present *Life Amongst the Giants*.

Content Warning

This book contains depictions of fantasy violence, genocide, mild injuries and blood, as well as references to famine and war.

Proceed with care.

Pronunciation Guide

acera	(uh-KEH-ruh)
Albian	(AL-bee-in)
Amphii	(am-fee)
andremedon	(an-DREH-meh-dawn)
aranid	(EH-rah-nid)
capaeman	(KAH-pay-man)
Copius	(KOPE-ee-us)
dreosaur	(DREY-o-sawr)
flavia	(FLAH-vee-ah)
iridescian	(ee-ri-DEH-see-in)
Koenig	(KO-nig)
leomus	(lee-O-mus)
Lyonis	(lee-AW-nis)
Maeko	(MAY-ko)
melvia	(MEL-vee-ah)
narecon	(nuh-RAY-ken)
Osia	(OH-see-ya)
Osinawa	(OH-see-nah-wah)
phii	(fee)
phypent	(FAI-pent)
Rostad	(RAW-stahd)
sangip	(SENG-gip)
scorofly	(SKOR-oh-flai)
styfisher	(STAI-fish-ur)
thornopine	(THOR-noh-pine)
vestia	(VES-tee-ah)
Zurec	(ZUR-ek)

The Giant Wilds

Members of Zurec

Lillian, 15	 *Mary, 14*

Seth, 32	 *Brianna, 30*	 *Miss May, 60*

Mia, 28	 *Kayla, 36*

Oscar, 9	 *Jen, 6*	 *Jan, 6*	 *Felix, 3*

Jamie, 21 *Albert, 14*

Trista, 7 *Max, 5*

Noah, 42	*Gigi, 30*	*Zoey, 29*	*Theo, 40*
Milo, 24	*Jess, 26*	*Bruno, 34*	*Thomas, 31*

Lina, 35	*Madilyn, 35*	*Julian, 35*

Elias, 37	*Finn, 29*	*Gabriel, 33*	*Archer, 28*
William, 34	*Robin, 39*	*Lance, 38*	*Carmen, 27*

Prologue
The Capaemen

boom... boom...

"Capaemen! It's the capaemen! Run for your lives!" The colossal *booms* echo through the forest, each step crashing like thunder. All around the clearing, people scramble to hide—screaming, crying, grabbing their children. In the panic, a little girl is knocked to the ground.

She sits on her knees, staring at the chaos in shock. This must be a dream. That's the only explanation. How could a perfectly ordinary day have become a nightmare so quickly? One minute ago, everyone was laughing. She was playing with her friends. The adults were relaxing in the cool shade of the canopy.

boom... boom...

Why are *they* here? They're not supposed to be here. This place is supposed to be safe—a sanctuary for humankind where they can live and hide in peace.

Boom... Boom...

In an instant, that peace has been destroyed.

Suddenly, someone grabs the little girl's hand. "Come with me!" they scream. She can't make out who it is, but she knows the voice. It's her mother. Her mother drags her in the opposite direction of the fleeing crowd. The little girl is sure they're not supposed to be going this way. She tries to speak up, but her voice won't come out.

"Mommy, where are we going?" another voice asks. Through her tear-stained vision, the girl makes out a second figure. It must be her younger brother. He sounds just as terrified as she is.

Boom Boom

The sound is deafening now, making it even harder to think. "The burrow isn't safe!" her mother's voice shouts. "I just know it. Come on, we're hiding in this bush."

She drags them through a mess of tangled branches and leaves. The needle-like sticks scratch her skin, growing more numerous as her mother drags them along. Deeper and deeper until hardly any light shines through the brambles. When she feels as if she's suffocating in the slew of sticks, the briar finally thins. Her mother lets them go.

The little girl's vision begins to clear. She takes in her surroundings. Sprigs and shoots weave together above her head, blocking out almost all light. All around them are walls of branches, but here is a clear patch of dirt. Here, it is isolated and so well hidden. It's like their own little cave, a secret base.

Her mother takes a seat in the dirt and pats her lap. Both children jump into it, clinging to her.

BOOM BOOM

Shadows pass through the cracks of light in their shelter. Chills erupt up and down the little girl's spine.

BOOM.

"They're here," her mother says. The girl has never seen her look this scared.

"Noooo," her brother cries. "You said the scary giants would never come here."

The mother strokes her son's head. "I know. I'm sorry, but I don't know what's going on either."

"Mommy, what's going to happen to us?" the little girl asks. She stares pleadingly into her mother's eyes, praying for a sign, searching for any sparkle, any shimmer of hope. She needs to see it, because if her mother believes it, she will too.

Instead, her mother stares blankly at her, eyes as vacant as a corpse. "I don't know, sweetie."

"Wh-What do you mean?" She grabs her mother's shirt. "We hide really well. We're careful. They won't find us, right?"

"I don't know. I really don't."

"How can you say that? There are lots of monsters, and we hide from them okay. How are the capaemen different?"

"Keep your voice down," her mother whispers. "We don't want them to hear."

The little girl sobs into her mother's shirt. "Please, Mommy. Tell me everything's going to be okay."

"I can't promise that baby. Not with capaemen. You know what they are, what they do. They're very smart and tremendously strong. But maybe... just maybe... if we hide here, they won't find us."

"Promise...?" she says through her sobs.

Her mother strokes her head. "Now, now. You know I can't promise that, but I can promise this: your mother will always protect you, to the very end."

1

Hide to Survive

Lillian

In the midst of a giant forest live the Zurec, a skittish clan whose traditions consist of avoiding bloodthirsty monsters and hiding in a hole.

Today is a day of hiding... again. The people of Zurec tremble in their underground hovel, hoping that the thunderous *thud* they heard earlier was only a tree branch. They sit slumped against the dirt walls, not daring to peek outside, let alone move, until sundown.

All except two.

Two young women, the last alive in their generation, walk down a dark stairway with only a single lantern to light their path. Their skinny shadows dance on the brown walls with the flicker of the lantern light, growing in size as they tread deeper and deeper into the cavern. They walk nearly in sync, the old floorboards groaning with each step. The girl on the left has round, sharp eyes as blue and ambitious as the sky above. The one on the right: eyes brown and kind, the most patient eyes in the world. As the only teenagers of Zurec, they're always together... and always restless.

"How long until my mom notices we're gone?" the girl on the right says.

"Eh, she probably won't. She's too busy freaking out," the one holding the lantern replies. She peers into the darkness ahead. The lantern illuminates the sandy tone of her skin and the bronze of her hair. The warped shadow trailing behind her makes her short haircut look like a frizzy mess on top of her head.

"Hey, Lillian..." the other girl whispers. Her voice bounces off the narrow walls.

The athletically built girl holding the lantern turns to her friend. The other girl stands a head shorter than Lillian, whose frame is slim and tall. The lantern reveals her face: round, with an undefined jawbone and high rosy cheeks. Tucked behind a headband, her shoulder-length blonde hair looks almost orange under the lantern's light. She clutches her most prized possession, a necklace with a wooden pendant of a tree hanging from it, with glued-on stones as the leaves. Her brown eyes flicker with worry.

"What, Mary?" Lillian replies. She can't hide the annoyance in her tone.

"What do you think is out there?" The blonde girl points to the surface, her hand shaking. She can't stop glancing around, even though there's nothing to see here. The walls and ceiling are rotting redwood, and the stairs are the same, withering away from years of disuse.

"Probably a plant eater," Lillian replies. She stays focused on what's ahead, waiting for the tunnel to end.

"What? No. We wouldn't hide from that," the blonde says. Now, she looks irritated.

"Oh, yes, we would. It's happened before," Lillian adds. Their clan hides from everything bigger than them, so they're usually below ground. They say it's for survival, and they're probably right. Still, Lillian has to believe there's more to life than this. That's why she doesn't break her focus on the tunnel. They're almost there.

"Well, even plant eaters can be dangerous. It's better to be careful than crushed, after all."

Lillian rolls her eyes. "Really, Mary? Quoting your mom?" The way she sees it, Zurec is a little *too* careful. They bolt underground at a single *boom*. It could be a giant monster or a tree branch falling to the forest floor. They flee too quickly to know. It's sad, quite frankly.

"Hey, it's a good saying, and true too," Mary continues. "You know, you really should try to listen to my mother. She gives great advice."

"Riggghhht. Like how we shouldn't sneak down here again, but you went with me anyway?"

"Oh, come on. You *begged* me to come."

Lillian smirks. "Did not. You were dying for something to do." Before Mary can make a rebuttal, the lantern's light expands, illuminating a huge room. "Yes, we're here!" Lillian says. The faint scent of firewood hits her nostrils. The smell of the forge. It's such a comforting scent.

In Lillian's opinion, the forge is the best room in the burrow. Unlike the cramped bedrooms and crowded storage spaces, the forge is easy to walk through. Their ancestors kept it in excellent condition. The floor is made of smooth grey stone, and the wooden shelves lining the walls remain straight and sturdy. A large metal table occupies the center of the room. In the corner, a rusty anvil sits next to a furnace. The furnace is made of greyish-brown hardened clay with a round oven opening. Inside the opening is a metal grate and a dusty pile of coal. Coming out of the top of the oven is a long pipe leading to the surface. Of course, no smoke has pumped out of it in years.

"So, can you tell me why we're here already?" Mary asks.

Lillian bolts into the room, refusing to acknowledge her friend's question. In all honesty, she didn't hear half of it. She's too focused on showing her what she found. *Please, please still be here,* the eager girl thinks to herself.

Shelves of various boxed items line the walls of the small cavern, from shafts, to spearheads, to blocks of stone and glass bottles of adhesive for dagger-making. Lillian runs her hand across the boxes as she walks. Some of the weapons may look cool, but most pieces in these boxes aren't special. Rickety sticks and shafts and no metal to speak of. They get the job done, but she won't settle for that. She wants something quality, like the weapons she grew up reading about. Luckily, she's been here a lot, and after a tireless search, she has found something that fits her standards perfectly.

Under the box in the very corner of the forge is... *Yes! Still here!* Lillian grabs the object from under the bottom shelf. Eagerly, she sprints to the metal table in the middle of the room and places it gently on top.

"Take a look, Mary," Lillian says, smiling from ear to ear.

"Ohhhhh!" Mary gasps, her eyebrows raising in interest. It bears the design of a classic Zurec spear, but this one is different. Better.

"This is going to be my weapon when I become a surveyor," Lillian says proudly. The spear is about five feet long, with a shaft made of polished redwood. This shaft won't break, not for a long time. Bands carved into the wood mark where one would place their hands. What's more, wavy etchings cover every inch of the shaft, highlighting a myriad of shades of red that would otherwise be hidden in the grain. It reminds her of tree bark. Unlike the bands, this pattern appears to be for decoration only—so different from the utilitarian make of most of their weapons. It has two spearheads, one on each end of the shaft, but one is bigger than the other. The blades are made of a luminous metal, not stone, although Lillian can't tell what kind of metal it is.

"How did you find this?" Mary asks.

"It was in the back, under some crates. I'm surprised no one else is using it."

"It looks like it just came out of the fire."

Lillian ogles the spear, looking closer at its mysterious luster. In the torch-light it glows red, as if still hot from its forging fire. She picks it up. The spear feels heavy in her hands, truly a relic of Zurec's great past. She thinks of the process they might have used to make such a weapon. The temperature of the fire would have had to be just right. Next to the oven sits an old set of bellows. That would have been used to blow air into the furnace, meticulously stoking its flames. Lillian would have loved to see that in action, but there isn't anyone left who knows how.

She plucks the lantern from its place on the table and holds the larger spearhead closer to the light. The mysterious metal reacts to the change.

"Woahhhh," Mary gawks. "It's turning all different colors!"

"Yeah. I've never seen anything do this." The eager girl moves the blade back and forth, closer and farther from the lantern, watching it turn bright shades of red, orange, and yellow, reflecting the flickering fire. The bright colors dance across the forge walls, bathing the cavern and the girls in a kaleidoscope of lights they have never seen before. It feels almost magical.

"It's perfect for you," Mary says, her eyes sparkling. "But will your dad let you keep it?"

Lillian frowns. She fixes her gaze on the dusty wooden ceiling, still dancing with lights. "Not sure."

"If you bring this back up, they'll know you've been sneaking down here again," Mary says dismally.

"I know." Lillian crosses her arms. If they bring this up the stairs now, her father will be the least of her worries. She wonders how Mary's mother will react. Lillian's so close to leaving the burrow. Does she really want to sabotage all of that for this spear? This odd and very awesome spear? She stares at it. It glows a strange combination of colors now—bright orange with dark green in the center. Where the green came from, she has no idea. Still, the blades themselves look as if they could cut through steel. She would certainly fight better with this spear. Plus, leaving it to rot in this collapsing forge would be a shame.

"I really like it," Lillian asserts. "Why would they let such a valuable weapon collect dust down here? It doesn't make any sense."

"Maybe it's a keepsake?" Mary suggests. "We won't know unless we ask."

"That's true. And I want to know. You'll back me up, right?"

Mary smiles. "I'm always on your side."

Lillian's blue eyes brighten. "I knew I could count on you." That's why she brought Mary down here in the first place. She knew she'd understand. She's the only one who ever does. With newly acquired confidence, she grabs the spear and heads up the stairs.

The girls try to walk as slowly as possible, savoring their time together. Mary fiddles with her headband. "You know, if we both try to convince the adults to let you keep it, I bet even your dad will come around."

Lillian rolls her eyes. "Yeah, sure. If he even shows up." Ever since he became the chief, he is always gone. She wishes she could explore the Giant Wilds with him. The vast canopy of gargantuan swaying leaves, the mossy terrain, the river so clear one can see every rock at the bottom. The sunny flower fields and dark root caves. She wants to explore it all with her father, with the surveyors. Instead, she's stuck every day in these cramped halls, her unkempt hair and tattered clothes coated in dust. To make matters worse, every time the surveyors return, her dad pretends she doesn't exist. Always too busy, even for his own daughter.

Suddenly, something touches Lillian's shoulder. Mary stares at her with concern. Lillian didn't realize she'd been lost in a world of her own. "Seriously, it's going to be okay. The Red Eclipse is soon. You'll be with them in no time," Mary says as if reading her mind.

"Yeah. You're right."

Mary smiles widely. "I'm proud of you, Lillian. This is the first step to—"

CREEEAAAAKKK

From above, a familiar sound cuts Mary off. Followed by a—

CRASH!

"Th-That's the burrow door!" the blonde shrieks.

"And it sounds like someone opened it in a hurry," Lillian adds.

The girls sprint up the stairs.

⁂

"What do you think is going on?" Lillian asks.

"Whatever it is, it's bad. I've never heard the door open in such a rush," Mary says between panicked breaths.

When the girls emerge into the mud room, the first person they see is Mary's mother. Her hands are clamped over her mouth, and her white hair stands on end. At the far end of a small tunnel that slopes gradually upward, light streams into the burrow. The trapdoor is open, and a group of people rush in. Lo and behold, Lillian's dad stands at the front. The surveyors are back.

As the surveyors clamber down the narrow tunnel into the burrow, some collapse into the dirt. All are caked in sweat. They look like they just sprinted across half the Giant Wilds. Lillian's eyes lock on her father. He looks nervous. That's not like him at all.

Her dad stands in the center of the group, his bronze hair dripping with sweat. His hair is longer than Lillian's, reaching his shoulders. Being the second largest in the community, he's exactly seven feet tall. He has an air of authority to go with that imposing size too, because he possesses a trait rare amongst their people: optimism. No matter what befalls them, he always finds the bright side. He keeps them hopeful. However, the only emotion he's showing now is fear. His sharp hazel eyes are wide and darting about the room. Sweat drips off his thick beard and onto his armor.

"Lock the door, now!" Lillian's dad commands. "And make sure it's camouflaged!" A *creeaakkk* and a *SLAM* follow from above. The last of the surveyors trickle into the cavern from the exit tunnel, just as out of breath. Clan members emerge from various hiding spots in the mud room, trembling.

"Seth, what's going on?" Mary's mother, Miss May, asks. The children of Zurec surround her. She wraps her arms around them and whispers words of comfort.

Seth places a hand on his large forehead. There's a pause, as if no one knows what to say next. Mary clutches her necklace; she does that when she's nervous. The surveyors' fear seems to have spread throughout the room, rendering everyone speechless. Lillian doesn't understand why. They don't even know what has happened yet.

She decides to speak up. "You met with Albian, right?" The surveyors of both clans ran into each other a while ago, and neither wanted to fight, so negotiations were arranged. Still, there are many ways that could have gone wrong. "How did the peace talk go? Did they attack?"

Some surveyors flinch at the name "Albian."

Seth grits his teeth. "I'd like to tell you how the conversation went, but it kind of... didn't happen at all."

"What does that mean?" Mary's mother asks. She keeps her arms around the children.

"They... *They're* the ones who were attacked, not us," Seth says. He seems to struggle to find those words.

"By whom?" Lillian asks. There aren't many enemies in the forest, other than the monsters.

"Just spit it out," Mary's mother urges. "I can't take this suspense."

The chief sighs, scratching his sweaty beard. "Lillian, Miss May... you're right. I should just say it." He takes a deep breath, and the surveyors wince.

"It was the capaemen."

Collective gasps echo throughout the cavern, followed by a flurry of questions. Lillian's heart sinks. Capaemen? This deep in the forest? They come so infrequently that most of the adults of Zurec have never seen one before. How could they be here, much less attack the people nearest them? "Let me finish," Seth commands the sea of voices. The panicked conversations immediately stop. "We made it to Albian's burrow, only to find the door torn from the ground. That... that only could have been done by *them*."

"Th-That's a pretty wild assumption," Miss May comments. "Are you sure?"

"Yes. I wouldn't be saying this if I were not."

"I-It could have been another neighboring enemy. Rostad? We don't know what they're up to these days."

"The door was torn from the ground, Miss May!" the chief shouts.

Mary's mother shuts her mouth. The people of Zurec converse in hushed tones, expressing their fears. The children begin to cry, and Miss May holds them tighter. Lillian turns to Mary. Tears swell in her friend's brown eyes. "A-Albian is only a few hours away. They're close. So close... to us."

"You're right." That thought chills her to the bone. Why Albian, and why now? It doesn't make any sense. The capaemen have never been interested in them, and why would they? They're a tiny clan in the middle of the woods.

"We haven't checked their burrow," the chief continues. "We were too busy running. I was afraid *they* were still nearby. I'm sure it's not good, but we should go back and search it just in case. The gatherers will leave in two days to check. While they're doing that, the surveyors will check that our bunkers are secure, and we will keep on the lookout for capaemen. When everyone returns, we'll... decide what to do next." Sighs of relief echo through the cavern. "But..."

Lillian holds her breath.

"... if you hear anything suspicious, hide immediately," Seth directs.

Lillian nearly lets out a groan. They do that anyway. How is that going to help?

"And when you hide, wait much longer to go back outside. We can never be too careful with capaemen," the chief finishes.

With that, the meeting ends. Everyone separates into groups, and Seth gathers his surveyors to discuss the plan for their next mission. Soon, Lillian will be in that huddle. She just needs to wait a little longer.

She sighs and checks on Mary. The blonde's eyes are watery, but she still musters a smile. "H-Hey... on the bright side, at least we still get to go outside."

"Yeah," Lillian says. She's hardly thinking of that now. Something about this doesn't feel right. Their ancestors moved to the Giant Wilds specifically *because* capaemen don't hunt here. Why are they doing it now? This makes Lillian's spear problem feel so trivial. She stares at the weapon. It still glows orange, matching the torchlight. With it, a fire burns in her heart.

Even after this grim news, Lillian's dream remains the same. In fact, she wants it even more now. She's tired of hiding and relying on others to care for her. Her father needs her help. All the surveyors do. She's trained. She's learned. She's ready. She *will* join the surveyors.

Still, a thought burns in the back of Lillian's mind, making her tremble. It threatens the bravery she's worked so hard to conjure. *No, don't think about that.* She tries to put it out of her mind, but it doesn't budge. It's as rooted as the trees.

"A-Albian is only a few hours away," Mary had said. It's true, and everyone knows it. They're too afraid to say it or even think about it. But if the capaemen are hunting again, then...

We're next.

2

A Giant's World Bathed in Red

Lillian

Lillian tosses and turns all night. Even after yesterday's grim news, she doesn't wake. In her deep slumber, the strangest dream consumes her.

She's on an adventure with the surveyors, feeling the mossy forest floor squish under her shoes. The intense sun warms her skin. The trees sway to a gentle breeze, and the plants go along with them. The smell of earth and morning dew permeates the air. To make things even sweeter, Lillian's father lets her walk by his side. On one of his shoulder plates is a colored sigil—the sigil of Zurec. His is one of a kind, made only for the chief to wear. She hopes one day, it will become hers. They laugh together, and no one interrupts their conversation. It's silly talk about fighting monsters, but it's their talk. A bonding moment with her father. She cherishes every second.

But their fun is short-lived.

Suddenly, a faint *boom* echoes through the canopy.

The *boom* sounds again, this time twice as loud. This one is too big to fight. They'll have to hide until it passes.

Boom...

Four times as loud. Lillian's ears ring. Seth commands the surveyors to find a place to hide. They scatter, hiding in bushes, under tree roots, and anywhere else they can find.

BOOM

The sound punches her eardrums. She covers her ears to quell the pain. It doesn't help at all. She and her father are now the only people who haven't run for cover. Lillian wants to, but she can't get her body to move. Her ears throb, ruining her focus. She looks around frantically. Where are the rest of the surveyors hiding? She can't even catch a glimpse of one. They're either great at hiding, or they disappeared altogether. "Dad, I think we've gotta—" Lillian turns toward her father, but the spot where he was standing is empty.

BOOM

The sound pierces her aching head. It's as if it were being run through with a dagger. "Dad?" Lillian calls. "Where are you?" Her legs are rooted to the ground. Why can't she get them to move?

BOOM.

The now colossal sound knocks Lillian to the ground. A shadow grows over her, blocking the sun. It's too big. She can't fight. She can't run.

"Lillian... Hey Lillian..." a faded voice says. Where is that coming from? Is the creature speaking? "Lillian... LILLIAN!" the voice screams. "Lillian, WAKE UP!"

Lillian's blue eyes fly open in the real world. Her entire body is drenched in sweat. She notes her tan undershirt, leomus-skin tank top, and leomus leggings. All soaked. She should probably change, but Mary yanks her off her bed. "Come on, come on! By the Wilds, you're such a heavy sleeper! We're going to miss it!" She drags a half-asleep Lillian into and up the hallway.

"Miss what?" the tired girl asks, her vision beginning to clear. Flashes of that terrifying dream echo through her mind, like the enormous footsteps of the creature that pursued her.

"You mean, you don't know? It's what you've been waiting for! Come on!" She tightens her grip on Lillian's arm.

Only one thing can make Mary this eager. "Is it the eclipse?"

"Yes, sleepyhead! Everyone else is already out there. No one was able to wake you up!" It's happening quicker than she thought. This is amazing. Lillian yanks her arm out of Mary's grasp and sprints ahead. "Heyyy!" her friend calls.

With her friend trailing behind her, Lillian runs through the main hallway, the mud room, and out the exit tunnel, throwing the heavy trapdoor open. It falls to the ground behind her with a huge *clank*. A pillar of red light hits her.

The day of change has finally come.

As young Lillian Zurec joins the crowd, she can't help but smile.

Everyone in the clearing stares in awe at the sight above, from her dad's stoic right-hand men to the great warriors who are usually training when off-duty. No matter how many times they see this crimson light, it never gets boring. This is one of the few times all thirty members of their community can assemble in one place: the surveyors, the gatherers, the caretaker, and all the children. They take a break from survival for just a few minutes to enjoy this sight—the symbol of the new year.

The eyes of the children sparkle red as they focus intently on the sky. "Don't look directly at it!" Miss May scolds. All the children snap back at once, instead staring at the massive redwood trees. They've got to be at least one thousand feet tall. Their long roots twist and turn all over the forest floor. Bright-green moss covers the roots and can be seen growing from the base of the trees all the way to the top. Red light bathes the canopy above, making the forest look even brighter.

Lillian takes short glances at the red moon, making sure not to damage her eyesight. It slowly moves farther in front of the orange sun as if about to devour it. Mary catches up to her, her eyes sparkling with just as much wonder as the children. She spins around, taking in the sight of the forest. "Gets me every time," she says, twirling in a pillar of crimson light.

It's finally been a year.

Lillian locks eyes with Miss May, who's sticking close to the children. Being sixty as of today, the caretaker is the oldest member of Zurec by far. Her hair is white. Her face, neck, and hands are wrinkled and always clenched. She notices Lillian, and it's as if her worry increases tenfold. She scowls. She's always disapproved of her willful behavior.

Lillian ignores the caretaker. She won't let her ruin this day. She looks at Mary. The blonde is smiling, but there is fear in her eyes. She clutches her necklace again, a common habit when she's scared.

Lillian places a hand on her friend's shoulder. They stare at the crimson light together. It feels colder and colder as the sunlight disappears behind the red moon. But instead of stopping halfway, it keeps going.

She can't believe her eyes. "Oh my Wilds, is it a full one?"

Mary nods faintly. Her jaw twitches as if she has something to say, but no sound comes from her mouth. Lillian's heart springs with excitement. "This only happens once every two decades, right?"

The blonde nods again. Her eyes are locked on the eclipse. That can't be good for her, but it is an incredible occasion. This is the second—maybe even third—total eclipse for the adults, but for the girls and children, it's their first. They won't see this again for another twenty years. Who knows what will happen in such a massive stretch of time?

As the final sliver of the sun is extinguished, the world plunges into darkness. This darkness is strange, but doesn't feel dangerous. It's like a shadow—if a shadow could be pleasant—gently cloaking the forest. It feels almost peaceful.

Lillian has always been told that darkness is dangerous. One should be wary of what one cannot see and what they do not know. But at this moment, she is not afraid. She feels almost... relaxed. Relaxed in the middle of the Giant Wilds? Now, isn't that ironic. Everyone else is on their guard, but this is one of the few times Lillian feels at peace with herself. Not everything here is out to get them. She wants to believe there is still beauty in this brutal world, if only for a fleeting moment.

A few more moments pass before a speck of light appears from behind the red moon. The eclipse is ending almost as quickly as it began. "Aww, it's almost over," Mary says. "We won't see another one like that for twenty years."

"You're right," Lillian says. "What a way to end my childhood."

"You know I'll support you no matter what," Mary mentions. Her eyebrows furrow with concern. There's a "but" coming. "But oh man, it came so fast. A-Are you sure you want to go now? I mean, we just found out about the capaemen yesterday. This could be more dangerous than we thought." Her eyes are pleading.

Lillian stifles a sigh. She understands why her friend is worried, but the danger doesn't change a thing. In fact, it makes her want to go more. She must help the surveyors. She must help her dad when he needs it most. "Mary," she begins, "we've..." but her mind shifts to the giant from her dream, making her forget what she was going to say. Is that what she dreamed of? A capaeman? She's never seen one before. Kayla has drawn diagrams in the books she writes for their library, but she's not the best artist, so those aren't reliable. She wonders if she would have seen one in her dream if Mary hadn't woken her up. The thought makes her shudder.

"What?" Mary asks, bringing Lillian back to the real world. "We've what?"

Lillian stares at her hands. The red light is fading, and she has a feeling the next three hundred fifty days will be the worst for survival, perhaps the most challenging year in their history. Still, she is a warrior, and warriors face their foes without fear. She's tired of cowering in a hole. Now is the time for action. "We've faced impossible danger before and survived. Besides, if things are going to get bad, I'd rather be fighting than waiting in the burrow."

"Lillian, you could die," Mary says. She gazes up at the sky. The emerging sun brightens her blonde hair. She twiddles it with one hand and clutches her necklace with the other. "How can you not be afraid?"

Lillian takes a deep breath. It's not like she feels no fear at all. She's afraid—very afraid—but she won't let it stop her. "The surveyors face death every day, regardless of the capaemen. If I die, well, at least my life had meaning." She thinks of the surveyors' exploration stories. They've encountered loads of creatures big and small, met other clans, and traversed the more shadowy areas of the forest, finding everything from beautiful waterfalls to hidden caves. She will finally see the world—plus, she'll get to help her family while doing it. It is worth the danger. If she dies in the process, at least she got to live a little. "Honestly, I'd rather die up here than live down there any longer."

Mary's eyes widen. She looks as if she's about to cry, but she smiles instead. "Well then, let's just hope you'll have your trusty spear when you go out there. Try to visit often. And please, don't die."

Lillian claps Mary's shoulder. "Oh, come on. You and I both know I'm too stubborn to die."

The girls stare at the canopy. The sun has disappeared behind a gigantic cloud. Lillian wonders how far away the sun is and how close she can get before she burns. She smiles. *What a dangerous thought.* What's with this burning need in her chest? Shouldn't she prioritize survival, like the rest of the clan? Mary seems to value it, and Miss May has hammered survival instincts into both girls ever since they could walk. Lillian should be happy that she's alive, like everyone else. So, where did she get this urge from? This urge for... something more?

Mary throws her arms around her, interrupting her reverie again. "I-I mean it. I wouldn't be able to handle it if you died."

Lillian reluctantly returns the gesture. She's not a hugger, but she knows Mary is upset. "I told you, I'm stubborn. I will come back alive."

Mary lets go. She glances at Seth's group, who are standing across the clearing. They pack their backpacks and strap their weapons to them. "Well, it can't be long before the surveyors head out on another mission. You should talk to them. It's now or never. Want me to get the spear?" She looks like she wants to say more but stops herself.

"Not now. Let's take this one step at a time." Her friend nods and leaves Lillian alone.

The surveyors are gathered in a circle by a giant root. Seth laughs loudly about something and throws his arms around his closest confidants, Elias and William. Elias rolls his narrow eyes at the joke, clearly not entertained. Meanwhile, William, who's almost as large as Seth, laughs huskily. The two men high-five each other. It's good to see her dad smiling, especially after yesterday. Lillian approaches them, hoping to learn what they're laughing so hard about.

"H-Hey, Dad," she interrupts. The whole circle immediately falls silent. Twelve pairs of eyes rest on her, including her father's.

"Oh, Lillian!" Seth says as if noticing her now. She's caught off guard by his response. Did he forget about her? There's no way he'd forget his only daughter's coming-of-age, right? Lillian squares her shoulders, remembering what Mary said. *It's now or never.*

"I would like to join the surveyors."

Seth's eyes soften in realization. He really did forget. "Give us a moment alone," he bids the group. Lillian holds her breath. The tone became so serious the second she approached them. Now, he wants to talk to her alone. This can't be good. Seth breaks away from the circle, and she follows. The two of them walk to the large tree root nearby. They climb onto it and take a seat. Once they're comfortable, Seth places his head in his hands. He looks so frustrated. Lillian thinks to break the silence but can't. She's afraid she'll say something wrong, and he'll... Well, he'll grow more distant than he already is.

Lillian taps her knee, trying to distract herself until he speaks. Mary plays with the children by the burrow door, and Miss May sits on a tree root, a smirk on her face. The children call that spot "doodoo rock" because it looks more like a red boulder than a root, and more like animal poop than a boulder. She never understood the fun of giving it a name. It's just an odd-looking root. That's all.

Lillian's father shifts. Immediately, her attention darts back to him. Seth takes a deep breath in, and she holds hers. "This has been quite the year, huh?" he says, smiling nervously. Now that Seth is looking directly at her, Lillian realizes deep bags are under his eyes. How long has it been since he's slept?

"I-I guess so," she replies.

"It has been rough. The good news is we've lost fewer people than usual." He places his chin in his hand, his eyes wandering. They soften when he sees the kids with Mary.

He's ignoring the dreosaur in the room. Lillian can't blame him, though. With everything they've been through, he must be overwhelmed. She only hopes he'll let her help. "Anyway," her father continues, his tone darkening, "things are going to get much more dangerous now."

"I know. I'm ready. I can handle it," Lillian says, looking unwaveringly into her father's stern eyes. They are a light hazel, so different from her sky blue.

"I don't know if you can," Seth says.

"What does that mean?" Her voice cracks. The nerves are getting to her.

"What I mean is... being a surveyor just became perilous, more than usual. Our job is to scope the forest, looking for danger and killing monsters. I'll have the gatherers check out Albian's burrow and bury the dead. That place probably won't be attacked again. They'll be safer than us. As for the surveyors, well, we've got to do what's best: survey."

"Meaning...?" She doesn't like where this is going.

"After we check on our bunkers, we will look for them. Not attack, not be seen, but we've got to see what they're up to. Where they've been in the forest, where they may go next."

Lillian's heart skips a beat. "Dad, that's—"

"Unbelievably dangerous? Foolish? A terrible idea? Trust me, I've gotten plenty of that from the others, but just because we've avoided the capaemen for years does not mean we have to keep doing it. It worked before, but that's because they were never here before. We must find out what they're up to. We have to know..." He pauses for a moment, staring at the children. "We *have* to know when they'll strike next."

Lillian's jaw drops. Of course, he knows they're next. Everyone knows. They're just too afraid to say it. "Dad, that's..." She can't help but chuckle a little. "That sounds exactly like a plan *you'd* come up with."

"What's that supposed to mean?" Still, he laughs too. "It is a very *me* plan, isn't it? I was up all night thinking about it. Knowing they are after us is terrifying, but we can't just give up. If we can find out where they'll strike next, we can move before they do."

Lillian understands where he's coming from, but she's on a mission. She grabs his hand and takes a deep breath. "Dad, this plan doesn't scare me. I—"

"Oh, I had a feeling it wouldn't," he interrupts. "You're determined to follow in my footsteps, aren't you?" His tone suddenly turns condescending. She doesn't like it. "Lillian, this clan is dying. You don't want to inherit it."

"What? You just said we'd survive. We always do, and when we do, we'll need a new chief one day. With Mary becoming caretaker, I'm the only option for it, and no one can train me but you. You know that!"

Seth shakes his head. "We will survive for now; that much is true. But what about when my generation is gone? It will only be you, Mary, and a few children left. Even if you were chief, you wouldn't be chief of much. A few decades later, there won't be a Zurec clan anymore. You and whoever's left will probably join another burrow. Maybe Rostad will let you if you—"

"Seriously, Dad? Rostad?" She's angry at the mere thought. Those people are wild cards—at least, that's what all the adults say. No one ever knows what they're up to.

"Or you could become rogues. Travel around the Wilds a bit. By then, you and Mary would be old enough to make that decision. Our ancestors traveled. Who says you can't?"

"Dad, do you even know what you're saying? Sure, things look bad now, but we can turn this around. If you would only let me help you—"

Seth clenches his fists. "How, exactly, could we turn this around? I love you, Lillian, but you know nothing about the world. You know nothing about the events of the famine, the reason we're in this position. You were only a baby, but it doesn't matter because it is not your burden to bear."

Lillian hangs her head, watching her legs dangle over the root. What her father says is true. They lost all of their history books during that grim period, so she has only learned vague stories of Zurec's past. She knows it was bad and that a lot of people died, so she can see how her dad has such a cynical attitude. She sees things differently, though. No matter how big the age gap is between her and the adults, no matter what happened in their past, this is still her burrow. *Their* home. "But these are my people too, Dad. The future is all our burden, especially Mary's and mine."

Her father places a hand on her shoulder. His hazel eyes are filled with pity. "I understand, but becoming chief doesn't have to be. I want you to learn more about the world. That's why you should join the gatherers first."

Lillian flinches. She wasn't expecting that. "What? Why them?"

"I want you to see another perspective. Brianna will train you well, I'm sure."

"But I want to go with you!" she shouts. Across the clearing, everyone stops what they're doing. Mary stares with worry, Miss May with a frown. Lillian ignores them.

Seth lets out a frustrated sigh. "Trust me, the gatherers will be plenty for your first time. It's gotten more dangerous to be one of them too, you know?"

"But I—"

"This is not up for debate, Lillian. I've thought a lot about this. I've already talked to Brianna about it. It's decided. If after a year or so you still want to be a surveyor, and train to be chief, then so be it. I will recruit you. Assuming we don't all die before then." Seth laughs at that. Lillian doesn't.

She crosses her arms. "You want me to wait... a whole year?"

The chief nods.

"Why? I know what I want. You have to believe me!"

"I said this isn't up for debate!" Seth shouts. Everyone in the clearing stares. Lillian freezes. Her dad has never yelled at her before.

"You will join the gatherers, and you will listen to Brianna. Understood?" he says through gritted teeth.

"Dad, please—"

"Enough from you, or I'll tell Miss May to keep you in the burrow for a year instead. I'm sure she would *love* to do it."

Lillian shuts her mouth. *By the Wilds, anything but that.*

"Alright, that's settled then," the chief says, hopping off the tree root. He doesn't look back. Not even once. He didn't forget about her, but this is somehow worse. The gatherers, really? She hardly knows any of them.

Lillian stares at her feet, swinging them back and forth. Her shadow, so small in this giant forest, blends with the shadows of the swaying leaves. She was so close to joining the surveyors; then the capaemen had to rear their disgusting heads. Although he probably still would have done this, capaemen or not. What a convenient excuse to keep the distance between them. Distance that has no business being there.

As Seth's shadow moves farther and farther away, it blends with the shade of the trees, fitting in perfectly, unlike her. That was the first conversation they've had in months, and soon he'll leave her again. Every time he leaves, she's unsure if he'll return.

Still sitting on the root, Lillian watches her dad rejoin the surveyors. He tousles Elias' hair. The man pushes him away playfully. She burns with jealousy. How can he think joining him isn't what she needs? It's all she's talked about her whole life. She knows she won't change her mind. She'll prove that to him. Maybe then she will stop feeling so restless.

3

Forest of Monsters

Lillian

With the grim news they learned yesterday, Seth informs the people of Zurec to take the day off. It's a rare sight to have everyone in the burrow, but a welcome one. Especially since most people retire to their rooms, leaving things peaceful and quiet. Even Miss May isn't in the mood to teach, so classes and combat training are canceled. Lillian is bummed not to train, but it should give her time to catch up on sleep.

At least, that's what she thought. Instead, she spends most of the day comforting Mary. The girls go back and forth between the kitchen and their room, grabbing snacks and discussing the capaemen. Mary is still frantic about the news and talks nonstop about how they all could be doomed, but eventually, as evening falls in the Wilds, they both fall asleep for the night.

As she slumbers, Lillian has the same strange capaeman dream. However, just as she is about to see the giant, she wakes up again.

Lillian gasps. The nightmare was just as hair-raising as the night before. Once she realizes she is awake, she tries to calm herself. *It isn't real.* What is real is their mission for today. For the first time, she's going to Albian's burrow. Due to the two groups' rocky past, Zurec always had reason to be nervous about treading into their territory, but now the stakes have changed. Instead of being attacked by human enemies, they could be crushed by giants. The gatherers will have to be stealthy, and Lillian must do her best not to slow them down. This isn't how she imagined her first mission. She thought it would be a thrilling adventure, filling her with passion. Instead, she's drowning in dread. She must stay vigilant, but most of all, she cannot make mistakes. Her future as chief is counting on it.

It is still pitch-black in the bedroom. It must be early if Miss May hasn't lit any torches. Lillian thinks of going back to bed, but she doesn't want to have that dream again. Besides, if no one is awake now, they will be soon. Until then, she'll do some warm-up swings. Lillian slips out of bed, then grabs her armor and weaponry, trying not to wake the caretaker or Mary. Sharing a room sucks.

Out in the hallway, Lillian straps on her hide armor. First come the shoulder and forearm plates, next the breastplate, and then the calf and shin guards. She straps her bow, quiver, and pack to her back. Finally, she secures the most important part, a leomus-hide, arm-length shield, to her right arm. She loves this piece. It bears the Zurec sigil, a twist of lines with two spears crossed over the middle. She has had this set for a long time. She can't wait to use it on a real adventure.

There isn't much to the burrow. The walls, floors, and ceilings are all redwood. Horizontal wood beams positioned every few feet support the rotting roof, and occasionally Lillian spots teeny-tiny roots poking through the cracks in the boards. Lining either side of the hallway are wooden doors to bedrooms that other Zurec folks share. Behind her, at the back of the hall, are three doorways: the storeroom and kitchen on the left, and the washroom on the right. Ahead, the hallway opens into the mud room. Grabbing her two-headed spear, she heads to it.

The mud room is the largest cavern in the burrow—well, next to the forge. A few torches are already lit. On one side is the exit tunnel, a narrow corridor that slopes up to the surface. Near it, Brianna converses with Miss May. Even though no other gatherers have entered the room, Brianna stands here in full armor. Her red hair is tied back in a ponytail, and her Zurec sigil is painted in color on her shield, signifying her leadership. Her pale skin, littered with freckles, looks almost pink in the dim lighting, and naturally, she is ripped from head to toe. Traveling through the Giant Wilds every day is bound to make one strong, but she looks like she does extra training on the side. Perhaps it's because she takes her role as leader so seriously.

So, Lillian wasn't the first one awake. She should have known. Brianna seems punctual, and no one wakes up before Miss May.

The caretaker notices Lillian and rushes over. She scans her from head to toe. "Are you all set?" In Lillian's left hand is her spear. It glows red today. Miss May stares at it. Her eyebrows raise. Lillian holds her breath. With all the chaos, she forgot to tell her. She's in so much trouble.

The caretaker's next words seem nervous, like she's forcing herself to say them. "Lillian, are you sure you have everything?"

Lillian takes a moment to respond. Did Miss May just completely skip over the spear? *The* Miss May, who won't even let her go to the forge in their own burrow? She opens her mouth to ask but then spots a group of gatherers entering the room. Most are already wearing their armor, made from the hides of animals ranging from dark orange to brown to green. Earthy colors help them blend into the forest better. Among the arriving warriors, a spunky woman named Gigi, a gatherer, and her sister Carmen, a surveyor, hug each other goodbye. Meanwhile, other warriors file up the exit tunnel, led by Theo, one of the gatherers' best fighters. He moves to open the trapdoor.

The questions will have to come later. "Yes, I have everything I need. Now can I go?"

"Are you sure? You need a canteen of water, first-aid supplies, your bow, and arrows." She glances at the spear, then quickly looks away. "Oh, and you've tightened your armor, made sure it fits well? It looks like it does, but you can never be too careful. Better to be careful than crushed, after all."

Lillian rolls her eyes. "Miss May, I'm fine. I have everything." She stares at the door.

"Do not roll your eyes at me, missy! I just want to make sure you're safe."

"Don't worry. I will be." Safe as she can be in the Giant Wilds.

"Okay. Seth allowed this, so I'm sure you'll be fine. Ugh, but I swear something is missing. What is it? Drat. Well, I can't keep you waiting forever. Please be safe and listen to Brianna. Don't treat her the way you treat me, please. If you don't listen to her, you could die. That's much worse than anything I could do."

"I know. Don't worry, I'll listen," she responds quickly. She turns to the door, but it's too late.

"Lillian!" the voice of Mary interrupts. "Oh, thank goodness! You haven't left yet. I wanted to say goodbye." She throws her arms around her friend. Her blonde hair is unbrushed. Lillian inhales a few strands.

She coughs. "Hey, Mary."

"Hey, Mary? Yeah, hey to you too. If I hadn't woken up, would you have left without saying anything?"

"I'll be back later. It's no big deal." She manages to wriggle out of the hug.

"No big—" her friend stops short. "Oh, never mind. Just remember your promise to me: come back alive. When you get back, tell me everything. Don't leave a single thing out!"

"No problem," the new gatherer replies. She'll probably want to talk all about it when she gets back. "Now, let me go. They're waiting for me."

"I hope you didn't forget anything," Mary says, scanning her.

"Come on, you're just like Miss May," Lillian teases.

Mary's eyebrows raise. She looks at her mother with realization. "Hey Mom, doesn't she need a dagger?"

"Oh! That's it! Thank you, dear. Lillian, you forgot a dagger. I'll get one. Oh, I have just the piece." The caretaker skips to their bedroom.

Lillian peers at the exit and sighs. All the gatherers are outside by now. "Will I ever make it out?"

"I'm sure she won't be long. She's just trying to help." Mary smiles, but there's pain in her gaze.

"Right..." She thinks of asking the blonde what's wrong, but she doesn't want to be stuck here longer.

Luckily, Miss May returns quickly, holding a strange dagger. It's a little longer and thinner than a traditional Zurec dagger, and the sheath is made of black scales instead of hide. The waist strap is also black. Lillian's eyes widen. Another incredible piece she didn't know about?

The caretaker unsheathes the blade. The metal looks pristine. The base of the handle is in the shape of a round leaf, just like the leaves in the forest, and the hilt appears to have markings on it, although she can't make them out from here. "What kind of dagger is *that*?" Lillian asks, forgetting all about the people outside.

Miss May looks at it like a distant memory. "It's mine."

"This is *your* dagger?" Lillian asks. She's never seen a weapon so beautiful—other than the color-changing spear.

The caretaker's face expresses a mixture of nostalgia and sadness. "Yes, I wanted you to have it when you joined the surveyors, but that's been... delayed."

It feels as if the weapon is calling to her, just like the spear. "I-I can really have this?"

The caretaker's wrinkled lips curl into a full smile. "It's a relic of our past. One of the last ones we have left. I think you should have it."

She hands her the dagger. Lillian holds it up. She catches the reflection of her freckled, oval-shaped face and triangular jawline in its blade. The text *Property of May* is inscribed on the handle. This reminds her of the markings on her own spear. However, in the spear's case, those are more of a bark-like pattern for decoration. Here, it's a whole message. Why don't they personalize weapons like this anymore?

"It's yours now," the caretaker says, her smile fading to her usual frown. "If you use it regularly, which I know you will, sharpen it once a week. There's an old sharpening stone in the storeroom, so don't go sneaking into the forge again. I will show you where it is later. Also, make sure it doesn't get wet. Too much water could fray the sheath and handle. Are you listening?"

Lillian jumps. "Y-Yes. I'm listening."

"What did I say?" the caretaker remarks, her thin eyebrows furrowing in frustration.

"Uhhh, take good care of it."

"And what else?" Miss May asks.

Lillian smiles guiltily.

The caretaker sighs. "I *said* sharpen it once a week. I'll show you where the stone is later, and make sure it doesn't get wet."

"Got it." The warrior straps her new dagger to her waist. It looks fantastic with her hide armor—black on burnt orange. She makes eye contact with Mary, but instead of looking impressed, she seems dismayed. That's strange.

"Mom..." Mary says, "you had something like this this whole time?"

"Yes, I was waiting for Lillian to go on her first mission. Then I'd give it to her. Doesn't it look so lovely? Give us a spin, will you Lillian?"

"Not a chance."

"Well, it was worth a try."

"I..." Mary looks like she wants to speak up. Instead, she bites her lip. Does she want to say something or not?

"Well, we've wasted enough time," the caretaker continues. "Before you go, I have one more piece of advice: life can be... overwhelming. When you have too much on your mind, take it one step at a time."

"Got it." Before anyone can say anything else, Lillian rushes out of the burrow. At this point, the gatherers may leave her behind. She slams the door behind her.

When I have too much on my mind, take it one step at a time. She's heard that one before. It's her favorite saying. It's simple and will help her keep calm no matter what life throws at her. At least... she hopes so. The dream flashes through her mind again. *Focus, Lillian*, she thinks. *No time for fear now.*

The second Lillian joins them, the gatherers depart. No one says anything about her taking so long. Then again, they all know Miss May. She must have done this on each of their first days, too.

Lillian takes one last glance at the burrow. The door is camouflaged in the underbrush, keeping enemy groups from finding it. Now, it serves another purpose: hiding from capaemen. It'll at least keep them safe for a while, right? She shudders. No one knows the answer to that.

The clearing behind her is so familiar. That beautiful ring of crimson roots surrounds a giant redwood tree. The trapdoor beneath it is the only entrance and exit for their burrow, and she has so many memories from right outside it: learning to sew with Miss May, falling into dead leaves and mud during training, reluctantly playing hide-and-seek with the children... She was never fond of games, but Mary always made her participate. Now, she's leaving it all behind. She turns back around, facing the scores of giant redwoods ahead, bathed in the fog and soft light of early morning. This route may be familiar to the surveyors and gatherers, but it's brand new to her.

As they abandon the clearing, the roots of the giant trees begin to twist together. Bushes and brambles create obstacles that slow their pace, yet the gatherers press on, climbing over and under the vegetation intuitively. This is something familiar, at least. Lillian remembers doing this on their journeys to the river. That is a trip everyone takes part in. On those treks, they make sure to maintain cover as much as possible—always mindful that they are prey. She should have guessed it would be no different here.

The leader, Brianna, strides at the front, leading them on their twisting path. Her red ponytail sways as she moves, and even her elbows are covered with freckles. Lillian wonders how Brianna feels about her being rejected by the surveyors in favor of the gatherers. If Lillian can impress her, maybe she'd talk to Seth. If she doesn't impress her, she definitely will. Lillian takes a deep breath. She *must* do well.

"We'll be taking a detour to Bunker Two after we gather supplies for medicine. We're running low," the redhead announces.

The others nod as if this is their normal routine.

"Will we be staying there overnight?" Lillian asks. She tries not to sound too excited. This is normal for her fellow gatherers, but it's a milestone for her. It would be her first overnight trip.

"Yes. We'll stay there. We'll head to Albian's burrow tomorrow, but we'll be back home by the afternoon. Sound good to you?"

Lillian nods. She's never been to a bunker before. They're only used by the surveyors and gatherers. She's curious to see what it's like, but then a thought occurs: this will be the longest she's been separated from Mary.

She looks around anxiously. If they get there in the evening, who will she talk to during dinner? Who will she lay her mat by when it's time to go to sleep? She knows everyone here by name but isn't close to any of them. Walking at the front with Brianna is a man named Thomas. He has a light complexion and dark hair, and he's not very talkative. She knows he has a love of reading, which Lillian does not. They wouldn't have much to talk about. She shifts her gaze to other members. Noah, the oldest member of Zurec after Miss May, pensively studies the canopy as he walks. He's nice, but Lillian feels awkward talking to any of the older adults. They are all so quiet and closed off. It's hard to blame them, though; those in their forties have experienced more hardship than anyone. Trailing at the back are a married couple, Jess and Milo. Jess is a short, brown-haired girl, while Milo is a tall, muscular blonde. They wear matching orange and brown animal skins, both from a leomus. She's never seen them not together, so they're out too. It would be too awkward being a third wheel. Lillian scans for other members but is swiftly interrupted.

"So, are you nervous?" a shrill voice asks. A small figure takes a place walking next to her. It's the medic, Mia: a petite girl with dark-umber skin who always wears her shoulder-length, tight curls in a puff on top of her head. She carries a backpack nearly twice her size and about ready to burst at the seams. It looks like it's way too heavy, but she doesn't seem to have a problem with it.

"Not really," Lillian answers. She usually avoids talking to Mia, but she can't go anywhere right now.

"Oh, come on. You've got to be a little scared. My goodness, I was sooo nervous my first time. I mean, everything is *huge* here. Have you seen an aranid? Ugh, those are the worst! I once ran into a web and one jumped straight at my face. I slashed at it with my spear, and its blood and guts got everywhere! The worst part was that we were miles from the river, so I couldn't get it off for an entire day. I smelled so terrible no one could sleep."

Yeah, Lillian likes to avoid this particular member, not because she hates her. She doesn't hate anyone in their community, but if anything irritates Lillian, it's people who talk a lot. "Uh-huh," she says, pretending she's listening.

"Then there was this other time when another aranid scuttled by my legs. I mean, it was so fast! If it had been after me, I wouldn't have noticed until it had me, and those jaws, huge! I guess my point with all of this is that I hate bugs. I hate them so much. Where was I going with this? Oh yeah, there's no way you're not nervous, Lillian. You don't need to act tough for us. Tell us how you really feel."

The group climbs over a dead log. Instead of this conversation, Lillian listens to the birds chirping hundreds of feet above. How does she feel? If anything, she feels like she needs some peace and quiet. The other gatherers barely acknowledge her. Why does Mia have to be different?

After an hour of listening to Mia's ramblings, the gatherers approach a gigantic clearing, where the canopy opens to the bright-blue sky. Scores of flowers sway in the light breeze. Their colors range from yellow to orange to red. If Lillian can remember correctly, the tall yellow ones—flavias—are good for anti-itch cream and other topical medicines. The orange and red flowers, vestias and sangips, are used for dyes. She was forced to read all about that stuff as a kid in *Giant Wilds: Plants and Medicines*. She hopes she never has to touch that book again.

"We only need a few," Brianna says. "I'd say about five will do." Five gatherers come forward: Mia, Milo, Jess, Thomas, and the largest man in the whole of Zurec, Bruno. He and Mia seem deep in conversation as they do their job. It's no surprise since they're married as well. The flavia flowers they cut are nearly eight feet tall, yet each person slices the stem with their dagger effortlessly and throws the tall plant over their shoulder. Bruno carries three at once and even offers to take the one his wife has. She refuses, but it was kind of him to ask.

"Alright, let's go," the leader says. No nonsense, no time wasted. Lillian likes this. They follow Brianna through a giant cluster of weeds, towering far above even Bruno's head. The redhead unsheathes her dagger, slashing at the plants.

Above Lillian, a scorofly flutters by. Being a foot-long, narrow-winged bug with a massive stinger for a tail, it's a good thing they usually ignore people. Crawling on the forest floor are tiny scavenger phiis, insects that feed off corpses. They're about as big as the palm of Lillian's hand, and the smallest creatures in the Giant Wilds. Lillian's careful not to step on them. They make an ugly crunching noise when crushed.

BZZZZZZ

Suddenly, a fly the length of a forearm lands on Mia's head. It digs its slimy legs into her thick bun. "Eww! Go away! Go away!" She screeches, swatting at the insect. Her husband rushes to help her, but there's no need. Realizing the medic's hair is not a flower, the creature quickly takes off. In her panic, Mia drops her yellow flower. She quickly picks it up and then locks eyes with Lillian. Her face is the epitome of horror. "I hate this place."

Luckily for Mia, it isn't long before Brianna slices through the last of the weeds, and they make their way out of the clearing. Just like that, the forest blackens under a dense canopy. The gatherers carefully pick their way through the roots. Lillian is reminded of the Red Eclipse, but this time, it puts her on edge. Even the birds sound eerie here. There are fewer bugs here, sure, but more predators. She fingers her spear.

rustle rustle

The gatherers freeze. It's the pitter-patter of footsteps, the crunching of leaves many feet away. Everyone readies their weapons. Some hold their spears. Others draw their bows. Those holding flowers drop them. No one makes a sound. Lillian silences her breathing and pays close attention to her senses like she was taught. She can hear everything: the soft wind rustling through the trees, the birds chirping, the bugs chittering at each other as if in a constant battle for who can chitter the loudest. She hones in on the sound of the footsteps, growing closer and closer. It's coming from the left, but her heart is the most audible noise by far. It pounds quicker the longer they stand here, waiting to see what will emerge. She knows this feeling; it's adrenaline. She hopes a fight breaks out. She wants to test everything she's learned.

As if reading each other's minds, the gatherers create a V formation facing the footsteps. Brianna stands at the vertex alongside Theo. The archers, including Jess and Milo, are at the back. Lillian scrambles to a spot near the middle. She holds her spear to her chest.

rustle rustle...

When she sees what emerges, her body stiffens. They stride on all fours, their fur bathed in shadow. Some have faded stripes on their hides, while others are a solid tawny color. They walk in sync, their long saber teeth sticking out of their mouths like daggers. Even from here, Lillian can tell they're massive, standing at least five feet tall on all fours. If they stood up on their hind legs, they would dwarf her. She's only six feet three. This is the leomus, the creature whose hide she is wearing, that almost everyone is wearing. She wonders if they'll notice.

"Do not engage," Brianna whispers, keeping her head forward. "Only if they attack first."

As with the gatherers, it's obvious who the pack leader is. A slightly larger leomus stands at the front. Its stripes are much more defined, its yellow eyes larger and fiercer, and its saber teeth longer. The rest of the pack looks at it as if asking what to do next. The long whiskers of the pack leader twitch, and it growls, glaring at Brianna. Those yellow eyes grow brighter with fury the more they stare. Still, Brianna doesn't budge an inch.

If this were the surveyors, a fight would have broken out already. However, the gatherers try to avoid fighting at all costs. Lillian's body is shaking. She's trained for this her whole life. She thought she'd be ready, eager even, to fight monsters. Now that she's face-to-face with them, she isn't so sure.

"You know nothing about the world," her father's voice says in her head.

No, I must prove him wrong. She takes deep breaths, trying to stop the shaking.

The alpha makes the first move, charging at Brianna. The rest of the pack follows immediately. Lillian leaps backward. They're faster than she thought. Those massive hind legs are perfect for lunging.

A fight breaks out instantly. A smaller leomus weaves through the chaos and charges straight at Lillian, its fangs bared. Lillian hops out of the way, holding up her spear to block its claw strikes. It wheels around in a matter of seconds, charging at her again. She parries its strikes, running in circles around the beast, her body giving into instinct. Fear takes a back seat to adrenaline, and she realizes she *can* do this. She's quick enough, smart enough. She's smaller than her opponent, but that shouldn't matter if she can dodge its attacks. Dodge and counter: the basics of spear combat.

The longer Lillian fights, the more aware she becomes. She notices the twitch of the monster's shoulders as it slashes at her with its claws, the tensing of its back legs before it charges forward. Everything makes subtle movements before attacking, and this leomus is no exception. She feels incredible in this moment—like she can do anything.

That is until the leomus begins to read her too. It charges again, but this time feels different. Its eyes aren't focused on biting or tearing into her flesh. Instead, they're looking down.

The creature pounces on her spear and knocks it out of her hands. Lillian's weapon launches into the air, getting lost in the flurry of spears slashing and arrows flying. Suddenly, she's on the ground.

She searches frantically for her spear and spots it several feet away. She won't get to it in time. At the same moment, a terrifying thought occurs. *I'm going to die.* Her life flashes before her eyes; all the time she spent sneaking into the forge, reading about weaponry, and beating both Mary and Miss May in training multiple times—all of it is about to be crushed right now. Killed on her first mission. How disgraceful. She wonders what her dad will think. But then, in that same second, Mary's face flashes through her mind. She promised her she wouldn't die. She can't break a promise.

Lillian's eyes fall on her dagger.

As the leomus lunges for her neck, saber teeth ready to tear, Lillian draws her dagger and shoves it into its mouth sideways. The monster gnashes its teeth around the cold steel in a frenzy, still trying to reach her face. Blood drips from its jaw and also from her right hand, which presses right on the blade of the dagger, keeping those teeth only inches away from her neck. With all of her strength, Lillian pushes her arms up and slashes the monster's cheek open. The metal dagger slices through its flesh with ease. It roars furiously, but this won't be enough. In a second, the monster's surprise will fade, and it'll overpower her. *What do I do now?* She has seconds. She must think fast.

sshhiink!

Or must she?

From above, a stone spear plunges into the leomus' head and exits just as quickly. The beast's eyes roll to the back of its skull, and it collapses right on top of Lillian. Standing over her, armor splattered with blood, is Brianna. Wordlessly, she grabs Lillian's arm and pulls her out from under the leomus.

"Fall back! Toward the bushes," she commands. Seemingly in a flash, the gatherers have regrouped. Lillian spots her spear several feet away. She lunges for it and swiftly joins the others. They're in a line formation, pacing backward toward the bushes. A wave of relief rushes over Lillian. It's reassuring to have a person on either side of her. On her right side is Brianna, whose technique would easily land her a spot in the surveyors. On her left is Mia. Her face is focused and determined. She parries the strikes of the monsters with incredible precision. Even Mia is better at this than her. She really does have a long way to go.

A leomus strikes from Lillian's right side, but she blocks it with the shield on her arm. The claws dig into the shield, getting stuck. She shakes them out, and Brianna swiftly kills the creature.

As the gatherers continue to fall back, a shadow creeps over the group. They're almost entirely within the bushes. It will be harder for the pack to pursue them there. They duck and weave through the brambles, and the pack slows down. Finally, when the gatherers reach the middle of the brush, the pack stops completely, tangled in the shoots. They look to their alpha. It glares at Brianna, then turns to make its way out of the brush. The rest of the pack follows.

As quickly as it began, it's over. Everyone lowers their weapons, sighing in relief. "Well, that was strange," Brianna says.

"How so?" Lillian asks between exhausted breaths. She can't believe how much happened in only a few minutes.

"This isn't their territory, but they acted like it was. Why have they claimed the territory between our land and Albi—" She stops short, her eyes widening.

"It's because they're gone," Mia mumbles. "By the Wilds, they really must all be dead. Otherwise, the leomus would never attack us here." Lillian's heart sinks. Even the animals are acting weird, thanks to the capaemen.

"Don't jump to conclusions, Mia," Brianna says. "We'll be at Bunker Two in a couple of hours. When we get there, let's take the rest of the day to chop up and preserve the flavias. While we do that, you can patch up Lillian's injury. Then—"

"Wait, Lillian is *injured?*"

"Don't interrupt me," Brianna continues, irritated. "We'll stay over at the bunker, wake up tomorrow, and judge the Albian situation when we arrive at their burrow. We don't know anything yet." But even she sounds nervous.

This adventure isn't going as Lillian hoped.

4

The Human, the Acera, and an Impossible Threat

Mary

"Come on! You can do better than that." Mary Zurec's mother stands over her with a disappointed scowl. She points a wooden spear at her daughter, her ponytail shining white in the sun. For the third time, Mary has landed butt-first in the moss. Why can't she get this right?

"Something on your mind, sweetie?" she asks. She holds her hand out. Mary takes it, and her mother pulls her up. She thinks of Lillian leaving this morning. The brunette didn't notice, but Mary's mom was acting strange. Her overprotective self was still there, but it had a nervous edge. She kept glancing at Lillian's spear yet said nothing. That was even stranger.

Mary dusts herself off. "Yeah, there is something. The spear Lillian had, why didn't you say anything about it?"

Her mother's face grows hard. "You two snuck into the forge again." Mary nods guiltily. "I should have known she'd find it. I told Seth to throw that thing away years ago. I'm sorry, but I didn't have the heart to tell her."

"Tell her what?" the curious girl asks.

"It was..." Mary's anxiety rises. The caretaker *never* hesitates. Her mother sighs and takes a seat on a tree root just barely jutting out of the ground. She pats the spot next to her. Mary scrambles over, trying not to look nervous and failing miserably. "It was her mother's," she says sadly. "She asked me to give it to Lillian on her fifteenth birthday."

Mary gasps. "Why would *she* do that?"

The caretaker stares at her daughter, her pale-blue eyes distant. "Despite her selfishness, I think Emilia still cared for Lillian." Mary scoffs. That woman doesn't deserve any favors. She left when Lillian was a baby, all because some collective of rogues seemed better than Zurec. If it weren't for Mary's mom, who breastfed both of them, Lillian wouldn't have made it. She cared for them even as most of Zurec died of starvation. At least, that's how the story goes. No wonder the spear was hidden, but sadly, Lillian managed to find it anyway—like she was *destined* for it. She can see why her mom didn't want to say anything.

Still, Mary must know, what exactly did Lillian's mother say? She left her husband with only a note, yet she talked to the caretaker? The image of that woman requesting such a thing before abandoning her child is disgusting. Mary musters the courage to ask more questions, but before she can, her mother speaks.

"I know that look. This was a bad idea. I don't want to be here all day. You should be training, not chit-chatting."

"But Mommm! Just a few questions. I *have* to know."

Her mother stands and raises her spear. "I don't want to talk about this anymore. Let's keep this between us. Come on, back to training." Mary groans. When her mother decides something, there's no changing her mind. She takes a defensive stance, ready to spar. Her mother's scowl deepens. "You know, you should try to be more offensive. Maybe then you'd win."

"M-More offense?"

"Yes, Lillian is obsessed with offense. Even though she sometimes wins, I have to tell her to stop being so reckless, but you're the opposite. You need to be bolder. It's funny; I raised you both. How did that happen?"

"I-I don't—"

"You're too timid, Mary. Now that Lillian is gone, we're going to fix that. I'll have to go harder on you. Act like this fight is real and you're trying to take me down."

"What? It will never be real. I'm a caretaker, not a fighter," Mary says. She doesn't know why her mother is teaching her this now. She couldn't have cared less when Lillian was around. They only sparred with each other.

Her mom looks disappointed. "I know you don't like to fight, but I think you should learn before you turn fifteen next eclipse, just in case."

"What's the point? I'm going to be the caretaker, right? They don't fight." That's why her mother gave Lillian the dagger, not her.

"You will become the next caretaker, but not right now. I'm not going to drop dead anytime soon. I have a few good years left, at least. Plus, we don't know what's going to happen, especially with the return of, well, *them*."

Mary gulps. The capaemen. She was awake all night thinking about them.

"I will not have a weak daughter in this chaos. So, come on. Come at me with everything you've got. We're getting you in shape."

Mary raises her spear. "O-Okay!"

They train until evening breaks. The canopy grows darker. "Oh man, I'm beat," her mother says. "Time to turn in for the night. Let's join the others." She heads to the trapdoor, pulling on the latch. It seems she wasn't exaggerating her exhaustion. She tries to lift the door, but it doesn't budge. It takes both of them together to pry the door open. They head down the hall and into the mud room.

There isn't much to the mud room. Its wooden floor is always muddy, hence its name. The room is an open cavern with a leomus-skin rug in the middle. The rug is stained brown from the careless trampling of folks darting in and out. This is the place where important meetings happen. It's also where her mom's crafting, botany, history, and other classes take place, and where she reads them books about the Giant Wilds. She holds classes here when the weather is bad or a creature stomps about where it doesn't belong. There are many pleasant memories here—and many where Lillian got her into trouble, but even those are held fondly in Mary's heart.

Sitting in a circle on the darkened rug are the children and a surveyor named Kayla. Sewing supplies surround the children, and Kayla is buried in a book, her sandy hair sitting in a nest on her head. Her three-year-old son Felix doesn't look much better, but he seems happy enough. He sits in her lap, poking the rug with a stick. Excluding Mary, there are only four kids in Zurec: Felix, a pair of identical twin girls who only speak to each other, and a black-haired boy who trembles over his sewing. He looks as if he's about to cry. Only two torches are lit, but Mary's mom fixes that, walking about the room and re-lighting the other six. "Why were you working in such dim lighting?"

"Huh?" the surveyor asks, looking up from her book. "Oh yeah, that."

"Yes. Isn't this so much better?" her mother sits on the rug.

"Lots. Lets me see my book better."

"How's the baby?" she asks.

"Which one?"

The caretaker scowls and points at her belly.

"Oh yeah, this one. He's wonderful. You know, he's been kicking a lot lately. I think he's ready to come out soon."

Mary settles down next to her mother. "How do you know it's a 'he'?"

"I just do," Kayla says, not looking up from her book.

"Well, how have the children been doing with their crafts?" her mother asks. "I asked you to teach them while Mary and I were sparring, remember?"

"Oh yeah, they're good," Kayla says nonchalantly.

Mary and Miss May look around the room, and it's not good. It's not good at all. The anxious boy's stitches are too far apart, and the twins, Jen and Jan, aren't even sewing. They're just taking turns stabbing the felt with the needle. The mother and daughter sigh simultaneously. Mary helps the boy. Her mom takes the twins.

The black-haired boy's skin is paler than usual and his little eyes are full of fear. He's trying his best. The timid nine-year-old lost his parents very young, and he's been anxious ever since. He can't focus, and who can blame him? "Hey, Oscar, you can stop if you want to," Mary says.

"I-I can? Miss May won't get mad?"

"She won't. Right, Mom?" She gestures to the caretaker, who gives her a skeptical look.

"I have an idea. Let me read you all a story." Mary gets up and heads down the hall. She makes a left to the storeroom. It's a stuffy, cramped space full of rows of crowded shelves. They keep everything here, from medical supplies to weapons to jarred food preserves. It used to be a bedroom, but when the old storeroom collapsed years ago, Zurec made do with what they had. Mary navigates the shelves until, *Bingo!* She finds the books.

Running her fingers along the spines, she spots Kayla's *Giant Wilds: Plants and Medicines*, *Giant Wilds: Creatures*, *Giant Wilds: Seasons*, and *Outside the Wilds: What We Know*—that book is very thin. Most of the books here are written by Kayla, but there is one that her people have had forever. It miraculously survived the cavern collapse twenty years ago, and the famine war with Albian. It's a true treasure. One of the last stories left from Zurec's past, and, and...

It isn't here, Mary thinks.

A memory snaps into her head at that moment. *Oh yeah! I decided to reread it about a week ago. It must be in our room,* she thinks. She rushes to her quarters. Down the hall and through the second door on the right is their room—Miss May, Mary, and Lillian's quarters. Mary opens the old door with a *creeaakkk.*

In the room are three beds, one against each wall. Her mother's is to the left, with her clothes nicely folded into her trunk and her bed made. Lillian's bed is near the back. There isn't much to Lillian's side of the room. All she keeps near is a trunk full of clothes, a backpack of medicine, and her unkempt bed. Her pillow and sheets lie strewn on the wooden floor. There's no need to pick them up; they always end up down there.

Mary envies the simplicity of Lillian's side. She looks at her part of the room and feels immediately overwhelmed by piles of unfinished projects. Some aren't even hers. She just stole them from the storeroom for inspiration. Mary tiptoes to her pile of junk. *Now, where is it?*

She glances at the top of her bed. Sitting on it is an embroidery ring with a small strip of brown fabric in it. That's the most important project. She won't lose it before she finishes it. It's a gift for Lillian. She wishes she could have done it before the eclipse, but that has passed. She'll need to keep working on it. She'll give it to her soon. Now, the book.

Mary rummages through the mayhem on the floor, and after sifting through several piles of junk, she spots it. The corner of a book sticks out from under a pile of clay dolls. She plucks it from the pile and dusts it off. If her mom found out she was treating the book this way, she'd be in big trouble—better put it back on the shelves after this.

As she emerges to rejoin the others, the silence in the room is palpable. Everyone looks at her expectantly. "Is it *The Adventures of Cecilia and Alida?*" the caretaker asks, her eyebrows raised. "You never get tired of that story, do you?"

Mary shakes her head. "It's one of my favorites." She sits in the circle. The children scooch in so they can see the pictures.

"It's my favorite too!" Oscar yells.

"And mine," Jen says.

"Me too," Jan responds. The twins have dark skin, a cloud of soft coils on their heads, and brown eyes. They're basically copies of their mother, Mia, and they're so alike at their young age that it's difficult to tell them apart. Whenever they speak, they speak together.

"Well, I'm glad it's everyone's favorite," Mary states. She feels a warm sense of nostalgia every time she looks at this book. She and Lillian would make her mother read this story over and over again when they were little. On the cover, there's an illustration of a woman flying high in the sky. She rides a massive winged beast called an acera. It has rubbery, brown skin, a wide mouth, a slender body with a long pointed tail, and bulging eyes. The acera looks almost happy in the picture—happy to be carrying the woman on its back.

Mary opens the book. The pages are wrinkled and worn, and the illustrations are faded, but it's still in pretty good shape for its age. It's much better crafted than the books they have today. The first page contains a drawing of the woman on the acera. She points a spear at a pack of leomus. They look terrified.

Mary clears her throat. "Okay, are you all ready?" The kids nod eagerly. She begins to read. Her story voice is loud and confident.

"Once upon a time, there was a very strong warrior named Cecilia, but Cecilia wasn't strong by herself. She was strong because of her trusted partner, Alida. Alida was her acera. She was big and could easily carry Cecilia. With Alida, Cecilia could fly high in the sky, higher than even the tallest creatures. Even the capaemen looked like bugs from her view in the sky."

"Even the capaemen! So cool!" Oscar says, his brown eyes sparkling.

From there, Mary dives into the story. She reads everything passionately, from Cecilia and Alida helping their clan, to the fight with the fearsome narecon and their tragic separation. She tears up a little every time she reads about how Alida sacrifices herself for Cecilia. As a child, it made her so sad, but she knows this story has a happy ending. Their reunion is a beautiful scene, with a gorgeous illustration of Cecilia hugging her acera and Alida licking her in return. She begs Alida never to leave her again because life without her is torture. A wonderful ending, and something so rare in the real world. Maybe that's why everyone likes it so much.

Before the final line of the story, Mary pauses for dramatic effect. The children hold their breath. "With that, the duo soared into the sky. Apart, they can go far, but together they can do anything." Everyone claps. Mary smiles.

"Again, again!" Oscar pleas.

"No," Miss May says, "that's enough for today." She looks at Kayla, who's scribbling in her journal. "Kayla, what are you writing?"

"Oh, I just started it this week. It doesn't have much yet. It's called *Capaemen: What We Know*," she says, steadying her son. The toddler won't stop bouncing.

"Wow, that is bound to be a good one," her mom remarks, "especially since all the books we had on them have been lost. That reminds me, we need to have a talk about capaemen."

"Wonderful, I'll take notes," Kayla says, readying her pen.

"No! I don't want to talk about the scary giants. I want to read the story again," Oscar says, pouting. The twins nod in agreement.

"Kids, you've heard that story a hundred times. This is more important," the caretaker says.

"But—"

"Mary can reread it later. Right, Mary?"

She nods.

"Noooo," the twins say simultaneously.

"Don't argue. This is an important conversation. Besides, I'm getting tired. If I sit through that story again, I'll be too sleepy to tell *my* story. Did you know I've seen a capaeman with my own eyes?" Everyone flinches, even Kayla. She's seen a capaeman? Mary is offended she's never heard of this. "Well, it's true. It was back before any of you were born, but I won't be able to tell the story if Mary reads *The Adventures of Cecilia and Alida* again."

"Fine," Oscar says, crossing his arms. Everyone leans in, morbid curiosity taking over. The caretaker takes a deep breath. "You can't know how scary they are until you've seen one. You can't know how big they are until you hear their thunderous footsteps. They stand tall enough to touch the low branches of the redwood trees. I was only a girl, new to the gatherers, when I saw one. It had to be at least fifty feet tall. Its shadow stretched across miles of forest floor. In the face of such a threat, the leader of the gatherers, Brianna's late father, had no idea what to do. We stood there, frozen in place. Luckily, it passed. It did not see us."

Mary clutches her necklace. The stones glued to it feel ice-cold in her hand. "And then what happened?"

"We talked about it. It was a terrifying yet strangely surreal experience. They look a lot like us, yet also very different."

"Do they wear clothes?" a child interjects.

Her mother chuckles. "Yes, Oscar, but their clothes are different from ours."

"Can they talk?" Jen and Jan ask at the same time.

"I think so, but none are eager to have a conversation with us."

"They have scales for skin, right?" Mary adds. She vaguely remembers some stories she was told as a kid and some doodles Kayla made. They seem to be reptilian.

"Yes. They look like people, but with scales for skin and claws for hands. This one had its back turned, luckily. If it were facing us, it could have seen us. I think it was just passing through for whatever reason. Thank the Wilds it wasn't hunting. Back then, we'd see very few of them. They live down south, outside the forest."

Mary shudders even thinking about it.

"They never cared about us. So why do you think they're after us now?" Kayla asks.

"Maybe Albian made a mistake and was seen? Still though, that doesn't add up. From what I remember, the capaemen do kill humans they encounter outside the forest, but they don't bother with those who hide, at least not here. It would make sense if it were Rostad. They live farther south, but the capaemen rarely come as deep into the woods as we are. They've never cared to."

Mary's mind races. It's hard to reach this part of the Wilds, even as a giant. What has them so riled up? She was taught they would always be safe from the capaemen, but it turns out that isn't true.

"There are many things that don't add up," the surveyor chimes in. "I hope the gatherers can find out more." She rubs her huge belly. "And I hope... that my children don't have to grow up terrified of the capaemen. I'm sick of this. All of it." Mary frowns. It would be wonderful if there were a place where they could live in peace forever, but that's not the way this world works.

"I agree, Kayla," the caretaker says somberly. "At any rate, we must be extra careful now. Every day, I'll check on the trapdoor and make sure the camouflage hasn't worn off. If anything stomps by, we hide. Do not leave stuff outside. If they spot something that's ours, it could lead them straight to us. Do you understand?"

The children nod, terrified. Mary scooches over to Oscar, who's looking paler and paler by the minute. She wraps her arms around him. He shivers in them, sniffling. He's trying not to cry. "It'll be okay. We're Zurec. We always survive," she whispers.

Her mother stares at them. "I'm sorry. I wish we could have talked about something happier, but you all need to know what's at stake here. Well, that's all I have for you. The rest of the night is free. You can reread the story." She stands up, stretches, and heads down the hall.

All the children instantly look to Mary. "Read it again! Read it again!"

But now her mind is racing. She's not sure if she can get into character now. She stands, awkwardly holding the book in her arms. "How about we read it again first thing tomorrow morning?"

"Noooooo," the children cry simultaneously.

"I'm so sorry. I didn't sleep well last night, so I'd like to get a head start tonight. First thing tomorrow, I promise. I'll even let you wake me up."

"Pleeeaaase? The book isn't that long," Oscar pleads.

"I, uh..." Mary feels like she is about to cry. She doesn't want the children to see that. She casts a fleeting glance at Kayla. *Help me.*

"I think hearing the story in the morning is a good idea. You know why? Because..." the woman improvises, "I'm going to tell you a true story. It's about how Chief Seth took on a thornopine burrower all by himself."

"Woahhhhh," the kids say.

"Let's go to my room. I'll tell you all about it."

"Okay!"

On the way out, Kayla winks at Mary.

"Thank you," she mouths. She rushes to her room.

As Mary settles under the blankets of her messy bed, she stares at the ceiling. She can't get her mother's story out of her head. Something that big is after them, and Lillian is out there in the Wilds where anything can happen. By tomorrow, the gatherers should make it to Albian's burrow. She wonders what they'll find there.

Most of all, she hopes they'll be okay.

5

Trapped and Frozen

Lillian

Bunker Two is very cramped. Lillian didn't think it would be only one room—one stuffy room with a pile of junk sitting at the back. She hardly had any space to lay down her mat, much less sleep. She knew the shelters wouldn't be as big as the burrow, but she certainly wasn't expecting this.

As morning breaks, the gatherers crawl out of the narrow entrance one by one. When Lillian finally gets outside, she stretches. Her back cracks with a loud *pop*. Standing on a tree root in front of her is Brianna. She stares at the canopy, her expression blank. Lillian decides to join her.

The redhead takes a deep breath, taking in the spring air. "I'm not sure if you're ready for what we may find there."

"I guess we'll find out," Lillian says. After yesterday, she feels like anything could happen.

"How's your hand?"

The girl turns her attention to her right palm. Yesterday, Mia disinfected it and wrapped it in a tight tan bandage. She had forgotten about it until now. It doesn't even hurt anymore. "I've had much worse. I'll be fine in a few days."

"I guess you have," Brianna says with concern. She must remember what happened when Lillian was little. It was one of the first times she snuck into the forge on her own, and it went horribly wrong. Eight-year-old Lillian accidentally knocked a box of dagger blades off the top shelf. The blades rained down on her. She managed to deflect most of them with her arms, but in the end, she still had cuts all over her body. Some of them bled a lot, but instead of crying, she ran up the stairs and got help from Miss May, as well as an earful.

It only took a few weeks to heal, and once she was better, she snuck into the forge again. Most people would be traumatized from that experience, but Lillian wasn't. People get hurt all the time. Why was it such a big deal just because she was a kid? It was fine then, and it's fine now.

"You *are* resilient. I'll give you that," Brianna says. Yeah, she's thinking of the same memory. "Maybe you'll be fine today, even if we see something... grim."

Lillian frowns, but this is what she's been training for. It may look slightly different than she imagined, but she's still a warrior. "I'll be okay. No matter what, we stick together, right?"

"Right," the redhead says. "I'm glad you're with us."

"Me too. Oh, and thank you for saving me yesterday." She feels like a disgrace, having to be saved like that, but she tries to play it cool. The last thing she needs is the gatherers looking down on her.

"Don't thank me. It's what we do. We support each other."

"So, you won't tell my dad?"

Brianna raises an eyebrow. "Why would I? It was one mistake. We've all been there. Just do better next time, and don't lose that spear. It's one of a kind." She hops off the root.

"What do you mean by that?" Lillian asks. She holds up her spear to the light. It shimmers green, reflecting the leaves. "Do you know where it came from?"

"That isn't my story to tell." The redhead walks away. It's clear Lillian won't get anything else out of her. *What did she mean by that?* Nevertheless, someone else must know. She'll find out soon enough.

With the chittering of the forest echoing in the background, the gatherers prepare to move out. Mia changes the bandages of another injured gatherer. She has a nasty gash on her arm. Her skin is light brown, eyes narrow and dark, and her long hair cascades down her right shoulder. She talks about people in the surveyors, causing some to narrow their eyes at her—Zoey, the burrow gossip. She and Mia are a terrible combination. Together, nothing is ever quiet. Lillian's lucky her injury is minor, or she may have been stuck between them.

Once everyone is ready, they travel straight to Albian's burrow, with Mia and Zoey excitedly talking to each other. After a few minutes, Brianna tells them to stop. So instead, the girls start whispering. Eventually, other gatherers, including Gigi and Jess, join in, and no one else intervenes. Lillian doesn't mind it. She can hardly hear them anyway.

The moss squelches under the Zurec people's shoes, sending water vapor into the air. It must have rained after the leomus fight. As they traverse deeper into the forest, the trees become thicker and the girls finally stop talking. This place is covered in shadow, with only a few specks of light breaking through the canopy. It puts everyone on edge. Mia tightens her grip on her spear. Brianna stiffens slightly. They enter an enormous, foggy clearing surrounded by gnarled tree roots. The roots sprawl and tangle over and under each other along the perimeter as if encaging them. Species of lichen thrive in this rarefied patch of sun, latching onto the roots, causing their red bark to grow paler and drier; it's a den of death. Lillian shivers. She wants to run.

As the gatherers approach the center of the gigantic clearing, they spot a large round piece of wood. Attached are several large metal hinges partially camouflaged under clumps of moss. Lillian's breath catches in her throat. This is a burrow door, much like their own. How did it get all the way over here? Isn't it supposed to be, well, covering a burrow? Her eyes focus on the metal hinges, and her heartbeat thrums in her ears. The thick metal that's supposed to hold the door in place has been bent and broken. Some hinges hold on by a thread, but stains in the wood reveal where others were completely severed. Whatever did this is strong enough to bend metal. Her father was right.

Brianna bends over, placing her hand on the door. She moves it over the camouflage, all the way to the broken hinges.

No human could have fought against this and lived.

Some of the gatherers are already beginning to panic. Others ready their weapons as if anticipating an attack. Mia's dark eyes are so wide they look like they're about to pop out of her head.

"Let's move on," Brianna says as if snapping herself out of a trance. "Seth already told us about this. We shouldn't dwell on it."

"It's... awful. It... It looks like it's been thrown into the middle of the clearing. N-No human is strong enough to do this. It's *them.* It was definitely—"

"Enough, Mia," their leader interrupts. "We know."

Mia fiddles with her backpack strap. "I'm sorry." Brianna makes her way toward one of the trees. The gatherers wordlessly follow. It's the largest in the clearing, and a massive, gaping hole is under it. This must be the burrow.

Lillian's senses heighten. The nearer they get, the more her heart pounds. Somehow, she knows something bad is over there. Something very bad. The smell of rotting tree bark carries through the heavy breeze. The roots of this tree are higher and thicker, like walls. If some members of Albian are still alive, those would be the perfect places to hide for an ambush. Seth must be sure they're all gone for him to send the gatherers here. Otherwise, they could be in trouble. Although, humans should be Lillian's last concern right now.

"O-Oh my goodness!" Mia screams suddenly. "Over there!" Lillian follows her finger. When she sees what the medic is pointing at, she wants to vomit.

Only feet away from them, lying face down, is a person; well, it used to be. Now it's nothing but a corpse sinking into the moss. Tiny scavenger phiis crawl all over it, and the smell, it's unreal. It burns Lillian's nostrils and stings her eyes. She has never smelled something so horrible in her life. She doesn't look away, though.

Brianna grabs a cloth from her bag and uses it to examine the body. "Her neck is broken. No... more like, it's been *shattered*. I don't think there's a single bone in her neck that isn't crushed."

Lillian feels like she can't breathe. She can't imagine what that woman must have seen before she died. On her back is the Albian sigil, which is much like Zurec's, but with one spear crossed over it instead of two. That confirms it. Something horrific happened, but if it were capaemen, then why is this woman all alone?

Clutched in the woman's right hand is a dagger. It's spotless. Perhaps she tried to fight back. If so, she didn't get far. Her neck must have been like a twig to *them*. Lillian feels her own neck—how fragile and vulnerable it was when the leomus almost bit into it. How fragile it still is now.

Even after seeing that, Brianna keeps going. The others follow, barely holding it together as they approach the hole. There it is: Albian's base. Bile rises in Lillian's throat, but she pushes it down. This is her mission; she must go through with it.

Inside, the air feels almost as thick as water, and it burns her eyes. She gasps. It's as if a furnace has been set ablaze in her chest. What happened to this place? She's reminded of something Miss May explained once: *"You can't let the fire burn for too long. In a burrow, too much smoke can become poison."* Is this smoke pollution? No, it wouldn't sting like this.

They creep through the entrance hallway and soon emerge in the main room of this burrow. The sight in front of them is horrific. At least ten people are on the floor, still as statues and pale as bone. Some lean against a wall with their arms around each other. Others lie sprawled in the dirt, their eyes wide open. At first, Lillian thinks they are alive, but the way their eyes have sunken into their skulls extinguishes that hope. It feels like a moment frozen in time: a moment in which these people, huddled in clusters, are forever in agony. Lillian's head throbs.

"Let's leave, right *now*," their leader says urgently. They sprint outside without hesitation.

Lillian stumbles out, falling into a coughing fit. Her lungs feel like they're about to explode. Tears run down her face. "Wh-What was *that*, Brianna?" Mia croaks. She grips a tree root for support. Her husband rushes over to comfort her.

"My guess? Poison," Brianna responds.

Poison, Lillian thinks. *Like a poisonous plant?* That wasn't ordinary smoke. It must have been made specifically to kill people who live underground. Zurec knows so little about the capaemen; could they have made that? Lillian doesn't know how it would work. She's not sure she *wants* to know.

"This is bad. This is very bad," Brianna says, unable to hide her panic.

"This was calculated. Against something like that... how do we... how can we...?" Even Mia is at a loss for words.

Brianna takes a seat on the ground, catching her breath. A circle gathers around her. "What... now?" Lillian asks breathlessly.

"We report to Seth. His fears are true." The atmosphere is heavy with despair.

"And then?" Mia manages.

The young warrior wracks her brain. There must be a way to help. "My dad was talking about moving burrows. Bunker One is the farthest north and we almost never use it. Maybe we can—"

"That's for him to decide," Brianna interrupts. She gets up, brushing the dust off her clothes. "Come on, we're heading back."

No one even stops to entertain it. Not the leader of the gatherers, nor even the most talkative members. Mia is avoiding eye contact. Lillian doesn't understand what is wrong with her idea. If they move north, they'll be farther away from the capaemen. It's at least better than staying put. She rushes toward Brianna. "Wait, you won't even think about it? Why?"

"I'm not the chief. I don't make those kinds of decisions."

"But you do lead the gatherers. You can—"

rustle rustle

She's interrupted by a sudden noise. It emanates from the bushes nearby. *Not again*, Lillian thinks. She's not ready for another fight. The gatherers ready their weapons. Lillian draws her spear.

What emerges is not a monster, but two children.

Two kids, who can't be any older than eight, cautiously approach the gatherers. It's a boy and a girl. The little boy looks younger, but he is the one leading. He drags the girl along, his small hand clasped in hers. They look alike, with dark-brown hair, round faces, almond-shaped eyes, and deep-tawny skin like smooth clay. Their torn hide clothes are coated in mud. The little girl stares blankly as if in a trance. The boy looks more aware but is on the verge of tears.

Mia is the first to get to them. She bends over, unable to mask her relief. "Hi, there. Who are you two?"

The boy immediately breaks into tears. "P-Please help us, miss. W-We're thirsty and hungry." The little girl stands like a statue.

"Oh, goodness! Let's see. I have some snacks in my bag; hold on." The medic swings her huge pack off her shoulders and rummages through it.

"What clan are you from?" Brianna asks. Her tone has become gentler.

"A-Albian," the boy says, sniffling. Lillian's eyebrows furrow. How is that possible? They're little kids.

"Albian? Can you tell us what happened?" Brianna asks evenly.

The boy chokes on his tears. "I think... I think... everyone's dead." He looks at the little girl, who stares at nothing. She hasn't said a word nor looked at a single person this whole time. It's like she's not even here.

Mia hands each of the children a piece of dried fruit. The boy gobbles it up. The girl takes it but doesn't look at it. "Don't worry, it's not poisoned." Slowly, the girl raises the fruit to her mouth. She takes a tiny bite and chews sluggishly.

Brianna bends down and places her hands on the kids' shoulders. "What are your names?"

"I'm Max, and this is Trista," he sniffles. "Do you have a place to sleep? We're so tired."

"Right this way," Brianna says. She heads in the direction of Zurec's burrow. Lillian notices the faces of the gatherers. They seem less harrowed, as if seeing the children has made their sorrow disappear. These children are from an enemy clan, but they survived somehow. In a land filled with death, now they have hope.

The children follow as best they can, but it's clear they're too exhausted. Mia moves her backpack to her chest, letting the girl, Trista, jump onto her back. The boy, Max, pokes Lillian. "Up." Lillian stares at him, bewildered. Can't he ask anyone else? He pouts, noticing her reluctance. She sighs, slinging her backpack to one shoulder and letting him climb up. He's light. They must be right about hardly eating. She has so many questions, but this situation is delicate. They are traumatized. She'll start small.

"How old are you two?"

"I'm five. My sister's seven." Lillian glances at Trista. The little girl has already fallen asleep on Mia's back. "What clan are you from?" Max asks.

Lillian isn't sure she should answer. Would it make him scared? Well, he will find out anyway, so it doesn't matter. "Zurec."

"Z-Zurec? Oh no, you're the bad guys! Let me go, let me go!" He struggles against Lillian's grip. She tightens her arms, but then he starts punching and kicking. "Let me go, monster!"

Trista jolts awake. "What's going on?"

"They're Zurec! They're Zurec!"

The girl begins to cry. "Please don't hurt us."

Brianna steps in. "Lillian, let the boy go." She does as her boss asks, trying her best to place him gently on the forest floor, but his struggling makes him fall. He lands butt-first in the moss. This only makes him cry louder. "It's okay," Brianna says kindly. "We may have been enemies in the past, but we aren't anymore. Your burrow is gone, and we want to help."

The boy wipes his face. "R-Really?"

"Yes. I mean, look around. Do we seem like bad guys?" Max stands up, his legs shaking. He studies each of the eleven members of the gatherers, lingering on Lillian for a minute as if she could be a bad guy. She shouldn't have said anything.

"No, you look nice."

"Trust your gut," Brianna says. "Bad guys look bad. Do we?" The boy shakes his head. Trista yawns and goes back to sleep. That's clearly enough for her.

As they start walking again, the boy grabs Lillian's hand. His little green eyes stare at her pleadingly. "Up." Lillian raises her eyebrows. The boy was fighting her moments ago. Now he wants her to carry him again? She will never understand children.

As they leave the dark part of the forest, Max falls asleep on her back. He snores softly. That's bound to get annoying soon, so she tries to ignore it. As they get closer and closer to the burrow, more light streams through the canopy. The afternoon sun warms Lillian's skin. Eventually, climbing over tree roots with the boy gets very tiring. Mia hands the little girl to Brianna, but when Lillian tries to hand Max off, he clings to her and cries. She has no idea how the child became so attached to her, but she respects his wishes and keeps carrying him.

They arrive at the burrow in the evening. When Lillian sees that familiar clearing, she sighs in relief. She's been sweating buckets for hours. She can't wait to sleep in her cozy bed near Mary and Miss May.

Mary... Miss May...

Gazing at the familiar clearing, this place she has always called home, her two-day journey finally sinks in. Slowly, she puts the boy down. *That... really happened*, Lillian thinks. The images of the bodies, the foul stench taking over her senses. Her knees feel weak.

"Oh no! Are you okay, miss?" Max asks. Lillian looks at him. She hates how helpless she feels, but for some reason, the boy's dirty, mangy face gives her comfort. She would give anything to see what he's seen, even if it was horrifying. They must find out how they survived, and fast. It's their only lead on how the capaemen work.

She opens her mouth, but all she can say is, "I'm fine. You're safe now." It isn't her place to ask them what happened. She'll let Mary and Miss May do it. After all, those two are good with children. If anyone can find out the truth, it's them.

6

Miracle Children

Mary

"Lillian!" Mary screams. It feels like it's been weeks since she's seen her. She throws her arms around her.

"Hey, Mary." Her voice is low and even, and there's a bandage around her hand.

"Oh my Wilds! Are you hurt? How did this happen?"

The brunette looks away. "We've got a lot to catch up on."

"What's going on?" Mary's mother shrieks. "Who are these children?" Mary looks around, keeping her arms around her friend. Standing next to Brianna are a little boy and girl she's never seen before. Their shirts are torn and ragged, and their dark hair is matted and dirty. One glance at their clothes is enough to tell how much they've been through. Less than a glance at their faces, and she knows it was hell.

Brianna's voice fades into the background as she explains what happened. It must have been bad, but Mary is only focused on one thing. "Lillian, tell me what happened."

Light returns to her friend's eyes. "I'm fine. You should worry about them."

"My mom's got them! I'm here for *you*. By the Wilds, there's blood on your clothes. Did something attack you? Are you injured anywhere else? Did you... did you see the *capaemen*?"

"Yes, no, and no," she answers frankly. "Now, can you let me go?"

"No! You must be traumatized," Mary says, tightening her hug. She knows what Lillian is trying to do. She downplays anything negative or traumatic.

Her friend pushes her away. "I'm fine. Don't worry about me. You should focus on those children." She's trying to change the subject. That's another one of her tactics. Mary won't fall for it.

"Mary, can you help me out?" her mother interrupts. Mary turns to see the caretaker escorting the strange children to the burrow.

"I can't. I need to—"

"Help them," Lillian says. "I'm okay, really. They're the ones who need you."

"Fine. I'll talk to you later." They take the children down the tunnel and into the washroom first. Like most spaces in the burrow, there isn't much to it. Dirty towels hang on wooden wall hooks and sit in piles on the floor. Wooden stalls containing simple toilets line the left wall of the room. On the right wall are three large tubs of water, a cabinet storing herbs and soap powder, and several wooden buckets. People use those bathtubs in the winter when it's hard to go outside. Otherwise, they bathe in the river. But Mary knows why they're here: these kids are so dirty, it could affect their health. They need a bath right now.

The kids cooperate during bath time, even though Mary and her mother are complete strangers. They seem grateful to be clean and don't complain about anything, not the overly aromatic scent of the soap nor the rough bristles of the cleansing brushes on their skin. They're silent for all of it—a far cry from the children of Zurec.

It isn't long before the kids are out of the washroom and heading back down the hall. Her mom even took the liberty of picking a change of clothes for them. They belong to Oscar, but they can always make him new ones.

On the way back to their bedroom, they briefly pass the well room. The space has a dugout leading to an aquifer. Atop the dugout is a small well with a worn rope attached to a pulley. This is one of the ways they get water. One pulls the water up, takes it to the kitchen to be boiled and purified, and then finally stores it. Mary thinks of stopping by the kitchen for a drink, but she'll have to wait until later. They must deal with these children first.

Entering their shared room, her mother takes a seat on her bed with the boy, and Mary sits on the floor, facing the girl. "Mary, this is Trista and her brother, Max. They're from Albian."

The girl's heart skips a beat. "D-Did you say Albian?" No wonder Lillian was so insistent on helping them. It's a miracle they are alive. She cannot imagine what they must have been through. She looks at her mother. The caretaker is scowling as usual, but there's a determined glint in her eyes. Mary knows what that means. They need information—anything they can get on the capaemen. She takes a deep breath. *Okay, I can do this.* "Hey, I hope you're feeling better.

I'm Mary, Miss May's daughter. She's the caretaker here. You two must be hungry. Could I get you a snack?"

The boy shakes his head. "No. The doctor girl already gave us lots. I just wanna go to sleep."

"Doctor girl? Oh, you must mean Mia." That sounds just like her. After all, Mia does have two children of her own. Jen and Jan did not inherit their mother's talkative side, thank goodness.

"Yes, she was very nice," he says. "Can we go to sleep now?" It looks like they haven't slept in days. The little girl has at least three layers of bags under her eyes and the boy is holding onto Miss May's arm just to stay upright. Mary knows the burrow needs information, but is now the right time?

Her mother stares at her expectantly. She clearly doesn't want to wait any longer. Then why doesn't she ask them? Why does it have to be Mary? She takes another deep breath. She should rip off the bandage. The girl hasn't talked, so she'll ask the boy. If he starts crying, she will stop. "Max, I know this is hard for you, but can you tell us your story?"

His little eyes widen. "M-My story?"

"You and your sister. How did you get here?"

He clings to her mother's arm. "Th-The gatherers found us." The caretaker moves her hand in circles, encouraging Mary to go on.

"How did they find you?" she asks next. She'll still take this slow. They can work backward from the moment they were found to the capaemen.

"Th-The bush. We hid in it for three days," Max explains. "It was so hard. We didn't sleep at all. Then we saw the nice Zurec people."

"What were you doing in the bush?"

"It was the only safe place. The burrow was, the burrow was..." The boy trails off, tears falling down his cheeks.

"Don't ask him. He had his eyes closed the whole time," Trista interrupts.

Mary turns her attention to the little girl. "I understand why. Did you close yours too?"

She shakes her head, then says darkly, "They died. All of them."

Mary's eyes widen in horror. She had a feeling this was the case, but she is still surprised to hear it. She was holding out hope that maybe the surveyors were mistaken. "Do you remember how?"

"You know! The capaemen killed them. Can I go to sleep now?" she snaps.

"Of course, we'll let you sleep. It's just—"

"Yeah yeah, could you stop acting nice? I know why you're helping us. You don't wanna be next. Well, guess what? There's nothing you can do. We're all gonna die. I'm going to sleep now." The little girl hops into Lillian's bed, pulling the sheets over her head.

"E-Excuse me, that's not—"

"I don't care. I'm going to *sleep*," she growls. Mary's jaw hangs open. She has never heard a child talk like that before. Her mom would never let that slide, even with Lillian. Although, looking at her mom's face now, she'd tolerate anything given where these children came from. She gently tucks Max into her bed. He knocks out instantly.

"I'm sorry, Mom. They're tired. We should talk to them later," Mary says. She feels terrible for having done that. She wishes her mother would have waited.

The caretaker pats her on the head. "Yes, we'll talk to them later. You did a good job."

"Thanks. I should check on Lillian now." She looks into her mother's pale-blue eyes. No words pass between them; her face says it all. Miss May is just as terrified as she is.

"Of course. Go help Lillian."

⤞⤝

Her brunette friend waits in the mud room with the others. Some of the oldest gatherers, Noah, Theo, and Bruno, trade stories about people in Zurec who have died. Mary tries to listen in, but they converse in a whisper as if they don't want to be overheard. It's always been like this when it comes to their past. It must be too traumatic to explain the famine to the younger generation. Dozens of people died at once, an amount Mary can't begin to imagine. She probably wouldn't understand. She tries not to dwell on it and instead focuses on her melancholy friend.

Lillian stands alone, as out of place as a flower in winter. Her lips are curled into a slight smile, but her eyes are somber. Bothered. Mary grabs her hand. "Come on, let's talk in private."

"No, I want to stay. What happened with the children?" Lillian whispers.

"I can tell you what happened when we get out of here. Mom will fill in the others. Come on." She's not about to take no for an answer. She tightens her grip on Lillian's hand, dragging her down the hall.

"We passed our room. Where are we going?" she asks, looking backward.

"The kids are asleep in there. Let's go to the storeroom."

Mary dislikes the storeroom, but it's the only place they will have privacy. She leads Lillian toward the food shelving. She likes this part of the room. The shelves create a narrow corridor, blocking them from view of anyone who might walk in. Mary sits opposite Lillian on the dirty floor. Those sky-blue eyes are bloodshot and vacant. It horrifies Mary to see her this way. Even after a grueling day of training, Lillian would practice her spear swings on her own. She would train until she dropped every day. Now, she looks like she doesn't want to touch her spear. It was left behind in the mud room.

"So, uh..." Mary stares at the wall. At the end of the overcrowded shelves, a single torch is lit. It casts a shadow over her friend's face, making her look even drearier. Maybe she should start slow, like with the kids. "How's the spear?" *Really, Mary?* she thinks. Of all the things she could have brought up, why did that come out?

The question seems to work, though. For just a second, there is a spark in her friend's eyes. "It's great."

"Oh really? I'm so glad it worked out. I was scared Mom wouldn't let you have it." She tries not to think about the truth behind Lillian's spear.

"I was too, and I can see why."

Mary's smile falls. "What's that supposed to mean? No one's worked harder than you. You deserve a great weapon, and to be in the gatherers."

"I... didn't do well on our first expedition," Lillian mumbles. Her freckled face is wracked with pain. She hates failing more than anyone, so this must be hurting her deeply.

She grabs her friend's hands. "Please, tell me everything."

Lillian starts from the beginning. She recounts the terrifying leomus attack from which she got her injury and the claustrophobic size of Bunker Two. Her friend's brush with death makes Mary's heart drop, but she doesn't interrupt. Lillian continues with their journey through the dark forest up to their arrival at Albian's clearing. But when she gets there, she stops.

"Go on," the curious girl says. She's terrified, but she must hear the rest. Lillian takes a deep breath. She describes the trapdoor torn off its hinges, the dead woman, and what the burrow looked like inside. The more she talks, the harder Mary finds it to breathe. She doesn't understand how her friend is so calm right now. Lillian has always been stoic, something Mary could never be.

"So, that's what happened," her friend finishes. "I know it's a lot, but hey, at least I'm not dead."

Mary feels sick to her stomach—all those people... gone overnight. Not only did her best friend almost die, but she witnessed a massacre, all on her first mission. Does she even realize how staggering that is?

"What happened with the kids?" Lillian asks, as if not bothered at all.

Now she's trying to change the subject. At most, Mary has one question left. She'd better make it count. "Before that, umm, please tell me, and answer honestly: are you okay? That was... a lot."

The warrior nods. "Why wouldn't I be? Death happens all the time. I just have to get used to it."

Mary swallows. "I... wouldn't put it like that."

"Are you going to tell me about the kids or not?" Lillian says angrily.

She can't push this further. "Okay. Yeah. The boy, Max, was sweet, but Trista wasn't great. When we finally got her speaking, she was rude and very... doomsday. She basically told us that we're all going to die and there's nothing we can do about it. Then she took your bed."

"Wait, she took *my bed*?"

Mary grins. Is that seriously what she got from that? "I mean, she's been through a lot. Still, that's no excuse to be mean to people who took her in."

The brunette crosses her arms. "Where am I going to sleep?"

"Wow, you're *really* torn up about this," Mary says sarcastically. "Don't worry. We can sleep in my bed."

She rolls her eyes. "Sounds great."

"Hey! It won't be that bad. We used to do it as kids. We can do it now."

"We were *smaller* as kids. This is going to suck."

"Oh, come on! Would you rather sleep on the floor?"

"Hey, I never said that." They both laugh. For a faint moment, Mary is reminded of old times. There was a time when all they had to worry about was studying, training, and hiding in the burrow. The adults took care of everything else. Why does that feel so long ago? It's only been a few days since they heard about the capaemen, but it feels like it's been weeks, months even—almost like time has ground to a halt. People used to smile and have fun. There's hardly any of that now. Everyone is on edge. Mary is barely sleeping.

Lillian's eyes glaze over again. She must be deep in thought too. "What do you think my dad will do about the kids?"

"I'm not sure. We'll have to wait until he gets back," Mary says. Seth is kind, but his whimsical plans make him as unpredictable as a phypent.

"Waiting," her friend sighs. "We're always waiting."

Mary frowns. It's true.

step step step...

The sound of footsteps echoes down the hall. "Hey Lillian, you in here?" the monotone voice of Brianna asks.

"Yeah." If Seth is a phypent, then Brianna is a thornopine burrower. She's beautiful, but it's hard to read her. There is no way to know if she will leave one alone or use her thorns.

"We're leaving first thing tomorrow morning. Don't be late." The footsteps immediately fade away. She says everything with such aloofness. It makes Mary nervous. Still, she gives Lillian a fake smile, trying to stay casual. "Wow, leaving already? You just got here."

"Par for the course," her friend responds. She stands. "I should get ready for bed."

"I–I'll come with you."

As the girls change into their loose linen nightgowns and makeshift slippers, Mary thinks again of their childhood. As a child, she always had terrible nightmares. Whenever she had one, she would crawl into Lillian's bed. Her friend was irritated at first but got used to it. Mary was grateful for that. For some reason, the energetic brunette had a way of calming her down. She's excited for tonight. Maybe she'll be able to sleep.

The girls brush their teeth over an empty bucket. When they're done, it's finally time to head to bed. The bedroom is pitch-black, the only light coming from the crack under the door. Lillian leaps over Mary's junk pile, slamming into the bed. It groans loudly. "Lillian!" Mary whispers urgently.

She giggles.

"What is wrong with you? Don't wake them up." Mary tiptoes through her stuff, gently slipping under the covers. She notices the embroidery ring with the strip of brown fabric still in it. That's Lillian's gift! She can't let her see that. She casually knocks it to the floor. Luckily, her friend doesn't notice.

The second Lillian's head hits the pillow, she is out like a light. *How do you do that?* Mary wants to ask. Every time she closes her eyes, her thoughts race.

Lillian will leave again tomorrow. With what's been going on, who knows what could happen next? This could be the last time she—no. She won't go there. Her friend promised that she would survive.

Tomorrow, Mary will be left alone with the kids. Her mother said she needed a break. She is taking a more hands-off approach, letting Mary take care of everyone while she cleans the burrow rooms. It must be for training; after all, Mary will tend to all the children someday. Still, her mother could give her a break after today. Mary doesn't mind cleaning, especially if that means she gets to stop reading *The Adventures of Cecilia and Alida*. She loves that story, but if she must narrate it to the kids one more time, her head will explode.

That isn't even the biggest problem. What if one day their home were attacked, just like Albian? She shudders. No, she can't think that way. She must think positively, or she will never fall asleep.

It doesn't matter anyway. From what Lillian said, if the capaemen find them, it'll be over quickly. All her worries won't matter. There will only be death.

No! Think positive. Think positive. Come on, Mary, you can do this. Lillian is already fast asleep. She's probably dreaming by now. *Clear your mind, Mary. You've got this.* She tries to think like Lillian, keeping all those nasty thoughts at bay. Finally, with her best friend next to her, she drifts off.

7

The Clan That Has It All

Lillian

Lillian wakes up early again. She doesn't want to be late for her next mission, but there's one problem: Mary is still knocked out. It's great that she's asleep, and Lillian doesn't want to wake her. However, the blonde doesn't make that easy; her arms are wrapped tightly around Lillian. She tries to pry them off, but her friend's grip is too strong. She quickly gets frustrated and pushes her. Mary's eyes flutter open. Her pupils are dilated, as if Lillian pulled her out of a bad dream.

"Good morning, you two," Miss May says. She sits on her bed, combing her white hair. On her trunk is a lantern. The flame casts its shadows on the walls. The boy, Max, is still asleep in her bed. It looks like Trista is too, bundled in Lillian's sheets. Lillian narrows her round eyes. The disrespect is ridiculous.

Mary yawns. "Good morning."

"Morning." Lillian throws her feet off the bed and rummages through her friend's junk for the gatherer gear she left there last night. She quickly puts it on, staring at the mess. "Mary, when are you going to clean this?"

"Hey, I need all this stuff," she says, pouting.

Lillian throws the blonde a skeptical look. There are pieces of parchment, clay dolls, pottery, empty jars, unfinished sewing projects, and some stuff she doesn't even recognize. "You don't *need* any of this."

"Lillian is right. Clean up your space, Mary," Miss May says, although not with her usual passion. Even she has given up. "Also, Lillian, you'd better get ready. The gatherers move fast."

"Right." She heads toward the door.

"Wait, I'm coming with you," Mary says.

"Oh no you don't," the caretaker interrupts. "You're getting more sleep. I'm very worried about you."

"Mom, I slept well last night, I swear." This is an obvious lie.

The caretaker frowns. "Even if that were true, you could use more sleep. I know how you are.

Lillian sees where Miss May is coming from. She's been worried too, but she knows Mary is utterly bored in the burrow. She should help her out if only to break up her monotonous routine. "How about this? Mary will see me off, then she can come right back here and go back to sleep. You said the gatherers move fast, right? It shouldn't take long."

The caretaker sighs. "Fine, then. Go on, girls." The girls rush out the door before the caretaker can change her mind.

"Thanks for the save. I wouldn't have been able to go back to sleep anyway," Mary whispers.

"I know." It's a miracle she slept as long as she did. Then again, the two of them used to sleep together as kids. Maybe it's comforting to her.

As they enter the mud room, Lillian realizes Miss May was right. Most of the gatherers are already awake and geared up. It seems they are only missing a few people, including Mia and Jess. Brianna sits near the exit, the torchlight illuminating the freckles on her arms. Her left shoulder plate has the Zurec sigil etched into it. Lillian glances at the shield on her own right arm. It also has the sigil, but it's very faded. Maybe she can get Mary to carve it back in.

The redhead waves at the girls. They approach her. Faint light shines through the trapdoor above. If Lillian were to guess, the sun has just risen. "So, we're going back to Albian's base today," Brianna says.

Lillian's heart sinks into her stomach. Did she hear that right? They have learned all they need. There's no need to go back. "Why?"

"It sounds bad, but we need to. It will haunt us forever if we don't give those people a proper burial."

"That's a good point," Mary says. "They may have been our enemies, but they still deserve that much. Just be safe and watch Lillian. You know she can be reckless." She gives her a concerned smile.

Lillian rolls her eyes. "I *told* you I'm fine."

"She's a good fighter. Better than I was at her age," Brianna says nonchalantly.

The warrior shakes her head. "You had to save me, remember?"

"Didn't I tell you that wasn't a big deal? We can help each other, you know. Although, if you want me to nitpick, you should have stuck to the rear. Let the more experienced fighters take the front and middle. Didn't Miss May teach you that?" She nods guiltily. Miss May told her a long time ago, but at the moment, she didn't remember. She wanted to see what a real fight was like, and that nearly got her killed.

"My goodness! Lillian, *not* following orders? What a surprise," Mary teases. Lillian slugs her shoulder. "Ouch! Hey, you can't deny the truth."

It isn't long before the rest of the gatherers arrive in the main room. Mia is the last. She stumbles in, her backpack overflowing. Jess carries a wooden bottle and frantically tries to stuff it into the already-bursting bag. "Come on, you can do it!" Mia encourages. "We need that extra disinfectant." Lillian could beg to differ.

Mary hugs her goodbye. It's one of her suffocating hugs. "Be safe, please."

"I will, now let go," the warrior says. She knows Mary's not used to her leaving, but geez. She *needs* to get used to it. Lillian did it with her dad. She never wanted him to go, but he always left anyway. She would cling to his leg, cry, and beg. She was so pathetic. One day, she gave up and felt much better. She wonders what he's up to now. *"We're going to look for them. Not attack, not be seen, but we've got to see what they're up to."* She hopes the surveyors have found more clues than the gatherers so far. Right now, their only leads are two traumatized children, and they are hardly talking. She doesn't like their odds. Maybe they will find something else today while they bury the bodies.

Wow, could it get any more desperate? Lillian thinks.

The trek to Albian's burrow seems much faster this time, probably because they skip the detour to Bunker Two. Brianna stands in the clearing of death, staring at the hole ahead. "Here's the plan. Grab whatever you can find—moss, dirt, anything really—and throw it in the hole. We're burying the entire burrow."

"Huh? The whole burrow?" Lillian asks. Most of the poison gas should have dissipated by now. They can get the bodies out and create proper graves. Why would she want to collapse the whole place?

"It may sound strange to some of you," the redhead goes on. "After all, I bet they have stuff we could use, but that feels wrong to me. We should bury them with all their stuff. Let ashes return to ashes."

They stare at the body of the woman just outside of the hole. It's still there, but it's almost a skeleton now. The scavenger phiis work fast. "We should throw her in the burrow with her family," Brianna says, but just as she moves to pick up the body, a voice interrupts her.

"Get out!"

In a split second, everyone's weapons are drawn. It is a human voice, but that does not mean its owner is friendly. Lillian draws her spear. She hopes she can use it correctly this time. *Is it a survivor?* she thinks. She hopes that's not the case. It would complicate things, considering they took their children.

Brianna paces slowly toward the burrow. As the gatherers follow her closer to it, Lillian spots two people coming out.

"Get out!" the same deep voice says again. "Go back to where ya came from, you stinkin' rogues."

The first person, an adult woman, emerges from the hole. "Well, I didn't like you much either. Good riddance, jerk!" She crosses her arms and scowls. This woman is massive—tall and buff. She wears tight grey clothing, her muscles bulging through the silky fabric. She has pitch-black hair, brown skin, full lips, and a diamond-shaped jaw. Her narrow eyes are a piercing green. Lillian can see them all the way from their spot in the clearing.

The second person is a young boy. He stands a few inches shorter than Lillian, but he might be her age. The boy has black hair just like the woman, and long bangs that cover the right side of his face. The left side is juvenile and a little rounder than the woman's. His skin is the same shade of brown and he is dressed in the same peculiar silver clothing. Lillian guesses they're siblings. She rubs her eyes to make sure they aren't broken. She cannot believe it. She's never seen a boy her age before.

The boy follows the woman silently until he spots the gatherers, at which point his visible eye widens. He pulls out two weapons, his face turning to stone. Lillian thought she had a fast draw, but this boy beats her by a mile. One second, he was empty-handed. The next, he has two crescent-shaped blades in his hands and has taken a strange stance. "Jamie," the boy says, glancing at the woman.

The woman glares at the gatherers, then places two fingers in her mouth, and two low whistles escape her lips. "Come on, Amphii! Damn, where is she?" She draws her weapons: dual blades shaped like crescents, the same as the boy's except a bit larger. She smiles crookedly. "What now? Are you their reinforcements?"

"Are you from Albian?" Brianna asks calmly.

"From what now?" It's as if she has never heard the name.

Lillian doubts they're Albian, and judging by the look on their leader's face, Brianna doesn't think so either. Their faces are without a single blemish. The woman wears a golden, circular clip in her hair, holding up a bun, and the boy wears a messy ponytail. Not to mention their grey and tight clothes covering nearly their entire bodies. Around each of their waists is a corset loaded with sharp, foreign objects. Whoever they are, they're not from the Wilds.

"They're rogues," Brianna says. "Where are you from?"

"Osi—" the boy begins to say.

The woman punches him on the shoulder. "Why should we tell *you*?" She's confident, and sort of scary. Meanwhile, the boy is small and seems harmless. They could take him, but Lillian is unsure what the woman can do. Still, right now, there are eleven gatherers versus two of them. If this gets ugly, they will have the upper hand. Then again, who was she whistling for? If they have allies, the gatherers could be in trouble. These two mysterious rogues clearly don't like them already. Lillian can think of multiple ways this could go south, and easily. There are too many unknown variables.

"We don't fight unless we have to. If you aren't Albian, you may leave." Brianna is still so calm.

The woman raises her eyebrows. "You mean, you don't want to kill us?"

"Kill you? You haven't done anything."

The woman sheathes her weapons. "Woah! You guys are a lot nicer than the jerks down there." She points a thumb at the boy. "Yo, Albert. Put away your weapons."

The boy slips the crescent blades into the sheaths on his belt. He looks directly at Lillian, his single dark eye wide with... is that curiosity? Fascination?

clomp clomp clomp...

Before she can figure that out, more company emerges from the burrow. A group this time. The rogues, Jamie and Albert, sprint away from them as if they're poison. They now stand halfway between the two groups, glancing back and forth from Zurec to the strangers from the hole. Their weapons are out again. They're so nimble, moving in the blink of an eye. Lillian burns with jealousy.

At the front of the new group is another boy. He also looks young. He is even taller than the woman and has a commanding presence about him. This must be the owner of the deep voice they heard earlier. His skin is pale, and his hair a bark brown. Spiky black armor sits on his shoulders, and in his right hand is a long blade with a curve at the end. Lillian's breath catches in her throat. That's a scimitar, the weapon of Rostad. He holds the blade down, but Lillian raises her weapon anyway. Rostad has been a wild card since the famine. No one is sure whether they are friend or foe.

Behind the boy, more and more people stream out of the burrow, scimitars in hand, black armor glinting in the sunlight. He gestures for them to stay where they are. Lillian wonders how leadership works in this clan. He seems too young for his position.

He points his scimitar at Brianna. "We've got guests. The Zurec clan, I'm guessing?"

"That's right," she responds, "and you're Rostad?"

"A part of it," he brags. The people blocking the burrow entrance are now at least twenty strong, nearly double the gatherers' size.

"What are you doing so far from your burrow?" Brianna asks. Her stone-cold expression is unflinching.

"Albian is dead. What do ya think we're doing? They have good stuff." His eyes drift to the ground. A few feet away from him is the skeleton. He scoffs at it. Brianna shows a flicker of anger. She wanted to bury Albian with all of their belongings intact. Instead, these jerks are here looting and disrespecting the dead. This is outrageous. Lillian fumes right along with her.

Just as quickly, the redhead returns to her stoic self. "I see, so what—"

"I'm done with questions," the boy interrupts. "This is our turf now. Get your *dying* clan out of here." Brianna clenches her teeth. Lillian balls her fists. She is only seconds away from going ballistic on this blockhead. How dare he disrespect them so blatantly? "Honestly, I don't know how y'all are still standing. It's annoying. Well, at least Albian is dead. I'm sure you're just jumping with joy about that. Too bad their burrow is so close to yours. The *capaemen* are closing in." He smiles crookedly, amused by the horrified expressions.

Enraged, Lillian lunges, but Brianna grabs her arm, returning her to her senses. She shakes her head slowly. They're outnumbered. Now's not the time to fight; now's the time to run. The gatherers back away slowly. The mysterious rogues, Jamie and Albert, follow.

"That's right. Run away." The boy raises both of his arms, gesturing to his huge group. "Flee like the backstabbing *cowards* ya are."

"Shut your damn mouth!" the female rogue blurts. She points a scythe at him. "They're leaving, okay? So you can stroke each other's massive egos once all of us are gone. I can't wait until karma catches up to you and you all get eaten by a massive andremedon."

The boy's jaw drops. "Jamie!" Albert scolds. "Don't insult them. We should leave."

"Yeah. Let's get out of this awful place. It reeks of insolence," Jamie sneers. Together, they all run out of the clearing.

8

Rogues from the Waterlands

Lillian

The gatherers run as fast as they can. Rostad does not follow. Lillian can't stop glancing at Jamie and Albert. The rogues are still with them. After running for a while, over and under tree roots, through bushes and brambles, and past scores of redwood trees, Brianna slows down. They stop in a small clearing.

The redhead eyes the two strangers. "Why are you following us?"

Jamie places her hands on her hips. "Isn't it obvious? We're trying to get away from those jerks too."

"You could have gone anywhere else," Mia says. Brianna raises a finger. The medic closes her mouth.

"You didn't have to follow us to do that," she continues.

"Well, that's not the only reason. I like you guys. You have the honor of accepting *me* into your ranks." Did Lillian hear that right?

Their leader scratches her head. "*We* have the honor? Tell me, why would it be *our* honor to accept *you*?"

"Well, I heard you're low on members." The air tenses. The way the rogue said that so casually is irksome. "Too harsh? Sorry, my brother Albert and I haven't talked to people in a while," Jamie continues. "Look, we've been searching for a clan to join. You guys seem nice. Much nicer than anyone else we've met, especially those Rostad pricks. You interested?"

Brianna regains her composure quickly. "Okay, but why us?"

An awkward pause ensues. Jamie crosses her arms, staring at the redhead as if she's dense. She may have stood up for them a few minutes ago, but that doesn't give her the right to be this condescending. Who does she think she is,

62

following them and demanding to join their clan? Meanwhile, her brother isn't saying anything. He stares at the shadowy canopy, lost in a world of his own.

"I just said I like you guys," Jamie says. "Shouldn't that be enough?"

More silence.

"Wow. Tough crowd. Fine, then. Look, we're from very far away. We've been traveling for a long time and are ready to settle. Right, Albert?" She nudges the boy. He smiles awkwardly.

"Where, exactly, are you from?" Brianna asks, studying their grey clothes. The make is incredible, way better than anything Zurec can do. It's very strange that people like them want to join. It would be amazing if they were telling the truth, but Lillian can't help but suspect ulterior motives.

Jamie scans the group, her lips curling into a scowl. "Where are we from? You wouldn't know it. Trust me."

Lillian crosses her arms. *Wow. She's not even going to explain.* That's definitely suspicious. The boy, Albert, still doesn't speak.

"You're probably right," their leader says, her tone still even. "We're an isolated group. We haven't seen a rogue in over twenty years, much less one who wanted to stay. So, I ask again, why do you really want to join us?"

Jamie smirks. "Honestly, it's just a hunch." Brianna raises an eyebrow. "A hunch that you are good people and would be a good fit for Albert and me." She claps her brother on the back. He glares at her.

Zoey is the first to react. She leans to her left and whispers to Theo and Thomas, no doubt sharing her disdain for the rogues' audacity. The men frown in agreement.

"That's all?" Brianna asks suspiciously.

"Yup. That's all. What do you say?"

"Why were you at Albian's burrow?" Brianna asks, changing her tactic. That's a good question. If they won't tell them where they are from, maybe they'll say why they are here.

"We were traveling through when we spotted the door torn from the ground. Came to investigate. We found, well, all of them dead. Then, living people entered from the deeper part of the burrow. We asked whether they knew the ones who died, and they immediately started being rude to us. I don't like them."

"That's something we can agree on," Brianna adds.

So, that's what happened back there, Lillian thinks. That was her first impression of Rostad, and theirs too. So far, she can see why Zurec has avoided them all this time.

"You got an answer for me now?" Jamie asks impatiently.

Brianna sighs, clearly thinking hard. "It isn't my call to make." The members who were whispering narrow their eyes at her as if they were expecting her to say no. Even though she isn't chief, they would have listened. Apparently, when Lillian's grandfather died, Brianna was the clan's first choice for chief, but she turned it down. As a result, Seth got the role instead. This is something that's always been baffling to Lillian. This woman had a chance to lead the whole clan but instead decided to head a smaller group with the gatherers. If it were Lillian, she would have jumped at the opportunity.

"Huh? You made me answer all those questions when it isn't even your call? Who's the chief then?" Jamie scans the crowd. "They aren't here, are they?"

Brianna shakes her head. "I'm afraid not."

"Well then, take me to them. I'm sure I can gain their approval," Jamie says resolutely. That confidence keeps building. It's annoying, but at the same time, Lillian can't help but admire it.

Brianna sighs in resignation. She must have realized how valuable they could be. "Are you really interested? You'd better not be messing with us."

Jamie crosses her arms. "I would never kid about something like this. I'm dead serious."

The lead gatherer smirks. "Alright, follow me." She turns, her thick red ponytail bobbing behind her.

Just like that, they are on the move again. This feels very strange. Under normal circumstances, Lillian doubts the gatherers would let two strangers follow them, but these are desperate times. Still, it would be risky to head back to the burrow. "Brianna, where are we going?"

"Bunker Two again. We have important supplies to grab." Lillian exhales almost too loudly. Good, they're at least being a little careful. She should take this time to get to know the rogues and determine if they're telling the truth. She walks alongside them.

"Jamie and Albert, huh?" Up close, she notices more details about the two warriors. There is a certain elegance to Jamie's physique. The metal corset around her waist greatly compliments her sculpted torso. The corset is loaded with all sorts of strange weapons, all slightly bigger than the palm of Lillian's hand. What an odd way to hold weapons, but it looks great.

"Yeah, those are our names," she says, noticing Lillian's wandering eyes.

"I'm Lillian. It's nice to meet you."

Jamie nods slightly, keeping her gaze forward.

"W-Where are you from?" Lillian ventures.

"Yes, where?" The leader has taken a spot on the other side of the rogues, studying them both intently. Jamie and Albert turn, surprised. "Brianna." She sticks out her hand.

Jamie hesitates, then shakes.

"Look, you say you're dead serious about joining us. If that is the case, then we need to establish *trust*. You really should tell us where you're from. We've heard of a few places. We may know where it is."

"Osina—" Albert tries to speak, but his sister elbows him. "Hey!"

"It's a place very far away from here. Like I said, you wouldn't know it."

Lillian dislikes how stubborn she's being. Her people may not know much about the wider world, but they can learn. "Brianna is right. You never know. Try us."

"Hmph. It's an island off the coast of Lyonis. A rather large one at that. That's where we're from."

"Osinawa," her brother finishes.

Island? Coast? Lyonis? Osinawa? This is much harder than she thought. She makes eye contact with Brianna, but she looks just as stumped. The other gatherers, who are obviously listening in, also seem confused. "What's an island?" Lillian asks.

Jamie places her face in her palm. "I told you, Albert, the locals here won't understand these terms." The boy shrugs. He drifts over to Lillian, getting uncomfortably close. She can smell his sweat from here. He reeks, but at least she can see his face more clearly. A black piece of cloth is underneath his bangs, covering his right eye—an eyepatch. That must be why he wears his hair like that.

"An island is a piece of land surrounded by water," he says, leaning even closer.

Lillian's nose burns. She leans away. "S-Surrounded by water?" She thinks of the Crystal River. Sometimes rocks jut out of the water. Is that what he means? If so, they must be from a very small place. Or maybe the river is so big that there are lands in between. She can't even imagine it.

"Yeah, that water is called the sea," he smirks.

"Oh, so the sea is like a giant river?"

"Uhh, no. Man, you guys don't know anything." He pokes her forehead playfully.

"I-I'm willing to learn!" She won't be ignorant. Not anymore.

"That's the spirit." He nudges Jamie. "I like this one, sis."

"Hmm, she's not bad." The green-eyed woman looks skeptically at the rest of the gatherers, then back to Lillian. "Hey, kid."

"Y-Yes?" She responds, stiffening. When Jamie looks directly at her, Lillian feels so small.

"What's your chief like? I mean, how accepting are they?"

"Well..." She thinks of Mia, who is the child of a rogue Zurec once took in. Apparently, Mia's father had to pass a few tests before he could join, but that was back when the clan was much bigger. There's no doubt the rules are much laxer now. They need all the help they can get. "We're pretty accepting. I'm sure the chief will give you some sort of test, but it shouldn't be hard."

"Yeah, they'll pass for sure," Mia interrupts. Lillian wondered when she would chime in. She looked like she was dying to speak. "Hello! I'm Mia. Thank you for standing up for us back there, even though it could have gotten us killed. If you hadn't said anything, I might have ripped that snarky boy's—well, you get the picture."

"Yo, I'm Jamie, and this is Albert. I'm sure we'll pass your test with no problem at all."

"Oh yes! My dad passed the tests, and that was back when we had a wayyy stricter chief. This one is so laid back. I know you'll get in. Oh, it's been so long since we've had rogues! This is so exciting." The medic places a hand on her cheek, lost in a memory.

"Sounds good to me. Who's the chief, and how do we earn their trust?"

"His name is Seth. Hmm, if I remember correctly, the previous chief had a rigorous program; part of it included going on multiple missions with different groups who each had their own set of questions. Oh, but I doubt you'll have to do all of that! Seth hated how long that process was. Let's see, first, he will probably interview you at least. You know, to make sure you're decent human beings and share our values. Second, he loves to spar. He'll want to fight you both—to gauge your strength and strategy. Can't have any useless people joining us now, can we?"

Jamie smiles, flashing a set of pearly white teeth. "I like this already. I'd love to see how your chief fights."

"Oh, he's strong. The strongest. And clever. I'd be surprised if you lasted ten seconds."

Her hands drift to her scythes. "Is that a challenge?"

Lillian has never seen her father fight, but she has heard stories: how he can take on two leomus simultaneously and once soloed a thornopine by targeting its weak spots. He even managed to lead a young andremedon, one of the fiercest predators in the Giant Wilds, into a deadly trap. Its foot got caught in a tight cluster of roots, and the surveyors were able to kill it. Her dad has seen countless battles. What has this woman done? Sure, she has some fancy weapons and looks like she can handle herself in combat, but Seth would still kick her teeth in. Lillian would like to see that.

"Wow, so confident!" Mia says. "Hey Brianna, Seth *must* let them join. Put in a good word, okay? He likes you." Brianna doesn't respond.

For a couple of hours, Jamie and Albert get to know each member of the gatherers. On occasion, Albert glances at Lillian, then looks away, pretending he didn't see her. How odd. Is this how boys her age act? He seems so on edge. Meanwhile, his sister is already acting like she has belonged for years. A small crowd gathers around her, listening intently to one story after another. There is no way to know whether anything she's saying is true, but her audience devours the stories like a reading of *The Adventures of Cecilia and Alida*. It's interesting to watch.

After a while, Lillian grows tired of walking. It took them about five hours to get to Albian's burrow. Now they are walking northward again, in the direction of Bunker Two. She's never walked this long in one day before. As she climbs over perhaps the thousandth tree root, it begins to get colder. The sunlight is fading. She wipes the sweat off her forehead, hoping for a break soon. Meanwhile, the two rogues don't seem tired at all. How often do they walk for this long? Well, they are from far away, so probably a lot.

Even as evening sets in, Brianna forges ahead. *Guess she knows best*, Lillian thinks to herself. She looks to Mia, whose breaths have become shallow. Her backpack is weighing her down. She reaches into the side pocket of her pack, pulling out a canteen of water. Realizing how thirsty she is, Lillian does the same, taking her tiny pack off her shoulders and chugging from her canteen. She hopes they get to Bunker Two soon because she's almost out of water.

⁂

As the sun sets, they stop next to an ancient redwood tree. It is so old that giant mushroom heads peek out of its roots. Brianna bends down and brushes piles of dirt off a spot on the ground. This reveals the familiar circular door, just big enough for one person to crawl in at a time. Lillian exhales. Bunker Two.

She never thought she'd be happy to see the place. One by one, they crawl inside. Lillian, Jamie, and Albert are the last to go in.

Inside, their heads nearly touch the ceiling, especially Jamie's, which seems only an inch away from bonking it. At least she doesn't have to stand in a permanent slouch like Bruno. Brianna drifts around, lighting the torches on the walls. The small cavern has a large brown carpet in the center and a tiny hallway off to the side, which leads to a storage room. That's all there is to the place.

After she finishes lighting up the room, Brianna grabs a mat and everyone else follows suit. That is, except for Mia, who rummages through everything in storage. It's unclear what she's looking for.

Lillian's stomach growls. She hasn't eaten since this morning. "Rations in the back," Brianna says as if reading the young girl's mind.

"Thanks."

"Oh, can I come? I'm hungry too," Albert says.

"That's fine," the redhead replies.

"Sweet." He follows Lillian to the back.

The storage room is filled with the stench of rotting wood, much like the main burrow. It makes Lillian feel at home. She grabs a small bowl from the bottom shelf and removes the lid. It's full of dried berries cut into thin strips. She gathers several long pieces and hands the bowl to Albert. He immediately shoves two into his mouth. Next, they grab their mats.

Sitting on their beds, the girl and the rogue scarf down their meal. He eats a little faster than her, which is very impressive. She's never seen someone beat her at eating. Lillian glances at Brianna, who is staring intently. The redhead winks at them. She has no idea what that's supposed to mean.

Jamie sits against the wall nearby, her eyes closed. "Hey Jamie, we have a bed for you over here," Lillian says.

The rogue opens one eye and then stands. Slowly, she unstraps her corset and scythes, placing them against the wall. "Gonna be honest, I'm not very tired."

"Me neither," Lillian says. It's a lie, but she wants to keep talking to them. She looks around the room. Most people are still awake, having their own conversations. Zoey has started a huddle. Most of the gatherers sit in it, telling stories. Meanwhile, Thomas lies on a mat buried in a book. He must have brought it with him from the burrow. It's titled *Capaemen: What We Know*. It's very thin, more of a pamphlet, really, and Lillian's never seen it before. Kayla must have written a new one. At any rate, everyone is doing their own thing. It won't bother anyone if they stay up.

"What happened to your hand?" Albert asks.

Lillian holds up her bandaged palm. She nearly forgot the wrappings were there. "Encounter with a leomus. Things went south."

"Oh, that must suck." He tries to keep talking, but his voice turns hoarse. "Hey," he croaks with difficulty, "you got any water? I'm out." Lillian rummages through her bag, handing him her canteen. He chugs the rest of it.

Rude, she thinks.

"Sorry about that," his sister says. "We ran out of water. We'd go get more, but Amphii is still out hunting, so we can't travel far."

"Amphii?" Lillian asks. Did they have another person with them? They have a strange name.

"Yeah, she's our acera," Jamie says.

"Acera?" She knows what that means. It's the name of the creature in that story they used to read.

"Look, I'm sure you've probably never heard of it, but an acera is—"

"No, no. I have. I know what it is!" Lillian says eagerly.

"Wait, you do?" She looks so surprised it's offensive.

"Yeah. We have records—stories that tell us about the outside world. Aceras are usually brown, with huge wings, round faces, and stubby legs, right?"

"See, I told you. They're isolated, but they're not clueless," Albert says.

Jamie's mouth is still open. "Wow, I wasn't expecting that."

Lillian can hardly hide her excitement. This is straight out of her favorite fantasy story. Cecilia was so strong on Alida. "You two have a real acera? Like, you can fly and stuff?" The two of them nod as if that were a regular thing. All the gatherers have stopped what they're doing, staring at the rogues with dropped jaws. Lillian said that too loud.

"That's amazing! You *have* to take me flying sometime." She looks around, and the Zurec people are now looking at her as if she just grew an andremedon tail. *Come on, they must want to fly on one too.* Everyone grew up reading that story. Maybe they don't believe Jamie is telling the truth. That's fair; they've only just met. Still, Lillian doesn't think the rogues would lie about something like this. It's too specific. Brianna seems to think so too, as she observes the trio with a light smirk instead of a judgmental frown.

"Of course, we'll take you flying. I'm sure your chief will accept us, since I'm going to beat him," Jamie says confidently. Her brother lets out an exasperated sigh and sprawls out on his back. He has probably had enough of that ego to last several lifetimes.

"What makes you think you can beat him?" Lillian asks. Her annoyance has been replaced with curiosity.

"I'm strong. You'll see."

"No aceras allowed."

"Oh, I know that. That just wouldn't be fair. Amphii will be watching from the sidelines like a good girl. Assuming she returns from hunting by then. I'll whistle for her again in the morning."

"I can't wait to meet her," Lillian says. She is practically bouncing on her mat. A real-life Alida and a real-life Cecilia too. She's unsure where Albert fits in this metaphor, but it's still amazing. She's always wanted an acera, but she wasn't sure they were real.

Jamie lays flat on her mat, staring at the dirt ceiling. Lillian lies down too. The rogues lie on either side of her, and Albert is already asleep. He may fall asleep faster than her. She rolls her eyes. She takes great pride in that. Meanwhile, his sister fixes her gaze on Lillian's spear, propped against the wall near Jamie's corset. "So familiar," she whispers. "What's it made of?"

Lillian frowns. "I don't know. The shaft is redwood, but you're asking about the metal, right?"

"Yes. I've never seen it before."

"Really? Haven't you and your brother been all over the world?"

"No," Jamie says. "The world is bigger than you or even I know. We could spend our whole lives exploring it and never see it all."

"Seriously?" She can't comprehend it. After all, to Zurec, this forest *is* the world.

"It's a giant's world, so yeah, I'm serious. Anyway, how did you get the spear? That metal... I've seen something like that before, but it was different where I'm from. I wonder if they have the same purpose."

"Purpose? What do you mean?"

She goes silent for a moment. When she finally speaks again, her tone is much darker. "That isn't something I want to talk about right now."

"Oh... okay. I found it in the forge in our burrow. It was hidden under some boxes. No one was using it."

"Even stranger. Hmm, someone in your clan must know what it is. It's so different from your other spears. Have you tried asking around?"

"No one seems to know anything." That's not entirely true, but those who do aren't speaking up. She glances at the gatherers, but they seem to be busy again.

The story circle has restarted, and Brianna and Mia lie beside one another, not saying a word. It's strange how no one has said anything. *Someone* must have left it in the forge, even if it was long ago. Lillian has been wanting to ask her dad, but he and the surveyors have yet to return from their mission. Miss May knew something but wouldn't talk. She has no idea why, but it's okay as long as she gets to keep the spear.

Jamie yawns. "No one? Maybe it's a relic. It's pretty. I like how it changes colors."

"Thanks." She wants to keep it more than anything, but she doesn't deserve it. After all, she can't even make proper use of it.

They both stop talking, staring at the dirt ceiling as it incrementally shifts from brown to black. Someone is blowing out all the torches. Eventually, Lillian can't even see her own hands anymore.

What an unbelievable day. They found Rostad and two rogues. Lately, it's been one piece of bad news after another. It's nice to finally have some good news. Jamie and Albert seem nice. She was skeptical at first, but she doesn't think they are going to hurt anyone. Besides, they have bigger problems to worry about. Lillian shivers at the thought of all those people, frozen in terror. They must have had no idea what was going on, and then they were dead. It is so appalling Lillian can hardly think about it. She tries to put it out of her mind.

"Hey," Jamie says, breaking the silence. "Why are you the only young person here?"

"Huh?" Lillian asks.

"Don't get me wrong. The people here aren't that old. It's just that there's obviously a huge gap between them and you."

"Oh yeah..." She trails off. Another story about death. How will she explain this?

Jamie yawns. "Oh, never mind. That's a personal question. I'm sure I'll learn later." She whispers the next part. "By the way, Albert is about your age. I'll be keeping an eye on the two of you." Lillian looks at her skeptically. She's not sure what she means by that. "Anyway," Jamie says, "I like you. We should be friends."

"Thanks?" It's an odd time to say that, but she's flattered. As a kid, she wanted nothing more than to be like Cecilia. Now she's met a real-life version of her—at least, she thinks so. "I, um, like you too?"

"Hah! What's not to like?"

Lillian turns over, pretending to fall asleep. That attitude is going to take some getting used to. Nonetheless, this day has been incredible. She can't wait to go back home and see Mary's reaction to all of this. She will freak out when she sees the real-life Cecilia and Alida.

As the warrior drifts to sleep, she dreams of flying like the hero from the story. If that doesn't make one feel invincible, she doesn't know what will.

9

The Crystal River

Mary

"With that, the duo soared into the sky. Apart they can go far, but together they can do anything," Mary says, finishing *The Adventures of Cecilia and Alida* for at least the twentieth time.

"Woo-hoo!" Oscar screams, clapping. "Again, again!"

"Yes, again!" the twins say simultaneously.

Mary closes the book. "Now, let's not get too hasty. A good story is best enjoyed when you have time to reflect on it." *More like when the narrator has time to regain her sanity.*

"Aww, no fair. Can you at least read the part when—" but Oscar cuts off, his eyes darting to the hallway. Mary turns her head and spots Trista in the hall. Her little arms are crossed, and a big pout is etched on her face. Her brother Max lingers behind her.

"That story was trash," she says.

"Hey, you don't even know it, Albian girl." Oscar sticks out his tongue.

"Oscar!" Mary scolds. "That isn't nice." She studies Trista. The little girl doesn't seem offended.

"It's all mushy and gushy and happy. Sorry to break it to you, but the world's not like that," the little girl says.

"Hey, it can be," Oscar argues, rage boiling in his little brown eyes.

"It isn't. Ever. Even when you're happy, it's fake. Trust me."

Mary dashes to Trista. "Now Trista, isn't that too negative?"

She shrugs Mary off. "No, it's realistic."

"How about we talk about this in the other room?" She can't believe someone so young is saying something so hurtful. She glances at Max, trying to see if he agrees, but all he does is stare at the floor.

"Don't even bother. I'm going back to sleep," Trista says. She grabs her brother's hand and storms back into their bedroom. Mary stands there, unsure if she should follow or tend to the other children.

creeaaaakkk

She doesn't have much time to think about it, as the trapdoor is opening. The first to enter the mud room is Chief Seth, followed by the surveyors clad in hide armor. Some of their spears are stained with blood. "Seth!" Mary scans the group, making sure none of them are missing. "You're all alive. That's great."

"Of course we are," the chief responds. "Where's Miss May?" Mary points to the back. Seth nods.

"What happened on your journey this time?" she asks, looking at the rest of the group. They ignore her, heading to their rooms. She sighs. *Oh well. I guess I'll ask Mom after they brief her.* She checks on the three children, who seem just as curious as her. "We'll find out later," she tells them, smiling.

After another five readings of the children's story, Mary's mother finally comes out of their room. Following her are Seth and all the surveyors, still fully armed.

"Wh-What's going on?" Mary asks. Even the caretaker is geared up. She holds her old spear from her gatherer days and wears a complete set of Zurec armor. Her white hair is tied in a ponytail, and her eyes are stony—a warrior's eyes. She looks at least ten years younger, almost like she fits in with the adults. Mary sometimes forgets the twenty-year age gap between her mother and the second-oldest members of the community. It must get lonely being the only clan elder.

Her mother gives her a faint smirk. "What does it look like? Get geared up, Mary. We're going to the Crystal River."

The Crystal River? Mary stares at her dirt-caked hands. She could use a bath. Not to mention everyone else. They all stink.

"Oh, and I've already let Max know. He's getting ready, but Trista... You're the best with her. Can you get her out of bed?" her mom asks.

Mary sighs internally. *Here we go again.* She looks to the children for support, but they aren't paying attention. They're too busy jumping up and down with excitement. "Of course, I'll go get her."

"I know you can do it," her mother encourages.

Mary makes her way into their room. The small lump that is Trista rests under the blankets of Lillian's bed. "Hey, Trista," she says, placing a hand on the bulge.

"I don't wanna go," she whines. The lump scrunches a bit.

"Well, you have to. I know you and Max just washed up, but you're still stinky. The river is so much better for getting clean. Now, get out from under there."

"No, I don't wanna," the little girl says, her voice cracking.

"Well, would you rather stay here, all alone?"

The lump that is Trista freezes. Then, slowly, she lifts the covers off her head, revealing bloodshot eyes. Her brown-black hair sits in a tangled nest, covering parts of her face. "I'm fine alone."

The poor girl melts Mary's heart. She wishes she could know more about what happened to her and her brother. Baby steps, though. "We're going with the surveyors. It's the safest we could be. You've got to get out sometime, right?"

Trista sniffles. "It's never safe. Don't lie to me."

"No, but—" What can she say? They all know it's true. She decides to take a page from Lillian's book. "What's the fun of life without a little risk, right?"

"Huh, fun?"

"Yeah, if we didn't have sadness, happiness wouldn't be as sweet. I think... I think it's the same for danger. If we don't have risk, what's so great about being safe?"

The little girl looks at her quizzically. "I don't get it."

Mary pats her head. That's too complicated for someone her age. "Oh, forget it. How about this? Let's have a competition. Count all the bugs and creatures you see on our adventure. I'll count too. Whoever has the most when we get home will be the winner."

Trista's face lights up. "What do I get if I win?"

"Hmm, let's see. I'll make you something. Anything you want," Mary says.

"You're on! And if you win, I'll uh, I'll..." She stretches out her arms. "I'll give you a big hug!"

"That sounds wonderful," Mary says, chuckling. She heads toward the door. "You coming?"

"Yes!" Trista says excitedly.

On her way out, however, Mary realizes she forgot something. She rushes back into the room, grabs a sack, and stuffs it with her dirty clothes. Then she glances over at Lillian's side. She should do her laundry too, since she isn't here.

Mary stuffs Lillian's clothes in the sack. That girl wears the same thing every day, so her dirty laundry is half the size but smells twice as bad. Mary recoils at the scent. Closing the sack, the hurried girl rushes to the storeroom to find some armor. She straps it on. Arms, shoulders, shins, knees. She straps a shield onto her arm, then grabs one of the extra spears: a small, stone-tipped one. It'll do. Lastly, she removes her fur headband and ties up her hair, making a messy ponytail. Mary heads to the mud room, ready to go.

After shutting the trapdoor, Seth leads the way. Mary, her mom, and the children walk in the middle of the group, with surveyors stationed in front and behind them. Poor little Trista can't stop shivering, and her brother clings to the caretaker. At least one thing is working well. A large beetle crawls on the ground near their feet. "One," Trista mumbles. Her mother glances in her direction, those blue eyes full of approval. Mary nods. Frankly, she doesn't deserve the praise. It wasn't that hard.

As the spring air hits her, the caretaker's daughter feels she can finally breathe again. A leaf falls from the canopy. She watches it drift toward the ground. It has a long way to go.

Her peace is short-lived, as someone grabs her arm. The black-haired boy with warm brown eyes stares up at her, moving his tiny legs as fast as he can to keep up with Mary's long strides. His muddy shoes look like they need to be replaced. He sniffs. "Hi, Mary."

"Hey, Oscar," Mary says, tousling his hair.

"Stop it!" he says, slapping her hand away, although he smiles as he does it. On Mary's other side, someone tugs at her shirt. She looks down to see dark-brown hair and green eyes. It's Trista's brother, Max. When did he get away from her mother?

"Hi, Mary."

Mary messes with his hair too. "How are you holding up?"

"I'm okay," the little boy says. He stares at the bushes nearby as if something is going to jump out of them. Mary quickly realizes Oscar is doing the same thing.

"Now boys..." Their little eyes fall on her. "It is not your job to watch for monsters. Let the surveyors do that." The surveyors have made a circle around them. When it comes to the Giant Wilds, Mary couldn't feel any safer.

As they walk, the plants gradually get thicker and greener. The canopy above becomes more crowded, letting in less sunlight. Birds chirp from its branches, and bugs fly by, their wings shimmering in what little light is left. Admiring the beauty of the forest, Mary feels almost relaxed. That is until she spots something massive bursting through the leaves above.

fwoosh fwoosh

She recognizes it immediately: a light-yellow beak, dagger-like talons, and scaly brown wings spread wide. Even without being able to spot a single, curved horn on its forehead from this distance, Mary is sure what this menacing creature is. It's a narecon—exactly like the one that separated Cecilia and Alida in the story. "Duck into that root," Seth commands. He says it just loud enough for the group to hear, but not so loud as to startle the flying predator above.

The surveyors rush the children into a nearby root cave. These become more common as one nears the river. Some wood-eating bug species like to make these caves, and although they damage the trees, they are fantastic hiding spots for Zurec. They rarely stretch on for long, but it's hard for anything to ambush them inside one. Even if the creature circling overhead did attack, the surveyors would have the advantage. Still, Mary's heart pounds in her chest as Oscar and Max throw their arms around her.

The caretaker, Kayla, Mary, and the children huddle together on the cavern floor while the surveyors stand closer to the entrance. Mary pats Max's back. "It's okay," she whispers. "They will protect us." It's not like this hasn't happened before. The surveyors have protected them from forest beasts countless times: leomus, phypents, thornopine burrowers, and even a young andremedon once. Narecons are difficult to fight against, though. They are tactful predators that ambush from the sky with lightning speed.

Mary peers past the terrified children at the surveyors, stationed at the ready. Some of them stand farther into the cave, closer to the children. In the low light, she can make out the silhouettes of Carmen and William. William usually flanks Seth, but right now he bends down next to Kayla, his wife, assuring her that he will protect their burgeoning little family. He places one hand on Felix and the other on her belly. She nods resolutely.

Meanwhile, Seth and his friend Elias stand at the entrance. They watch the canopy without a hint of fear in their stances. It has only been seconds since they've hidden, but each moment feels like an hour. Mary bites her lower lip.

What those two men are doing is risky, although they should have enough time to duck into the cave if the narecon were to swoop down. Still, even the thought of that is terrifying. They are endangering their lives just to keep watch. Mary could never be a surveyor.

She's glad Lillian isn't one of them either.

Mary watches Seth and Elias, waiting impatiently for them to give a sign. Then, to her relief, their chief raises his hand and makes a beckoning gesture.

"It has passed," he says. "We're safe."

The group breathes a collective sigh of relief. Mary and her mother guide the children back outside, but Trista still seems to think they're in danger. She stares southward with dread. "Hey, it's okay. We're safe now," Mary reassures her.

The little girl doesn't respond.

Abruptly, Mary remembers something. Hadn't Trista said she hid in a bush from the capaemen? It's not the same thing, but having to hide from sudden danger... *Oh no*, she thinks. This event must have triggered those memories. Now Trista must be regretting coming outside with them. Mary must think fast. She needs to remind her of the bright side of things, not to let her spiral. "Hey, how many bugs have you seen so far?"

"What?" Trista asks. It's as if she's forgotten.

"Remember our competition?"

"Oh yeah!" She scans the ground.

Crisis averted, and just in time. The Crystal River is only a half hour away from their burrow. "We should be there soon," Mary says.

"Really? That's fast. It's really far from my old home," Max responds. He has made his way over to the two of them, clearly to check on his sister. "The trip was always hard."

"It was?" Come to think of it, according to the maps Kayla has drawn, Albian is pretty far away from the river. A couple of hours, at least. Mary recalls what she knows about Albian's history with her people. Their homes are so far away from each other. To think, during the famine, they once infiltrated Zurec's burrow and collapsed many of its rooms. That is all over now, though—thanks to the capaemen. Things can change so quickly, just like the current of the river.

"Yeah," Max continues, "but my mommy told me to be brave..." He looks at his sister as if asking for her approval. Trista glares at him, her little fists clenching. Max averts his eyes, kicking up mounds of dirt as he walks. Mary wonders what that exchange was about. She wishes she could see into their minds, figure out exactly what happened to them.

whoooooossshhh

The familiar *whoosh* of flowing water rises from ahead. *Almost there!*

When they reach the river, the chief has everyone put their stuff down near some algae-covered boulders. Mary throws off her backpack and laundry sack. She rolls out her shoulders. Oscar and Max return to the caretaker, their nerves melting away at the prospect of playing in the river. The kids strip to their underwear. "Swimming! It's time to go swimming!"

The river is a sight to behold. Even though Mary has seen it a hundred times, it always takes her breath away. The red roots of the thousand-foot trees twist and tangle into the water. Many tall plants arch over the bank, their leaves reflecting off the clear surface. No matter the depth, one can see straight to the bottom, hence the name Crystal River. A plethora of multicolored rocks litter the river floor, their beauty illuminated by the bright-orange sun. They shimmer and shine as the leaves sway above. If Mary looks far down at the riverbed, she can sometimes spot giant fish swimming by. They usually travel in pods, following the river's flow. She hopes she sees some today.

The river must be miles wide because from this bank, the other side looks so far away. From this distance, the thousand-foot trees look like saplings. A thick fog obscures the plants beneath them, bathing the forest floor in shadow. Zurec has never ventured to the other side of the river. All Mary's been told is that evil lurks there. She's not sure what that means, but she trusts the adults. If they say so, it must be true.

The kids and caretaker always bathe first while the surveyors stand guard. To get ready, Mary removes her armor and throws off her U-neck top and leggings, leaving on only her bra and underwear. Next, she removes her necklace and bracelets, and gently places them on her bag. The breeze chills her bare skin.

As Mary steps into the water, she gets more chills. The freezing cold temperature prickles her skin like a million needles. She'll get used to it, though. Everyone stays in the shallow end, rubbing the dirt off their arms and legs. It is said that those who try to swim to the middle will be eaten by a giant fish. Mary chuckles. She's swam in the deep end before. Well, not the deepest part of the river, not even close, but she does like to venture where her toes can't touch. She used to compete with Lillian for who could swim the fastest. Mary always won. It's one of the few things she's better at than her.

The blonde dunks her head under the surface. In the water, her hair follows the current. The light, southward flow is relaxing. She opens her eyes and searches for the prettiest stones, gathering several before coming up for air. These will make for great pieces of jewelry.

At the surface, she spots the children. The boys, Oscar and Max, splash the girls. Behind them, Kayla and Miss May watch, smiling. Eventually, Trista gets fed up with their shenanigans and splashes them even harder. This starts an all-out war. The twins gang up on Oscar and Felix, while Trista and Max have the most intense splashing competition Mary has ever seen. It ends with the sister tackling her brother into the water. Kayla quickly wades over, throwing her off him. "Don't do that! Do you want your brother to drown?" Then she casts a glance at the boys and twins. "Take it easy! Felix is only three. Too young for a splash war."

"They started it!" Trista screams. "They need to say they're sorry."

"Bath time is over," her mother intervenes. "If you have time to goof off, you must be clean. Mary, come on out." And just as quickly as their fun began, they must get out. The adults drag the kids out of the river. They kick and scream, but it doesn't do much. When Mary emerges from the water, her mother hands her a used towel. She dries her hair and tries to keep mud from sticking to her bare feet, at least until she can get to her shoes.

As the children dress, the younger surveyors—those in their late twenties and early thirties—strip down and head in. The people in their late thirties to early forties stay on the shore. So does Seth. He glances at Mary then quickly looks away. She's not sure why.

As Mary changes, the first group of surveyors bathe. They scrub their skin rapidly with washcloths and then do a quick dunk under the water. They are always so efficient. None of them talk to each other, either. Mary can see why; they could be attacked at any time. They need to stay focused. A few of the surveyors rarely talk to others anyway. Finn, for instance, prefers the company of her equally shy husband, Gabriel. They bathe next to each other in silence. Meanwhile, Carmen is already wading back toward the shore, squeezing water out of the long side of her hair. The other side is shaved—an odd but compelling look. She reminds Mary of Lillian, if Lillian actually listened to orders. She is one of the strongest warriors in the surveyors, and she's great at her job. Since she's so focused, she rarely socializes.

After changing, Mary throws her laundry sack over her shoulder, grabs a washboard, and finds a shallow area along the riverbank away from the group. She positions the washboard over the river and grabs a jar of soap powder from her bag. They make this by grinding down specific plants picked by the gatherers. Dashing the powder over a fur-bristled brush, Mary begins scrubbing. As she gets busy, someone approaches her. "Doing my daughter's laundry again, huh?" Mary's head jolts up to face the chief. He takes a seat beside her. No one else is around, not even William or Elias. How strange. Seth doesn't talk to Lillian much, but he talks even less to Mary. This is as rare as a capaeman sighting.

The chief strokes his stubbled chin. "What would she do without you?"

Mary chuckles. "I wonder that every day. How did the mission go?"

"It was a wash. We don't have the first idea how to track capaemen."

She tries to focus on scrubbing Lillian's stinky shirt. This is just too weird. "It's in times like these I wish we were better allies with Rostad. You know, the clan down south? They see capaemen all the time. They could help us."

Mary nods again. Rostad is also weird. They haven't been in contact with Zurec for decades, yet everyone walks on eggshells when it comes to them. It's natural to fear what one doesn't know, but Mary still finds it strange that no one has suggested talking to them. After all, they're the only other humans left in the Wilds—Zurec's only potential ally against a massive threat. What does she know, though? She's only the caretaker's daughter. She isn't qualified to think about these things, and she can never understand the trauma her family endured before she was even born. She almost feels guilty about it.

"Anyway, I'm not here to chat. Although, I'm sure you already know that," he continues.

"I figured," she says coldly. He wants something from her.

"Have you told Lillian about her spear yet?"

Mary nearly tears the shirt she's cleaning in half. She was expecting many things, but not this. "No... why?"

"Well, when she finds out, I want it to come from you."

Mary remembers what her mom said: "*It was her mother's. She asked me to give it to Lillian on her fifteenth birthday.*" Lillian's horrible mother who left with another clan.

She doesn't know much about that group—only that they came from outside the Wilds, and when they left, Emilia went with them. So *that's* why Seth is here. He wants to shirk his fatherly responsibilities... again. She grits her teeth.

"Why do you want *me* to tell her?"

"Honestly, she'd take it best from you. The rest of us would make her angry. Please, I don't ask much of you," Seth begs, looking very uncomfortable.

She squeezes the water out of the shirt. "Why did we even have it here anyway, if it belonged to that horrible woman?"

"That's my fault," he says sadly. "I couldn't throw it away."

Mary sighs. She's heard the story. Not only did Lillian's mother leave her, but she said goodbye to Seth in a letter. It destroyed him. This is a sensitive topic for Seth; maybe it is best if she breaks the news. "Okay, I guess I'll do it."

"Thank you, Mary." He stands. "The surveyors and I will head out again tomorrow morning." With that, he leaves. He got what he came for.

This is a part of her responsibilities as the future caretaker: to take on the role of a parent. She just wonders how she's going to go about it. Lillian will be furious no matter what, but is there a way to make her *less* furious? Mary tries not to think about it for now. She's got enough on her mind.

As the future caretaker finishes washing the clothes, she stares at the Crystal River. She wonders how Lillian is doing right now. Maybe the gatherers have had better luck than the surveyors. She sure hopes so, but she also hopes not. That may put Lillian in more danger. More than anything, she wants her closest friend to be safe. That can't be too much to ask for.

Soon, the final group of surveyors bathes, and before they know it, it's time to go home. Mary stuffs the wet clothing in her sack. It's ready to be hung up when they get home.

As they leave, Mary takes one last glimpse at the river. She has no idea when they'll be back. With how rapidly things are changing, she doesn't know about anything anymore. She hopes the surveyors find a lead. Or maybe she can get answers out of Trista and Max. Trista seems to listen to her and no one else. Only she can do it. Yes, she *has* to.

If they don't find a way to stop what's coming, they are all doomed.

10

The Bird Stained with Black and Red

Lillian

At first light, the gatherers stream outside one by one. No one wants to be in Bunker Two any longer than they must. Aboveground, a cool breeze twists through the trees. Lillian is one of the first out of the burrow. When the company awoke, she bundled up her mat and leaped over everyone to stuff it back in the storage room. She *had* to get out. The air is so thick in there it's hard to breathe.

Right behind her, someone follows. "Good morning, Giant Wilds!" the confident voice of Jamie says.

Albert stumbles after her. "Good morning." He claps Lillian on the shoulder.

"Hey," she replies.

"So, excited to go back home?" he asks.

"I guess," she says, staring at her feet. Despite yesterday, she's still nervous about bringing these strangers home. By the looks of the other Zurec members, she's not the only one feeling that way. They stay a distance away but are watching the rogues closely. One mistake, and she's sure the gatherers will tear them away from Lillian.

Albert sighs deeply. "Oh, man. I can't wait to sleep in an actual burrow. Jamie and I have been sleeping in the trees. I can't believe we're not dead. Well, more like how *I'm* not dead. My sister is invincible."

"You've been sleeping in the trees? How?" Lillian asks, trying to act like she doesn't notice the watchful eyes of her kin.

"Ahem!" Jamie interrupts. She throws an arm around her brother. "Albert. New home. New start. Please spare these poor people your self-deprecating jokes."

"Oh, but Jamie, I simply pale in comparison to you. You don't have *a-cera* in the world." He winks at Lillian.

Jamie's face flushes. She wraps her arm around his neck. "Really? A pun? You want to die?"

Albert struggles in her choke hold. "That's why... I said it," he wheezes. "Jamie... can't... *breathe.*" Lillian laughs. His sister seems like a handful.

Jamie releases her stranglehold. "Don't encourage him. He'll never stop."

"Oh, come on, that was funny. Maybe it isn't him. Maybe you need to loosen up a bit, because I think you *a-cera* a little too much." She smiles slyly.

The woman's jaw drops. "By the plains, I've been betrayed. How could you cross to his side like that?"

Albert throws an arm around Lillian. "I knew this clan would be a great fit! How does it feel to lose for once, sister?"

"I didn't lose—" but she stops in the middle. "Let's change the subject. Tell us, Lillian, what is your main burrow like? Will we be going there soon?"

As she forms an answer, the gatherers begin to move. "The burrow is much bigger than any of the bunkers. It has lots of bedrooms, a much bigger storeroom, and a forge if you take the stairs far underground. As for when we're going back, I think that's our next destination. Today."

"Sweet! So, I take it you trust us now? I knew you would."

Lillian scoffs. For crying out loud, they just met. "I wouldn't go that far. You still have a test to pass, and I have no idea what the surveyors will think either." She glances at the gatherers walking behind them. Jamie and Albert must have noticed their skeptical gazes. Brianna is observing them like a phypent stalks its prey. Lillian is sure she's speaking for all the gatherers when she says this: "We need help, sure, but we've just met, and trust takes time."

"Oh..." For once, Jamie doesn't have much to say.

"That's fair," Albert finishes, glancing at the other gatherers. At least one of them has noticed. "We're willing to wait as long as it takes." Their faces have grown grim. They are avoiding eye contact with Lillian as if she said something terrible. She doesn't understand why. She only told them the truth.

After a period of uncomfortable silence, Jamie drifts away from her brother and Lillian. She starts a conversation with Brianna, and soon enough, they are talking up a storm. Other more chatty gatherers like Mia and Zoey join in, and soon there is a whole group around the two of them. Lillian has never seen Brianna speak this much before.

Meanwhile, she walks by Albert, still in silence. She has so many questions, but that cold look in his single eye is making her hesitate to ask. She wonders if they've seen anywhere more beautiful than the Giant Wilds. The outside world is so big. There's got to be something that beats this place. She looks down at the moss under her shoes, then up at the swirling red and brown of the trees. The leaves look so small up there. Hundreds sit scattered on the forest floor, slowly crumbling to pieces, and they're huge. Still, it's all the same. Red trees, big roots, and moss—lots and lots of moss. She often fantasized about adventuring with the surveyors, exploring new environments, and expanding their knowledge of the Giant Wilds, but that's not the duty of the gatherers. They circle the same few places, picking up materials. It isn't a bad job, but it will get boring fast.

Lillian stares at the mysterious boy. He has been to so many places; the Giant Wilds must be so boring to him. He stares into the distance, his face unreadable. She decides she's tired of the silence. "Hey, can you tell me what the waterlands are like?" She hopes she said that right.

"Waterlands? Oh, you mean the ocean," Albert responds, still in a daze. "It's beautiful, but a pain in the rear to cross. My sister and I left Osinawa when I was young, so I don't remember much about the ocean, only that I got tired of it very fast."

"Did you fly across it on that acera you have?"

"Oh no! No way. Amphii can't fly for that long. We would have fallen into that endless water hole and died."

"How did you do it, then?"

"We, uh... Heh. Well..." He scratches the back of his head. "We stowed away on a ship."

"What is—"

"Ships are huge structures that float and travel on water. My sister, Amphii, and I got on the back of a huge cargo ship. The crew had no idea."

"Woah! People have things like that in the outside world?" A glimmer of hope ignites in Lillian's eyes. Maybe the outside world isn't as terrible as she thought.

"No, not people."

At first, she doesn't get what he means. Not people? Lillian's eyes widen. "Oh... I see. Wait, you rode on a *capaeman* ship?!"

"I know. For the record, it was Jamie's idea. It was easy to hide in the cargo of the ship. They have way too much stuff. So, it worked out, and it was more than worth it to get away from home."

"You wanted to leave so badly that you snuck onto a capaeman ship?" Lillian asks, still unable to believe it.

His eye glazes over much more than before. "Yeah."

"What made you take such a huge risk?"

"Please, not that. I'll talk about anything else."

Lillian swallows her curiosity. Something terrible must have happened to make them cross the ocean like that. She understands there may be some things they don't want to talk about. After all, she's not eager to mention the famine, nor Albian. She changes the subject. "Okay, what were they like? The capaemen, I mean?"

"Huh? Why do you want to know *that*?" He backs away a little.

"Call it morbid curiosity." He doesn't look like he believes her. "Okay, fine," she continues. "I do have a reason. Our clan... we're in trouble. They're after us, and we don't have the first idea how to survive. The first thing I thought when I met you both was that you might know something. Anything will help."

Albert grits his teeth. "Damn it, why do they have to be *everywhere* we go? No matter where we run, they are always there. They hunt us relentlessly, and for what?" Before Lillian can make sense of what he said, they're interrupted.

fwoosh fwoosh

It sounds like the beating of wings. Could that be the acera? Jamie lets out a loud gasp. "That's not Amphii! We're under attack!"

"Get down!" Brianna commands. As she says that, the creature lands right on top of them.

⁕ ⁕

Screaming erupts from the gatherers. The monster swoops straight into the middle of the group. Its back faces Lillian, so she can't see anything but the wings and a long pointy tail. The wings, each one longer than Lillian's entire body, are jet-black, unlike anything she's ever seen or read about. Lillian draws her bow but has no idea how she's going to use it. The wings beat up and down, blowing huge gusts of wind in all directions. The creature is so big that simply moving seems like an attack. Lillian digs her heels into the ground, trying not to be blown away. If she fired an arrow now, it would just go flying.

The gatherers must have already realized this. They drew their spears first, and Theo and Brianna are already rushing the monster. Next to Lillian, Albert draws his scythes and runs around the gargantuan wings. He's heading for the front. She follows him, ditching her bow in favor of her spear. It shines black. Now's not the time to panic. If they can get in view of its head, they can figure out what it is—maybe even kill it. She can redeem herself from the leomus fight.

SCREEEEEEE

Before they can reach its front, a piercing sound comes out of the creature. Lillian doubles over, covering her ears. She's never heard anything like that before, and it's so loud that her ears might burst.

Following it is another sound: Jamie's whistle. She's calling for her acera again. "Amphii! We're in big trouble. Please!"

Albert places two fingers in his mouth, letting out a whistle louder than Jamie's. "Come on!" he yells.

The gatherers attempt to fight the creature as it swats them away like flies. They fall to the ground left and right but quickly get back up again. "This is not normal!" Mia screams. Her husband, Bruno, shields her with his massive body, keeping her from blowing away in the gusts from the bird's flapping wings.

Then, just as soon as it landed, the creature takes off again. An even bigger gust of wind slams into them like a thunderclap. This time, Lillian is knocked to the ground, but she doesn't take her eyes off the monster. As it ascends, her eyes lock on its massive claws. When she sees what's in them, time seems to slow down.

In the talons is a mangled human body. Blood rains in thick, viscous droplets toward the ground. "Noah!" Mia screams.

The eldest of the gatherers has died.

Miss May helped raise him, and ever since then he has been with the gatherers, guiding Brianna as she navigated leadership and helping train new members. Most of what Lillian knows about him has been observational. They never talked, but still, he's a part of her family.

Flashes of Albian's burrow move through Lillian's head. Her elbows buckle under her. That is what will happen to her if she fights back: she will end up a bloodied corpse—a memory frozen in agony.

Calm down, Lillian. Now's not the time to think about that. You must be strong.

This is the reality of the Giant Wilds. Lillian was... prepared for this. This is not their first loss, either. People die all the time. This is still better, yes, much better than being in the burrow. She tries to take in the forest air, now filled with dust. When did it get so hard to breathe? She feels just like she did when she brought Max home, except much worse. *Breathe, Lillian.* She must stand up and fight. Fight for what they've lost. *Stand,* she thinks, but her body isn't listening.

"Hey," Albert grabs her hand and yanks her up. She looks into his single eye. Again, there's no warmth in his expression. "This is no time to be scared. Mourn later, fight now."

That snaps her out of it. She looks up, and the monster is still above them. Logically, it should retreat now. It already has a meal. However, as it flies higher and higher, its talons loosen on the corpse.

thud.

Noah's lifeless body crashes onto the forest floor. This isn't how birds hunt. Lillian knew something was off about this monster. Now she's sure of it. She studies the creature. It has pitch-black, gargantuan wings for front limbs and long clawed talons for back ones. Protruding from either side of its angular head are two spiked horns, each next to two crimson eyes, giving it four eyes in total. Contrasted against its black scales, the beak is the most noticeable part: a dark-yellow color, like rotting teeth.

It looks like a narecon, but their feathery scales are usually brown, not *black.* They don't have two horns, and they never get this big. This beast is nearly twice the size of a regular narecon. Also, none attack this aggressively. At most, they snatch one person and fly away. This one just threw away its meal, and its four eyes still look so hungry.

It's in this for the kill.

First, the leomus were acting strange, now this. Why is it so riled up? The surveyors may have been able to fight it, but the gatherers aren't equipped for this. At this rate...

Jamie whistles twice again. "Amphii, please! People are dying!" The narecon plunges toward them again.

SCRAAAAA

Another cry echoes through the Giant Wilds, but not from the narecon this time. Lillian glances at Jamie, who stays close, her fingers still in her mouth. "I'm over here, Amphii!" She whistles again, but this attracts more than just the acera's attention. The black beast changes direction, diving straight for her. She moves out of the way in the nick of time. Brianna slashes underneath its wing.

Together, she and the gatherers push the creature back, but its sharp talons slash at them, one slicing straight through the shoulder of a gatherer. She falls to the ground, but the pack keeps pushing. In the chaos, Lillian can't tell who it is, but she has a feeling they just lost another person.

"Surround it and slash whatever you can. Weaken it!" Brianna commands.

At their leader's order, the gatherers regroup and form a circle around the beast, spears slashing every which way. Lillian and Albert join the circle. She goes for a wing, but every one of her attacks misses. How can something so massive move so quickly? She looks around; no one's having much luck.

"Close the circle. Slowly. It either has to fight us or fly away!"

One step at a time, the circle constricts. Next to Lillian, Albert pulls something out of his corset. He throws them at the creature. The hand-sized, star-shaped blades glint silver as they fly. One lodges in a wing. The other bounces off the narecon's scales and lands uselessly on the ground. "Oops, I'm out of practice," Albert says. His tone is a lot lighter than earlier.

As if realizing what the humans are trying to do, the narecon raises its gargantuan wings again and takes flight. This pushes the gatherers back, but no one falls over this time.

"Ha, it's retreating! Not so big and bad now, huh?" Albert hollers. But the narecon doesn't look like it's flying *away*. More like... recalibrating. It hovers midair, then screeches again.

SCREEEEEEE

Albert's smile drops. "Uh-oh."

"We have to ground it. Archers, draw your bows!" Brianna screams. Milo, the best archer of the gatherers, already has his bow drawn. The other gatherers hurry to catch up. Meanwhile, Jamie still stands outside the circle, her fingers in her mouth. She blows one last whistle.

WHUMPF

A large figure lands behind her, sending moss and dust flying into the air. It looks almost exactly like the winged creature from *The Adventures of Cecilia and Alida*. It cranes its neck toward their scaly adversary and growls, one of its legs wrapped protectively around Jamie. From one glance, Lillian can tell it is quite a bit smaller than the narecon. It also looks very odd. Its light-brown skin is soft, yet hairless and somehow reflects the canopy light. Its legs are long yet muscular, and it has flat, almost webbed feet. Its face is round and slightly pudgy, with huge bulging eyes. It growls again, revealing layered rows of sharp teeth. Its tongue is long and pointed.

"Amphii, that's a good girl. Now let's teach this bird a lesson." Jamie steps onto the acera's wing like it's the most natural thing in the world, hopping into a saddle on top. It's as if Cecilia and Alida leaped straight out of their storybook.

From a sheath in the saddle, Jamie pulls out the biggest scythe Lillian has ever seen. This one has a chain attached to it. Then, the rogue clicks her tongue twice: a command. Amphii spreads her brown wings and soars into the air, charging at the narecon. The two monsters dart through the trees like lightning.

"Damn, she left me behind again. I wanted to go," Albert says. He still stands next to Lillian. "Don't worry, guys, she's got this." Brianna and the other warriors watch in disbelief as Jamie's chain scythe flies around like a whip. Now it's turned into a hunt, with the black bird fleeing through the mess of tree branches and the acera following close behind, that deadly whip repeatedly flying toward the monster. Some thinner branches break clean off the surrounding trees, crashing to the floor below.

"Get back here, you coward!" Jamie screams. Sometimes Lillian can see the massive scythe glinting in the sun. Other times she only sees its outline through the leaves—a rope of death shooting out of the shadow of a woman on an acera. Such a sight would make Mary pass out.

However, there is one thing Lillian can't stop thinking about: if they are so much like Cecilia and Alida, then can they take down that narecon? In the story, Cecilia and her acera lost to the narecon and got separated. There's something different about these two, though. Amphii is much bigger than Alida, and Jamie's weapon is terrifyingly bizarre. It must have been made to fight monsters.

As Lillian's mind struggles to keep up, Jamie's whip of death hits something vital, and the narecon screeches. A silhouette of liquid bursts from its body. Then it crashes through the slew of branches and lands on the forest floor with a colossal *BOOM*.

Wordlessly, the warriors rush to the crash site. Over and under a few roots, past a couple of trees, and there it is in a tiny clearing.

Jamie and her acera are already there. She treads down Amphii's wing and lands gracefully on the ground. Then, she draws her smaller scythes. She walks calmly toward the creature.

The gatherers ready their spears, but Brianna holds up a hand. She looks from Jamie to the black narecon, then to her again, and nods. The warrior nods back as if they've made some silent agreement. The rogue creeps closer to what is left of the monster. It breathes haggardly, its beak hanging open. It looks as if it's been torn apart, scythe-sized gashes puncturing its ribcage and stomach.

Rib bones stick out at various sickening angles. Its deep-red blood pollutes the moss, which soaks it up like water.

Jamie walks past the monster's scrunched-up wings, standing over its head. The head is so massive that it reaches half her height, but she doesn't seem frightened at all. She frowns as if pitying the creature, but that only lasts a second. She raises her two weapons. The narecon closes its eyes as if accepting its fate.

The scythes rend the monster's neck into three fleshy pieces.

It's over. Jamie somberly walks away from the corpse, her weapons dripping with blood. She tries to wipe the spatters off her face, but it's no use. The blood is everywhere.

There is a pause as everyone takes in what happened. This is more than just the story coming to life. Jamie slaughtered that narecon. She isn't Cecilia—she's *better*.

Cheering breaks out. The gatherers run toward her, embracing her like a savior. Albert stays by Lillian's side. He elbows her. "You're gawking."

"Am not!" She closes her mouth, realizing it was hanging open.

As Jamie accepts the praise, Amphii lays on the ground, her round head between her legs. She is so disciplined. "How do you train her to do that?" Lillian asks Albert.

"If you raise an acera from birth, they'll be loyal forever." He puts his arm around her. "Pretty cool, right?"

She tenses. She feels so ashamed. She was useless in this fight too.

After the cheering dies down and the gatherers refocus, Brianna directs them to bury the bodies. The atmosphere immediately turns dismal. For a moment, they forgot about the tragedy that took place. Now, they've snapped back to reality. The gatherers have gone from eleven people to nine. Her heart sinking, Lillian and the others make their way to the small clearing where the battle began. There on the forest floor is the mangled body of Noah. In his chest cavity are deep claw wounds, and right next to him...

Gigi lays face-up on the forest floor, her eyes staring at the canopy and cheeks stained with tears. Her short dark hair is stained red. The narecon's talons tore through her collarbone, shattered the left side of her ribs, and stopped at the base of her stomach. She must have bled out rapidly. She lies frozen in agony, just like the bodies of Albian.

Zoey screams mournfully, collapsing over the body of her friend, and Mia sobs right along with her. She gently runs her hand over Gigi's face, closing her eyes.

Meanwhile, Brianna and some of the older men take care of Noah. Theo and Bruno are amongst the eldest of the gatherers, and they help her bury him. They find a spot under a tree root and pull short shovels out of their backpacks. Lillian takes another glance at the women with Gigi, and they're taking her to the same place. Meanwhile, Lillian can't even move. She is shocked that some brought shovels, that they prepared for people to die. Then, something taps her shoulder.

She flinches at the touch, then turns around to see that it's the rogues. They must feel out of place too. The three of them stand separately from the others, eyes wide, words absent.

Finally, one of the siblings speaks. "It doesn't get any easier, does it?" Albert says.

"No," Jamie responds. There isn't a hint of pride in her voice. She genuinely feels bad for the gatherers. "It *never* gets easier." Lillian swallows. She thought she was prepared for this, but she doesn't even know how to help.

Before she knows it, the gatherers finish burying their friends and make their way over to the detached trio. Half of their faces are stained with tears. Mia, Zoey, Jess, and Milo are still crying. Despite all of that, they stare at Lillian with sympathy. Brianna places a hand on her shoulder and looks her straight in the eyes. "We're going to be okay. I swear, we will protect you."

Lillian's breath catches in her throat. This is the last thing she wants. She is supposed to protect herself, not be protected. That's the whole reason she fights in the first place. Still, she can't utter a word in the face of such tragedy. All she can do is make eye contact with Jamie and Albert.

What they just faced is unlike anything Zurec has seen before, yet Jamie and her acera easily took it down. Without them, there surely would have been many more deaths. She doesn't want to admit it, but they may be their only hope. How can she become as strong as them?

One thing's for sure; whatever just happened, Lillian is in way over her head. They all are.

11

The Rogues and the Ticking Dawn

Mary

Trista is a very aggravating girl. Mary can't blame her. She has been through a lot.

Still, isn't there a point when enough is enough? Where is Kayla's book for this? *How Much Trouble is Too Much Trouble from a Child Traumatized by Capaemen.* She could use something like that right now. Or maybe just *How to Get Children to Listen.* Or even... Lillian. She misses her. Her harshness may make Trista listen.

The little girl is curled under a bundle of sheets, still as a rock. She's as hard to move as one, too. Mary takes a deep breath. Showing impatience may make the child more upset. Then there's no way she'll get her out of bed. "It's almost noon. Everyone's waiting. Don't you want some fresh air?" she says tenderly, rubbing what she thinks is Trista's shoulder.

"No!" she yells.

"Okay, how about this: if you get out of bed, I'll let you have a snack. How do dried red berries sound?"

"No!"

"Trista, you can't live in this bed forever. There's a great wide world out there. We've gotta prepare you to survive in—"

"No!"

Mary crosses her arms. "You know, ever since we went to the Crystal River you've been even—"

"No no no no no!"

"What do you mean 'no no no no no'?" she asks. More than one "no." Maybe she can make some headway here.

"I already went outside. Besides, I won the bug-counting competition. You don't get to tell me what to do!"

Mary sits on the bed. That competition was just to get Trista to go outside, but maybe she should have tried to win. If she had known the girl would act like this, she would have. "Trista, I agreed to make you something. I didn't say you could do anything you wanted." Come to think of it, she still needs to finish her present for Lillian.

"Then make my dolly and leave me alone. I told you I want a warrior princess!"

"So, you did like the story of Cecilia and Alida, huh?" Mary asks.

"No! I don't want it to be her. Just a warrior princess."

She sighs. She's getting nowhere. "Trista, do you want to talk about why you won't come out? I've found that talking can—"

"No! Go away!"

"I won't go away. Why are you so upset?"

"Because." The bundle of sheets tenses.

"Because what?"

"Because *they're* out there."

Mary rubs the girl's shoulder again. "Sweetie..." but she can't find the words.

"Not even inside is safe. Nowhere is." The little girl says as if reading Mary's mind.

"Now that's just not true. The burrow is—"

"Especially not the burrow!" the child screams, throwing the blankets off. Her eyes are red.

Speechless, Mary does the only thing she can do. She gets under the covers and hugs the girl. Trista cries softly into her shirt. "It's okay. It's okay," she mumbles, rubbing the girl's dark hair. "I know it's hard, but we can't give up. We'll find a way out of this."

Several moments pass. Mary stares up at the roots hanging from the ceiling. She wonders when the wooden planks holding this place up will collapse. It's only a matter of time. She thinks of Lillian. If Zurec could leave this place, she would jump at the opportunity, but they have nowhere else to go. The Giant Wilds are crawling with monsters, and outside them is capaeman territory. No matter how she looks at it, they're trapped.

"I shouldn't be alive," the child says in barely a whisper.

"*What?* No. Don't think that way," Mary replies, horrified.

"It's true, though."

"No, that's not true at all. Look, I know our clans were enemies, but you're one of us now. Now and forever. You're not a burden—"

"No no no!" the girl says, holding her head. "No no no no no!" Trista's tiny body begins to shake, and her breathing speeds up. Realizing she's gone too far, Mary backtracks.

"L-Let's not talk about the hard things anymore. And you know what, you don't have to go to class today. Also, I'll stay inside with you. We can talk about cool things all day. Like, what's the best meal you've ever had? What's your favorite animal? And, uh, how do you keep your hair so pretty?" So much for getting her out of bed.

Trista's breathing slows, and she sniffles. "You think my hair is pretty?"

"Yes, very much so! It's so glossy, and the dark brown matches your eyes perfectly."

Her arms tighten around Mary's waist. "Thank you. You're the nicest person here." The future caretaker closes her eyes. Thank goodness she got out of that one.

⚜ ⚜

A while later, Mary wakes up to voices echoing from the main room. *I fell asleep?* she thinks. *Oh no, for how long?* Are the gatherers back?

As Mary tries deciphering the cluster of voices, she gently untangles herself from Trista. The little girl stays fast asleep, feeling her hair and grinning. Mary smiles. She's glad they both got some sleep.

The caretaker's daughter stumbles down the dark hall and into the mud room. To one side, her mother and Kayla speak with Brianna in fervent, hushed tones, aware of the children within earshot next to them. That can't be good. Then, Mary spots a few gatherers: Zoey, Mia, and Theo. They look down. Mary knows that gaze—they must have lost people. She begins to panic, frantically scanning the group, until finally, she spots Lillian. Thank the Wilds, she's okay, but she's talking to two people Mary has never seen before. By the looks of them, they are not from the Giant Wilds.

"Lillian!" She jumps into her arms, nearly knocking her over. "I missed you so much. You wouldn't believe—"

"You wouldn't believe what happened," Lillian interrupts, pushing Mary out of the hug. "I... have so much to catch you up on." She seems dismayed as well.

"Y-Yes!" her friend says. Nervously, she looks around at the gatherers again, and now she knows who is missing. Noah, the second eldest after Miss May, is gone. So is Gigi, Carmen's sister. The surveyors are gone right now, but when they return they will be heartbroken. Mary doesn't even have time to process these deaths, however, because of the two strangers standing by Lillian. They haven't had guests in so long, and if they're here, the gatherers must trust them.

The two strangers, a woman and a young man, stare at the girls. She can't read their expressions. "W-Who are these two?" Mary asks. The woman scrubs her face and clothes with a rag. The rag is soaked with blood. That's unnerving, to say the least. The male, who's relatively short, slumps against the wall. Mary thought she was short at five feet eleven, but this boy is a few inches shorter than that. Her eyes lock with his left one; the other is hidden by a curtain of black hair. He must be young. Could he be the same age as her? Mary can't tell with all that hair in his face.

"This is Jamie," Lillian gestures to the woman wiping the blood, "and this is Albert." She gestures to him.

"Uh, welcome!" She shakes their hands, hoping she doesn't look too nervous. "M-My name is Mary. Bestest friend of Lillian since forever. We're the only people of our generation, so it's amazing to meet new friends. Especially someone close to our age. How old are you, Albert?"

"Fourteen," he answers.

"Amazing!" she blurts. "I'm fourteen, too." It's a boy! A real boy her age. She never thought she'd see one.

"Cool," he says, smiling, but the smile doesn't reach his eye.

"And I'm twenty-one," Jamie says, pointing to herself. "Brianna told me about the generation gap. Looks like I'm a bit in-between too. The youngest adult here is twenty-four."

"Hey, I'm an adult," Lillian says.

"I mean *real* adults, sweetie," she responds condescendingly.

Mary raises an eyebrow. "Anyway, where are you two from?"

"Osi—" Albert begins to speak, but Jamie elbows him, cutting him off. "Come on!" he yells.

"It's a place very far away from here, surrounded by water," Lillian explains. "They don't like to talk about it."

"I see. That's alright," Mary says, glaring at Jamie. There was no need to cut him off.

"My word!" someone screams. Mary's mother, Kayla, and the children are now rushing across the dusty carpet to greet the new people. Max looks better today. At least he shows up to class, unlike his sister. Kayla has a book tightly clutched in her arms. Mary recognizes the black cover immediately and feels nauseous. *The Adventures of Cecilia and Alida.* If she has to read that one more time, she will explode.

"New recruits. How wonderful!" her mother says, shaking both of their hands at the same time. Her enthusiastic handshake rocks the strangers back and forth. When she lets go, her gaze falls on Albert. She leans in a little too close, studying him. Then she tries to lift his bangs.

He slaps her hand away. "Wh-What are you doing?"

"How old are you?" Mary's mom asks, her eyes wide. She's still way too close. It's clearly making the boy uncomfortable.

"F-Fourteen."

"I see!" she says, looking from him to her daughter with raised eyebrows.

Horror rises in Mary's chest. "Mom," she says, smiling, "let's not overwhelm them, okay? We don't want to scare them away." If Noah and Gigi are dead, they need new people now more than ever. She badly wants someone to fill her in on what happened, but given the chaos, she'll have to wait.

"I agree," Jamie says, placing her hands on her hips. "First things first: where are our rooms?"

"Rooms?" the caretaker asks. "Oh, well, we can't give you permanent lodging until Chief Seth decides whether you may join the clan. He isn't back yet."

"What, so we've got to sleep in the trees tonight? Come on, I saved your whole—"

"You," her mother interrupts loudly, cutting off whatever arrogant thing Jamie was about to say. "You can use Noah and his late wife's room tonight," she concludes at her regular volume. With a sad smile, she adds, "Please, follow me."

It has been a few weeks since anyone has died. Still, Mary should have known it would happen sooner or later. She didn't know Noah and Gigi well, but they were a part of the family—a family that's getting smaller and smaller. Tears well in her eyes. She looks to Lillian. Her face says, *It's a long story, and I'd really like to tell you.* Mary needs to hear it.

Mary, Lillian, Jamie, and Albert follow Miss May to the room. As they walk, the children seize their chance to greet the newcomers. They feel their silky grey clothes. "So cool. So cool!" Max says, his little green eyes sparkling. His hands drift to Jamie's corset.

She slaps them away. "Hey, no touching, kid. They're sharp."

"Okay," he says sadly. He drifts to Albert, who isn't protesting the children's curiosity. Jen and Jan tug on his sleeves while Oscar yanks his belt. He laughs uncomfortably.

"Hey, stop that. It's rude," Lillian says, pulling one of the twins off him. The children scatter away from her.

"Yeah guys, leave them alone," Mary says. Albert sighs in relief, fixing his belt.

"Are you superheroes? Like Cecilia?" Oscar asks.

Before Mary can answer, Jamie speaks in that loud voice again. "Of course we are. We hail from the faraway island of Osinawa. We travel the world fighting monsters."

The children cheer, throwing out question after question. They all talk at once, so it's impossible to discern who is asking what. Jamie just smiles and pats their little heads. One of them reaches for her corset again, and she slaps their hand away. "No touching." That corset does look cool. It's loaded with all sorts of weapons Mary doesn't recognize, all made of metal. They aren't lying about being from far away.

As the group descends the hall, it gets darker. "Man, not good lighting in this place, huh?" Jamie says.

"We don't light the halls too much," her mom explains. "The smoke pollutes the air."

"I see. I've never seen halls so narrow," Jamie says. Mary's getting sick and tired of this lady's condescending tone. She clearly thinks she is superior to everyone. That is not a good attitude to have when they're letting her stay here. What is her problem?

Finally, the caretaker stops in front of a rickety redwood door. She jimmies it open. "This one gets stuck a lot. Sorry." The door creaks open to reveal a tiny room with a bed on either side. The first looks very lived-in. One of its legs is cracked, and the blankets are bundled in a large ball on top of the mattress. Noah's trunk is wide open, and clothes are strewn all over the floor. Clearly, he was not a neat freak. Mary can relate.

The second one is perfectly made, with the sheets tucked under the mattress and pillow. The entire bed is coated in a thick layer of dust. "Noah once shared this room with his wife, but she died long before he did. I suppose now they can be together, at least," her mother says grimly. "Here, I'll get the clothes out of here. You two make yourselves at home."

Jamie and Albert drift inside, both staring at the dusty, neat bed. Although clothes are strewn all about the room, none of them are anywhere near it. Noah must have respected his wife. She died during the famine.

"I call the made bed!" Jamie screams, jumping onto it. Dust billows into the air.

"Hey, no fair," her brother complains.

The caretaker gathers a bundle of clothes and strides out of the room, elbowing Lillian out of the doorway. Mary glances at all the clothes still on the floor. "Come on, Lillian, let's help Mom." Lillian nods faintly.

"She's your mom?" Albert asks.

Mary crouches to the ground, picking up the clothes. "Yeah."

"Ah, that makes sense," he says, heading to Noah's bed. He unbundles the blankets, spreading them across the mattress as neatly as possible.

"What do you mean?"

"He means you're both high-strung. He can see the family resemblance," Lillian teases.

"Hey!"

Albert chuckles. "No, it's not like that. It's just that you two look alike. I should ask though, why do you have brown eyes?"

Mary blinks. "Huh? Uh, I got them from my dad I think." It's been a long time since she's thought about him.

"Blonde hair and brown eyes. That's a rare combo. Really *Pops* out to me." Jamie groans. Mary isn't quite sure why. All she knows is he emphasized the word "pops."

Lillian chuckles. "Good one!"

Albert winks at her. Then he turns around and sits on his newly made bed, observing Mary with a huge smile. "Don't look upset. It's pretty."

"Th-Thank you," Mary says nervously.

"Tell me, are you married, Mary?"

Her face flushes. "H-Huh? Is that a joke, or..."

"Eh, partially. I also haven't seen a girl in a long time, other than my crazy sister. I've got to know what my chances are."

Her grip tightens around the clothing, and heat rises in her cheeks. "Um, uh..." She looks to Lillian, who now seems very fixated on the floor, then to Jamie, whose hand is on one of her weapons. She looks ready to strike. What did Mary do? It's Albert asking these offhand questions, not her! "M-My hands are full. I-I'm going to go p-put these away. Uh, see you in a minute!" She rushes out of the room.

Mary takes a right in the hallway instead of a left. She quickly turns around. *No, silly. Storeroom is this way*, she thinks to herself.

When she enters the crowded storeroom, she spots her mother's pale hair between the shelves. She quickly shuffles over to her. "Hey Mom, where do I put these?" she asks, a nervous edge in her voice.

"Ah, in this basket. I'll wash the dirty ones the next time we go to the river. Are you okay, dear? You're looking, well, very *red*."

"I-I'm fine!" She stuffs the bundle of clothes in the basket.

"No, you're not sweetie. Tell me what's wrong," her mother says.

Oh no, why does she have to know me so well? Mary thinks. "Albert makes some terrible jokes," she says before rushing out of the room.

Okay, that may have been a bad idea. Now her mother is going to ask what he did. He hasn't done anything wrong. Just, *marriage*? Mary never imagined getting a chance at that. She always thought she'd be stuck with Lillian forever. Her heart pounds harder in her chest as she gets closer and closer to Jamie and Albert's quarters. As she's about to enter the room, she bumps into Lillian.

"Oh, hey," Mary says.

"Wow, you're out of it today," her friend says, bending down to grab some clothes she dropped.

"Yeah, sorry," she says, helping Lillian pick them up.

"Getting enough sleep?"

"Of course not. You know me." She lets out a very forced laugh.

"Please hang in there," her friend says as she heads down the hall.

"I will."

Back in the room, Jamie looks less murderous than before. She scans Mary up and down before scoffing and falling back onto her pillow. Albert has lain down too, looking disappointed. What happened in the ten seconds Mary was gone? She decides not to ask. She continues to clean up the room. "Need help with that?" Albert asks grumpily.

She scans the room and shakes her head. The only thing left is the trunk. "No, we're almost done."

"Alright," he says, shoving his face into his new pillow. They must be exhausted from their long journey. Mary should get out of their way. She takes the last bundle of clothes, including Jamie's bloody towel, and quietly leaves the room, closing the rickety door behind her.

After dropping off the last of the clothes, Mary heads back to her quarters. She really should check on Trista. She wonders if the fussy girl is still asleep.

That would be a blessing. Oh, no. What is she thinking? The girl should be awake by now. They need to teach her something today.

Her mother and Lillian have already returned to the room. Both stand around Lillian's bed, staring at the lump under the sheets that is Trista. Oh, no. It's worse than she thought. Her friend probably wants to rest after her adventure, yet the little girl is in her bed.

The caretaker turns around, her face contorted with annoyance. She gestures for Mary to come. Her expression says, *Please help us out.* Her daughter nods, rushing to Trista's side.

She has to do this all over again. This time with an audience.

12

A Fight for the Ages

Mary

"Hey, Trista," Mary says, placing a hand on the bundle of blankets. "You managed to skip the day, so you don't need to worry now. We're not trying to make you go outside. Lillian just needs her bed back." She looks to her friend. The brunette scowls.

Trista sniffles. The blankets muffle the sound. "Promise?"

"Yes, I promise. It's dark out now. None of us are outside." Mary rubs the bundle of sheets.

"It's... it's night?" the little girl says, poking her tiny head out. She's been crying again.

"Yes."

Trista pops out of the sheets, throwing her little arms around Mary. "I'm scared. I can't sleep at night. That's why I stay here all day."

That is something the two of them share. Still, she must ask. "Why can't you sleep?"

"*They* came for us at dawn."

As if Mary didn't have enough reasons to lie awake at night. She looks to her mother for support. Her tired blue eyes are wide with fear. She doesn't know what to do either. That makes Mary even more nervous. Before Seth left, he told them the surveyors' last mission was a wash. They don't know the first thing about tracking capaemen. No one knows what to do. She wishes they still had the library. It probably contained tons of records on the capaemen, but even if so, they are long gone.

She's got to question more. Trista just revealed something crucial. "You said they came at dawn? Do you think they always do that?"

"I don't know," she mumbles.

"Is there anything else you can tell us? Any details will help."

Disappointingly, she shakes her head. That's all they will get from her, but it is better than nothing.

Miss May lights up. "So, they attacked at dawn? That means they might do it again. Thank you. I'll tell the chief the second he gets back." She hurries out of the room.

One would think this would lift her spirits, but Lillian simply glares at Trista. "Can I have my bed back?"

Trista looks up at the brunette with fear. She is much bigger than the little girl, with her tall stature and toned shoulders. She must not realize how intimidating she looks to a kid. Of course, she wouldn't. She's Lillian. It's up to Mary to fix this.

"It's okay. You can sleep with me."

The little girl shakes her head. "I'll just sleep with Kayla and my brother." She throws her little feet off the bed and rushes out of the room without another word.

Lillian jumps onto her bed without a care. "Guess she doesn't like me much."

"Well, with the way you were glaring at her, who can blame her?"

"Glaring? I wasn't glaring. I was just annoyed."

"Yeah. You were glaring at her. You know, you could be a little bit nicer. She's just a kid."

"Just a kid who knows a heck of a lot about the life-or-death situation we're in and says *nothing*."

Mary shuts her mouth. She can't argue with that. Even she is growing frustrated. She gets that the kid is traumatized, but she also doesn't care whether they live or die. All that running, that snarky attitude, the hiding under the blankets; Mary must find a way to lift her spirits, or they will never get answers.

Ugh, she groans internally. With all these worries swirling in her mind, she'll never fall asleep. *Forget all that.* She needs to focus on the now, and on the positives. When the surveyors return, Seth will likely provide a test for the newcomers. She looks forward to that. Until then, she'll get some sleep.

Mary is in darkness. No matter where she looks, she can't see a thing—just an empty black void.

"Come on, Mary," a voice says. It's her own voice speaking back to her. "Everyone's waiting. Don't you want some fresh air?"

"No!" she screams. Now, she's under a bundle of sheets. She's too scared to leave.

"Come on, you know you want to get out of here."

"No, I don't! I want to stay here forever." The Mary outside of the sheets is scary. She doesn't want to listen to her. She will get her killed.

"You know that isn't true. You wish you could leave."

"No! I'm going to become the caretaker. I don't want to leave. Not now, not ever." That's right. That is her destiny: taking care of people like Trista and the kids, forever. It's safe. It's what she's good at. Lillian's the one who wants to leave, not her.

The other Mary goes silent. Thank goodness. Now, there is peace.

Before she knows it, someone is shaking her awake. "Mary! The surveyors are back. You don't want to miss this!" Lillian says.

"Miss what?" she asks, her eyes half-open.

"My dad questioned the new recruits, and he loves them. He wants to fight them now!"

At the mention of Seth, Mary jolts awake. "W-What? The surveyors are back?" Even she is excited about this. She wonders how the rogues will rise to his challenge.

"Let's go!" Lillian drags her friend out of bed. She doesn't even have time to think about brushing her hair before they're down the hall. Lillian throws open the trapdoor, letting in the forest sunlight. The morning light blinds Mary. Outside, the people of Zurec stand in a cluster, mumbling to each other.

"Never seen a rogue like that before."

"Dual wielders. No idea how to fight that. Hope Seth will be okay."

"He's going to win. He's *much* more experienced."

Still dragging Mary along, Lillian pushes their way to the front of the crowd. But the sight near the front makes Mary do a double take.

There, surrounded by the children, is a giant winged beast. It purrs as the children climb all over its grand wings. Its large round eyes stay fixated on Jamie and Albert, who watch close by. It handles the children gently, even as they tug, pull, and walk all over it. Tears well in Mary's eyes. It looks exactly like Alida, depicted in the illustrations of their favorite childhood story. She's got to be dreaming. This is too good to be true.

"Is that... an acera?"

"It sure is," Jamie answers, taking a spot next to them. Her outfit has changed from the grey suit to Zurec hide. Even though she still has her weapons and corset, she looks much less intimidating in this outfit—less regal and more human. Mary likes this look on her. "May made me change," Jamie says as if reading her mind. "Too much blood on my clothes."

It sounds weird hearing her mother's name without the "Miss" title before it. Not even the chief calls her that. "People call her Miss May," she retorts.

"Really? She seems fine with it. After all, she didn't raise my brother and me. Plus, I'm not a fan of honorifics."

"Did she *say* she was okay with it?"

The rogue snickers. "She said it was charming." Mary sighs. That does sound like something her mother would say.

"She looks angry, sis. Maybe we should call her Miss May. After all, she *may* like that more," Albert says. His sister scoffs. Mary is liking the boy more and more. Anyone who puts that look on Jamie's face is a friend of hers. She sure hopes the chief can bring that ego down. She's rooting for him in the match.

Across the clearing, Seth sits on a gnarled tree root. He sharpens his double-headed spear with a metal rod. Brianna and several other surveyors sit chatting with him. His usual entourage, Elias and William, hype him up for the fight. Nodding along is Lance, the best fighter in the surveyors, and his buddy Archer. Mary isn't sure why they are friends. Lance is a tiny, calm man, while Archer is a lanky hothead. She has never seen their antics, but she's heard about them. One is too reckless in battle, and the other is always bailing him out. Perhaps that's another reason Lillian's dad didn't let her join the surveyors; he didn't want her to turn out like that.

Come to think of it, all of the surveyors are present except for Carmen. Mary's face falls. She already knows the reason why. Someone must have informed her of her sister's death. She must be alone somewhere.

Before Mary can observe more, Jamie speaks again. "This is going to be easy." Albert rolls his eyes, but Lillian's eyes are sparkling. She doesn't realize this woman is an egomaniac.

Mary takes a deep breath. No matter how much the rogue grinds her gears, she can't get angry. They have an acera. Zurec needs them. "Okay, we know how Jamie feels. Albert, how do you think you'll do?"

The boy smiles awkwardly. "Really bad."

"Oh? Why?"

"I just suck." That leaves no room for conversation, but they're out of time anyway. In the distance, Seth hops off his tree root and makes his way to the middle of the clearing. Jamie meets him halfway. The two face off several feet apart, and the crowd falls silent. Albert heads over to the acera, grabbing hold of its reigns. Mary isn't sure why until Jamie draws her weapons. The acera grows restless in response. It clearly has a very deep attachment to its rider, much like Cecilia and Alida.

"So, who do you think is going to win?" Lillian whispers.

"Seth. For sure," Mary says.

"I'm betting on Jamie." Mary's jaw drops. Lillian *idolizes* her father. Has she found a new idol in Jamie? No, that's impossible. "You should have seen her yesterday. She defeated a narecon on her own."

"What?" Mary says a little too loud. Some of the crowd turns toward her. She smiles awkwardly.

Seth squares his broad shoulders and holds up his spear. Because of his hulking form, he wields one of the biggest spears ever made. Its tips are made of sharpened metal, and the shaft is whitewood, from the branch of a rare tree in the Giant Wilds. It is said to be somewhere along the bank of the Crystal River. Spears like that haven't been made since before the forge shut down.

"I hope you're ready to lose," Jamie taunts. Mary cringes. No one talks to Seth like that.

The chief laughs. "Now that's what I like to hear."

Mary's mom makes her way to the front of the crowd, standing perpendicular to the face-off. "Before the fight begins, it is customary for me to go over the rules. Shallow cuts and bruises are legal, but this is with real weapons, so don't seriously injure or kill each other. I have enough work as it is. I don't want to waste my time patching you two up."

"Got it. I won't waste your time," Jamie says.

The caretaker seems to ignore that. "The victor will be decided when one person is on the ground for more than three seconds or when one is able to land a lethal blow, in theory. I cannot stress enough that if you're about to land a lethal blow, you should stop right there. You have won the fight."

"I'm not going to kill him, May. Don't worry." The woman takes a strange stance, gripping her dual scythes.

"Yeah, I'll take it easy on her," Seth says, smirking. He holds his spear across his chest.

"Alright then," Miss May says, raising her hand. Before she even gives the command for them to begin, both of the warriors charge. The caretaker puts her hand back down, sighing.

In a flash, vastly different weapons clash against one another. Jamie's dual scythes hook around the shaft of Seth's spear. Mary should have known she would do that. She's trying to disarm him. Knowing exactly what she's doing, Seth shifts his weight backward, dragging her weapons with him. Jamie unhooks them and leaps away. She smiles, amused.

She chases after him, unleashing a swift flurry of dual attacks. The second her first scythe comes down, the other is right behind it. Her strikes blur into each other, making the two scythes look like a single weapon. She slowly pushes Seth backward to one of the giant redwood trees. Due to his size, however, he only budges a couple of inches at a time, and the precise strikes from those scythes are countered by his spear. He may not look it, but he is quick enough to counter every one of Jamie's attacks. He predicts every strike no matter the angle, and that isn't easy; Jamie doesn't have a pattern. At least, not one easy to pick up. Mary's mouth hangs open. She thought Lillian was tough. She thought her mother was tough, but they are nothing compared to these two. No wasted movement. It's incredible.

Seth continues to parry the scythe strikes, using his immense size and strength to his advantage, but he slowly loses ground. If he continues to fight on the defensive, he'll end up backed against a tree. He may have no choice, though; Jamie's speed is overwhelming.

Despite his disadvantage, Seth is still smiling. Isn't he afraid of losing in front of his clan? He is supposed to be an example for everyone. Mary looks around. Some people look anxious. Others are in awe. Brianna seems the most worried, which is surprising.

Meanwhile, the children near the acera are clearly confused. Trista is finally out, her arms around Kayla's waist. Max holds her hand. This must be difficult for them to follow. Heck, it's hard enough for Mary to follow. She wonders if Lillian is doing any better. The brunette's eyes sparkle. Nothing could tear them away from this fight. Of course, she is enjoying this the most.

Seth is getting knocked back farther. That is very strange. Before, he was hardly budging an inch. Now Jamie's strikes are knocking him back several feet at a time. They are nearing the tree. Is Seth getting tired? No, that can't be right. He's still blocking every strike.

Seth's steps seem to grow heavy from all the blows, his feet sinking into the moss, yet still, he stands his ground. Among the flurry of attacks, Mary manages to catch a glance at Jamie's face. She's smiling. That's surprising. Isn't his resilience irritating her?

Mary would believe this could go on forever if it weren't for the approaching tree. There is no weakness in either of their stances. No openings. If Jamie had any, she'd be on the ground right now. Same for Seth.

They're only a few feet away from the tree. Seth will be backed up against it any minute—a couple more feet. Jamie knocks him back again. And again. And again. Why is he letting her knock him back that much? Is it his plan to lose?

Finally, he's inches away from the trunk. Jamie's attacks continue relentlessly. The surveyors and gatherers place their hands on their mouths. Mary's heart pounds through her chest. Is this how it ends?

The following happens in less than a second. Jamie raises one of her scythes to finish the match. But then, with stunning agility for his size, Seth twists his body and leaps sideways, narrowly dodging the attack. Jamie's scythe lodges in the bark, and she lets it go, losing a weapon.

Without missing a beat, Seth hops over a tree root. Jamie follows. The smile on her face has vanished. Once she is on top of the root, just before she descends to meet him, Seth swipes his spear at her feet, knocking her off the root entirely. Mary gasps. Usually being on higher ground gives you the advantage. That's probably what Jamie thought too. However, being lower, Seth was able to do what spears do best: knock people off-balance. Jamie tumbles to the ground. "One—" her mother counts.

Before she gets to two, Jamie is back on her feet. Covered in dirt and clearly angry, she charges at the chief. However, without her dual strikes, he fends her off easily.

The next part happens so quickly Mary hardly has time to comprehend it. A shiny piece of metal launches from Jamie's free hand. It lodges in a chink in Seth's armor but doesn't slow him down at all. He changes his spear's angle and strikes Jamie on her unarmed side. She tumbles to the ground. Seth points the larger blade of his spear at her neck. She drops her weapons.

The crowd is silent. It's incredible how quickly that went down: how many decisions were made in mere minutes. Mary always overthinks and hesitates. She could never hope to be this good.

The chief lowers his spear and offers a calloused hand to Jamie. "Now *that* was entertaining." The rogue takes it, and Seth pulls her into a very tight hug. Her arms stiffen. She looks like she's suffocating. Luckily, he lets her go quickly.

"Welcome to Zurec."

13

The Scouts

Mary

"And the victor is Seth!" Mary's mother announces. Cheers erupt from the group. Immediately, a crowd forms around Seth, with Brianna being the first to hug him. Mia's voice rises above the din. "Out of the way! I've got to treat his wound."

Meanwhile, Jamie's only fans seem to be Lillian, the acera, and her brother. Mary has a feeling Albert's only there because he has to be. Despite this, the warrior smiles proudly. Her acera is the first to greet her, nuzzling her with its round nose.

"Down, girl," Jamie says, chuckling. It backs off immediately. "That's a good girl, Amphii."

"I haven't had a fight that intense in a while," she continues, "and I haven't lost in forever." She turns her brother around and digs through his backpack. From it, she pulls a small handkerchief and wipes the dirt off her face.

"Who else have you lost to?" Lillian asks.

Mary wonders if her friend knows how starry-eyed she looks. Knowing Lillian, she does not.

"You wouldn't know them."

"Still, you can tell me about them?" the brunette begs.

"Another day, kid. I'm beat," Jamie says, stretching. She heads to the redwood tree and pulls out her scythe. It isn't damaged. What an incredible weapon.

When she returns, Lillian is the first to speak. "Can we spar?"

"You want me to train you? Oh, of course you do. You loved that fight, didn't you?" The brunette nods enthusiastically. "Well, since I'm now a proud

member of Zurec, I'd be happy to take a pupil or two under my wing. Jamie...
Zurec. Yeah, I like the ring of that. I'll use that from now on." Meanwhile, Albert
pretends he isn't a part of the conversation. He scratches Amphii's head. She
seems to like that a lot. "Mary, you look like you could sharpen your skills too.
Want to train under me?"

Mary scoffs and walks away. She's had enough of this. "Hey, where are you
going?" Lillian asks.

"I'm, uh, not feeling well." Yeah, that's a good enough excuse.

She immediately bumps into her mother. In the caretaker's wrinkled hands
is a bloody cloth. Mary tries to smile. She doesn't want her mother asking about
what just went down. "Oh! Mary," she says, "can you give this back to Jamie?"
Her mother opens the cloth. Inside is a small metal blade. Well, more like a ring
of six blades. This one doesn't even have a handle. The hole in the middle is
what one would grab to throw it if she had to guess. One of its blades is still
stained with Seth's blood.

"Y-Yeah. I'll return it," Mary says, gritting her teeth. Great. She just walked
away. Now, she must go back.

If her mother notices her bad mood, she doesn't show it. "Thank you, Mary.
Oh, I have so much to do today. Albert surely will pass Seth's test, too. You
know what that means? They need Zurec sigils. I've got to get started on those.
Oh, this is so exciting! Don't you think?"

"Yeah," her daughter deadpans. She quickly turns back to the rogues.

"Oh, change your mind?" Jamie says when she sees Mary approach.

She is tempted to throw the little blade star at her but restrains herself. "No.
My mother just wanted me to bring you this."

"Good," the warrior says, plucking the star out of the cloth. "These are hard
to make. Thanks for returning it."

Mary nods, but as she starts to leave again, Seth makes an announcement.
"I'm ready to battle the other one now. Come on up, Albert!" The boy's face
flushes. This isn't going to go well.

He takes his hand off Amphii and saunters over. The acera whines.

"Seth! Shouldn't you wait? You're wounded," Mia says.

"Nah. I'll be fine. What, do you think I'll lose?" The entire clan shakes their
heads. Albert grows paler.

"The bleeding has stopped. I'm good." He takes his spot in the clearing
again, gesturing to Albert. "Come on, kid. I want to eat lunch soon." The boy
walks to the center of the clearing, his arms stiff as boards. He's so much smaller
than his sister, and compared to Seth, he looks like a child.

When he comes face-to-face with the chief, he draws his scythes, taking the same stance as Jamie. Since Mary's mother is in the burrow now, Brianna takes over as referee. She stands confidently between the two men, her red ponytail swaying in the breeze. "As you know, no lethal hits. Shallow cuts are legal. Fall to the ground for three seconds or more, and you lose. If your opponent nearly lands a lethal blow, you lose. Ready, set, go!"

Brianna's rapid-fire speech catches Albert off guard. Seth attacks immediately, knocking the boy to the ground. "One, two—" He's about to go for the lethal strike when Albert rolls out of the way and springs back onto his feet. He's quick, which makes sense for his size. His dual scythes move like Jamie's, but with less precision. Instead of losing his ground, Seth pushes Albert back. He looks scared but still blocks the hits.

For this fight, Seth is much more offensive, slashing back and forth with his spear. This reminds Mary of sparring with Lillian. In this case, Lillian is Seth and Mary is Albert. He stands no chance. Still, he's lasting longer than she thought he would.

The chief's heavy attacks knock the boy back farther and farther, but he stays rooted. Then Seth goes for his leg. The boy falls to the ground. "Albert! Come on, you can do better than that," his sister yells. That's uncalled for. She shouldn't distract him.

"One, two—" Brianna counts, but the boy gets back on his feet again, and suddenly, the air around him shifts. Mary feels a chill go down her spine. She's not sure why. This is just a young boy, so why does he suddenly look so... cold?

In half a second, his attacks change. They land faster, more precise, more like his sister. He knocks Seth back and gains some ground. The chief is so surprised he lets him do it. Mary trembles. She is afraid of him. She isn't sure why, but she is. Even the chief looks aghast. Albert dashes toward him, his bangs blowing sideways, revealing an eyepatch underneath. His single eye is glassy and vacant, almost as if possessed.

With each strike of the boy's scythes, he becomes more precise, more deadly. Seth reverts to defense. Each of Albert's strikes blurs into the next, making his scythes look like one weapon. His shaggy hair falls in and out of his face, but it doesn't distract him at all.

"Yeah, that's the spirit, Albert!" Jamie cheers. As if his sister's voice is a wake-up call, the boy hesitates. Seth knocks him to the ground. This time, he does not get up. His head hangs as if in shame.

"One, two, three, you're out," Brianna announces. The audience claps but does not cheer. The air still feels ominous.

Seth bends down, offering a hand to his opponent. "You did well." Albert takes it, and the chief pulls him up like he weighs nothing. "We've got to get more meat on your bones, kid. Also, more sparring, lots of sparring, but you've got skills. Don't be afraid to use them." He claps the boy on the back. "Welcome to Zurec."

Lillian and Jamie run straight to the boy. Mary isn't far behind. She wants to know what that was all about. It didn't feel right. "What happened?" Lillian asks.

"I, uh, don't know," he says, a forced laugh escaping his lips.

"You were doing good there for a minute," Lillian says. "Like, *wow*. I'd like to spar with you sometime."

"M-Me? No, I'm no good. You saw it."

"Nonsense," Mary intervenes. "It's like Seth said. You just need more strength and more practice." She smiles, grabbing one of his hands. It's more calloused than her own, which surprises her. She's no warrior, but she's been exercising her whole life. Whatever he and his sister have been through must have been hell. She felt it all in that moment of coldness. "You were really good, but what happened toward the end—"

Albert yanks his hand away, cutting her off. "Right. You're right. I need to get better."

Okay, that was a mistake, she thinks. She shouldn't have brought that up. It's clearly personal.

"Practice with me," Lillian says, grabbing his other hand. With her, he doesn't yank away. Mary takes a deep breath. Saved by her friend yet again.

Soon, Jamie joins in, throwing an arm around Lillian and her brother. "Yes, we'll all practice together, with me as the teacher, of course. I'm so excited!" Both roll their eyes this time.

"Hey Lillian!" Brianna calls. She stands several feet away, the gatherers clustered around her. "We're having a meeting. Come here."

Lillian nods. "We'll spar later." Now Mary is alone with them. She wants to walk away, but that would make things even more awkward.

"You sure you don't want to join us, Mary?" Jamie asks, a condescending smirk on her face.

Keep your cool, Mary, she thinks. "I'm good. I'm Miss May's daughter, you know. Going to be the next caretaker. Very important job. I've got to focus on that."

"I do know. May talks very fondly about you. Sure, caretaking is important, but fighting is even more so. You know, your mother was once a warrior herself. You could be too."

"No, I'm not a warrior," Mary says, looking at the canopy.

"Not a—" Jamie starts. "That's impossible. We're all warriors. That's how we stay alive, after all."

"I know how to fight. I just... don't like it."

"Hmm, fair enough. But my offer still stands. This world is cruel and unpredictable. You never know when you'll need to fight. You've got to learn to like it."

Mary clenches her fists. "No, I have a job. I don't need to 'learn to like' anything."

Jamie crosses her arms. "Wow, you're just as stubborn as Lillian."

"Huh?" Mary is baffled. That's impossible. She follows the rules; she doesn't complain. That is the opposite of stubborn.

"Jamie, Albert, may I have a word?" It's Seth. Mary exhales. He has saved her too. Seth approaches the rogues, followed by the eleven other surveyors.

"Sir," Jamie responds. "Umm, is that what we're supposed to call you?" At least she is respectful to the chief, probably because he won.

"Just Seth is fine. Now that you've joined the ranks, I have an idea as to your role."

"Whatever it is, I can do it," Jamie says. Her brother shoots her a quizzical look.

The chief takes a deep breath, his stress lines showing again. He looks at Amphii. The acera licks the underside of her wings, her long pink tongue leaving saliva all over her skin. "Recently," the chief starts, "a neighboring clan, who lived in the burrow where the gatherers found you two, was attacked by capaemen."

"I know. Albert and I saw that. It's why we stopped by. We wanted to know what was going on in this forest," Jamie says. Is it just Mary, or did fear flicker in her eyes? Maybe she is afraid of something after all. "We ran into Rostad, but they were not very friendly. I'm glad we came across you guys. Once we saw you, we knew you were who we'd been looking for. People like you are very rare."

"Rare how?"

"You're kind. You genuinely care for and help each other. That kind of thing is seldom seen in this world."

"I appreciate it. We try to stay optimistic around here." Behind him, Elias clears his throat. Seth glances at the surveyors, then turns back to the rogues awkwardly. Does he seem nervous? Then, she spots Carmen standing near the front of the group with crossed arms. Her eyes are red and puffy. The burrow lost a member when Gigi died, but it's different for her. She lost a sister. "And…" Seth continues, "that kindness often depends on trust. When we spoke this morning, I noticed the two of you are quite private about your past. Trust me, I understand. Sometimes rogues seek a fresh start, to put the past behind them. We'll let you do that, but only if you publicly answer a few more questions."

The surveyors glance between the chief and the new members with guarded expressions. This must have been their suggestion. After all, even with the rogues' help, people still died. Grief can make people distrustful, even spiteful. Carmen sniffs. A group of three, Lina, Madilyn, and Julian, lean forward eagerly. If Zoey is the gatherers' gossip, those three are the surveyors' snoopers.

"Why did you leave your original home?" Seth starts.

The siblings break eye contact.

"You don't need to go into details, but a general reason would be nice. It would… put folks at ease."

Jamie smirks a little at that comment. "Okay, well, it's because… they died."

The mood immediately drops, and some surveyors turn their heads to Carmen. She is looking intensely at the rogues, eyes wide and brows knit upward. Her mouth hangs open slightly.

Jamie's brother speaks next. "The capaemen found us. My sister and I managed to escape in time, but none of the others made it out."

"Oh. If I knew that, I… I'm sorry to make you recall it," Seth says. He seems hesitant and looks to the surveyors. They all gesture for him to keep going, and Carmen nods in approval. "Did your whole clan have aceras, or did you find yours on your travels?"

"They all had them," Jamie says. "I know what you're thinking. You're wondering how we can help with your… current problem. The answer is, not much."

"Anything you can do, we'd be grateful for. It's been generations since the capaemen attacked our people, so we know practically nothing about them. But since we're so close to Albian's former territory, we're probably next. I want to find a way to avoid that."

Jamie's face grows grave as stone. "What would you have us do?"

"If you can, I'd like you and your brother to keep tabs on the capaemen. You can fly, so you'd be able to cover more ground. Tell me, would that be within your skill set?"

Both of them nod.

"Thank you. The surveyors and I have been trying to figure out how to track them, but we've made no progress. It'll be great if you can collect some intelligence."

Jamie says her next words carefully. "What, *exactly,* do you want to know?"

"Their general patterns, schedule during the day. How they are tracking us, how many there are, and especially how close they are. When they find us, we'll have to evacuate everyone to a bunker."

Mary gulps. He said *when* they find them. So, it really is inevitable.

Jamie nods slowly. "Go on."

"That's all. Check in with me regularly. For the next few days, we'll be surveying the rest of Albian's territory. We've been looking for signs of capaemen there, and it's a lot of ground to cover. We can rendezvous after that, and based on which areas you've checked, we'll decide where to survey next. I guess you could say I've started a new unit. Your skills would be best on their own, not with the surveyors nor the gatherers. We'll call you... the scouts. How do you like it?"

The siblings look at each other, then back to Seth. "Whatever helps this clan survive. I'm so sorry you have to go through this. It's always hell." Jamie's green eyes have dimmed considerably.

"I take it you know a few things about them, then?" Seth asks.

The warrior tenses. This is the first time Mary has seen her flinch. She *is* afraid of them. "Y-Yes, we probably know more than you do."

Seth sits in the grass and gestures for everyone to join him. They form a circle. The other surveyors are completely silent; they are waiting for more. Both the siblings' eyes are wide, as if caught in a nightmare. Jamie looks to the canopy, her black hair glistening in a pillar of sunlight. "You know, this forest is much more beautiful than the one we're from."

"Wait, are you telling the full story?" Albert asks, shaking.

"I am." She stares at the ground. "I appreciate your respect for our past, Seth, but we belong to this community now, and we like you guys. We shouldn't be keeping secrets."

In that moment, Lillian runs over, apparently done with her meeting. "What's going on?" Her father places a finger on his lips. The girl closes her mouth and sits down.

"The people of our original home were a particular type of assassins, trained to kill our enemies. We called ourselves Osia, but we weren't the only ones who used that name. There were other groups across Osinawa, all like us. We lived separately but had one agenda: killing capaemen." No one responds. They just lean in closer. "The Osia Coalition and the capaemen had been at war for a long time. I didn't get to participate, though; I was thirteen when the capaemen found us. I had only just learned to ride an acera. Albert was six."

Tears well in Jamie's eyes. She tries to continue, but her breath catches in her throat. Her brother places a hand on her shoulder. "My turn."

"Much like those kids you found, we were the only survivors. After that, we traveled through Osinawa, across the ocean, and into Lyonis—that's this place. We were looking for a place to settle, jumping from one clan to another for years. None truly stuck."

The whole group is silent for a few minutes. Not even Lillian, who's naturally curious, has anything to say. Mary cannot even imagine going through what they did. Losing their family that young, traveling across the world, trying to join total strangers? It sounds like a nightmare.

Finally, after several awkward moments, Seth breaks the silence. "I'm sorry you had to go through that. Forgive me, but I have to ask now: if your people killed them before, does that mean you know how to do it?"

Her face flushes. "Like I said earlier, we can't help you with that. I know how, but it would be impossible alone. You'd need a team of me's and Amphii's to stand a chance."

"I see. I was mostly asking as a last resort, but now we know that isn't an option. It's probably for the best. Killing them will only make them angry. Anyway, continue."

"R-Right. Here's what Osia knew about them: the capaemen that target humans are called hunters. They are specially trained to kill and scarily good at it."

"Hunters." They have a name for themselves. Mary never thought of that.

"The hunters travel from place to place, searching for people to kill. That's how they found our home. I'm sure that's the case for Zurec, too."

"But why now?" Seth asks, his expression pleading. Even he can't mask his desperation.

"It could be for many reasons. Some humans pissed them off, perhaps. Or they could be doing it for sport." Mary gags. They murder people for fun? Why does that not surprise her?

"That's... comforting," Seth says sarcastically. "So, how can we stop a hunter without using violence?"

Jamie stares at him, eyes blank. "That's just it. You can't. Once it has set its sights on a target, it will never relent. Only killing them will stop them." Silence falls over the group. Seth places his head in his hands, clearly overwhelmed. Lillian glares at the ground, her eyes wide with fury. Mary sympathizes with that.

"So," Mary says, surprised to hear her own voice, "all we can do is run?" The siblings nod dejectedly.

The chief looks like he's thinking hard. Everyone leans in, waiting for him to say something. It's a lose-lose situation, yet their leader still must make a decision. What a heavy mantle it is, being chief.

"Well then," Seth starts. "if this is how it has to be, then so be it!" He stands up and walks to the center of the circle. "We won't lie down and take this. We're Zurec. We always survive. We'll just keep running until they give up. Jamie, Albert, you're still willing to track them, right? No confrontation, just observation. That's all you need to do."

"O-Of course," she responds. She stares at the chief with shock and admiration. Everyone does.

"Then from now on, you are the scouts," he says proudly. "I'll have Kayla and our tactician, Robin, go over our maps of the terrain and its territorial boundaries with you tonight. As long as you can keep tabs on them, we'll figure out the rest. It'll be okay."

Jamie nods but avoids eye contact. Still, that doesn't seem to faze him.

"This meeting is over," the chief announces. He heads for the trapdoor. "Get some rest today, everyone. The surveyors and gatherers leave first thing tomorrow." He looks at Jamie and Albert. "And so do the *scouts*."

Only Seth could devise such a dicey plan *and* do so with a smile. There are so many ways it could go wrong, but for the sake of their future, Mary hopes it works.

14

Journey through the Trees

Lillian

That night Lillian has a wild dream.

She is Jamie. She brings her scythes down with deadly accuracy. Her dad blocks every attack, yet he's losing ground. She's actually a match against him. Now, he'll have to let her join the surveyors. However, just as she begins gaining ground, something blows her away. She goes flying, exactly like how Jamie flew off that root. *No!* She was so close.

The sudden ending jolts Lillian awake. Standing above her is a figure in grey. She rubs her eyes, clearing her vision. It's Jamie, back in her signature clothes. Miss May must have finished washing them.

The rogue puts a finger to her lips. In her left hand is a torch, the only light source in the room. Lillian sits up and whispers, "What's going on?"

"Let's get out of here," Jamie says a little too loudly.

The warrior who almost beat her father wants her to go somewhere. Who is she to say no?

Out in the mud room, Jamie's brother leans against the dirty wall. All the torches are lit, creating a ring of fire around the room. "Alright, now we can talk," Jamie says.

"About what?" She's already wide awake.

"Albert and I are about to leave for our scouting mission. We were wondering if you wanted to come."

"This early?" Lillian asks. It isn't even dawn. No one else has left yet.

"I wanted to ask before people start waking up. You seemed so interested. We can at least show you what it's like to sit on Amphii's saddle. So, you in or out?"

Her eyes widen. She wants to ride on that acera, but her dad won't even let her join the surveyors. There is no way he'd let her do something this risky. "You want me to go with you? Why?"

"We like you, that's why. I think you should learn more about the world."

Albert smiles. "Yeah, Amphii can fit up to three people. Although she will move a bit slower."

Lillian grins. Her dad said the same thing: how he wants her to see the world. The thought of riding on an acera, a *real* acera, makes Lillian's heart flutter, but she shakes her head. "I can't." She can't believe she said it. A few weeks ago, she wouldn't have hesitated to say yes, but things have changed now. She had a meeting with the gatherers yesterday. They have a mission to scout the forest and note the plants that are blooming. She can't disappoint Brianna.

"A shame," Jamie muses. "Would you feel better if you asked permission? You're a gatherer, right? What was your leader's name? Umm, Brittany?"

"Brianna."

"Yeah. If she lets you come, it's all good right?" Lillian places a hand on her chin. Brianna would absolutely say no, but there's no harm in asking. Then another thought occurs: Jamie and Albert are tracking the capaemen. She hardly knows how to fight monsters. She would only slow them down.

"It's not like we're fighting," Jamie continues, as if reading her mind. "Just watching. It's going to be super boring, and I don't want to be stuck with my brother all day."

Albert crosses his arms. "Love you too, sis."

"Besides," his sister goes on, "you've never seen one before, right?"

Albian flashes through Lillian's mind. "Are you serious? They could kill us, like, instantly. Why would I want to see that?"

Both the siblings' faces harden. Jamie stares at the dusty ceiling. "Oh, I *hate* them. Don't get me wrong." She forces a smile. "I guess you can say Albert and I need some moral support. So come on, what do you say?"

Lillian looks toward the exit. Despite the danger, she *is* curious. If Mary were awake, she would be scolding her right now. *"What are you thinking? I'm already worried about you all the time. Now you want to see capaemen? What is wrong with you?"*

"If you can miraculously get Brianna to say yes, then fine, I'll go," she finds herself saying. Mary's scolding gets louder.

"Go where?" someone interrupts.

Lillian could recognize that stoic voice anywhere. "Brianna?"

The redhead emerges from the hall. "Good morning."

"Damn, we're out of time," Jamie says out loud.

"Trying to steal my new recruit, I see?"

"Hey, she wants to go. Right, Lillian?"

She nods faintly.

"Oh really? Then why does she look so nervous?"

Albert places a hand on her shoulder. "Lillian? It's okay if you don't want to go."

She meets his single eye. Somehow, it eases her nerves. She thinks of the acera—how Jamie soared gracefully through the sky. It looked like so much fun. "I do. I want to go."

Brianna raises an eyebrow. "You sure?"

"Yes, please let me go." She isn't sure if it'll work, but she should at least try. With Brianna, she has a lot better chance than with her dad.

"Sounds dangerous. Seth wouldn't like it."

Lillian remembers what her dad said on the day of the eclipse. "No, I think it's okay. He said I should learn about the world, right? Well, these two are offering to fly me across the Giant Wilds. What's a better learning experience than that?"

The leader of the gatherers shrugs. "Clever girl. I'm jealous. The gatherers never get to have this much fun." She looks to the Osian assassins, her face hardening. "Just observation, right? You'll be safe on that acera, watching from a distance?"

Jamie nods.

"How can I say no to that? You guys go ahead and leave. I'll let them know where you went. When you're done, head over to Bunker Three. It's along the river, near the place we bathe. Lillian knows the spot. We'll be there by nightfall."

Lillian holds back her shock. Not only did her superior say yes, but she offered to tell the others for her. Won't that get them both in trouble?

As if reading her mind, Brianna says, "It's okay, Lillian. I accepted you into the gatherers because Seth told me to. He wants you to be safe, as all fathers do, but he also wants you to see the world. He can't have both. If I'd had a chance to see more than just this boring forest at your age, I would have jumped at it. Yeah, it's dangerous, but that's what makes it fun." She lets out a rare smile. Lillian can't hide her awe. She had no idea the leader of the gatherers was so adventurous. "Just for today, I will let you go. I'll tell Seth and Miss May *after* you've already left."

"Will they really be—"

"Okay with it? I doubt it, but I'll make a good case for you. If they're still mad after that, I'll take the blame. They can't stay mad at me for long. After all, we do work together."

"I like you, Brianna," Jamie says, patting her on the back. "That sounds like a plan. We'll go out, then meet you at the river bunker by nightfall. Let's get ready to go."

creeaakkk

Someone is opening a door. Brianna's face falls. "Go. I think Miss May is waking up." With that, the trio grabs their armor and rushes out of the burrow.

⁕⁕⁕

The Wilds are chilly today. A few trees away, a thornopine burrower hobbles with its young in tow. It's a round, rodent-like creature. Not dangerous to them, unless someone is bold enough to bother its young. The little thornlets resemble tiny brown balls from this distance. Their thorns haven't grown in yet. Lillian smiles. It's always interesting seeing what's out in the morning.

Jamie whistles twice. The high-pitched sound echoes through the canopy. Only seconds later, her acera bursts through the trees and touches down into the clearing. Lillian will never get used to that sight. The creature's marvelous wings beating through the wind, tossing debris into the air as she lands. She is straight out of a fantasy. Lillian has to thank Brianna for this when she gets back. The woman has done her a real solid.

The acera lowers her wings, and Jamie gracefully steps on, sitting at the front of the saddle. "Albert, give her a hand getting on."

"Okay." The boy grabs Lillian's hand. His hand is calloused and rough, the hands of a warrior. She's jealous. She wishes she could have trained more.

Amphii purrs a little when they step on her wing. It feels oddly delicate, like it could break under her weight. "You're doing great," Albert encourages. "Tread lightly. If you step too hard it'll hurt her."

Lillian makes each step as light as a feather. When they reach the creature's back, Albert hops onto the back of the saddle and then reaches out a hand. He hoists Lillian to the spot between them. "This is the safest spot to ride. If anything happens, I'll be the first to fall off, then Jamie, then you," the boy jokes.

"What's the point of that? Once your sister falls off, I'm done for." They both laugh.

"Albert, are you two wearing your seatbelts?" Jamie sounds annoyed.

"Yes, *Mom*," her brother mocks. He wraps a leather belt around Lillian's waist, fastening it into place. "This thing will save your life. You don't fall off as easy."

"Good to know." She's trying her best not to sound nervous and failing miserably. It feels strange, sitting on an animal; nothing like solid ground. Amphii makes subtle moves, breathing and fidgeting. She stiffens. If it's this unstable now, what will it feel like in the air?

Jamie grabs the reigns of the animal. "Alright, you ready?" Lillian nods reluctantly.

The rogue makes a clicking noise with her tongue, doing it twice in rapid succession. On that command, the acera's gargantuan wings stretch as wide as a tree trunk and lift into the air.

With the first beat of those wings, there is a jolt, then another jolt, as the ground gets farther and farther away. Immediately, the world begins to spin, but then Albert wraps his arms around her. "I know, first time flying sucks. Just keep your body still. Oh, and don't look at the ground. I did that my first time, like the chump I am." She tries her best to look at anything but the ground as the bile rises in her throat.

Once they get near the branches of the thousand-foot trees, the acera's flying begins to stabilize. Lillian never realized just how big the tree branches are. They look much smaller from below. Up here, she can see the brambles twist and turn amongst each other, creating an endless sea of red and brown. Is it just her, or is it warmer here too? They pass through a break in the foliage, causing Lillian to squint in the bright light, and she realizes the sun is closer. She hopes they don't hit it. It would be very hot.

She tries to look ahead, but that only makes things worse. Every time they are about to run into a branch, they dodge it last second, making Lillian's head spin. Plus, the wind hurts her face. She buries it in Jamie's back. The rogue keeps her head forward as if this were the most natural thing in the world. She seems perfectly content with Amphii's speed, and the whiplash doesn't bother her at all. How many years of training does it take to get used to this? One? Two? Ten? Well, however many, Lillian wants to do it. This is incredible.

"This is unreal!" she screams through the wind.

"You're doing great," Albert reassures her, his grip tightening around her waist. Lillian nearly forgot his arms were there. His warmth is welcome in this freezing wind.

Suddenly, Amphii begins to slow down. Lillian feels the bumpiness again. The animal bounces up and down in the air as she slows her flying. The world blurs. "This is the hardest part," Albert says. The creature beats her wings, touching down on a thick tree branch. She lands with a loud *thud* and Lillian turns green.

Jamie is the first to unbuckle her seatbelt. "Okay, be extra careful here, since we're not on the ground."

Both the siblings help Lillian out of her seatbelt, but she cannot move from the saddle. "No. I'm going to fall."

"You won't fall," Jamie says. "This is a big tree branch. I could run up and down this and be fine. Heck, I could fall over and be fine."

They yank on each of her arms. "Why is this so scary?" she asks.

"You get used to it," Albert says.

Reluctantly, the girl tries to stand. Her body lurches over in response. The siblings stabilize her. "Take it one step at a time," Jamie says.

Even though her body protests severely, Lillian takes a single step onto the acera's wing. Amphii sits perfectly still, her wings lain flat on the tree branch and her head down in submission. Her large round eyes stare at them with fascination.

It's as if Lillian's body weighs a thousand pounds. It feels impossible just to lift her feet. If it were not for Albert and Jamie urging her along at her sides, she wouldn't be able to move at all. Slowly but surely, they make their way down the wing.

When they take the final step off, the animal makes a slight screeching noise, then folds her wings. Lillian is surprised at how stable the tree branch feels—almost like solid ground, except actual ground is ironically a lot mushier than this tree. There is moss on many of the branches, including this one. They stand on a particularly thick patch of it.

Suddenly, her two support beams let go of her. Lillian stumbles and catches herself. "Hey!"

"See, you're fine," Jamie says. "We wouldn't land anywhere you couldn't walk."

For the final time, the girl's face turns green. She crawls to the edge of the branch and throws up off the side.

"I'm sorry," she says, coughing.

Jamie pats her back. "It's okay."

"It's cool. I did that my first time too," Albert says.

"I didn't," his sister brags.

"Yes, that's because you are *perfect*, sister," he says sarcastically.

"Shut up, Albert."

After retching over the side of the tree branch, Lillian gets her first look at the ground. Her eyes widen. She can see everything from here: the path the moss, lichens, and fungi take as they creep up and down the thousand-foot trees. From this height, she can see how they scale their trunks, numerous long branches, and even their giant round leaves. From the gaps in the canopy, hundreds of pillars of sunlight rain down, illuminating the many greens, oranges, and browns of the Giant Wilds. Bushes, flowers, and even more moss coat the forest floor, and the gargantuan redwood roots paint abstract patterns across it. Finally, far in the distance, she spots something huge: an enormous four-legged creature with a long pointed tail and a very tall neck. Artificial moss and leaves cover the skin of the beast. It blends into the forest as it stomps by.

"A dreosaur," Lillian mumbles. She remembers it from Kayla's creature book. She's never seen one in the flesh before. They are the biggest herbivores in the Giant Wilds.

Albert crouches down next to her. "Amazing, right?"

Jamie takes a seat next to Amphii. "We humans have such a limited view of the world. Luckily, we have gals like Amphii to help fix that. Isn't that right, girl?" Amphii nuzzles Jamie's face, then curls her massive tail around her protectively.

Lillian makes her way to the other side of the branch, trying to get a better view of the dreosaur. It moves incredibly slowly, each step landing with a *boom*. It must be hard to move such a massive body.

"You've never seen anything like this, have you?" Albert asks. She had forgotten he's still beside her. The girl nods faintly, fixated on the dreosaur. They sit in silence, watching each of its powerful strides until it disappears into the distance. That thing can probably travel wherever it wants without worrying, except for encountering the occasional andremedon. Those predators can be vicious. Lillian looks at her tiny body. Why did she have to be born a human? She is so vulnerable. She's so *weak*. How can she explore the world like this?

"Why the long face?" Albert asks.

"What does the outside world look like?" she finds herself asking.

"Huh? You mean outside this forest?"

She nods.

"That's a vague question, you know."

"How so?"

"There's a lot in this world. Vast treeless plains, thick jungles, the ocean. That kind of stuff."

"Okay, then tell me what outside this forest looks like," Lillian says.

"You mean, right outside?" he asks.

She nods, staring at their beautiful view from the trees.

"Out there are grass plains, mostly. There is a town, though."

"A town?"

"You know, a place where capaemen live," he says darkly.

"Oh."

"Yeah."

There is a short pause. Then Lillian turns back to him. "Is that all?"

"Pretty much."

She pouts. She had hoped there would be more to it than that. Then again, what was she expecting? Vast scores of berry bushes as far as the eye can see? A river even more beautiful than the Crystal River? Perhaps, a place where humans can live in peace? None of that is real.

"Trust me, we're safest in the Wilds," Albert says. "If you think it's brutal here, it's ten times worse out there. There's a reason most clans choose to hide in forests."

"Lots of cover?" Lillian asks.

"Exactly." They sit in silence for a few minutes, a soft breeze blowing. She remembers the story the siblings shared yesterday. They've seen so many places. If Albert says they are safest here, he's probably right. Still, Lillian wishes he weren't. She hopes that somewhere, somehow, there is a better place than this. Is that realistic? Probably not, but even as an idea, it gives her comfort.

After a short while, Jamie breaks the silence. "Alright, ready to move on? This time we won't stop until we find a capaeman. Or Amphii gets tired, of course." She strokes the acera's nose.

Lillian practically jumps out of her spot, then realizes how high she is and wobbles a bit. "I-I'm ready!"

"I am too," Albert says darkly. He must have been lost in thought.

It's much easier to climb on the acera this time. Maybe getting used to flying won't be as hard as she thought. At least, that's what Lillian thinks until the creature shoots up into the air again, sending her guts on yet another spiral. Albert wraps his arms around her again. She appreciates the security, but her stomach is empty now. She has nothing to lose. The branches pass by like lightning. Looking around makes her sick, but she keeps doing it. If she forces herself to look around, she'll get less sick over time. At least, she thinks so.

"Hey, you don't have to do that," Albert says.

"It's cool. I feel—" she gags, cutting off her sentence, "just fine."

"Really? Because you're turning green again."

Heat rises to her cheeks. "I-I am?"

"Yeah, you look like the forest floor right now," he teases.

"Hey!" She elbows him. He laughs.

Jamie was serious about not stopping. It feels like forever riding on the back of the acera, seeing the trees blur by. As they stay in the air longer, Lillian begins to feel less sick. Or is it just that she's feeling numb? She can't tell. Either way, looking around has become a little easier. Now, she can watch for capaemen like the other two, but what exactly is she looking for? A very big person? It feels wrong to call them that, but that's the only description she has ever gotten. Why is that? Some of the older people must have seen one before, but they never talk about it.

"Doing okay?" Albert asks. She nods, scanning their surroundings. She tries to look on both sides of the acera—cover all the ground—but it's no use. Everything is moving too fast. How will they know if they see one? She assumes Jamie's eyes have had some sort of extensive training that Lillian's eyes cannot even fathom. Otherwise, she should slow down the acera because they won't find anything like this.

Or so she thinks.

whoooooossshhh

Even with the whipping of the wind, a familiar sound roars through the trees. Lillian looks down toward the ground and sees nothing but water. They're flying over the Crystal River. Now that Lillian can see the river from the sky, she can finally fathom how big it is. There must be a mile of water between one bank and the other. If they could somehow walk across it, reaching the other side would take them half an hour. Flying on Amphii would take only minutes.

"Why are we at the river?" Lillian asks.

"Just a hunch," Jamie responds.

"Good call, sis. We aren't the only ones who find this place beautiful. There might be one here." She nods, her gaze fixated on the river.

Amphii continues to fly beneath the canopy. Patches of sunlight flash by like lightning. Still, Lillian keeps her gaze fixed ahead. She's afraid if she looks away even for a second, she will miss something big.

What passes by next, however, is something she could *never* miss.

15

The Healer by the River

Lillian

Slumped against one of the giant trees is a human figure. But the way Lillian catches sight of it even from the air terrifies her. The creature is so massive it would be impossible not to notice.

Jamie reacts first, yanking on Amphii's reigns. The acera soars deeper into the trees and settles on a branch surrounded by leaves.

"Why are we landing here?" Lillian asks.

"Capaemen have really good eyesight," Jamie says.

Chills run up and down her spine. *Of course* they do. "But how are we going to see it?"

"Easy, we find an opening," Albert adds. He grabs her wrist and walks her down the branch. Then, he stops in front of a small gap in the leaves. From this opening, Lillian has a perfect view of the rushing river and the forest floor, not to mention the colossus below.

As Lillian studies the giant, her heart pounds through her ears. It leans against a whitewood tree, its back hunched over and clawed hands at work on something. It has side-swept black hair, brown skin, and square shoulders. Maybe it's a male. She doesn't know for sure, though. It wears a loose, green jacket and tan slacks. Lillian cannot place what material the clothes are made of. They seem out of this world.

The giant looks so peaceful. Nearby forest critters chitter away without a care. It's as if they are not bothered at all by its presence. From so high up in the trees, Lillian can almost convince herself that the humanoid figure is... the same size as a regular person.

That's the problem, though. From this high, humans should look like bugs. If the giant looks normal from here, she can't imagine how it would look from the ground. She shivers at the thought.

"So, what do you think?" Albert whispers. Lillian hears the words, but she doesn't process them. She wants to burn this image into her head. This is what the enemy looks like. *This* is what is after her family. "Hey, Albert to Lily. Come in, Lily." He shakes her back and forth.

"Why are you calling me that?" she asks, irritated.

"What do you think of the capaeman?"

She notes its human-like features. "It looks kind of like you."

"What? I'm not that ugly. How dare you."

"I mean, age-wise. It has to be about our age, don't you think?" She's only seen two male teenagers—Albert and the awful Rostad boy—so she can't be sure, but she has a feeling she's right.

"First of all, you have no way of knowing that. For all we know, that monster could be a hundred years old. Also, I don't have scales for skin."

Lillian thinks of commenting on that joke, but she's too surprised by what he said after it. "Scales for skin?"

"Yeah, it's hard to tell from here, but their skin is made of scales. Hard as stone too. Even if you have the numbers, they're still damn hard to kill." Lillian squints, trying to make out the texture of the capaeman's skin. It wears long sleeves, so the only skin exposed is its hands and face. The pillars of light from the canopy are so tiny compared to its gigantic body that any gleam against it is nominal, but in particularly bright patches, its skin does look odd. It is almost as if its skin is... shimmering in the sunlight. If Lillian could get closer, she's sure she'd be able to see the scales. If only getting closer didn't mean death.

"Jamie, how are you holding up?" Albert asks.

For a moment Lillian's focus breaks, and she checks on the rogue. Jamie lays cuddled against her acera, her body shaking. "I-I'm fine, Albert." She isn't even looking at the capaeman, yet her eyes are wide with fear.

"No, you're not. Look, if you want to leave—"

"N-No! Not until we get a clue. W-We've got to see if—if this one's hostile or not."

"Well, if you say so," her brother responds, concern in his tone.

"What's up with her?" Lillian whispers.

"Ever since our people were killed, she gets like this. Best not to ask her about it. She won't give you a straight answer."

Lillian nods, glad to fixate on the capaeman again. Suddenly, the giant's hands freeze, and it looks up, leaning its head against the white tree trunk. She can finally see its face.

The capaeman's face is heart-shaped with defined cheeks. Its eyes are a deep green, like the shadowy zones of the forest—much darker than the green of any human's eyes, and, whereas a human iris is surrounded by white, this capaeman's iris takes up its entire eye. It has reptilian slits for pupils. Despite the shockingly alien gaze, she can read its expression. It seems deep in thought, lost in a world of its own. This is nothing like how she pictured the capaemen. For some reason, she always imagined them as more monster than human, but this one looks more human than monster.

Next to her, Albert gasps. "What's that in its hands?" Lillian's attention turns to the hands. Cupped gently in them is a small creature with little flightless wings and a tiny beak. It does not appear to be moving. She guesses it to be a baby styfisher, a local species at the river. They are about five feet tall, only about a foot and a half shorter than the average human. The capaeman must have killed it.

No... it's moving.

Gently, the capaeman lowers the creature to the ground and places a finger on one of its little legs. Lillian squints. Is the creature wearing bandages? The leg twitches, and the creature squawks. It attempts to get up, wobbling on its injured leg.

The giant smiles kindly, watching as the styfisher limps around. It falls clumsily over, but before its face can hit the dirt, the giant's hand catches it. It scoops the creature back up, cradling it in its hands. Lillian feels like she can't breathe. This capaeman... is treating such a small creature... with *kindness*. It has tended to its wounds so gently. Is this really the same kind of creature that killed Albian? The images of those bodies slumped over and not moving haunt Lillian's mind. So do the mangled body of Noah and the frozen, hopeless eyes of Gigi. They did not die by a capaeman's hand, but they are gone, nonetheless. She tries her best not to think about them, but sometimes they appear when she lies down to sleep, or when she dreams.

She wonders if the rogues can shed some light on this. She looks at Albert, and to her surprise, Jamie is standing beside him. Her dark skin is so pale it looks unhealthy. Her brother looks at her, waiting for her to say something. "Let's leave," she mumbles.

"Huh?" Lillian asks. It seems too soon. Don't they need to wait for clues? Clues as to how the capaemen could be hunting them? Then again, this one doesn't seem to be hunting at all.

"There's nothing here. Let's find another one." Without even being told, Amphii spreads her wings into a walkway again, ready for them to climb onto her back.

"W-What do you think of this?" Lillian asks as they make their way onto the acera.

"Don't be deceived, Lillian," Jamie responds. "All we know right now is that this one isn't doing anything. Trust me when I say that they are monsters, no matter how nice they appear."

Something doesn't feel right. Sure, the capaeman looks scary, but it seems it couldn't care less about hunting. On the contrary, it was helping an injured animal. Miss May said that some capaemen just pass through the forest, and the rogues explained that the hunters are specialists. They train to kill. So, does that mean some capaemen don't care about humans at all? Maybe this one is like that. Still dangerous, but not a hunter. They could stand to observe it a little longer. "There's no need to leave so quickly," Lillian says. "If it isn't doing anything, maybe we can learn something."

Albert scoffs. "Regardless of what it's doing, it's just as dangerous. Besides, we're looking for hunters, remember? We have to see what they're up to. We don't have time for curiosity."

"Yeah," his sister chimes in. "The only reason my brother and I have survived this long is because we *don't* wonder. We only learn what we need to know. So, trash that curious attitude of yours before it gets you killed."

"But—"

"Don't get your hopes up, Lillian," Albert interrupts. "It's our enemy, no matter how innocent it looks." The siblings' scathing words do nothing to quell Lillian's curiosity. They are probably right, but she can't help but sense there is something she's missing. That capaeman wasn't terrorizing the forest. It was just sitting by the river. It even helped an animal. Why was it doing that?

No, what's wrong with me? She should not question such things when the capaemen are trying to kill them. Just because it was nice to an animal does not mean it would be to them. She will bury her curiosity. That's what is best for everyone.

⚕

The group spends a few more hours flying, with no luck. Before Lillian knows it, the light in the forest begins to fade. They have been riding on the acera so long, her butt aches. Her muscles feel stiff and sore. She will have to stretch when they get to the bunker.

"Sis, are we heading home soon?" Albert asks. They have been flying near the edge of the Wilds, around what Lillian presumes to be Rostad's territory. It's a good place to check, as it's closer to capaeman domain. "I think Bridget wanted us to meet her by the river bunker."

"It's *Brianna*, and she said something like that. Unfortunately, that's back down the path we came. I'm sooo eager to go past the tree where we saw a capaeman. I'm sure that won't go wrong at all."

Lillian gulps. She only now realizes how close Bunker Three is to that whitewood tree. Is it safe for them to stay there now?

Albert's arms tighten around her waist. "Don't we need to warn them?"

"Yeah, they'll need to abandon that bunker."

"Abandon it?" Lillian asks. "That seems extreme."

"No, it isn't," Jamie says grimly. "It's perfectly reasonable. If any capaeman is nearby, we should abandon ship."

"Abandon... ship?"

"It's an expression. Don't worry about it," Albert explains. "The important thing is, we need to find the gatherers. Right now."

"That's what I'm trying to do. Damn, I guess we need to go near the whitewood after all. They might already be there."

"On the bright side," her brother adds, "it's probably gone by now. They don't stay out when it gets dark."

"True."

Time passes. Eventually, Lillian can hear the river over the whipping wind. A deep, fast-flowing part of the river comes into view. A few minutes later, a short waterfall appears, and on the bank next to it, the whitewood tree. Lillian's heart skips a beat seeing it again, but the capaeman isn't there anymore. Thank the Wilds.

From that point, the sound of the river starts to increase. They pass a section of rapids. "We're almost there," Jamie says over the roar. Gradually, the rapids reduce in size until they finally peter out, replaced by a smooth, moderate current. They reach the site of Bunker Three in seconds. It sits between the rapids and Zurec's favorite bathing spot. In the distance, Lillian spots the shallow riverbed where she and Mary used to splash each other, and the deeper water where they would dive for new stones for Mary's jewelry. So many fond memories. From here, those places look so small, so insignificant in the massive Giant Wilds. All the places she has been, all the things she has done so far, are tiny compared to the scale of the world. If there's anything she has learned from leaving the burrow, it's that she knows nothing. Jamie and Albert have made that painfully clear.

Jamie pulls on the reigns and moves Amphii to land, and for a moment Lillian wonders why, until she spots a group of people making their way through a field of red flowers. They grow next to the ferns of the riverbank. At the front of the group is a long red ponytail.

They have found the gatherers.

They circle to the front of the group and land slowly, making sure not to startle them. At first, the group draws their weapons, but when they spot the trio, they lower them. Brianna looks worn out. There are bags under her eyes, and she carries a basket full of giant crimson berries. "Good evening. How was your trip?"

Jamie is the first to hop off of the acera. "Hey. It was a wash. We didn't find any clues, but Lillian had fun, I think."

"Well, that's good at least," Mia comments. "Because when Seth and Miss May found out what you pulled, they weren't happy."

The other gatherers nod, disappointment etched on their faces, and suddenly Lillian is wracked with guilt. "I'm sorry. Was it bad? Are we both in trouble?"

"Don't worry. I took care of it. Mia is exaggerating," Brianna explains. "Miss May gave me a stern talking to, but she's at least open to the idea. Seth was mainly angry because we didn't ask permission, and he wants to talk to you about it. The surveyors will be gone for a few days though, so we have time."

"So, she can continue to fly with us?" Jamie asks.

The leader of the gatherers nods. Others, however, seem miffed. Mia is obviously dying to say something but refrains from it. Meanwhile, Theo stares daggers at her, Bruno has his eyebrows raised, and Zoey simply cocks her head.

Lillian tries to steer the subject. "We saw a capaeman. It was uh, well, it was by the whitewood tree." She's unsure if she was supposed to say that, but they deserve to know.

Brianna's face flushes. "That doesn't sound like nothing. Are we safe?"

"We should be for the night," Jamie explains, narrowing her eyes, "but let's wake up extra early and abandon the bunker tomorrow."

"Okay, is there anything else we should know?" She looks around. The other gatherers seem exhausted. They carry loads of supplies, from herbs to fruits to berries. It is clearly weighing them down. "Oh, never mind. We're almost at the bunker. Let's talk in there," Brianna says.

The bunker is only a few dozen trees down from the whitewood. Like Bunker Two, the entrance is small, barely wide enough to fit one person at a time. The gatherers are carrying a lot, so Lillian and Jamie unlatch and open the door. It creaks open. The redwood is so rotten it feels fragile in Lillian's hands. Maybe they should abandon this place.

When they settle in the bunker, having lit the torches and laid out sleeping mats, Mia passes out one glass jar and three fist-sized red berries to each person. They all sit in a circle.

"What are we doing?" Lillian asks, staring at the glass. This is a valuable object. With the forge no longer in use, they can no longer make glass.

"We're making jam," Mia responds. "We had a very nice haul of berries today. We've got to restock on rations. So, newcomers, this is how you do it." She pulls out a cylindrical, blunt object made of wood. "You take a pestle, and one at a time, grind the berries into your jar. Then, stir in some nectar from that container in the center. That'll give the jam its texture. If you fill up one, I'll get you another. Oh, and please, try not to break the jars. We have a limited supply."

"I've done this before," Jamie adds. "It's pretty easy. You use melvia flowers for the nectar, right?"

"We do! They can be found in the northern part of the Wilds. We haven't picked any in forever, though. Their nectar never expires. Anyway," the medic continues, "once everyone is done, we can get a good night's sleep, and then flee in the morning. Oh my, Brianna, what will we take from the bunker? There are so many useful supplies here. I'd hate to abandon them."

The redhead is already crushing her berries. "Whatever we can carry. If we have to, we can take two trips. We just need to be careful."

"You're right. I can't believe one of them was so close by. Jamie, what do you think it was doing here? A-Are we going to be okay?"

All eyes immediately fall on the scouts. Lillian stares at them expectantly as well. They dodged her questions about the capaeman earlier. Maybe they'll shed some light on things now.

As she mashes her berries, Jamie recalls the whole story, from how they found the capaeman, to specific details about its appearance and behavior. Lillian is surprised by how many details Jamie remembers, considering she was hiding in the leaves the whole time. She conveniently leaves out that part.

"So, I'd say from what we know, that one isn't a hunter—meaning it's not after us—but it might be around the forest a lot, especially near the river. We need to be careful."

Lillian opens her mouth but then closes it. She wants to add other important details: how it looked young, how it hung out by the river without a care, and how it cared for an injured styfisher. Are these details her clan would care about? She doesn't think so, but she doesn't like how Jamie glossed over them either. Considering what Zurec believes about capaemen, this should be discussed, right?

"Not as bad as I thought," Brianna responds. "If you do find a hunter, let us know immediately. I'll let Seth know about what the three of you found today. No bathing by the river for a while."

Then again, maybe Lillian is overthinking it. All that matters is that capaeman is not a hunter. It isn't in the way of their survival, end of story. She remembers Jamie's words when she asked too many questions: *Trash that curious attitude of yours before it gets you killed.* She has no right to question that advice. After all, she knows nothing about the world.

Lillian mixes the nectar in and twists the wooden lid shut on her jar, trying to distract herself. She can't believe she's never made this before. Given all the crafts and cooking they learned with Miss May, one would think they'd learn to make preserves too. Maybe it's just a gatherer thing. Either way, she's proud of her creation. She moves the jar around. The red inches around the container. It has a gelatinous texture. Lillian stuffs it in her backpack.

"Oh, can we keep them?" Albert asks, seeing what she's doing.

"If you want," Brianna says. "Just make sure to return the jar. We should have plenty of jam to go around." Many gatherers have already finished multiple bottles.

"Sweet," the boy responds. He stuffs his jar in his black backpack.

It isn't long before everyone has finished. Mia sits at the back of the room, shoving herbs into more jars. Sweat beads on her forehead.

"Mia, I'm about to blow out the torches. Might want to finish up," Brianna mentions, staring disapprovingly.

"W-Wait, no! I'm not done yet."

"If we wait for you to be done, we'll be up all night." She drifts about the room, blowing out the torches one by one. Even though she grew up sleeping underground, Lillian has never liked the pitch-black that follows the lights going out. Not even a sliver of moonlight can shine through the bunker door. They are completely closed off in here. She breathes in the stuffy air. It smells of dirt and burning wood. On her right, she can hear Jamie and Albert stirring, likely settling into their beds. No words pass between them.

She can't help but think of what they saw today. Maybe they're also thinking about that capaeman, sitting peacefully by the riverbank. It looked almost... human. If the two species are that similar, then why do they hunt humans? None of what happened today makes sense.

Doesn't make sense, or you can't make sense of it? she thinks.

For once, it takes Lillian forever to fall asleep. She twists and turns repeatedly, like a log stuck in the river. Capaemen are evil. That's the end of it.

So why can't she let this go?

16

Cornered

Lillian

Lillian is out of the bunker first thing in the morning. The less time she spends in that claustrophobic space, the better.

In the Giant Wilds, mist fills the air. She sits on a tree root, watching the light shimmer on the river's surface and munching on some dried vegetables. After yesterday, she is starving. She thought of eating the jam but decided to save it for later. It doesn't take up much room in her backpack.

As she eats, Lillian studies the river's flow. This part of the river is interesting, as it is the midpoint between Zurec's peaceful bathing spot and the roaring rapids. Here, plant life encroaches on the river more than usual. She finds it fascinating how the water builds pressure as it moves south, dodging the obstacle course of tree roots.

It isn't long before her peace is interrupted. The trapdoor creaks open, and Brianna emerges. One by one, the other gatherers follow her until there is a small crowd around Lillian.

The leader of the gatherers already has her spear in hand. Her eyes dart around in every direction. "Good morning."

"Morning," Lillian says, food still in her mouth.

The rest of the gatherers have their arms full of food sacks, containers of medicine, and large stacks of wood. It seems they've taken everything they can carry. Mia is hauling too many bags for her tiny form. Her knees are bent, and sweat trickles down her forehead. Still, the medic smiles at Lillian. She can respect her for that.

Brianna's green eyes keep darting around. "Still want to go with Jamie and Albert today? Otherwise, we could use another hand." She hasn't looked at her once.

"I'm good," Lillian replies. "I think they like me traveling with them."

"I think so too. Okay, we're off then. Stay safe."

"I will."

With that, the gatherers leave. Lillian watches them slowly fade into the misty forest, and she is alone again. The warrior stares at the river. It flows with a massive, never-ending *whoosh*. It's oddly peaceful. The river may go up and down, but the sound of its flow never changes. The roots of the nearby redwood tree twist and tangle into the water. A distance ahead of those roots, an adult styfisher floats through the water currents. From a distance, it seems small, but she isn't fooled. She knows a full-grown styfisher can stand up to fifteen feet tall. The creature dives below the water briefly, catching a massive fish in its beak and swallowing it with one gulp. Its feathers are a darker color than the one from yesterday—the one that was with the capaeman. That one was about the size of a human, yet the giant cared for it so gently. Helping a creature so much smaller than oneself must take a lot of skill. It's astounding that those massive creatures have that. She wonders what else they don't know about capaemen. To think that yesterday it was just a few trees down. The whitewood isn't even a ten-minute walk from here. Terrifying.

"Lily. Hey!" Albert says.

"Wh-What?" The sound of the assassin boy's voice startles her. She didn't hear him come out of the bunker.

He takes a seat next to her. "Whatcha thinking about, Lily?"

"I said don't call me that."

"But it's cute. Why don't you like it?"

"I have a name. It's Lillian."

"And Lily is a nickname. It's kind of like a shorter version of your name." She sighs. She doesn't have the mental space to argue. "There you go again," Albert says.

"Huh?"

"Drifting off. What's got you thinking so much?"

"Sorry, I've been a bit spacey lately."

"You've been spacey since I met you," he teases. "That's beside the point, though." She bites her lip, wondering if she should tell him. "It's about the capaeman, isn't it?"

Lillian jumps. "How did you know?"

"It was all over your face. Don't worry, I've been thinking about it too. It was so close. The sooner we get out of here, the better." He pauses, staring at the distant styfisher as if it's going to attack them.

"You know they only hunt fish, right?" Lillian says, pointing at the creature. "It isn't dangerous." She's not sure why she's explaining this, but she feels she has to.

"I know, but you can never be too cautious," Albert responds flatly.

"It's just fishing. It's not going to hurt us. Don't worry."

The boy falls silent, watching the styfisher disappear into the distant water. Lillian watches it with him, not knowing what to say next. No matter how hard she tries, she can't stop thinking about the capaeman from yesterday. That wasn't how she imagined them. The giant wasn't terrorizing the forest. It wasn't looking for humans to kill, and it was kind to the animals. Jamie and Albert didn't even comment on that. They didn't wonder if it were strange. They just moved on, as if it was any other capaeman.

After the awkward pause, Albert finally speaks. "Look, I know what you're thinking right now. I was like that too, before I saw what they're capable of. Heck, even Jamie is terrified—more so than me. I still haven't—"

"Good morning, scouts!" Jamie interrupts.

Not again. He was clearly about to say something important. Lillian crosses her arms. "Hey."

The overenthusiastic sister throws her arms around the both of them. "How's it going this morning? Did you two sleep well?"

"Yeah," Albert says.

"No," Lillian says at the same time.

"Great!" She isn't even listening. "We should get going as soon as possible. I'll whistle for Amphii." She takes some distance from them, places two fingers in her mouth, and lets out two loud whistles.

A few minutes pass. No response.

"Huh. Well, we are close to the river. Maybe she can't hear us. Come on guys, we're taking a hike." She gestures for them to follow. They pick up their packs and trail behind Jamie until the river is a quiet hum in the distance. They arrive in a small clearing full of sunlight. Red flowers grow in clusters, swaying back and forth in the wind. Their scent fills the air. Jamie climbs onto a tree root. "Okay, she'll have to hear us here." She whistles again.

This time, Amphii arrives within seconds. She must have been waiting for them. She lands quickly and nuzzles her head up to Jamie, purring loudly.

"Aww, who's a good girl? You are, you are." She scratches the side of the acera's head. Amphii stomps her foot.

"So," Lillian says, "how are we going to search for the capaemen today?"

Jamie's face darkens. "Same as yesterday. Why do you ask?"

"Just... want to know the plan." Oh no, she's said too much again.

"Right. Well, the plan is to find a different capaeman. Not the one from yesterday."

"Jamie, you're shaking... really bad," Albert says. His face has also grown stony.

"H-Huh? I-I'm not afraid. I'm wary, just as a-anyone else would be. They're monsters. They killed our people, remember?"

"Yes, I was there," he retorts. Lillian closes her mouth. She really did say too much. Curse her curiosity. "I was there, Jamie, and I'm not nearly as afraid as you are. You think I don't remember the massacre, but I do. I remember every awful second of that day, yet it's you who's always quaking in her boots. I'd get it if it were both of us, or just me. You've always been stronger than me. But you? Why are you more afraid of something than I am, huh?"

"Albert, I've said not to push this," Jamie says through gritted teeth.

"You've always been like this. Why?" her brother says coldly. This is something they have talked about before. All Lillian can do is listen. It isn't her place to intervene.

"I told you. I was thirteen. You were six. You may think you remember, but I remember more clearly than you do. That's why I'm afraid." Fury burns in Albert's brown eye. It's as if he has heard that explanation a million times. "End of story, Albert," Jamie says.

Albert clenches his fists and takes a seat on Amphii. "Well, we should get ready to go."

Jamie follows. "Yes, we should."

Lillian stands still, her mouth open. These siblings have more baggage than anyone else she knows. She doesn't know what it's all about but knows it's not good. She almost regrets not going with the gatherers. "Hurry up," Jamie says. The warrior nods, meandering toward Amphii's outstretched wings. At the same time, the bushes to her left rustle a bit. She spots it from the corner of her eye and quickly unstraps her spear from her back. What monster is it this time?

Out of the bushes emerges a small creature, barely shorter than Lillian. It has two little webbed feet, tiny flightless wings, wide round eyes, and a pointed beak. Its tan feathers stick up high on top of its head. A baby styfisher. Is it related to the one they saw a few minutes ago?

The styfisher stops, staring at the humans. It quacks and cocks its huge head. Its wide eyes look so innocent—just curious to see what was going on. It isn't a threat. Not at all.

So why has the atmosphere grown so cold?

She turns back to the siblings. They look like they're about to scream but are holding it in. Jamie's face contorts with terror so strong it spreads to Lillian. Chills run down her spine. Then, she makes the connection.

Yesterday, that capaeman had a styfisher. It can't be the same one, though. Many styfishers live by the river. It could be another baby alone without its mom, and in the same place the capaeman was in yesterday, and... *Oh no.*

Lillian spots a bandage wrapped around the creature's leg. She can't believe she didn't notice it until now. The styfisher waddles toward her, its flightless wings twitching. The capaeman could be anywhere, but she can't get her body to move.

It runs in circles around her as if the injury doesn't affect it. Where is the capaeman? The boy that cared for this bird? Maybe it's not here. Maybe after caring for the styfisher, it took off. Yeah, that must be it.

"Lillian! What in the Wilds are you doing? Get over here!" Albert says. This snaps her out of her stupor. She *has* to move. She makes her way to the acera, but then the styfisher jumps in her way.

It quacks, pecking her arm. "Ow!" Lillian screams. She tries to go around it again. It jumps in her way, thinking she's playing. Its little beak opens and closes as it quacks with glee. She tries to move it out of the way, but it stays rooted. It may be shorter than her, but it's heftier.

Then she hears the sound. Faint at first.

boom... boom...

Steady, rhythmic, an animal with two feet. And it is enormous. "Move, you stupid animal!" Lillian says, panicking. Jamie's grip tightens around the reigns, and she watches the canopy as if ready to take off at any minute.

Boom... Boom...

Twice as loud.

"It's coming! Get over here, NOW!" Albert screams at the top of his lungs. The styfisher still won't move. It keeps bounding in her way as if this is a game. Lillian moves right, left, backward, forward—it still blocks the way. Its feathers twitch with excitement.

Boom Boom

Four times as loud. Her ears ring. If this is the capaeman, it's close now. She's out of time. This styfisher may be a friendly, tame creature, but survival comes first. The warrior raises her spear. "I'm sorry!"

BOOM.

The colossal sound makes Lillian stumble. In the next second, two things happen simultaneously. First, Amphii spreads her wings and flies away without her. "Jamie, no!" Albert screams.

Second, a shadow descends over her.

⁂

Lillian lowers her spear, and the styfisher hobbles up to her, nuzzling her shoulder. She can't even move. Did Jamie and Albert leave her? Just like that?

The shadow over her shifts, shaking the ground. Lillian's breath catches in her throat. Her feet feel glued to the moss. How can she survive this? *Think. Think.* She can't outrun it. Her only means of getting away just took off without her. How could Jamie do that to her? *Think.* There has to be another way. She clutches her spear in her left hand. Can she fight? No, that's preposterous. Not something this big. She would need an army.

The styfisher quacks at her, as if now sensing her distress. It looks up at the shadow, then at Lillian, then up at it again.

"I see you have acquired a new friend," a voice booms. Immediately, Lillian knows that isn't the voice of a human. It's too low and distorted. Again, the bodies of Albian flash through her mind. *I'm next*, she thinks with horror. No. Get it under control. *You've got to think logically,* she thinks to herself. There must be a way to make it out alive.

"Return," the voice says. At first, Lillian thinks it's talking to her. However, at the command, the styfisher runs behind Lillian, back to its guardian. "Now, what is a human doing in this place?" the voice asks. It still sounds strange, like a man's voice mixed with an animal's. There is a low growl in its inflection. Now that Lillian has heard it a few times, she begins to make out the tone. It sounds very condescending. Like Miss May when she gives her a scolding. "Trying to murder the styfisher too. How typical."

Lillian's knees buckle, but she stiffens, steadying herself. She will stay standing. If she is to die here, she will do it with dignity. Still, she never thought this was how she would die. There's still so much she wants to do—so much she wants to see.

"But you hesitated to kill it. You had ample time to do so." It speaks so strangely. She doesn't understand some of the words it says, but what she comprehends the least is... why is she still alive? It's almost like it is attempting to talk to her. "Do you speak, human? Or is what I have overheard only a rumor?"

Lillian takes in a deep breath. "The styfisher..." she trails off, her breath catching in her throat. Her body isn't listening to her. Her heart thumps so loudly it feels like her ears are about to explode. She wracks her brain, trying to find a way out of this situation.

Then, a sudden calmness washes over her. *That's it*, she thinks. *There is no way out. It's impossible*. There is no way she will survive this. That means... she can say whatever she wants, and it won't matter. She may die here, but she is going to die fighting. "The styfisher wouldn't get out of my way. I was prepared to do whatever I had to," she says loudly.

"I see, you were attempting to flee." The shadow shifts, and the wind wavers. With every word, the air vibrates. With every movement, the world rumbles. Lillian shuts her eyes tight. At any moment, she could be crushed. She wonders if she will feel the pain or if it'll be over too quickly to register. She hopes for the latter.

The rumbling stops, followed by deafening silence. All she can hear is the river flowing in the distance. Lillian wonders what Jamie and Albert are doing right now. Did they flee, or are they hiding in the trees, designing a plan to rescue her? They wouldn't abandon her, right? Right?

"How do you survive, being so little?" the capaeman asks. It's still asking questions. Why? Come to think of it, this all feels very surreal. Lillian could be dreaming right now. Yeah, she'll wake up any minute. This is like that nightmare she had before the Red Eclipse. There is no way she would end up in this situation in real life. She's not meant to die here. She's meant to join the surveyors someday. She has to prove to her dad that she is worthy of becoming chief. There's no way this is real. Maybe seeing the capaeman's face will wake her up. Slowly, Lillian turns around. She just needs one more push.

The second her eyes fall on the creature, Lillian staggers backward but doesn't fall. She will not fall. She takes in the sight, knees bent, breaths haggard.

A humanoid mountain towers over her, its shadow blocking out the sun. Even the red flowers, which shined so brightly before, are now bathed in shadow. The capaeman has taken a seat on the ground, its legs crossed. It is so massive, her height barely reaches its knee. Up close like this, Lillian can finally see its scales. They crowd in rows up and down its face, neck, chest, and hands. The scales, brown in tint, complement its black hair and dark-green eyes. Its vertical pupils dilate and constrict. Lillian cannot tell what it is thinking. These giants must be either emotionless or very stoic, like Brianna.

The warrior takes a deep breath. This is not a dream after all. "What do you want from me?"

The boy's gaze shifts toward the river. The styfisher is sitting in its hands. It squawks with excitement, as if being there isn't dangerous. "I suppose... I simply want you to answer my questions."

That's an odd answer. Still, this is an opening. It's now or never. "If I do that, will you let me go?"

The capaeman snaps its gaze back, almost too quickly for its size. "You are a human. Why would I do that?"

Lillian's legs almost collapse again. Its gaze is piercing, almost as if peering into her soul. She can't stop trembling. "B-Because I mean you no harm?"

It makes a growling sound, almost like a chortle. "Hmph, what an obvious lie. Especially with that weapon in your hand." Those soulless green eyes glare at Lillian's spear, but why? She glances at it. It shimmers red, reflecting the red flowers all around them. If that isn't a sign she is going to die, she doesn't know what is.

The capaeman points a giant finger at her spear. "That metal is very rare, you know."

"I know *nothing* about it," Lillian says. Why would the capaeman be threatened by her spear? It's a toothpick to it.

"How did humans as primitive as you acquire *that*?" it asks, completely ignoring what she said.

Primitive. She's never heard that word before, but it sounds insulting. Something about how this thing is talking rubs her the wrong way. "*Primitive?*"

The giant's expression remains blank. "Yes. Do you not know what that means?"

"I know full well! Listen, you... capaeman!" She grasps her spear and points it at the giant. "I don't like these games. If you're going to kill me, just do it already." The capaeman's eyes widen, then its lips turn upward, showing a full set of pointed teeth. Where a human's canines would be, the teeth are a little longer—a pair of fangs. As if capaemen didn't look deadly enough.

Lillian braces herself.

But instead of attacking her, the capaeman lets out what can only be described as a laugh. The sound booms through the Giant Wilds, no doubt alerting anyone nearby to get the heck out of here. Lillian clasps her hands over her ears. The sound is so loud the ground itself shakes. "You are *amusing*. You wish for death?"

Lillian takes her hands off her ears. "No, of course not, but you said it yourself. You won't let me go. That leaves only one option." The capaeman's face falls. Where there was a smile, there is now darkness. She's such a fool. Why did she say that? She is practically asking to die.

Then, it shakes its head. "Do not be absurd. There is more than just one option. You are human, but you do not seem to be a threat."

It's Lillian's turn to laugh now. "What? Me? A threat? To you? Who's really being *absurd* here?"

The capaeman smirks. It's a strange sight, watching those scales move as its face does. "Fair point." Lillian regains control of her body. This giant... It isn't going to harm her. If it wanted to, it would have done so already. She may even be able to get some answers.

"It is Lionel, by the way."

"Huh?"

"My name is Lionel. Do not call me *capaeman*." Lillian raises her eyebrows. She didn't even think about that. "*Yes*, we have names," Lionel says as if reading her mind. "What is yours?"

Her name catches in her throat. None of this makes any sense.

"Do *you* possess names?"

She nods faintly, but only one thing is on her mind. She wants answers. For the first time, Lillian willingly makes eye contact with the capaeman. If he can glare into her soul, she can right back. "Lionel, what are you doing here? What are the *capaemen* doing here?"

Lionel's face is unreadable. He strokes the styfisher, now fast asleep in his hands.

She has really done it this time. No one—*no one*—would ask a question so reckless, except for her. She remembers what Jamie said— *"They are monsters, no matter how nice they appear,"*—and what Albert told her— *"It's our enemy, no matter how innocent it looks."* Despite their warnings and everything she's ever been taught, for some reason, she had to ask. She wants to know more, even if it kills her. Lillian wonders whether she's lost her mind or if this is how she's always been.

The capaeman stares at the horizon. The sun is climbing toward the canopy. "I must head back soon." With that, Lionel stands.

"Wh-What are you doing?" she shouts, hoping he can hear her from up there.

"I am leaving," the capaeman says. "I have decided to let you go."

If Lillian thought he was tall before, that's nothing compared to now. It was so easy to gaze down at him from the trees yesterday. He looked so much smaller from far above. Now, standing in this capaeman's shadow, she feels like such a fool. He makes the redwood trees look almost normal. To him, this is not the Giant Wilds. She wonders what capaemen call this place. The Regular Wilds? Just, the Wilds?

Those huge feet lift off the ground, and the capaeman leaves. The sound of his footsteps echoes through the trees. "Wait," Lillian says. She can't believe she's saying it. He freezes, the echo fading almost instantly.

"You haven't answered my question."

He doesn't turn around, but his head tilts up. Not even he is tall enough to reach the canopy. "If you ever wish to talk more, I will be by the river." With that, Lionel starts walking again, the *boom*s picking up pace. They thrum in Lillian's ears. The giant travels farther and farther away from her until finally, he disappears into the forest.

Lillian falls to her knees.

17

The Girl Who Survived

Lillian

As the low *boom*s of Lionel's footsteps fade, Lillian's eyes grow heavier. She can hardly see her shaking hands. What just happened... was impossible. She had a conversation with a capaeman, a real one, and she is alive. This goes way beyond anything she was prepared for. The capaeman... It, no, *he* said he would give her answers. Could that be true?

"If you ever wish to talk more, I will be by the river."

flap flap flap

She hears something, but it seems so far away. It's as if she is in another world entirely. After such a strange encounter, perhaps she is. Then something warm envelops her. "Lillian, are you okay?" the voice of Albert asks. "By the Wilds, I thought you were going to die."

"She didn't, thank goodness," Jamie chimes in. She sounds even farther away than Albert. "We've got to leave this place."

"Jamie! Can't we take a break? Lillian is traumatized."

"A break? It could come back at any minute."

"I doubt that. Besides, she wouldn't be like this in the first place if *you* hadn't abandoned her."

"T-T—" Lillian tries to speak, but sound fails to come out again. That's Jamie and Albert. Her friends. Or at least she thought. They left her with... with that *thing*. That capaeman boy could easily have killed her, and they didn't even try to rescue her.

"What is it?" the siblings say together.

She takes deep breaths. Slowly, her vision begins to clear. Now is not the time to pass out. She looks up at the two warriors. They stare at her, wide-eyed.

146

Their expressions are a mixture of worry and guilt. Lillian wants to yell at them. She wants to scream and scold and give them a piece of her mind, but she doesn't have any energy left. All she can manage is one phrase. "T-Take me home."

"But—" Jamie starts.

"I said, take me home. I want to go home. Now."

"Fine, then," Jamie says, "but don't tell anyone about this, alright?"

"What? Why?" This seems like something everyone should know about. If the capaeman boy were willing to talk to her again, his information could prove invaluable. They could learn how the capaemen operate, how the hunters found Albian, and maybe even their strengths and weaknesses. Most of all, they could find out why. Why are the capaemen hunting them again?

"What do you mean, why?" Jamie shouts. "Do you really think they'd understand?"

"Understand what?" Lillian asks. She's not following. They've been desperate for any information they can get. Now, for some unknown reason, a capaeman is willing to give it to them. What's not to understand?

"If you tell them what happened here, there's no way Brianna would let you keep traveling with us," Jamie says.

That's what she's worried about? This woman needs to get her priorities straight. Lillian's energy returns. Maybe it's the rage igniting inside her. She stands, meeting the close-minded woman's eyes. "We have bigger things to worry about than that."

Those once-confident eyes are now full of fear. "Don't... Don't tell me you actually believe what it said?"

"You heard?" Lillian asks. She hadn't thought about it until now, but they must not have gone far. They were probably watching... waiting to see if that capaeman would kill her. That must have been terrifying.

"It was lying, Lillian. It wants to use you."

"How do you know that?"

"I think I know what my sister is getting at," Albert intervenes. "We've been all across the world, and if there's one thing we've learned on our travels, it's that capaemen only care about one thing: themselves. Whatever it was trying to do, it can't be good."

"And what if you're wrong? What if it actually wants to talk to us? The information he has could save lives. Maybe it's worth—"

"Trusting them is *never* worth it!" Jamie shouts. "Humans and capaemen have been enemies for generations, and those giants can end your life with the wave of a hand. They see us as beneath them and that will *never* change. I don't know why it spared you, but Albert's right. The reason can't be good. You will *not* meet with it. You will *not* talk to it again."

"But what if—"

"Don't be fooled, Lillian. It wants you to let your guard down, because the second you do it will figure out the location of Zurec. Then, once your usefulness has run dry, it will take away everything you love."

Chills run down Lillian's spine. She didn't think about that. Maybe Jamie is right. After all, the capaeman did talk down to her, and he was clearly thinking about killing her. That isn't even close to friendly. Not to mention the rogues have more experience with capaemen than Lillian. They've been outside the Wilds: to the plains, across the waterlands, to distant places she can only dream of. Who is she to question *them*?

Albert places a hand on her shoulder. "I'm grateful you're okay, but don't ever think a capaeman will help us. They are our enemy. It's always been this way."

Lillian balls her fists. Deep down she knows he's right. She felt so helpless, so insignificant compared to that giant. It was awful. All she wants to do is be strong, but everything that has happened has only proven how weak she is.

Albert hugs her, jolting her out of her stupor. He stinks of dust and sweat, but he is comforting, nonetheless. "I know it's a lot, but it's okay. We're going to stay far away from it from now on. I'm sorry we left you behind. It won't happen again."

Jamie scoffs. "Next time get on the damn acera like I told you to. Oh, and also, I meant what I said earlier. We can't mention this to the others."

Lillian crosses her arms. "Fine. I won't say anything, but don't you ever abandon me again."

The rogue smiles. "It's a deal."

With that, the trio mounts the acera, ready to fly back home.

⸎ ⸎

It feels strange arriving back at the burrow. When they reunited with the gatherers, it was a blur. When they walked home together, that too was a blur. Lillian remembers talking to Albert about... something to do with the waterlands? It was a pointless conversation—only to pass time. They couldn't talk about what's really on her mind. It's for the best. The people of Zurec have enough on their plates. The last thing they need is to hear about another one of Lillian's screw-ups.

When she spots the clearing of the burrow, that beautiful ring of red roots surrounding a giant redwood tree, Lillian can hardly believe it is real. The leaves sway in the evening wind, bathed in fading sunlight. It's as if this whole time she has been in a nightmare, and she is just now waking up. She feels groggy and disoriented. All she wants to do is lie down. Maybe some sleep will clear her head.

Mary won't let her do that, however. The second they open the trapdoor and enter the mud room, her flighty friend will be waiting for her, wanting to hear every detail of their adventure. The only problem is that she can't tell her everything this time. Imagine how her best friend would react if she did. Mary would cling to her and never let go. Miss May would ban her from leaving the burrow ever again. Not to mention Brianna and Seth... the disappointment they'd feel. She sighs. Now she's realizing why the siblings want to keep this a secret.

The next thing Lillian knows, Brianna is opening the trapdoor. They head inside, following her in a single file. Lillian sticks to the back, biting her lower lip. She doesn't have time to strategize. They enter the mud room, and Mary is right there. She's sitting on the floor reading a book to the kids. Lillian recognizes it as *Zurec: A Brief History*. She never liked that one. It's filled with dry, vague information about where they came from and where they plan to go. Lillian could only sit through it because it was short, covering events from the past couple of decades alone. After all, the clan did lose their detailed records.

The second the blonde spots Lillian, she shoots up. She throws her arms around her, squeezing out what little life she has left. "I'm so happy to see you!"

"It's only been..." Lillian wheezes, "two days." The girl doesn't listen. Of course not, she's excited. Lillian can understand that. When she used to stay in the burrow every day, life felt like punishment. They milked every bit of entertainment they could get. She'll humor Mary, just as she's done before. She'll tell her how it felt to fly on the acera and about seeing the capaeman boy, but not meeting him. She doesn't want the poor girl to have a heart attack.

However, what Mary says next throws her for a loop. "I heard you left with the scouts. Why didn't you tell us first?" There is betrayal in her friend's eyes.

Lillian's heart sinks with guilt. When she left, she didn't think of how Mary would feel, only how she'd react. "I-I knew you wouldn't say yes."

"Of course, we wouldn't have!" she shouts. "That was so dangerous, but that's just like you, isn't it? Leaping straight into danger, despite our warnings."

Lillian can't tell if Mary is angry or worried. Perhaps it's a little bit of both. "I'm sorry I didn't tell you. That was wrong, but I swear traveling with Jamie and Albert is safe. Safer than being with the gatherers, even. Plus, I've already learned so much. Don't you want to hear about our first mission? It was eventful!" This isn't a lie. Ordinarily, it would be safe to travel with the rogues. They just made a mistake. They should move on and focus on what went well.

Predictably, the girl's brown eyes light up. "Eventful, really? Okay, but you've got to tell me everything. Don't leave a single detail out, and I may forgive you."

"Done," Lillian says with a smile, but her chest tightens. *It's for a good cause,* she thinks.

"Gatherers, scouts, welcome back! Any news?" Miss May asks from across the room. Good, a distraction. Lillian feels relieved until the caretaker looks at her, narrowing her eyes. Her expression says it all: *We'll talk later.* She is definitely in for a lecture, but that hardly matters to her right now.

Mary stares at Lillian, her eyes wide with curiosity. "Lillian?"

She wracks her brain for a plan. How can she talk about Lionel without her face contorting with confusion? "Uhh..." Everyone else is gathering in a circle across the room. "Here, the scouts will tell you about him! I-I mean it." Lillian curses herself for that slip-up as she invites Mary to listen.

In the circle, the caretaker and Kayla stare intently at the warriors. Trying to avoid Mary's gaze, Lillian spots Albert sticking outside the group. She wishes she could hide like that.

"We saw a capaeman," Jamie begins. "No, it isn't a threat, so don't worry. I don't think this one was a hunter. We'll keep looking. Oh, but stay away from the river. That capaeman likes to hang out around there, so you should steer clear of the area until we know it's safe."

Mary's jaw drops. She is not satisfied with that story, but before she can respond, Brianna jumps in. "What Jamie said is the gist of it. Miss May, I will fill you in on the details later. We could use some rest."

The caretaker nods. "O-Of course. I'm sorry for being hasty. You've had a long day. Let's all get some shut-eye."

The redhead nods and heads to her quarters. The rest, including Jamie and Albert, follow. All she gets on their way out is a glare from Jamie. It's as if she is telling Lillian, *"Don't fess up,"* but she isn't sticking around to help. How can she do this without them? Even the kids head into Kayla's room. What was once a bustling mud room is now empty and quiet. Lillian stares at the hall, wondering if she can retreat too.

Mary grabs her arm. No such luck. "That was strange... wasn't it?"

Lillian sighs loudly. "Yeah, they're both weird. You get used to it."

"Let's sit down a second. I want to hear from your point of view. What happened when you saw the capaeman?" She sits on the dirty carpet, patting the spot in front of her.

Lillian swallows and reluctantly sits next to her friend. What can she tell her without getting kicked out of the scouts? She will have to choose her words carefully. "It was... eye-opening."

Mary leans in. "What was it doing? Nothing good, I imagine."

"It wasn't doing anything *diabolical*, actually. It was just... sitting there."

"That's it? Just sitting by the river?"

"Yeah, it had a baby styfisher with it. That was strange." Lillian shifts around awkwardly, not knowing what to say next.

"A *baby* styfisher?" Mary says, her face darkening with worry. "It must have been torturing the poor thing. I'm sure that was horrible to watch."

"What? No, he wasn't torturing it," she finds herself explaining. "I mean, uh, *it* was actually very gentle with the creature. In fact, we think it was nursing it back to health."

"You keep saying *he*," Mary says suspiciously. "Was the capaeman... a male?"

Lillian nods. "It's strange... I thought they'd be plotting to take us down every waking moment, but I think there's more to them than meets the eye." *Stop, Lillian*, she thinks. *You're going to give it away.* For some reason though, she feels she needs to say this. "It was treating that animal so gently, even though it was much smaller. It had no reason to help it, but it did so anyway. I'm not saying they would do the same with us." She pauses again, remembering how he spared her. "But... but all I'm saying is they may be *different* than we think."

Mary is silent for a few seconds. Her mouth hangs open as if she has no idea what to say next.

"I know," Lillian continues. "It sounds weird, but I can't stop thinking about it."

Then, her friend places a hand on her shoulder. She looks serious, as if someone died. "Lillian, that is impossible."

"I thought the same thing, but—"

"But nothing. Look, I know you tend to see things in bright lights, but it isn't like that. This world is brutal. We should focus on surviving and not *anything* more."

When Mary says those words, Lillian remembers what she said after the Red Eclipse about wanting more. Is that it? Is that the reason she cannot let this go? Because she's hoping that capaeman has the answers? If so, she has to shut that down *now*. The stakes are too high. What was she thinking, that she would meet him at the river again and he would tell her everything she's ever wanted to know? That's a fantasy. Mary is right. Heck, Jamie is probably right too. That capaeman intends to use her, plain and simple. "I... understand," she mumbles.

"Aww," Mary says, leaning in for a hug. The girls embrace. "I know you want to see the best in everything, but we've got to trust the adults. They know more than we do. Besides, if capaemen were secretly good, don't you think our ancestors would have found that out a long time ago?"

"Yeah..." Lillian answers, "you're right." Oddly enough, she feels a little better. Zurec has spent nearly a hundred years in these Wilds. Who is she to go against a century of historical proof? Not only that, but the rogues from beyond the Wilds too?

Her friend lets go of her. "Don't worry about this anymore, okay? Let's change the subject. I can't believe we lost Bunker Three. That was my favorite one."

Lillian chuckles. "That's the only one you've gotten near."

"Right, because it's so close to where we swim." The blonde pauses. She looks like she is thinking hard. Maybe she hasn't dropped it after all. "You know... we went to the river the other day. Wish you had been there. It's not the same without someone to race, and now we have to stay away from there..."

"Hey, you always won anyway," Lillian teases nervously.

"Heck yeah, I always win. Something I am very proud of, by the way." She stops again.

"What's wrong?"

"I, uh, did your laundry. It's folded in your trunk."

"Oh, thank you. You didn't have to do that." Lillian wonders why she bothered. There's no need to do her laundry often. She wears the same outfit for at least a week before changing.

"You're so busy. I wanted to help out."

"Is there... anything I can help you with in return?" She dislikes when someone does her a favor.

Mary sighs. "Ugh, it's Trista. She's being so difficult. She throws a tantrum every day to stay out of craft class. She refuses to sit with the other kids for story time, and when we try to force her, she bickers with everyone. And she refuses to tell us anything about how she and Max survived. I'm glad you and the scouts have had better luck, because we haven't found out anything."

Lillian pats her on the back. She's no good at comforting others or giving advice, but she'll try. "It sucks that she's being difficult. I mean, there are lives on the line here."

"I know, right? I mean, if I saw what she saw, I would be eager to make sure no one else had to be hurt like that. I don't know what her problem is."

If I saw what she saw, Lillian thinks. Her head pounds. What did young Trista see? It certainly wasn't a capaeman trying to talk to her. They were trying to *kill* her. Lillian is traumatized enough from one being somewhat friendly. She can't imagine what Trista must have gone through—a *true* brush with death. And here she is, keeping her mouth shut about everything. "Hey, maybe she has a good reason. That kind of thing can be traumatizing, you know?"

"Huh? That's a one-eighty; you, empathizing with people? When did this happen?"

"I guess I've gotten a new perspective from these past few days," Lillian says. She tries to sound nonchalant, but it comes out shaky.

Mary sighs. "Haven't we all. I'm trying to understand her, but I also want to know what she's hiding, you know?"

"Y-Yeah. I get that," the warrior stammers.

"Anyway, you look tired. Sorry for keeping you up. You probably want to get some sleep, right?" Lillian nods, only now realizing how tired she is. To think, just earlier today... No. She's not thinking about that anymore. Sleep. She needs that. Tomorrow is a new day, and she will put this all behind her.

"Okay, cool. Let's go to bed. I could use some sleep too. Oh, and by the way, Trista sleeps with Kayla now, so your bed is free and ready for you."

"That's good news."

As the girls get ready for bed, they don't say another word to each other. Lillian isn't sure if it's a lucky break or if Mary knows she is hiding something. Either way, she is grateful for the silence.

She needs time to think.

18

Built-Up Secrets

Mary

Mary has a strange feeling about last night. Is there something Lillian is not sharing? No, that can't be it. She told her about the capaeman by the river. Still, she looked so on edge, as if something were deeply bothering her. It must be the narecon attack. If watching Gigi and Noah die has taken such a toll on the gatherers, Mary can only imagine how her fifteen-year-old friend must feel.

"What story will you read this time, Mary?" Oscar asks, tugging on her sleeve. She had forgotten he was there. The twins sit next to him, leaning in. Even Trista and Max are here, but they aren't paying attention, of course.

Mary did not get much sleep last night, as usual. To make things worse, by the time she woke up it was bright and early, and her mother asked her to watch the kids. She can't count how many times that has happened. Things used to be different with Lillian around. None of the children bothered her so as long as they were together. Now, it's like Mary is already the new caretaker.

She can't blame her mother for giving her more time with them. Watching a bunch of kids for sixteen hours straight can be... exhausting to say the least. Maybe, in some way, this is a test—to see how well Mary would do as the caretaker. She cannot let her down.

Mary stares at the book she has grabbed for the children. *Zurec: A Brief History* by Kayla Zurec. The author's three-year-old son, little Felix, sits right next to her. He pokes the mud room rug with his stick. Mary thinks to take it away so he can listen to the story but decides against it. If someone tries to take the stick, he throws a tantrum. She does not have the energy to deal with that today.

She holds up the book. "We'll continue with the history of our clan."

Oscar pouts. "What? That book *again*? We just heard it yesterday."

"But we didn't get to finish it. Besides, you've heard *The Adventures of Cecilia and Alida* hundreds of times, and you're not tired of that one."

"That's because that story is fun. This one is boring," Oscar complains. His hair sits in a tangled nest on his head. No one remembered to brush it this morning. She'll have to take care of that too.

Mary sighs. "Look, since Trista and Max have joined us, they need to learn about our history. It won't take long. It's short anyway. Now, let's start from the beginning since I'm certain not all of you were listening." Besides, she doesn't want to hunt for another book.

"Aww but—"

"I can always teach lessons instead," Mary threatens. This shuts Oscar up. The twins shake their heads in disagreement. If there is anything the children don't like, it's having to learn new things. They would rather have Mary read a story over and over than learn to read it themselves. "Alright, Trista, Max, I want you to pay attention."

Max nods. He looks like he's trying, at least. Trista rolls her eyes. "Yeah, whatever."

"Alright, here we go." Mary breathes in and opens the book to the first page. Below the title, the neat text reads *Kayla Zurec, Year Ninety-Three*. She wrote this three years ago. "Hundreds of years ago, our ancestors fled from the north to find a new place to live. They were so tired. Tired of fighting. Tired of the deaths..."

Mary becomes engrossed in the story, telling of Zurec's adventure across the plains, through valleys and forests, and finally, into the Giant Wilds. It is incredible that their ancestors came from so far away. She cannot imagine such a massive journey. How many must have died to give them peace? They fought for this burrow, for this home.

Mary pauses, thinking of Lillian. She was trying to hide it, but she seemed terrified when she talked about that capaeman by the river. Could that be the reason she was so nervous? No, that doesn't make sense. After all, her friend said all that ludicrous stuff about capaemen being secretly good. Why did she say that?

"What's wrong?" Oscar asks. He's grabbing her sleeve again.

She takes a deep breath. "Nothing. Let's continue." At this point in the book, there is a considerable gap. From the Year of Arrival to Year Eighty, all that is written is, "When our ancestors finally settled in the Giant Wilds, there were several decades of peace. The clans of the Giant Wilds were not friends, but they left each other alone."

Lillian never liked this part. Mary recalls when her ever-curious friend asked her mother about the time skip. *"You're almost sixty years old!"* Lillian said. *"You've got to know something that happened during those years. I know it's hard to talk about it, but we're not kids anymore."*

She remembers her mother's response too. *"All the interesting things happened when I was too young to remember. Besides, it doesn't matter where we came from, only where we are going."*

That was her answer every time and the response of the rest of the adults. So eventually, Lillian stopped asking. It's a shame that the hurt overshadows the memories. Mary would like to know about her mother's youth, but it's as if the famine war severed her from her younger self. And Kayla's recollection of events is so vague. Not that that is her fault; the rains buried all their detailed records. Still, it's good for the kids to know, so she moves on to the next chapter anyway. This one is about Seth's father.

"Next was Year Eighty-Two since Zurec settled in the Giant Wilds. It was the era of Chief Darrel's command and the start of the great rains. The Crystal River overflowed and destroyed most of Zurec's bunkers. The rooms of our old burrow could not take all the water and collapsed. We lost many people, but that was only the beginning of our grief. We took over the hovel of a thornopine burrower and made it Zurec's new home, rebuilding as much as we could. Among the lost bunkers, three were able to be saved, allowing us to rebuild our influence slowly. However, even though we made a new home, the rains had drowned the plants and scared away the animals. Soon after, a famine swept the Giant Wilds. Albian, once our greatest ally, became our enemy. While Zurec remained ever peaceful in the face of such scarcity, Albian became aggressive, ruthlessly raiding us for our resources and... Trista, are you paying attention?"

The little girl stares at the ceiling with her finger in her nose. Her brown eyes are blank. "Trista?"

"What?"

"Trista, this is important."

"Hah hah! You were picking your nose," Oscar says.

Trista stands up. "Was not!"

"Was too."

"Was not!"

"Was too!"

Mary thinks of breaking up this squabble but buries her head in the book instead. She shouldn't have expected them to take this seriously.

"Nose picker, nose picker!"

"I am not! You're a nose picker."

"Oh yeah, then why were you picking your nose, nose picker?"

"I saw it," Jen says.

"Me too," Jan adds.

"Then you guys need to get your eyes checked because I'm not a nose picker!" Trista screams.

"Are too!"

"Am not!"

"Are too," the twins say simultaneously.

"Am not! Am not am not am not am not."

"Are you okay, Mary?" Max asks over the chaos. He places a hand on her arm, his little eyes full of concern.

"I-I'm fine. Just tired." She forces a smile. How unprofessional of her, getting frustrated like this. Max doesn't seem convinced, but it doesn't matter. Someone has finally arrived to save her.

"What is going on here?" Miss May asks angrily. The kids immediately stop their screaming match, staring at the caretaker with fear. "Tell me what's going on, right now." The children point fingers at each other, no one willing to take the blame. Her mom understands the situation immediately. "Trista, if you're going to pick your nose, don't do it in front of people."

"But I didn't—"

"Oscar, Jen, Jan, it's not nice to gang up on a fellow member of your clan. Apologize to Trista right now."

"But—"

"I'm not asking," she says sternly. The twins apologize first, followed by a very insincere apology from Oscar. Trista pouts. "There, now was that so hard? Oh, and Mary, dear." She switches her attention to her daughter. Mary looks up from the book. "Have you been getting enough sleep?"

"You know the answer to that."

"You will take a nap immediately. I'll take over." Finally, she's taking a turn. It's about time. Mary leaves immediately, and as she heads to their bedroom, she sees the door creak open. A droopy-eyed Lillian makes her way into the hall. She looks so... worn out.

"Good morning." She tries to look happy to see her. If she looks upset, it will only make her friend feel worse.

The brunette stares right through the wall. "Morning." She ambles down the hall.

"Wh-Where are you going?"

"To get some fresh air."

"I-I'll join you." She doubts Lillian wants the company, but it is precisely when she doesn't want it that she needs it the most. She's stubborn. She doesn't express herself well. She needs her.

"Where do you think you're going?" her mother asks as they make their way across the mud room.

"Outside. We won't go far. Lillian wants some air."

The caretaker crosses her arms. "What about your nap, young lady?"

"I can nap later. Please?" Mary anxiously signals to Lillian with her eyes, hoping her mom gets the message. She is exhausted, but she barely gets to see her friend these days.

"Fine, then. But if you hear anything, get back inside right away."

"Of course."

They head up the exit tunnel to the massive door. Lillian pushes it, but it won't budge. How strange; she is usually strong enough to move it. Her body is so sluggish today, as if she's carrying one hundred pounds on her back. Mary helps her.

The sunlight is always blinding when they open the door, but the air is cool and refreshing. The strong scent of morning dew and moss hangs in the air. Mary lets it cool her skin. It's been several weeks since spring hit, and there is a pleasant breeze in the Giant Wilds today. Mary's blonde hair moves with the wind. As usual, Lillian's hair falls in her face. It's at that odd length where she can't tie it up, but she also can't stop it from being a mess. She seems to like it that way. Either that or she cares that little.

Immediately, Lillian starts walking, the foliage squishing under her shoes. That's when Mary realizes they are not alone. Across the clearing are the former rogues. Jamie scrubs her acera's amphibian-like skin with a washcloth, and the boy, Albert, holds a bucket. He still has those long bangs in his face. It's odd that they don't bother him.

"Hey guys," Lillian says with a little more energy. "Giving Amphii a bath?"

"Well, sort of," Jamie says. "She doesn't like us touching her face, like, *at all*."

"Guess she can't *face* the fact that she has eye boogers, can you girl?" Albert scratches the acera on the side of her head. She purrs.

Lillian laughs. She joins them, borrowing a washcloth from Jamie. All Mary can do is watch. They seem to have a sense of camaraderie that they didn't before.

Albert splashes the brunette with the water. Her jaw drops. "Oh no you *didn't.*"

"What are you going to do about it, Lily?"

"I said don't call me that!" She chases him. They run in circles around the acera, laughing.

They've become this close after just one mission? Then again, it was a hard one. *"Eye-opening,"* as Lillian described. Well, Mary is not about to be left out. She runs opposite Lillian, cornering Albert. He freaks out, pouring water all over her head. "Hey!" she says, laughing. Her hair is soaked.

"You brought that on yourself," the boy says.

"Having fun?" someone interrupts. It's her mother. She, Kayla, and the gatherers have come out of the burrow, the kids following closely behind them.

"Mom, what's going on?" Mary asks.

"It is a lovely day, and the gatherers have some free time. Let's do some training. It's been a while."

The little kids groan as Brianna hands out wooden poles. Everyone has come out of the burrow except Trista. That's not a surprise. Not even Mary can get her to come outside. She guesses her mother has given up too. The stubborn little girl has finally won.

"Hey, this is a perfect opportunity," Jamie says, throwing an arm around Lillian. "How about you spar with me? You said you wanted to learn from the best." The girl nods, her eyes full of wonder. Mary doesn't understand it. Sure, they are acera warriors from outside the Giant Wilds, but that doesn't mean they should worship them.

"What about me?" Albert asks.

"You can spar with, uhh, blondie here. You up for that, blondie?"

Mary clenches her fists. *Blondie? Seriously?* But she swallows her anger. It would be in poor form to lose it in front of the gatherers and the kids. Not to mention Lillian, who looks up to Jamie so much. "Sure," she says, forcing a smile. "I'll spar with Albert."

It isn't long before the training begins. Out in the clearing, the children train with different gatherers. Nine-year-old Oscar practices swinging a child-sized wooden spear with Mia and Jess. He is about at the age where they can start teaching Zurec's technique, although he is a slow learner. He keeps stabbing with the spear instead of swinging. Mia looks at the end of her wits, but Jess patiently corrects him. Mary can see why they paired up.

The twins train separately, and they do not seem happy about it. Jen seems to be doing better than Jan—at least *she* can keep hold of her weapon. Milo encourages her to keep going, trying to improve the speed of her swings. Meanwhile, the pole keeps flying out of Jan's hands, and Thomas is no help. He keeps flitting between teaching and writing in a journal, Kayla-style. Sure, he likes to read and write, but is now the best time?

Finally, Max learns dodging techniques with Brianna. Their exercise is basically a two-person game of tag; Brianna blocks Max as he runs for a knotted tree root that represents base. "Rooaarrr!" Brianna stomps toward him like a monster. Suddenly, the little boy falls to the ground, trembling. The redhead stops. "Hey, it's okay. It's not real." She helps Max up. "I'm sorry, I forgot about..."

Mary had nearly forgotten about that too. Unlike his sister, little Max acts like nothing is wrong. It's easy to forget he went through the same thing as Trista.

Meanwhile, Zoey, Theo, and Bruno abstain from training. Theo and Bruno tried to spar at first but quickly gave up. The three of them, along with Kayla, now sit in a circle across the clearing, apparently sharing stories about Noah and Gigi. That's what Mary overheard her mother saying as she went to join them. Mary wonders what stories they are telling. She didn't know Gigi or Noah well, but she wishes she had. She wishes she could understand the gatherers' pain, commiserate with them. Instead, she stays with Lillian and the two former rogues, somewhat outside the rest of the community.

Lillian and Jamie have already started their match. The brunette charges at the rogue, but she easily predicts her moves and parries. This doesn't seem to faze Lillian though, as she goes straight for another attack. Mary wishes she had that kind of confidence, but with more strategy. She remembers what her mother said: that Lillian is too reckless while she is too cautious. How strange that they were raised by the same person but have completely different fighting styles. She examines her opponent. She'll have to be better than she has been if she wants a chance at winning.

Mary takes an offensive stance. "Albert, are you ready?"

The boy draws his scythes. "Ready as I'll ever be. You move first."

Trying to imitate her friend's reckless abandon, she charges at the boy. However, unlike Lillian, she doesn't come in head-on. She runs to his left, trying to attack in his blind spot. She thought she was moving quickly, but Albert is faster, parrying her immediately. Mary backs away. She's not used to offense.

Albert does not pursue her. Instead, he takes that same stance again.

"You won't come after me?"

The assassin shakes his head. "You're the defensive type. You should step out of your comfort zone."

"Oh, um, thanks." She composes herself. *You can do this, Mary. It's just sparring. It's no big deal.* She notes the hair all over the right side of his face, covering an eyepatch. He must have a huge blind spot there. She'll try striking to his right next.

Mary charges again, this time trying to stay to his right, but she's still at a huge disadvantage. His foreign fighting style is something she has never faced before. How did Seth so easily parry his strikes, not to mention his sister's? With dual blades, every attack comes from two directions at once, which is hard to block with a spear. The surveyors are on another level.

Even though she does much better this time, it isn't long before Mary is knocked to the ground. Albert reaches toward her, smiling. "Good job."

Mary takes his hand. "Don't lie to me."

"I'm not lying. You're doing pretty good, especially with that thing." He points at the wooden spear.

"Probably should have brought something better." She smiles, picking up her flimsy weapon.

"Too late now. Let's go again."

They spar until evening breaks. By the time the sun sets, Mary is sore and caked in sweat. All the other warriors have gone inside, yet Albert is hardly sweating. He looks like he could go all night. What are these rogues made of?

She glances at Lillian. That girl is not doing much better. The young warrior stands, knees buckled, using her spear as support. She looks exhausted. "One more... time," she mumbles.

"Absolutely not. The last couple of attempts were pathetic. You're too exhausted," Jamie says.

"Did I... do good?" she says between exhausted breaths. "Do you think I've... improved?"

"I'd say so. Next time, we'll work on your defense. You rely too much on offense. I'd know. I have the same habit." It almost seems like she's praising Lillian. Mary didn't think that show-off was capable of complements.

Jamie yawns. "Let's turn in, guys. Even I am starting to get a little tired. We should get some sleep. The gatherers and scouts leave first thing tomorrow morning." Albert drifts over to the two of them, and they talk like they've all known each other for years. Again, Mary can't help but feel left out. That feeling that she's missing something drifts into her head again, like a bug buzzing where it doesn't belong.

Mary walks toward them, suspicious. "You all seem close."

Lillian's blue eyes flicker for just a second. What was that emotion? Nervousness? Fear? It was something bad. "Yeah, guess we get along pretty well."

"Is it fun, riding on an acera?"

The second she asks that, Lillian's face lights up. She goes on about the wind in her hair and the view of the Wilds from the sky, telling tales of walking on trees and seeing a dreosaur from the canopy. It reminds Mary of her favorite childhood story—almost enough to make her want to read it again. The siblings simply smile, happy their new friend is having a good time.

Maybe she is just being paranoid. Nothing bad happened. Lillian learned to ride on an acera and... saw a capaeman from a safe distance. This is a positive learning experience for her. Yeah, everything is alright. They will just... see how this pans out.

As long as Lillian is safe, it'll be okay.

19

The Hunter by the Burrow

Lillian

They have been searching for three days now. Lillian sits sandwiched between Albert and Jamie on the acera, feeling the whiplash across her hands and body. Her stomach isn't protesting anymore. She is already getting used to flying. She wishes she could have her own acera. Unfortunately, that's nothing but a dream.

Lillian is glad Jamie got her up earlier than everyone else. They've been staying in the burrow between missions, and Mary has been bothering them nonstop. She can't tell if it's because she suspects something or is genuinely trying to get closer to the rogues. Either way, she can't find out what happened at the river. Her friend is stressed enough as it is. Imagine how she would react if she found out what Lillian saw—what Jamie and Albert let happen. She remembers that capaeman, Lionel. *"If you ever wish to talk more, I will be by the river."*

No, stop thinking about that. A capaeman would never help them. They're the enemy. So, there's nothing to say to Mary. Nothing at all.

"Do you think we'll find another capaeman?" Albert asks over the wind.

"Maybe," Jamie answers. "They're not exactly hard to spot. Plus, we're searching farther south today."

It's not long before they make their next stop, a younger tree covered with mushrooms. They land on its thickest branch, hundreds of feet above the forest floor. When they land, Amphii pants heavily, her eyes half-closed. Carrying all these people isn't easy for her. When Lillian gets off the acera's back, her stomach lurches, but she keeps her food down this time. "So, why the stop?" she asks. "Well, other than Amphii."

"Breakfast break," Jamie explains. "Also, just look at that view." She points to a massive figure in the distance. It isn't a capaeman, but it is certainly a sight to see.

The creature must be at least thirty feet tall. It stands on two massive legs with an enormous tail shaped like a whip. Its two arms look like sticks, but any thoracic feebleness is more than made up for by its head—or, really, its mouth. The creature's jaw is long and rectangular with clusters of razor-sharp teeth. This one appears to be a male, as its feathery scales display several bright shades of red and orange. Kayla's book, *Giant Wilds: Creatures*, states that these large predators grow colorful feathers in the spring, which is mating season. Lillian knows exactly what sort of creature this is.

"An andremedon. I've never seen one in person."

Jamie opens her backpack and passes around some edible leaves. "This is the top predator in the Wilds, I gather?"

Lillian takes a bite from her leaves. They have a strong, refreshing taste. "Yeah. Definitely the top. They prey on young dreosaurs. Not like the one we saw, but still."

"Makes sense," she says with a full mouth. "You know, these creatures are much bigger in the plains."

"T-They get *bigger*?" Lillian nearly spits out her food.

"Oh yeah. The andremedon and the dreosaur. Albert and I have seen similar subspecies all over the place. Let's see, I think the biggest dreosaur can be two hundred feet. The andremedons are up to seventy. Am I getting that right, Albert?"

"Yeah, I think so," her brother answers. He has already scarfed down his meal. "Hey, what do you think would happen if that thing ate me?" He gazes at the andremedon. It sniffs the air, searching for its next meal.

"Umm, you'd die. Horribly," Jamie says, rolling her eyes.

"But, like, would I die instantly, or would I get to see the inside of its stomach? I bet its stomach is as big as a burrow."

"I doubt it," his sister says. "Why are you talking about this?"

He shrugs. "Just curious."

They watch the monster until it stomps away, at which point Jamie promptly leads them back onto Amphii's back. "That's a good girl. You've been so great lately," she says, patting the acera's head. Amphii purrs.

"Still looking for capaemen?" Lillian asks as she straps herself into the saddle.

"Yeah. If they're hunting, then they'll be out in the forest a lot. Some come around every day. Hunters take their jobs very seriously. All we need to do is fly around until we spot one."

Lillian gulps. "And the last one we saw—"

"—wasn't what we're looking for. Are you still thinking about that?"

The girl nods shamefully.

"Look, I'm sorry we left you behind. But to be fair, you wouldn't get on the acera."

"Jamie!" Albert yells.

"What? It's true. If it were me, I would have killed that styfisher and hopped on when I had the chance. You're too soft. We've got to work on that."

Lillian grits her teeth. "But what if I had killed it and still didn't make it in time? Would you have abandoned me then?" The siblings pause, their eyes widening.

Lillian doesn't say it out loud, but she knows what would have happened if she killed that styfisher. The capaeman would have shown no mercy. He seemed to have an attachment to the animal, one she does not understand. "Did you have a plan to rescue me, or were you going to let me die?"

Albert is the first to speak. "I... I wanted to fly down and rescue you, but I was not the one with the reigns."

"That would have gotten us *all* killed," Jamie says. "Look, it was the right call, okay? Everyone survived. Can we just move on?"

"Of course, *you'd* say that," her brother comments. "You'll do anything but apologize."

The air grows heavier. Lillian regrets bringing this up. The two siblings are going to fight and she will be stuck in the middle, and it's all because she can't let it go. Her survival was a miracle, a fluke, that's all. Now, she gets to ride on an acera with people from outside the Giant Wilds. It's a dream come true. She cannot jeopardize that. "Hey, we've got a mission, remember? Let's focus on that. I'm sorry for bringing this up. It won't happen again."

"It's okay," Albert says. "I guess none of us can understand what happened."

His sister's eyes narrow. "We should just forget about it. Now, let's go. We've got a hunter to find."

They spend the next few hours flying, taking small breaks now and then so Amphii can rest. Then, as the sun gives way to late afternoon, they finally find something.

They've been heading south this whole time, so they may be near Rostad's base. Lillian remembers the first time she saw Rostad at Albian's burrow. Those awful people had no respect for Zurec, only scathing words filled with resentment. She has no idea why they were so mean to them. They haven't done anything. They hadn't even seen each other in years, but at least one good thing came out of it: they found Jamie and Albert.

Lillian doesn't have to think about Rostad for long. Out of the corner of her eye, she spots a massive figure. At first, she thinks it is a tree, but she swears she saw a flash of white. That's not right. There are sparse whitewood trees, but even those have patches of brown. The white Lillian just saw was so bright, it was nearly blinding. That was *not* a tree. It seems Jamie noticed the figure too, as she swerves the acera to the left and away from it. "Where are we going?"

No answer.

"It's another one," she says finally, looking back at Albert. His face has grown grim. Jamie tugs the reigns upward, and Amphii flies deeper into the leaves.

The thought of seeing a capaeman again makes Lillian's stomach lurch. That gargantuan size, the scales, the fangs... Suddenly, the world is spinning more than usual as they fly. So far, they've seen a strange capaeman boy with a styfisher. Now what will they see?

Finally, Amphii begins to slow, then lands on a large thick tree branch. This one is much higher than the previous ones and at an upward angle. Lillian is scared to step off the acera. She looks toward the ground way below. "Where is—"

Jamie shushes her, and the siblings help Lillian down the acera's wing. They are shivering more than her. Amphii stays close to the group, her tail wrapped around them protectively. The air is stifling.

"Why do we need to be quiet? Can they hear really well too?" Lillian whispers.

"No. It's just Jamie being paranoid again," Albert answers.

"Am not."

The group finds a gap in the leaves they can safely look through. Another human-like creature stands in a clearing below. When Lillian's eyes settle on it, she feels as though her heart has stopped. Its eyes are closed, and the palms of its hands are held out. Surrounding it at no more than shin height are roots and bushes, which are like caves and hills to humans. What is it doing, just standing there? All she knows is the more she looks at it, the more fear she feels. Pins and needles prickle her skin. This one is different from the one by the river. *Very* different.

This capaeman is also a male with large, broad shoulders and shaven dark hair. Its skin has the same brown scales as the previous giant, but that is where the similarity ends. In hindsight, Lillian now knows the boy was comparatively tall and lanky. This capaeman is massive. It looks like it could topple a redwood tree on its own.

Lillian hears no chittering in the forest—only silence. The bugs and birds are too scared to chirp—too frightened of it noticing them. The capaeman wears a white shirt, loose around the arms, and tucked into a tan pair of pants. The pants are littered with pockets stuffed with foreign metal tools. She doesn't want to know what those are for.

Finally, Lillian musters up the courage to scan its face. It looks like a man in his early fifties, only ten years younger than Miss May. Humans don't usually live past their sixties around here, but capaemen probably have different rules. After all, few things can kill them.

She studies its body language, wondering what it is doing. The giant stands in the middle of the Wilds, motionless, eyes closed and hands out. How strange.

"Wow, you're surprisingly calm," Albert whispers.

"I am?" Lillian asks, her eyes locked on the giant. She wonders what color its eyes are. Are they that deep green of the previous capaeman, or something different?

Yes, you're very calm," he says with a nervous edge. She glances at him briefly. Sweat glistens on his face, and his breathing is erratic. "This one is dangerous."

As soon as he says that, the capaeman's eyelids twitch. Lillian leans in. The giant opens its eyes very slowly, and what she sees shatters her calm facade.

Orange. Like the sun. This capaeman has bright-orange eyes. She focuses, trying to make out more features. They are a bit narrower than the other capaeman's eyes, and they too have long black slits for pupils. It was harder to see the slits in the boy's dark eyes, but they are clear as day against these irises. The giant's gaze burns with a cold, subtle rage. This is what Lillian imagined when she thought of a capaeman. This thing looks like it can kill.

"Jamie, what do you think it's doing?" Albert whispers.

No response. Lillian checks on her. The terrified woman clings to Amphii's tail, shaking like a leaf. "I'm... fine."

"No, you're not fine. We've stayed long enough. We can leave if you want," her brother says.

She stubbornly shakes her head. "No, this one's the real deal. We have to see what it's up to."

"Jamie…"

Lillian turns her attention back to the clearing. She tries to read the giant's facial expression. There's got to be something she can see in those blank orange eyes, but the more she reads into them, the more she wants to run.

Without changing its glassy expression, the giant raises two fingers to its lips and blows a roaring whistle. The sound rattles Lillian's bones. It's much deeper than human whistling, and much louder, echoing through the trees for miles.

Slowly, the capaeman puts its arm down and steps forward. Its footsteps crush the forest debris with massive *boom*s. Lillian moves sideways on the tree branch, following its path, making sure she keeps sight of it. It stops again and holds out an arm, onto which a black, winged creature lands. She recognizes it immediately.

A black narecon.

Lillian freezes. She can't believe what she is seeing. *So that's why that narecon was acting so weird.* That narecon they killed belonged to a capaeman—to *this* capaeman.

In that instant, everything happens at once. Jamie finally speaks. "Damn it! It can smell us. We have to go!" The narecon looks in their direction and caws. The capaeman's head jolts upward, those orange eyes piercing their hiding spot. Now that it's looking directly at them, Lillian's fascination fades. There isn't a hint of emotion in those eyes. Staying will bring death. The three of them rush onto Amphii, who takes off before they can even buckle their seatbelts. The acera doesn't need Jamie's command now. She knows. They all know.

They must get out of here as fast as possible.

20

The Hunter Stained with White and Red

Lillian

"I'm so sorry! I should have noticed sooner," Jamie shouts over the wind. Amphii is tired from carrying three people, but that doesn't stop her now. She zips through the trees as if her life depends on it.

Lillian dares to look behind her and sees a great black shadow chasing them. Adrenaline courses through her veins. She thinks back to their first encounter with one of these beasts a few days ago. *That's why the narecon attacked us but left those it killed behind.* She didn't think capaemen could train animals, but she should have.

"It was a hunting bird! How could I be so thoughtless?" Jamie continues.

"To be fair, I didn't notice either," Albert says.

"Damn, they always use different animals! Why do they do that?"

"What are you talking about?" Lillian asks. She can hardly hear her voice over the wind.

"This means that thing is a pro. Damn it, it's a pro! What is it doing here?"

The composed and confident Jamie that Lillian's been getting to know is no longer here, and that terrifies her. "Jamie, please tell me what's going on."

"Hunters have different levels," Albert explains. "There are amateurs, inter-mediates, and professionals. At least that's what my sister and I call them."

"A pro shouldn't be here! This place is remote and isolated, and the people are so weak."

"Hey!" Lillian shouts.

"No offense, but she's right," Albert says. "Let me explain more. Professional hunters command animals. They can use them to sniff us out." She thinks back to the last black narecon. If Jamie hadn't been there, she has no idea how many more people would have died.

"I thought here we could escape that hell. Damn, why do they have to be everywhere? It will find the burrow within a matter of days!"

Lillian's breath catches in her throat. *Days? That can't be right. We've got to have more time than that.* She looks back at the narecon chasing them. It seems to have fallen behind a bit. Amphii is really flying for her life—for all of their lives.

"You're right. No one is safe," Albert confirms.

"Wait, slow down," Lillian says. "What do you mean a couple of days? Also, how do you know this one is a pro?"

"Did that look like an amateur to you?" Jamie asks.

She shakes her head vigorously. If looks could kill, she would be dead already. The look in the giant's eyes alone made Lillian want to give up. They were pure evil, through and through.

"Trust me, Albert and I know a pro when we see one. Our home was destroyed by them. They have this look—the look of a seasoned killer."

"What?"

"The Osia Coalition were expert capaemen assassins," Jamie's brother explains. "It only makes sense that they'd send the pros on us, but here..."

SCREEEEEEE

The narecon screeches from behind. Jamie draws her giant scythe from Amphii's saddle. "No more time to talk!" In sync with her rider, Amphii turns to face their foe. The narecon has caught up with them. Lillian wanted to see what it was like to fight in the air; now she has a front-row seat.

Jamie launches her scythe at the creature. It flies backward, narrowly avoiding the weapon. Amphii doesn't waste any time though. She charges, causing all the people on board to lurch forward. If Lillian were not strapped in, she would have fallen off. Airsickness begins to take hold again. She clutches her stomach, trying to keep it together. Albert hugs her tightly.

The narecon switches from attacking to fleeing. It didn't take long for it to realize that it was outclassed. Jamie pulls her scythe back and goes for another strike. It misses by a long shot. That scythe must have been made for situations like this: high above ground with no chance to retrieve a lost weapon mid-battle. Now that Lillian has a closer look at it, she realizes the blade is serrated. There are miniature dips in it so that when the blade pierces flesh, it will dig in and rip out large chunks of the enemy.

Amphii continues the chase until the narecon flies downward through the trees. The acera tries to follow, growling angrily, but Jamie pulls on her reigns. Why did they stop? She's killed one before.

Lillian stops wondering that as soon as she gazes below.

Standing on the forest floor is the orange-eyed capaeman. The narecon lands on its shoulder, its gargantuan body dwarfed by the size of the capaeman. It bows its head in submission. The giant looks at it, those eyes glassy and emotionless. It hasn't spotted them yet, and Jamie is not about to let it either. Just as fast as when they were flying away from the narecon, Amphii takes off. As they bob and weave through the trees, Lillian comes to another realization.

We were flying, she thinks. They were going so fast the trees were blurring together, yet that capaeman could keep up with them. No wonder everyone is so afraid. If they were on foot, there would be no way to outrun one. Lillian thinks of her family. None of them have animals on which to escape.

Lillian shakes her head. *No, I can't panic. That won't do any good.* She decides to distract herself. Thinking too much about this will only cloud her mind. "Where are we headed now?"

"As far away from here as possible," Jamie says shakily.

"You said we only have a couple of days, right? We have to warn the clan."

"Yes, and we'll get there, but we have to make sure we've lost the capaeman first."

"How will we do that?"

"We're going to fly around a while," Albert explains. "If we go in circles for a few hours, we should lose it. Then we'll be safe to head back to the burrow."

A few more hours of this? The wind, which was so pleasant earlier, now pricks Lillian's skin like needles. She hoped they would take a break after this, but no such luck.

"Of course, we'll stop and rest from time to time. You know Amphii will get tired," Albert says as if reading her mind.

"Thank goodness," Lillian responds.

"Damn, this is bad. This is so bad," Jamie says.

"I know," her brother agrees.

"How bad?"

"The hunter saw Amphii. I'm sure of it. That's going to make things so much worse. I'm so sorry." The Osian warrior grips the reigns of her acera tightly.

"Please, tell me more. I want to be prepared."

"They treat people with aceras much more seriously," she continues. There's no telling what it'll do now. We tried to help, but we've only made things worse."

"What? No way. We wouldn't know any of this if you two hadn't shown up," Lillian says, placing a hand on her shoulder. The warrior does not respond. She keeps her gaze ahead, watching as Amphii weaves through the tree branches. "Guys? There's got to be a way through this. We can warn everyone and escape. It's going to be okay, right?"

Neither of the siblings answer.

⚜

After what seems like forever, Jamie finally turns them on a straight path toward the river.

"Shouldn't we fly back to the burrow to warn everyone?" Lillian asks.

"Amphii's been flying since daybreak. I don't think she can go far past the bunker," Jamie says. Lillian looks at the acera. They did have to take double the breaks this afternoon.

The sun is beginning to set. On their way, they spot the gatherers walking across the terrain, their tiny figures looking no bigger than insects. Is this how the capaemen see them? They are no different than the bugs that roam the land.

Amphii touches down next to them. This time, no one draws their weapons. They seem much too tired, and their hands are too full. "Hey, scouts," Brianna says. "Any updates?"

None of the scouts, not even Jamie, can hide their defeated expressions. Lillian unbuckles herself and walks down Amphii's wing, grateful to be on solid ground again. The siblings stay rooted on the acera. "What happened?" the leader asks again, her face growing frigid.

The girl looks to the acera warriors. Jamie clings to Amphii's reigns so tight her knuckles are turning pale, and Albert stares at Lillian like he's waiting for her to say something. She takes a deep breath. It's up to her. "Brianna, let's hurry back. We need to evacuate everyone."

The redhead's face turns pale as bone. "Why?"

Lillian looks at the ground, wondering how to word everything she has seen. "It's a long story. Just know we're not safe in the burrow anymore. We have to move somewhere safer."

"Is Bunker Two still safe? It's a bit of a walk, but better than the river one," Brianna says.

"It won't be for much longer."

"Then we will let Miss May know when we get back to the burrow. Come on, everyone, let's hurry home."

The leader of the gatherers beckons the group to keep walking. They make their way toward the main burrow. On the way, Lillian tells them about the terrifying encounter. She describes the orange-eyed capaeman and its connection to the black narecons. She tells them that Albert and Jamie believe he's a pro, and that means they do not have long. The deeper she delves into the story, the more apprehensive the gatherers become. She feels bad bringing them such terrible news, but they need to know.

When Lillian finishes, the gatherers look from side to side as if expecting the hunter to pop out of the trees any minute. More experienced fighters like Theo already have their weapons out.

Brianna simply stares forward, her expression a mixture of rage and fear. It's rare to see her show this much emotion. "Maybe it was a bad idea to let you go with them. When Seth finds out—"

"What do you mean? He won't make her leave the scouts, will he?" Jamie interrupts. She and Albert are still on Amphii. The acera walks with the group like she is one of the gatherers. She seems proud of it too.

"Well—"

"We *need* Lillian. Without her, we wouldn't have gotten as much info as we did," the acera warrior says. Her brother looks at her skeptically. She elbows him, trying to get him to play along. "Albert and I are terrified of capaemen because of our past, but on our mission, Lillian stayed calm. I don't know how she does it, but it lets me think clearly. Without her, it would be hard to do this job."

"Yeah, Jamie really loses her wits around giants," Albert adds. His sister elbows him much harder. "Oww!"

"So please let her travel with us," she finishes.

Brianna turns to Lillian. "Is this true?"

The girl's mouth hangs open. How can they say those things? She's been nothing but a burden this whole time. "Well, I—"

"Of course, it's true," Jamie answers.

"I'm asking *her*," Brianna says. Her tone is a warning.

Lillian realizes she has a choice to make. Either lie about how helpful she has been and keep flying with the scouts, or tell the truth and rejoin the gatherers, where many more boring errands await. It's a no-brainer. "We've been fine."

"Fine? You don't sound fine."

"I-I am." Why can't she stop shaking? She's safe. That's what matters, so she can keep traveling with Jamie and Albert. That is what she wants.

Brianna places a hand on her shoulder. "Lillian, if this is too much for you, you can always rejoin us. All you have to do is tell me."

"I-I..." She looks at the rogues and then at the gatherers. Why is she acting like this? She's going to ruin everything. Now, all the gatherers look concerned. She must say something. "A-Albert told me I'm good at staying calm in the face of danger. I think that's what they were talking about."

"That's good," Brianna says.

"That hunter, it was different from the other capaeman we saw. They could tell. I could too. I think I have a... sense for these things."

The gatherers are clearly not convinced. She must think of something more to say, something to convince them, but her mouth is dry. She still can't stop thinking about the capaeman by the river. What if... against all odds, he was telling the truth? It could be their only hope. If so, she shouldn't keep it a secret.

"Odds are, we only have a few days before the hunter finds us. We should focus on preparing the clan to evacuate. Let Lillian think for a little while. I'm sure she will make the right decision," Albert says, trying to help.

"Of course. That should be our main focus," the leader of the gatherers responds. "That's why I must do this: since Lillian cannot make up her mind, I will do it for her. The two of you had a close call with that hunter. I thought you could keep her safe, but that doesn't seem to be the case. She'll need to stick with us for now."

"What?" Lillian shouts. "No, you heard them. They need me."

"Yeah," Jamie says. "No need to be hasty. We can keep her safe." Her brother says nothing.

"Well, Lillian clearly does not feel the same way and hasn't for a while. Did something else happen? You've been acting weird since your first mission." The three of them freeze. She thought they were keeping the secret well, but apparently not. She's never been good at lying to her family. "I won't let you go back with the scouts until you tell me everything. That's the job: scout and *report*. Do not leave anything out," the leader of the gatherers says with finality.

"There really wasn't anything—" Jamie tries to say, but Brianna cuts her off.

"I've heard enough out of you. It's Lillian's turn to speak."

The girl takes a deep breath. She has no choice. "There might have been... another incident."

"Go on."

Although the siblings stare with disapproval, she tells the gatherers the story. How on that fateful morning, she talked to a capaeman. "Wait... a capaeman tried to *talk* to you?" Mia says. "This is unheard of. Unprecedented. It doesn't make any sen—"

"Yes, Mia," Brianna says. "It doesn't make sense, but you're missing the point. You two... You *let* this happen?"

Jamie and Albert nod shamefully. Suddenly, they are out of excuses. The other gatherers are fuming. Bruno makes his way over, standing between Lillian and them, glaring at the siblings. Zoey talks to the other gatherers, calling this a "betrayal." Most of them nod in agreement.

"I entrusted you with the safety of one of our children, one of the last ones we have, and you let her be seen by a capaeman?" It's chilling to see Brianna angry.

"They didn't let it happen!" Lillian snaps. She cannot let them get in trouble. "It was *my* fault. I refused to get on the acera because I was too scared. They tried to drag me on, but I wouldn't listen. Then, the capaeman cornered me. They had no choice but to flee. They did everything they could to rescue me, but—"

"I've heard enough!" Brianna shouts. Everyone falls silent. "No matter whose fault it was, they still had a mission to protect you and they *failed*. We can never let this happen again. Lillian, you are out of the scouts, for good."

"But you said—"

"I don't care what I said. Your safety was completely compromised, and I will *not* leave your life up to chance again. That would betray everything we stand for."

Lillian closes her mouth. She tried to fix things, and again, she only made it worse. She thought that maybe if she told them about the capaeman, they would be curious like her. That they too might wonder whether he was lying, but no. It's only she who is curious. It's only she who wonders.

Everyone else cares only about survival.

A few minutes later, they make it to the burrow. Night has fallen, and so have Lillian's spirits. Is she naïve for wondering? Is she radical for hoping? Is she wrong... for wanting something more?

The air is thick with disappointment. Hardly anyone talks, and Lillian heads into the burrow close to last. She knows the storm that's about to hit and dreads it. It's over. There's no way Brianna will not report this to Miss May and in turn, the whole of Zurec. The caretaker will never let her go outside again. She completely blew it.

But that may not even matter with a professional hunter after them. If they don't escape in time, nothing will matter. How have the capaemen so completely and utterly backed them into a corner in just a matter of weeks? Why do all this after they had left them alone for generations?

As they enter the mud room, Lillian feels almost relieved that no one is there. They must have gone to sleep, but that won't last long. One of them must have heard the trapdoor open. They will come to greet them soon, and with that, Lillian loses her freedom.

The worst part is, she might have had a chance to get answers, but now she will never reach them.

"If you ever wish to talk more, I will be by the river."

Why did he spare her life? There is no explanation, at least from what Zurec believes about capaemen.

"Once your usefulness has run dry, it will take away everything you love."

Is that really it? Was the capaeman trying to manipulate her? That doesn't make sense either. What use would he have for her? She knows nothing.

No, she can't go down this thornopine hole again. It will drive her up the wall. She should be focused on survival, just like everyone else.

Maybe then, she will finally feel like she belongs.

21

Secrets Revealed, Reason Concealed

Mary

After teaching the children for a little while, Mary's mom dumps the kids on her again. She should have known this would happen. Her mother and Kayla have been going back and forth between the well room and kitchen, restocking their water supply. It's been a while since they've maintained the well, so she supposes it's a good excuse. Still, Mary wishes her mother would switch jobs with her, at least on occasion. She loves cooking, even if it's just boiling water. Besides, she could use the time to think. Perhaps then she'd have less sleepless nights.

It doesn't matter too much tonight though, as everyone is up. The sun has already set outside, yet the children are still bouncing around, and Mary lacks the energy to stop them. Instead, she lets them play in the bedroom.

Mary sits on the floor, watching the twins shuffle through the pile of junk by her bed as if it is a treasure trove. Usually this would irritate her, but Jen and Jan's passion as they rummage through her stuff is too cute to stop.

She just finished telling a story. This time, it is not from a book. It's a surveyor story—when Seth took down a thornopine burrower. Mary thought a hopeful story would help lift the dreary atmosphere of the burrow. She was wrong. Little Oscar sits in Mary's lap. "I don't feel safe here," he mumbles.

"Well, your feeling is right," Trista says, crossing her arms.

Mary glares at Trista. *Don't you do this now, young lady.* Trista's brother sits next to her, lost in a world of his own. The siblings have been through the same trauma, but they handle it so differently.

"Shut up, Trista," Oscar says. Trista sticks out her tongue.

Mary tries to redirect. "Anyway—"

"Can we play outside tomorrow?" Oscar asks. He stares at Mary, his eyes pleading. He can be annoying, but she does feel bad for the kid. His parents died not long after he was born.

Mary shakes her head. "Please know we're only trying to keep you safe."

"We got to go outside with the gatherers. Why can't we do it again?"

"That was different. The gatherers can protect you much better. With Kayla, Miss May, and me, well, that would be too dangerous."

"It wasn't before," Oscar says. "Before, we got to play outside every day." The future caretaker sighs. How can she begin to explain the danger of this situation to a child? At first, they were scared and listened well. Now, they have grown restless, and she can't blame them. She never thought she'd miss being outside. Being confined to the burrow is torture.

"You're fools. All of you," Trista says. "The burrow isn't safe. Nowhere is."

"Trista," Mary says. She reaches for her, but the little girl slaps her hand away.

"I'm going to my room." She gets up, clearly intent on hiding in Kayla's bed... again.

"Now you just wait right—"

"What are you going to do about it, huh? Put me in timeout? Well, that would be better than this. Goodbye!" She storms out the door. Wordlessly, Max gets up to follow her. Mary doesn't stop him.

"It's okay. She's not worth your time," Oscar says.

"Now, that's not true," Mary begins, but she is interrupted again when the twins pull quite the find from her pile.

"Woahhh, this is so pretty! Look, Jen."

"Wowwww."

In Jan's hands is the headband Mary's been working on for weeks—a gift for Lillian. She finally finished it. She had placed it on the end of her bedframe, but it must have fallen onto the floor during the night.

"Can I have this, Mary?" Jan asks.

"No, I want it!" Jen says, trying to snatch the headband from her sister.

Mary reaches over, taking it away from both of them. "I'm sorry, but this is not for either of you. It's a gift for Lillian." She stares at it: a brown strip of fabric embroidered with the Zurec sigil. The sigil consists of a dark-brown circle with two double-headed spears diagonally crossed over it. Topping all of that is an ochre infinite loop, shaped sort of like a plus sign. As a bit of a personal touch,

Mary made the tips of the spears all the colors of the rainbow to represent Lillian's spear. It was not easy finding dyes for all of that thread.

She made this for Lillian partly as a gift and partly to get that hair of hers under control. Mary's headband keeps her hair out of her eyes. This one will help her friend too.

"Boo, why did you make something for *her*?" Jen asks, scowling.

"Because she's my best friend," Mary says.

"But she's mean," Jan says.

The caretaker-in-training takes a deep breath. *She's not like that on purpose*, Mary thinks. She can be cold sometimes, but it's never intentional. She prefers to keep to herself, and that is okay.

That is... perfectly okay.

She remembers the last time they really talked. Something was clearly bothering her. At first, Mary thought she was being paranoid, but for the past couple of days Lillian has continued to act weird. Is she really keeping secrets?

creeaaaakkk

As Mary wonders about Lillian, a familiar sound comes from the mud room. The trapdoor is opening. The children scramble out of the room, eager for anything remotely entertaining. Mary follows closely behind. Is it the surveyors or the gatherers?

She knows who it is the second she sees red hair. The gatherers are back, which means so is Lillian. Mary clutches the headband in her hands. She wants to give it to her now, but she has a strange feeling about their return. They don't usually come back at night.

The gatherers' expressions are etched with fear. Mary's heart pounds as she remembers the last time she saw that look. It was when the surveyors came to tell them Albian was dead.

Her mother hurries down the hall to greet the group. She looks them up and down. "Thank goodness. No one is dead this time." Mary spots Jamie and Albert. As usual, they stick to the back of the group. They look like they've seen a ghost. It is the first time she has seen Jamie scared, and it does not feel cathartic like she thought it would. Instead, terror rises in her chest. If the Osian assassins are terrified...

Kayla and her son rush into the room. "What's going on?"

Now everyone is here.

The people of Zurec look to the gatherers. Brianna, Mia, Lillian—all their faces look so grim. So, it's bad. Who is going to tell them? Brianna sighs deeply, and all eyes fall on her. "Miss May, you may want to sit down."

"I-Is it that serious?" the caretaker stammers.

"Deadly so. We'll have to evacuate the burrow." Gasps echo throughout the mud room. The caretaker turns bone white. Kayla holds her steady. "When the scouts were on their mission, they spotted a hunter. It's worse than we thought. Remember the narecon we encountered on our way back from Albian's burrow? Well, it turns out it wasn't there by coincidence. The black narecons are under the command of a capaeman, and if one was that close..."

"Then we don't have much time," Jamie finishes. "Honestly, I'm surprised we've lasted this long. That one is no amateur."

The caretaker places a hand on her head, tears in her eyes. "Wh-Where should we go? Wh-When do we leave? How much time do we have? We've lived here... for so long. I never thought we would have to..." She stops when she sees the looks on the children's faces. Oscar has begun to cry, and the twins do not look much better. Kayla leads them all into her room.

"I'm sorry," Brianna says. "I should have warned you first, so the kids wouldn't have to hear that."

"No," her mom answers. "They were going to hear about it regardless. So... what do we do?"

Mary's mind races. They must leave the burrow. That has never happened before. For generations, they have been safe here. Now, all of that is crumbling. Her life, all their lives, are about to change completely. She meets Lillian's eyes. She wonders whether her friend is feeling the same, but her expression is blank. The girl stares at the floor as if in another world. Mary's heart pounds. When Lillian shuts down like this...

"Here's the plan," Brianna continues. "First thing tomorrow morning, Jamie and Albert will find the surveyors and bring them back here. Seth will figure out where we go. He has the final say as usual, but I will advise him that we go to Bunker Two. It's our only real option. In the meantime, we hunker down. No one goes outside under any circumstances until the surveyors return."

"That's a bad idea!" a small voice screams. Mary turns to see Trista standing in the hall. Kayla has grabbed her arm and is trying to lead her back to their room, but the little girl won't budge. "You need to leave. Right now. The burrow isn't safe. Soon, they'll poison everyone!"

This is the first time the girl has shown care for anyone or anything. It is also the only time she has willingly talked about what happened. Why now? "They know more than you think. If we want to live, we gotta act different. We have to be... unpre-unpredictable." The little girl stammers on that last word. She must have just learned it.

No one knows how to respond except her little brother, who slowly approaches her. He takes his sister's hand and stares out at the clan, resolute. "It's true."

The kids' absolute statement hangs in the air.

"You have a point, little ones," Jamie says shakily. "Maybe we can escape if we do something they can't predict. So far, we've acted the way many people have before. We must come up with a plan they won't see coming, and I think the best person to come up with that plan is... well, it's Seth. This clan has an astute chief, and I think he would understand what you mean, umm..."

"Trista," the little girl says. "That's my name."

"And I'm Max."

"Trista and Max. Right. New plan, everyone. Albert and I will bring the surveyors back as soon as possible. I swear, we'll get them back here by tomorrow afternoon at the latest. We'll tell Seth about what Trista said. Whatever he decides, we will leave first thing." She gazes at Brianna as if pleading for her approval.

"Fine, then," the leader of the gatherers says. "Go. We will discuss your punishment when you return."

"Thank you so much." With that, Jamie and her brother rush out of the burrow.

"Punishment?" her mother asks. "What did they do?"

Brianna glares at Lillian. "May we... talk in private? Just, you, me, and her."

"Okay," the caretaker says, her frown deepening.

The gatherers go to their rooms, leaving the four of them alone. Mary refuses to budge, and the three of them stare at her.

"Mary, dear, she said just us three," her mother says.

"I know," she retorts. "But I'm not leaving."

Lillian's eyes widen. "M-Mary, this is very—"

"Important? I know. That's why you're not leaving me out. What has been going on with you?"

The brunette sighs. "Please, let her stay. She'll eavesdrop anyway."

"Fine," Brianna says. "Let's sit down."

They gather in a small circle on the rug. As Brianna and Lillian tell the story, Mary cannot believe her ears.

"I'm very sorry. The story I'm about to tell, it's... partially my fault," Brianna begins. "I was negligent as Lillian's guardian, and because of that, she was put in danger." Mary stares at her friend. It's as if the life has been slowly draining out of her, ever since the other day. The day she came back... changed.

"An incident occurred by the river with the scouts four days ago. I was not made aware of it until today. I'm still not sure how they managed to lose track of her like this, but the fact remains... Lillian almost died thanks to their irresponsibility, and my neglect."

The color drains from Miss May's face. "Wh-What?"

Almost... died? In her first couple of weeks in the outside world, she joined the scouts, almost died because of them, and... she didn't say anything?

"The capaeman that the scouts spotted by the river, it... cornered Lillian. Jamie and Albert were supposed to keep her close, but in that moment, they did not. We're not sure why, but it didn't harm her. It just spoke to her and let her go. It's a miracle she survived."

Mary's heart drops. No way did she hear that right.

"You mean to tell me..." her mom says, shaking, "...that Lillian encountered a capaeman? Not only that, but she was left *alone* with it?"

"That's correct," Brianna confirms. "It was a lapse in my judgment. I am very sorry."

"H-How is that possible? We've seen a few, sure, but no one in the history of Zurec has ever talked to one and lived to tell the tale."

"I don't understand it myself," Lillian says, "but... please don't punish Jamie and Albert. It wasn't their fault. Besides, I'm okay. That's all that matters, right?"

"Wh-Why didn't you tell me?" Mary asks. She's afraid to hear the answer.

Lillian avoids her gaze. "I... I didn't want to make a big deal of it."

"Make a big deal of it? What are you talking about? This is a *massive* deal." Now, their conversation the other day makes sense. She was doubting the capaemen's villainy because one of them *talked* to her. Why didn't she say that?

"I-I know, and I'm sorry. I couldn't tell anybody. It was too hard."

"N-Not even your best friend? I thought you trusted me."

"Mary, it's not that I don't. I just..." She hesitates.

Mary dislikes the look on her friend's face. "You just... what?"

"You've been stressed enough. I didn't want to make things worse."

"Worse for me or *yourself?*"

Her friend pauses again.

"Mary," Brianna intervenes, "Lillian has been through a lot. Don't be hard on her."

Mary clenches her fists. "We've all been through a lot. The least we can do is trust each other. Aren't you mad that she didn't tell anyone?"

"Mary, dear," her mother says, "why don't you go pack? The two of you can sort this out later. For now, we need to discuss her punishment."

"What? Punishment?" The brunette looks taken aback. She shouldn't be. Of course, she would be disciplined too. Brianna pulled a lot of strings for her to be with the scouts, yet Lillian was still careless.

"Whatever punishment she receives, I will take it as well," Brianna says shamefully.

"No," Miss May counters. "It was not your fault. You've been honest with us." The redhead nods abjectly. The caretaker turns back to her daughter, raising her eyebrows. "Dear?"

"Fine, I'll go," Mary says. "But this isn't over." She heads to their room.

Mary closes the creaky door and collapses onto her bed. She doesn't understand it. How can they share everything one day and keep secrets from each other the next? There has to be a reason. Yeah, Lillian has done stupid things before, and they always made up. Everything is going to be okay.

The girl gets up, needing to distract herself. She's too restless to try sleeping yet. She has to pack. Mary drags a small backpack out of her pile of junk. She picks through all her stuff, her anxiety building. *What kind of outfits should I bring? I only have room for one or two, and I have so many clothes. Can't forget my personal hygiene stuff either. Oh dear, that takes up a lot of room already. I also have that dolly project I was working on for Trista. Will that fit?... Yes, but it might get crushed. She'd be mad.* As she stuffs it in her backpack with everything else, something falls out of her pocket.

It's the headband. Should she give it to her? Of course, she should. She worked hard on it. It would be a shame for that to go to waste. Tears well in Mary's eyes. So much has happened in the span of a few weeks. Albian was killed, Jamie and Albert joined Zurec, Lillian became a scout and *talked* to a *capaeman.* What has Mary been doing this whole time?

Trying to entertain the children and failing.

She is so useless. She couldn't even get Trista to give them clues. She's been a poor excuse for a caretaker and apparently, an untrustworthy friend too.

creeaakkk

Slowly, the rickety door to their room opens. "Hey, can we talk?" Lillian asks.

Mary sits on her bed next to her overflowing backpack, the gift in her hands. "Yeah, we need to." Her friend stares at her for a few seconds, then heads to her bed and packs her backpack. It only takes her a few minutes before it's ready. She places her spear next to it. The blades glow orange in the torchlight.

"I made this headband for you," Mary says, holding it up.

Lillian stares at the gift blankly. "That's nice of you."

"I've been so worried about you. It was supposed to be for the Red Eclipse. I wanted to make something special for you to remember me by, out in the Wilds, but things have been so hectic. I'm sorry it took so long to finish." She brings the headband to her. "May I?"

The brunette leans in. "Sure."

She wraps the piece of cloth around Lillian's head. Now, the Zurec sigil sits proudly on her friend's forehead. The headband holds down her hair, making it look a little neater. "It looks good," Mary says. "Do you... like it?"

Lillian pats her head, then pulls her top layers of hair out of the headband, messing it up again. Now the only visible part is the sigil on her forehead. "Yeah, it's nice."

Mary frowns. "You know you can use it to handle that messy haircut of yours, right?"

"I like it like this."

"I see." When did it get so hard to talk to her? Was it when Jamie and Albert arrived? No... it was before then. She has been acting differently since she joined the gatherers. Mary takes a seat next to her friend. "Lillian... why didn't you tell me what happened to you?"

Her friend's lip quivers. "I guess I was... afraid."

"Afraid of what?"

"You have enough going on. I didn't want you to, you know, freak out."

"What does *that* mean?" Mary doesn't like the way she said that.

"Well, I mean, you're always worrying about me. I don't want you to do that."

"And you think withholding the truth accomplishes that?"

"I was trying to protect you. Besides, what does it matter whether you know every detail of my life anyway?" Her tone is turning hostile.

Mary's heart sinks. Why is Lillian angry all of a sudden? "I'm your friend. There's nothing wrong with me knowing about your life."

"Can everyone stop breathing down my neck for like, five seconds? I don't even have time to think. It's like none of you trust me to do anything, not even brush my own hair. I will never become a good warrior if everyone keeps suffocating me like this!"

Mary's jaw drops. Her friend finds her... suffocating?

"Why are you so eager to know every detail of my life anyway? You have your own."

"Because you're so reckless!" Mary snaps. "I can't help but worry about you, and neither can they. You never listen to the adults, you always start trouble, and when you fight, you charge without thinking. It's like you don't care about your own life at all."

"Of course I care!" Lillian shouts. "I want to survive, just like everyone else. Why wouldn't I? The only difference between you and me is that I want something more. Only surviving is agony. I want to *live*."

"What does that even mean? How can you live if you don't have regard for your own life? If you... if you let yourself be cornered by a capaeman? It's like you have a death wish. So yeah, I worry about you. I care. Because *someone* has to."

Her friend sighs. "You know what I think? I think you're jealous. Deep down, you hate it here, but you don't want to admit that. So, you cling to me. You live your life through mine because you're too afraid to face the fact that you *hate* yours."

Mary gasps, tears welling in her eyes.

Lillian's face softens. "Mary, I'm sorry. I didn't mean—"

"N-No, I know what you meant," she says, getting up. "My life is empty and yours is great, huh? That's why my mom gave you her dagger. It's why you got that spear. You're special, and I'm not. You've made that painfully clear."

"Please, let me—"

"Just shut up!" Mary screams. "This conversation is over. Let's just pack and get ready to uproot our lives."

As the two of them finish packing, there's nothing but silence. Mary can't even look at her friend right now—if she can call her that. Their whole lives, it has always been "Lillian this, Lillian that." Despite that, Mary tried to be supportive because that's what friends do. Turns out, her supposed "friend" doesn't even want that. She finds her *suffocating*. Mary feels crushed for caring.

Tomorrow, they are leaving the burrow, starting a new life. So, from now on, Mary will stay out of her hair. Maybe then Lillian will realize how valuable she is. Yes, she will regret this. Mary is sure of it.

22

The Fight Before the Storm

Lillian

Lillian imagined many reactions from Mary, but this is the worst-case scenario. They've fought before, but never like this. That was much worse than Albert and Jamie's arguments. She wants to apologize, but Mary told her to shut up. So, as they leave their beds and begin the day, they do it in silence.

Lillian hardly slept last night, and she doubts her friend did either. Every time she recalls their argument, her entire body boils with rage. She thought Mary was the one person who understood her, someone who would always have her back. It turns out she was wrong. Mary sees her the same way everyone else does: as a failure. As someone who needs to be looked after. She wants to know every detail about her life not because she cares, but because she wants to change her. Everyone wants to change Lillian. No one likes who she is. No one except... Jamie and Albert. Now she's lost them, along with her freedom. She wonders if Mary even cares.

The blonde shoves an absurd amount of stuff into a tiny bag. It seems she changed her mind about what she packed last night and is now desperately trying to save even more from their life in the burrow. It's not going to fit in there. Still, she huffs and puffs, sweat beating down her forehead, her expression filled with frustration. Lillian is certain it's not the bag she's mad at.

Suddenly, a knock comes from the redwood door. Miss May creeps in. "Are you girls ready? I'm sure Seth will be back soon." Her eyes dart between them. She came in last night well after the girls had gone to bed, but clearly, she heard their argument. The whole burrow must have. They were yelling so loud.

"No," Mary says. "Why in the Wilds are these bags so small?"

187

"Honey, you can't bring all of that with you. You'll hurt your back."

"Then what am I supposed to do?" the blonde says, tears welling in her eyes.

Her mother embraces her. "I'm sorry. I'm so sorry that we have to leave. It's hard for me too, but the capaemen are no joke." She lets go and smiles at both girls. "Wherever we go we will make a wonderful home, as long as we are together." Lillian has trouble believing that. Not just because of the pain in Miss May's eyes, but because of everything she and Mary have said. No matter where they are, Lillian is an outcast. She's too reckless. Too curious. Too… different.

"Now, Lillian," Miss May says, noticing the girl's expression. "You know this is for your own good. You have to learn to listen to the clan's rules, young lady. We only want to keep you safe."

"Right, okay." She is sick of talking about how much she screwed up. If only everyone would leave her alone.

"What is Lillian's punishment?" Mary asks.

"She'll be staying with us for a few months until she's ready to rejoin the gatherers. I have yet to ask Seth, but I'm sure he will agree. You and I are going to have our work cut out for us. She needs to learn self-discipline before she'll be allowed to leave again."

Mary chuckles. "Then she'll be here forever. Might as well make her the new caretaker." The two laugh. Lillian doesn't know what's so funny. They've imprisoned her, and for what? Wanting to see the world? Is that so wrong?

"Anyway," the caretaker says, "what were you two yelling about last night? It sounded nasty. If you're going to be living together for the next couple of months, you'll need to make up." Mary crosses her arms, refusing to look at either of them.

Lillian sighs. She did go too far in their argument, so she doesn't mind apologizing first. "I'm sorry. I didn't mean it when I said you were jealous. I was angry."

She scoffs. "It sounded like you meant it."

"I didn't. I let my anger get the better of me. You're great at caring for the kids, something I can't do."

Mary glares at her. "Because that's all that I am, right?"

"No!" She's taking this all wrong.

"Also, that wasn't even a full apology. What, are you not sorry for the rest of it? Keeping secrets from us? Saying I'm *suffocating* you."

"What? I didn't say that. I just said that we have two separate lives. Plus, you said some terrible things too."

"I only told you what you needed to hear," Mary seethes. "I'm looking out for you."

"Oh, come on," Miss May interrupts. "Just apologize, both of you. We have bigger things to worry about."

"Apologize, for what?" Mary snarls. "She's the one who should apologize to me."

"I already did," Lillian says through clenched teeth.

"A full apology."

As tensions rise, Miss May grows more and more nervous. "Well, you'll just have to figure this out yourselves. I must help the kids pack. They're panicking, you know. So, once you've sorted this out, we could really use your help." She hurries out of the room.

Lillian can't blame her for leaving. There is so much going on right now. This is hardly the time for a fight. She wishes she could leave too, but that somehow feels worse, like giving up. She doesn't want to give up. She wants to solve this. Lillian tries to meet Mary's eyes, but the blonde ignores her.

Maybe she should have been honest from the start. No, that doesn't feel right. Her friend would have freaked out regardless. What would have been the best move? How could she have avoided this fight?

CREEEAAAAKKK

That's the trapdoor. She can't take it here any longer. Lillian rushes toward the mud room, hoping it's the surveyors. Luckily, Mary doesn't follow her.

As the surveyors flood into the burrow, Lillian can tell what's about to happen. Seth walks with a great sense of urgency. The others follow behind him, weapons at the ready. With them are Jamie and Albert, who look incredibly on edge. They keep glancing back at the trapdoor as if expecting an attack.

Lillian is glad to see the two rogues. She wishes she could join them and escape from here, but her elders will no longer allow that. Lillian wishes she never met that capaeman. All it has brought her is trouble.

Seth fixes his armor. The Zurec sigil sits proudly on his shoulder plate. "Jamie, Albert, please head out again. I want you to survey the area. If you see anything suspicious, fly back and reroute us. We can't run into narecons now."

"Understood," Jamie responds.

Just like that, they turn to leave again. Will they be able to stay friends, with Lillian confined to a bunker? They will be so busy flying around, seeing the world, and she'll be underground rotting. As the two make their way up the exit tunnel, Albert locks eyes with Lillian. He smiles guiltily as if saying, *"I'm sorry you can't come with us."*

She feels completely and utterly helpless.

"As for everyone else," Seth says, "if you haven't already packed, do so now. We leave as soon as we can. We will be taking shelter in Bunker Two, which is a few hours' walk from here. If Jamie and Albert spot narecons near there, we'll move. The plan is to keep moving between Bunkers Two and One as needed."

"Wait, Bunker One? W-We haven't been there in years," Miss May interjects. For some reason, she sounds nervous.

"That hardly matters now," the chief says, looking her dead in the eyes. "If they become dangerous too, we'll move to our *other* shelters."

The caretaker grows pale. "Seth, we all promised not to—"

"If it comes to it, we will break that."

All of the adults fall dead silent. Even Elias, Seth's most skeptical friend, seems to know what's going on. Right now, something unspoken is passing amongst the adults, and Lillian does not like it. What does he mean by "other shelters"? Don't they only have four bases, including this burrow? Maybe there are backup shelters for emergencies. She wants to believe that, but she has a feeling it's wrong.

"Anyway," Seth says, his tone suddenly growing lighter, "as you can see, we've brought back some meat to share, but in light of this news, we don't have time to cook it. At the very least, this gives us something to look forward to in Bunker Two. If we survive today, we'll do a cookout tonight to celebrate. It's been too long." Only now does Lillian notice what some of the surveyors hold: Madilyn, Lance, Finn, and William have hemp sacks thrown over their shoulders. Some are stained with blood.

The last time they had a cookout, Noah and Gigi were there. Gigi gossiped with the girls while Noah took charge of roasting. He was the best at making sure the meat was cooked even and tender, and it tasted delicious. Perhaps they brought this food back to cook in their honor. Their expressions are sullen.

"We killed some of the leomus invading Albian's territory," the chief adds. "We thought the group could use some time to bond, especially with how much we've lost."

"Oh, Seth," Miss May says, "that's a sweet thought, but is it safe to cook with the capaemen out?"

"I asked the scouts, and it is. Relatively," Seth explains. "Capaemen need to sleep too."

"Well, maybe we can do it once we're safely at the bunker," the caretaker says, although she doesn't look hopeful.

"Do we really get to eat some?" Oscar asks eagerly.

"Meat! Meat! Meat!" the twins start chanting. "Can we have some, Uncle Robin?"

Bruno's brother Robin addresses the twins, twiddling his thick dark hair with his thumb. He is close to many of the surveyors but not any of the children. He's better with tactics than kids, especially overeager kids. Lillian almost feels excited too. They rarely eat meat, mainly because it's so hard to kill most creatures of the Giant Wilds. If they can make it to the bunker, this will be a much-needed treat.

"If we hurry, we can get there by sundown. Now, let's go!" the chief commands.

Everyone scrambles. Some surveyors rush to their rooms. Others stay, checking their backpacks. Lillian pats her bag. She has everything she needs: a hairbrush, toothbrush, several days' worth of clothing and food rations, and her weapons, of course. Her dagger is strapped to her waist while her bow, quiver, and spear are on her back. She has tried not to look at the spear since... the incident. She can't see it the same after what that capaeman said. *That metal is very rare, you know.*

"Hey Lillian," someone says.

Lillian almost double-takes when she sees who spoke. Her dad stands next to her, his arms crossed and a disappointed look on his face.

Oh no. They've filled him in, she thinks.

"I just got done speaking with Brianna," he says threateningly. "I am very disappointed in you." Here it comes. There is no worse punishment than what he's about to say.

"Miss May thinks you should stay in the bunker for a while, but I don't think that's fair."

Yup, makes sense. He talked to Miss May and agreed to, wait, no. What did he just say?

"It's a great way to keep you safe, but you won't learn from it. Otherwise, you would have learned from the fifteen years you were there already."

Finally! A voice of reason. "Yes, you're right. Please don't make me go back. I want to—"

"Right, yes. You want to join the surveyors. Honestly, we could use all the help we can get."

"I'll do anything else, just don't, wait..." Lillian trails off, realizing what her dad just said.

"What was I thinking? That Brianna would keep you out of danger better than I could? That the scouts would protect you from capaemen? I wanted you to be safe, but none of us are. So, if you want to join the surveyors, we'll take you and teach you to follow the rules."

"You mean, I can join the *surveyors*?"

"Yes. You will learn the ways of Zurec, or what's left of it anyway. I already talked to Miss May and Brianna about it. One isn't so thrilled. The other thinks it's a great idea. I'll let you guess who is who. Anyway, what do you say?"

This is all Lillian has ever wanted since she was a little kid. She dreamed about learning from her father, going on adventures, and becoming chief one day, but... but...

What is this feeling rising in her chest?

Learning from her father? He is so busy he hardly has time for her. He'll probably stick her with Elias or William and make them train her instead. That would be a massive disappointment, especially since she had hoped Jamie would become her trainer.

Adventures? Nothing compares to the feeling of being in the sky, the wind on her face, and the view of the forest below.

Becoming chief? The notion almost makes her laugh. Chief of what? Zurec is dying, and she... she...

"Lillian, are you okay?"

What is wrong with me?

"Haha, I'm sure it doesn't feel like much of a punishment, but you've been punished enough. I mean, talking to a capaeman? That must have been terrifying. By the way, you have to tell me how that happened. Lillian, are you still listening?"

"No," she says.

Seth raises an eyebrow. "No, you're not listening?"

"No, I..." she trails off, her thoughts racing.

"Still in shock? I'm sure it'll be overwhelming at first, but with enough training and discipline, you'll be—"

"Why now, Dad?" Lillian says, clenching her fists. "A couple weeks ago, I would have been over the moon if you said this to me, but now it feels wrong."

"Wrong? Isn't this what you've wanted your whole life?"

"It is, but..." The scouts changed her life. She didn't realize it until now, but they did. She is willing to deal with Jamie's antics if it means more acera rides. If it means more deep conversations with Albert, more bird's-eye views of the Giant Wilds.

Lillian takes a deep breath. Her past self screams for her to stop, but she can't. She must say this. "You wanted me to change. Well, congratulations, I have. Traveling with the scouts may have been dangerous, but I've learned more about the world than I ever thought I could. I like Jamie and Albert, and I love riding on their acera. I don't want to do anything else."

Seth makes an expression she has never seen him make before. It's a combination of shock and confusion.

"Please, let me rejoin the scouts. We made a mistake. It won't happen again, I swear."

"I..." Her father struggles to speak. This has taken him completely off guard. Lillian is surprised too. She wishes the surveyors were still what she wanted, but they aren't anymore. Maybe her dad will—

"No," he finishes.

Her heart sinks. "What?"

"Lillian, you cannot be serious. After sneaking off without my permission, making Brianna cover for you, and being seen by a capaeman, you think you can go back to the scouts?"

"Again, you wanted me to learn. I did."

"You almost *died*. That's what happened. No, I won't allow it. You join the surveyors or stay in the bunker. Those are your choices."

"But—"

"No buts." Seth glances down the hall. "Everyone's almost ready. We will discuss your decision later. I hope you join us. Don't be stubborn. This is for your own good."

As her father leaves again, Lillian feels worse than the last time they spoke. She thought that maybe because Seth saw Miss May's punishment as unfair, he would understand her, but again she was wrong.

He sees her the same way everyone else does. She should have known.

Seth's massive shadow dances on the torchlit walls, but instead of dwarfing hers per usual, it grows smaller as he walks farther away. Lillian remembers how she felt the first time he rejected her: the burning desire to be accepted, to be by her father's side with the surveyors.

Now, she doesn't know how to feel.

It isn't long before everyone is gathered in the mud room. It's strange seeing all the members of Zurec in armor. Even Mary and the kids are ready for combat. Lillian shivers at the thought of what they risk facing. Just being in the hunter's presence was overwhelming, as if it could kill her with a thought.

The clan heads west, in the direction of Bunker Two. The air smells heavily of dew, and the bits of sky visible through the canopy are grey and cloudy. It might rain. That won't bode well for Zurec. If it rains for too long, the foliage turns to mud, and people may get stuck.

The plan is simple: get everyone to the bunker before sundown. If they see anything giant, they will hide. Albert and Jamie are off who knows where, making sure no narecons are in the area. It's reassuring to know they will at least get a warning before an attack, assuming the acera warriors don't get ambushed themselves. So many things can go wrong with this plan, but they have no choice. They must leave.

Lillian walks alone, trying not to make eye contact with anyone. She's sure she is the laughingstock of the community. No one wants to talk to her, and who could blame them? Meanwhile, Mary walks with the caretaker and the kids. The strange Albian girl, Trista, clings to her. For once, Lillian takes pity on the girl. They both know how terrifying the capaemen can be.

Brianna and the gatherers stick to the rear while Seth and the surveyors take the front, safeguarding the caretaker and children between them. It's a good formation. It would defend against a ground attack from multiple angles, but would it stop a narecon?

No. It would not.

Lillian feels her back, making sure her spear is still there. She's been practicing her draw. Hopefully, if something does attack, she will be able to react quicker this time.

"Vigilant as ever, I see," someone says. She turns to her right to see the leader of the gatherers, Brianna. "Hey," she says, "I'm taking a break. How are you holding up?"

"You know the answer to that."

Brianna chuckles. "I think I do."

"I'm sorry I got you into this mess. Maybe I am too reckless after all."

"Come on, give me *some* credit. I'm the one who agreed to let you join the scouts, after all. I'm to blame too."

"Did you get punished?" Lillian asks.

The redhead shrugs. "Not really. Seth scolded me, is all. Told me it was a bad idea, and I shouldn't have stepped out of line like that. Hmm, he's right."

"Then why did you help me?"

Brianna slugs her on the shoulder. "Because you were miserable and I care about you. We all do. In our own ways."

Lillian looks around at the group. "I wish they'd listen to me like you do."

"I know this is hard to hear, but we really do want what's best for you. All of us. Don't forget that, okay?" Although she doesn't believe that, Lillian nods. She likes how Brianna's acting right now—less stoic and more human. She wonders what brought this change. "If you want my advice, join the surveyors. That's where I'd be if I weren't leading the gatherers. Seth is a great leader, and I'm sure it would be great for you two to spend time together."

"Thanks." She's reminded of how Brianna turned down the position of chief. Maybe it's because she thought Seth would be better at it. There's no way to know for sure unless she asks, but things are hectic right now, and there's so much on her mind. They'll have time to talk once everyone is safe at Bunker Two.

"We'll miss you in the gatherers, you know."

Lillian recalls her time with them and scoffs. "Come on, I was a nuisance, and you all know it."

"You were not. Everyone makes mistakes. What counts is what you do about them. And you, my girl, *never* give up."

She smiles. This is the only person who's listened to her all day. Maybe she can mention what's been bothering her. "Brianna, I—"

flap flap flap

Upon hearing the flapping of large wings, the surveyors and gatherers draw their weapons. Lillian draws her spear.

What touches down next to them is not a narecon, but an acera. "Jamie, Albert!" Seth yells. "What's the situation?"

Jamie is shivering. She clutches the acera's reigns, her eyes wide and jaw twitching. "Run."

"Run? Why? What's happening?"

She points in the direction the group is headed. "They're coming. Narecons. From the west. They're almost here. You need to run!"

"How many?" Seth asks, trying to keep it together.

"At least five of them, and the hunter, it's here too. I'm sorry. This is all my fault. The capaeman would never have treated you this seriously if it weren't for Albert and me."

"Which direction should we run?"

"The river. Bunker Three. It's our only option. Let's move, now!"

"You heard her. Let's go!" Seth commands.

The clan picks up the pace, ducking and jumping over tree roots, pushing through the plants. Amphii flies low overhead, watching, waiting. Sweat beads on Lillian's forehead as she runs with her spear in hand. Their enemies could appear anywhere at any time. If that happened, who would they kill first? Brianna? Miss May? Seth?

... Mary?

She glances back at her former friend. For the first time since their fight, Mary meets her eyes. She looks like she is about to fall apart. Lillian wishes she could comfort her. That she could tell her everything is going to be okay, but she doesn't know that. No one does.

SCREEEEEEE

Swooping down from the canopy are two black narecons.

23

The Hand or the River

Lillian

"Get out of here! We'll try to hold them off!" Jamie screams. Amphii shoots through the air, snarling. She is just as unhappy to see these narecons as the humans, but the terrible reality is that there are two narecons, and only one acera.

"This way, everyone!" Seth screams as the group sprints toward Bunker Three. The surveyors are now at the rear of the formation instead of the front. Do they plan to fight those things?

As if answering her question, Seth shouts, "Surveyors! Protect our family at all costs."

"Yes sir!" the surveyors say in unison, all except Kayla, who runs with Miss May and the children clutching her stomach. She has another life to worry about.

"Stay with me! All of you. Don't get separated," Miss May commands, her spear held up. She and Kayla herd the children, and together they run, now following the gatherers. Lillian wants to help the surveyors, but she gets the feeling she'd slow them down. She'd better stick by Mary and the others, make sure they're safe.

They duck under roots and blow through brambles. The children were slow before, but now they are going much quicker than Lillian thought possible.

"We're gonna die," Trista cries.

"No, we're not!" Mary shouts. "Just run! The surveyors and scouts will hold them off."

CRASH

A colossal crash reverberates from behind. One of the narecons has touched down. Its landing sends dust into the air and blood splattering. Lillian wants to scream, but no sound comes out. All she can do is watch as yet another limp body is mangled by a monster's claws.

"Elias!" Seth screams, but he composes himself quickly. "Keep fighting! Let them escape!" He, William, and the surveyor's best fighter, Lance, drive their spears into the beast while it's distracted with their dead friend. It screeches in agony.

All Lillian can do is run. It's what her dad wants. It's what the members of Zurec who are fighting and dying now would want. She'll only get in the way. At this moment, she finally realizes why her dad didn't want her to be a surveyor. *This* is the reality of their job. If there is ever any danger, they're the first to the frontline. They're the first to die.

Brianna leads the formation. She ducks over and under the tree roots with precision, but not so quickly that the caretaker and children can't keep up. They have a good strategy, with the surveyors fighting at the rear and the gatherers running forward. Still, more people will die before the day's end.

"Oh no, you don't," Jamie's voice echoes. "This is my clan, and you're not laying a hand on them, monster!" Amphii screeches right along with the Osian warrior. The sound of tearing flesh fills the air, giving Lillian both dread and hope. She hopes the wounded are the narecons and not more of her people. She must check, if only to put her mind at rest. The young warrior takes a glimpse back.

The scene is overwhelming. Jamie, Amphii, and Albert are covered in narecon blood. If she were to guess, they've already killed one, and now they're taking on the other. The second narecon is taking off, realizing it's outmatched. Madilyn, Robin, and other surveyors pull out their bows, but there isn't much they can do against those massive wings. With every flap, people go flying. Luckily, Jamie goes after it, but she can only be in so many places at once. There is now more than one body lying on the forest floor. Lillian turns away, not daring to check who they are.

"Step on it, everyone!" Miss May yells shrilly. "Get to Bunker Three!" Despite her old age, she carries little Felix in her arms as she guides the group through crisis. Bruno would have helped if he were not already carrying both of his daughters. Mia runs right by them, breathing haggardly as she sprints with her giant backpack.

With how quickly they are moving, they will make it in minutes. Still, a lot can happen in that amount of time. They have no idea whether that capaeman boy is by the river today. If he is, they could end up cornered. Not to mention the orange-eyed hunter. It could make an appearance at any time.

The surveyors fade farther into the distance, yet their screams seem to grow louder. Lillian can hear her father shouting orders but can't distinguish his words. A scream pierces the air. Is that Finn? Lillian isn't sure whether the shriek means she is hurt or someone she loves is. Still, it's horrifying to hear. That woman rarely speaks, much less cries out. She wants so badly to turn around, do something to help, but she'd be useless—and she'd make their sacrifices meaningless.

Why me? Lillian thinks with tears in her eyes. *Why do you all care so much? I'm not a good member of our clan. I'm not even a good friend.* The surveyors are laying down their lives for them without hesitation. They've seen what death is like. They've lost many friends to it, yet they still do it. They care about Zurec that much.

The sound of roaring water rises in the distance. Adrenaline courses through Lillian's veins like the river rapids. It's as if she has super speed, and time slows down around her. Every second feels like an hour. Every scream a reminder of who they've lost and who they stand to lose next. Their bodies frozen in agony and regret, never to move again. They have lost too much already. Will it ever end?

Out of the corner of her eye, Lillian spots blonde hair. Mary now sprints next to her. The girl looks like she is either about to vomit or faint, but she keeps up with the group. If this massacre is shaking Lillian, she can't even imagine what her empathetic friend must be feeling now.

"Hang in there…. Mary," Lillian says between breaths.

Mary forces a smile. "I'm okay," she huffs. "We must… get the children to safety." She drags the distraught Trista and Oscar along. Even in this chaos, Mary is still being Mary, putting on an act to make others feel better. She has always been so kind. Sure, she can be judgmental at times, but everyone has their faults. Mary is a good person.

Lillian dares to look behind her again and sees that some surveyors have caught up with them. She scans the group, trying to figure out who is missing: Elias of course, Gabriel, Lina, and… wait, where is her dad? She glances back and forth, searching desperately. Then, she meets William's gaze. There is blood splattered on his clothes. He shields Kayla as they press through a patch of brambles.

"Don't worry," his pregnant wife says, panting. "Seth is alive. He's just staying on the back line with the best fighters."

Lillian nods and snaps her focus forward. This means others may still be alive too. There's no need to note who's missing. It will only make her more terrified.

Jamie and Albert fly overhead, their acera covered in blood, but both alive. That's good. They might make it out of this.

But she thinks too soon.

From the front this time, two more black narecons swoop down. One goes straight for the middle of the formation. As it lands, it creates a gust of wind so strong that it knocks everyone to the ground, including Lillian and Mary. Their bodies crash onto the forest floor with a loud *thud*, separating them from the children. Lillian gazes up at the beast with dread. Its giant wings cast a shadow as it uses its beak and talons to tear into a surveyor's shoulder. Lillian recognizes him as Archer. The reckless man jumped in front of the kids at the last second. He collapses to the ground, his blood pooling into the moss. The children scream in horror. Miss May barks orders to keep running, but her words are drowned out in the carnage.

Almost all the gatherers have joined the fight. Brianna, Jess, Zoey, Theo, and Milo attack the narecon that killed Archer, while Jamie and Amphii take on the second one that just landed. Even Albert is fighting from the back of the acera, slicing its flesh with his smaller scythes as Amphii charges at the beast. No one is safe anymore.

"Girls!" the caretaker wails. She and Kayla have gathered the children in one spot and are beckoning the girls to follow. Lillian forces her feet to move and grabs Mary. With the caretaker, children, and remaining adults, they sprint to the river.

The scene is now a war zone. Blood splatters as a narecon finishes with one surveyor and goes for a gatherer next. It is so overwhelming Lillian can't tell who is dying anymore. Screaming emanates from every direction. All she knows is they are sacrificing themselves for *them*. They die in hopes that their loved ones will reach Bunker Three safely.

Lillian forces herself to look ahead. If she keeps taking in the scene, it will destroy her. How many people are dead? Five? Ten? More than that? To think the narecons have done this much damage, and their commander isn't even here. If that *hunter* finds them, there won't be a Zurec anymore.

The river's roar grows louder and the forest foliage thicker. Their group is almost at Bunker Three. If they could make it a little farther without getting ambushed again, they may save the children. *Please, at least let us save them,* Lillian thinks. Zurec cannot die here. Not after all they've fought for.

whooooossshhh

Finally, the river overtakes the sounds of the chaos. The thick foliage makes way for algae-covered rocks and muddy moss. Then, the familiar roots of Bunker Three's tree come into view. "We're almost there!" Mia shouts.

The second they reach the trapdoor, Bruno throws it open and gestures for the children to go in first. They rush down the hole, with Jen and Jan fighting on the way down.

"We don't have time for this. Get in, girls!" Miss May screams.

"One at a time!" Mia shouts. Despite Mia's instruction, her daughters end up squeezing down the narrow corridor together. When the children have all entered, Kayla goes next. Then, Bruno gestures for the two teenagers to enter, and Lillian points at Mary. If either of them makes it out of this, she wants it to be her.

"No," Mary says, "you go first."

The warrior crosses her arms. "I thought you hated me."

"I don't hate you. I was mad. Now, get in the bunker so we can talk about this."

"I won't. Not until you're safe."

"It doesn't matter who goes first!" Miss May screams. She's already in the hallway. She reaches out a hand. "Just come on!"

Mary reaches for her mother's hand. Good. There isn't enough time to argue.

SCRAAAAAA

Before their hands can touch, another narecon lets out its sickening cry.

⚜

There can be no denying it now. Two narecons attacked from behind, two from the front, and now a fifth narecon is swooping down upon them—these birds are herding them. Lillian has a creeping feeling that their ringleader is nearby, ready to massacre them once they are all in the same spot.

Bruno drops the trapdoor on Miss May. The caretaker screams from the other side, begging him to let the girls in, but then the narecon lands. It is smaller than the rest, but its landing still sends a massive gust of wind in all directions, knocking them away from the bunker.

The remaining members of Zurec run yet again. Lillian keeps a tight grip on her best friend's hand. No matter what happens, Mary cannot die. She *has to* protect her.

Bruno, Thomas, and Mia distract the narecon. There aren't enough of them to kill it.

"Find a place to hide!" Mia screeches. "We'll lead this one to the others. We'll be fine!" But Lillian knows that's a lie. As the pair run away, Lillian feels like she can't breathe, and not from the exertion. Now it is just the two of them. Behind them, Zurec warriors are dropping like insects, and the hunter isn't even here yet. The girls need to find shelter, and fast.

Lillian can hear the distant screaming of the warriors fighting the narecons. She hears Jamie yelling, and that gives her an inkling of hope. If they can get to all the narecons in time, some people might live. Still, there are many unknowns. She has no idea where her dad is. By the Wilds, she hopes he's okay.

The girls run south, treading along the bank of the river. Lillian knows south is the wrong way to go. It's toward capaemen territory, but the narecons leave them no choice; it's the bank or the beasts. They come across an elderly tree surrounded by a grove of giant ferns. Their massive leaves dangle over the water, which is picking up speed. This is where the river rapids begin, leading down to the whitewood tree. The last thing Lillian wants is to take Mary back to that place, so they'll need to find a hiding spot here.

Lillian swings her backpack off and straps her spear back onto it. She ran with it in hand this whole time, but now is not the time to fight. As she secures the spear, its metal tips glow bright blue, like water.

Next, she checks on her friend, and her heart skips a beat. Mary's stare has gone completely blank, and she drags behind, only able to keep up because of their clasped hands.

"Mary, are you okay?" Lillian asks. The girl winces. "I'm so sorry! I swear, we'll get to safety soon." She stares at the ferns, and as they grow closer, the *whoosh* of the river quickens. Perhaps hiding near the rapids is a good thing. If they make any noise, it will be hard to hear. All she hopes is they can get there before another narecon arrives.

boom... boom...

Then, the sound of something even worse echoes through the forest.

Boom... Boom...

Two feet, not four.

Boom Boom

It's coming from the south, straight toward them.

And it's almost here.

In an instant, a gargantuan figure comes into view. It is about five trees away from them and has yet to see them. However, if they can see it, it can find them. Lillian's last run-in with the hunter taught her that much.

BOOM.

The sound punches Lillian's ear drums. That, on top of the chaos around them, makes it impossible to think clearly. She looks at Mary. It is only the two of them now, and the ferns are only several feet away, but her friend won't budge.

Mary stares at the distant capaeman, her eyes glassy. Her hand is clutched around her necklace. "Mary, come on. We need to hide," Lillian says.

No response.

Backed by the soundtrack of screaming, the capaeman steps gracefully through the forest in calf-high combat boots, its face completely expression-less. Instead of light colors, it now wears a black shirt and loose camouflage pants. Strange gadgets, probably all made for death, stick out of a toolbelt in place of its pants pockets. It is like this giant was born for this, as if surrounded by the suffering of her people is where it is most at home. In the shadow of the canopy, its eyes are a bloody orange.

Lillian forces Mary to move. If they can get to the center of the fern cluster and hide under the roots of that old tree, they won't be seen.

rustle rustle

She pushes through the stalks of the massive plants, even as they make terrifyingly obvious rustling sounds. She winces with each step, and with every *rustle*, looks up at the capaeman in the distance. Now it is just... standing in a clearing. Its eyes are closed and hands held outward, much like the last time she saw it.

Lillian has no idea why the hunter is doing that, but it gives them their best chance.

rustle rustle

They move faster, growing closer to the old tree at the center, which may have a root cave if they're lucky.

rustle rustle

She drags her unresponsive friend. *We're going to make it. We're going to—*
snap!

Only too late does Lillian realize her mistake. This is an old tree. It's bound to have big rotting branches surrounding its base. And she just stepped on one, snapping it in half.

The capaeman's head whips in their direction.

Oh no oh no oh no—

She is such a fool. It closed its eyes because it was listening—waiting for its prey to move. In her rush to get them to safety, she led it straight to them. Lillian sprints through the tangle of ferns, still dragging Mary behind her.

BOOM BOOM

The capaeman is running toward them. How many strides will it take for it to reach them? Twenty? Ten? Less? Lillian breaks for it, shoving through the ferns, desperate to reach the tree's roots. They only have seconds before it crushes them.

"That thing is a pro. Damn it, it's a pro!" Jamie had said. Lillian was such a fool for believing they had a chance.

BOOM BOOM BOOM BOOM

The warrior's mind moves a million miles an hour as she scours the area for anywhere they can hide. Then, she spots something. It looks like a human-sized hole in the ground, but Lillian knows it is more. She can see gnawed bark as far as six inches down the hollowed-out root, then nothing but darkness.

The girls leap into the opening.

They tumble down the corridor, the river roaring in the background. The cave drops down diagonally, and they clumsily tumble, scraping themselves on loose wood and bruising on the uneven floor. Finally, they land on flat ground, or at least something that feels like it.

Lillian gets up, her body already aching. "You... okay?"

"Y-Yeah..." her friend finally responds.

They hear a large *rumble* from above. It must be looking for them. They don't have long. "Is it... r-really still chasing us?" Mary asks.

"Afraid so. This one's a pro. I bet it can get us even from this cave." Light streams down the bumpy entryway from which they arrived. The cave smells of water-soaked wood, and the *WHOOSH* of the river is deafening. The river likely has flown through here many times, which would explain how this cave formed in the first place. That, and the wood-eating bugs. Some crawl on the walls even now, their pincher-like mouths chewing away.

"No.. No... How could this... How could this..." Mary shakes violently.

Lillian rushes over, hugging her tight. "It's okay. It's okay."

"We're going to die, aren't we?"

"I don't know. All I know is I'm going to fight, and I will keep fighting, no matter what. So, don't you give up either." Lillian has no idea how they can possibly get out of this, but she is still breathing, so she won't give up. Then, Miss May's slogan rings through her head: *"Remember, one step at a time."* If she studies her surroundings bit by bit, she may be able to find a way out of this, or at least a way for Mary. Yes, *she* at least, must live.

Mary collapses onto her knees. "It's hopeless. We can't run. We can't hide."

rrrrrumble

From the surface, another reverb. Lillian has no idea what the capaeman is doing, but she knows it won't be good for them. She must think.

WHOOOOOSSSHHH

Ugh! It's hard to concentrate with the river going so fast. Then she smells something. Something... foul. The odor instantly reminds her of Albian. The huddled bodies in their burrow, frozen in agony and pale as bone.

Horrifyingly, Mary begins to cough. "Wh-What is this smell?"

The poison gas, Lillian thinks to herself. *We're out of time.* The hunter is using the same methods it used with Albian. No, they can't go out like this. The gas burns her throat, clouding her mind. Very soon, thinking will become impossible. In this situation, the capaeman wins either way; if they climb back the way they came, it will be waiting for them, but if they stay here, they'll die. How can they get out of this?

Lillian stares at her friend, who is now coughing violently. Her own eyes and throat feel like they have been stuffed with hot coals. *No,* she thinks. *Not like this.*

"Are we—" Mary says through her coughs, "—going to die?"

Lillian recalls those frozen bodies in Albian. Some looked terrified, like they had no idea what was going on. Others were clutching their loved ones as if accepting the inevitable. She will *never* accept such a fate. They still have so much to see, so much time to live.

The warrior listens to the river because that's all she can hear right now.

Wait... the river.

"Lillian," Mary coughs. "I'm sorry. I'm so sorry." Lillian looks deeper into the cave. Some caves can have two openings.

She has an idea, a reckless idea.

"You're so strong. Stronger than all of us. You don't deserve to go out like this," her friend says through her wheezing.

Lillian listens closely. The *WHOOSH* seems to increase deeper into the cave, so perhaps there is an exit on the other side. There will be rapids, but it's their only hope now. The warrior grabs Mary's hand.

"What are you doing?"

"I think I found a way out of here," Lillian says.

"You... did?" The blonde's eyes are drooping. They must hurry.

"Yes, you're going to live, okay? I'll make sure you live." As they go deeper and deeper, the cave grows brighter. This is either the smartest or the most absurd idea Lillian has ever had. On the one hand, the capaeman could be right outside and they could walk straight to their deaths. On the other, it may not have anticipated this exit existing, or may be too busy trying to smoke them out. It's a gamble with their lives on the line, but a risk they must take.

As they emerge, Lillian is surprised by how far into the river this path trails. They now stand on a huge healthy root sprawling across rushing water. It seems that it wrapped around the root cave as it grew. At one point it dips straight below the surface, so they can't follow it anywhere, but still, she thought this exit would be much worse. Below, the river flows incredibly fast, bashing against jagged rocks. If they fall in here, it will carry them across miles of the Giant Wilds. That is, if they don't get torn apart first. Lillian glances at Mary. This girl is the best swimmer in Zurec. If anyone can make it, it's her.

Mary's knees buckle. She won't last much longer.

boom...

The hunter, somewhere behind them. Lillian doesn't bother to search for it. There's only one way to make it out of this now, even if the ending is tragic. She only has seconds to prepare.

"Mary, I'm sorry too. That fight was pointless," Lillian says, staring at the rocky rapids below.

"It was, wasn't it?" her friend says through tears. "I love you, Lillian. I only want what's best for you."

The warrior nods. "I know, and I love you too."

Then, the hunter spots them. It's only dozens of feet away, a distance that must be nothing to a capaeman. The second its eyes lock on the girls, it launches into action. In one powerful stride, the capaeman is towering over them, its massive form casting a shadow over the two tiny girls. Lillian glares at it—staring at an insurmountable mountain. Even as those fiery eyes pierce her soul, chill her to the bone, make her want to run and never stop, the warrior does not break her gaze. Lillian wants this capaeman to know that she hates it and will *never* give it what it wants.

It's time. She knows what she must do. She suspected it the moment they entered that cave.

Lillian throws her arms around Mary, turning her away from the giant. She should not have to look at that monster. "Keep fighting, Mary," the warrior says with finality.

As the capaeman's hand shoots down at them, Lillian glares straight at it and, back first, plunges with Mary into the river.

24

Despair and Hope

Lillian

The girls crash into the jagged rocks below. Lillian can feel them tearing through her flesh, and the cold water pierces her skin like a million tiny needles. The pain is coming from so many places that she can't tell where she's been hurt, but it doesn't matter. She has done her part. Because of her sacrifice, Mary won't be hurt by the rocks.

But her friend opens her eyes only to see blood all around them—Lillian's blood. Mary screams, letting hundreds of air bubbles out of her mouth. Lillian closes it with her palm, but right at that moment, they hit another rock. Lillian, being underneath Mary, takes the brunt of the hit. Icy water seeps into the open flesh on the back of her leg, sending chills throughout her entire body. Mary clings to her, her eyes frantic. She is trying to save her, but it's no use. This wound is fatal.

You must live. Forget about me, Lillian thinks. With that, she pushes her best friend away. She disappears in the current. *There, I've done my part.* Lillian tries to let go, to let the water fill her lungs and slowly overtake her.

But... why won't she open her mouth?

The pressure from the water... It's so painful. She needs air, but she's losing control. Her body is spinning in all directions and it throbs from hitting the rocks. It would be easier to die here. So why does she still hold her breath?

She has watched so many people die. There was... There was so much blood... so much screaming, and...

"We'll lead this one to the others. We'll be fine!"

Those were Mia's last words before she plunged into the battle, knowing it could be her last. Her family has sacrificed so much, all so they could live. And here Lillian is, throwing away that future.

By the Wilds... I don't want to die.

A new strength surging within her, Lillian pushes her feet against a river rock and shoots to the surface, inhaling a life-saving breath of air.

Lillian glides right, staying with the current but slowly making her way to shore. It's a dangerous move. She should stay with the current until it slows, but that is also dangerous. The longer she stays in the depths of the Crystal River, the more likely she is to pass out. Who knows how much blood she has lost?

The warrior keeps her eyes open in the frigid water. It's deeper now, so the rocks aren't hitting her anymore. Below her, colored stones flash by; some smooth, some jagged. She's reminded of Mary's rock-collecting hobby. Wherever that girl is, she had better survive.

The warrior lifts her head above the water, gasping for a second. *Just keep swimming right,* she coaches herself. *Toward shore, but don't fight the current.* She can do this.

Suddenly, a sharp pain erupts in Lillian's shin. Her body jerks upward. That must have been another rock. Why did that hurt so much? Isn't she still wearing her shin guards? The warrior plunges her head back under the water and glances at her legs. Both of her shin guards have fallen off. What else has she lost? She feels her back. The spear is still there, somehow, but her bow is gone.

Lillian keeps swimming, adrenaline coursing through her veins. She will not die here. She must get out, find Mary, then get back to Zurec. They'll be glad to know both girls are alive. What was she thinking, sacrificing herself? She's strong. She can make it out of this.

Finally, the shore is looking closer, but now the water is shallower. She'll really have to watch for rocks now. The current shows no sign of slowing. Lillian lifts her head above the surface, deciding to float and paddle rather than stroke through it. She's getting lightheaded, but she can't swim straight to shore. The water is moving too fast. It's better to move with the current, gradually drifting to her right toward shallower water.

Ahead of Lillian lies a cluster of boulders. Her body slams against one, knocking the wind out of her. She swallows water, pain erupting in her lungs, but remains still, using her upper body strength to keep her head above the water. This is the best place to crawl onto land. Clawing for anything to keep her from slipping around the boulder and floating farther downstream, Lillian grips a jagged groove in the rock. It digs into her hand. She doesn't care. The warrior pulls herself halfway out of the river, hacking up water.

She pulls herself up farther, yanking with all her strength. Blood oozes from her hand and down the side of the rock, but she keeps fighting. Finally, she manages to put her foot in another groove and drag herself on top of the stone.

Now that she can see the rest of the river, Lillian is glad she stopped when she did. She spots a small waterfall in the distance. A leaf falls, landing on the surface of the river. The current swirls around and submerges it, dragging it over the cliffside. That could have been her. She hopes Mary got out in time.

Lillian turns toward the land, trying to figure out the best path. Dense foliage covers the shore. She has no idea what could be in there. She looks back at her immediate surroundings. Near the cluster of river rocks, a massive set of tree roots arches upward. They must belong to an ancient tree, as there seem to be hundreds of roots intersecting one another. They go straight into the river and sprawl all over the shore. Tracing the roots' path backward, Lillian finds a tree next to the waterfall. She notes its distinctive color. White. *The whitewood tree,* Lillian thinks to herself. This is where she saw that capaeman for the first time.

A small opening at the base of the tree is a root cave, small enough for her to crawl in. Ironically, this tree could be her saving grace. Her open wounds are an invitation to the animals of the forest. Lillian hops from boulder to boulder, determined to reach the cave. Right as she is about to reach it, she slips and falls, plunging into the mud.

The warrior forces her aching body to stand. She forgot how slippery algae can be, and these rocks are covered in it. Lillian tries to wipe the mud off, but it's no use. She trudges through the riverbed and into the cave.

The inside of the cave is larger than she expected. Being near the tree's center, this cave is not just a single, hollowed-out root but a woven mesh of roots. Light shines down in tiny pillars through the mesh, making the path ahead slightly visible. Her shoes make strange *plip* and *plop* noises as she hobbles through the darkness. Lillian can only imagine how deep these roots go underground. She heaves, the pain of her injuries catching up with her. *No, I must keep going. I must find help.* The warrior shivers violently. Although she is finally out of the icy river, it's still freezing in here. The ceiling drips with water.

drip.

drop.

drip... drop.

A familiar pitter-patter echoes through the cave, then quickly picks up. In a matter of seconds, water begins leaking through the holes in the roots. It has begun to rain.

This is bad. This is very bad.

Not only are Lillian's first-aid supplies completely soaked, but now there is no way of drying them out to treat her wounds. How is she going to get out of this? Zurec is scattered. Mary is somewhere along the river. Jamie and Albert are whoknows where, and, and... *that hunter* could be anywhere. Lillian hopes the members of Zurec found some damn good hiding spots, but what if they didn't? What if she finds a way out of this and then—No, Lillian can't think about that. Her body will freeze up, and she will never make it out.

CR-ACK!

Thunder explodes outside. Will it even be safe to travel? When it rains in the Giant Wilds, it rains hard, usually for a few days. The forest floor becomes a squishy trap of mud and puddles.

As these thoughts race through her mind, Lillian approaches what looks like the exit of the cave. Light shines in front of her, growing brighter and brighter. *Thank goodness.*

However, the second the daylight hits her, she collapses. Why is she so weak all of a sudden?

drop

drip... drop

drip drop

Finally, Lillian looks at her legs and gasps. On her left shin is a massive bruise. It's already turning a dark purple. And on the right...

How is she even standing on *this*?

A massive chunk of tangled, open flesh bleeds all over the ground. Her shoes are thoroughly soaked in blood. The warrior looks behind her. A trail of red leads down the path she took.

Lillian's vision begins to blur.

No, this can't be happening.

The warrior throws off her breastplate and shirt. Hands shaking, she fumbles for her dagger and uses it to tear a long thin strip off the shirt. She then wraps her shirt around her leg and secures it with the fabric strip. It hardly stops the bleeding, but it's better than nothing. It may buy her some time. Time to—

Time to do what? Her consciousness is slipping away.

The warrior slides down the cave wall and wraps her arms around her waist. Her bloodied hands stain her undershirt. *It's no use.* Her father, the caretaker, her best friend... She'll never see them again. And she was so mean to them. She wonders where they are right now. Her father is undoubtedly alive. Miss May is in the bunker, and Mary...

She pushed her away—literally.

She is such a fool. Maybe she deserves to die. After all, this is a world where only the strong survive. Lillian has proven time and time again that she can't handle this world. She's too reckless, too curious, too... *weak.*

Lillian wanted to see the outside world so she could save people. That's the reason she tried to join the surveyors. That's why she begrudgingly became a gatherer, and then a scout. All she wants is to save her family, but she is powerless.

The "warrior" squeezes her eyes shut, wondering whether she deserves such a title. She has been nothing but useless. A selfish burden on everyone. Now, she will pay the price.

"Lillian..."

A voice echoes in her head. Mary's voice.

"Lillian..."

She hopes Mary survived. That girl *has* a purpose, unlike her.

"I-I mean it. I wouldn't be able to handle it if you died."

"I told you, I'm stubborn." Now it's her voice, responding to Mary.

"You, my girl, never *give up."* Brianna now.

"One step at a time." That's Miss May.

What would the people who supported her say if they saw her now? What would Noah, Gigi, Elias, Archer, and all those who have died think? If she gives up, it debases their sacrifice. This is not like her. She *never* gives up. She isn't about to start now. The warrior stands even though she should be unable to do so. Pain jolts through her body. It feels like she is carrying a hundred pounds—no, more than that. Every fiber of her being is protesting against her, but she can still move. She can at least get outside. And then, and then...

No, don't think ahead. One step at a time. The goal right now is to get outside. Even if she dies here, she will die fighting—kicking and screaming to the very end, like a true member of Zurec. Lillian limps, her head pounding, but she refuses to yield. She will *never* yield.

As the warrior approaches the exit, she smiles and steps straight into the rain.

It has really begun to pour now. As rain hits the ground, each droplet sends huge puffs of vapor into the air. All Lillian can smell is the thick scent of moisture and mud. Her shoes sink into the foliage. With all this water, traversing the land will take even more effort. She won't make it, but she will at least try. As a tiny human in this giant world, she has no control over the powers that be, but she can take control of herself.

The warrior summons all her strength just to walk forward. She feels like she's living the literal version of "one step at a time." With each step, Lillian feels heavier and heavier. Trudging through the mud would be bad enough if she were healthy, but now it feels impossible. Her legs scream in protest. Blood seeps through her shirt wrapped around her bad leg. Her left hand is bleeding too, from hanging onto the rock. Who knows where else she is wounded?

Heh. It really is hopeless. Even so, the warrior smiles. Everything else has fallen apart. She won't lose her will too.

boom... boom...

Then she hears a familiar sound.

Boom... Boom...

A bipedal creature. Another capaeman, and it's close. It's either the orange-eyed capaeman, or...

No. It can't be the hunter. It wouldn't pursue them down the river, not with the rest of Zurec fighting the narecons. Lillian looks at the cave from which she just emerged, then up at the whitewood tree. This is where she saw the green-eyed boy for the first time. She could never forget that name or what he said that day.

Boom Boom

If that is him, this could be her only chance.

Yet she hesitates. If she calls out his name, and he shows up, she's as good as dead. That's what everyone says. That's what her people have always believed. Before Zurec settled in this forest, they were running from the capaemen. They are the most powerful monsters in the world. Who is she to think this one is different? No, she can't call *him*. It would go against everything.

Boom Boom

Her knees buckle, and she nearly falls face-first into the mud.

BOOM BOOM

If she doesn't get help soon, she will die, but if she trusts a capaeman, she also may die. The warrior smirks morbidly. A "maybe" is better than a certainty.

"Lionel!" she shouts through the rain.

Silence. Her heart pounds through her chest. She should stop. This isn't just impulsive. This is *self-destructive*. "Lionel!" Lillian screams with all the strength her tiny body can muster. "Lionel, please! Lionel!"

Still silence. She just heard the footsteps. Why did they stop? Was it her imagination? No, it couldn't have been.

As the rain splatters on her shoulders, Lillian tries to move, but her body stays still as a statue. And she feels cold... so cold.

This is her last chance. Taking in all the breath she can muster, she lets out one final scream. "LIONELLL!" She collapses to her knees.

BOOM BOOM BOOM BOOM—

Finally, the footsteps quicken, getting closer and closer. Lillian stares into the misty forest, hope rising in her chest. She doesn't even blink for fear of passing out. A gargantuan figure emerges from behind the thousand-foot trees, knocking away everything in its path. Standing thirty feet away is Lionel, the capaeman she met—the one who said he could help.

He looks like he's in shock. "It is... you." Much more slowly now, he approaches her, his footsteps *boom*ing over the rain. The capaeman looms over her. He bends down slowly, holding above his head an object Lillian has never seen before. It looks like some sort of rain shield, and before she knows it, the massive thing is protecting her as well. Lillian exhales, so glad to get a break.

The green-eyed capaeman stares at her in silence, his eyebrows raised.

"You are... dying," he says finally, and reaches toward her. The hand is nearly as long as her entire body. Lillian recoils as it grows closer. The capaeman's face falls, quickly changing from concern to disdain. "What did you attempt, a leap into the river?"

Still acting smug, even now?

"Why did you call for me?" the capaeman asks. He seems genuinely curious, as if their last conversation didn't even happen.

"You said... you wanted to help... right?" Lillian says through gasping breaths.

Lionel nods slightly. "I did not think you would be unwise enough to ask."

With all her strength, Lillian stands. Her legs quake as she forces them to support her injured body one last time. "Well, here I am. Are you going to help me or not?"

"Do not put weight on those legs. Do you wish to die quicker?"

She laughs. "You know, you've asked that before, and the answer is no." The second Lillian says that, she falls over again. However, before she can hit the ground, something warm catches her. She's so out of it she doesn't even have the energy to be scared. Everything is blurry, including the hand that holds her now.

With just two fingers, Lionel puts pressure on her bleeding leg. "I might be able to save you, but I make no promises. Also, I cannot do it here. I will have to take you outside of the Crimson Forest."

Lillian gazes at her torn-up leg. There is already a cloth wrapped around it.

"Are you hearing me, human? You may never return."

"N-Never return? Why?"

"Your chances of survival are slim," he speaks so bluntly.

"And you..." Lillian says. "Can you help me?"

"Indeed, I can, but I cannot guarantee your safety if you live."

She laughs weakly. Her safety has never been guaranteed. "Is that all? I'd rather take a slim chance than no chance."

The capaeman makes a low growling sound. "Laughing, at a time like this? You truly are heedless." Suddenly, Lillian shoots into the air: ten, twenty, thirty, forty feet. The pace is so dizzying it makes riding on Amphii seem easy. She tries to stay awake, but her will is slipping.

She's tired... so tired.

Maybe she'll close her eyes, just for a second.

Yeah, just a second. She'll wake up soon.

25

Blood in the Rapids

Mary

As they plunge into the river, all Mary sees is blood. The horrid red substance surrounds them like a deep, blinding fog. That's *Lillian's* blood, and there is so much of it. Mary screams under the water. The sound is muffled and pathetic, barely audible. Then, as if more concerned for her safety, Lillian covers Mary's mouth. The two girls jolt downward again, slamming into even more rocks. She doesn't feel it, but she knows her friend did. Even more blood pools around them.

Lillian is acting as a human shield.

Without medical attention, she'll die. Mary must not let go.

But horrifyingly, her friend pushes her away, a light smile on her face. It's as if she is saying, *"Go. Forget about me."* Then, just as suddenly as the blood unfurled, it dissipates.

Her best friend has vanished.

No no no. Where is she? Mary *must* find her. Alone and bleeding, Lillian won't last an hour out here. The girl scans the riverbed, watching the colored rocks pass by below, but she doesn't see a thing. The Crystal River is miles wide and who knows how long. The odds of finding her friend are slim to none. Still, Mary keeps her eyes wide open and her head below water as she drifts with the current. She doesn't dare blink. She doesn't dare breathe even as her chest burns. The pain surges up her throat, threatening to push all the air from her lungs. She swallows, but that only makes it worse. If she doesn't take a breath, she is going to drown.

Mary's head bobs to the surface, just for a second. She looks around, and Lillian isn't here either. Maybe she found a way to shore, as wild as that is. If anyone can do it, that girl can.

Or maybe she's already sunk to the bottom of the river, never to be seen again.

No! I can't think that way, Mary screams in her head. Desperately, she dunks her head back under, looking for a clue, an inkling that her friend is still alive. This cannot be happening. Yesterday, she and Lillian got into a fight. It was the nastiest fight they'd ever had, and it ended with them hardly speaking. This *can't* be how it ends. Mary wants to hold her friend in her arms, heal her wounds, and get back to the way things were. She has a sinking feeling. One that, if she lets it take over, will send her to the bottom of the river...

The panicked girl sucks in more air and dives back under the fast-flowing water, but the second she does, her knee runs straight into a rock.

Mary's body tumbles out of control. The girl spins and spins at a dizzying pace, and she can't tell which direction is up. All those people... dead in a single afternoon. Now, if she doesn't get out of this, she'll join them. Would that be such a bad thing? If Lillian is gone, what does she even have to live for? This world is as dizzying and confusing as the current sweeping her away.

What if she lets go?

She closes her eyes to the swirling chaos around her.

But before everything goes black, something makes them flutter right back open.

Bubbles are floating upward. Mary reaches toward them, letting out a short breath. The air effortlessly floats to the surface. *That's it. Air always goes up,* Mary thinks. Just as seeds fall from the trees, air always leaves water. That's how she'll get out of this tailspin.

The girl straightens out her body and pushes off the bottom of the river, shooting in the direction of the bubbles. She splashes to the surface, taking a gasp of the Giant Wilds breeze. What a senseless thought. She wouldn't be any help to Lillian dead.

She *must* get to shore. Then, they will find each other. It's at a time like this when Mary is grateful to be the best swimmer she knows. Even so, the current is still at whiplash speed. She can navigate it alright, but she doubts getting to shore will be easy right now. *The current will slow. I have to be patient,* Mary thinks to herself.

She keeps her eyes wide open as she swims, scanning the colorful rocks tens of feet below. On occasion, she spots a river creature. One of them holds up its claws, pinching in her direction. She keeps her distance. The last thing she needs is her arms chopped off.

Although the water is cold as ice, her blood boils. All that is on her mind now is survival. If Lillian still lives, and she is not there to help her, Mary will never forgive herself. She also has to survive for Zurec. Her mother, who had Mary by a miracle; the children, who without her will drive Miss May up the wall; Mia, Brianna, the surveyors, the gatherers—even Seth. He may keep his distance, but Mary sees straight through that. That man cares deeply about both of them. If he knew how close they are to death...

The image of that hunter flashes in Mary's mind. The girls made *one* wrong move. Snapping one old stick was all it took. The capaeman was looming over them in only a few strides, ready to crush them like bugs. The hands of the giant reminded her of the gripping teeth of an andremedon, absolute and all-powerful. Once one is in those jaws, they're done for. There is nothing one can do to escape. The capaemen are death itself.

When they were on that root, Mary could hardly speak. If Lillian hadn't been there, if she hadn't been so quick on her feet, they would both be dead right now. The reckless girl may not think much, but when she does, she has incredible instincts. Her ability to stay calm under pressure is something Mary has always admired about her. She only wishes that her friend didn't let go.

As the girl drifts, her shoulder pads begin to loosen. She already lost her shield and spear in the current. She doesn't mind losing the armor either. All Mary cares about is making it out of this river. The best way to do that is to carry the least weight possible. She undoes the straps of her shoulder plates, then her knee and shin guards, but the weight of her backpack is exhausting her too. She gets rid of that as well, watching as it sinks to the rocky bottom. All those hours of packing... for nothing. It's almost comical.

Mary keeps her body as still as possible, in sync with the current. *I am a leaf,* she thinks. A leaf floating on the surface of the water. Not worth paying any attention to. Yes, a leaf that is—

A leaf that is drowning.

The current picks up. Mary didn't think it could go any faster, but it does. She looks ahead and sees the river cut off, but she's smart enough to know that's not really its end. *No, not a waterfall.*

She's already in its pull. There is nothing that can stop it now. The current swirls and drags her deeper into the water. Mary keeps her body still and chest strong. She won't be able to take a breath for a while. That is, if she survives the fall.

Before the girl knows it, the water guides her over the edge of a small cliff. She turns herself around, trying to land with her legs. *Protect the head and neck.*

Luckily, the fall is shorter than she thought. It is several feet, more of a brief drop than a waterfall. Still, the waters slam her tiny body into the pools below, and she plunges to the bottom. The water is shallower than she expected. Pain erupts from Mary's legs, but she forces them to push off the bottom. When her head emerges from the water, she gasps.

Mary knows she doesn't have much longer. Her breaths are becoming more frequent, and her eyes are growing heavy. Just how far has she drifted? She doesn't want to know. All she needs to think about is getting out of this river safely. Then, she will take the next step. *"One step at a time,"* her mother always says.

Finally, the current begins to slow. Mary tries to swim to shore, but it's much harder than she thought. The river fights her with every kick, every movement of her arms. She kicks harder, her tired muscles whining in protest. *Come on! Just a little longer, and I'll get to rest.* She remembers the faces of Trista, Max, and the other kids. Those children have lost too much. Mary won't let them lose anyone else.

She struggles to shore. First swimming, then crawling through the muddy bank. Her will to live propels her forward until finally, she's on land. Mary catches her breath, her arms and legs sinking in the mud. The forest is clouded with fog, permeating the air with the scent of mist.

Then, she hears the pitter-patter of water.

Rain falls in the Giant Wilds. Great. This is just perfect. Travel is nearly impossible when it rains. She will have to find shelter, but where? She looks around. All she can see are clusters of giant ferns and a large boulder. That won't do. If any of those wretched black birds flew by, they would see her. Then, behind the boulder, she spots the hollow carcass of a fallen tree. It's old, grey, and looks as if it could crumble to pieces any minute. Still, Mary crawls toward it, knowing she doesn't have much of a choice.

As she grows nearer to the hollowed-out tree, fatigue sets in. Mary has never run, let alone swum, so much in her life. Sure, they have a workout regimen, but it's nothing like sprinting from narecons, not to mention a capaeman. Her eyes droop, and she quickly forces them open. *No, now is not the time to close my eyes!* Where is this drowsiness when she's trying to sleep? She swears it comes at the worst times.

Finally, the girl's hands touch bark, and she climbs into the dead tree, collapsing onto its bumpy surface. The rain pours outside and a chill sets in.

She hoped she would warm up when she emerged from the river, but no such luck. The girl shivers as the rain quickens to a deafening roar. Her mind drifts away. This is the farthest she has ever been from home, and now she can't even move. What a tragedy. This is why Mary never wanted to leave the burrow. The world is a dangerous place, unfit for humanity. If she sleeps now, even for a few minutes, will something eat her for lunch? She isn't sure, but still, her consciousness fades.

Just for a second. I'll close my eyes just for a second, the girl thinks. She needs to regain some strength to get home, wherever that is. *I'll wake up... soon.*

Mary drifts on the edge of consciousness. She is not quite asleep, but not awake either. The rain roars outside, filling the dead tree with the scent of wet bark. It feels like she has been here for hours, or has it only been a few minutes? There's no way to tell. To make things more confusing, she begins to hear voices.

"Who in the Wilds is this?" a masculine teenage voice says.

"By the plains! It's a girl!" This one sounds slightly higher and grainier, like they're ready to scold someone.

"A girl? Woahhh, she's out cold, y'all. What should we do?" Now, a third. This one is the deepest voice. It sounds a little like Seth's. Maybe she is dreaming of the surveyors.

"Dang, she's really cute. What clan do ya suppose she's from?" the high voice says.

"Don't know. Don't see a sigil. She's really banged up though."

"What happened?"

Wait, this isn't a dream. She fell in the river and now is passed out in a tree. Whatever is going on outside, it's *real.* Mary's eyes flutter open. Through her blurred vision, she sees three figures standing in the rain.

"Hey, she's awake!" the deep voice says. As Mary's vision clears, she sees a big-boned man with a long dark beard peering at her. His skin is an onyx brown, like the dark loam found in some corners of the forest. Even though he's huge, his face is rounder and younger than his physique suggests. His eyes are a soft brown but sharp, with a clever spark in them.

Mary sits up, her heart sinking. She has no idea who these people are, nor whether they are friends or enemies. They look a little strange, with their black, scaly armor and spears with curved blades. *The armor must be phypent-skin?* she guesses. Based on how they're studying her, they are just as wary as she is. She could never take them in a fight, nor does she want to, so she must look as non-threatening as possible.

"Looks like she can move. What should we do, boss?" This man is the owner of the higher voice. He looks a bit younger than the one with the beard but is definitely still an adult. He is also tall but lankier, with a diamond-shaped face, messy blonde hair, and narrow grey eyes. Blonde stubble litters his cheeks. He glares at her as if she has done something wrong.

"Well, she's awake. Let's ask her a few questions." The third man is only a teenager, clearly younger than his friends, but he is somehow more striking than them. He stands in the middle of the trio, his shoulders squared. He's tall and muscular, with a triangular jawbone, side-swept dark hair, and piercing blue eyes, even brighter than Lillian's. He strolls toward Mary, the muscles in his legs tensing with every decisive step. Mary notices herself taking in every detail of this boy, from the confident way he walks to his gorgeous, sly smile, which he is clearly aiming at her. Her heart flutters in a strange way. It isn't just out of fear. It's... something else.

The boy comes right up to her and bends down, his face too close for comfort. Water drips off his shining dark hair. "Hey there. What's a pretty girl like you doing here?" Mary tries to say something, but all that comes out is a small gasp. Other than Albert, she has never seen a boy her age. She has no idea what to do.

But then, his eyes fall on her clothes, and that smile quickly becomes a scowl. "Wait a minute. You're Zurec, aren't ya?" The disdain in his tone makes Mary flinch.

On the boy's shoulder is a circle with two curve-bladed spears crossed over it. Centered atop that are two black loops intertwining with one another: the symbol for infinity. Mary remembers who they are. She may have never seen them with her own eyes, but she's read about them. Plenty of times.

They are Rostad.

Mary scooches away from him. She can't believe she drifted this far down the river. "Y-Yes, I'm from Zurec, but I swear, I mean you no harm!" The boy's blue eyes turn hard as stone. His friends each place a hand on their weapons. "L-Look," Mary says, "I-I don't have any weapons, see? I couldn't hurt you even if I wanted to. So please, just let me go."

"You're trespassing," the boy says, his face now inches from hers. "This is *our* territory. Your kind *isn't* welcome." Mary hates the way he says that. What's wrong with Zurec? They haven't done anything to them. Still, she swallows her pride. There's got to be something she can say that will make them listen to her and see her as a friend, not an enemy. Then, she can ask them to help her find Lillian. The poor girl must be crumpled up somewhere, bleeding and alone. Mary is the only one who knows she is in danger. She doesn't have time for this.

"For the second time," the boy continues, his face still inches away, "you're *trespassing*. What are ya doing here, Zurec girl?"

"I-I—" Mary wracks her brain for something. The two men in the back are growing impatient. The large one glares at her while the blonde looks ready to strike. This will be her last chance. They don't sympathize with her, so asking for help directly is out of the question. She must be cleverer than that. If she were in their shoes, what would she want to hear most? What does almost every community value?

Then, it hits her. The girl stands, faking confidence. "My clan was attacked, and you're next. I have some valuable information your chief will want to hear."

The boy raises an eyebrow. "Really now?" He looks to his colleagues as if asking for approval.

"Vivian would wanna see her," the large man says. "Even if she is lying, we should hear her out." Mary lets out a breath of relief. Even *they* must be starved for answers.

The boy gives her some space, seeming to consider what she said. "Well, I guess it's your lucky day, *girl*." He practically spits out the word. Then, he grabs her by the arm and drags her along with them.

"Wait!" Mary screams. "Let go of me! My friend is in danger. We got separated. I *must* find her."

"Not our problem," the blonde man adds. They have surrounded her, making sure she doesn't escape. There's nothing she can do but follow. She stares at the muddy ground, watching the rain splatter around her feet. The rain has slowed considerably. Tiny droplets run down her legs, which are covered with brand-new bruises. Mary can only imagine how much worse Lillian is, and she can't help her. She feels like such a fool for believing she could.

She can't even save herself.

26

New Traditions, New Suspicions

Mary

The Rostad boy grips Mary's arm so hard she is losing circulation. The men surround her as they walk, the boy in the front and his lackeys on her left and right. Even if she could break free of this iron grip, there is nowhere to run. Besides, based on the way the men are dressed, they are surveyors, or something like them. They could easily catch up to her. *I'm so weak,* Mary thinks, tears in her eyes.

They tread through the forest, moving farther away from the river, away from Lillian. With each step they take, Mary's heart breaks a little more. How will her friend survive without her? Even this group of able-bodied people are having trouble traversing the rain-soaked forest. They trek slowly, avoiding mud pits and loose bundles of moss.

"Pick up the pace, would ya?" the boy gripping her arm says. "We don't have all day. The rains could return any second."

"I-I'm doing my best," Mary responds, her voice raspy. Her body feels as if it has been hit by a falling tree branch.

"Hey, I know she's Zurec, but don't be so cruel, Steven," the man to her left says. He's the big man with a long dark beard and deep-brown skin. He must be as big as Seth, and his clothes make him look even larger: spiked black epaulets, a massive metal chest plate, and a long fur cape with a forked tail at the end. She isn't sure of the utility of the outfit, except to look intimidating. Still, despite his hulking appearance, there is a glint of pity in the man's dark eyes. This is Mary's spark of hope.

"Please, let me go," she says as nicely as possible. "I'm not going to run. I can't anyway."

224

The boy, Steven, scoffs and releases his grip. "Fine, but if ya try anything—"

"I won't," Mary interrupts. "I know you're suspicious of me. Let me prove you wrong. I'll cooperate."

"Well, at least she has *some* sense," the blonde man says. Out of the three, this one is the most trouble. Mary can sense it. He looked like he wanted to kill her the second he realized she was Zurec. Now, he keeps the most distance despite her being completely at their mercy. His chest plate is much smaller than the big guy's, and he also wears shoulder spikes. The only significant difference between his outfit and the other man's is the Rostad sigil. The blonde wears it on his belt like a badge of honor. Meanwhile, the big guy has his sigil woven into the back of his cape. Both seem prideful but in vastly different ways. Mary's certain they get along like oil and water.

Meanwhile, Steven seems the most underdressed out of the three. It's ironic, considering he is their leader. He has the same armor but lacks a fur cape. However, there is a Rostad sigil on both of his shoulders, designed in a way that reminds Mary of Seth. The chief's symbol is of much higher quality than that of other Zurec members. It's a work of art painted onto his shoulder plate in full color. The Rostad sigils are similar, except in more whites and greys.

After a few minutes of treading in silence, Steven speaks again. "So, why are ya here? Zurec hasn't encroached on our territory in decades."

An opening? Mary didn't think she would get a chance to explain herself. "M-My people were attacked by a capaeman. I..." She trails off, remembering how close she was to death. "We, I mean uh, my friend and I jumped into the river to escape it."

"You expect us to believe that?" the blonde man asks. "The rapids should have torn ya apart. Come up with a better lie than that."

"It's the truth!" Mary shouts, losing her composure. "My friend is still back there, bleeding. Please, if you let me help her—"

Steven crosses his arms. "We don't have time to go back. If what ya said is true, we'd be walking straight into a capaeman attack. Plus, it's harder to travel because of the rain. I hate to be the one to say it, but if your friend's still over there and bleeding, then she's *dead*."

Mary stops walking. All three of the men turn to look at her. The blonde one places a hand on his weapon, but she doesn't care. "H-How can you say that?" Tears stream down her face like waterfalls, dripping off her chin until her eyes are red and puffy. She knows she shouldn't be crying in front of the enemy, but she's not strong enough to stop.

"Keep fighting, Mary," her friend said.

How could she do this to me? Lillian should know Mary well enough to realize this is the last thing she wants. Sacrificing herself to save her... What a ridiculous thing to do. Everyone knows Lillian is more valuable. That's why her mother gave her the dagger. She has ambition, drive, and skill. All Mary has is the ability to take care of kids. That's all she will *ever* be good for.

"Good going, Steven. Ya made her cry," the big man scolds.

"Come on, Zane. How was I supposed to know it's a sore subject? People die all the time. Most are numb to it."

"She must be barely fifteen, if that. Give her a break. It's not as if ya didn't act the same two years ago."

The boy scratches his head. "Hey, don't bring up ancient history. Two years is a long time. I'm grown now."

"Riiigghhtt."

A hand touches Mary's shoulder. It's the big man, Zane. "Hey, if you're telling the truth, it'll be okay. Our chief isn't so cruel that she'd kill a little girl for no reason. So, don't ya worry."

"If you don't kill me, what will you do with me?" She may be naive, but she's not dumb. There are fates worse than death.

"That's for the chief to decide," Steven interjects. "Until then, you're our prisoner, so ya'd better—"

boom...

As a familiar *boom*ing sound echoes through the forest, Mary's heart skips a beat. "It's one of *them*," the blonde man says. "Hide!" The group sprints to a nearby cluster of tall plants with large roof-like leaves. They duck down, concealing themselves amidst the lanky stems.

Steven places a hand firmly on Mary's shoulder. "Stay down."

"O-Okay," she whispers.

Boom Boom

This one is coming so fast it makes Mary's blood turn cold. Haven't they done enough?

BOOM BOOM BOOM—

The sound shakes the Giant Wilds. Absolute. All-powerful.

Then, in almost an instant, an enormous figure passes through the trees. This is not the same capaeman as that hunter. It is shorter and skinnier, with messy black hair and a green jacket with grey-striped cuffs. Its eyes are wide as if afraid. There is something clutched in its hands as it runs, but Mary cannot make it out. Whatever it is doing, it cannot be good.

The giant passes in a blink, its earth-shaking footsteps echoing in the distance of the forest. Steven exhales in relief. "That was close. I've never seen one run so fast. How in the Wilds can they even do that? They're so freakin' big."

"No idea, man," Zane answers. "They're getting bolder. That can't bode well."

"Let's get back home," Steven declares, helping Mary up. "I'm not in the mood for more surprises today." Neither is Mary, but she has a feeling the surprises aren't going to stop any time soon.

Especially since she is about to walk into the leomus' den.

⸎ ⸎

After hours of walking, Mary sees mushrooms.

Fungi are everywhere. They grow in clusters on trees, roots, and all over the ground, towering over the group like ferns. Their shadows have taken over the forest floor, making way for thick moss to thrive. The mushrooms come in all shades of brown, red, orange, and yellow. Some blend in almost perfectly with the trees. Others are so dark brown that they stick out like a sapling in winter. Mary has studied fungi before, but she's never seen anything like this.

Finally, the boys slow down, stopping by an impressively wide-roofed mushroom. Its red top covers nearly half the clearing. Steven approaches the stalk of the fungus, bends down, and grips a handle buried in the dirt. A familiar *creak*ing sound emanates from the ground. He is lifting the door to Rostad's burrow.

Mary is about to enter an entirely different world.

She heard about the last time Rostad met Zurec. They flat-out insulted them, saying they were an extinct people worthy of nothing. They even rejected Jamie and Albert, who wanted to join them before they found Zurec. Mary wonders why they wouldn't accept the Osian assassins, perhaps because of Rostad's apparent disdain for foreigners. For some reason, these three hate her because she is from Zurec. What will the other members think? If they are anything like the blonde man, she could be killed no matter what she does.

"Howdy everyone, we're back!" Steven announces.

As they enter Rostad's main hall, Mary gasps loudly. It is magnificent. A polished hardwood floor stretches across a vast open space, much bigger than their dingy mud room. Every several feet, a massive wooden pillar feeds up into the ceiling. At the top of each column is a Rostad sigil, masterfully etched into the wood. Tacked to the pillars are a plethora of paintings depicting so many incredible things. She notices one in which people throw spears at a leomus pack and another of a thornopine burrower with its thornlets. A phypent stalks the burrower from behind, its fangs bared.

Dozens of new faces stare at them warily. Some are teenagers, some are adults, and a couple look even older than her mother. How they have lived this long, Mary has no idea. All she knows is that during the famine, Rostad was doing fine. Somehow, they survived with hundreds of people. They must have hoarded a secret food stash that neither Zurec nor Albian knew about, something Mary resents them for to this day.

Each was performing some sort of crafting task, from wood whittling to basket weaving to sewing. That is until Steven and his crew arrived. Now, they glare at Mary like she's a scavenger phii eating where it doesn't belong. The blatant hatred in their eyes is unnerving. It makes her want to shrink into a hole and never come out.

"Who the heck is that?" one of the elderly people asks. He leans against a pillar, staring at Mary like she were something he scraped off his shoe.

"She's Zurec," Steven says. Collective gasps echo throughout the great cavern, followed by highly offensive comments.

"Are ya crazy? That's the enemy!"

"I'm surprised they're still around."

"She's broken and battered. What can she even do?"

"Still, Steven should'a known better than this."

"We should kill her."

"Calm down, everyone," Steven says. The crowd immediately goes silent. "Yes, she's from Zurec, but she's just a young girl. The capaemen attacked them. She's got valuable information to share with Chief Vivian. The chief'll decide what to do with her after that." The crowd murmurs, clearly unconvinced, but no one questions Steven's authority. He can't be much older than her. What did he do to demand such respect?

"Well, s'long as Vivian's involved, we'll let her through," the old man says again. They talk a little differently from Zurec. It's strange to hear.

"It'll be fine. Chief Vivian adores me," Steven says with a smile. With that, Mary is dragged to their next destination.

Past the room of paintings is a long branching hallway. She is baffled by how many directions there are. How does anyone know where they are going with so many pathways? Zurec's burrow was small but straightforward. She wonders if their old burrow used to be the same as this incredible space. She can't even imagine.

The artwork continues, even down these halls. Although now, instead of animals, they depict weapons painted in black. All the blades have a curve, from their spears to their swords, which Mary remembers are called scimitars. Everything is so bizarre here. She catches a glimpse of some nearby rooms but can't make out most of their utilities. Some have long tables surrounded by chairs, while others are filled with... digging tools? They seem to have a room for every purpose imaginable.

As they go deeper down the hall, Mary sees some familiar sights too. She spots storage shelves, beds, and what looks like a huge kitchen. Zurec's kitchen is so tiny that only a few people can work there at a time, but this one has tons of people. Some chop up giant vegetables and fruits, while others roast various dishes in massive furnaces. Each oven has its own metal grate for cooking and a thick pipe leading up to the ceiling. That must be what takes the smoke to the surface.

Another thing Mary is baffled by is the size of the food they cook. Some fruits lean against the wall, nearly touching the ceiling. The sheer size of them makes Mary stop in her tracks. How did they get food so large? Is there a magical tree somewhere nearby?

Steven pushes her. "Keep going. We're almost there." The girl snaps her gaze forward. She forgot why she was here. "Where are we going?"

"To Chief Vivian's quarters."

"I see," Mary says, unable to hide the fear in her tone.

"Don't worry. She probably won't hurt you," Zane says.

"Or she will," the blonde man adds, staring daggers at Zane. It seems they're having a silent argument.

"Come on, the girl's already walking on eggshells. Don't be a jerk, Alec."

The blonde man, Alec, rolls his eyes. "I'm not a jerk. I'm realistic. Why are we acting like Chief Vivian is this ray of sunshine? She has no—"

"Come on, boys," Steven intervenes, "she's not gonna kill her. Well, probably. In the end, she always makes the right call."

"*You* brought her to the burrow. She knows where we live now. If Vivian doesn't approve, what do ya think is gonna—"

Before the pompous jerk can finish his sentence, Zane punches him in the back. The force of the big guy's punch is so strong it nearly knocks the skinny man to the floor. It's satisfying to watch. Alec holds up a fist. "Why, you—"

Zane crosses his beefy arms. "Ya want to go? Let's do it."

"Hey, no fighting. You'll never win anyway, Alec," Steven intercedes, but he's smiling as if this is entertaining.

All it makes Mary feel is sick to her stomach. Is this what young men are like? Some of the men of Zurec would get into squabbles, but it never escalated to blows. The men are older and prefer to sort things out with words, not fists. What happens when a man doesn't have that experience? Based on Steven's reaction, they must get into fights all the time. That sounds pointless and tiring.

With all the banter and squabbling, it isn't long before the group reaches the end of the hall. Somehow, this place is even nicer than all the rooms prior. Mary didn't realize that was possible. As they step down polished redwood stairs, the hallway expands, ending with a pair of double doors. The doors look as if they've been newly carved from the tree they came from. They are not rotting like the ones in Zurec's burrow, and most beautiful of all, they're a glistening white. They must have gathered branches from the whitewood tree by the river to make these doors.

Alec grabs one of the metal handles, which is shaped like a lever. The whitewood doors open smoothly, without a single *creak*, and as if Mary weren't in awe enough, the room itself is even more extravagant.

The walls and ceiling are made of three different kinds of timber, all stained and varnished with a bright, clear coat. One type of lumber is the common redwood, the next is whitewood, and the third is a brown material she's never seen before. They have been hammered in planks, forming a pleasant three-color pattern. As they transition to the ceiling, the planks converge into a singular point, like triangular slices.

In the center of the room is a grand, two-person bed with a comforter made of leomus fur. Logs etched with engravings frame the bed. Surrounding the bedframe are many shiny foreign instruments in all colors of the rainbow. Some are round, some are angular, and some are sharp. The strangest thing about these objects is that they are gigantic, too big to be used by people. Why would Rostad make tools this large?

"Vivian! Got someone here to meet ya," Steven announces. Mary's head shoots to the left side of the room, where there is a large desk with a very nice chair. At the desk sits the biggest woman Mary has ever seen: broad, bulky shoulders, clay-brown skin, and long, grey-streaked black hair in a thick cascade down her back. When she stands, she looks like a giant. Her arms are wider than Mary's head, and her face is round and undefined. It's hard to tell the difference between her chin and neck. She wears a scaly top, baggy black pants, and a furry jacket tied about her waist. On her shoulder is a sash with the Rostad sigil embroidered in grey and white. Her eyes—so brown they're almost black—settle on Mary with a gaze cold as a phypent. Even without armor, her presence is overwhelming.

The chief smirks slightly. "Ah, ya brought a girl home." Her voice is a lot deeper than any woman's voice Mary has ever heard.

"Her name is Mary," Steven says sneeringly. He is several inches shorter than Chief Vivian and several decades younger, but he talks to her like they are old friends.

"Mary? What a lovely name." It should be a compliment, but it doesn't sound like one. She said it too slowly. The chief walks in circles around Mary, taking in every detail. It doesn't help that she is nearly a foot taller than her.

"My dear, are you from Zurec?"

The girl swallows. "Y-Yes, I am."

Chief Vivian looks Mary straight in the eyes, her expression unreadable. "What brought ya here, young lady?"

Mary clutches her necklace. This question has multiple layers, and if she doesn't answer it just right, she's in trouble. "I was brought here to share valuable information about the capaemen. My people were attacked, and we are afraid Rostad is next."

"I see, and why do ya care about us now?"

"E-Excuse me?"

"I repeat, why do ya care? The Rostad and Zurec clans have been living separately for decades now. Ya have narry a reason to come here just to warn us about the capaemen. Plus, we already know about them." Mary meets Zane's eyes, but he clearly has no intention of helping her. The boys stand on the other side of the room, soaking up the interrogation like it's a compelling book.

"I, uh—"

"Honey, ya look like a thornopine pup caught in a trap. You weren't brought here of your own free will, were ya?"

Shamefully, she shakes her head.

"So, I ask again, what brought ya here?"

Sweat beads on Mary's forehead. It's as if every minute she talks to this woman, it gets slightly hotter. "My friend and I jumped in the river to escape a capaeman attack. We got separated, and I swam a little too far. Then, I ended up on the shore of your territory. I'm so sorry. This was all a huge mistake. Please, let me go back to my family, and you will never hear from us again."

Chief Vivian clicks her tongue, clearly not impressed. "*You,* of all people, should know it ain't gonna be that simple."

"It isn't? I swear, I'm not—"

The chief gets right in Mary's face, practically spitting out her next words. "It's as if you have forgotten, but we *never* forget. Y'all think you can waltz in here and tell us what's what, but Rostad remembers."

Mary backs away, practically by instinct. "I don't know what you're talking about."

As if puzzled, the chief leans back. "Really now?" Finally, the girl gets a bit of breathing room. She exhales, trying to clear her head. She is doing a terrible job convincing them she should live. What would Lillian do in this situation? She would probably start an argument with Chief Vivian, escalating everything. No, if Mary wants them to let her go, she must be smarter than that.

The chief sighs. It's a long, deep sound. "Steven, she's either a great liar or absolutely clueless. Where did ya find her again?"

"By the river. It's exactly as she said."

"Hmm," she says. "We have no use for her. Throw her in—"

"Wait!" Mary interrupts. "If you get rid of me, you won't get to make use of the acera warriors we have in Zurec. They know how to track capaemen. They've been keeping tabs on the hunter for weeks."

"Are ya kidding?" Chief Vivian says, clearly growing impatient. "Now you're just making things up from children's fables. Steven, throw—"

"It isn't made up!" Mary shouts. "Perhaps some of your people have seen them before. They're two silver-clothed warriors with dual scythes. *They* have an acera."

"Nonsense. You're wasting my time—"

Before the chief can continue, Steven intervenes. "Come to think of it, we did see people like that. Chief Vivian, with all due respect, if she's telling the truth, they could change the game." The chief's face falls. "I mean, no matter how little we like to admit it, we *are* in trouble. If Zurec has found a way to track the capaemen, that at least warrants an investigation, right?"

"Hmm, I think ya might have a point," she admits finally. "Very well, then. I'll hand this over to you, Steven. Tell the surveyors to find Zurec. Once they do, take this girl with ya and see if she's lying." The chief leans in again, whispering in the boy's ear. She must think Mary can't hear her like this, but her voice is so loud the sound is clear as day. "If she is a liar, show no mercy to her or her clan."

"Yes, sir," Steven says obediently. He reaches to grab his prisoner.

She slaps his hand away. "And? What if I'm *not* lying?"

The tower of a woman looks almost impressed. She must not have been expecting Mary to have some bark. "We will cross that bridge when we come to it, now won't we?"

27

A Murky History

Mary

"We will cross that bridge when we come to it, *now won't we?"* Mary despises the sound of that. It's a non-answer.

The chief of Rostad sits back down at her desk, clearly done talking. The boys escort Mary out of the room. She goes quietly, fuming on the inside. The chief didn't listen to her at all. That brute of a woman was more interested in intimidating her than learning the truth. She can't understand it. Here they are with a common enemy, and she hardly gave Mary the time of day. The only thing these people care about is themselves. Would the rogues even agree to help people like these? She could see Jamie picking a fight with Vivian, which would no doubt spark a war between the clans. That's the last thing they need. Why did she have to bring *them* up?

Steven seems deep in thought, probably thinking of what to do with her. Now he has the power—whether that's a good or bad thing, Mary can't tell. He calls someone over from one of the rooms and pulls out a small piece of parchment. He hands it to the man and whispers in his ear. The man nods and rushes down the hall. There's no way to tell what that means.

"Huh, that went well," Zane says when they have gained some distance from the chief's room.

"I suppose it did," Steven adds as if surprised. He looks relaxed for the first time. "Are ya alright? You know, you're one of the only ones I've seen talk to her like that and get away with it. Perhaps there's some hope for ya after all."

She scoffs. "I don't know what you're talking about."

234

"Me neither," Alec says. "If ya ask me, she's dug herself into a deeper hole. The chief despises those who don't follow the rules. Even if the girl is tellin' the truth, people'll be watching her now."

Steven crosses his arms. "Come on, she doesn't seem like the type to make trouble. I believe her story."

"Huh, ya believe her now? What, because Mommy Chief took a shine to her? You have no ability to think for yourself."

"She ain't my mom, Alec. You know that."

"Might as well be, with how she gives ya special treatment and all." The two devolve into an argument, and Mary wishes she could plug her ears. She misses home so much, but the more she thinks about it, the worse she feels. No matter how much she wants it to, life will never return to normal. That thought alone is enough to crush her, so she tries to distract herself. They pass several doors that seem to connect to one massive room. Inside is a plethora of high-quality weapons. Some sit on shelves, while others are mounted to the walls. That is a room Lillian would love.

Lillian...

No, that's a terrible distraction.

There is another room right next door. This one is filled with furnaces. People hammer away at new blades, the forging fires blazing.

That's worse, Mary thinks. She turns to the other side of the hall.

There is another huge room. Lining the shelves of this room are more books than she has ever seen. She is drawn to it like a fly to a campfire. She could read these books for years and still never get through them all. Finally, something that is uniquely her.

Zane's husky voice fills the hall. "I know, pretty cool right? You can look after we drop ya off in your room."

"My... room?" the girl asks, puzzled. She still feels like a prisoner.

"Yeah, we gotta find out where Zurec is before we can meet with them. Don't ya worry. We're familiar with their territory. It won't take us long, a day or two at most. While we're gone, you can take a peek at the library. So long as ya freshen up in your room first."

Mary sniffs her armpit and gags. "Wow, I'm so sorry."

"It's alright. Heck, I'd smell awful too if I took a mud dive in that nasty riverbank. Freshen up, and we'll come grab ya when we've located them."

As Alec and Steven continue their pointless argument, the big guy leads Mary to a vacant room only a few doors down from the library. The door's finish is like the walls in Chief Vivian's quarters—pristine, varnished redwood. When Zane turns the doorknob, it opens smoothly.

Inside is a room about half the size of the mud room. It has everything from a rug to a trunk to a beautifully crafted wooden bed. There's a large bucket in the corner filled with water. Next to it is a stool and a small table with herbs and a soap jar. Those items are undoubtedly for cleaning, and they are all for her. That isn't even the most mind-blowing thing about this room; the floor is made of wood, but the walls are stone. Mary runs her hand over the sanded rocks, unable to believe it.

"This is one of our newer rooms," Zane says, noticing her awe. "We've been trying new building styles, though people've been hesitant to move to them. Probably because it's inconvenient."

"It's perfect," she says without thinking.

The big man laughs. It's a surprisingly pleasant sound. "Well, don't get too comfortable. It's only temporary. Glad one of Steven's guys could put this together last minute. Don't ya worry. Those herbs are new. Just picked yesterday."

"*Steven* did this?" She recalls a few minutes ago when he whispered to that man. That must have been what that guy left to do.

"I'm sure it's hard to believe, but he's a pretty great guy when ya get to know him. A stickler for the rules, it's true, but he's got a good heart." Mary clasps her hands together, admiring the room. Did she judge him too harshly? "Anyway, I gotta go. Get some rest," Zane says, closing the door gently.

The girl takes a seat on the bed, her head spinning. In the center of her pillow, she spots a note. It's a tiny piece of parchment folded in half—the same one she saw Steven write on and hand to the man. Mary picks it up. On the outside in neat print are the words:

MESSAGE FROM STEVEN ROSTAD,
LEADER OF THE SURVEYORS SPECIALIZED UNIT

She unfolds it warily. Inside, a scribbled note reads:

Lay low here until I come get you. Tracking Zurec should not take long, but if it does, do not leave this room without Zane or Alec. The people don't trust ya.

That means the library is off-limits, unless Mary wants someone breathing down her neck while she reads. She'll rest in here until someone shows up. At least she's not being treated like a prisoner. Again, Mary wonders why these people bear such animosity toward Zurec. She remembers what Chief Vivian said to her: *"Rostad remembers."* Remembers what? The two clans don't have much of a history together.

Mary rubs the pendant of her necklace, feeling the stones under her thumb. She cannot believe that this morning, she was in the burrow with her family. Everything—evacuating the burrow, being attacked by narecons, Lillian sacrificing herself so they could escape the hunter, getting captured by Rostad—all happened in one day. One single, life-changing day.

Mary collapses onto a very soft pillow, her entire body aching. She didn't realize how exhausted she was until just now. The scent of herbs permeates the air, reminding her of home. It's making her sleepy. She can rest here, just for a little while. After all, there's not much else to do.

As she closes her eyes, she sees the river rapids. *Lillian,* Mary thinks, *I'm so sorry. I can't help you right now, but wherever you are, please be safe.* She's safe somewhere. She has to be. They were in the water when Lillian was wounded, so maybe there wasn't as much blood as Mary thought. Yeah, it all happened so quickly. Her friend isn't dead. She can't be.

⁕ ⁕ ⁕

Mary is running down a root cave. No, not running. She's being dragged. Lillian is ahead of her, dashing straight into the mist even though they can hardly see two inches in front of them. How does she do it?

They stop. Here, the root overlooks the river. The roaring sound of the water crashing against the rocks is overwhelming. Mary can't even think straight, yet her friend looks so calm. She stares at the jagged boulders, her face unwavering. It is impossible to tell what she's thinking when she's like this. All Mary knows is she can feel a destructive presence looming closer and closer the more they waste time.

"It's better this way," Lillian says, her eyes locked on the rocks.

"Wh-What do you mean?"

"You've always held me back. This way, you won't anymore." Lillian doesn't give her time for more questions. Instead, she grabs Mary against her will, and together they dive into the river.

Mary wakes up caked in sweat. Her chest is heaving and the blankets are soaked. She has no idea what that was. She doesn't want to think about it.

Luckily, she doesn't have to. Sitting by her bedside is Steven. His thick eyebrows are raised, looking almost concerned. Mary resets her headband. It's rude for him to come in here while she is sleeping. "What do *you* want?"

"I was trying to wake ya up, but you kept talking in your sleep."

Blood rises in her round cheeks. She didn't know she did that. As if not noticing her embarrassment, Steven keeps talking. "Anyway, we found Zurec."

"Already? That was fast. I thought it'd take at least a day."

He stares at her. "Uhh, it did. It's late morning. You slept all night. Even now, it was hard to get ya up."

"What? No, how could I—" Her heart crawls into her throat. It's been over twenty-eight hours. Over a day since she was separated from her best friend. "D-Did you find anyone else? By the river, maybe?"

"We hardly searched the river. Our intel is a little dated, but I don't think Zurec has many bunkers there. Where they're at is farther west. Why do ya ask?"

Mary doesn't know how to respond. Does that mean Lillian is okay or not? She could be hiding out somewhere, or she could have gone back to their main burrow. Or she never left the Crystal River... There is no way to know, and it's killing her inside.

"I brought some armor I think will fit ya," Steven continues. He must not notice the look on her face. Either that or he doesn't care. "Put it on, and we'll head out."

Mary glances at the end of her bed. Sitting by her feet is her own set of black phypent-skin armor paired with a metal-tipped spear. There is an exaggerated curve to the blade. "No, I can't take this. It's too much."

The boy crosses his arms. "We don't want ya to get killed on the way there. That would ruin any chance of negotiations."

"B-But I can't fight. This armor is useless on me."

"It's useful in keeping you *alive*. That's all I care about. Now, get changed. I'll be waiting in the hall." He leaves as if in a hurry.

Now Mary is alone with her thoughts again. She focuses on strapping on her armor. It fastens a little differently than Zurec's, so it takes her a moment to figure out. Once she gets most of it on, she heads to the water bucket.

She looks like a different person in this reflection. Her blonde hair sits in tangled tufts around her face, and her eyes are worn. A battered and broken girl in foreign armor. She takes her headband off and glances around the room. *Looks like they forgot to bring me a hairbrush,* Mary thinks.

Not to mention, she lost her backpack in the river. All that packing and worrying was for nothing. She has nothing now, nothing but what Rostad provides.

She does the best she can, tying the messy blonde strands into a ponytail. The headband looks good like this, even with the frizz in her hair. Next, Mary rubs some soap on her arms and rinses them off with water. Since she slept so long, she had no time to get clean. At least the scent of these plants will cover up her river stench. It's all she can do until they find her people.

I'm going home, she thinks. Home, wherever that is now. She's going to see her mother, Seth, Brianna, and the kids. She should be happy, yet all she feels is worried.

knock knock

"Hey," Steven's voice says from the other side of the door, "are ya almost done? We've gotta go if we want to arrive before sunset."

"Coming!" she yells.

A group of strangers stands in the hall behind Steven. There must be at least twenty of them, far more than what's left of Zurec's surveyors. Mary bites her lip. If things go wrong today, it will be catastrophic for her people.

"Alright everyone, let's head out," Steven orders. "Remember, do not engage the enemy unless I give the okay. We are working under the assumption that what this girl said is true. We will find the acera warriors and make a deal with them. Understood?"

"Yes, sir," many people say at once. Even so, there is some murmuring of doubt in the back. Mary can't make out what they are saying from here, but she knows it's about her. No one here trusts her. A single slip-up, and they will notice.

As the surveyors leave the burrow, crossing the forest of mushrooms, Mary feels incredibly guilty. She's always relying on Zurec to sort out her mess: on Seth's clever tongue and her mother's protection. If they don't do well, they're in trouble, all because she was too afraid to exit the river sooner. To make matters worse, it will take them a little over seven hours to get to the bunker. That's more than enough time for her to spiral.

Eventually, the mushrooms end, revealing a sea of roots and moss. As they trek deeper into the forest, the scenery becomes more familiar. The annoying roots and bushes—always hard to traverse—and the chittering of monsters in the canopy put Mary on edge. They may sound pleasant, but they could attack any time, and she will be helpless to resist. What a fool she was, thinking she could avoid danger for the rest of her life, hiding in the burrow and caring for the children forever. The dream that she could be at peace with her family? That's all it is—a dream.

After what feels like endless walking, voices begin echoing through the trees. Children playing, and—

"Now Oscar, stop pulling Trista's hair. It's rude." Her mother. That's her mother's voice.

Mary wants to run to her. To jump into her arms and never let go, but she stops herself. Steven walks in front of her, and Alec and Zane flank either side of him. Their capes billow in the breeze. She can't just run to her family. She is surrounded by enemies.

The massive group emerges from the underbrush and into the clearing of what must be a bunker location. At the sight of them, Miss May turns white. "Get behind me, kids! Max, go get the adults. Now!" The little boy scrambles to the bunker door, leaping inside.

"You remember who we are, Miss Caretaker," Steven says mockingly. "How flattering." Mary shoots him a hostile look.

Her mother isn't concerned with that comment. Instead, her eyes have fallen on her only daughter, recognition lighting up her face. "M-Mary, darling? You're alive?"

"Mom—" She moves without thinking, but Steven throws an arm in front of her.

"This is your daughter? That'll make things easier, then. Where are your acera warriors? If they exist, we want a word."

"And what, you won't hand her over until they show up?" She has never seen her so furious before. Rostad sparks rage that Mary didn't even know her mother had.

The gatherers emerge from the burrow, starting with Brianna. There are so few of them that it brings tears to Mary's eyes. Despite their numbers, they rush in front of the caretaker and children, brandishing their spears. Among the survivors are the medic Mia, her husband Bruno, the level-headed Jess, the fighter Theo, and... wait, *that's* it. There are only five gatherers left.

Only five of them... and no sign of Lillian.

"What are you doing here?" the redhead snarls. "We had an agreement. Why are you breaking it?"

"Because times have changed," Steven says condescendingly. "You have something we need. So, give us that, and ya get the girl. Easy, right?" Mary's head feels like it is about to explode. What agreement? Also, Steven has completely changed his tune. The same person who gave her a room and armor is now deriding her clan. Her family. Why? They've suffered enough as it is.

"Fine. What do you want?" Brianna growls.

"We want—"

WHUMPF

Before Steven can start, a ginormous winged beast descends from above. On it is a saddle, and atop that saddle...

Jamie and Albert.

The duo leap off Amphii, drawing their scythes as quickly as lightning. Rostad responds in kind. There's about to be a fight.

Without thinking, Mary leaps between the two groups, holding out her hands on either side. "WAIT!" she screams. Rostad and Zurec stop, all eyes falling on her. "We don't have to fight. We have the same goal. Rostad wants to use Jamie and Albert's intel to help them avoid the capaemen."

"Really, then why are they armed to the teeth?" Jamie asks. The two rogues grip their scythes tightly, ready to strike at any moment. Amphii growls, reflecting their anger.

"They're... real," Steven murmurs, ogling the acera. He looks exactly like Mary did when she first saw her room: speechless. The rest of the Rostad people are the same, mouths gaping open like children.

"By the Wilds, not *you* again," Jamie says with disdain. "You very rudely rejected us last time. Why are you giving us googly eyes now? You had your chance, *Rostad boy*."

"We had no clue y'all were this powerful," Steven responds, his eyes locked on Amphii. "We've made a huge mistake. The two of ya don't belong here, you belong—"

"Can it, boy," Jamie interrupts. "You think we want to work with you after what you did? No chance. Go crawl back in your hole and die for all I care." The other Zurec people seem to agree, especially Brianna, who is fuming. That's so unlike her.

Wait... those guys who insulted Zurec after the Albian massacre, were they... *Steven's* group? Mary glares at him in disgust. It does sound like something he would do.

"Now, what is all this commotion?" a new voice says. All eyes fall on a massive figure: broad shoulders, a wide stubbly chin, and long brown hair.

Following him are his right-hand William, the tactician Robin, the warrior Lance, and the steadfast Carmen. This must be what's left of the surveyors. Mary can't even speak. They have lost so many.

The chief of Zurec enters the center of the dispute and crosses his arms, his colored sigil worn proudly for all to see. Even with the phypent-clad Rostad on one side and acera warriors on another, Chief Seth still stands out. "Surveyors of Rostad," he says calmly.

"You're the chief?" Steven asks. Suddenly, he's nervous.

"Why are you here?"

The boy is unable to meet his eyes. Even though he has no reason to be scared, he still is. *That's* the power of their chief. "We, uh, we're here because we have the same goal. We're the only two clans left. We should work together to escape the capaemen."

Seth's hazel eyes have no light in them. Is it just Mary, or does he appear much more worn than usual? His armor is crooked, and layers of bags are under his eyes. "You want... a truce? After all this time?"

Steven nods. He's sure changed his tune from when they first arrived.

"Okay. Let's do it. We have nothing to lose, right?" He agreed so quickly. Mary thought this would be more of a struggle, but it wasn't. This should be good news, but as she studies Seth's glassy, lifeless eyes she can't help but feel dread. It's as if he's given up. No, that can't be right. The chief *never* gives up.

The people of Zurec lower their weapons. Even Jamie and Albert begrudgingly sheathe their scythes. "Give us a day to prepare, then bring your chief. We'll tell you all the capaemen's recent activity, but only on one condition: Mary stays with us."

"Sounds fair to me," Steven says. "After all, she was telling the truth." The second they signal that she can leave, Mary dives into her mother's arms.

"Baby!" she screams, already sobbing. "I thought you were dead. I'm so relieved, I..." She pauses, scanning the Rostad group. "Where's Lillian?"

Mary freezes.

Her mother grabs her shoulders. "Honey, where is *Lillian*? Where is the other girl I raised?"

So, she's not here after all. Mary is speechless.

"Where is she?" Brianna repeats, her green eyes wide. "Don't tell me that she—"

"I don't know!" Mary screams. "I don't know, okay? All I know is that we fell in the river, the rocks were sharp, and there was... there was so much blood. She shielded me with her own body."

The atmosphere is the epitome of despair, as it dawns on everyone what Mary means. Mia looks as if she's about to pass out, and Jess steadies her even as tears fall down her own face. Meanwhile, William stares at Seth as if waiting for him to fall apart.

"We'll, uh, head back to our territory now," Steven says, retreating. "We'll be back tomorrow. Be ready, okay?" With that awkward goodbye, Rostad disappears into the underbrush, but Mary is hardly thinking of them anymore. What's in front of her is her worst nightmare.

"No..." Seth mumbles. "It can't be."

"I'm sorry," she says. "I tried to save her. I did everything I could."

"So, she's gone then?" Lillian's father says, choking on the words.

"I don't know, maybe she..." but Mary can't finish her sentence. Maybe she what? Is there any way she could have survived the Giant Wilds, alone and injured, in the middle of an attack?

Mary's mom collapses to her knees, whaling. Brianna and Bruno try to comfort her, but she's inconsolable. Screaming and crying and hitting the ground with her fists. Meanwhile, the children are sobbing, and Kayla tries to keep them together. All the while, Seth stares straight ahead, his face blank.

No. They're acting like she's dead. She can't be, not after everything. Mary looks at Lillian's father. He's an optimist. Surely, he will agree with her.

"Seth? Seth?" Mary says, shaking him. "Say something, please. Tell me we're going to be alright. Tell me everything will be okay, and that Zurec will survive. We always do, right? Lillian, she's stubborn. There's a chance she's alive. I-If anyone could find a way, it's her."

No response. He doesn't even look at her.

"Seth, I'm begging you! Answer me! Please give me one of your pep talks. Tell me what to do. There must be a way to save her. We must have hope, like you said. We can't give up, I'll—"

"If what you said is true, she's gone," Jamie interrupts. The rogues look strangely serious for people who should be mourning. Jamie is still stern as ever, while her brother hides behind his hair, his face concealed. It's almost as if they don't care.

"No, no, that can't be..." Mary says, but she's believing it less and less.

"She's *dead*," the woman growls. "She's dead, and we're all *screwed*." Finally, Mary collapses as well, too exhausted to deny it.

Lillian is dead, and it's all her fault.

28

Worlds Collide

Lillian

Lillian had such a wild dream. The narecon commander with the cold, orange eyes found her family. The hunter chased them down, and Lillian sacrificed herself to save Mary. The pain was unbearable. Survival instinct took over and...

She asked that strange capaeman boy, Lionel, for help. How absurd. There is no way any capaeman would help her. They are natural enemies. Is she still holding on to that ridiculous hope—that feeling that capaemen may not be all they seem? She needs to let that go.

Luckily, Lillian is back in reality now.

She is on an adventure with the gatherers. The trees stand tall and unmoving, and the plants below are eerily still. The clouds block out the sun. The smell of dirt and dew permeates the air, and the forest is coated in a creepy fog. It may rain again. Wait, again? No, that happened in Lillian's dream, not in real life. To make things even stranger, the gatherers walk so fast she can't keep up. Jess, Zoey, and Milo disappear into the thick fog. Then, Mia and Bruno. Then Brianna. She tries to run after them, but her legs won't move.

What's the point? They'll never accept me anyway.

Now, she can't spot any of the gatherers in the mist. Lillian stands alone and lost. Fear rises in her chest. Sure, her family doesn't understand her, and they try to run her life, but she doesn't want to be alone. Being alone is so much scarier. "Hello?" she calls into the fog. "Anyone?"

Nothing. The silence hurts her more than a thousand scathing words. This is not what she wanted. "I'm sorry I've been so bad," she says. "I just want to make my own decisions. I don't need to be protected all the time. I should learn to stand on my own."

More silence. Lillian feels a crushing loneliness. "Please!" she shouts. "Anyone, please, listen to me!"

Suddenly, a faint *boom* echoes through the canopy. Something big is coming.

The *boom* reverberates again, this time twice as loud. This is not a creature she can fight. She'll have to run or hide. Those are her only options.

But are they? Is the world really that bleak?

Boom...

Four times as loud. Lillian's ears ring. In the distance, Brianna yells something at the gatherers. Lillian tries to go toward them but can't see through the fog. She doesn't even know which direction the voice came from.

Boom Boom

The sound punches Lillian's ear drums. She clasps her hands over her head, but it doesn't help. She wants to hide, but again, her body won't budge. She looks around frantically. Where are the rest of the gatherers hiding? It's impossible to tell, as she's still blinded by the fog. Think, think. She's running out of time. "Brianna, Mia? Where are you?" Lillian forces herself forward. First, she walks. Then her steps quickly escalate to a run. Still, no matter how much she runs, it feels like she's getting nowhere. The fog remains thick as ever, and there isn't a tree in sight.

BOOM BOOM

The sound pierces her aching head. "Guys?" Lillian calls as her running becomes a full-on sprint. "I don't want to be alone!"

Suddenly, her legs are rooted to the ground again. Why can't she move?

BOOM.

The colossal sound knocks Lillian to the ground and a shadow looms over her. A gust of icy air hits her, and her body freezes in terror. This creature, whatever it is, is too big to fight. She's a dead woman now.

"Lillian..." a thunderous voice says. Where is that coming from? She still can't see anything. "I can help you," the voice says. It's not human, but what choice does she have? She glances every which way, searching for the source of the voice. Finally, when she dares look upward, she sees the origin of the shadow. The second it comes into view, the fog clears.

Towering over her with a rain shield in hand is Lionel. Lillian tries to speak but has no words. He is so massive his mere presence makes her speechless.

Lionel doesn't seem to mind her silence. He reaches out a clawed hand as if inviting her to come with him. He has the same look she saw him give that styfisher. Is such kindness even possible?

Before Lillian can find out, she wakes up, her body caked in sweat.

But this isn't her bed.

The sheets are warm and fluffy, and the mattress is so soft she feels like she is floating on a cloud. *Am I still dreaming?* Lillian thinks. As the warrior sits up, she is overwhelmed with aches and pains, especially in her legs. It's as if they're being stabbed repeatedly.

Then, the memories return. The orange-eyed capaemen, the narecons, the surveyors and gatherers, all the deaths, all the blood...

... and the river.

What she just woke up from, *that* was the dream. *This* is reality.

Lillian glances around, her heart pounding through her ears. She is in a dark, enclosed space. The room is enormous, and the walls look so odd. They are made from wood, and instead of being in the shape of a circle, like the mud room, they make a box shape. The only objects in the room are the bed she is in, her backpack, and a giant roll of white bandages. The roll is bigger than her entire body. It looks like it's been used.

Lillian throws the sheets off her legs, and the sight makes her gasp. Her legs are completely wrapped up. The right leg that was bleeding is now thick with bandages, and the left leg with the bruise has a splint attached, holding it straight. She scans the rest of her body. There are bandages around her right shoulder and on her left palm. The white bandages are the only clue she was once bleeding. Not a drop of red in sight. Even her bedsheets are clean. How is this possible?

"I might be able to save you, but I make no promises." Lionel said that when he found her. To survive, Lillian took the gamble of a lifetime. Which means...

She isn't in the Giant Wilds anymore. She is wherever Lionel took her. As the warrior realizes what that means, she is wracked with fear.

Lillian is now in the capaemen's world.

Slowly, the warrior forces her aching body out of bed, but as soon as she stands, she falls over. She pushes up on the hard wooden ground, her body screaming in protest. *I have to figure out where I am,* she thinks. In her struggle, Lillian grabs something she didn't know was there. It feels like the shaft of a spear.

Thank goodness, her spear is okay. But as she uses it to stand, she notices something different. It lacks blades, and the shaft is made of a different type of wood.

This isn't her spear. It's a walking stick. Lillian glances around the dark room. Her reflective spear is nowhere to be seen. She pats her waist. Her dagger is missing too. Lionel stole from her? Why? A capaeman has no need for her little weapons. They would be toothpicks to him. She limps forward, using the stick as support. She must find an exit to this strange place. There is an exit, right?

There don't seem to be doors or openings, but a faint light is coming from one of the walls. The light shines through each of its corners as if that wall isn't glued to the others. Could she push it out of the way? It's too big, but she at least needs to try. Lillian leans against the wall, pushing with all her might, and unexpectedly, it swings right open. The wall swerves away from Lillian as if fleeing, but it doesn't fall. Instead, it stays attached to the room by several metal bolts.

This is a cabinet—a *mega* cabinet.

Just as quickly as it swung away, the door comes back. Lillian catches it, holding it open. She's breathing so much heavier than usual. If she were healthy, this would be easy, but she can hardly stand. All she can do is take a peek out the cabinet door.

The room outside must be at least a thousand times bigger. Stretching out below her is a giant metal table, which curiously stretches wall to wall over a giant chair. Instead of the burrow's muddy brown, this place has grey walls. They appear to be dyed somehow. On every wall, there is something new to take in.

The left wall contains silver shelves taller than most plants of the Giant Wilds. The shelves are lined with gadgets and tools she's never seen before. On the wall opposite Lillian is a gargantuan wooden door and another table and chair, also covered in strange junk. Finally, entirely making up the right wall is a megaton of glass, so much it makes her head spin. Square panes of glass are organized in an enormous grid, which stretches across the entire wall and ceiling. Instead of meeting at a sharp angle, the two surfaces are essentially made one, connected by a wide curve in the glass grid. Through the ceiling, she can see stars in the sky. The moon is a bright and beautiful blue.

Yet somehow, even though it's nighttime, the room is filled with light. Lillian squints at the left side of the room. Over the shelves are some very bright lights. Could those be a capaeman torch of some kind?

jiggle jiggle

Before Lillian can take in more of the room, the knob on the giant door turns. Her heart crawls into her throat. *Click.* The door swings open, and Lillian retreats into the cabinet, the wood *slamming* behind her. She winces at the loud sound.

There is silence, then the sound of a closing door. Then, silence again. Lillian feels like she's suffocating. Her legs shake, and her shoulders slump. She flattens herself against a wall for dear life. One hand clutching her walking stick, one over her mouth to quiet her panicked breaths.

boom boom boom—

Footsteps.

boom, creeeaaakkk.

The capaeman must be sitting. Lillian doesn't make a sound. She has no idea what kind of danger she's in right now. She has no plan, no way to act. This is the worst feeling in the world.

"Are you... awake?" Lillian nearly forgot how deep Lionel's voice is. It rattles the cabinet a little. At least she knows that the capaeman outside this door is Lionel. She looks at her legs again. She cannot believe he saved her. Everyone in her life, including the rogues, said a capaeman would never help a human, but is that true? Jamie's words ring in her mind.

"Once your usefulness has run dry, it will take away everything you love."

Is he trying to use her in some way? To trick her into giving away information about her clan? Somehow, that doesn't feel right. If he wanted to use her, why put this much effort into helping her? The bed, the bandages, the walking stick—this isn't what someone evil would do. What if... what if he is different?

No, Lillian must remain vigilant. She can't let her guard down. This *thing* could kill her at any time, and she still doesn't know what it wants.

"I heard the cupboard door. You know, your legs are in no condition for bearing weight." He's still talking. She should answer, but she's not sure what to say. What does one say to a giant who saved their life under mysterious circumstances? Kayla hasn't written any books about that. "If you do not answer, I am opening the cupboard."

Lillian's knees buckle. "N-No!" she screams out of instinct. "I-I'm awake, okay?"

There is a *rumble*, and then another *creak*. He must have sat back down. "Hmph, how fortunate. You are alive. I was minutes away from burying you in the yard, you know."

"What? Why would you do that?"

"You have been asleep for three days, and you are so small I cannot feel your pulse. I was unsure whether you were alive or dead."

"Th-Three days?" It's nighttime, so Lillian thought it may have been a few hours, but *days*? She has never slept that long in her entire life. What could be going on in the Giant Wilds? Is her family alive? It dawns on her that she has no way of finding out.

"Frankly, I doubted you would make it. This is fascinating. Do humans heal more quickly than us? Or perhaps the environment in which you were raised is the principal factor? The Crimson Forest is a harsh place to subsist, even for stronger flora and fauna."

Lillian's mind spins. She didn't understand half of that.

"I do not possess enough knowledge about the human species to synthesize a concrete answer. Perhaps you can fill in some gaps?"

"Maybe if you speak English?" Lillian blurts. The second she says it, she regrets it.

"Excuse me? I speak perfect English. Quite rude of you to say such a thing. I saved your life. I had no obligation to do so."

Lillian leans her head against the wall. Should she ask? Would he even give her an answer? Before she can decide, she's already speaking. "Why did you save me, anyway?"

There is a long pause. She wonders if that was wrong to ask.

"You..." Lionel trails off. "You were practically *begging* for my help. How could I not oblige?"

She doesn't like that answer. "I'm going to be honest. We're supposed to be enemies, right?" If there is anything Lillian hates more than having no control, it's beating around the bush.

"*Yes*," the capaemen says coldly, "we are."

The words send a chill up and down Lillian's spine. "Then why? Why didn't you just kill me?"

"I suppose it is... fascination. Yes, that is it. We do not know much about the human species, and I would prefer to know more."

That also doesn't sit right. If he wants something, he does not need to ask nicely, especially if they're enemies. She chooses to drop it, though. It's clear

Lionel has no intention of giving a straight answer. She should change the subject. "If I answer your questions, will you let me go?"

"Perhaps. As I said, nothing is certain here."

"Why?"

"Reasons you cannot understand."

Lillian is reminded of how her elders talked down to her. They shouldn't expect her to learn if they don't explain anything. "Try me."

There is a low growl, followed by what she can only describe as a sigh. It sounds deep and husky, with a hint of frustration. "Quite the nosy human, you are."

The warrior laughs. "I've been called worse."

"Fine, then. I shall tell you this. To be honest, I do not trust you. Wherever humans go, chaos and destruction follow. You are like little armies of death."

"Is that why you took my weapons away?"

"A small price to pay for your life, were it not?" Lionel says flatly.

"Why do you even want to talk to me if you don't trust me?"

"Again, I am curious. Do not make me repeat myself." Lillian places a hand on her head. It's like talking to a rock. At least she doesn't have to see him. She can speak her mind with less fear, being in the darkness of this cabinet.

"I believe I am overdue for some answers," the capaeman boy says condescendingly.

"Sure, ask away," Lillian says. She's not getting anywhere anyway.

"Why do humans have skin as protection for their internal organs instead of scales? It seems quite impractical. Other species share a similar fragility, but it is usually traded for an evolutionary advantage. Based on what I know, however, humans gain little to no advantage from this adaptation. Surely, you would benefit from a tougher exterior shell, no?"

Never mind, Lillian can't do this. Not at all. Maybe if she had paid more attention to Kayla's books on biology, but she was never checked in during those lessons. Even if she had been, she has a feeling it wouldn't have helped much with this. It's like they're speaking different languages.

"Another quandary: why is it that we look so similar? I mean, there are some differences in physique, such as body size, pupil shape, skin type, as well as intelligence—"

"Excuse me? Are you calling me stupid?"

"Well, you certainly aren't bright." Lillian scoffs. She can't believe the superiority complex of this giant. It might be worse than Jamie's. Although come to think of it, she's not sure why she's surprised. If Lillian were that strong, she might have an inflated ego too. "Do not take offense to that. It is a fact," Lionel says simply.

"Right, just like it's a *fact* that we bring death and destruction. You know, for someone smarter than me, you sure spew a lot of nonsense."

Another growl. Maybe Lillian went too far this time. She doesn't care, though. This giant is getting on her nerves. "It... isn't... nonsense," the capaeman says slowly.

"Come on, like *we* could hurt *you*. If anything, capaemen are the ones who cause death and destruction." She bites her tongue, thinking of Albian and... the river. What is she doing right now, talking to a creature capable of *that*? She could die instantly if he so much as lifted a finger. What fate would he choose for her? Crushed? Torn apart? Poisoned, like so many others?

The weight of Lillian's decision at the river finally dawns on her. She is in a giant cabinet in a capaeman's home in who knows where. She may never see her friends or family again. In a way, this is much worse than her situation back home. No, it *is* worse. At least they cared. They did what they thought was best for her. If she makes one wrong move with Lionel, she's dead. Heck, it may not even matter what she does. She might die no matter what. Her breathing grows heavy again. *No no no, I can't freak out now. I can't show fear. That will make it worse. Think.*

Not all hope is lost; she hasn't explored the room yet. *Remember, Lillian, one step at a time.* For now, she will keep the capaeman entertained enough not to kill her. Then, when he leaves, she'll look for a way out. This place is huge. There's got to be a crack she could slip through. Then, when she gets outside...

... She has no weapons, and she can hardly walk.

No, don't think that far. If she managed to escape, her situation outside would probably be better anyway. Anything would be better than here, where she has no control over her fate.

Come to think of it, Lionel has been silent for a while. Is he already thinking of...

"H-Hey, are you still there?" she asks nervously.

"I am," the capaeman says. "I will head out now. I will return shortly. In the meantime, get some rest. I don't want to have to fix your legs again." With a few *boom*s, a *slam*, and a *click*, Lionel leaves the room. The instant she's alone, Lillian crawls over to her bed, grabs the fluffy pillow, and screams into it.

That was too close. She has no time to waste. She must find an exit. She must... She must...

But she feels so light-headed. She lost so much blood in the river. Her body must be in overdrive just to keep her awake. *No, push through the pain,* Lillian thinks, but it isn't working. The warrior lies against the wall again, feeling defeated.

This was a terrible idea.

Or was it?

After all, she *is* still alive. That's much more than the others thought would happen if she ever talked to Lionel again. He could have opened the cabinet, but he didn't. He could have demanded answers from her, threatening her life, but he didn't. He didn't have to save her at all, but he did. Why?

Lillian places her head in her hands. All this doubt is awful. She won't be able to make the decision best for her survival. What would the others do? They wouldn't trust a word Lionel said, and they'd get the heck out of this place as soon as possible.

But why does that feel wrong, too?

Lillian yawns. She is struggling to keep her eyes open.

She'll worry about this later. It seems she's safe for now, and that's good enough.

29

The Winds of Change

Mary

Mary almost misses the privacy of that Rostad room. She is grateful Seth negotiated her rescue, but there's no denying that Bunker Two is a poor replacement for Zurec's main burrow. Heck, she'd prefer Bunker Three over this. It's a shame her people were only able to hide there during the attack.

The entire place is barely bigger than the mud room. There is hardly space to sleep, much less take care of personal hygiene. Mary lays on a poorly crafted mat that barely separates her from the dirt. The children are fast asleep, their clothes tear-stained. Most people didn't sleep last night. They lost someone—someone they were desperately trying to protect.

Mary never closed her eyes, not for a second. For hours, she couldn't stop crying. At first, loudly with her mother, and then, when most had cried themselves to sleep, her tears continued to fall in silence. What happened at the river repeated on a loop in her head as she rolled back and forth on her mat. It feels as if she's been torn to pieces. No amount of physical pain can compare to the ache in her chest now. To her dried-out eyes, which refuse to shed any more tears. To the massive, gaping hole in her heart that will never be filled.

As morning dawns, Brianna drifts gracefully about the room, lighting each torch one by one. Slowly, the members of Zurec crawl out of their beds, their bodies sluggish and eyes worn. Mary doesn't move a muscle. She's not sure she can. Even though this bed is terrible and the blanket hardly provides any warmth, she snuggles beneath it. She wishes she could lie here forever and forget about this ruthless world.

creeaakkk

253

The trapdoor opens slowly, letting in light from the surface. Trista groans. She slept right next to Mary and stayed awake the longest, holding the distraught teenager's hand and telling her things would be okay. The little girl, whom Mary should be guiding and protecting, comforted her. It's shameful. She should be the one comforting the children.

Mary is a caretaker. That is her purpose. She isn't good for anything else, but Lillian...

Lillian could have become anything she set her mind to, but now she's gone. It happened so quickly. There is so much more Mary wanted to say to her. So many things she wanted to do together. Now, they will never have another chance.

As Mary wallows in her grief, the chief's voice fills the room. "Good morning... everyone," Seth says gloomily. He utters the words without a hint of confidence. "Let's get ready, okay? Rostad could show up any minute, and we want to look... presentable."

Forget presentable. Mary can't even get out of bed.

Something touches her shoulder. It feels like two little hands trying to shake her awake. "Hey Mary," the voice of Trista says, "it's time to get up. Everyone is getting ready."

"What's the point?" she finds herself mumbling. "They can do it without me."

"Don't be that way. If you're sad, it makes us all sad."

Mary peeks out from under the covers. "Really?"

"Yeah, let's play a game. Whoever can smile the most wins." Trista places her fingers on the corners of Mary's mouth, pushing it into a smile.

The grieving girl sits up. "Look at you, getting *me* out of bed. You're growing up fast." She tousles the little girl's hair. Trista giggles.

The children get ready with Miss May and Kayla. Some obediently change into their day clothes, while others mess around. Oscar is off task today. He whips one of the twins in the back with a pair of pants and then runs away. The caretaker lacks the energy to stop him. It's up to her daughter yet again.

"Hey!" Jan screams. She moves to chase him, but Mary blocks her.

"Let's not fight," she says gently. "Today is a big day, and everyone must be on their best behavior. Oscar, get back here and put your pants on. I will not tolerate any shenanigans today." Her mother beams with approval. They have never sounded so alike.

"Yes, Miss Mary," the boy responds.

Miss Mary, she thinks. It has a nice ring to it. Reminded of her purpose, the future caretaker ties her hair back and straps on some armor. Luckily, there was an extra set close to her size in the storage room. She glances at the Rostad armor and fancy curved spear she borrowed. She won't put that on, no matter how great it is.

With that, everyone is ready to go. The last of Zurec exits the bunker, emerging into the Giant Wilds.

It is extra windy today. Usually, the trees protect them from harsh weather and extreme temperatures like this, but the wind is so strong it whips through the leaves. Bushes and ferns shake back and forth, and everyone's hair is a mess. Even Jamie, who stands by her acera with her brother, has trouble securing her bun. After a few frustrating minutes, she lets her hair fall by her sides. Mary never realized how long it is. It goes all the way to the small of her back.

The rogues look about as disheveled as everyone else, so they must not have slept well either. Somehow, that's a comfort. When Jamie complained how cramped the burrow was last night, and then left with her brother in frustration, Mary wanted to scream. Now is not the time to complain and run off. They should be sticking together, not sleeping in trees or who knows where.

Albert stands next to his sister, still hiding behind his hair. He hasn't said a single word since he found out about Lillian.

"Is everyone here?" Seth asks. He scans the crowd, which is less of a crowd and more of a small group. Jess and William's eyes are bloodshot. They lost their sister, Zoey. Mia tries to comfort them, but they shrug her off. Meanwhile, Lance sits with Robin, repeatedly insisting that Archer's death was his fault. Mary catches something about not being able to "bail him out this time." Robin just shakes his head and keeps an arm around him. His husband Theo, usually so present, absentmindedly draws lines in the dirt with the butt of his spear, eyes unfocused. So many friends were lost. As of now, there are only ten people left who can fight. Not ten gatherers, not ten surveyors—ten people in total.

The chief sighs. "Yeah, I guess this is everybody." Zurec has dwindled from thirty-two people to a mere twenty-one. They lost *eleven* people in the attack, including Lillian. It's a miracle they didn't lose more. No, not a miracle; the acera warriors standing a distance away are the reason so many survived. Mary hates feeling like she owes them anything. That woman doesn't need any more reasons to be cocky.

Still, even with their help, some sustained serious injuries. Bruno's right arm is in a sling. He won't be swinging his spear any time soon. Jess has bloodstained bandages around her shoulder, and her brother William has them on both forearms. She cries in his embrace, going on about how her husband sacrificed himself for her. They all look so demoralized.

"Chief Seth, I hate to bring this up now," Mia says, her dark-brown eyes darting around nervously, "but we ran out of food this morning. Who are the surveyors and gatherers now? Because after this, we need to go out and get more food. Plus, the injured were not able to rest properly last night. We've run out of clean bandages. Maybe we could—"

Brianna places a hand on the medic's shoulder. "Not now, Mia." They stare at the chief.

Lillian's father averts his gaze from the two women. "No, it's okay. Mia brings up some good points. We will talk about it after we get through this. Let's just... meet with Rostad first. One step at a time."

"O-Okay, I'm sorry," the medic mumbles.

The chief takes a seat on a root, looking like he's on the verge of collapse. The others keep their distance as if allergic to him. Even his closest friends stay away. No one has ever seen him like this. His hair is a raggedy mess, his armor is still crooked, and there is a new layer of bags under his eyes. He grips his spear as if trying to snap it in half. Slowly, Mary approaches him.

... But what can she say? His only daughter is dead, and he ignored her for most of her life. The guilt he feels must be immeasurable. Mary stops in her tracks. She would only make him feel worse.

Instead, she does what she knows best. She entertains the children until Rostad arrives: chasing them, telling stories, and playing hide-and-seek, all while keeping a convincing smile. She can't show her sadness. If she is upset, they will be too.

It's good to smile, even if it's fake. It's good to laugh, even if it's forced. After all, what else can she do? There are people who need her, and so long as they need her, she will continue to smile.

"Ready or not, here I come!" Mary says, uncovering her eyes. Looking across the clearing, she can already see little Max's hair sticking up from behind a giant leaf. "Oh wow, you all hide so well. I have no idea where to start. I guess I'll check... under this root!" She darts to the nearest root, knowing no one is there. Then, several feet away, she hears the laugh of one of the twins.

"Now, who's that giggling? You don't want to give away your position, because I'm a big bad phypent and I'll—" She jumps into a patch of moss, ambushing Jen and Jan. "I'll eat you up! Nom nom nom." The girls squeal and try to run, but Mary already has them clutched in her arms. "Muahaha, you can never escape me!"

As she says that, genuine fear emerges in Jen's eyes. The future caretaker lets them go, thinking she may have gone too far, but then the little girl grabs her sister's sleeve and points across the clearing.

Strolling out of the brush are fifty Rostad warriors. Women and men of all sizes have hostile looks etched on their faces. Some have war paint splattered on their cheeks. Several pair their black armor with capes embroidered with the Rostad sigil, while others have drawn the sigil on their massive arms.

Mary rushes into the clearing, taking a spot near her mother, who hardly acknowledges her. Once the warriors are only a few feet away from the Zurec people, Chief Vivian, standing proudly at the front of her army, raises a hand. They stop, pounding their curved spears into the ground in unison.

Wind whips through the forest.

Chief Vivian is the first to speak. "Wow, is this really all that's left of y'all?"

Standing directly in front of her, Seth responds with an even "Yes."

The chief straps her weapon to her back. The rest of the warriors do the same. That should be taken as a sign of good faith, but it feels more like an insult. It's as if they are saying, "*We could take you easily, so we don't need to be prepared.*" Despite this, all the adults on Zurec's side keep straight faces. They are one mind, thinking together—all except Jamie and Albert, whose eyes are filled with rage.

"So, these are the famous acera warriors," the chief of Rostad says, making her way toward them. Jamie holds one arm in front of her brother and the other over her weapon. Vivian is bigger than even her, and it's clearly intimidating the siblings. Their acera growls softly.

"Easy there," the chief says. She holds out her palms for the creature to sniff. At first, Amphii hesitates, but then her rider nods in approval. The acera leans in and takes a considerable whiff of Vivian's hands. Seeming satisfied, she nuzzles them. "That's a good girl. Ya know, it's been so long since we've seen an acera. Thought they all left the Wilds."

"What do you mean?" Jamie asks. "They aren't native to here."

The hulking woman gives Jamie a quizzical look as if she said something strange. Then, her attention shifts back to Seth. "Pretty lucky ya found an acera. Although, it's quite ironic for y'all to rely on one of those. The Zurec people used to be prideful. Now I see only a shadow."

Chief Seth frowns. "Your clan sure has grown. It's impressive." Chief Vivian's brow furrows. The expression is matched by the warriors flanking her, including the ones Mary met yesterday. They have drifted closer to their chief, hands on the scimitars attached to their hips. Mary glances around and realizes too late that the Rostad people aren't just in front, but all around them, forming a massive circle. Chills run down her spine. There's nowhere to run.

"Anyhow," the chief of Rostad continues, "how do these acera warriors work? Give me their strategy."

"You should ask them," Seth says. "They have names, you know."

Brianna shoots him an alarming look. This is delicate. He should know that, yet he's biting down like a leomus.

Vivian's dark eyes narrow. "Fine. Girl, what do you and the little one do to track the capaemen?"

"Little one" must refer to Albert. He shrinks away as if trying to disappear from this conversation. Mary also wishes she could vanish. First, they lose nearly a dozen people to that hunter, and now they're forced to negotiate with people who don't care whether they live or die. It's all because of her. If only Mary had been more careful when swimming down the river; none of this would have happened.

Jamie squares her shoulders, trying to look intimidating. "First, you answer some questions for me. Why did you treat us so horribly when we first met? It's despicable how your people behaved."

"What are you going on about?"

The rogue points at Steven, who stands close to Vivian's side. "It was a group led by that boy. He told us to, and I quote, 'Go back to where you came from, you stinking rogues.'"

For the first time, the chief's expression changes. She looks almost disappointed in Steven, who shrugs nervously. She shakes her head at him. "I'm sorry about my subordinate. Ya see he's still young, and sometimes he messes up. It was a mistake turning you two away."

Jamie cocks her head, surprised by the apology.

"Let's get back to the matter at hand. Tell me, acera warriors, how do you track the capaemen? How soon do ya know when they'll attack, and what strategies do you use to avoid them?"

This time, the Osian warrior answers the question. She discloses where they are from, their experience observing capaemen, and how they can tell when one is about to attack. Every member of Rostad is engaged the entire time. The respect they pay the warriors just because they're useful puts a bad taste in Mary's mouth. People shouldn't extend kindness to others just because they have something to gain. It should be a given.

"So, that's about it," Jamie finishes. "Tell me, chief of Rostad, is that a good enough answer for you? Remember, you'd better treat Zurec with respect, or we won't work for you at all." Her boldness never ceases to baffle Mary. Still, in this case it may be a good thing.

The chief smirks. It's an odd sight on her stony face. "Wow, ya sure are something. I have no more questions. Chief of Zurec, let's talk terms."

All eyes fall on Seth. Usually, he would stand tall even with hundreds of people staring him down, but right now he doesn't look like himself. His shoulders are slightly slumped, and he doesn't move his hair out of his face no matter how much the wind messes it up. "Yes. What do you want?"

"It's quite simple. In exchange for sparing your lives, we want updates from your acera warriors. Warnings about the capaemen and whatnot."

"That's all?" Seth asks.

"That's all."

He glances around, noting that they are surrounded. "I'm surprised you don't want more."

What are you doing? Mary thinks. Now's the time to bargain. The acera warriors are valuable, and they could be getting things Zurec needs: food, fresh hides, medical supplies. After all, Mia said just this morning that they're running low on everything. The few survivors are standing in the clearing, bleeding through their bandages. Mary bites her lip in frustration. She can't believe she's thinking about this and he isn't. The other adults are clearly questioning it too. Her mother's eyes are wide, and Brianna looks on the verge of intervening.

"What more could we take?" Chief Vivian says bluntly. "You've already lost everything. By the looks of it, you'll be the last chief of Zurec, won't you?"

At that moment, Mary sees something she thought she'd never witness: Seth is shaking. "Y-Yeah... I guess this is a triumphant moment for you, huh?"

Brianna grabs his arm as if begging him to stop. He ignores her, seeming to grow more agitated with each moment.

"I must say, I reckoned it would be," Vivian says, "but it's mostly sad. I never expected y'all to go out with a whimper."

The members of Rostad murmur amongst themselves in agreement. Mary hears a lot of "pathetic," "sad," and "they deserve it." She clenches her fists.

"Right," Seth says. "Well, if the capaemen have anything to say about it, I'm sure your people aren't far behind."

Chief Vivian freezes. "What did you just say?"

The murmurs quickly turn to growls. Some members of Rostad draw their weapons. Miss May unstraps her spear and shoves her daughter behind her. Mary can't believe her ears. It's as if their chief wants a fight. He hasn't been the same since he heard about Lillian. It's as if all the optimism and strength that made him such a good leader has drained away. He is in no shape to negotiate.

Before fighting can erupt, Brianna leaps in front of Seth. "He didn't mean it!" The Rostad people hesitate. "You are right, Chief Vivian. You see, Chief Seth has just lost his only daughter. He's sorry for speaking out of turn. It isn't like him."

"... And who are you?"

"My name is Brianna, leader of the gatherers," she says calmly and cordially. "I will speak on Chief Seth's behalf. Mia, please check him over. He is unwell."

"You got it, boss!" the medic says, dragging Seth to the back of the group.

"Finally," Vivian says. "You look like you know what you're doing. Let's talk, Miss Brianna."

The women sit on two adjacent tree roots facing each other, and they talk for what seems like forever. First, they discuss the acera warriors' role as "the scouts." Chief Vivian asks for an account of the capaemen's movements to date. Brianna makes eye contact with Jamie and Albert. They nod, so she recaps the gatherers' first trip to Albian's burrow, the black narecon attack, the giant by the Crystal River, the scouts' encounter with the hunter, and—very briefly for the sake of the traumatized faces amongst Zurec—the attack on their burrow. Mary and the others listen apprehensively, and the hostility in the air eases a bit. It seems the chief of Rostad is willing to give them one more chance. It's all up to Brianna now.

"Tell me, head of gatherers, what do you want in return for the acera warriors' help?"

The redhead leans in, clasping her hands together. "With respect, Chief Vivian, that is not the right question to ask. Think about it. We are on two different sides of the Giant Wilds. It would be difficult for them to give news to both of us."

"What are ya saying?"

"Your clan is certainly strong, but the capaemen are even stronger. For the next couple of weeks, we all will be on high alert. Why not do it together?"

Mary's breath catches in her throat. She was expecting Brianna to ask for something, but this... There's no way they will go for it. She remembers the disdainful gazes of those people in Rostad's burrow. The thought of having to be around them again makes her blood boil.

The chief of Rostad pauses. She says her next words slowly and carefully. "Young lady, are you requesting an alliance?"

"Not requesting. Persuading," Brianna responds confidently. "You think the acera warriors are the only useful people, but everyone here has a special skill. We have fighters, medics, writers, and cartographers. Plus, our surveyors ran a perimeter sweep after the Albian massacre, and the scouts have seen more than one capaeman in our territory. We can tell you where they were and what they were doing."

"We hardly care about where the capaemen were, only where they'll strike next. As for those skills ya mentioned, all those things will get done by the capable people of Rostad. There are hardly any of ya left anyway. We do not need y'all."

"I disagree. For a situation like this, you need everyone you can find—every piece of information you can get."

Vivian seems to consider this, to the surprise of both groups. "After everything, why should we help you?"

"You said it yourself. We are a shadow of what we once were. Don't think of it as helping Zurec. Instead, see it as people banding together to survive. We have never faced a threat this massive."

The two continue to talk. For a moment, it seems as if Vivian is about to give in, but that changes when she glances at her colleagues. Many of them are scowling and shaking their heads. Steven's friend Alec waves his hand over his neck, signaling her to stop. In that moment, she sighs, her face falling.

"I say, I do respect you Miss Brianna, but..." A gust of wind surges through the Giant Wilds. The chief of Rostad stays still as a statue, her mane of hair blowing behind her hardened expression. "We can't just forget everything your people have done." Her people? Mary has no idea what she's talking about.

Tension spikes yet again. Brianna seems to be at a loss for words. That must have been her last idea.

"But," Vivian continues, "there is one way. We've been constructing some new rooms in the burrow, yet people have been slow to move in. It won't be permanent by any stretch, but we may be able to host ya if you move to that section and follow some rules."

"Chief Vivian, what are you—" Alec tries to speak, but his boss cuts him off.

"It ain't ideal, but then again, none of this is. Most of the burrow will be off-limits. If any members of Zurec poke around where they aren't welcome, they'll be punished, and if we think anyone is a threat..." She places a hand on her scimitar. "This agreement is done for."

There is an eerie stillness. Mary wishes she could crawl under her bed sheets and never come out. It doesn't matter that the mats are uncomfortable or that the bunker is cramped. It's *theirs*. They are free to do what they want. If Brianna takes this deal, they'll basically be prisoners—well-fed and housed, but prisoners nonetheless.

What did they do to deserve this? Is Mary missing something?

"Well, what do ya say?" Chief Vivian asks, clearly growing impatient.

"I..." The redhead glances at her colleagues, but everyone in Zurec is speechless. Even Seth waits patiently for her response. She clenches her jaw. "We accept your terms. Hopefully, with enough time, we can begin to trust each other, and there will be no need for those rules."

"I wouldn't count on it," the chief says, standing. "We'll be back in five days to escort you to our burrow. Be ready by then."

As the chief turns to leave, her army follows, disappearing into the windy forest. They aren't surrounded anymore, but Mary has never felt more trapped.

She's no longer Rostad's prisoner.

Now, they *all* are.

30

The Capaemen's World

Lillian

Darkness.

Lillian's been in nothing but darkness for five days. Or more? No, it must be five. Lionel has come in consistently each day: a few hours in the morning and then several in the evening. There was one night when he didn't even leave to sleep. Instead, he passed out face-down on the table. When that happened, Lillian came out of the cabinet and watched the night for a while. She was terrified he might wake up, but capaemen sleep like the dead.

Now, Lillian is in darkness again. She does sit-ups against the cabinet wall, wondering if she will ever see the outside. She has been trying to keep in shape, but it isn't easy with her legs so messed up. Nonetheless, Lillian doesn't stop. It would be helpful if this room had a torch. Then she wouldn't have to exercise in the dark. She never thought she would miss the burrow, but here she is, longing for its coziness. She misses the warmth of her family, but even if she could leave this place, there is no guarantee she'd return to them. In fact, the chances are almost zero. The hunter has destroyed their home by now, and whoever is left has fled. She hopes at least some made it out alive. Please, Mary at least...

creeaakkk

Suddenly, Lillian hears a chair being moved, followed by *boom*ing footsteps.

click.

Lionel has left the room again. He must have finished his morning work. Lillian stops her sit-ups. Now is her chance. He likely won't return until the evening, so she can leave the cabinet. She must continue to explore the giant room and find a way out. Her life depends on it.

Using the walking stick as support, Lillian hobbles to the cabinet door, pushing it open. At first, she cracks it and glances around. Shiny gadgets and trinkets are strewn about the tables. Next to them are clusters of giant tools. Lionel likes making things. As for what he's building, she hasn't the foggiest idea.

The warrior slips out the door, careful not to put too much pressure on her legs as she lands on the enormous table several feet below. The table shines silver in the sunlight. It blows Lillian's mind how almost everything in this room is made of metal or glass. Both materials are hard to get in the Giant Wilds, but the capaemen have them in abundance. She burns with jealousy. If Zurec could have even a fraction of these materials, they would be much better off.

Slowly, Lillian limps across the table, sweat beating down her forehead. It gets so hot around midday, with the sun shining directly through the glass ceiling. She squints at it. The bright-orange light nearly blinds her. How can Lionel stand this heat? How can he survive with no canopy? With hardly a tree in sight? Through the gridded glass panes, she can see sparse short trees in groves of grass. In the far distance, beyond the grass plains, is a forest of red trees. The trees are so tall they grow straight into the clouds. *That* must be the Giant Wilds. It's farther away than it looks, but it's there. Home is within sight.

Focus, Lillian, she thinks. *We need to find a way outside first.*

She scans the incredibly long table. It spans the entirety of the wall and, curiously, appears to be attached to it. Next to the cabinet is a massive metal structure that dips deep into the table. On the bottom is an open drain. Lillian isn't sure where it leads, but it reminds her of the toilets and bathtubs in Zurec's burrow, so she has started throwing all waste down that drain. She hopes the drain leads somewhere far underground, like Zurec's. If she is wrong about that, she's not sure she could justify her behavior to Lionel.

Besides the massive tub, the table has tools and gadgets as far as the eye can see. Maybe the glass wall has an opening? No. It seems solid as a rock. Lillian keeps moving forward. If anywhere would have an escape route, it would probably be one of the walls, but where?

The two cabinets above the sink are shorter, leaving some grey wall space open. In that space hangs a shiny disk with the numbers one through fourteen marked around its edge. Two black arrows, each roughly the size of Lillian's spear, protrude from its center. That isn't what she's looking for. Plus, the ticking sound it makes creeps her out, so she moves on.

Then she spots something in the upper righthand corner where the grey wall meets the glass one. There is a structure she doesn't recognize. She limps toward it.

It appears to be a rectangular metal plate attached to the wall, and as Lillian gets closer, she swears a draft is coming from it. Could that be wind from outside? She hobbles to the corner, staring up at the structure.

Yes, this contraption does indeed have openings in it, but they're too small: rows of narrow shutters spouting cool air. Not to mention it's about ten feet above Lillian. She couldn't reach it even if she jumped.

The warrior looks around. There's got to be something she can push in front of it for a boost. Even if she can't get out, the air coming from that spot on the wall would be relieving. She's already dripping with sweat.

Lillian scans the table and spots a box along the glass wall. It's only feet away from the cold air and doesn't seem too big. She makes her way to it.

But pushing the box is a lot harder than it looks. What is it filled with, rocks? No, it's probably more metal. Lillian heaves, and her legs scream in protest. She collapses on the table. She is getting nowhere.

boom boom

And in that moment, footsteps echo from the other side of the giant door.

"No no no, not now," Lillian says. She glances at the cabinet. It's on the other side of the room, way too far away for her to reach it in time. Where else can she hide?

The warrior dives behind the box. She's facing the glass wall, which makes her even hotter, but at least Lionel won't see her.

The door opens and closes with a massive *slam*. Lillian winces. The capaeman makes his way to his usual spot, which happens to be right next to her. Lillian stays frozen as a statue. There is nowhere else to hide.

"By the waters, Maeko," Lionel says, seemingly to himself. He collapses into his chair and slams something onto the table. The entire structure shakes.

Clearly angry for some reason, Lionel works on a new project. Lillian can't see what it is from here, but it must be huge, as usual. She can't get caught now. Who knows what he does when he's angry?

"Hey human, you awake?" he says loudly.

Lillian clasps her hands over her mouth. She can't answer that.

The capaeman makes a sound that can only be described as a scoff and then gets back to work. With each movement, the table shakes. Between that and the heat, Lillian wants to throw up, but she chokes it down. She is already halfway through her food supply, including that jam she made with the gatherers. She can't afford to lose her meal.

Lionel continues to work on whatever he's building. There's still much anger in his movements. "By the earth, where's the latch apparatus?" There is some rummaging. Lillian looks at the box she's leaning on. If what he's looking for is in there, she may be screwed.

As soon as she thinks that, the box moves, and she collapses onto the table. She jinxed it.

Glaring at her, box in hand, is Lionel.

⊱ ⊰

Lionel gasps. "What in the winds?" Lillian shuffles away, trying to put as much distance between them as possible, but soon hits the wall. There's nowhere else to go.

The capaeman sighs and puts the box down. "How the... How the stars did you get over here?" Lionel's presence is suffocating, especially this close. He stares at her, those slits for pupils dilating and contracting. His scales shimmer in the sunlight. Behind his lips she can see his razor-sharp teeth, and his voice makes the table vibrate. "Are you hurt anywhere? Let me—"

He reaches toward her and Lillian sees her life flash before her eyes. "Get away from me!" The capaeman freezes, his eyes widening. Then, slowly, he pulls his hand away.

Immediately, Lillian regrets saying that. She sounded so afraid. How could she show such weakness in the face of the enemy? Now, she will be at a disadvantage. She can't do anything right.

But Lionel doesn't have the reaction she expected. Instead of getting angry or questioning her, he picks up his chair and moves it to the other side of the room. Then, he sits back down.

"Is this an improvement?" He looks nervous. Why would *he* be scared? "I apologize for frightening you. You simply surprised me. That is all."

Now that she has some space, Lillian can breathe again. This capaeman... His actions make no sense. One moment, he says he doesn't care and that they're enemies. The next, he keeps his distance when she asks. Lillian stands, clinging to the walking stick for support. "What is your deal?"

"Pardon?" Lionel asks.

"One minute, you act like I'm dangerous. Then you try to help me. It doesn't make any sense."

He places a clawed hand on his chin. "You asked me to help you. Are you not grateful?"

"Then you say things like that! I'm sorry, but it's hard to feel grateful when I'm trapped here. Do I even get to leave? Do I even have a future anymore?" The capaeman pauses, his stare going blank. "Sure, I'm glad you saved me, but if this is the price, I can't pay it. I would rather be dead." It's a terrible thing to say, but it's true. She cannot take more hours alone in the dark. She must know if she is going to be okay.

Lionel grimaces.

Again, not what she was expecting.

"I have thought of taking you home, but to do that I would need to know the location of your hovel. Would you be willing to share such information with me?"

The color drains from Lillian's face. She remembers what happened when Lionel was close to the burrow. They evacuated immediately. He is a danger to all of them, so *knowing* where they live? Absolutely out of the question. "Are you kidding?"

"That is the reaction I predicted you would have. So, inform me, how am I supposed to free you if I do not know where to take you?"

"I can get there myself. Just drop me by the river. That isn't hard."

"Human, you can hardly walk. Do not expect me to believe such nonsense." Lillian stares down at her legs. The wrappings have held up nicely, but she can barely move without the stick Lionel gave her. She would be eaten alive in the Giant Wilds. She knows that, but...

She wishes it weren't true.

"If you have some other method to get home safely, I am open to it," Lionel says, "but I did not put so much effort into saving you just to let you run off and die."

"Why do you even care?"

He looks at the door, grimacing again. "I am not entirely sure. I am taking a huge risk helping you."

"How?" the warrior asks. As far as she can see, the only one at risk is her.

"That is... complicated."

That's no excuse. She can learn if given the chance. "Try me."

Lionel sighs. "I cannot fathom where you get this audacity. Very well. I shall humor you again. Humans and capaemen have a murky history, to say the least."

"Tell me something I don't know." Lillian pulls up an object. She is unsure what it is, but it's flat, so she sits on it. The heat is sweltering, and most annoyingly, Lionel seems completely unbothered by it.

"For generations, our two species have been at war. Humans all over the world have invaded, burned cities, slaughtered entire families. They are ruthless, savage, and spare no brutality. We only do what we must to defend ourselves. To keep our loved ones safe."

Lillian can't believe what she's hearing. In no way are *they* a threat to *them*. Maybe it's different outside the Wilds, but not here. "I don't know about the outside world, but *we* just want to live in peace. Why are the capaemen targeting us?"

"Really? You are completely free of fault? Please. All humans are a threat at one point or another."

"If you really believed that, you wouldn't have saved me," Lillian says.

The capaeman bares his fangs. "I remind you, I did that out of fascination, nothing more."

"I. Don't. Believe you," she says slowly.

Lionel stands, glaring at her. Lillian winces. She may have gone too far. "Do you want proof? I can show you. Every place in the world that is at war with humans. All the lives that have been affected." He heads out the door and slams it shut. Lillian gets chills. What in the Wilds just happened? Did she seriously challenge a capaeman again? Maybe Mary was right. She does crave death.

Shortly, Lionel returns, holding the most massive piece of paper Lillian has ever seen, although it looks different from Zurec's paper. This parchment has a glossy sheen to it. Lionel takes a seat and spreads it out so she can see it. Lillian's eyes widen.

It's a map. A gigantic map.

Is this... the world? She scans it, looking for anything she can recognize. Most of the words are meaningless, but one stands out to her.

"You see, this is called a map. It displays every country and territory on Copius, and important geographical features as well. If you look here—"

"Osinawa," Lillian says, pointing at a landmass that seems to be on its own.

"You..." Lionel says, shocked. "You can read?" For the first time in a while, she looks directly at the capaeman. Those dark-green eyes stare at her in disbelief.

Lillian can't help but feel a sense of pride. "Of course, I can read. We're not *savages* like you seem to think."

"How... is that possible?" The fact he is in such disbelief is insulting.

"We aren't dumb."

"Hmm, what does this say?" He points to the next closest piece of land to Osinawa, across the sea.

She squints. It's hard to see from here. "Ly-Lyonis."

"And here? To the right of Lyonis?"

"Zad-Zaddia?"

"And up here?" This time he points above Lyonis.

"Koenig." She has never heard of these places, but she can read them. Zurec has a few maps left, mostly of the Giant Wilds, but those maps have taught her enough. She somewhat understands what's on this parchment.

Lionel leans back in his chair. "Well, this is quite unexpected. What else could you possibly know?"

"Hey! I know a lot. I know how to forage for food, to cook, to hunt. I know how to find clean water even in a drought and the medicinal and practical uses of plants. It may come as a surprise, but I have a life, and living requires knowing things."

"Survival skills. Indeed that adds up, considering the environment you are from." He looks deep in thought.

Lillian grits her teeth. It's a little more than just "survival skills" that she knows, but she decides to let that go. This capaeman wouldn't understand.

She stares at the island of Osinawa. This map shows its location, but she can't tell its distance. It must be incredibly far, according to Jamie and Albert. Even so, she wants to know more about it. The siblings were very general when they told her, but maybe *he* won't be.

"Hey, so what about Osinawa? What's it like?" Lillian asks.

"Why do you wish to know that?"

"Just curious."

"Very well, then. We will begin with Osinawa."

As Lillian stares at the map, Lionel tells an incredibly detailed story about the land of Osinawa—how it is an island surrounded by a sea of monsters even the capaemen have trouble fighting. On the island, there are many towns of capaemen and lush forests called jungles. Apparently, the humans there are "vicious" and like to hide in these jungles to attack. Little does he realize Lillian knows whom he's talking about: the Osia Coalition. Jamie and Albert's original clan.

As Lionel explains, he marks places on the map that humans have attacked, and it's a lot of them. Lillian takes in every word, every detail. She feels like a fool for taking his word so seriously, but why would he lie? Plus, the map is right here, and he is being so specific about which areas have fighting and which don't.

"In conclusion, Osinawa is a harsh place to live. The locals have the choice of either living by jungles filled with vicious humans, or next to the inactive volcano, whose past eruptions have caused the area around it to be arid and nearly unlivable. The situation there is much worse than here, in Lyonis."

"That place?" Lillian asks, pointing at the piece named "Lyonis." "This is where we are?"

"Indeed. This town and the Crimson Forest are located approximately here."

Lillian stares at the spot at which Lionel is pointing. It's at the center of the piece of land, right next to its label. There is an area in green labeled "Crimson Forest," and outside it is another place labeled "Rouge Town."

"It's so small," the warrior says in disbelief.

The capaeman nods. "This world is much bigger than you know."

Lillian knows the world is big. Jamie and Albert told her so, but until this moment, she didn't imagine just *how* big. The Giant Wilds is but a tiny splotch on the map. Knowing this, her life feels insignificant.

Lionel rolls up the map. "So, do you now understand why I hesitate to trust you?"

The warrior raises her eyebrows. She nearly forgot about that. "No, not really."

The capaeman groans. It has a slight growl to it, like an animal about to attack. "Are you serious? Did you not listen to a single word I said?"

"I was listening. I still don't get it, though. You're so much stronger than us. You have no reason to be scared."

Lionel places his head in his hands. "You... are... *insufferable.*"

"Right back at you," Lillian retorts. He told her so much but failed to answer her most important questions.

"Hey..." Lionel says. "Your name, what is it?"

Lillian jumps. It is only now that she realizes she knows his name, but he doesn't know hers. "Why do you want to know?"

"You know mine. Is it not only fair?"

He is evading the question again. Still, she feels obligated to answer. "It's Lillian."

"Lillian? How strange. Sounds like my name."

Come to think of it, it does.

"Well, Lillian," Lionel continues. "You seem to be ignorant of just about everything. Allow me to help with that. I cannot take you to the Crimson Forest, but there are other places to see."

He takes a step closer and reaches out his hand. Lillian backs away.

Lionel's face falls, and he backs away again. "Another time, then." With that, he gathers a bunch of appliances in his arms and leaves the room. She has a feeling he won't be back for a while.

Alone again, she processes what happened. They just had a conversation as if they were not enemy species.

How is that possible?

Lillian stares out the glass wall at the setting sun in the distance. They talked for so long it's already evening. She and Mary used to have conversations like this—ones that would go on forever but felt like the blink of an eye. She misses her. She misses all of them.

Mary, please don't be dead. Even if Lillian can never make it back, even if it turns out she is trapped here forever, she hopes her best friend can lead a full life. That those who sacrificed themselves won't have done so in vain, and the rest of Zurec somehow find a way to escape. She wishes she could tell every one of them that she is sorry for everything, but she can't now. All she can do is stare out the window and long for what could have been.

That, and find out what Lionel is all about.

For the first time, the thought of him coming back through that door doesn't terrify her.

If by some miracle, he turns out to be a good person...

... then that will change *everything*.

31

Fresh Wounds

Mary

Five days after negotiations, a group of Rostad surveyors arrive at the bunker.

Steven leads them. Mary can't tell if he is annoyed or thankful for the job. Nonetheless, this group is much less intimidating than the last one—only about thirty strong and led by a teenager. Chief Vivian must be convinced that Zurec is not a threat. Painfully, she's right.

The Giant Wilds are much less windy today. The air is clean, and the sun streaming through the canopy is pleasantly warm. The mud from the rains has dried, and the forest is now as it was—as if the massacre and the river never happened.

Mary wishes it were that easy to forget. Then, she wouldn't have this ache in her chest.

Speaking of mourning, Seth is last to exit the bunker. He does not wear his chief sigil today, as if he's ashamed of it. What's left of the surveyors form their own group away from him. Brianna tries to comfort him, but he shoos her away, saying he would prefer to be alone. She drifts to the front of the gathering, greeting Rostad.

Steven scoffs at her. "This'd better not take too long. We want to get back before sundown."

Brianna crosses her arms. "How long will it take to get to your burrow?"

"Seven hours," Zane answers. He is a pleasant person to see again. He may be intimidating, but he is kinder than the others.

Brianna seems to recognize this, as she directs her next question at him. "Will you go over the rules again so we can follow them correctly?"

"Of course. When we get to the burrow, you will come in through the north entrance. We've already set up a barricade at the end of the hall. That's where ya ain't allowed to cross. You also can't enter or leave from any of the other entrances. There's three others, one for each cardinal direction. You're more than welcome to come and go from the north entrance. Joining outside events is also allowed, but only if the group lets ya. As far as food, it will be provided from the kitchen. You can gather your own food if ya want, but we have plenty. Any questions?"

Her eyes narrow, considering everything. Finally, she says, "No, that sounds... clear."

They may be going into a gilded cage, but it's a cage, nonetheless. Mary cannot fathom why they're being treated this way. All she can recall is something Chief Vivian said to her when they first met: *"Rostad remembers."* They keep implying there is something Zurec did, but there is nothing in her clan's history that justifies this treatment, unless...

Unless someone's been lying.

Mary's eyes drift across the clearing, searching for hints. Most of the members of Zurec seem resentful of the arrangement... or remorseful? Mary can't tell. Kayla carries her son in her arms and stares at the forest floor. Mia and Bruno briefly make eye contact with her, then immediately break her gaze. Meanwhile, the rogues and their acera slink near the back, keeping their distance from everyone else. They should be the life of the meeting, yet Jamie and Albert are isolated. There is something off about them. Mary sensed it ever since they found out about Lillian. Perhaps they care more about her death than they're letting on, or maybe they hate Rostad that much. Nonetheless, their behavior is a problem. It might cause conflict later.

Finally, Jamie tucks her hair behind her ear and speaks. "So, the trip will take seven hours?"

Zane and some others nod.

"Alright, my brother and I will head out then. We've got to do our jobs. We'll catch up with you later."

All too quickly, the siblings hop on Amphii and fly off. They seemed way too eager to leave. Mary glares at them as they disappear into the canopy. They could at least offer to follow them in case of danger.

"Alright, y'all!" Steven announces. "Everyone looks ready. Let's move out."

"Yes sir!" the surveyors shout.

The next few hours feel like days. Mary has made this journey once before, but in the tense, dead air, it feels like an eternity. The people of Rostad stick to the front, quietly talking to each other, and Zurec trails behind silently. Even the children are behaving, clearly terrified of their captors. Some cling to Miss May and Kayla, while others make their way over to Mary.

"Up," Trista says, raising her arms.

The future caretaker sighs. "Hop on."

The little girl climbs onto her back then falls straight to sleep. She must be exhausted.

As they traverse the forest, Mary's thoughts drift. The only thing she can think about is how this can go wrong. Only she has seen what Rostad's burrow is like—the hatred those people hold. All it takes is a few prejudiced people, and they're in big trouble. They are walking a tightrope, one so flimsy that it might just snap even if they tread right.

"Hey, are you doing alright?" a familiar voice asks.

Mary flinches. She wasn't expecting someone to talk to her, especially this person. "Seth?"

Lillian's father smirks. "The one and only."

"You look... better," she says awkwardly.

"Here, let me help you." He lifts the half-asleep Trista and lets her cling to his back instead.

Mary rolls out her shoulders. "What do you think... of all this?"

"I'm not sure how it's going to go, honestly," he says warily. "This is a shaky deal. I don't know what Brianna was thinking trying to be friends, but she did save us, which is better than what I could do."

"Do you think we'll fight again?"

"It's possible. We've... never gotten along in the past."

"Because they're unpredictable?"

"Yeah, exactly. That's the reason." He too avoids her gaze.

Mary raises an eyebrow. "What's on your mind?"

"Nothing. At least, nothing important."

They walk in silence.

Again, something feels off, but she can't place what.

When they finally arrive at the mushroom entrance, it does feel like a prison. The Rostad surveyors usher them inside, shutting the redwood doors on them.

Each room is bigger than the next, with those same stone walls. At first, the group is in awe, but when they reach the end of the hall, that amazement quickly dissipates.

All her family gets is one short hallway. Cutting them off from the rest of the burrow is a gate made of redwood and metal. There is a small handle on its left side that, if lifted, would open the gate, but no one dares to touch it. That handle is not meant for them.

Instead, the people of Zurec explore their new rooms.

The rooms are completely empty. They have more than enough space for everyone to sleep, yet there is nowhere to cook, craft, study, or even hang out. Brianna immediately designates one of the largest rooms as "the new mud room," but it isn't the same. It's isolated in a corner near the barricade, and there's no comfortable way to sit on the hard floors.

"Okay everyone," Brianna says, "this will take some getting used to, but let's start by picking rooms. Then we'll go out in groups and make new furniture for them." She clearly wasn't expecting them to have nothing.

Mary is surprised too. After all, Steven's friend had a room ready for her so quickly. They have no shortage of supplies. Maybe it isn't that they can't provide furniture, but that they don't want to. There was much debate behind Chief Vivian's decision. She can't even imagine how the people here reacted. Suddenly, Mary is grateful for the gate at the end of the hall. That may be the one thing keeping them safe.

creeaakkk

As she thinks of the barricade, it opens from the other side. Mary backs away, and so do the others. Entering their part of the burrow are Steven and his friends. In their arms are mats and blankets, which they promptly place against the walls. "Afternoon, Mary and Zurec," Zane says. "Sorry for the delay. Here's what ya get for now. We got more guys coming later with your meals."

It isn't much, but at least they will be able to sleep.

Mary meets Steven's eyes for a second, but he promptly looks away. She wonders if he feels guilty for how he treated her now that they've established somewhat of an alliance. Before she can study him further, his group drops the last of the supplies and immediately leaves, closing the gate behind them.

Their sentence begins.

Mary observes everyone, making sure they are alright. Brianna is already dividing up supplies and reassuring people. Many, including Mia, narrow their eyes at her. Carmen gives her a particularly nasty look before taking a room to herself. No one questions her. In a little over a week, she lost her sister *and* her husband. Robin and his husband Theo claim a room, grumbling in hushed tones as they exit the hall. All the while, the former leader of the gatherers pretends not to notice the searing stares. That must take a lot of strength.

Meanwhile, Kayla, William, and Mary's mother usher the children to a room where they will all sleep together. Kayla's husband has been sticking by her lately. The expecting pair are wary of this place. They glance back and forth between the entrance and the hall. Unlike the main parts of the burrow, there are no charming drawings on these walls. They are like a blank canvas waiting to be painted on.

Finally, Seth slinks to the back of the group, refusing to take supplies or chat with anyone. Eventually, Brianna makes her way over to him and forces him to take a bundle of blankets.

"Take them," Mary overhears her saying.

"Trust me, I can sleep anywhere. Just give me the floor, and I'll be fine."

"No, you need rest," Brianna urges. "You more than any of us."

There's an awkward pause.

"Please," she continues. "We need you."

"You have things taken care of," he says with a smirk. "Honestly, you should have taken the chief position when you had the chance. I've done nothing but screw up."

"No, Seth. You're just—" Brianna tries to respond, but it's too late. He has already claimed one of the rooms, closing the door behind him. She sighs. "At least he took the blankets."

"Don't worry," Mary says, approaching her. "He'll bounce back. He's just stubborn, like his daughter."

The redhead's face falls at the mention of Lillian, and immediately Mary realizes she has made a mistake. "I'm sorry," she says urgently.

"Don't be. The wounds are still fresh. That's all." The woman walks away without another word.

Mary silently chastises herself. Ever since the attack, she has been terrible at comforting anyone. Not only that, but because of her they are now at the mercy of an enemy who could turn on them at any moment. All she's tried to do is help, yet she keeps failing. She wonders what Lillian would do in this situation, but the mere thought of her former friend wracks her body with pain.

She's gone, Mary, the girl thinks. *She's gone, so stop thinking about her.*

Trying to find a distraction, she heads to the room where her mother and the others went. Maybe she could tell the children a story. She knocks on the door. Instead of letting her in, her mom slips out the door with a finger to her lips.

"Darling, you should be resting."

"You know me," she says with a smile. "I've got to make sure everyone is okay. So, let me in."

"No," she declares. "It's my turn to be the caretaker. Thank you for giving me a break, honey, but you need to mourn now. You... *We* have all suffered a grievous loss."

Tears well in Mary's eyes. "That's why I should help you! You aren't okay either. None of us are, so let's support each other."

Her mother places a hand on her daughter's face. "You've always been so wonderful and kind, but I'll be alright. I've suffered more loss than anyone. This is new to you. Take some time to be alone to process your feelings. The room next door is empty. You may have it to yourself."

The tears become uncontrollable, falling down Mary's cheeks. "No, I'm okay. I swear I'm fine, as long as I'm h-helping people."

Her mom gently wraps her arms around her. The crying devolves into sobs, and her mother helps her walk to her room, sets up the bed, and tucks her in just as she did when Mary was little.

The girl clings to her mother, not caring if it's childish.

Without being the caretaker, without Lillian, what does she even have anymore?

⁕⁕⁕

Mary wakes up in a daze. Her mother is no longer in the room with her, and her pillow is wet with tears.

She must have cried herself to sleep.

To her surprise, the bed isn't the only thing in the room anymore. She now has a desk, a bucket of water with more soap powder, and a mysterious sack sitting in the corner. She eagerly rummages through it, finding a hairbrush, toothbrush, and a change of clothes. There are even some labor-intensive items like a glass bottle of mouthwash (made from certain plants in the Giant Wilds) and cleaning tools made of bones. Lastly, Mary pulls out a weapon with a traditional Rostad curved blade.

She stares at the scimitar skeptically. There is no way they would give her a weapon, not with how wary Rostad has been of Zurec. On the end of the sheath, she spots a small note:

Before you throw this away, trust me, it isn't useless with you.
I think you'll like it if you give it a go.
– Steven

She smirks. Maybe he does feel bad after all. She places her new sword with the change of clothes, ready to try everything on.

Mary stares at her reflection in the water. Although the clothes are darker than she is used to, with that signature Rostad black, it isn't a bad outfit. She admires how the macabre style looks on her. The black contrasts her pale skin and light hair strikingly. To finish off the look, she fastens her hair into a ponytail. She then takes her dirty clothes and washes them in the bucket.

knock knock

Just then, someone arrives at the door. "Who is it?" she asks nervously. She hopes it isn't someone difficult to talk to, like Seth or Brianna. Her mood has finally improved.

"M-May I come in?" the voice of Trista asks meekly.

"O-Oh, of course!"

The little girl creeps into the room as if she isn't supposed to be here. She looks Mary up and down. "Aren't those Rostad clothes?"

"Yeah, but mine were dirty."

"I... see," she says, clearly uncomfortable.

Mary sits on her bed, patting the spot next to her. "What did you want to see me for?"

Trista stays standing. "Are you okay?"

"I'm fine," she says with a smile. "What about you?"

Finally, the little girl hobbles over, taking the spot next to her. "I don't like it here."

"Me neither," Mary says gloomily, "but what choice do we have?"

There is a pause between the two girls. Trista is clearly thinking about their situation, something Mary has tried to avoid as much as possible. She recalls what happened earlier. Maybe her mother is right; she can't evade this forever. "What's on your mind?"

Trista bites her lower lip. "A lot."

"You can talk to me," she reassures her. "What are you the most worried about? Let's start with that."

"It... It's the bad guys."

"You mean Rostad?"

"No, they're just mean. I mean the real bad guys."

"Oh..." she mumbles. Memories from the river flash through her head. She grits her teeth, trying not to get emotional around the kid.

Trista seems deep in thought until finally, she says, "Why are the birds here now?"

"Huh? What do you mean?" Jamie told them hunting animals are common with capaemen. *Especially with a hunter that knows what it's doing.* She shudders.

"They didn't have them before. Why now?"

Mary's eyes widen. "Wait, you mean when your burrow was attacked, there weren't any narecons?"

"It was already so horrible without them!" the little girl screams. "Why? Why is it worse? Why why why? They already..."

"Trista, calm down. It's okay."

She holds her head, her eyes squeezed shut. "They were... I was... I shouldn't be alive."

Mary gently hugs the distraught little girl. "We've been over this. You don't have to feel bad for surviving. Your family wouldn't want that."

"No! You don't understand. It was right there. We should have died!"

"What was there?" she asks fearfully. She has wanted to know how two Albian kids survived a capaeman attack for ages, but gave up a while ago.

"It... It..." The little girl trips over her speech as if she can't find the right words. "No no no! It makes no sense."

Growing impatient, Mary urges her. "Just explain it as best you can. What happened?"

"I..." Suddenly, she turns eerily calm. Her next words are full of hatred. "It didn't kill us... on *purpose.*"

Shivers run down Mary's spine. She can't believe what she's hearing. "Are you saying... that the hunter saw you and *spared* you?"

The little girl nods slowly.

Trista is right. That doesn't make any sense. The hunter slaughtered Albian mercilessly, yet kept she and Max alive? Capaemen have ruthlessly hunted humans without respite for years. There is no reason they would spare anyone, unless...

Mary has a chilling thought but doesn't want to say it in front of Trista.

"Hey, are you okay?" the little girl asks, grabbing her hand.

Mary throws her arms around her. "That must have been horrible. I'm so sorry. Don't worry, I won't ask about this anymore. If you feel comfortable sharing, tell me. Otherwise, you don't have to remember. You won't *ever* have to."

No wonder neither sibling shared this before. With Albian having been their enemy, some might have thought they were dangerous and not let them take shelter. She is sure at least Theo and Lance would have been skeptical. Others, like Elias and Carmen, would have turned accusatory, believing they were spies for the capaemen. Plus, the gossips of both the surveyors and gatherers would have asked invasive questions. Now that Mary has seen an attack for herself, she knows how horrible that would be. She doesn't want to recall those memories.

Trista hugs her back. "Thank you," she whispers. "Please don't tell anyone. Things are already bad."

Mary hesitates. Since the siblings joined them, Zurec has been in direct danger multiple times. The gatherers were attacked by a narecon on their way back from Albian's burrow. It could be a coincidence, but if what Trista says is true, it is more likely because of them somehow. She can't begin to comprehend how the capaemen used the children, but they must have in some way. If Mary were in their shoes, she wouldn't want anyone to know either. It is not their fault. They don't deserve to be punished for it. Finally, she nods in agreement.

The little girl breathes a sigh of relief. "I don't wanna talk about this anymore. How's my dolly doing?"

Mary snaps out of her thoughts. "You're... what?"

The little girl lets go. "You forgot, didn't you?"

Realization dawns, and the memory returns. "Oh... that." She doesn't know how to say she lost it in the river. She lost *everything* in the river.

"Remember, I want a warrior princess. When will it be done?"

"Uhhh..." she smiles guiltily. "Give me a few days." Mary will have to start over, but that's okay. She has a feeling that for the next few days, she will have a lot of free time.

32

The Fountain of Rouge Town

Lillian

The past several days have been confusing, to say the least. On the one hand, Lillian has learned so much. Back at the burrow, it felt like everyone was regurgitating the same boring information.

On the other hand, she has been trapped in the same place for almost two weeks. In that way, the burrow and this place are the same. She's stuck learning about the world but never seeing it—doing the same thing every day. Being told that the outside world is dangerous, she should stay and rot here. The only change is her captor.

The warrior stares at the rising moon through the glass ceiling. It isn't all bad. She can gaze at the moon and stars without care. When Lillian lived in the Giant Wilds, she rarely saw the blue moon. There were too many nocturnal monsters. Lillian envies the capaemen. They live in these massive houses and never have to worry about danger.

Lionel sits halfway across the room from her, tinkering away at another device. She's grown used to his presence. He is still terrifying, but Lillian can at least stand to be in the same room as him. He even brought a cloth for her to sit on while they talk. It protects her from the scorching metal table, which she appreciates.

Lionel is always so focused when he works. Whenever he tinkers with something, he doesn't speak to Lillian unless she says something first. At times, she is grateful for the silence. It gives her time to think.

But right now, she is restless. All she's been doing for the past several days is eating, sleeping, and talking to Lionel. She can hardly even exercise with her injuries. The boredom is killing her.

"Hey, what are you working on?" Lillian asks.

Lionel doesn't look at her. "My brother Maeko broke the mixer yet again. I am trying to salvage what is left."

"The... mixer?"

"Indeed. Do you see this big glass pitcher? It goes on top of the blades on this device, which are supposed to spin, turning any food into a drink in seconds."

Lillian's eyes widen. "Huh." They often used grains and nuts to make soup and mush in the burrow, but depending on the ingredients, the grinding could take what felt like hours to Lillian. To think that in mere seconds...

"It is quite nifty, that is for certain," the capaeman says nonchalantly. "We possess all sorts of devices that make our lives easier."

Lillian studies the machine. Maybe there's a way to replicate it, but much smaller? She can see how the pitcher and blades would work but has no idea how those blades could spin fast enough to turn food into liquid instantly. That is, until Lionel pushes something on the base of the device.

VROOMMMMMM

The sound is deafening.

Quickly, Lionel turns the machine off, but it's too late. Lillian's ears are already ringing.

"I apologize," the capaeman says. "On the bright side, it appears I have fixed it."

"How..." Lillian says, trying to talk through the ringing. "How do the blades spin *that* fast?"

"That is quite complicated, but I am sure you will make me explain anyway. To put it in simple terms, it runs on a source of energy called electricity. Electricity runs throughout the country, all over the continent actually, giving every device in the entire world the power to function. This mixer has something called a battery, so for a time it can run on stored power. That is how you saw it activate without it being plugged into a power source."

Lillian's jaw hangs open. She didn't get any of that.

The capaeman sighs. "We found a way to transform fire into a more concentrated form, and that fire is called electricity. It fuels almost everything in our homes. That's why there are lights in this room, and why these blades spin."

"Ohhhhh, why didn't you say so?" Lillian says. "That makes much more sense."

Lionel stares at the mixer, seeming lost in thought. He does this very often. They'll be talking, and then he suddenly stops and stares into space.

"Hey," he says, "are you not starving? I can bring you something to eat if you wish."

Lillian's stomach grumbles. She ran out of the snacks she was rationing this morning but didn't want to ask for any. Honestly, she's not sure she can trust capaeman food, but she may have no choice at this point. "What do you eat?"

"Hmm," he says. "Andremedon feet, dreosaur teeth, scavenger phii soup, fried aranids, thorns from a thornopine burrower, oh and let us not forget charred fish eyeballs. Those are a delicacy."

Lillian turns green. She'd rather starve to death.

The corners of Lionel's lips slowly curl upward; then he bursts out laughing. The sound fills the entire room.

"Wh-What? Why are you laughing?" She has never seen him smile before. Honestly, with the fangs, it's unnerving.

"You are so gullible! Did you seriously think we consume such things? We are not monsters. Well, fish eyeballs are okay when cooked a certain way, but I digress. Would you like a piece of fruit to start out with? That is simple enough that you should enjoy it."

Now she's feeling paranoid. "It's not poisoned, is it?"

Lionel raises an eyebrow. "By the earth, of course not. Do you truly think I would keep you here this long just to poison you? What would I gain from that?"

The warrior shrugs.

"I will return shortly," the capaeman says. He stretches, then slips out the door.

After a few minutes, Lionel comes back. "Ugh, Maeko is incredibly annoying."

"Your brother?" Lillian asks.

"Indeed. I am the only one who possesses a key to this room, but he is still quite nosy. I may need to spend less time here. He is growing suspicious."

The warrior freezes. Come to think of it, she has heard mysterious footsteps outside the door before, but she always assumed it was Lionel. To think there's another capaeman in this house only one wall away...

"Are you sure I'm safe here?" Lillian finds herself asking.

"Sure is a rather strong word," the capaeman responds. "It is not as if there are no ways to get in, but it would be very difficult. After all, this is my space. It is no doubt the safest place in the house."

That's the best answer she's going to get from him. At least he seems sincere. She wonders what would happen if his brother found out about her. She can hardly handle Lionel, but another capaeman? She can't imagine it. Still, Lillian is curious. Do capaeman families work the same way human ones do? Certainly not. Otherwise, there would be many more capaemen here.

"What's your brother like?" Lillian asks.

"Little. Irritating. Kind of like you."

"Hey!"

"Well, not quite as little as you, but just as dense. He has the audacity to ignorantly speak on matters about which he knows nothing, and no sense of boundaries. In that, you two are *certainly* similar."

Lillian gasps. "Wooowww, that's rich, coming from someone determined to teach me all about the capaeman's side of things but tunes out when I talk about humans. If you ask me, you're the dense one. A bit egotistical too. No, never mind, *a lot* egotistical."

Lionel scoffs. "Sounds like someone does not want to eat." He holds up the biggest fruit Lillian has ever seen.

Her mouth waters, but she crosses her arms and looks away. *Stand your ground, Lillian.*

The capaeman waves the fruit around. "This is called a mangroe. Sweet and fragrant on the outside, juicy and filling on the inside. Incredibly rich in vitamin D and potassium as well, not that you would know what those are. The point is, it will fill you right up."

Lillian doesn't move. She stands by what she says, even as her stomach grumbles.

Lionel sighs and moves toward the giant metal tub next to the cabinet. She wonders why. All that has is a drain. Does he plan on throwing the fruit away? That is such a waste of food. She shuffles toward the tub, her legs aching.

But instead of throwing the fruit down the drain, Lionel flips a switch at the top of the tub, and a miracle happens.

Water gushes out of a metal pipe sticking over the top of the tub, flowing as fast as the Crystal River.

Lillian feels her parched throat. She ran out of water recently, so this is like a treasure trove. "Wh-What's happening?" Her first thought is that there's a well connected to this device, but that doesn't add up. It'd have to feed directly into the river to flow that heavily.

Lionel runs the fruit under the water and stares at Lillian, dumbfounded. "Do you not have faucets either? I keep forgetting how primitive you are."

There's that word again. *Primitive.* "I can't tell if that's an observation or an insult," she responds, raising her eyebrows.

"Do you not know what primitive means after all?" Lionel looks at her expression and sighs. "It is not necessarily a derogatory word. It simply means a group of people whose technology is far behind what is standard. The majority of humans fall into that category."

She thinks about this for a moment. Sure, her clan has lost some technology over the years, but to be considered "primitive"? That's too far. "Yeah, that sounds insulting. Who decides what this 'standard' is anyway?"

"I uh..." He pauses as if not knowing how to answer. "Well, running water is a staple of an advanced society. That and electricity. Everyone knows that."

Unsatisfied with that answer, Lillian tries to form a rebuttal, but then Lionel flips the faucet switch, and the water stops.

Her heart sinks. "Um, hello?! That was water! Why did you stop it?"

"Umm, because I am finished washing the fruit. Why are you panicking?"

"You stopped the water!"

With a flick of his wrist, Lionel flips the switch again, and the water returns.

Lillian gasps. "It's back!" It's incredible how this thing works. It beats pulling up a bucket every time.

"Of course it is, stupid. Look, the supply is endless, so feel free to use this to wash up any time you want. Also, that drain leads to the sewers, so feel free to, well, uh, you can use this faucet for anything you need, okay?"

It takes her a moment to realize what Lionel means. When it clicks, Lillian nearly sighs in relief. She had already been using that tub for waste because it resembled the washroom back at home, but she had no idea it had water too. A device that pumps *endless* water. Incredible.

"I am begging you, when you can, use this to wash up. I can smell you from here." Lionel says.

Lillian turns bright red. He's got to be messing with her. She changed her shirt not long after she got here. There's no way she smells that bad. She sniffs her clothes and winces.

She *is* that bad.

That's so embarrassing. Now, she wants to crawl into the cabinet and never come out.

"I'm, uh, sorry about that," Lillian says awkwardly.

Lionel laughs and hands her a piece of fruit. "Here, is this enough for you?"

Grateful for the change of subject, Lillian takes the slice. It's more than enough. There's no way she could eat all of this in one sitting. She sits on her cloth on the table, staring at it.

The skin of the fruit is yellow, while the inside is orange. She has never had this big of a meal, well, *ever*. Zurec always rations their food, so no one gets more than they can spare. Looking at this fruit, the warrior thinks of all the ways she could store it. The empty fruit jar in her bag would certainly be helpful.

But she doesn't *have* to do that.

There must be so much more food where this came from—an endless amount she could never eat in her entire lifetime. Just like the water from the faucet and just like that fire Lionel calls electricity.

She takes a bite of the fruit. Delicious. Of course, it is.

If her people could have even a fraction of this food, they wouldn't have starved to death during the rains. They wouldn't be in such dire straits. Lillian watches Lionel sit back in his chair, eating the rest of the fruit. He does it without a care in the world—for him, there's plenty more where that came from. If Lionel wanted to, he could save so many lives, so why doesn't he?

This world... It doesn't make any sense.

They eat in silence for a few minutes, watching the blue moon. She is still baffled that it is so common to see the moon here. The capaeman world is so different than her own. Lillian puts down the fruit. For the first time, she's full, and she didn't even finish it.

Lionel has finished his meal as well. "Hey, it is late, but would you like to go somewhere? You are surely sick of being cooped up here." Again, with that offer. The capaeman boy has offered to take her somewhere multiple times now. The problem is Lillian won't let him touch her. She's already vulnerable just being near him. Letting him pick her up would be way too risky.

"I see you are still hesitant," Lionel says. "If I wanted to hurt you, I would have done it already. Why can you not trust me?"

Lillian grimaces. She can think of a million reasons. "Don't say that. Do you have any idea what you look like to me?"

The capaeman stares at his hands as if realizing how big he is. Then, wordlessly, he leaves the room. Did she scare him off? For someone so cocky, he sure does scare easily. Every time she says something serious, he leaves the room. Makes it hard to learn anything useful.

But to Lillian's surprise, Lionel returns only seconds later, holding a giant sack. He places it on the table several feet away from Lillian and then backs away. "I have concocted a plan," the capaeman says. "You get in the backpack, then I can pick it up and take you somewhere. This way, we do not have to make contact. You have no reason to be scared. Just get in the bag, and I will take care of the rest."

Lillian raises an eyebrow. Does he have any idea how suspicious that sounds?

Lionel places a hand on his forehead. "Okay, that sounded strange. I promise I am not trying to kidnap you or anything. Maybe this was a bad idea."

Now it's her turn to burst out laughing.

"W-Why are you laughing?" Lionel asks, dumbfounded.

"Watching you fumble around like this," Lillian says, still laughing. "It's hilarious. I didn't know capaemen could get nervous."

He looks appalled. "Excuse me? I don't know what you're on about. Look, I am doing you a favor. You're growing restless being stuck in this room. When we leave, try not to make any noise. I'm going out of my way to help you here. Do not inconvenience me."

"Riiiggghhtt," she teases. "Like *I* could hamper *you*."

Lionel crosses his arms. "Do you wish to leave or not?"

"I'll get in. Just give me a minute."

Lillian limps toward the bag, her heart pounding. She cannot believe she's doing this, but her need for fresh air well exceeds her fear. Besides, Lionel does have a point. If he wanted to hurt her, he would have done it already. It's going to be okay. She just needs to get in the sack.

Yeah, that sounds weird.

Still, she opens the drawstring and crawls in. For a moment, all she hears is silence, and all she sees is brown fabric. The inside of the bag smells like twine.

Then her body jolts upward, and she shoots high in the air.

There's no going back now.

⚜

It feels like forever before they reach their destination. Riding in the bag is so much worse than being on an acera. With each step, Lillian's body bounces into the air. It takes everything she has not to vomit.

Then, finally, Lionel places the bag on solid ground.

"We have arrived. You may come out." Lillian forces the sack open and tumbles outside. Never has she been so grateful to feel solid ground.

"You appear to be sick," Lionel says.

She glares at him. "You don't say."

Lillian is grateful he's keeping his distance. He sits on a bench well enough away from her, allowing her to catch her breath. She can see her hands, blurry and spread out. The surface underneath them appears to be made of some kind of stone, and she can hear running water. The *WHOOOSSHH* is so loud Lillian can hardly think straight.

"Do not worry," Lionel says. "People rarely come around here at night. You are free to look around. On the off chance someone does show up, I will make sure they do not see you."

Finally, the warrior manages to catch her breath enough to take in the scenery, and it is breathtaking.

She is on a raised platform made of stone. The stone arches all the way around in a massive circle, and in the center is an endless amount of water. It flows up in a spout and crashes into a lake down below. The water is so clear she can see the bottom, and just like the Crystal River, stones of every color in the rainbow glisten down there. It almost feels like home.

"This is called a fountain," Lionel says. "It too has endless water, but it is more for decoration than drinking."

Lillian is too occupied to respond. Being careful not to aggravate her injuries, she crawls to the water and cups it in her hands.

But the taste isn't what she expects.

It burns her throat, and the shock from the pain makes her body keel over, plunging into the water.

Lillian tries to move her legs, but they are too weak to swim. She tries to open her eyes, but the strange water sears into them like a thousand needles. She's sinking quickly and she can hardly keep her eyes open. Why is this water poisonous? Why would Lionel take her to such a terrible place?

Just as she begins to wonder if he is trying to kill her, something warm envelops her, and she shoots right back out of the water.

Lillian coughs violently, trying to regain her vision.

"You buffoon!" Lionel scolds. "Do not jump in the water. It's chlorinated."

The warrior massages her throat, trying to make the pain go away. As her vision clears, she notices she's not touching the ground. She rubs her eyes and realizes she is surrounded by brown scales. They are warm, even in the cool night breeze, but all she feels is fear.

"P-Put me down!"

"Oh! I apologize," Lionel says as if realizing it now.

Gently, the capaeman places her back on the stone wall of the fountain. "Are you... alright?"

Lillian coughs. "Yeah, no thanks to you."

"Hey, I saved you. Can you not show a tiny bit of gratitude?"

She can't be grateful if he didn't even warn her about the water in the first place. That's pretty backward. Still, when Lionel picked her up it didn't feel the way she thought it would. So, it *was* real. When Lionel rescued her, shielded her from the rain, and stopped her bleeding, his hands were warm then too. It is incredible how someone so giant can be so gentle.

Finally, Lillian's voice begins to clear. "Why didn't you tell me the water was poisoned?"

"I didn't think you would be ignorant enough to jump in. On the bright side, chlorine is quite cleansing. You should be clean now."

"How is poison cleansing?" Lillian asks. "You have a funny way of looking at things."

"It's not poison. It is simply chlorine. Chlorine is a substance mixed into water not meant for drinking. It keeps it clean and free of pests."

"Is it some kind of soap?"

"I'm surprised you know what that is, and no, not exactly. Although it does contain similar cleansing properties."

She is too tired to understand. All Lillian needs to know is that he wasn't trying to kill her. At least not for now. That's good enough for her.

The warrior scans her surroundings a little more. There are benches all around this fountain. Flattened pieces of stone are cemented into the ground, making a path toward the trees. Like the Giant Wilds, these trees are hundreds of feet tall and a blazing crimson. Lillian almost believes she is home.

Yes, this place does look like home if not for the silhouettes of glass houses in the distance. To think, each of those shadows houses at least one capaeman. Terrifying, how many there are.

"May I... ask you something?" Lionel says. His face has grown grim.

"Sure," Lillian says cautiously.

"Please tell me... how are *you* supposed to be a threat?"

The warrior sighs. She should have known it would be an insult. "Rude, but what do you mean?"

"We have been at war with humans for generations, yet I cannot fathom why. You are so weak and ignorant. I mean, I had to fish you out of the fountain just now. Yet, there are people afraid of your species. I cannot comprehend it."

"I can't either," Lillian says dolefully. It is awful to admit, but it's true. "My people have been peaceful for generations, yet the capaemen are attacking. It doesn't make any sense. I can't speak to those in Osinawa or wherever, but here, we aren't a threat to you. We just want to live in peace."

Lionel's eyes widen. For once, there is understanding in them. "Is that really true?"

She nods. "Why would I lie to you?"

The capaeman hangs his head. "I'm... not sure what to believe anymore."

Lillian cannot believe what she's hearing. Lionel has no idea some humans are peaceful. Does that mean he really doesn't know? He doesn't know how much people suffer because of the capaemen?

How is that even possible? They aren't isolated like Zurec. They have access to everything they could ever want. There is no way they couldn't know what they're doing, but Lionel is acting like this is news to him. She is reminded of the stories Miss May used to tell her—how capaeman are evil, and there is nothing more to them. She also remembers Jamie and Albert's warnings—how they always have ill intent no matter what. Looking at Lionel, she knows that can't be true. He's not harming or manipulating her. Perhaps, this whole time, he has been conflicted inside too. Some way, somehow, there has been a huge misunderstanding. They both think the other is evil, but it isn't that clear-cut.

At a fountain in the middle of a giant's town, a human and a capaeman begin to realize that the world is not what it seems.

And the revelation is crushing.

Because if capaemen aren't evil, then why are they doing this?

33

Collapse

Mary

It has been a week.

An entire week since they moved in with Rostad, and all Mary has done is work on Trista's gift and read. Steven has been sneaking in books for her, along with clothes, jewelry, and even a new set of armor. She doesn't need most of this stuff, yet he keeps sending it anyway. She is beginning to wonder if he has a crush on her. *Come on,* Mary thinks, *him liking me? Ridiculous. We're from rival clans.* She opens the latest gift, which contains books and a handwritten note, as usual. The message reads:

> *Last batch for a while. A rather large group of people is against*
> *us helping y'all. We've been dealing with that. Hope to visit soon.*
> *— Steven*

She never fails to crack a smile. Although she's seen him a total of zero times this week, the gifts and notes have been entertaining. She takes the books out of the bag and scans the titles. One seems like a basic biology book: *Trees of the Giant Wilds.* Another is for crafting: *The Many Uses of Glass.* These are cool and all, but it's the final one that catches her eye. The cover is an illustration of people pointing their spears into the air. Above them is a second group of people on... aceras? This must be a fictional book. However, it is titled *History of the Giant Wilds.*

Mary immediately reads the back cover. She's never seen a history book that wasn't written by Kayla. She scans the synopsis, spotting familiar stories such as the clan Lillian's mother left with and the beginning of the famine. Halfway through the passage, she stops on one line: *Read the true story of how the clans came to be and how Zurec and Albian betrayed Rostad, destroying the Ancestral Alliance.*

Mary's jaw drops to the floor. This cannot be real. They must have made this up, yet she opens the book. Skimming the pages, at first the story is familiar. It more or less aligns with what her mother taught her: *Long ago, the Zurec people immigrated to the Giant Wilds. They wanted to escape the capaemen once and for all and live a life of peace.* However, instead of continuing with the story of peace, it takes a turn.

> *YEAR FORTY-ONE: THE SPLIT*
> *For the first forty years in the Giant Wilds, Zurec was one large clan, but given time and differences in opinion, it crumbled. Year Forty-One was The Split. Several groups left Zurec and became clans in their own right. They fought frequently. Some died out, others persevered. The most powerful amongst them by far was Zurec, the original. They had a strong drive to reunite the fragmented groups—to become the one Zurec people once again.*

Mary flips through the pages, reading the events that follow with more fervor than she has read anything ever before. *The Split marked the beginning of the Freedom Wars. Some allied with Zurec. Others opposed them...* She jumps ahead, skimming. Year Forty-Four: the end of the Freedom Wars, Zurec's defeat...Years Forty-Five to Seventy-Five: a time of shaky peace, the Lillian Era—

She freezes on the name of her former best friend.

> *Chief Lillian of Zurec did not believe that the disparate clans should be reunified. Instead, she worked with the four other clans of the Giant Wilds, now dubbed Rostad, Albian, Nurem, and Civare. They established territories and ushered in an era of relative harmony. This lasted for thirty years.*
> *That is until she retired and named her son, Darrel, the new chief.*

Mary struggles to breathe. This is so detailed, and now there's a chief named Lillian? The adults would have told them about this. Yeah, this isn't real. If it were, Lillian would have had a great-grandmother she didn't even know about, one she was clearly *named* after.

No, this is just fiction. A lie, she thinks as she keeps reading.

YEAR SEVENTY-SIX: THE NEW ARRIVALS
Around the time Zurec changed leadership, new people came to the Giant Wilds. They had technology beyond anyone's wildest dreams and rode aceras. Previously, aceras were believed to be a myth, but Silver dissolved that idea. Everyone was curious about them.
Everyone... except for Zurec.
Silver had come to the Giant Wilds for one purpose and one alone: to slay the capaemen of the neighboring town. This went against the very reason everyone's ancestors migrated to the Wilds in the first place. So, Chief Darrel protested against the operation. Chiefs Vivian of Rostad and Camille of Albian agreed with him and urged the people of Silver to back down. What was at first a civil debate quickly devolved into fighting, as neither side was willing to compromise their principles. One year later, Darrel had had enough and did something drastic.

YEAR SEVENTY-SEVEN: THE RIVER WAR
Unknown to their allies, the Zurec people snuck into Silver's territory on the east side of the river. They slayed their aceras in the dead of night—

knock knock!
A rap on the door makes Mary jump in her seat. Then, without warning, it opens. She slams the book shut and shoves it under her mattress. At the same time, her mother slips through the door.

Mary stares at her mother, unable to hide the alarm in her expression. She didn't see that, did she?

Miss May raises an eyebrow. "Are you alright, dear?"

"Y-Yes! I'm fine," her daughter says, forcing a smile.

Usually, her mother would press the issue, but she seems distracted. "There's a protest happening at the gate. Everyone's heading outside to escape. Come on, we've got to go."

"Why are they protesting?" she asks. "Did we do something wrong?"

"Well, uh... You know what, you should see for yourself." Her mother leads her into the hall. The second Mary sees the barricade, her heart drops.

On the other side of the gate is Alec. A crowd of people surround him, and they look furious. Some hit their scimitars into the walls, making a rhythmic *clank*ing sound. "Come on in, Zurec! I dare ya," the scrawny man says, clenching his fists around the bars of the gate.

"We can't," Brianna says calmly. "That would break our agreement."

"Those acera warriors have been useless. They've found nothing. That means you've got no right to be here. We oughta break down this gate."

"Yeah!" some agree.

"Traitors!"

"Tear it down!"

The *clank*ing grows louder.

"Under whose authority are you here?" Brianna asks, getting close to the barricade. "Did Chief Vivian tell you to do this?"

"She's a coward. Gone too soft to do what needs to be done," Alec snarls. The others readily agree. Some start pushing on the gate. Brianna, Bruno, and Theo push back, holding it steady. Meanwhile, Seth, Kayla, and the former surveyors encourage the children to flee, ushering them toward the exit. At this rate, the gate is going to collapse. Mary can't even imagine the horror that would ensue if that happened. She thinks of moving closer to mediate the situation but stops herself. The last thing they need is her making things worse. These people look ready to kill them. Why? Does the strange book have an answer?

No, she thinks, *it isn't true. It can't be.* First of all, Zurec was brutal in that story—nothing like the peace-loving adults she knows. Secondly, *if* the book were true, that would mean her family lied to her about most of their history. They wouldn't do that, would they?

"Now, what's all this commotion?" a familiar voice echoes over the chaos. Shoving his way to the front of the mob is Steven. He is fully clad in his Rostad armor, as if ready to go somewhere. "Did Vivian order this?"

"No, but—"

He interrupts Alec before he can continue. "Then you ain't got the authority to be here. Step back."

Zane is close behind, his arms crossed and a frown etched on his face. "How long has this been going on?"

"About an hour," Brianna answers. "They've been blocking supplies from being delivered."

"A shame." Zane turns to the mob. "Y'all are getting on our nerves. Another incident like this, and there will be punishment."

"Punishment? For us? Are ya kidding me? You're the ones who let Zurec in our midst. Our people are restless, and it's all been for naught. Those acera foreigners are completely worthless!"

"We get your complaints," Steven answers, his face inches from Alec's. "The acera warriors are outside. We were about to talk to them, but we won't get nothing done if y'all keep terrorizing the Zurec people." In the presence of an authority figure, the cowardly blonde slinks back like a phypent, the others reluctantly following suit. Mary has a feeling that's not the last they'll see of him, but they have bigger things to worry about.

Steven and Zane open the gate and enter Zurec's hallway. The people back away, all except Mary, who waves. The boy pretends not to notice her, addressing the whole group instead. "Let's head outside now. We can't leave them waiting too long."

With fungi growing on roots and towering high above them, this doesn't feel like the Giant Wilds. They're in a foreign forest, to which they may never be welcome. Standing under the roof of a massive brown mushroom are the acera warriors, Seth, and the former Zurec surveyors. Kayla and Robin comfort the children, who are crying about the mob. The rest of Zurec joins them. This time, it is the two Rostad people who stick out. Still, they stand proud and firm, staring up at the rogues.

"The situation has been dealt with for now, but it won't last. Are ya sure you have no new updates?" Steven asks. He is clearly frustrated.

"I'm sorry, but we don't," Jamie says through gritted teeth. She and her brother are still seated on Amphii, ready to take off any minute. The acera looks around nervously under the roof of the mushroom. These two haven't even been sleeping in the burrow, which has no doubt fanned the flames of their situation. Mary's beginning to wonder why they joined their clan in the first place if all they plan to do is spend time away from them.

"Come on," Steven says impatiently, "you've got to have *something*."

"I don't," the woman confirms. "Why are you so insistent, boy? We agreed to this ridiculous deal. The least you can do is show a tiny bit of respect."

"*Respect?* All you've been is arrogant and rude. I will not show respect to *you*."

"Why you—" she starts. The acera growls with her.

Then, Zane steps between them. "We're off topic. Look, Jamie, Albert, the burrow situation is dire. People want answers. After all, that's why we agreed to house Zurec in the first place. If ya can't deliver, then we can't placate the problem, and your friends will be in danger."

A light breeze blows through the following silence. What's left of Zurec stands frozen in place. It's evident from their petrified faces that they all fear for their lives.

Jamie grips the reigns of her acera, grinding her teeth. Then, slowly, she speaks. "Fine, I'll tell you this. We haven't seen anything. There was a lot of activity in the forest before the attack on Zurec, but now, nothing. That can only mean two things. One: the hunters are taking a break. They do this from time to time, but trust me when I say they will come back. They always do."

"And the second option?" Steven asks, clearly concerned.

She takes a deep breath. "This is the worst-case scenario, but the second possibility is they're planning something big. If they already know how large Rostad is, they could take us all out in one fell swoop."

"What? How is that possible?"

"Trust me, they are *more* than capable of it."

Another pause. Steven stares at the forest floor, defeated. "This... does not bode well."

"If it makes you feel better," Jamie says, "I think it's more likely the first option." She doesn't meet his eyes when she says that.

"Good," he responds, not noticing. "I can work with this for now. I'll report that the hunters are on break, but you'd better get us something solid soon, or your friends will pay the price."

The siblings nod grimly. Albert hasn't said a word. Come to think of it, he hasn't spoken to anyone all week. All he does is hide behind his hair and his boisterous sister. He was full of life when Lillian was still around. Was she that important to them?

And her family? Will they ever recover?

Mary knows the answer to that, and she hates it. Ever since her best friend left and they lost half the adults, the atmosphere of Zurec has been bleak. She observes Seth as he converses with who's left of the surveyors. They all have grim looks on their faces and speak in low voices, glancing around as they do so. Whatever they are talking about, they don't want anyone else to hear. It didn't used to be like this. Before, everyone was open. They had hope and optimism.

But is that even true? Mary wavers. Moments from her underground upbringing flash through her mind: fervent whispers in shadowy corners, the dodged questions about their past. Her family's sorrow may be deep and fresh, but that caginess is old news. Although, one can't blame others for how they cope with trauma, right?

Why would Steven give her that book if it were fake? He wouldn't lie to her. Then again, neither would her family. Mary clasps her hands over her head. What would Lillian do? She was always great under pressure.

Lillian would march over to the dismayed adults and confront them. She wouldn't bother deliberating over whether the book is fake, not with a way to know for sure right in front of her.

Jamie and Albert leave again, flying past the tall mushroom caps and disappearing into the canopy. They will take any excuse not to be here, all because their flying buddy is dead. Mary understands that they miss Lillian, but at the same time they have a job to do. They don't even seem to be trying. No one in Zurec is. They're just going through the motions.

Mary should have been the one to take the brunt of those rocks. Look at what's happened to everyone because *she* survived instead of Lillian. She doesn't even have the courage to find out the truth about that book. She wishes she could go back in time and sacrifice herself instead, but she can't. All she can do is continue to be useless.

Steven glares at the break in the canopy through which the scouts disappeared, then quickly turns back toward the burrow entrance. Mary follows, fists clenched. Everything's so screwed up, and she doesn't know how to fix it.

However, watching Steven trudge ahead of her with both rage and purpose, she hatches an idea.

If she asks *him* about the book, what will he say?

⊱ ⊰

Chief Vivian is already in the hall. She stands just inside the gate, leaning against the wall. It's wide open, but only she is here. The crowd that was here before has disappeared, likely because of her arrival. "Hey, you'd better have something for us."

"We do," Brianna says. She is the spokesperson for the clan these days.

"Good, because I can't hold them back much longer. In a way, they do got a point. You've got to deliver on your end of the deal."

The redhead takes a deep breath. "The reason why you haven't received news is because there isn't much to tell. There've been no capaemen sightings.

297

Sometimes, hunters take breaks. This is a good time for us to stock up on resources and plan for when they return."

The chief huffs, the sound echoing down the hall. "Are ya kidding me? How is *that* all they've got?"

"Another possibility is that they're planning something," Steven blurts. He's not as dull as he looks. He must have noticed Jamie's lack of eye contact when she said that option was less likely. "They may know we're here and that we're a big population. If they've figured that out, then they're planning something big. That's why the acera warriors haven't spotted anything the past week."

Chief Vivian raises an eyebrow. "Really now? Well, that doesn't bode well for us."

"No, it doesn't."

The people of Zurec wait nervously for the Rostad chief's final verdict. She crosses her arms and rests her head on the wall. Even faced with news as grim as this, her expression is the same.

Finally, after several agonizing seconds, she speaks. "I'll tell them the hunters are on break, but the break won't last long. I'll let them know we've got to stock up on food and other necessities, so we can be prepared for when they next strike. That should placate them for now. Oh, and Steven?"

"Sir?" the boy asks obediently.

"Get a squad together tomorrow and grab as much food as you can get ahold of. You know where."

"You can count on me."

The chief nods and heads back to Rostad's side of the hall, closing the gate behind her. Mary wonders what she meant when she told Steven, *"You know where."* There is so much she doesn't understand. Could it have something to do with how Rostad survived the famine? She hasn't read that part of the book yet—*if* the book is true.

Zurec and Albian betrayed Rostad...

That's what the back cover read. When does that take place? What happens to Silver after their aceras are slain? She *must* know, even if it is fiction.

"Hey, what's wrong?" Steven asks. He is standing right next to her, and the nearest people are Robin and Theo. The couple stands at the end of the hall, having a private conversation.

No one is listening right now.

"I... don't know," Mary says, gritting her teeth. "I'm so confused. Why did you send me that book?"

"Ya needed to know the truth. Why else?"

Mary's eyes widen. "That can't be right. Zurec is peaceful. We always have been, and all those events, all those clans... The history I learned wasn't that complicated. For most of it, nothing happened. Not until recently."

Steven crosses his arms. "Are those seriously the lies you were fed? Geez, ya think they'd come up with something better than that. Did you really believe we had almost one hundred years of history with hardly anything happening? Hate to break it to ya, but that ain't how people work. They fight over territory, resources, and especially beliefs. *Your* kin, they were the worst of them."

"No!" she shouts. Robin and Theo eye her but then go back to their conversation. "That doesn't make any sense. My people are kind and good. All we've ever cared about is survival, and any conflict we've had we tried to negotiate peacefully."

The Rostad boy frowns and glares at the Zurec members at the end of the hall. "I'm sorry, but that just isn't true. I don't know why they lied to ya, but they did, and they still are now. Have ya read about the famine yet?"

She shakes her head.

"Do it now. Once you do, it'll all come together."

The girl clenches her fists. What was she expecting when she asked Steven? That he would tell her it was all a joke? He believes everything depicted in that book, but that doesn't mean she should. "Why should I trust your word? If history can be faked, then what if your book is exaggerated, or the writers made up things?"

Steven's eyes light up. "How *dare* you! My people are not liars. Yours are. You're just too stubborn to see it. Open your eyes, Mary. Deep down, you know something's been off. We've got to hate each other for a reason, right?"

"Shut up!" Mary screeches. She storms up the hall, not wanting to believe a word, even as her heart sinks. As she nears her room, she realizes her door is open.

Who has entered her bedroom?

Mary rounds the corner to find her bed in disarray. The spot where she'd hidden the book is completely exposed, and perched on the edge of her mattress is her mother. Most horrifyingly, *History of the Giant Wilds* is in her hands.

"Mary... what is *this*?"

She must have seen her hide it after all. "Mom, I—"

She shoots up from her seat. "*Who* gave this to you?"

"It was me," Steven intervenes, appearing in the doorway. "She deserves to know."

"That is not for *you* to decide!" she shouts.

"Then whose decision is it? Yours? Some good that's done."

"Be quiet, both of you!" Mary screams, shutting her eyes tight. "I don't know what to believe anymore. All I know is something has been off, but I still trust my people. I don't believe you'd lie about something so important. So, please tell me, Mom, that book is false, right?"

The caretaker's wrinkled hands clench so tightly around the book they turn bone white. "Yes. It's made up. Now, tell that boy to get out of here."

Mary meets Steven's eyes and is surprised to see his expression is pleading. She looks between them, desperately wanting to believe her mother, but Steven may be right. She knows her mother, and she wouldn't act this way if she had nothing to hide. Plus, if nothing happened between the clans in almost a hundred years, the events of the past several days, especially today, make no sense. "Okay, Mom, I will let this go, but only if you answer one simple question."

The caretaker frowns. "Why do I have to do that?"

She takes a deep breath. "If the book isn't true, why are you so worried about me reading it?"

Her mom's mouth hangs wide open.

"It is real. So, you erased our history? Why?"

She does not answer.

"Mom, what really happened during the famine?"

The caretaker's face turns red with rage. "It doesn't matter. We've moved on."

"Really, and do you think Rostad feels the same about that? I mean, they've been so *friendly*, haven't they?"

"Don't you dare use that tone with me, young lady!" she snaps. "You were only a baby back then. You would never understand!" Tears well in Mary's eyes. Do they see her that way? Too naïve to handle reality? "Baby, I'm sorry. I didn't mean—"

Before she can continue, her daughter sprints out of the room. Mary's entire body feels on fire, blazing in an inferno yet simultaneously withering away. She is infuriated, yet deeply heartbroken. Even in the wake of all this tragedy, they see her as a child in need of coddling. Sure, Mary isn't as valuable as most people in her community, but she doesn't deserve this. She... She *and Lillian* have been lied to.

Mary stomps down the hall, ignores Robin and Theo as they ask where she's going, throws open the trapdoor, and *SLAMS* it behind her. She collapses onto a mushroom cap, bringing her knees to her chest. Everything that could go wrong has gone wrong, and it doesn't look like it will stop any time soon. She feels like her mind is crumbling.

creeaakkk

Unsurprisingly, the door opens again and she hears one person's footsteps approaching her. *Great*, she thinks, *she's come to scold me.* Mary braces herself.

"Hey," the voice of Steven says.

The girl wheels around to find the boy has taken a seat next to her. "What? Why are you here?"

"Well, ya did run off. Someone had to find you, and your mother seemed... preoccupied."

Tears pool in her eyes. She doesn't want anyone to see her like this, much less *him*. "I thought you were mad at me. Just go away. I'm fine."

"I was a little, but after seeing that fight, I get it. You trusted them. After all, they did raise ya. Can't blame you for snapping at me like you did."

"Why have you done this?" she cries. "Why do you even care? Why the gifts? Why talk to me at all?"

"Woahhh," he responds calmly. "Slow it down. I can only answer one at a time. Are ya saying you didn't like my gifts?"

"No—I don't know. Why were you so eager for me to know the truth?"

"They had no right to do that to you," Steven says. "Ya know that, right?"

She grits her teeth. "I don't know. I don't know their reasons. I'm not sure of anything anymore."

Evening is settling in over the Giant Wilds. The sun sinks slowly behind the giant leaves, and birds fly through the brambles, making their way back to their nests. Mary wishes she had a home to return to, but that too has been taken away. Unable to hold them back anymore, the tears stream down her face. She buries her head in her knees.

"Woah," Steven says. "That bad, huh? Then again, I can't blame ya."

"It's all so wrong," she mumbles through her sobs.

"What was that?"

"This... this is wrong. How could... how could things go so horribly in such little time?" There is no response. "I can't take this anymore," Mary sobs. "Not the lies or the deaths. I want things to go back to the way they were. How do I go back? How?"

A long pause.

Then, an arm wraps around her back. "You can't."

The girl raises her head, the mushroom-filled forest settling into view. There are more fungi than moss here, which she still hasn't grown accustomed to. She leans her head on Steven's shoulder. Right now, she doesn't care that they are from enemy clans. She needs someone to lean on, and he is the closest right now.

"My..." the boy starts, taking a deep breath, "my folks died when I was young. I barely knew them. When I moved in with the caretaker, I didn't get along with the other kids. Back then, Rostad was digging out a new burrow, the one we call home now. Although she had led the clan for decades, Vivian wasn't very popular back then. Her decisions were... controversial, making her an outsider in her own home. She took a liking to me, a poor orphaned boy with no friends. She practically raised me, and I guess she saw something in me, because she named me as her successor."

Mary sniffles. "Why are you telling me this?"

"I guess what I'm trying to say is, I can relate. To loss, I mean."

She stares in the direction of the river. "You know loss? Then, may I ask you something?"

"What is it?"

"I've seen people die before, but when *she* died, it was different. Everything and everyone changed. How do you deal with losing someone... who used to mean everything to you?" Steven goes stiff. He must not know how to respond. She should have known. It's a loaded question, one even her mother wouldn't be able to answer. How can she expect a teenage boy to do so?

She is about to take it back, but then he speaks.

"I just... go on an adventure."

"What?" Mary was expecting a few different answers, but not that.

"An adventure. The surveyors and I get up to the wildest things, and it's kept me going. When we lose somebody, we don't cry. We act. We provide for those still around, and I think doing that is a comfort. Either way, it's better than sitting around moping." Mary doesn't completely understand, but still, her eyes light up with hope. For the first time since Lillian, there is a fluttering in her chest. She wants to hear more about this "adventure" method.

"Yeah, no matter what happens, ya gotta keep moving. It may seem disrespectful to the dead, but think of it this way: would your friend want you to spend your life sad and miserable?"

Lillian's last words play in her head.

"Keep fighting, Mary."

She shakes her head. "No. In fact, she'd be mad at me if she saw me now. She'd say, 'What are you doing? Keep moving.' Or maybe something like, 'Stop crying over me. I'm not worth it.'"

"Wow, sounds like ya knew her well."

She wipes her tears with her shirt. "We were practically sisters."

The two take comfort in each other's arms as they stare into the vast world beyond. The sky has turned a marvelous melody of colors: yellow, orange, pink, and purple. The colors are so bold they permeate the leaves of the canopy, making them glow. Mary has never seen a sunset before. Her family always goes inside before then, but even with the leaves blocking most of the colored sky, she knows it is beyond her wildest dreams.

"Does it really work?" Mary asks after a long time.

Steven looks at her and confidently responds, "Yes. It gives purpose even to the purposeless."

"But I..." She trails off, remembering the role she was raised for. "I was training to be a caretaker, and only that."

"Huh? Why would they make you do that?"

Mary thinks about it, then sighs. "It was my idea. I'm... not good at fighting or adventuring."

"Oh, come on now. You were pretty tough to escape a *capaeman* and swim all the way into our territory. I reckon you're better than ya think. You should join us sometime."

"On a surveyor mission?"

"Yeah."

"I'd be completely useless."

He squeezes her shoulder. "No, you wouldn't. We could use all the help we can get. Besides, we've had newbies before. It's no biggie."

"Really?" she asks. She doesn't know why Steven thinks that way about her, but he does. After all, why did he send her that scimitar and armor?

"Really. I think if ya gave it a chance, it would help you... with everything."

Mary smiles, enamored by how the colors of the sunset reflect off his beautiful blue eyes. The old Mary would never consider Steven's offer, but after what's happened, she is willing to try anything—whatever will distract her from this agony in her chest, from this feeling that she has no one to turn to and no purpose.

"Okay. Maybe I'll come with you, one of these days."

34

Riverside Chat

Lillian

As days turn into weeks, Lillian loses track of time. It's been at least two weeks. She can't imagine what her family must have gone through in that time—if they're alive. It's been so long since she has seen Mary, or any human for that matter. She has almost become used to Lionel. After going to the fountain with him, they've been spending a lot of time together. In the mornings, Lionel comes in to check on her. Then, they leave to explore the town. When they return in the evening, Lionel works on a project, and they talk about the world. He has been more receptive to Lillian's questions but still tunes out when she talks about herself.

Traveling in Lionel's bag, Lillian has now seen many places in the capaeman town. They've been to the fountain, a giant library, a dome made entirely of glass, a colorful flower garden, and a place called a "market." There were astronomical amounts of food there.

Despite all the time she has spent with Lionel, there's still a divide between them. He talks to her all day about how the capaemen work, but the second anything personal comes up, he shuts down.

Lillian contemplates all of this as she wakes in the morning, staring up at the smooth wood ceiling—funny how it's really just the bottom of a cabinet shelf. She slips out of her plush bed and pushes the cabinet door open. She's walking much better now. She doesn't even need the stick if she moves slowly.

The girl climbs onto the table, glancing at the orange sun shining through the glass ceiling. Apparently, that glass isn't the same type of glass they make in Zurec. It is something called "tempered glass," which is much stronger. The glass dome they visited had many capaeman laying on long chairs, basking in the sun. They sure love to do that.

As usual, it feels like a furnace in the workshop. Sweat beads down Lillian's forehead. She misses the canopy of the Giant Wilds. It protected them from the sun, which shines so harshly. She never even knew.

It's not long before Lionel arrives for his morning visit. He closes the door silently as if trying to avoid something. The only other person in the house is his brother, Maeko. They occasionally hear his voice from the other side of the door.

"Good morning," Lionel says.

"Hey," Lillian responds. She wonders where they are going today. Lionel has a giant backpack over his shoulder and a massive dagger on his waist. It's the first time she has seen him armed. What need would a capaeman have for a weapon? They are powerful enough on their own.

"Let us go somewhere new today," he says, his eyes darting about.

"Is everything okay?" Lillian asks. She has never seen him like this. The sight of that dagger, which is bigger than her entire body, puts her on edge.

"Everything is fine," Lionel says in a steely tone. "We simply need to get out of here for the afternoon."

"It doesn't seem fine."

"Look, you'll like this place. It is gorgeous." He places the travel sack on the table near Lillian. "Now come on. Get in." Lillian backs away slowly. There is definitely something wrong. "Do not be afraid," the capaeman says. "We've done this a dozen times."

"Tell me what's going on."

Lionel sighs loudly. "Always have to be difficult, don't you? If you must know, my brother has been growing suspicious over the past couple of weeks. He's wondering what I get up to for long hours in here. Now, he wishes to use this room. This place may belong primarily to me, but I cannot keep him out forever. That will raise even greater suspicion."

Lillian crosses her arms. "I know about your brother. Why didn't you just tell me?"

The capaeman rolls his eyes. She didn't know they could do that with those massive irises. "It is because I'm in a hurry, okay? Now, will you accompany me or not?"

Something still feels wrong, but Lillian has enjoyed all their trips so far. She has learned things about the outside world she never could have dreamed of back in Zurec, and Lionel has never done anything to hurt her. This time won't be any different, right?

Her eyes lock on the dagger. "Why do you need that?"

The capaeman glances at his belt, then places a hand on the weapon. "The place where we are headed is technically in the plains. It is rare, but sometimes even we are attacked."

"The monsters there are *that* strong?" Suddenly, Lillian wonders if she should take her chances hiding from his brother.

"It is simply a precaution. As I said, it rarely happens. Even on the off chance it does, I can take them down. I know how to fight."

Lillian stares at him, dumbfounded. Why does he know how to fight? From their adventures, she's learned that most capaemen don't. They do not focus on survival. They do something called "working." It's where they pick something they like to do and get something called "venna" in exchange. The whole system is a little confusing, but venna coins can be exchanged for all sorts of things. They don't need to hunt or fight monsters to get it, so why? Somehow, each question Lionel answers only raises more.

The capaeman growls impatiently. "What is with that look on your face? I said I'm in a hurry. Come on."

"I-I want a weapon too." It's a long shot, but if they're going somewhere dangerous, she wants to be prepared.

The capaeman groans. "Fine." He rummages through a box on the table, the same box Lillian hid behind when Lionel first caught her outside the cabinet. Out of it, he pulls a stick-like object. A thin metal rod sticks out of a thick handle and ends by narrowing into a flat, dull tip. If that is meant to be her weapon, she'd rather go unarmed. It doesn't look like it could do much, not that she could even carry it.

Instead of handing it to her, Lionel sticks the blunt end into the metal shutters in the corner of the room. Carefully, he removes four screws from each end of the shutters and peels the entire metal structure off the wall. A blast of cold air rushes into the room. Lillian takes a deep breath, relieved.

Lionel reaches into the wall. There seems to be a crawlspace behind those shutters, and it's deep—at least the length of his arm.

"Here," he says, holding out his hand. In it is something Lillian thought she'd never see again: black hilt, black handle, and only half the size of Lionel's pinkie.

"M-My dagger." She snatches it and holds it in her arms. "Thank the Wilds it's okay!" Miss May told her not to get it wet, but it happened anyway. Flashes of the Crystal River permeate her mind, making her think of her family. She wonders how the survivors are doing. By now, they probably think she is dead. If only she could send a message to them, but she can't. It could put them in danger.

"There, now we are both armed. Let's go." Lionel begins screwing the shutters back on the wall.

"Wait!" she yells. "Don't close that. It isn't scorching in here for once."

The capaeman raises an eyebrow. "Scorching? It feels fine to me."

Her jaw drops. "Are you *kidding* me? I feel like I've been baking."

Lionel places a hand on his chin, thinking. "Oh! I apologize. I did not even take heat into account. Your species is mammalian, so you must be more sensitive to temperature. On the contrary, we are more in between classifications. Fascinating, the differences between us."

"Yeah, yeah. So, can you leave the air shutters open? I could really use it."

"Air *vent*. And I can do better than that." Lionel puts the "vent" back on the wall and turns a small dial on one of its corners. In the next few minutes, the room cools down drastically. Now it feels less like a scorching hellscape and more like the shade of the Giant Wilds.

They can manipulate temperature too? She should have known. "Why didn't you do that sooner?"

"You never asked. Now, can we—"

Before Lionel can continue, the doorknob on the other side of the room jiggles. "Hey! You said I could use the room now. What is taking so long?"

Maeko. He has a higher and lighter voice than his brother, but a capaeman's voice all the same. Its frequency causes the tables to vibrate. "Just a moment!" Lionel yells. He turns to Lillian and quietly says, "We are out of time. Let's go. Now." She scrambles into the bag, which Lionel immediately scoops up.

Lillian can feel his every step. In only a couple of strides, they are opening the door.

"Finally," the voice of Maeko says. "What is the matter with you lately?" He sounds so close he's practically breathing on her. Lillian clasps a hand over her mouth, trying not to move a single muscle. Suddenly, she is glad she's leaving with Lionel. Hiding from his brother would be a nightmare.

"None of your business," Lionel says coldly. "The room is all yours now. Try not to destroy it while I am away."

"Where are you off to?" Maeko asks, frustration in his massive voice.

"Again, none of your business."

"It's the Crimson Forest again, is it not? That place is dangerous, you know—"

"I am aware," Lionel interrupts. "I enjoy reading there. The creek is peaceful. Do not worry. I am fully capable of taking care of myself."

There is a short period of silence. Then his brother speaks again. "Well, when you return, we must go to the market. We are running out of food. I am not going alone this time. You have been cooped up in your workshop all day, every day. It is unhealthy."

"I'll keep that in mind," Lionel responds irritably.

They start moving again. Lillian takes a deep breath, relieved, but part of her feels pity for Maeko. That's a cold way to treat his family. It reminds her of how she used to act. Hearing it from an outside perspective is eye-opening.

⁂

As the breeze blows through the small holes in the fabric, Lillian's mind wanders. There is no way they'll go to the Giant Wilds, right? She can't get her hopes up. What would her community even look like now, after the attack? She shivers, remembering the orange-eyed hunter. She has tried not to think about him or the attack... all the screaming, the slashing, the bloodshed. After all, there's nothing she can do right now.

But one day, she will have to go back. She'll return to the Wilds, and to her tragically monotonous life of survival and overprotective guardians. That is, *if* they are alive. If not...

No, she can't think about that.

whooooosshh

Lillian hears a familiar sound. She must be dreaming. There's no way Lionel would take her here, but the sound is unmistakable. *That's the river.* Slowly, the bag lowers until Lillian can feel solid ground. The air smells of local plants and dewdrops. She dares to hope as she opens the drawstrings of the pack.

But the sight before them is unlike anything she's ever seen.

They stand in a clearing, surrounded by tall grass and wildflowers. She can hear a river, but she can't see it. She's too short. Lionel kneels, observing the scene.

This reminds Lillian of the first time they met. They were also in a clearing surrounded by wildflowers. Except this place only has one brown-barked tree, which stands behind them, providing much-needed shade. Right now, Lionel wears the same ridiculous expression as when they first talked: condescending fascination. This time, however, there is a glint of kindness in those dark-green eyes. It's mind-blowing how things have changed in the past few weeks.

"What has you in such deep thought?" Lionel asks quietly. It must be their equivalent of a whisper.

"Why so quiet?" she wonders.

"Oh, you cannot see them?" He props his backpack upright. "Here, climb onto this if you can." Lillian makes the journey up the backpack while Lionel stares in the distance. He seems fixated on whatever lies ahead, not breaking his gaze to check on her once. The warrior climbs faster, curious.

When she sees it, she nearly falls off the massive heap of fabric.

It must be thousands of feet away, but she can see it clearly since the land is so flat. Trudging through the tall grass, on the other side of a massive river, is the largest andremedon she has ever seen. The apex predator of the Giant Wilds. Its long jaw hangs open, revealing several rows of dagger-like teeth. The grass barely touches its ankles, and as it walks by one of the rare trees, it reaches half its height—magnitudes bigger than the andremedons of the Giant Wilds. The light from the orange sun shimmers off its feathery scales, revealing a swirling pattern of gold and green. It is mesmerizing.

Its talons and teeth are just as terrifying as its scales are beautiful. The monster brings its long jaws down and tears into the carcass of another giant creature. Lillian didn't realize the corpse was there until she saw the blood on the andremedon's fangs. They rip through flesh as if it's paper. The poor beast it killed had no chance.

"Incredible." Lionel fumbles through his backpack, nearly knocking Lillian off of it. She falls face-first onto the fabric. "I apologize. I must take down some notes."

"Don't be so careless!"

"Again, I apologize. I have been waiting to observe an andremedon hunting up close. It is such a rarefied sight. I suppose you are good luck. Just remember, we need to be quiet, and we cannot move until it leaves. Not even I could take on such a foe. That thing is *much* bigger than me."

The warrior takes a seat, staring at the monster and its prey. If Lillian squints, she can see red trees growing thicker in the distance. That's the Giant Wilds. She is so close, yet so far away.

"I never thought I would see such a perfect specimen. My knowledge of the plains creatures will surely expand from this," Lionel says while writing.

She doesn't get what's so interesting about this. "Things like this happen in the Giant Wilds all the time. What's got you so excited?"

"The... Giant Wilds?" Lionel snickers. "What a silly name."

"It's not silly! It's what we call the forest. It's where I grew up."

"Oh, you mean the Crimson Forest? That is its proper name, you know."

"Proper name? I think Giant Wilds is just fine."

"But it is not giant. It is a rather small forest, as far as nature preserves are concerned."

Lillian rolls her eyes. "Well, I can see why you'd say that. You *are* a giant."

Lionel puts down his pen. "I find that offensive. I am not a giant. You are simply a very small person." This makes her head spin. Lillian has never thought of it that way, but who's really the odd one out? Her entire life, *everything* has been bigger than her. The trees, the plants, the animals... Even animals at the bottom of the food chain are larger. Well, most of them.

Maybe the world is rightsized, and *they* are the "abnormalities."

As Lillian watches the andremedon ravage the giant corpse, helplessness creeps in yet again. How is she supposed to be strong when everything is bigger than her? She tries and tries, yet she still has to rely on others to get by. It's embarrassing.

"I wonder," Lionel says, "what is the evolutionary advantage to being as minuscule as you are?"

"Huh? English please?"

"Biologists have been trying to figure it out for centuries, but there is not much to go on. Humans are weak in practically every sense of the word. Your only redeeming quality seems to be your intelligence, but being small can only get you so far. It almost seems like your species is not entirely fit for this world."

"Excuse me?" Lillian snaps. She's almost as furious as when he called them primitive. "You have no basis for that. You know nothing about us."

The capaeman looks directly at her, eyebrows raised. "I meant no offense. I am simply stating an observation."

The warrior scoffs. "Well, offense taken. You know, I'm sick and tired of hearing you blather on about your species but always insult mine. Can't we have a real conversation for once?"

Lionel's reptilian eyes widen, and he slams his notebook shut.

Normally, Lillian would be afraid now—afraid she crossed the line, but this time she isn't. She thinks back to when they first traveled together to that beautiful fountain with the tiled stones. There, Lionel showed real emotion. He showed empathy for her, and for just a second, she thought he would open up.

Then, the following day, he arrived acting the same as he always has. Nothing's changed. She wonders if it ever will.

The capaeman is lost in thought. He would have left the room by this point, but he can't here. They can't get up until that andremedon leaves. He is a sitting styfisher—trapped here with Lillian, and she is loving that.

"Are you ready to talk to me for real now?"

Lionel lets out a loud sigh. "Let us sit by the tree. This may take a while." The capaeman scooches backward, resting his head against the brown tree. Lillian makes her way down the backpack and joins him, climbing onto a root. She swings her dangling feet back and forth, waiting for him to speak. Lionel stares at the sky.

Lillian grows nervous. It's like that time when her father was about to tell her bad news. She silently sat on that root near the burrow, waiting for him to speak. That feels like years ago now, even though timewise it has been a little over a month.

"My mother..." Lionel starts. "She would have loved to see this."

"Your mother?" There's reason to be nervous, after all. Moms are her least favorite topic.

"Yes, she was a biologist. Exactly like me. We used to rescue endangered species and nurse them back to health."

"Must be nice. My mom left me when I was a baby." Lillian doesn't know why she is saying this. Usually, she would never bring it up.

"Truly? That is awful. My mother died when I was young. I was primarily raised by family friends."

Lillian hangs her head. She is no stranger to death, so she knows how much it hurts. "I'm sorry. That must have been terrible."

"It was a long time ago. It is alright," Lionel says softly. "I would argue your situation is worse. My mother did not want to leave. She died." Lillian bites her lip. She doesn't know how to respond to that. To her, knowing her mother is alive somewhere is comforting, even though she would slap her if they ever met. The capaeman takes a deep breath. "I can somewhat empathize with you. My father skipped out on raising us after our mother died. After a while, he came back. I suppose he was tired of being a world-class jerk. He is still around now, but I hardly see him anymore."

"Really?" She can't believe what she's hearing. "My dad skipped raising me too. He thinks leading the burrow is more important."

Lionel laughs. "Perhaps we are not so different after all."

Lillian laughs with him. "I was thinking the same thing."

In this moment, Lillian wonders if she should ask something. A question has been on her mind for so long, but she has been too terrified of Lionel to bring it up. However, as she gazes at the swaying, round leaves above, she doesn't feel the slightest bit of fear. She cannot believe he's evil, no matter what the others said.

The warrior takes a deep breath. This is for her people, but mostly, this is for her. She has to know. "Lionel, it's my turn to ask something important."

"What is it?"

In the distance, the andremedon licks blood off its fangs. Lillian swallows.

"You seem to know a lot about humans. At least, the problems the capaemen have with us. Tell me... do you know... do you know why the hunters are after us?"

There is an incredibly long pause. Lillian observes Lionel the whole time, waiting impatiently for an answer. First, his eyes widen. Then, he shuts them tightly and clenches his fists. He clenches them so tightly that his claws dig into his hands. Then finally, after a deep, hulking breath, he speaks.

"Indeed, you deserve an answer. I am not involved with the hunters, but I do know this: the hunters came to this town because of a complaint. A group of humans was seen stealing from the local market. People do not like their goods being taken, so they called the hunters."

"They came to *kill* us because *one group* stole some food?"

Lionel nods somberly.

"What in the Wilds is wrong with you people? I've seen how much you eat. You have plenty to spare. How could something so minor..." She remembers the horrors she's been through: the faces of Albian frozen in death, her people desperately fending off the narecons, Mary's scream underwater after Lillian did the unthinkable. All of that started... because one group of *tiny* people stole something?

"That is simply their policy. If they find humans, they kill them."

"Even if they are innocent? My people didn't steal anything. It must have been another clan." There's only one that could have done it. Only one is close enough to the edge of the Giant Wilds.

"There *are* no innocent humans. That is what *they* believe."

Lillian feels sick.

To capaemen, humans aren't even human—they are animals. No, less than that. They're *pests*. They're worth nothing. It's a miracle Lionel bothered to save her. It's a miracle they connected at all. Because she's right; the capaemen are not evil. They just care *that* little. They see humans as beneath them. If they step out of line even once, they will be crushed.

She wants to stand up, scream at Lionel, and ask him why it has to be this way— especially with what they've learned about each other. However, when she tries to open her mouth, no sound comes out. She feels sicker than when she rode Amphii for the first time. Since the attack on Albian, everyone has been wondering why... Why are the capaemen hunting them now, after all this time? Lillian thought the answer would give meaning to the senseless slaughter of her people, but it doesn't. The reason is so miniscule. To the capaemen, they mean nothing.

Somehow, that is so much worse than them being evil.

After quite a bit of time passes, Lionel begins to move, packing his stuff. "The andremedon is gone. We should get going. I must go grocery shopping with my brother today."

Lillian nods, but she feels like she's not even in her body. It's as if she were a scavenger phii clamoring across the ground, not even significant enough for other creatures to avoid stepping on her. However, even in her melancholy, one glimmer of hope remains. If this is how capaemen feel about humans, why is Lionel different?

That's the only thing keeping her going—that one burning question.

It's the one thing that gives her hope.

35

Breaking Point

Mary

Mary wakes up in her room and is grateful for the privacy. She's been avoiding everyone but the children for the past two weeks, and her life has felt like a living hell. What could go wrong did go wrong, and now she can't deny it anymore—her family lied to her. They left so many details out of their history, it's basically a made-up story. She has no idea who the people who raised her are, and that utterly terrifies her.

The girl forces herself out of bed, her head throbbing. She glances at the pile of books stacked on top of one another. Missing from the top of the stack is *History of the Giant Wilds*. Her mother took it away. She will never get to read its ending—never know what became of Silver, nor what truly happened during the famine.

Mary has considered asking some other people in Zurec. Maybe Brianna or Seth will talk, but she has an eerie feeling there is an agreement between all the adults. After all, their fake accounts of the events have been consistent, as if they planned it together. Now, they are avoiding her together as well. The surveyors and gatherers hang out in circles, idly passing the time. Carmen and Seth have mostly stuck to their respective rooms, only coming out to grab food. By now, the news of Mary's discovery must have spread, but none have come forward to give her an explanation. For a little while, she wondered if they had a good reason for lying, but now she's not so sure. Mary remembers what her mother once told Lillian: *"All the interesting things happened when I was too young to remember."*

Mary was a fool for believing that.

"Absolutely not!" Before she can think further, a voice interrupts her. Curious, Mary presses her ear against the door. "Get out. What's the point of the barrier if you keep barging your way in?" her mother yells. Mary clenches her fist at the voice. That is the last person she wants to hear from.

"I get that," Steven says defensively. "We're only here to ask one thing. Then we'll be out of your hair."

Come to think of it, Steven was more than eager to talk about what happened. If anyone will tell her the whole story, it's him. Mary carefully opens the door, creeping into the hall. Next to the makeshift barrier, her mom fumes at a pair of uninvited guests. "Are you kidding me?" she seethes. "You want to ask a favor after that mob?"

"Everyone's alright, aren't they? Chief Vivian's more than capable of handling those people."

"They almost broke through the gate!" Mary's breath catches in her throat as she remembers what almost happened two weeks ago. Why did that happen? Why are they so determined to keep the reason from her?

She grabs the caretaker's arm. "Mom, what are you doing?"

"O-Oh, you're awake. I was just telling these hooligans to get out." Steven and Zane cross their arms.

"Why?" she asks. "They've done nothing but help."

"I wouldn't call their lack of boundaries helping. Go back to your room, Mary. I'll handle this."

She doesn't move.

"Did you hear me? I said go back to bed."

Mary shakes her head slowly. "I won't."

Her mother growls. "The adults have this handled. Now—"

"I think she should stay," Steven says.

"I didn't ask *you*."

"Well, I don't care about your opinion, so..."

The caretaker clenches her fists.

Mary grabs her mother's shoulder. "Why are you two here?"

"Thought ya might want to know there are a few openings for the mission today. We're looking for volunteers."

"Volunteers? For what?"

"My sect of the surveyors is a little... special," Steven explains. "Sometimes we do odd jobs, checking on neighboring groups and such. Other missions are a bit more interesting."

"Why would you even—" the caretaker starts, but her daughter cuts her off.

"What do you mean by *interesting?*" She dislikes how he's beating around the bush, especially after these two weeks. People should say what they mean, not hide the truth through white lies. She's sick of it.

"I was getting to that," the boy says. "You remember those giant fruits you saw in the kitchen, don't ya? Want to guess where they're from?"

The girl shuffles through the memories from her first tour of Rostad's burrow. The kitchen stood out like a flower in winter. She had never seen anything like those fruits. They were massive, some taller than a whole person. Now that she thinks about it, there is no way those are native to this forest. Mary's heart drops. "Those aren't from the Giant Wilds. They're from *outside*. That's how you survived the famine."

Steven's lips curl upward. "Clever girl. Back then we had nothing, so we had to be crafty. Now, 'borrowing' is a tradition. Out there, there's more food than you can imagine, so it's easy pickings."

"But isn't that extremely dangerous?" Mary asks, her heart pounding at the mere thought. "If even one of *them* saw you—"

"We're careful," Zane says. "No one has ever been followed or killed. Don't ya worry."

"Absolutely not!" her mother shrieks. "You won't get anyone from Zurec to do that. It's ludicrous!"

The boy turns to the caretaker's daughter. "Mary? It's up to you."

She feels sick to her stomach. When Steven told her the surveyors went on adventures, she never thought he meant this. Still, she doesn't want to say no either, not after what they shared at sunset weeks ago. Besides, she misses his letters. She wonders why he stopped sending them.

"We wouldn't be asking if we weren't desperate," Zane confesses. "It's just that no one wants to go, what with the recent movements of the capaemen. We need volunteers."

"All these years, *this* is how you got your food? You don't think it's the least bit dangerous?" her mother seethes.

"*You* have no right to judge us," Steven says, gritting his teeth. "We did what we had to do to survive, just like Zurec did." The caretaker frowns but doesn't say anything else.

Mary clenches her fists. She wants more than anything to know what Zurec did—what cruel action they took after slaying those aceras—aceras that could have helped them in this time of attack. Her mother is keeping that secret even now. Seeing the determined look on the caretaker's face, Mary doubts she would get that answer out of her in a million years. She's tempted to leave with Steven. After all, he hasn't treated her like a thoughtless child.

"All we want is a few more people to go. We'll handle the rest. I've been doing this for years. I swear, nothing bad will happen on my watch," Steven says confidently. Despite Miss May's stubborn protests, he still tries to convince her.

"You need to leave," Mary's mother growls, taking a hostile step toward the boys. "You've caused us enough pain. Under no circumstances is anyone going with you."

"Look, I know our people aren't the kindest to ya. That must be unpleasant," Zane says, trying to intervene, "but we're here asking for a truce. We shouldn't let the past divide us now."

"You know what I think?" Mary's mother says. "I think you're only saying that because you *need* us now. You need volunteers for that mission so you can keep feeding your massive populace who hates us. I'm sure that once that's done, you'll go right back to pretending we don't *matter*."

"Mom!" Mary yells. "Stop it. That's too far."

"What?" She is clearly surprised. Her daughter has never spoken to her that way.

"I'll go," she says with finality.

"Huh?" everyone says in unison. Steven must not have been expecting her to agree. To be honest, she didn't either.

"You heard me," Mary says. "I'll go. Someone has to."

"No! No one should—"

"Nothing will get better if we keep avoiding each other!" Mary yells. "I'm so sick of this. Whatever petty disagreement you two are having, get over it. We must try to get along, now more than ever."

"Mary, it's not petty—"

"Then what is going on? Because I have no idea how you could hold so much hatred toward these people, even before the mob! You've told me nothing, and do you think I'm so dense that I don't know something is up? I'll give you one last chance, Mother. Tell me why you're so determined to keep me away from Rostad. No more lies!"

"Mary..." she says, clasping her hands together. "We had a good reason to do what we did. So don't you—"

"Then what's the reason?"

"Now is not a good time!" she shouts. "Go back to your room. We'll discuss this later."

Her rage boiling over, Mary walks straight up to her mother. "You've been lying to me my whole life, and you want me to *wait*? It's already been two weeks. How much longer do I need to wait before you stop treating me like a child? Another fourteen years?" Her mom's face falls as if *she* were the one who's been betrayed. This only makes the girl's anger tunnel deeper. She's about to explode when—

"Am I interrupting something?" a deep voice asks.

"Seth. No, I was just telling my daughter that she cannot leave on a dangerous mission with Rostad surveyors, and now she refuses to return to her room. My my, if I didn't have eyes, I'd mistake you for Lillian, young lady." Mary flinches at the name.

Their chief lets out a hearty laugh. "Wait, Mary wants to do what now? That's the greatest thing I've heard all week!"

"Don't encourage her!" her mother responds, horrified. Mary is glad to see their chief outside his room for a reason other than food but enraged that her mother has changed the subject. She has no intention of explaining herself.

Seth firmly grips her shoulder. "Look Mary, I'm proud of you for gaining some grit, but now isn't the time. We need to be sure everyone is in one place. We don't know what will happen next."

She slaps his hand away. "Yeah, I'm sure you'd say that. I bet you're the one who ordered everyone to lie to us, aren't you? Well, I know the truth. Tell me, Seth, why did you hide our real history?" The Zurec chief's face falls.

"It's time we stopped putting this off. Miss May, I know we made a vow, but I don't think we can keep it now. Leave us. I'll handle this."

"Wait, Seth, she's not ready for—"

"It doesn't matter whether she's ready or not. We must tell her, or someone else will." His eyes narrow at Steven and Zane.

"I..." Her mother is trembling. "Fine. Go." She walks past them, heading back to her quarters without another word.

Mary almost feels guilty, but quickly remembers that she's the one who has been lied to. She has every right to act this way. Unfalteringly, she meets Seth's eyes. "This had better be the truth, and only the truth."

He nods earnestly. "Let's go outside. Get some fresh air."

⚜

They leave the burrow and sit on a fungi-infested root. Seth stares in the direction of the river, a slight frown on his face. "I still can't believe she's gone."

Mary's lower lip trembles. "Me neither. Nothing has been the same."

"I should have been there for her. Instead, everything we did pushed her farther away."

Mary cannot deny that. Their chief always prioritized the clan over his daughter. It hurt Lillian every day, and now that she is gone, the guilt must be eating away at her dad like a scavenger phii devouring a corpse. He looks much better today, almost like his old self, but she knows better than to believe he has recovered. Like her, he must have moved past the worst of the grief, and now he is putting on a brave face for everyone else.

"But enough about that," Seth says, steering back to the subject at hand. "Perhaps this was a bad decision, perhaps it wasn't, but after everything that happened, we wanted to start over."

"Why? Is what we did that bad?"

He runs a hand over the Zurec sigil on his arm. "My dad, Lillian's grandfather, cared about the community, but he was irrational. He did all sorts of awful things, including betraying Rostad. Chief Camille of Albian may have played a part in the plan, but Dad arranged it. We used to be part of an alliance, fighting a great war I don't want to get into right now."

Mary frowns. "The war against Silver, right?"

Seth looks away, clearly uncomfortable. "Yeah, that's the one."

"I don't know the full story of that either. I wish I had the book to fill me in on it."

"So that's where you learned this from... Miss May returned it to the Rostad people. It was wrong of your mother to take it away. Please understand, she's just scared. We all are—"

"*You're* scared? I'm terrified! Do you want to know where I stopped reading before she took it? Zurec killed Silver's aceras just because they disagreed with their capaeman-slaying philosophy. You said we were peacekeepers. That's anything *but* peaceful."

Seth freezes as if caught in a nightmare. "I, uh... so you know about that too."

"What happened after that?"

He stares off into the distance. "It's not something any of us want to remember." Mary throws him a bitter look. The second their eyes meet, he sighs. "But you deserve to know. That action sparked the River War. Nurem and Civare allied with Silver and moved to the other side of the river with them. They formed the Silver Coalition. Meanwhile, Albian and Rostad agreed more with Zurec's ideals, even if our methods were, well... barbaric. We believed our ancestors were right and that we should never mess with the capaemen. So, we created the Ancestral Alliance.

"Thanks to most of their aceras being gone, the Ancestral Alliance had an advantage, but the war was still hard-fought. Many people died, including dear friends of mine..." He trails off, shaking. Come to think of it, neither Seth nor her mom have ever talked about the people they've lost. Sure, there have been mentions in passing, but nothing else about them. They really do want to forget.

"Half of my generation died, and most of your mother's. They sacrificed themselves so we could live and finally, two bitter years later, the Ancestral Alliance was nearly victorious."

"Nearly?" Mary asks. There's more to this story, and judging by the look on Seth's face, it gets worse.

"The Silver Coalition grew desperate, and one night, they came and took a hostage."

Her eyes widen. "Who was it?" A breeze blows through the Giant Wilds, and even as it whips past them, Mary feels as if all has fallen silent. She is hanging on the chief's every word.

"It was... my wife. They took Emilia. She was only a couple months pregnant with Lillian at the time."

"Emilia? Is that why she left?" But then, that wouldn't make any sense. Lillian would have been born as a member of Silver.

"No, we negotiated with the Silver Coalition, naturally. We agreed to a cease-fire, and they promised to leave the Giant Wilds the next fall. There was... some kind of migration they planned on traveling with. I'm not sure what they meant, but we agreed to the terms. After all, she was dear to me and my father and was carrying my child. We got Emilia back, but when she returned, she wasn't the same. She would often sneak out at night and not come back until morning. Then, right after she gave birth to Lillian, she..." He trails off again. Mary stays silent. It's all coming together now. "She... had fallen in love with her captor. Once she gave birth to Lillian, she went to him. Then she left with Silver."

"Wow..." is all Mary can say.

She hates Lillian's mom even more now. What heartless monster abandons her husband and child because she has fallen for another? No wonder Seth never talks about her. He must blame himself for Emilia leaving. She places a hand on his shoulder. "It wasn't your fault. I hope you know that."

He brushes her hand away. "I'd rather not talk about it."

She nods respectfully. "Of course."

"Anyway, do you have any more questions?"

Mary pauses momentarily, wondering if it would be cruel to ask him to continue. Then, she remembers their lies. This never should have been kept from her in the first place, and she has every right to know what happened next. "I want to know about the famine. What happened to the Ancestral Alliance?" *Why does Rostad hate us so much?* she thinks.

"Right. Our recent history." Seth seems worn out but obliges anyway. "Not long after Silver left, rains swept the Giant Wilds. At first, we worked together to survive, but once the plants started dying, we quickly ran out of food. Chief Darrel became desperate, and so did Camille and Vivian. We knew one was bound to betray the other eventually, and my dad was determined for us to end up on top.

"We aren't the peaceful people you've come to know. For most of Zurec's history, we sought out strength and glory. This time was no exception. After our victory against the Silver Coalition, Vivian began to doubt Darrel's leadership. Meetings between the clans were growing tense because Rostad regretted what we did to win. We feared another war was on the horizon, so my dad formed a plan. He arranged a meeting between all three clans to discuss how they would get food moving forward, but it was a lie. Once the meeting started, we and Albian attacked Rostad. Then, we raided their burrow, forcing them to leave everything behind."

Mary scooches away from him. This contradicts everything she has come to know about the adults. To think they were capable of such horrors... She can't even imagine it. She doesn't want to believe it, but it makes sense. Why else would Rostad hold such seething hatred for them? Only a decade and a half ago, Zurec killed their people and took their home. "Th-That's horrible. How could you *do* that?"

"It was not our proudest moment, that's for sure. But it is how you and Lillian survived. If it were not for that food, we all would have starved, and neither of you would be here today. Well, I guess it's only you now, but still."

"Okay, but why have you all been lying about it for years?"

"Because all Zurec has ever done led to misery. Eventually, we ran into the same problem and began fighting with Albian for resources too. This is the part of the story you know."

She clenches her teeth. They told her bits and pieces, but she has the whole picture now. "Let me guess, Chief Darrel decided to attack them?"

Seth winces. "Yeah... again, he wasn't the best guy. By that point even I was beginning to question him. Brianna, Elias, William, and I tried to reason with him, to stop the bloodshed, but he refused to listen. Eventually, Brianna stood up to him, and I openly supported her, but that only made things worse. Infighting started within Zurec, and even more people died. We were forced to back down. I hate to say it, but it was a relief when someone from Albian took my father out. Only then were we able to move forward."

Mary doesn't know what to say. On the one hand, she wants to empathize with Seth. His dad must have had an overwhelming hold on the community. On the other hand, he tried to stop it too late. Not only that, but there was infighting. That means some of the adults agreed with Darrel's decisions, at least a little. The thought makes her sick. "So, we were the aggressors. *We* are the reason for Rostad and Albian's animosity toward us, and you went along with it. You *all* did. What, did you want to escape from your mistakes or something? Is that why you kept this from us?"

"You've hit the nail on the head there. We didn't want our children to carry the burden of our mistakes, and by the end of our war with Albian, we had little left. We wanted you all to be able to start over, free from everything."

"What does that even mean?" Mary asks, her anger bubbling to the surface. "Just because you lie about it doesn't make it go away. What made you think we'd be happier like this?" She recalls how Lillian lied about the scouts and seeing a capaeman. No matter how she tried to hide it, the truth eventually came out. Truth matters. How can they forge a better future without knowing what happened in their past?

"You weren't there back then," Seth says. "We were devastated after it ended, and no one wanted to remember. It nearly destroyed us."

"So, this was never about us, was it?" she asks, but she already knows the answer. "You all wanted to escape your guilt, but you had no plan in the event that Rostad managed to survive, or if, I don't know, we talked to Albian for more than five seconds. I bet Trista knows more about our history than me. Denying our past isn't keeping us safe. It's dooming us."

The chief of Zurec doesn't respond.

Her entire life, she thought everything her family did was to protect their children, but it was really to preserve their bottom line. Following that realization, she is terrified to ask the next question, but she has no choice. "Were our records even destroyed, or did you lie about that too?"

He takes a deep breath. "Our main burrow was destroyed in the rains. We didn't lie about that, but... some of the extra bunkers up north still contain some records. I'm sorry. We should have—"

In that instant, Mary explodes. "Are you *kidding* me? All that time we spent in the burrow wondering about our past, and you knew the whole time? Not only that, but the Giant Wilds used to have people with aceras. Aceras! They could have been protecting us from the capaemen right now. Then, to add insult to injury, I learn we're the reason the other clans hate us. You betrayed the people of Rostad—your allies! They trusted you and you killed them! If you think hiding that fact from us means it never happened, you're wrong. Things don't just go away. I washed up on Rostad's doorstep and had to take their hatred without even knowing what we had done. I was so confused! A little, 'Hey, by the way, our people used to be evil,' would've helped. Geez, it's a miracle they took us in at all."

"Mary, you have to understand!" Seth shouts desperately. "When we did all those things to the Silver Coalition, it was to protect everyone. We couldn't have them sparking a war with the capaemen. The whole reason Zurec came to the Giant Wilds in the first place was to escape that. We couldn't have known the capaemen would attack after they left. And yes, our actions during the famine were horrible, but if we hadn't done what we did, everyone would have starved. Do we feel guilty for it? Absolutely, but we didn't see another choice! We aren't the reason for everything that's happened. We're just a part of it. War is messy and grey. You can't separate it into sides of good and evil. This isn't a children's fable."

Mary can't believe what she's hearing. They killed innocent aceras, betrayed their neighbors, and lied to their children, and now Seth's saying they didn't have a choice? "Ohhh, now you're trying to defend yourself? If you really believed that, you would have told Lillian and me the truth. Instead, you lied to us. Lillian *died* never knowing her own people! How can I trust any of you again?"

Seth's jaw falls open, and he leans away. He must not have been expecting this—the meek Mary yelling, showing genuine rage, but she's done with nice. All nice has done is bring lies and betrayal.

Mary leaps off the root and walks away. She trusted her people so much that she dedicated her whole life to following in her mother's footsteps. Now, all of that has shattered. Mary doesn't know what to do with herself, much less her family.

Only as she is leaving does Seth have the guts to speak again. "Mary, please wait—"

"If you care about me at all, you won't follow me," she declares.

Mary hears Seth get up, but then he sits back down. "Okay, please be safe." He seems to know exactly where she is going, yet he doesn't stop her. This is a first.

Maybe she was too harsh. Seth looked hurt, especially when Lillian was brought up. Perhaps if Mary turns around and they talk a little more, they'll come to an understanding. Then everything will be as it was, and...

She shakes her head. That thought is nothing but a dream. After a betrayal like this, there is no going back.

Mary approaches the entrance to Zurec's part of the burrow but walks past it. She can hear voices in the distance. The surveyors must be gathered at a different entrance, ready to leave. This is perfect. She won't have to search for them.

All alone, Mary approaches a group of Rostad people. They number only nine, which seems far too few for a mission outside the Giant Wilds.

"Hey, Steven," she says readily. Now she knows that everything he has shared with her is the truth.

"Mary! Are ya coming after all?" He stares at her eagerly.

"Yeah," she says, anger still in her tone. "Let's get out of here."

"Glad to have you," Zane says encouragingly. "What made ya change your mind?"

She stares at the ground, recalling the enraging conversation she just had. "I'm fed up with my family and need to get away. I don't care where."

"Well, come on then," Steven says, grabbing her hand. "I swear, you won't regret this."

Mary nods, and for the first time in weeks, she feels excited. She wants to move forward and discover the kind of person she is without Lillian, without her family controlling her. This may be the way to do it.

36

Mary's First "Borrowing"

Mary

At the end of the forest is a sea of grass. Mary didn't think grass could grow all in one place like this, nor did she imagine a land with so few trees. She shivers at the thought of crossing it. Who knows what could be lurking in there, waiting to gobble them up?

However, to her relief, the group does not go forward into the plains. Instead, they turn right and walk along the forest's edge. The line dividing the grove of trees and the flat grasslands is so sharp and immediate, almost as if an invisible barrier were purposefully placed between the two environments. It feels unreal, just like the way she is sweating.

The orange sun is clear in the bright sky. She has always viewed it through a covering of leaves, never out in the open like this. Seeing and feeling it now, Mary understands why her ancestors called the forest their home. The heat is sweltering. Her skin tingles as sweat drips down her chin.

Noticing her distress, Steven leans in and says quietly, "This is the worst part. Soon, we'll get to the bridge. Past it there's a grove of trees leading into the town."

"Wh-What do you mean by 'bridge'?" Mary asks. Floorboards can make a bridge over dirt, and roots can bridge over mud, but she doubts either of those is what he's talking about.

"It's something the capaemen built," Zane mentions. "It's incredible, goes all the way across the Crystal River. We don't have to swim or nothing."

whooooosssshhh

Just as he says that, Mary picks up the sound of the river in the distance. It flows more slowly than the rapids but faster than at Zurec's old bathing spot.

This part of the Crystal River flows outside the Giant Wilds—into completely new territory. She braces herself as the group leaves the forest's edge, creeping closer to the sound. Walking single file, they slowly push through clusters of grass, parting the brush like a curtain. Weeds bristle past Mary's arms and legs, making her body hair stand on end. Unlike in the Giant Wilds, the grass of the plains is twice her height. She doesn't even know how far it goes, only that it's tall enough to hide any manner of creature. She shudders. Even with Steven kindly grabbing her weapons and armor for her last minute, she doubts she could do anything about a monster home to *this* grass.

Luckily, the grass thins out rapidly, revealing a gigantic wooden structure twenty feet ahead. That must be the bridge.

She looks around. A cobbled path wide enough for a capaeman begins at the edge of the bridge and cuts through the plains, leading back to the forest's edge. From there, it turns, running along the forest's western edge in a curve. The path is massive and exposed. Mary can see why they came in from the east.

There's so much to take in, but the surveyors are already moving on. Their phypent-skin boots make heavy *clomp*ing sounds against the dark-colored boulders that make up the path. The massive rocks have been filed and cemented together, creating a smoothly traversable walkway. As they walk, the arched redwood structure ahead looms larger and larger until it consumes Mary's entire field of vision. The capaemen must have felled several trees to build that monstrosity. Humans could never hope to use a whole tree, but the capaemen must be different. Mary never once wondered about what they might be like, what they might be able to build.

Mary takes her first step onto the bridge, crossing into an alien world.

Gargantuan wooden planks are laid in neat rows under her feet. On either side of the structure are tall pillars with decorative, arched wooden beams seamlessly hammered into them. They must be tens of feet high—tall enough for a capaeman to put its hands on the rails. Between the beams, Mary catches a glimpse of water rushing below. She can't help but peer down at the river as it reflects the afternoon sun, but she quickly realizes that is a mistake.

The Crystal River is tens of feet below them, far enough down that falling into it would be painful, if not fatal. It only now occurs to her how high this bridge arches. She halts, breathing heavily.

The second Mary stops, Steven does too. "Hey, it's alright. This thing is super stable. You're not gonna fall."

"I-It's so high, a-and we're exposed out here." She recalls the root onto which she and Lillian escaped—how no ferns or trees protected them from the hunter's sight. If a capaeman happens to walk by now, they are dead.

"It's not so bad," Zane adds. "We've jumped off from here before, remember?"

Steven laughs as if that's a funny thing to recall. "Yeah, that was a close one. Luckily, the river peters out about a mile down from here. It wasn't a bad swim. Better than that capaeman seeing us." In response, Mary's knees buckle. Steven grabs her hand and drags her along. "But that ain't gonna happen today. It's alright. That was only once."

She is so terrified she can hardly speak. Then, noticing Steven walking ahead of her, holding the same hand that Lillian did on that fateful day, she takes a deep breath. Mary will not be a coward again. No matter how treacherous this mission is, she is going to be helpful.

Tearing her attention away from the bridge and the grim river below it, Mary looks up at the landscape ahead of the group and gasps. Steven was right; a grove of trees is on the other side. What she wasn't expecting is how beautiful it is.

At the end of the bridge, the stone path picks up again. It twists and turns in a phypent-like pattern, weaving through colorful trees. Here, the trees aren't only reddish. Shades of brown, orange, grey, and white all grow together. Planted beneath them are flowers, ranging in all colors of the rainbow. They sit in neat, purposeful rows. Some are in full bloom, while others are shy, their petals bundled together. Above them, bright-winged lightflies shimmer, enjoying the shade and flora. Mary's eyes sparkle at the twisting branches above. Even some of the trees are blossoming with flowers.

"We're almost to the orchard. There's much more cover there." Steven still has her hand, but he feels so far away, so insignificant compared to this incredible sight.

The leader of the surveyors drags her off the path and into a patch of bushes that run parallel to the flowerbeds. Here, their view of the "orchard" is much more limited. Mary burns the memory of it into her mind. It is the most amazing thing she has ever seen, and they haven't even reached the town yet.

The group sneaks through the bushes for several minutes. That is until a familiar sound makes them stop.

boom... boom...

Instantly, the entire group ducks underneath the giant flowers. It's as if they have done so a thousand times. Mary mirrors them.

"I want to play. It is not fair, Father!" a strange voice, bass and distorted, says.

"You will be able to soon, Son," a slightly heavier voice responds. "Only not inside the forest. Until the nice hunters are finished in there, our walks can only be along the edge, alright?"

"Why do they take so long?" the child asks impatiently. "Are humans not stupid?"

"They are very stupid," the dad responds nonchalantly, "but I have heard they are small. That makes them difficult to find. Regardless, it is nothing for us to worry about. You will be able to play in the forest again soon enough."

boom... boom...

The pair of capaemen continue walking toward the Giant Wilds, their footsteps fading in the distance.

With a finger to his lips, Steven ushers everyone forward. They continue.

What that capaeman child said chills Mary to the core. Even so young, they have a bloodlust for humans. It wants them to die quickly just so it can play in the Giant Wilds. That is so screwed up. Are they born evil?

For an hour, the group weaves through seemingly endless bushes. Mary cannot believe how much distance there is between here and the town. There is so much forestry as well, weaving into the capaeman-made paths seamlessly.

"What do ya think so far?" Steven asks, checking in on the Zurec girl.

Oddly enough, Mary smiles. "It's so beautiful here."

"Sure is," Zane adds. "We were enamored on our first mission too. Ended up coming back with nothing, but I guess saving our hides was a win."

"I'm sorry you had to learn to do this," Mary starts. "My clan had no right to do what they did."

"Nah, it ain't your fault," Steven says. "In a way, you were worse off than us. I still don't understand why they'd keep that from you."

Her face falls. "I don't know either. I really don't."

The group falls silent, everyone preferring to focus on the mission. What is there to say? They are in capaeman territory right now. All that matters is getting the food they need to survive the coming days. Mary is glad she can finally be a part of something, rather than staying in her room or with the children. All it took was running away from home into capaeman territory.

What am I doing? A twinge of panic pangs in her chest, but she pushes it away. She's already made her decision.

Eventually, the light ahead of the group grows as they near the end of the bushes. Steven pushes past the last branches, then stands tall and confident, gazing at what's ahead with a light smirk. Mary scrambles behind, curious to see what's beyond the horizon.

⋙⋘

Glass.

Capaeman homes are made of glass.

Not even in Mary's dreams did she imagine this.

In a valley below, surrounded by an open field, are rows upon rows of transparent houses. Some parts of the homes have solid walls, but most of them are at least fifty percent glass. It is shocking how much one can see through the grids of glass panes. Some capaemen are sitting at desks reading or writing. Others talk to each other, standing around bizarre appliances. Even more are empty, meaning those giants are stomping about someplace. The thought makes her shiver. "Creepy, right?" Zane remarks. "Do they not like privacy or something?"

Mary is at a loss for words. She cannot figure out how they built these. How many forges do they even have? It must have taken years—no, *decades*.

But she forgets they are giants. Maybe it took them no time at all. Rock paths stem off each house and then merge to form wide roads, like streams conjoining with a river. Mary wonders why they don't simply tread across the grass. It must only reach the calves of a capaeman. There is even a path right outside their hiding spot, leading south. In its direction, structures of all shapes and sizes stretch as far as the eye can see: some with flat roofs, some angular, others are pyramid-shaped. The rock paths cluster together in some places, forming rectangular, grassless clearings filled with even more foreign structures. The number of constructions is unfathomable. Is it out of necessity, or just because they like building things?

Steven points at one of the stone clearings. "Ya see that in the distance? That place with the giant tents and metal boxes?" Mary nods, her eyes wide. She is still speechless. "That's where we're headed."

She takes in the distant courtyard. They are standing on top of a hill, and that one seems only one more hill away. "I-Is there food there?"

"You'll see. It'll blow your mind."

"A-Are you sure this is safe?" Mary asks. She knows they've done this hundreds of times, but this is riskier than all the past Zurec missions combined. A wide path is ahead of them, and if they cross it, they'll have nowhere to hide. For a brief moment, she wonders if she should have stayed at home, but she shoos the thought away. If she had to spend one more minute in that small hallway with those liars, she would lose it.

"Y'all brace yourselves," Steven says, not answering her question. He points at the open road between them and the yard. "It's time for the home stretch." The surveyors secure their weapons and tighten their backpacks.

"Are we going to *run*?" Mary asks, her heart dropping.

"We're about to be out of cover," Zane explains. "We've gotta sprint for it, then we'll be at the market. This is the riskiest part."

She adjusts her headband. "There isn't a safer way?"

Steven shakes his head. "It'll only be for a minute. Trust me, okay?" The boy leader checks to see if everyone is ready. Then, he begins to count down. "Five, four, three, two..."

On "one," the entire group bursts forward, sprinting into the stony road. Even though she is less used to running, Mary keeps up with them, her body hot with adrenaline. It will take them seconds to reach the grassy end of the path at this speed, but those seconds feel like minutes. Mary's head darts around, and down the road she sees the houses planted next to each other one by one. They are perfectly lined up. To think each one contains at least one capaeman...

Then, they hit the grass. The relieving shade of a tree greets them. As the group slows to a halt, Mary doubles over, panting. A hand claps her on the back. "That was great!" Zane praises. "Mary, you've got more guts than ya give yourself credit for."

Steven smirks. "Ya know, many newbies fail that part. They get too scared and are left behind. We end up having to go get them later."

"Really?" Mary asks. She wonders if they are pulling her leg.

"Really," the boy says with no hesitation. "Now come on. If ya liked what you've seen so far, you're gonna love this!" They push through some weeds growing under the sparse trees that populate this spot. When they reach the crest of the hill, the scenery below opens up.

The few trees that currently shade them are the last things standing between them and their destination. There is only grassland beyond this point. And beyond that, the field of cobbled stones.

Mary's jaw drops at the sight. It is even more mind-blowing up close.

"This is where capaemen trade food," Steven explains. "Why they do that, we're not sure, but this is where we'll get our take." The area below is indeed full of food, so much neither Zurec nor Rostad could eat it all, not even in their entire lifetimes. The food sits in piles on tented tables organized in neat rows all over the valley, creating an easy path for visitors to cross. Standing at each table is a capaeman, handing out bags of food in exchange for something small and round. She can't see exactly what the objects they're trading are, but they glint in the sunlight.

That isn't all, though.

Surrounding the food-packed stalls are stacks upon stacks of wooden boxes, littered with hundreds of foods she's never seen before. Next to them are enormous metal boxes mounted on what look like black wheels, but are curiously... rubbery? Mary has no clue how those can bear such weight, especially when the bins are filled with even more crated food. Through the opened backs of the boxes, she can see enormous foods in every shape, color, and category imaginable: fruits, roots, beans, grains, and leafy greens. Mary's mouth waters. Beans aren't ready to harvest until midsummer in the Giant Wilds. Come to think of it, many of the produce here are out of season.

"Alright, the market ain't packed right now," Steven says. "We lucked out. Let's go."

"Wait, we're going directly down *there*?" she asks in horror. "That's a death wish!"

"Don't worry, we won't be going right in the middle of everything. We go off to the side and pluck a couple of fruits and vegetables from their containers," Zane reassures her. "In and out, no big deal. We do this all the time."

"O-Okay," she says, shaking. "I'll follow your lead."

"Move out. Don't waste a single second," their leader commands. The surveyors dash. Mary rushes to keep up, her breathing growing heavier and heavier. Right now, grass surrounds them, but the boxes will be their only cover when they reach the market. *"No big deal"?* They must be kidding.

Before Mary can catch her breath, the plants end, and the Rostad people dive behind a crate. All around, the *boom*s of capaemen footsteps echo.

"Too high," Steven mumbles, staring at the brim of the box they lean against. "Farther. Let's go."

The adventurers duck and dive past multiple crates, being extra careful that the capaemen at the stalls don't turn around. Mary copies their movements—if she doesn't, she's dead.

Finally, they come across a crate low to the ground, but they will be completely exposed if they try to hide behind it. From a capaeman's sky-high view, it could see them. They'll have to stay behind their current box until they have a perfect opening.

The only problem is that could take hours.

Steven gestures for them to crouch lower, and some sit on the ground. They talk amongst themselves as if it's a regular day in an ordinary place. Mary cannot believe they are being so casual about this. She can't stop shaking.

"Relax," Zane whispers, "they hardly come back here. Plus, we can jump behind the larger crates if things get bad." He gestures to a massive stack of them sitting on the edge of the courtyard. They are piled up near one of the giant metal boxes and nowhere near the tented stalls. "So long as we don't make any loud noises, we're safe."

She feels far from safe.

boom

Mary winces at the sound of another nearby footfall. The stone under her feet vibrates. "We have no need for this many mangroes. Put some back, would you?" the annoyed voice of a capaeman says.

"We can afford it," a second capaeman responds. Its voice is slightly higher than the first, but she's pretty sure they are both male. "What is with you lately? You seldom leave your workshop."

"So what? You have plenty of things to do. Just because I am your elder brother does not mean you need me for entertainment." By the Wilds, they're arguing. It is strange to hear. She didn't think capaemen *could* argue.

"Well, that is true, but I've never seen you take so long on a project. You have been repairing that mixer for weeks," the younger one says.

"By the earth, it is because *you* broke it, you know," the older one retaliates.

"It *never* takes you this long to fix anything."

"Excuse me, are the two of you going to purchase or…" a new voice asks. Those two capaemen are so deep in an argument that they seem to be irritating the others. Mary waves her hand at Steven. This is as good of a distraction as any.

The group springs into action, rolling over to the short crate. In it are red, oval-shaped fruits piled nearly a foot above the crate's edge.

"Okay," Zane whispers, "here's how you do it. Don't grab a fruit that has too many others sitting on top. Could cause an avalanche."

Some of them are as big as her bed. That would be quite an avalanche. "Got it," Mary says. She observes the experts. Half of the group heads to the left corner, the other to the right. The corner seems to be the best place to grab the produce. She reaches up to help the group nearest her but is too short to touch the fruit.

The younger capaemen growls. "This past month you've been so different. What in the waters happened?"

"Nothing," the elder says angrily. "It is none of your business. Don't you have anything better to do?"

"Nothing, you say? Then you would not mind if I used the workshop for a couple more days, would you?"

"Come now, you've already used it today."

"I would like to, *again*," it says accusingly.

The older one growls, then begins walking. Its *boom*ing footsteps seem to grow louder, nearer.

Mary's heart drops. It's just her imagination, right? It has no reason to come this way. Regardless, they've got to grab that fruit, right *now*. She jumps up to try to help, but this turns out to be a mistake.

In a split second, half the pile comes tumbling down.

"What in the winds?" the capaeman at the table says.

boom boom

The humans run for their lives. Dropping everything, they sprint toward a group of larger crates. Mary follows—that is, until something hits her from behind. She *slam*s to the ground.

It takes her a few seconds to realize a giant fruit is rolling over her. This one is a little smaller, about half the size of her bed. It isn't heavy enough to crush her, but it does hurt. "Hurry!" Steven says, pulling her up. He hastily guides the rolling fruit behind the maze of boxes, and together, they leap to safety.

boom boom boom boom

A few people peer around the corner of their hiding spot, Mary included.

Now they can *see* the capaemen.

"What the stars knocked this over? It is not even windy today," an older-looking female capaeman says. It wears an apron around its waist. This must be one of the managers of the food. It is massive, with a round, bulging belly and arms thicker than tree trunks. The mere sight of it makes Mary want to run and never look back.

"It appears that they simply fell," the older capaeman says. This one is boyish, with a tall and lanky build, which seems somewhat familiar.

"Hmph, someone was careless in stacking these," the market manager growls, placing the runaway fruits back in the box. It stomps back to the table.

The two boys still stand there. The second is smaller and shares its siblings' head of thick black hair, but it's turned toward the market, so Mary can't see its face. "Well, nothing to see here, I suppose." It walks away calmly.

Yet the tall one doesn't move.

What reason does it have to stay? After all, that one said the produce fell on its own. Mary claps a hand over her mouth, afraid she might scream. If that capaeman so much as walks in their direction...

"We have to stay hidden," Steven says. The others don't move a muscle.

The Crystal River flashes in Mary's mind: the moment the hunter spotted them. "No, we have to leave. Try to make it to the grass, where it's safer."

"Too risky," the boy counters. "If we rustle the grass, it could hear us."

"If it checks here, it will *definitely* see us," Mary says. "Trust me, I've faced a capaeman," and she only survived because they ran.

Steven doesn't argue, but he doesn't move either. Mary is unsure if she has a right to argue. After all, she is the reason they are in this situation. She panicked. She caused the pile to fall. Some people in the group side-eye her, clearly furious about this careless mistake and hesitant to follow her idea. Mary turns her attention back to the lingering giant, praying her blunder won't get them all killed.

The capaeman kneels, grabbing one of the fruits they tried to steal. It seems transfixed by it. Those inhuman green eyes squint at the produce. The giant's side-swept black hair falls into its face.

Yes, this one *is* familiar.

It's the same boy that was running on the day of Lillian's death. This giant is bad news. Who knows what it was doing back then?

It begins scanning the ground as if following a trail. Then, its head shoots in their direction. The surveyors sprint deeper into the boxes.

boom... boom...

The capaeman's all-powerful steps pound in their direction, and the humans dash as fast as they can, treading deeper into the maze of crates. Mary's first thought is they're going to be trapped. Eventually, two boxes will be shoulder to shoulder. Then they will have nowhere to run. She wishes they had listened to her and gone for the grass.

Boom... Boom...

After much ducking and rolling, her fears come true: a dead end. At the very least, the crates are stacked high here. It will be hard for anything to see them, but Mary shakes her fear.

This capaeman seems different. More observant than the others.

Boom Boom

The sound is growing closer. It must be searching.

BOOM.

A shadow swallows the little cracks of light that seep between the crates. Mary hears creaking and the rustling of fabric, as loud as tree branches in a storm. Then, deep, hulking breaths. It exhales slowly and evenly, calm as the deep zones of the river.

Steven grabs Mary's hand, looking her in the eyes. "It'll be okay."

She shakes her head. "How are you so sure?"

He wraps his arms around her. "It's not your fault, alright? Everyone makes mistakes."

Her whole body is shaking. "I shouldn't have come."

No one responds to this. They must be thinking the same thing as her—that she's a screw-up. Perhaps Zurec was right to keep her in a cycle of lies. Maybe in a twisted way, that was the best thing for her, because at least she'd be *alive*.

"Hey, Lionel!" the voice of the younger boy echoes. "What has you so transfixed? Get over here! I wish to go home."

"Oh, alright. I'll be there in a moment," the older capaeman responds. It sounds only inches away from them.

boom boom boom...

Miraculously, footsteps head in the opposite direction, back into the market. Mary exhales in relief. That younger capaeman unknowingly saved them, and not a moment too soon.

Steven untangles their arms. "See? We're okay," he reassures, but his tone is shaky. "Everyone, let's get out of here before it comes back."

No group has been in more agreement.

⁕⁕⁕

The farther they get from the market, the safer Mary feels. Guilt about what happened eats away at her, and even though her family is bound to be furious at her for leaving, she wants more than anything to go home.

The sun is beginning to set in the Giant Wilds.

"That was a close one," Steven says somberly.

"Yeah, but we've had closer ones," Zane adds. His kind, brown eyes meet Mary's, trying to reassure her.

She hangs her head. "I'm sorry."

"Don't be," the boy leader says, placing a hand on her shoulder. "Trust me when I say we've seen far worse screw-ups."

"Far worse? How?"

"Just trust us on that," Zane says. "No one's gonna be mad at ya for this. I mean, we got something out of it anyway." He gestures to the giant fruit.

Five people at the back of the group carry a plump, red produce on their backs. The fruit is oval-shaped with a massive, curved stem sticking out of it. Mary can think of multiple uses for the stem alone, but the fruit could feed several people for days. It's sure to help them in the week to come. She is almost glad it ran her over. Otherwise, Steven wouldn't have rolled it into their hiding spot, and they would have returned with nothing.

Maybe Zane is right. It could have been worse.

Heading back through the fungi forest, the group turns in a direction unfamiliar to Mary. They approach a root so far off the ground that it makes a massive curve, and underneath is the largest trapdoor she has ever seen.

The people with the fruit head in first, bringing it into the burrow with practiced ease. Zane and two others help them out, leaving only Mary and Steven.

"This is the southern entrance, leads to the kitchen," Steven explains. "This ain't our best take, but it's not the worst either. I think Vivian will be pleased, considering how small our scavenging group was today."

"That's good," Mary says. "Still, it's my fault. Without me, I'm sure you would have done much better."

The boy peers at her with soft, pained eyes. "Hey, ya got a minute? I've got something that may make ya feel better."

"Sure, why not," she says. "I have nothing better to do."

They end up making their way through the mushrooms until Steven finds a place for them to sit next to the Zurec entrance. There, they wait for the sun to set completely. Mary doesn't know what could possibly be different about the mushroom forest at dusk, but at the same time, she isn't eager to see her family anyway. So, she waits.

As the daylight in the Giant Wilds dwindles, something strange happens to the mushrooms. She swears they're glowing a little, or maybe it's a trick of the light.

However, as the Wilds continue to darken, the fungi indeed get brighter. Mary sits in silence, marveling at the phenomenon. She has never seen anything like this in her life.

Finally, the sky falls into complete blackness.

Yet, it isn't even dark outside. By the light of the mushrooms, she can see the entirety of the Giant Wilds just as clearly as if it were early dusk. Green, pink, purple, blue, and yellow—they glow in shades she's never seen before, stretching on for miles. Mary runs her hand across the cap they're sitting on, which blazes pink. It is oddly warm, like a campfire. "Wh-Why do they do this?"

"Don't know, but it's why we don't eat them," Steven adds.

"Yeah, I'd bet this stuff would be harmful."

"Look, I don't want you to feel bad about today," he says, smiling nervously.

Mary frowns, staring at her feet in the mushroom light. "It's too late for that."

"Ya know, if we had listened to you back there, we may not have had such a close call. I certainly feel bad about that."

"What?" Mary asks. "No, it was a stupid plan. We might have gotten caught."

"We *were* almost caught *by* hiding. Besides, your plan reminded me of Vivian. It's rare for her to go on an expedition, but when she does, she always comes up with fast plans like that. Tells us to keep moving, no matter what. The only reason I didn't listen to ya is because the other folks might not have followed."

"Yeah, they were mad."

"Only in the moment. They'll cool down, I swear. Again, we've had much worse blunders."

Mary can't imagine worse than today, so she tries to put it out of her mind. "Why did you want me to see this?" she asks, gesturing toward the glowing mushrooms.

Wordlessly, the boy grabs her hand and leads her away from their sitting area. Then he clasps both of her hands in his. By the Wilds, Steven could not look more handsome right now, his chiseled features illuminated by the lights. The colors dance in a rainbow in his stunning blue eyes, and his dark hair falls into his face. He smiles, and it's as if he is glowing too.

"There's something we do every year at the end of spring. It's called the Dance of the Glowing Mushrooms."

"A-A dance?" Mary stutters.

"Yeah, it goes something like this." He places his arms around her and steps from side to side.

Mary trips over his foot. "What are you doing?"

"Just follow my movements," he instructs. "There's usually music, but we'll have to wait until the real thing for that part." He leads her in a circle, moving one of their clasped hands in and out as they spin. It feels magical.

"How's this?" Steven asks.

"This is... fine," she says, breathless. "It's perfectly fine."

"Yeah?" He pulls her in, and for some reason, Mary feels excitement ripple through her body. She closes her eyes.

And he hugs her. "It's going to be alright."

"Oh, r-right," Mary responds, feeling strangely disappointed.

"I've got your back, okay?"

"Yeah," she says, but following that is a sense of dread. Out of everyone, he's the only person who has her back. The person she once hated is now her only ally.

Everything is far from alright.

37

The Capaemen of the Waterlands

Lillian

When they returned to the workshop, the capaeman and human did not say another word to each other. Lionel simply dropped Lillian off and left. It's already the morning of the next day, and he still has not returned. So, the warrior sits on her bed in the darkness of the cabinet, alone with her thoughts.

Lillian feels like a fool. Her ancestors cautioned against the capaemen for a reason. Saying they are evil is an oversimplification, but it is more or less accurate. After all, they see humans as less than animals. Well, most of them do.

Thinking of Lionel makes Lillian's head pound. On the one hand, he has been kind to her. On the other, he will never see her as an equal. He has made the latter as clear as the Crystal River. Still, she holds onto a faint hope that maybe what's happening goes deeper than that. Perhaps, ever so slowly, he is starting to realize the same thing she is: that humans and capaemen are not so different.

She has to believe that's what's happening. Otherwise, she'll lose it.

Lillian hugs her knees. She misses her family so badly: Brianna, Mia, Jamie, Albert, even her dad, Miss May, and Mary. She hopes with everything she has that they're alive. She hopes Jess, Milo, Bruno, Zoey, and all the gatherers and surveyors are alright too. She knows some of them are dead... but they can't all be gone, right? The problems she had with them before feel so insignificant now. In fact, she understands where they were coming from. In this brutal world, there is nothing more important than family. There is nothing more important than staying safe, than staying together. So despite her hope, or somehow along with it, Lillian feels like a fool for thinking things could be different. What is she going to do, change the minds of an entire species? That's impossible.

click

The door to the room opens and closes. Great, more confusion. That's just what she needs right now.

"Lillian?" the voice of Lionel calls.

Lillian throws the blanket over her head.

"Come on out. I have someplace special to show you. It will blow your mind."

She doesn't answer. She needs time to think, and Lionel's voice is making her headache worse.

"I noticed your walking has improved. It will not be long before I escort you home. I swear, this place is the best yet. We can only travel there in reasonable time by train."

Lillian stays silent. She doesn't know what to say. No place in the world could make up for what he told her yesterday. *"There are no innocent humans. That is what they believe."*

To make things worse, after telling her that, Lionel went utterly silent. No words of reassurance. Nothing about what he was thinking at all. It's like he believes that statement is true, that no human is innocent. But how could he, after everything they have been through?

boom... boom...

Lionel is coming closer. He must be right outside the cabinet. "Hey, are you alright?"

"How could I be alright?" she finally says. Lillian can't believe he would ask such a silly question. It's as if he has no idea how those words affected her.

There is a pause from the other side. She can almost see Lionel's thinking face. A hand on his chin and eyes in a half-squint. "You are still upset, huh?"

You don't say, Lillian thinks, but she doesn't say it out loud.

"Look, I hate to admit it, but what I said was true. As a matter of fact, I have been taking a massive risk even helping you. Do you know what they do to capaemen who help your kind?"

Another pause. Lionel takes a deep breath and exhales loudly.

"If a capaeman helps a human, they will be branded as a traitor. Their name will be announced on the radio for all to hear, and they can face a wide variety of punishments, from jail time to the death sentence. Even if they are not sentenced to die, when they return to the working world, everyone will see them as a criminal. It would be nearly impossible to find a job. Nearly impossible to regain a life."

"...Then why did you help me? And don't say it was fascination. That isn't a good enough reason to risk your life."

Lillian hears the heavy *squeeeaaak* of a chair dragging across the floor. Lionel must be sitting down.

"Because... 'when you see a life in trouble, it is your duty to save it, regardless of how small.' My mother used to say that."

"Even if it's the life of a human?" Lillian asks. "Clearly, you don't see us that way."

"That is false," Lionel says. "It pains me to admit. I used to think like that, but it is different now."

"Different how?"

The capaeman sighs loudly. "Please, just... come out. I would like to catch the train on time. I will show you what I mean when we arrive."

He seems all too eager to get out of here. Usually, Lillian would ask why he's in such a rush, which would inevitably become an argument, but she's too tired—tired of reality. Maybe another trip to a new place will be good for her. She cautiously pushes open the cabinet door. "Okay, but you'd better tell me more once we get there."

Lionel smiles at her. That's a rare sight. Maybe this place really will take her mind off things. Lillian crawls into his bag, and they're off to their next destination.

Perhaps the last one.

⚜ ⚜

After several minutes of walking, they arrive at a sea of voices. The voices grow louder and louder, until they surround them. One... two... three... No, more than that. There are dozens of capaemen all around them. The heat spikes as well. What is a "train," and why are so many capaemen swarming it? Lillian wishes she could see outside.

"Ticket, please," a gruff capaeman voice says.

"Certainly," Lionel responds. There is a strange beeping noise, and then Lionel resumes walking.

Behind them, Lillian hears that same gruff voice again. "Ticket, please."

"Oh, now where in the winds did I put that thing? Give me a moment," a female capaeman says. Her voice is shriller than the male's, but still way too low to be human. They have visited places with other capaemen before, but never this many. Lillian feels like she is on another planet.

"It is okay. We have almost arrived at the cabin," Lionel whispers.

The air changes again, cooling down significantly. Lillian sighs in relief. The crowd must be thinning, or maybe they've gone inside a building. It's impossible to tell. She can now hear individual conversations instead of cacophonous chatter. It is still bizarre, but she'll take it over the chaos.

"Mother!" a smaller, higher voice exclaims.

"What is it now?"

"How long until we arrive? I wish to swim."

"It will be up to an hour, dear. Sit tight."

"Nooooooo."

From another direction, Lillian picks up a different conversation.

"I love you so much. I cannot wait to spend the rest of my life with you," a female says.

"Oh, my darling, I'd move the moon and stars for you," a deeper female voice responds.

Romance—one of the few things Lillian cannot and *does not* want to understand. How strange that it happens with capaemen as well. If someone her age had been born in Zurec besides Mary, that could be them whispering sweet nothings to her. She's thankful she never had to deal with that. There are enough challenges to survival.

click.

clunk.

Finally, something slides open and then closes, cutting off all the voices. She's thankful for the silence.

"We can speak freely here," Lionel says as he places the pack on a cold surface.

Lillian busts out of the bag, taking a much-needed breath of fresh air. This room is even stranger than the workshop. She is on a giant white table with long padded chairs on either side. The chairs are dyed blue, and the walls dark grey. Where the capaemen get so much dye, she will never know.

The most astonishing thing about this room is the massive window. It reaches from the ceiling all the way to the tiled floor. Outside, hoards of capaemen bustle about. She's never seen this many capaemen, no, this many *people* in one place before. Some stand in line, handing pieces of paper to a man behind a desk. Others loiter on the pavement in small groups. Some talk passionately, their reptilian eyes wide with enthusiasm. Others are more reserved, with not so much as a toothy smile. Almost every capaeman seems to be wearing light-weight clothing, from dresses to short-shorts to tank tops, all unequivocally paired with close-toed boots. How odd.

"You can gaze outside as much as you wish," Lionel says. "This glass is one-way only. You can see them, but they cannot see you."

Lillian jumps. She almost forgot about Lionel sitting right next to her. He too is wearing different clothes than usual: a white short-sleeved shirt, black shorts, and black combat boots. He has one foot on the chair and the other under the table. His scales glimmer in the light from the window, and he watches Lillian with a fanged smile. Again, what is going on with him?

"This is called a train," the capaeman explains. "We use these to travel long distances. Very soon, we will start moving."

"You mean this whole thing..." Lillian looks around the room, "... is a form of *transportation*? Like an acera or a boat?"

"Heh, I am impressed you remember what a boat is, but it is not just this room. It has multiple private booths, rows of chairs for regular passengers, and I suppose you can also count the cargo hold. That part of the train carries the luggage. You are lucky. We have some of the best seats on this entire vehicle."

"How is that?"

"It is one of the few benefits my father provides. Plenty of coin." Lillian glances about the cabin, open-mouthed. This isn't the only room. There are multitudes more. There's no way she can fathom the scale of this device.

"Wow, the train has not even begun moving, and you look as though you are about to pass out," Lionel teases.

"Hey," she says, "this is all new to me!"

"I am glad you are having fun." Again, this isn't like him. He's hardly insulted her today, and there is a permanent grin on his face.

"Who are you and what have you done with Lionel?"

"Heyyy, what are you on about? I am exactly the same as always."

"Are not. You're *never* this nice."

Before he can respond, the entire building jolts. Lillian flies into the air but manages to catch herself on Lionel's backpack. Then, rapidly, the scenery outside begins to blur.

The train emits an almost deafening whistle, followed by a repeated *chugging* of machinery that feels like it's just below the floor.

They're going so fast that she can barely see what's outside. They quickly pass the town of glass buildings. This is way faster than Jamie's acera—than she thought anything could be. The plains south of the town blur together until they are a simple green blob with a blue sky. They certainly will get to their destination soon. They are practically teleporting there.

Yet Lionel undoes the strings on his pack and pulls out a book.

He looks like he's done this a million times. They truly are from two different worlds.

As the landscape whizzes by, Lillian thinks back to the time in the forge when she recovered that spear with Mary. The hope she felt when she saw it glimmering in the torchlight, and how that hope was extinguished by the bloody reality of the world. Yet, in a way, Lillian was right; there is more to existence than living in a burrow. The world is so massive that she could dedicate her whole life to exploring it and never see it all. Why are they hiding in a hole in a forest? Why are they—

The bodies of Albian appear in her mind again, followed by the narecons—the way they brutalized the warriors of her clan. She understands why Zurec chose to hide. Lillian knows that better than anyone else now. And yet...

She stares at Lionel. He seems deeply engrossed in that book, the same way the Zurec children become with a good story.

If there are more capaemen like him, maybe things can change.

⚜

It feels like forever before the train finally comes to a stop. The land of Lyonis stretches on for hundreds of miles, a measure of distance Lillian can't even begin to comprehend. Sometimes, forests pass by. The tree leaves aren't the same color as those in the Giant Wilds. They are light brown instead of green, and from what she can tell there isn't moss all over the place. It must be nice not having to worry about that stuff growing everywhere. She wonders what sort of humans live there, if any at all.

Rows of capaemen buildings juxtapose these forests: some made with their signature glass, and others larger—more private. It's almost always at these places that the train stops, letting off some passengers and welcoming new ones. Lillian observes everything that she can about them. They hold out slips of paper to be checked by a man behind a table, one by one. They too wear short clothing, and many drag hefty bags along. Some are families. Some are couples. Some are groups of friends, laughing and teasing each other. Wherever they're headed, it's a place everyone is excited about. Lillian grows eager.

About half an hour later, the train comes to another stop, and finally, Lionel closes his book. "Here already, are we? The ride feels faster and faster every occasion."

"Where exactly is 'here'?" Lillian asks, staring out the window. Other than a singular building with the sign *CONCESSIONS & SOUVENIRS* hanging over it, this place is complete wilderness. There are sparse trees, hills, and tall grass as far as the eye can see. The soil is a strange color: bright tan, just like Lillian's undershirt. She didn't realize how diverse different environments could be. It's one thing hearing Jamie and Albert describe it, and another being here herself.

"If I tell you where we are now, it will ruin the surprise," Lionel says. "Trust me, alright?"

The warrior crosses her arms. "Fine, but it better not take too long. I'm starting to get tired of that uncomfortable bag."

The capaeman laughs. "Fair enough."

The second they get off the train, Lillian hears dozens of voices, but unlike the last stop, that's not the loudest sound. The voices of the other passengers sound drowned out, muffled almost, by... water?

fwooosh... fwooosh...

It sounds like water flowing, but not in the way the river does. Instead of constantly roaring, the sound fades and grows rhythmically, as if the water were moving back and forth. It is intense yet somehow calming.

The next thing Lillian notices is a thickness in the air. It smells almost sour, and she can feel water vapor penetrating her pores. There must be a massive body of water nearby.

As they travel to this new and uncharted place, Lillian closes her eyes and listens to the sound of the water. She hardly feels the bounce of Lionel's steps anymore. She is one with the current, with the soothing scent of fresh air all around her. Lillian takes a deep breath in, and a lasting breath out. When she was a child, Miss May always told them to take deep breaths when stressed. Now, she's simply doing it to relax.

Then Lionel stops.

"Okay, we are in a fairly remote place now, but before I let you out, we need to set some ground rules."

"Sure," Lillian says a little too casually.

"First of all, no touching the water. I cannot guarantee I can save you if you fall in. Secondly, I will be on watch. If I see anyone coming, you are to get back in the bag immediately, no questions asked. This is far enough that it should be a safe spot, but keep in mind we are in a public space. Anyone could show up at any time. Have I made myself clear?"

"Crystal."

"Very well, then." Finally, he places the bag on the ground. Lillian pulls it open and is immediately blinded by the sun.

"It's so bright," she says. It's also swelteringly hot, almost as hot as the workshop before Lionel turned the air down.

"That is the reason I brought this along."

He holds something over her that gives her shade. When Lillian's eyes fall on the object, a wave of nostalgia hits.

"The—The rain shield."

Lionel laughs. "Rain shield? This is called an umbrella, and yeah, I suppose you have seen this one before, when we—"

"—when you saved my life."

Her eyes adjusting, Lillian stares at the breathtaking scenery. It's nothing but bright-blue water for miles, flowing in and out in that beautiful rhythmic pattern. She watches one swell of water rise, crest into a sharp peak, then curl and crash down upon itself. The water is endless, reminding her of the stories Jamie told her. Then, realization dawns.

This is it. This is the *ocean*.

It's even more beautiful than Jamie and Albert described. Lining the shore's edges are all sorts of things she has never seen before, from hard-shelled creatures scuttling across the grainy, tan soil, to colorful stones glinting just out of reach. Without thinking, Lillian moves forward into the sun. Mary would love those colored rocks. If only she could get close enough to—

"Lillian, NO!" Lionel screams.

Without warning, the water barrels straight at her, knocking her flat on the ground. The current is unbearably strong, almost like the river rapids. She tries to stand up, but it shoves her back down like her body weighs nothing. Luckily, Lionel's hand swoops in just before the water buries her.

Lillian sits in the capaeman's hands, hacking up water. Somehow, this tastes worse than the fountain.

"You are so dense! What did I just tell you?"

She smiles guiltily. "Yeah, that was my bad this time."

Lionel places her a safe distance away from the foamy, rolling water. The tan dirt sticks to her leg bandages, now soaked through. "What were you so transfixed on that you nearly ended your own life?" Lillian points at the colored rocks. In response, Lionel picks one up. This one is tiny, only slightly bigger than Lillian's hand. "This is called a seashell," he says, handing it to her. "They are the exoskeletons of sea creatures that have died. They come in thousands of different forms and colors. My mother and I used to collect them. That specimen you are holding is from a very small species of mollusk. They like to burrow right here in the sand. When the tide comes in, they scavenge beneath the waves. When the tide goes out, they are exposed to the sun, so they must quickly bury themselves before they dry out. As a result, it is quite common to find their exoskeletons around here. Many do not make it. Take a look."

Lillian stares at the "sand" beneath the clear water. As the "tide" goes out, many seashells that look exactly like hers are exposed, but then they wiggle from side to side, disappearing under the soil and leaving only the *pop!* of an air bubble behind. There must be thousands of them—getting exposed and then burying themselves, then getting exposed yet again. What a dreary existence, constantly evading certain death.

"At least we are not like them," Lionel states. "We get to relax on occasion. Even humans, right?"

She nods, staring at her shell. It's shaped like a long triangle and pure white all the way to the tip, which is a bright red. "These are so beautiful."

"I possess a collection back at home if you wish to see it. You would not believe what washes to the shore, especially after a storm."

He pauses for a moment as if realizing something.

"What's wrong?" Lillian asks.

"Nothing. I was simply remembering."

"Remembering what?"

"My family used to live here, but our house was destroyed in the hurricane—a long-lasting rainstorm," he explains. "It was a fierce one."

Lillian remembers Zurec's stories of the rains. "I've heard of the rains. I'd just been born when they happened, so I don't remember, but because of those rains most of our clan died. There were so many great people I never got to meet."

Lionel stares at her, his green eyes full of sympathy. "I did not even consider how the hurricane may have affected the humans. I... I too lost someone. My mother... She did not make it to the shelter in time."

"*That's* how she died?"

The capaeman nods grimly.

Dying in a storm... That's a brutal way to go, Lillian thinks, but she doesn't say it out loud. For a moment, they stare at the waves together. The water is such a gorgeous turquoise, and it stretches deep into the skyline. Lillian wonders if somewhere out there, there is the island of Osinawa, where Jamie and Albert came from. If so, then they truly did come a long way. She can't wait to tell them she's seen the ocean. They will freak out.

"Hey, wait a minute," Lionel says. "You said you were a newborn during the hurricane. How old are you exactly?"

"I'm fifteen," she answers.

"Fifteen? Impossible. You must be much older than that."

"Hey!" Lillian yells. He's back to insulting her. She should have known it was only a matter of time. "Wait, if you were alive during the rains, then how old are *you?*"

"I am thirty-two."

"THIRTY-TWO?" Lillian screeches. That's the same age as her dad. "But... but you look like you're my age."

"I most certainly am not. You are younger than my brother. No wonder you are so immature."

She taps her foot in the sand. "Come on, you were doing so well. What's with the insults again?"

Lionel smiles from ear to ear, showing his razor-sharp teeth. "I believe I can surmise what is happening here. Capaemen must age differently from humans, yet another thing we have learned about each other. Based on what you just told me, it seems I am twice the age you expected me to be, and you are half the age I expected of you. That can only mean one thing. Tell me, what is a human's average life expectancy?"

"I have no idea. We're too busy being eaten by monsters."

Lionel laughs. "You make a fair point. Well, at any rate, my species probably lives longer than yours."

"That doesn't surprise me." She remembers Albert's words when they first saw Lionel: *"For all we know, that monster could be a hundred years old."* He was off by seventy years, but the idea was on point. They must age differently due to their size.

Lillian turns her attention back to the water. She imagines swimming in the river with Mary again and regaling her with tales of the ocean. Mary would *flip.*

Then again... even if her family is alive, would she be able to tell them all she's learned? She looks at Lionel, whose scales glimmer in the sun. Maybe if they saw what he's really like, they could all be friends. They could strive for a better tomorrow. Is such a future possible?

"Hey," Lionel says, "I think I have hatched an idea."

"What is it?" Lillian asks, snapping out of her wishful thoughts.

"How would you like to walk down the beach, but not in the bag this time?"

"What do you mean?"

The capaeman reaches out his hand until it's only inches away from her. "Do you trust me?"

This time, Lillian doesn't shy away. She wasn't scared when he picked her up from the ocean, and she isn't now. A few weeks ago, she never thought she would get to this point, but here she is. This may be the wildest thing she's done yet.

"Yes. I trust you."

Carefully, the warrior steps onto the hand of the capaeman, who gently lifts her until she reaches his shoulder. Understanding his intent, Lillian steps off his hand and onto his shoulder, taking a seat. Once she's settled, Lionel begins to walk.

boom... boom...

As the *boom*s of Lionel's steps mix with the sound of the waves, Lillian feels more powerful than ever before. She can see the massive footprints he leaves in the sand as he walks, gaze great distances from his perspective high in the sky. The wind blows her bronze hair back. She stretches her arms out in the air, wanting to enjoy every minute.

So, this is how it feels to be a capaeman.

"Enjoying yourself?" Lionel asks.

This close, Lillian can see every scale on Lionel's face. They follow the curves of his cheeks, fanning up and out on his forehead. The scales vary in size depending on their location. The ones on his forehead are as big as Lillian's spread-out hand, while the scales around his nose and eyelids are half that size. Never in her life did she imagine she'd be this close to a capaeman. She sees what they see—feels what they feel, and it's all so... magical.

"You know," Lionel says, "there is something I tried to say previously, but I was unable to. I believe I can say it now."

He stops and gazes at the horizon. There is ocean as far as the eye can see, even from this high in the sky. The waves grow and crash in an instant—a beautiful cycle of rolling water.

"What they have told us about humans... it is wrong. You are so much like us, it is terrifying. I cannot imagine the hardship your people have gone through because of the misconception we have. I do not even know how it started. All I know is, well... I think if more people had the chance to meet you, they might change their minds too."

Lillian's eyes grow cloudy. "Do you... do you really mean that?"

The capaeman stares at the ocean with absolute certainty. "I do. I truly do." Lillian beams at the light glimmering off the waves, not knowing what else to say. This morning she believed the capaemen would always see them as nothing, yet here is a capaeman—changing—on the exact same day. This is a marvel, a miracle.

So... why does Lionel look so sad?

38

Peacekeepers, Warmongers, and the Outsiders

Mary

boom... boom...

Mary is dragged through the forest, trying to outrun an inescapable force. The figure holding her hand is too blurry to see. All she knows is she'd be dead without them. They pull her along, determined for both of them to survive. No matter what obstacle they come across, be it a log or dense foliage, they get past it hastily. Still, Mary knows they would be much faster if they let go of her hand. They might even be able to escape the giant.

Boom... Boom...

With her, they're sure to be caught. At the deafening sound of each *boom*, Mary's body grows stiffer, slower, and more burdensome.

whooooossshhh

The river roars ahead. They are approaching a dead end, yet the foggy figure still refuses to let go of her hand. Mary wants to do it for them, to free this person of her dead weight, but she cannot bring herself to yank her hand away.

She wants to live too. How cowardly.

Suddenly, they are on that fateful root arching over the rapids. The fog around the figure dissipates, revealing a familiar face.

Tall and lean, blue eyes, dark hair, and black armor.

It's Steven.

Boom Boom

"It'll be okay," he says, clasping his hands in hers.

A shadow cloaks them, and Mary begins to panic.

BOOM.

"Let me go," she begs. "I'm not worth it. Please, save yourself."

Steven wraps his arms around her, shielding her from having to see the unstoppable force of nature that looms above. "Keep fighting, Mary."

"No! Please, no! I can't take this anymore. Just let me die instead. I'm begging you!"

He doesn't listen to her, and together they plunge into the river, Steven taking the brunt of the boulders.

Mary shoots out of her bed, hyperventilating.

It was just a dream.

Just a dream. It doesn't mean anything, Mary thinks, her eyes shut tight.

She glances about her room, trying to distract herself. Although lacking the fancy furnishings, it reminds her of the first night she spent in Rostad's burrow. It was straight out of a fairy tale and a nightmare simultaneously.

The girl hangs her head. Now, *everything* is a nightmare.

Adventuring distracted her for a minute, but in the end, she still had to come home. She still has to face her family.

knock knock

Someone is at her door. Mary throws the covers over her head.

knock knock knock

She curls up in her sheets, hoping they'll go away.

"Mary?" her mother asks. "Are you awake?"

The sound of that voice makes her tremble with rage.

"Darling, can we talk?" She sounds dismayed, nothing like the irate person she was yesterday. Still, Mary can't let her in. She used to be the person she trusted the most in this world, but she raised her on lies.

"Please," her mother begs. "I'm sorry, baby. I heard about what happened after you talked to Seth. You're not in trouble. I blame myself."

"Go away!" Mary cries. This is all she wanted to hear the other day, but now it's too little too late.

"I got... caught up in our old ways," she continues. "I was determined to preserve them because they worked for so long. We should have told you the second we decided to meet with Rostad. That's when we couldn't keep the secret anymore."

Mary's eyes sting, but she couldn't conjure tears if she tried. She's already dried her eyes out mourning Lillian.

"Please, what can I do to make it up to you?" Her mother is persistent.

For a moment, she thinks about it. Mary tries to imagine how her family could make up for the lies, a way this could be over, but comes up short. Nothing can erase this. Her whole view of who they are was a lie. They weren't peacekeepers. They were warmongers. How can their relationship recover when her trust has been broken beyond repair?

"Excuse me, ma'am. Let me try." It's the voice of Steven. Mary wonders why he is here.

There is another *knock* at the door. "Mary, come on out. The acera warriors have arrived, and they have massive news to share. They want everyone to gather outside."

"What?" her mother's voice asks. "A-Are we safe?"

"Not sure. Haven't heard what they have to say. You should get everyone out of their rooms. They're refusing to speak until all of Zurec is there."

"A-Alright then." Her footsteps depart down the hall.

"Coast is clear," Steven confirms. "May I come in?"

"Fine," Mary says. Oddly enough, he is one of the few people who hasn't betrayed her. She doesn't want to jeopardize this relationship too.

The door opens and closes softly. She feels her bed shift as he sits on it.

"Rough night, huh?"

Finally, Mary lifts the covers off of herself. She sits up, revealing her bed-head and baggy eyes. "The worst. I had a horrible nightmare."

"Really, what was it about?"

She shifts around nervously. Usually, Mary keeps her dreams to herself, but she needs his confirmation. "You... sacrificed yourself to save me. It's ridiculous, right? There's no way you'd do that."

Steven stares at her for a moment. Then, he clears his throat and says, "Heh, yeah. Absolutely ridiculous. Why would I ever do that for *you*?"

Mary pushes him playfully. "You're such a jerk," and that's just the way she likes it. No one is allowed to sacrifice themself for her—not ever again.

Bantering, the two make their way out of her room and into the Giant Wilds.

⁂

Everyone is here—including some faces she'd rather not see. They've gathered around the same mushroom as the last time the acera warriors returned. The tiny Zurec group stands to one side of the mushroom, while Rostad's grand clan crowds the other. Mary spots Chief Vivian, Zane, and Alec amongst the Rostad people. She has not seen that jerk since the mob incident. To make things even worse, Steven greets all of them as if nothing happened.

Mary stands between the two groups, not knowing where to go.

"Hey, get over here," Steven tells her. She reluctantly approaches them, glaring at the lousy guy to his right.

"It's been a while," Alec says nonchalantly. "How've ya been?"

Mary's disdain quickly turns to annoyance. "Why are you so friendly all of a sudden?"

He scratches his head. "Heard about what happened to you. That must suck."

She raises an eyebrow. Is that all?

"Yeah, continue Alec," Zane encourages, his massive hand squeezing the guy's shoulder.

"And I'm s-sorry. I didn't know you weren't like those other folks."

Mary isn't a fan of that apology. It's like they're holding him at knifepoint. "Thanks," she says sardonically.

"Come on, you can do better than that," Steven says, clapping him on the back. "Heck, you've kept that wife and kid for years. I see you treating them kindly. You can do the same here." Mary places a hand over her mouth. *He* has a family? That's a tough plant to swallow.

"I-I'm doing my best, man," he says through gritted teeth.

As the boys devolve into bickering, Mary turns her attention elsewhere. Across the fungal field, Seth is observing her with a slight grin on his face. She's unsure what he has to be happy about, but it's nice he isn't angry after she took off yesterday. Her mom and Kayla play with the kids. The pregnant ex-surveyor does a great job distracting them. Mia fidgets impatiently, clearly nervous about the announcement. Bruno holds her in his arms. Meanwhile, Brianna, Robin, Theo, and Jess whisper to each other, clearly trying to figure out what news the acera warriors are about to break to them.

Standing on the roof of the massive mushroom are Jamie, Albert, and Amphii. The woman atop her steed takes a huge breath. "Attention, everyone!" The massive crowd falls silent immediately. "I believe the hunters are about to make their move. You must switch burrows immediately!"

The people murmur amongst themselves. The Rostad side says things like:

"Move?"

"We can't leave. We've been here for decades."

Meanwhile, the Zurec side:

"Not again."

"What does she mean by hunters? I thought there was only one." Mary thought so too.

"I know it will be hard to leave," Jamie continues, "but it is necessary. Once a hunter pinpoints the location of a burrow, it arrives and fills it with poison gas. Anyone unfortunate enough to still be inside would experience a painful death. They did this to both Albian and Zurec. We can assume they will do the same to you."

Several Rostad people gasp, followed by more murmuring. Chief Vivian does her best to keep the panicking to a minimum, but even she appears distressed. It only now occurs to Mary that Rostad has no idea how the capaemen will attack. They've never experienced it before. This is one of the few areas in which Zurec has a leg-up. She watches as the clans begin to converse, with Rostad asking them if what she said is true and the Zurec people somberly confirming it.

Mary stands in between, still not sure who to talk to.

"Calm down, everyone," Jamie announces, although she also seems disturbed. "The good news is, the capaemen only attack during the day. The first time, it was at dawn. The second was midday. It's already past those times now. They won't do well at night in forest terrain, so we have at least until tomorrow morning." Mary stares at the sky and is surprised to see where the light is. She's right. It is already past the afternoon. That means she slept all day.

"Did ya hear that, everyone?" Chief Vivian's voice reverberates over the turmoil. "We're gonna be alright. All we gotta do is pack up our stuff and leave before the sun rises tomorrow." She came up with a plan quickly, and it's working too. The panic is already dying down.

"Yes," Jamie responds. "Do that, and we'll keep a close watch. We'll let you know if anything changes." As the assembly begins to disperse, Mary hears more murmurs amongst the crowd, showing that the Rostad people aren't too trusting of those words. She can't blame them. After all, those two still have hardly interacted with anyone. They do the bare minimum for their job, then fly who knows where.

Mary shoves her way closer to the towering mushroom, wanting to know why the acera warriors have been avoiding them. She too feels distant from Zurec now; maybe they can find something in common.

"Jamie, Albert!" Mary calls. The peer at her quizzically. She stares at their towering figures. "Long time no talk."

Albert is the first to jump to the ground. "Hey Mary, how's it hanging?" He hugs her. The girl plugs her nose. Why does he reek so bad?

"Sorry about that," Jamie says, hopping down second. "Living in the trees isn't exactly good for personal hygiene." She leans in. "Albert, you stink. Please show the girl mercy and leave some space."

"O-Oh, whoops." He backs away.

"You seem chipper again," Mary observes. "I was worried. You've both been distant lately."

"Yeah, well…" Jamie trails off as if trying to find the words. "We don't really fit in. I guess we never have."

"You got along well with Lillian." They both flinch at the name.

"She was… different," Albert says gloomily. "She was kind of an outsider too." Mary grimaces. So, that's it then. That is the reason they've been avoiding everyone. Lillian was the glue that held them together, and now that she is gone, the rogues have no one with whom to connect. Still, it is odd that they haven't even tried. Mary and Albert got along fine in the beginning. Why didn't they try to talk to her? Is she not good enough?

"You know, I'm sure there are some people you'd get along with if you gave them a chance," Mary states.

Jamie seems irked by this. "Who, the prejudiced Rostad people? Those guys are terrible, and your people have been isolating themselves. Although, I can hardly blame them."

"Hey, Rostad isn't so bad. Well, some of them aren't. You could at least *try*."

The woman's face falls. "What do you mean by *that*?"

"All you've been doing is the bare minimum. How do you think that looks to them? I mean, we did make a deal."

"Are you on *their* side now?" Jamie seethes. "I'm starting to see why you and Lillian butted heads so much."

"What's that supposed to mean?" Mary fumes. She cannot believe this despicable woman used her late friend as an insult.

"Guys, calm down—"

"Shut up, Albert," his sister says. "Little girl, you may act like a goody-two-shoes, like you're here to help everyone, but I see straight through that. You are way too quick to judge people without even trying to see their side."

Mary turns bright red. "What? That doesn't make any sense! What is wrong with you?" Her entire life has been lived for others, yet this woman accuses her of being selfish. How dare she?

Her brother tugs on her sleeve. "Sis, that's way too far, even for you."

"You don't think that, right Albert?" Mary asks, seething.

"I uh..."

Why is he hesitating? It's a simple question. "You *don't*... right?"

"O-Of course not!" he blurts. "My sister and I should be going now, right?"

Jamie exhales and glares at the girl. "Yes, we shouldn't waste any more time." The two rush back onto their acera and take off without another word.

Mary is dumbfounded.

What the heck was that conversation? She has no idea how Lillian managed to get along with those two. She knows they have a tragic past, but still, how can Jamie say those things? How dare they judge her relationship with Lillian when they have only been around for a few weeks? They know nothing about it.

Mary storms back into her room, no longer in the mood for talking.

However, before she can close the door, she spots a familiar little figure standing nearby.

"Mary, you're back?" It's Trista. She stands against the wall next to her room.

"Hey, what's going on?"

Her tiny eyes are wide. "Can we talk?"

"Of course." She may be angry but can never say no to little Trista. She won't turn away anyone in need. That is just the kind of person she is, which is the opposite of selfish.

They sit on the bed together. The little girl seems like she's about to collapse. She sways back and forth, and her eyelids keep drooping. This is something they have in common: the inability to sleep.

"We're gonna die," she says blatantly.

"Wh-What?" Mary should be expecting this by now, but she's caught off guard by the little girl's bluntness every time. "Look, Trista, I know it seems hopeless, but we're prepared this time. We'll leave before it even gets a chance to attack."

"And what then?" she screeches. "We live happily ever after? There's nowhere else to go!" The little girl begins to cry. She keeps wiping the tears away, but more flow out like a waterfall. All Mary can do is throw her arms around her. "One of them will find us," the little girl mumbles. "That's for sure."

"One... of them?" Mary asks, her heart sinking. "Trista, are you saying there's more than one?"

She nods. "There's always been two. I thought you knew that."

Mary is at a loss for words. So, when Jamie said "hunters" earlier, it wasn't an accident. Why didn't the scouts tell them about a second hunter? She squeezes her bed sheets, sick and tired of the lies. Of course, they've been keeping things from her too. Who hasn't been keeping secrets? There's no way to know for sure. She could ask Trista for a description, but what good would it do? She would never tell her, what with how much trauma that would bring back. Even if she did tell her, there's no way to stop them, regardless of how many there are. That was made painfully clear when they were almost caught at the market.

Finally, Mary works up the guts to speak. "Only one attacked us last time. We didn't realize there were two. So, two of them attacked your burrow?"

The little girl nods, shaking. "I'm sorry. I didn't know it was only one that time."

"It's okay," she says, hugging her tighter. "You were safely taken to the bunker before the hunter appeared, but yeah, no one saw more than one."

"There were two at our burrow," she repeats. "Two attacked us."

"I believe you," Mary says, but she has a feeling that's not the reason Trista is repeating those words. "Do you..." she asks, staring at the stone ceiling. "Do you think the second one will return? Do you think they'll attack Rostad, along with the first?"

The little girl nuzzles up to her, tears still streaming down her face. "I don't know."

By the Wilds, Mary has no idea either.

39

Orange Eyes

Lillian

The night after the beach adventure, Lillian sleeps better than she has her entire life. In Lionel's workshop, nothing can hurt her. She is unsure she'll adapt well when she returns to the Giant Wilds. Her bed in the burrow is uncomfortable compared to the one Lionel made for her. No... It will be even worse when Lillian returns. They can't even live in the burrow anymore. She will be stuck sleeping on one of those thin bunker mats. If that happens, she will have many restless nights, just like Mary.

That time on the beach... Lillian will look back at that and see it as one of the greatest times of her life. When her journey started with the gatherers, she never thought she would live to see such wonders. Back then, her ambitions were trivial, so small, like her world. Now, Lillian has seen how the capaemen live their lives, and how much she is missing. She has even befriended one of them, which everyone told her was impossible. She wonders what else is possible in this gigantic and beautiful world.

Lillian sits up in her bed and smiles. She cannot wait to see Lionel today: to share their life experiences, to travel together. Lionel said he would take her back home very soon. If Lillian doesn't have much longer here, she wants to make the most of it. Before she returns to her dreary life in the Giant Wilds, she wants to keep living like a capaeman.

The warrior does some stretches, checking her injuries. Her hand and shoulder have almost completely healed, but her legs are still sore. She can walk on them well enough. She just needs to be careful and not move too fast. Lionel did an incredible job with first aid, and now Lillian knows why. He is a "biologist," a capaeman expert on plants and animals. What an amazing thing to do with one's life. It turns out that when not constantly hiding from monsters, they have time to do things purely out of passion. His knowledge of flora and fauna would make Kayla squeal with delight.

Lillian grabs her dagger and pack, then exits the cabinet, eagerly waiting for Lionel. She wants to see his seashell collection, maybe even take one home as a gift for Mary—if she survived. The jewelry that girl could make with such material would be incredible. She sits next to the massive window, gazing at the wild grass outside for a few minutes.

A half hour.

An *hour.*

Lionel does not arrive.

Lillian glances at the sun moving over the cloudless sky. Soon, it will be the afternoon. He should be here already. What's taking him so long?

She remembers how sad Lionel looked on the beach, when he told her he was wrong about humans. There is still something bothering him. It's frustrating trying to figure that boy out. They had a tender moment, yet he is still holding something back. Lillian has no idea what he could be sad about. This is good news! Capaemen and humans are similar. If others knew the truth, maybe things could change. Maybe her family wouldn't have to live in a monster-infested forest anymore.

There is nothing to be upset about. They're friends, and that is a wonderful thing.

When Lionel comes through that door, Lillian is going to ask him. She will ask why he's conflicted because he shouldn't be. Sure, the punishment may be severe if he is caught helping her, but they just won't get caught. Easy. Lillian is small. She can hide anywhere.

boom... boom...

At the sound of footsteps, Lillian's head jerks toward the door. Someone is coming down the hall. It must be Lionel. He's a little late, but that's okay. She sees the giant doorknob turn, but then it gets stuck. It has never done that before. Lionel always opens it easily. The door handle jimmies and shakes. Lillian stands up, a bad feeling crawling in her gut.

With a large *click*, the door swings open...

... and on the other side is not Lionel.

The boy is a little shorter than Lionel, and skinnier as well. He wears a white collared shirt and brown knee-length pants. Like Lionel, he has black hair, but unlike him, he has orange eyes. In his hand is a needle-shaped object—a lockpick.

This must be Maeko.

And he is looking straight at her.

When those orange eyes settle on Lillian, they widen with terror. The boy backs away, shaking. "A-A human?"

Lillian stays rooted to the table, not knowing what to do. Lionel said this place was safe, that he was the only one with a key, but he must not have predicted his brother could pick the lock. Could she talk to him, maybe calm him down? Then again, if she could do that, wouldn't Lionel have introduced them? Plus, those eyes... they look exactly like that hunter's. That must be a coincidence, right?

"A human in our house..." the capaeman mumbles. "A human in our house."

Lillian does not like how he is looking at her right now—like she's an aranid that set up a web where it doesn't belong. The warrior glances around, wondering if she can hide anywhere, but it wouldn't matter anyway. Maeko would see her do it.

The boy grits his razor-sharp teeth and approaches her slowly, his fists clenched. Lillian backs up but then hits the wall. She has nowhere to run.

But suddenly, the capaeman stops in the middle of the room as if afraid to come closer. "Where are the others?" he growls.

Others? Lillian has no idea what he's talking about. All she knows is up close, he looks even more like that hunter. *It's a coincidence. It's just a coincidence*, she thinks.

"Tell me!" Maeko roars.

The sound pierces Lillian's ear drums.

"Tell me right now, and your death will be swift!" That ultimatum shakes the earth.

Now fearing for her life, Lillian begins to speak. "Th-There's no need to kill me. I am not a threat. There is no one else. It's just me." She gestures to her bandaged legs. "I was hurt. Your brother is taking care of me."

"Liar!" the boy screams, taking a step closer. "I shouldn't trust a word you say. You're here to kill my brother, aren't you? Tell me, *where* are the others?"

"I said there are no others!" the warrior yells. "And I would never hurt your brother. He and I are friends. Just wait until he gets here. He'll explain—"

"Shut up!" Maeko roars. "Seriously, that is the best lie you can come up with? Pathetic."

"I'm not lying. Look at me. Do you really think I'm in a state to hurt anyone?"

"I will take no more lies!" As fast as lightning, he slams his hand on the table. Lillian narrowly dodges the attack, using her legs to launch herself away from the wall. They scream in pain, but she doesn't have time to feel it before Maeko's other hand plummets to greet her. She rolls to the side, avoiding another killer blow. The warrior sprints and jumps around the table, pushing objects in front of her, ducking and weaving through Lionel's projects, doing anything and everything to avoid Maeko's massive attacks.

But she can't avoid them forever.

As the warrior runs for her life, she knows she is being cornered, quite literally.

In only a few seconds, she is backed against the corner of the table, where the wall and glass panes meet, right next to the air duct. There is nowhere else to run.

Maeko raises a hand and swiftly brings it down. This will surely be a lethal blow.

Out of options, Lillian uses the only tactic she has left.

"PLEASE, MAEKO!" she screams at the top of her lungs.

When the capaeman hears his name, he hesitates, and not a moment too soon. His hand looms only inches away from Lillian's face. She stares at it in horror.

"Please... just let me explain. If you kill me, Lionel will be furious."

The giant hand doesn't retreat. Instead, it wraps around Lillian's body, pinning her arms to her sides. Now, she can't look away from those raging orange eyes. She can't even move her body.

"How do you know our names?" Maeko says coldly.

Looking at him this closely, it is impossible not to see the resemblance to the orange-eyed hunter. Same facial structure, same white shirt, same cold and lifeless stare. Could it be... Is it possible that hunter is—

"Answer me!" Maeko demands. She can smell his enraged breaths.

His grip around her body tightens, and Lillian can barely breathe. "I told you," she wheezes, "Lionel and I are friends. He saved my life."

His grip tightens again. "How can I be sure you are telling the truth?"

"C-Can't... breathe..." Lillian chokes. It's as if she's being squeezed to death by a phypent.

"You are liars. All of you. I would wager your little vermin friends are waiting in ambush, aren't they?"

The world begins to blur. No... this can't be how Lillian dies. She's the only one who knows the truth. She has to get back to her people. She *has* to tell them.

BOOM BOOM BOOM BOOM—

Suddenly, she hears footsteps. They are coming this way, and fast.

In an instant, Lionel appears, wrapping his arm around his brother's neck. "Let her go," he says in the coldest tone she has ever heard. "Now."

Lillian plummets to the table, gasping for air. By the time her vision clears, the boys are already throwing punches.

⁕⁕⁕

Maeko tackles Lionel, knocking a massive crate of tools to the floor. The materials scatter all around them. He tries to punch Lionel, but Lionel blocks with his arm. Lillian didn't realize capaemen could move so fast. Just as quickly as Lionel blocked, he returns with a punch of his own, landing square in Maeko's face. The boy staggers backward, rage in his eyes.

"What in the stars are you doing, Lionel?"

"Get. Out."

Maeko lunges, slamming him up against the shelves. The entire room shakes. "You're harboring a human? Have you lost your mind? When Father finds out—"

Before he can finish his sentence, Lionel pulls a similar move to Seth, sweeping his leg under Maeko's. The boy crashes on the hard floor with the most massive *BOOM* Lillian has ever heard. Her ears ring in agony.

"It's bad enough that you rummage through Father's stuff," Lionel remarks, "but mine too? Why can't you keep to yourself?"

Out of Maeko's nose drips a dark-garnet liquid. The substance is a few shades deeper than human blood but still crimson. He wipes it on the back of his hand. "I have done nothing wrong. You're the one who has crossed the line. So, this is why you've been blowing me off? To save this *pest*? You of all people..." He chuckles. "Now, isn't that *ironic*."

Lionel glances at Lillian, then looks back at his brother. "I said, *leave*. This has nothing to do with you."

The boy stands. He is clearly outmatched but still gets back up, determination in those eerie orange eyes. "When *he* finds out—"

The second he says that Lionel grabs his shirt collar. Maeko balls his fists. They're about to fight again.

"Calm down, both of you!" Lillian screams. She can't take this anymore.

Both of the giants' heads snap toward her. Even so, Lillian stands tall. She cannot falter now. She must speak her mind.

"My name is Lillian Zurec. I am from a small clan in the Crimson Forest. We are a pacifist group. We only fight the monsters that try to eat us, not capaemen. A while ago, I was mortally wounded. If it weren't for your brother, I would have died. I have no allies. It's just me. I've been here for the past couple of weeks. When I recover, Lionel will return me to the forest, and you'll never see me again. I swear, I mean no harm."

When she finishes, both of the boys stand frozen for a moment. Then, Lionel lets his brother go. Maeko rubs his neck. "There are no innocent humans."

"You're wrong," Lionel says. "It isn't as black and white as that. I know it is difficult to believe, but—"

"There are *no* innocent humans!" he repeats as if trying to convince himself.

"I used to think the same way about capaemen," Lillian says. "I thought you were all evil, but it turns out I was wrong. Why can't the reverse be true?"

Maeko stares at her, clenching his teeth. "Lionel, why won't it shut up?"

"Hey, *she* has a right to speak. Listen to her, just for a moment. She makes some valid points."

"What *happened* to you?" his brother asks. "You used to be incredible, following in Father's footsteps. Now look at you, fraternizing with the enemy. What happened to wiping out the humans? What was the point of that grueling training you went through? What is the point of even being in this backwater town? You're supposed to finish your training, yet here you are, throwing away everything he has done for you."

Lillian trembles with dread. "Lionel... what is he talking about?"

Maeko scoffs. "Can you shut it up already? You are more than capable."

Lionel clenches his fists. "I will not repeat myself again. Leave, Maeko."

"If you get rid of that *thing*, I will."

"What makes you believe you can order me around? You forget your place. Father left me in charge."

Maeko rolls his shoulders back, locking eyes with his brother. There is a coldness deep within that's all too familiar. "Get rid of it, or I will tell Father, and *he* will get rid of it for us."

Lionel staggers a little. "Come on, that is cruel, even for you. She hasn't done anything wrong."

"Oh, you very well know I'd do it. I am the nosy tattletale. I break things all the time. I'm a terrible brother, a thorn in your side, but you know what? I do not mind being any of those things if it means you stay safe. You know the law better than me. You are aware of what helping that human could do to you—could do to *us*. So, I suppose I am cruel. I say again, if you do not get rid of it, I *will* tell Father."

Lionel meets Lillian's eyes, his face falling.

Lillian backs away. There's no way he would do what she's thinking, right? They're friends. He saved her life and taught her about the world. But the person she sees right now... looks completely different from Lionel. That cold gaze, where has she seen that before?

The river flashes through her mind. How, before she took a dive with Mary, she locked eyes with Albian's killer. There was no life in them, only death, much like how Lionel is looking at her now.

Lillian looks back and forth between the two brothers. One with green eyes and the other with orange. No, it can't be. She refuses to believe it. She stares at Lionel pleadingly, and suddenly, life returns to his face.

"I will *not* do it," he declares. "By tomorrow, she will be out of this place. I will return her to the Crimson Forest, and everything shall be as it was. You have my word, brother."

His little brother gets right up in his face. "You want to spare it? You truly have gone soft."

Lionel doesn't even flinch. "This is my final offer. You will take it or leave it."

A growl escapes from Maeko's lips. "Fine, then. You will return it to the forest right *now*, and never, I mean NEVER, let a human in this house again. If you do that, I will forget this ever happened. Father will never have to know."

"It's a deal. Now leave us," Lionel says with finality.

Finally, Maeko exits, slamming the door behind him.

An eerie silence takes over the room, and finally, Lillian has time to think. Maeko was beyond furious, believing she was his enemy without a second thought, and when Lionel tried to reason with him, it seemed to amuse him. *"You of all people... Now, isn't that* ironic?" And this entire time, from when Lionel came in, to the look on his face now, he has seemed like a different person. For a moment, Lillian believed he was going to kill her.

The warrior tries her best to stand tall, to be brave. She takes a deep breath, knowing what she is about to ask will change everything, but she wants to hear it from him directly—no one else.

"Lionel, who are you?"

The capaeman turns toward her slowly, the look in his eyes exactly that of the hunter who killed Albian.

"My name is Lionel Thanamore, and I come from a long line of hunters."

40

The Capaeman Stained with Red

Lillian

"My name is Lionel Thanamore, *and I come from a long line of hunters."*

He studies Lillian, waiting for her reaction. She can't even move. Lionel has that same piercing stare as when they first met. She feels like it's tearing into her soul, threatening to destroy everything she cares about.

She can't believe she didn't see it sooner.

Observing no reaction, Lionel approaches the table. By instinct Lillian backs up, but loses her balance, falling backward. She wants to stand back up, but she can't move. Her body isn't listening to her. It's as if it has detached from her mind. *Deep breaths, Lillian,* she thinks. One can stay calm in any situation as long as they take deep breaths—so why won't her lungs listen to her? They tremble, just like the rest of her body. She can't get them to stop.

Lionel approaches her slowly, reaching out a hand. "Lillian, allow me to explain."

She scooches backward until she hits the wall. "D-Don't come near me!"

Lionel pulls his hand away. "I would never hurt you. You know that."

Lillian shakes her head. "Just... stay right there. Don't move."

The capaeman stands rooted to the floor. The look in his eyes is still cold as ice. "You hate me now, don't you?"

Lillian doesn't know how to answer that. This feels like a nightmare, one she can't wake up from no matter how hard she tries. The Lionel she's come to know could never be a hunter. It doesn't make any sense. The hunter she saw was cold and distant. Lionel is warm and kind, yet right now, he couldn't look further from the person she's come to know. It's like he's been hiding an entire other personality.

"Lillian," he says calmly, "I did not mean to deceive you. Sure, I hated humans at first, but that has changed."

"So, it's true?" Lillian says, nearly choking on her words. "You're a hunter too?"

"I'm not one anymore," Lionel responds. "and I would never do anything to hurt you." The capaeman tries to come closer, and Lillian flinches. "Lillian... when I saved you, I warned that there would be consequences. Yet, you agreed to come with me."

"You were a hunter," she repeats. "That's hardly a consequence, more like cruel and unusual punishment. What else have you been hiding from me?"

Emotion flickers in his eyes, and Lionel hangs his head, grimacing. "I... It's... nothing! I'm hiding nothing else."

"Stop lying to me. Your brother looks exactly like the hunter that killed our neighboring clan, and who went after my people. That can't be a coincidence. That capaeman with the orange eyes... he's your father, isn't he?"

Lionel slides to the floor, leaning on the messy tool shelf. "By the stars, how did everything become so screwed up?"

This is it. This is why Lionel has been so closed off, why he was a jerk to her in the beginning, and why he seemed so convinced humans were the evil ones. Why he... why he was so sad that day on the beach. He has been keeping a monstrous secret. The reason for Zurec's suffering is sitting right in front of her. "Was..." Lillian says, her voice shaking. "Was any of it real, or have you been toying with me this whole time?"

Lionel stares at her, his voice solemn. "Of course, it was real."

She can't meet his eyes. It is impossible to gauge whether he's telling the truth. If he is a hunter, then all of his behavior comes into question. Saving her life. The fountain, where he showed emotion for the first time. Their conversation while watching that andremedon. The beach... Their entire friendship, a lie. All for what? His own sick amusement?

The warrior thinks back to Albian's burrow—all of those bodies frozen in agony, the mangled woman outside, rotting in the sun. She thinks of the attack on Zurec—Jamie, Albert, and the surveyors desperately trying to fend off the narecons as the gatherers and children ran away. Then, the hunter by the river. Those cold, lifeless eyes demanded death.

"And you... you were on *his* side, weren't you?"

Lionel nods slowly.

With that, her trust shatters.

Lionel punches the shelf. The entire thing shakes. "It wasn't supposed to be this way. Why are you a good person? Why aren't you evil like they all said? Humans are supposed to be an inferior, vicious species. All your people have brought is war and death."

"*We've* brought death?" Lillian says, appalled. "My people were doing nothing but minding our own business. It was *him*... It was *your father* who started this chaos. Do you even realize the suffering he's caused? An entire group of people is dead. Tell me, did they deserve to die just because they're human?"

Lionel stares at the floor.

No, she won't let him shut down now.

"Well, say something! Why are you doing this to us? We've done nothing wrong!"

The capaeman scoffs. "I sided with my father because I did not know at the time. My whole life, I was raised to believe humans are inferior pests. How was I supposed to know that was wrong? I'm trying to do the right thing now."

"Trying to do the right thing? Like lying to and belittling me? You've got a twisted sense of right and wrong."

"No! I saved your life, remember? I tended your wounds. I sheltered you here despite the risk. I taught you about the world outside the Crimson Forest and even took you places. I didn't have to do any of that. If that is not doing the right thing, then I am unsure what is."

"What is *wrong* with you?" Lillian asks. "Why are you making up excuses, even now?"

"I..." Lionel's eyes widen, as if just realizing that. "I did not mean for it to turn out like this. I despise that look you're giving me."

Lillian hates that response. He has no right to have that pitiable expression on his face. He is *not* the victim here. Because of his dad, lives were destroyed, and, and...

And for some unearthly reason, he saved her life. What kind of backward nonsense is this?

"Why?" Lillian starts. "Why did you save me?"

"Huh? You know the reason. Because of—"

"Fascination? Your mother? Yeah, I'm not buying any of that. Give me the real reason." Lillian's head is spinning in circles. She is sick of all of this back-and-forth, this avoiding, this mystery. Now, she will accept nothing less than the truth. Lillian *deserves* the truth.

Lionel gazes at the glass ceiling, his green eyes reflecting the orange sun. "Why indeed? What I told you earlier was true. My mother always told me that if a life is in danger, and I have the capability to save it, then I should. My father was quite the opposite. He taught me to kill. He told me that if I didn't, then I was weak, and those I couldn't kill would murder the ones I love. I thought the hunters were heroes."

Lillian scoffs. "Like *we* could hurt *you*. I've never heard anything so ridiculous."

Those reptilian eyes narrow. "Hmph, you underestimate your own species, but I agree with you. Your people are innocent. I simply wish my father would see things the same way. His intentions are in the right place, but his way of going about it is all wrong."

"Are you... are you *seriously* defending him?" Lillian asks with horror. "That man is a monster."

"I understand where you're coming from, but you do not know my father like I do. He truly believes what he's doing is right and has saved people before."

"I don't buy that for a second!" Lillian shouts. "In no way is killing innocent people justified. Your dad has given you an extremely twisted view of things. Can't you see that?"

"Do not presume you know my father!" Lionel roars. "You know nothing. Nothing of the nuances between the human and capaeman races. I cannot fathom where you get the audacity to speak as you do, when all you know of the world is a tiny forest."

Lillian's heart sinks. She's never heard him speak so condescendingly, and that's saying something. So, that time on the beach was a lie too? When he said he was glad to have met her? Clearly, he still sees her as beneath him, as all other capaemen do.

But immediately after saying that, Lionel's eyes soften. "I apologize. That was... too far. It—It feels like my head is splitting in two. I cannot make sense of what's going on. It wasn't supposed to be this way. I was supposed to help you, witness that you were evil, and confirm my father was right. Instead, you showed me the opposite."

"So that's all I am to you, just an experiment to prove your father was right?"

"What? No! I—Ugh! That's not it at all! This is coming out all wrong. Look, all that matters is that I am different now. I was wrong about humans. You showed me that."

Lillian clenches her fists. "Yet you still try to justify your father's actions. Do you realize how hypocritical that is? Because of him, two innocent children became orphans. We had to tell them that their mother and father were *never* coming back, and they had to start a life with people who were formerly their enemy. Tell me again, how is that in any way justified? How can your father think that's 'doing the right thing'?"

"Wha-What did you say just now?" Lionel looks as if he's realized something. "Two... two orphaned kids?"

"Yes. A little girl and boy. They're the only ones left of Albian, by the way. We took them in, but they're traumatized. They lost their entire family."

"So, they are alive," the capaeman says under his breath. "Thank the stars."

The room spins as Lillian's heart pounds in her ears, louder and louder. "How... how do you *know* about them?"

Lionel meets her eyes, his lower jaw twitching. "Because *I'm* the one who spared their lives."

It's getting harder for Lillian to control her breathing. If her body was trembling before, it's nothing compared to now. "Then, that means..."

No, it can't be. Anything but that.

That cold gaze returns. "It means exactly what you suspect. It was me. I killed them. I killed the ones you call Albian."

⊰ ❧ ⊱

Lillian is overwhelmed with revulsion. So, Lionel *is* a hunter. He must have been lying a moment ago when he said he quit. This whole time, she has been living with a hunter, one of the hunters who started everything. How dare he pretend to be someone else.

"Lillian, please don't look at me like that," Lionel says. "I am not involved in that anymore, I swear. I have been conflicted ever since I spared the lives of those children. Our time together wasn't a lie, it—"

"How can I trust a *word* you say?!" Lillian interrupts. "You're a killer! You and your father are the reason for all of our suffering. I can't believe you're the one who saved my life. I can't believe I thought you were my friend!"

The capaeman hangs his head. "I cannot deny that. Honestly, you have every reason to hate me, so go ahead. I deserve it."

Lillian pauses. There he is with the pity party again. It makes her blood boil. "You don't have the right to feel sorry for yourself. You're supposed to be the bad guy, so act like it!"

"I am not like that anymore! I am so sorry for the part I played in that clan's death, and in your people's suffering. Every night, ever since we talked at the fountain, I've been conflicted. I was trying to figure out how you could possibly be bad, but I couldn't. Then... as we talked, it began to dawn on me that what I had done may have been wrong, but how was I supposed to face that? I spent my whole life believing humans were evil. Now, it feels like everything is falling apart!"

Lillian freezes, her anger halting for just a moment. She too feels like everything has shattered. Weeks ago, she never could have imagined meeting someone like Lionel, a capaeman willing to listen to her. He has turned her world upside down. He must have had a reason for sparing her the first time they met. One he still isn't telling her.

"It's fallen apart for me too," Lillian says. "Before I met you, I thought all capaemen were the enemy, yet on the day we met, you spared my life. That means the inner conflict you speak of... started long before you met me. It's the reason you saved those kids. So, what actually happened at Albian?"

Lionel's eyes widen. "No, please. Do not make me recall that."

"I visited their burrow and saw their remains with my own eyes. Ever since, I've wanted to know what happened. If you care about me at all, you'll tell me. I will accept no empty apologies, only the truth."

Lionel sighs loudly. "Very well. I will tell you what took place on that day."

"It was supposed to be a simple mission. We were to approach the burrow, spray the poison gas, and all inside would perish. The beginning went off without a hitch, but then my father, being as thorough as he is, said we should check the perimeter, just in case. We began searching under roots and shrubs, ensuring no humans escaped the burrow. Then, when I opened a bush, there *they* were.

"I had trained for that moment. I should not have hesitated, but I did. The mother was shielding her children with her own body and glaring at me as if *I* were the monster. It made no sense. I stared at them for a moment, wondering what to do. Then, suddenly, my father took notice of my hesitation.

"He approached the bush I was kneeling over. I knew I only had a few seconds, so I tried to hide them, but..."

Lillian has never seen Lionel in such pain. His eyes twitch as he stares at the sky. The orange sun shimmers in his pupils as if setting his green irises on fire. "The mother, she—she slashed me with a tiny dagger. Not enough to penetrate my scales, but it still stung. I managed to grab the kids and place them in my jacket pocket, but that only made their mother fight back more. I attempted to grab her again, but she kept attacking me. Then, my father arrived..."

Lillian opens her mouth but quickly closes it. She almost wants him to stop.

"By the stars, I'm a horrible person! I'm sorry. I'm so sorry!"

Lionel looks up at her, expecting a response. Lillian does not give one.

He continues.

"My father saw her and instructed me to finish the job. I tried to remind myself it was for a good cause, that I was justified in what I was about to do. So, I... I followed his orders. Then, when he wasn't looking, I placed the children back in the bush and left."

"The nightmares from that day still haunt me. I started spending time in the forest to get away from it all. Then, I met you. And then, that day in the rain..."

He trails off for a second as if remembering a fond dream.

"I told you I would help you, but I did not think you'd be mad enough to accept the offer. Now, here we are."

There is a pause as Lillian takes all of this in. The scattered pieces of the mystery of Albian are coming together. So, *that's* how those kids survived. That's the answer she and Mary searched for so tirelessly. The dead woman with the dagger in her hands... she must have been Trista and Max's mother. No wonder Trista wouldn't tell them what happened. How does one even describe that? Even if she could, no one would have believed her. Lillian knows she wouldn't.

The enigma that is Lionel is coming together too. This explains so many of the capaeman's actions: his hesitation to help her, his distant demeanor, his reluctance to reveal his personal life, and his unwillingness to listen to her stories about Zurec. There is a duality within Lionel, and because of that, he saved those kids.

But he also destroyed their lives.

Lillian feels sick. "So, that's the real reason you helped me? Because of guilt?"

"What? No, that's not it either."

"Then what is it?"

"I, uh..." He struggles to come up with an answer.

Lillian's patience has run out. Her jaw begins to twitch. Her breathing quickens, and she loses control of her body completely. Indescribable rage boils to the surface, taking over her entire being. "Why me? Why am *I* so special? You killed those kids' mother. Their entire family! Because of you... because of you and your father, my people don't have a future! Saving me does *nothing* to justify that. You can't make up for what you've done, so why? Why help me at all? Why pretend to be my friend?"

"—Because I care about you!" Lionel shouts.

Lillian goes silent. She was expecting many answers, but not that.

"I didn't realize it was happening until it was too late, but I care about you. I truly do. I wish for you to know that everything I said to you, about myself, about the world, it was all true."

"Even the part about not being involved with the hunters?"

"I—That was once! I quit training with them. Well, not officially, but—"

"About hardly seeing your father anymore?"

"Okay, yes, he lives here, but we hardly talk because of—"

"Are you even a biologist?"

"E-Everything else was true. You have to believe me!"

"Get out," Lillian says.

Lionel stands up. "Excuse me?"

"You heard me."

"But if you'd just let me explain—"

"I said, GET OUT!" she screams.

He backs toward the door, looking betrayed. "Lillian, *please* don't do this."

"I want you to leave. The sight of you makes me sick."

Lionel's eyes well up with tears. No, that's impossible. There is no way these *monsters* can cry. Then, quietly, he opens the door and closes it behind him, leaving Lillian all alone.

She pounds the table with her fist. She has been such a reckless fool. Lionel was lying to her the whole time, and she didn't even notice. She let her guard down, something a warrior should never do. It's because she brushed off her dad, spurned her family, and dismissed her ancestors' warnings about the capaemen that she's in this situation now. She has only herself to blame. The signs were all there. Lillian was just too stubborn to see them.

She dared to hope, and now she must pay the price.

Lillian stares around the room, holding back her tears. From here on out, she will rely on Lionel no more, including to get out of this place. She must find an escape route on her own before he returns.

Her eyes lock on the air vent in the corner.

Perfect.

41

What It Takes to Be a Warrior

Lillian

The warrior steels herself. She will not mourn what was lost because there was nothing there to begin with.

After a few minutes, Lillian finally manages to stand, her legs throbbing. She does some side stretches, toe touches, and rolls out her arms—all classic training warm-ups, but she won't be training today.

Lillian is doing this to assess the condition of her body because she will need a lot of strength to get out of here. She was able to run fine when Maeko attacked her, but that was on adrenaline. Now, after that nightmare, she is exhausted. She wants nothing more than to go back into the cabinet and fall asleep, but she can't.

There is no way she can stay here.

Her body shaking, the warrior looks out at the sunlit plains through the wall of glass panes. She hears the chirping of birds, muffled by the barrier. So close, yet so far. Lillian turns her gaze and peers up at the shutters in the corner of the room, ten feet above the countertop. She can probably climb if she doesn't do it for long, but running may be an issue. She hopes she doesn't bump into anything she'd have to run from, at least until she gets outside. *If* she can get outside.

With pain in every step, Lillian makes her way across the length of the table, searching for the tool to open the air vent. She'll need it to get the screws out of the wall, but it's nowhere to be seen. Lillian comes across Lionel's mixer. It lies on its side at the center of the table in eerie stillness, surrounded by the tools he used to fix it.

All that time they spent together, the adventures they had... She never thought it would end like this. For a moment, she had hope that things would change. How foolish of her. What made her, one tiny girl, believe she could change anything?

"You know nothing. Nothing of the nuances between the human and capae-man races."

Thinking of what he said makes Lillian boil with rage. She must make it out of here and get back to her family. Everything they did... It was to keep her safe. She didn't understand that at the time, but she does now.

Lillian shakes her head to clear it. *Focus, Lillian. Where's that vent tool?* There are plenty of sharp objects, but nothing with a blunt end. Lillian tries to remember where Lionel stashed the tool. Then, she spots a familiar box near the corner of the wall.

This box, bulky and a few feet taller than her, has been an incredible help. It's the same container Lillian hid behind when Lionel entered the room the first time she'd left the cabinet. She also ducked behind it when Maeko was trying to kill her.

The box is double-lidded, and when closed both lids meet in the center. Bracing herself, the warrior forces her injured legs to jump, but she has nothing to grab onto and falls back onto the table. *Oh no, I'm not giving up that easily.* She unsheathes her dagger and bends her knees again. This time, Lillian jumps higher, and when she reaches the top of the box, she plunges her dagger into it.

She pulls herself onto the left lid and then throws the right one open, revealing all sorts of tools and gadgets. Some look like weapons. Others are spherical, transparent objects containing strange liquid. Lillian won't even try to figure out what those are. She *has* to go. Luckily, the vent tool sits at the top of the pile. She grabs it with both hands and nearly stumbles off the box. It's heavier than she imagined, not to mention nearly her height. She places it next to her, then closes the left lid.

Now for the second problem: how to reach the air vent. She has an idea but cringes at the thought. This will hurt. Even so, she gently climbs off the box, leaving the tool on top. Once on the counter again, she braces her knees and ever so slowly pushes the container against the wall. Sweat beads down her forehead and her body screams in agony, but she presses on.

Once the box is directly underneath the vent, Lillian collapses onto one knee, panting. She is still so weak. That doesn't bode well. She will have to cross the plains to make it to the Giant Wilds. Sure, she's small enough to hide, but if she is spotted it's over.

The warrior takes one last look at the workshop. The sun shines brightly through the tempered glass, illuminating the shelves of tools. On the top shelf is a book—the same one that Lionel was reading when they went to the beach.

Lillian swallows her feelings. *Now's not the time to think about that.* Those—Those *hunters* are the reason her people are in this mess in the first place.

Lillian forces herself back on top of the box, grabs the tool, and shoves its blunt end into the first screw. It takes her a few tries to get it right, but eventually it falls out of the wall.

On to the next.

Once three screws have fallen onto the table, the shutters become loose enough for her to slip through. The warrior climbs into the vent.

Inside is a vast hallway of metal. The shimmering material is nailed to the walls, ceiling, and floor in layered sheets. What it took to build such a structure, no human can say. The metal tunnel is so long it's hard to see the end, and it's cold...

Lillian has the urge to turn back. This is way over her head. She has no idea where this tunnel leads. Still, she fights her fear. If she stays, her safety is not guaranteed.

Go. There is nothing behind you, she tells herself.

Several feet away, there sits a large cloth. In the middle of a hallway bathed in silver, it sticks out like a thornlet without its mother. Lillian lifts the fabric, but as she moves it, something clamors to the metal floor.

The first thing she spots is a shimmering blade, followed by a redwood shaft.

It's her spear.

The warrior grabs the weapon, clutching it as if her life depends on it. It glows a deep blue. Why did that capaeman return her dagger but leave the spear here?

Lillian grits her teeth. *He's not your friend. It doesn't matter.*

She continues down the cramped hall, holding her spear proudly. Soon, the light from the workshop fades, transitioning to a soft darkness. Not even her spear glows now. With no light to reflect, its otherworldly luster has grown dim. She needs a torch, like they use in the burrow. It would also keep her warm. The hall is as freezing as a snowy winter. Lillian wraps the cloth from her spear around her body.

As the warrior rounds the corner, the vent slants like a steep hill. She trudges up, stepping on the grooves between each metal panel to keep from sliding back down. The roof is not an ideal place to escape from, but beggars can't be choosers. Luckily, just as she thinks that the incline stops and veers left. Now, there's a new hall stretching for almost half a mile, and as flat as the plains. On the left side of the hall, light periodically streams into the vent in thin horizontal strips, making it easy to see what's ahead. Those must be shutters leading to other rooms. At the very end of the tunnel, the light is at its brightest. That must be the way out.

She can make it. Lillian can get out of here.

So why is her heart sinking?

The conversation with Lionel flashes through her head, just for a moment. The reveal that he's a hunter, that he helped kill Albian, the look on his face—

The warrior holds her head. *No, **don't think about that. I must get out of here. There's no other option.*** She shouldn't be here to begin with. Everything she has experienced and learned feels like a distant dream—a far-off fantasy that was never meant to be. It was built on lies.

Lillian approaches the first source of light, wondering what is in the room below. She should check all the rooms. That will ensure she finds the exit to this dreaded place.

flutter flutter

From the other side of the vent comes the sound of wings.

Wings? That doesn't make any sense.

The warrior peeks through the shutters. When she sees what's in the room, she feels sick to her stomach. This room is much smaller than the workshop yet much more deadly.

Sitting in cages hanging from the ceiling is a flock of black narecons: tens of them, fluttering and squawking. The tiny cells are hardly enough to contain their enormous wings, so they fight against the bars, repeatedly causing their cages to swing and bash against the wall. The sounds they make are deafening. The longer Lillian watches, the more they freak out.

flutter

CLANG!

SCREEEEEEE

Then it hits her. Her scent... It must be wafting through the vent.

They know she's here.

Lillian sprints down the hall, her shoes clanging against the cold metal. Still, she must put as much distance between her and those monsters as possible. They are all in that one room. To think, the reason for Zurec's torment was just a few walls away from her. It's repulsive.

That's even more of a reason to get out of here. Once Lillian escapes, she can cross the plains and find her way back to the Giant Wilds. Maybe she'll see a plains andremedon again, from a distance of course. She wonders what other notes *he* took on them.

"Trash that curious attitude of yours before it gets you killed," Jamie says in her head.

Lillian snaps out of it. What is *wrong* with her? Why does she keep thinking like this, even now? Everyone else she knows would head straight for the exit, never looking back. Especially after everything she's learned. It's because of *his* family that her clan has been suffering. That capaeman is her *enemy*. Plain and simple.

"I am not like that anymore! I am so sorry..."

Lillian shakes her head. No, what he did is unforgivable. As for the apologies, the excuses... They can't have been real. After all, if he lied about one thing, how can she know if anything was the truth?

The capaemen are monsters. Those narecons are proof.

The birds scream at her from their cages, but as the warrior hobbles down the dark hall, the squawks gradually fade.

The next pillar of light is ahead.

The girl turns her head away. She can't look in the next room. Who knows what untold horrors await?

clink-clink

But then she hears the clinking of glass. What could that be?

Before Lillian can stop herself, she is peering in.

This room is massive and filled with food. Fruits and vegetables sit in baskets on a gigantic stone table. Against the wall are all sorts of devices, which must be for cooking. Some are as big as the burrow's cramped storeroom, but one towers even taller than a capaeman. It appears to be a metal cabinet with two doors, and it makes a low humming noise. Lillian wonders what the device is for but can't stick around.

After all, Maeko is standing in the center of the place, washing dishes with running water. The capaeman boy's orange eyes simmer with rage, and so do Lillian's. He treated her like she was nothing. That is how they see humans. Deep down it's how Lionel must see her too. They are from two different worlds, ones that were never meant to collide.

click

Suddenly, she hears a door opening and closing. It must be Lionel. Lillian clenches her fists and backs away from the vent. She does not want to see him.

"Father! You've come home!" the voice of Maeko echoes.

Lillian falls against the wall. *No, it can't be.*

"How was your mission? I presume it went well?"

Lillian clasps her hands over her ears. She doesn't want to hear the horrors of this house. Not the hunter's voice, nor that of his obedient son, and certainly not about the massacres he's conducted—the families he's separated, the people he's slaughtered. How can they not realize what they are doing is wrong?

Humans are beneath them, that's why.

The warrior keeps going, more determined than ever.

"I love you, Lillian, but you know nothing about the world," Seth echoes.

I'm sorry, Dad, she thinks. She has been a terrible daughter and an even worse warrior. All those times her people tried to warn her... and she never listened.

One more room. Then she will see them again. *Don't look in the next place. Just pass it, and freedom awaits.*

But as the light approaches, Lillian can't help but take one little glance. Just one. It can't hurt, right? After all, she is still looking for a reliable exit.

The first thing she spots is a solid-green jacket hanging on the wall. Against that same wall, a desk, and sitting at that desk...

... is Lionel.

Lillian snaps her head back. *This is too much.* She has seen unspeakable terrors in this house. She can't see Lionel too. Not after...

She clenches her fists. Who is she kidding? It's her fault that this happened. She chose to take the ultimate risk—to travel where people never do. To be vulnerable in the face of their worst enemy. Making oneself vulnerable: that's the biggest mistake a warrior can make. Lillian should be ashamed of herself. Maybe being in the burrow forever is what she deserves. That's the only way she will survive her own curiosity. If she can make it home, she will take any punishment her people give, without complaint.

As she approaches the end of the tunnel, Lillian hears birds and bugs chittering in the evening. It really is the outside. The warrior sprints to the end of the hall, her spear shimmering green.

This vent is much rustier than the others, likely from years of exposure to the elements. Lillian jiggles the shutters, creating an opening small enough to squeeze through. The ground is hundreds of feet below, but vines twist and turn all over the wall, weaving in and out of its giant, colorful stones. She can easily climb down.

So, why is Lillian hesitating?

Her legs won't move. Sure, they throb in pain, but not severely enough that she needs a break. If she could get down, she could...

She could do what, exactly?

"It's like you have a death wish," Mary sneers.

Staring out at the vast grasslands, it dawns on her how hopeless this is. This plan is suicide. No single human survives the plains. The odds of her making it home are next to none.

The warrior collapses on the metal floor.

Hundreds of feet below, the grass sways in the wind as the day transitions from afternoon to evening. They remind her of how the flowers swayed in the field where she and Lionel first met, and in the plains with the andremedon. Back then, she felt so hopeful. Now she feels just like everyone else.

Lillian unties her headband and stares at it. Somehow, it survived this long. The embroidered sigil really is beautiful. A dark-brown circle, with two double-headed spears crossed over the center, and an ochre line twisting over it all in a four-leaf flower shape. The spear tips are all the colors of the rainbow.

There is a reason Lillian chose this spear, which is so different from the others. She grasps it in her left hand. The blades have turned orange as if mocking her. It is the color of the grueling sun and the same color that has almost meant her death not once, but twice.

"It's like you have a death wish," Mary repeats.

No, that's not true, Lillian thinks. Who cares if she has different methods from the others? At least she was trying something new. Making plans the same as they always have, cowering below ground and never changing, is what got Zurec into this situation. Plus, in everything Lillian tried, she did her best to make it out alive. She doesn't have a death wish.

She isn't reckless, impulsive, or out of control. She's just different.

If Lillian climbs down these vines and somehow manages to make it back home, everything will be as it was. She will be confined to a bunker, forced to take orders from those who have never been outside the forest, and probably die as a creature's next meal—or, worse still, be killed by the hunters. There is nothing they can do to fight them. They're sitting styfishers.

... Or are they?

Lillian looks back down the hall.

No, she thinks.

But her body moves on its own.

If this fails, which it probably will, she will never question authority again. She will return to the Giant Wilds and be a good little soldier just as the adults intended... until they inevitably are killed by the hunters.

But if it succeeds, they may have a fighting chance.

The warrior moves back down the hall, determination in each step. Her heart races. This goes against everything she's ever known, but Lillian cannot walk away without trying everything she can, even if it's hopeless. She just needs a glimpse. She needs to be sure that there is no future for her here. If she is to leave this place on her own, to trash her hopes and become an obedient clan member, she must verify without a shadow of doubt that a capaeman could never care about a human. Otherwise, her hesitation will never cease. Lionel acted like he cared, but it might have just been a game to him. He is probably working on a project right now—his expression blank, unfazed by the horrors he put her through.

Now at her destination, she peers through the shutters to Lionel's room. Yes, she is only confirming what she already knows, what her ancestors have been saying for years. That Lionel is—he's—

He's no longer at his desk. On the wall near the door is a massive picture. Lillian has no idea how the image is so detailed, but what it depicts catches her wandering eyes. It's a capaeman about Brianna's age, and in the crook of her left arm is a very young Lionel. He smiles widely in the photo, his green eyes sparkling with innocence. The woman, whose features match his perfectly, can only be his mother. Cupped in her right hand is a baby reptile. It has a bandage around its head.

Wait, was Lionel telling the truth about her being a biologist? Even if he was, that doesn't mean anything. Perhaps there were some little white truths amongst the lies, but for the most part—

Lillian's eyes lock on something else.

In the corner of the room is a basket filled with seashells. It's his collection, the same one he mentioned at the beach. The warrior pats her backpack. The shell he gave her is still in there. She considers removing it but can't bring herself to.

When Lionel came clean, he told her the whole story of Albian. He didn't have to do that. He didn't have to open up about his mother either. What kind of manipulation tactic is that?

She grimaces. *No, I can't get my hopes up. He's going to walk back through that door and be perfectly fine. I am insignificant. He said it himself.* She kneels by the vent, waiting patiently for Lionel to return.

After a few minutes, the door opens slowly.

This is it.

Lionel enters his room and quietly closes the door, leaning against it. In his hand is the tool Lillian used to open the vents. He knows she has escaped.

It's his own fault. He should have realized this would happen. What healthy person sticks around after finding out their friend is a killer?

Lionel stays against the door, his gaze locked on the tool. Slowly, he slides to the floor. The only thing Lillian can hear is his breathing. Even the air in the vent has gone silent. The capaeman begins to shake. He clasps his hands around the tool and grits his fangs.

No, this means nothing, Lillian thinks.

Then, water hits the hardwood floor. Tears run down Lionel's cheeks and crash to the ground like raindrops. He doesn't make a sound, but they continue to fall, forming puddles around him.

So, capaemen truly can cry.

She grips the metal shutters, staring down at him. Then, as if it's contagious, her eyes well up too. How ridiculous. Lillian hasn't cried since she was a little girl. There is no need for such emotion in a world where tragedy is constant. Yet the tears flow down her cheeks and onto her tank top. They won't stop.

She has been through hell, and in a way, so has he. The divide between their species affects more than just her people. It's hurting *everyone*.

That boy crying all alone down there, he's not a liar. He is a person... who lied. Who makes mistakes. Just like her, just like her family. *"It was one mistake. We've all been there. Just try to do better next time."* Brianna's voice now. She was the only one who understood, and Lillian took her for granted. If she returns home, she will thank her.

But for now, the warrior takes a deep breath. "Lionel," she says in a volume that will reach him.

The capaeman flinches, then slowly looks up toward the vent.

This is by far the craziest thing she's ever done. No, not crazy, brave.

This is the *bravest* thing Lillian has ever done.

42

Closure

Lillian

As the capaeman is alerted to her presence, Lillian stays rooted to her spot. The survivalist within screams for her to run—to turn back around and take her chances in the plains, but she ignores that voice. She now knows that voice is not hers, but rather an instinct instilled in her since childhood by a fading generation. Her dad said it himself. Their clan is dying, and everything is changing. So too must their way of life.

Lionel's eyes are bloodshot, and he still holds the tool. Clutching it tighter, he stands from the floor and looks around the room. "I must be hearing things."

This is Lillian's last chance to back out, yet she doesn't hesitate to speak. "No, you're not. I'm here."

Realizing it is really her, Lionel rushes to lock the door. "Lillian! Why would you return? My father is here." He takes a few steps toward the vent.

"Stay right where you are," Lillian demands. The capaeman freezes instantly, staring up at her warily. She is reminded of when she first saw him, safe in her view from the trees. This must be how Lionel feels around her every day. It isn't fair.

"Why have you returned?" he asks.

She pauses for a moment, recalling her plan. Will it really work?

"You're putting yourself in unnecessary danger," he continues. "Get out of here while you still can."

"Sure, I could run now, but what good would that do? Even if I made it back to the forest, it would still be the same situation as before. Probably worse, and it's all because of you and your father."

The capaeman frowns and looks away. "So, what is your purpose for returning then?"

Lillian hesitates a second time. Lionel has committed horrible acts, and according to what she was taught, that makes him evil. But the world isn't that simple. It's not black and white. It's a rainbow of radiant colors.

She remembers all the capaemen she saw on their travels—the ones who smiled and laughed with each other on their way to the beach. They don't spend every waking moment hunting human beings. They are not all monsters. Heck, even Lionel, a former hunter, learned to care about her. This past month has opened something she never thought possible. If Lillian leaves, that door will close.

"I'm here to make a deal."

Lionel looks back up at the shutters, eyebrows raised.

"You say you feel guilty for what you've done, and I believe you. Not everything you told me was a lie, and that means there is still hope."

"Hope? What are you on about? The sight of me makes you sick. You said it yourself."

Lillian's hands clench around the shutters. "I shouldn't have said that, but you shouldn't have lied to me."

The capaeman says nothing.

"I trusted you even though that meant risking my life, and this is how it ends? Tell me, Lionel, if you were one of *them* before you found me, then why did you spare me on the day we met?"

Lionel collapses back into his chair. He seems to be thinking hard about his response, as if it's a matter of life and death. "Honestly, when I saw you, ending your life was my first thought, but then I remembered what happened the last time I did that. So, I could not. Instead, I found myself interacting with you. You say the silliest things, you know. Most humans do not try to speak to us. They usually run away, scream, or both. I was telling the truth back then. I really did find it amusing."

Then, he clasps his hands together. "Now, somehow... we are here. I am sorry. I am so sorry. Is that what you want me to say? I did not mean to deceive you. I saved you because you asked that of me, and I found that interesting. Then this turned into so much more. Once I realized what was happening, it was too late. You were already beginning to trust me. I did not want to ruin that."

The capaeman gazes up at the vent, waiting for a response. Chilling air flows through the hallway, making Lillian clutch her shoulders. The cloth is still draped over them, but it's not enough. She breathes slowly and evenly, wondering what to say next. So many emotions are buzzing inside her head—rage, melancholy, dejection—but miraculously, not only bad ones. Despite everything, she does not hate Lionel. In fact, she understands why he did it. He was taught all humans were evil. How was he supposed to know any different, until she came into his life?

"Look, I haven't forgiven you, but the things I've learned, the places I've been, I never thought possible. You may have done those horrible things, but I can't believe you're a bad person. For the first time in my life, I have something specific to pin my hopes on, and I'm not ready to throw that away."

"So, it is not over?" Lionel asks hopefully. The tears in his eyes have dried.

"I don't... want it to be," Lillian says somberly, "but there's something we need to talk about first."

"Is this the deal you mentioned earlier? What is it?"

She braces herself, preparing for if he refuses. Although they care about each other, if Lionel can't do this, they have no future. She'll have to run back up this frigid hall and never return. "Promise me you will never go back to the hunters."

Lionel's reptilian eyes widen. "I already left. Why would you—"

"If you care about me, you won't go back. Ever. I know you can't control your father's actions, but you can control yourself."

His shoulders slump. Then, his face falls in submission. "That is no problem. There is no way I could go back anyway, not after you."

"I want to hear you say it."

Conviction in his dark-green eyes, Lionel stares straight at her and says, "I promise. I will *never* go back. I am on your side now."

Lillian breathes a sigh of relief. She knows he means it. After everything they've been through, from the river to the beach, she's come to know him—his way of speaking and mannerisms. When Lionel lies, he avoids eye contact and fidgets with his hands. In hindsight he is a terrible liar. Not very evil of him, if he's supposed to be the villain. He's just a boy who was likely coerced into following in his father's footsteps, and instead he helped a human. It's because of Lionel that she survived, and she will continue to survive now.

"Thank you for saying that. Now, the next part: I have a plan."

Fittingly, Lionel pulls a notebook and pen from his desk. "I am all ears."

For the first time, the warrior talks about Zurec, and the capaeman listens. He even jots down notes. She tells him about how they are overprotective but kind, strict but open-minded. She tells him about her dad—how he's optimistic despite the hopeless circumstances. Finally, she tells Lionel about how they're desperate for any leads on the capaemen and reveals her plan. "You're a capaeman who used to be a hunter. Not only are you powerful, but you have insider knowledge. After I return to the forest, we should meet every so often. When we do, tell me their plans. If we know ahead of time, we can escape."

The capaeman twirls the pen between his fingers. "That could succeed in theory, but what about your family? I know you said they are open-minded, but I hardly believe they would be willing to work with a former hunter."

Lillian gulps. "They will," she says. "I'll convince them." She'll warm them up to it, somehow. They're desperate, after all. This may be their only way out.

Lionel seems to ponder this for a moment. Then he places the pen and journal back on his desk. "Is this what you truly want? Is this what will help you?"

"I think it will. My people are capable, but what's holding us back is a lack of intel. If you could supply us with that, we can find a way to survive. Plus... we'll get to keep talking, and that's nice, right?" This friendship has changed Lillian's life, and she knows that if this works, it will change everything for Zurec... forever.

"Yes," Lionel responds. "It is."

The capaeman and human sit in silence for a moment as the sun sets through the glass ceiling. Lillian can hardly see it through the shutters, but she knows it's there. Lionel's room has a glass ceiling just like the workshop, and its sunsets are glorious. She is going to miss these. Zurec wouldn't dare stay out until sundown, but even if they did, there's no seeing these beautiful shades of yellow, orange, and pink through the canopy. She wants to view it through glass panes one last time.

"Hey, can you let me out?" Lillian asks, breaking the silence.

"What? Have you forgotten my father is home?"

"It'll be okay," she says. "You're here."

Lionel picks up the tool for the vent, but he doesn't leave his desk chair. "I know we are allies now, but you would benefit from... limited interaction with me."

There he goes with the pity party again. "How so? You're not a hunter anymore."

"I may no longer be one, but I come from a family of them. Every moment you stay here, you are more likely to die. My brother is in the kitchen. The narecons who hunt your kind are only a few doors away, and the door may be locked, but my father could still show up at any moment. You are surrounded by enemies here."

Lillian flinches at the mention of her adversaries, but she does not waver. "If I went out in the plains or the forest, it would be the same. I'm surrounded by enemies no matter where I go, and my family can't protect me anymore. At least here, I have one dependable ally."

The capaeman stands. "Wow, are circumstances really that desperate?"

He's *starting* to get it, finally. "They won't be for much longer," she says confidently. "Now, can you let me out of here? It's freezing."

Lionel's hands clench. "I cannot fathom how you stand to be near me after what I have done."

"Can we not think about that, just for the night?" Lillian asks, having enough. Part of her feels like they should talk about it more, but she wants to forget for a moment. Especially if all Lionel would do is wallow in self-pity; that wouldn't serve her. She wants her friend back. "Tomorrow, I'm going back home. This is the last night survival won't constantly be on my mind."

"You... do not want to discuss what took place?" he asks, sounding confused.

"Not anymore. I'm not saying everything is fixed, but just for tonight, can we pretend our last conversation never happened? I want to watch the sunset without worrying, one last time."

Lionel stands, a light smile on his face. "Well then, when you put it like that, I am happy to oblige."

boom... boom...

Before they can continue, footsteps echo down the hall. Lillian's heart skips a beat. "Stay where you are," Lionel whispers urgently.

boom boom boom...

Luckily, the steps quickly pass.

"Are you certain you want to come out?" he asks one last time.

"Yeah," Lillian answers. "I'm not afraid of them, not with you here."

Cautiously, the capaeman drags his chair against the wall and stands on it, giving him a boost to the vent. "Okay, then. Still, if anyone enters, hide immediately."

"Of course," Lillian answers. She can't wait to get out of this freezing metal can—to bask in the warmth of a capaeman home and talk with her friend. She'll cherish every moment of this night.

Because tomorrow, she'll see her clan again.

Lionel's room is even bigger than it looked from the vents. All around it are vivid depictions of nature, from the forest to the beach. Lillian is reminded of when she first saw him: sitting peacefully by the river with a styfisher he'd saved. That little thing got her into a heap of trouble, trying to play with her when Jamie and Albert were fleeing. Although, looking back at it now, maybe the styfisher was trying to tell her something. *"Hey! You look like my friend. Can we be friends too?"* Lillian smiles at the thought. How silly. There's no way it was trying to get them to meet. It's just an animal.

"What are you grinning about?" Lionel asks.

The capaeman sits with his legs crossed on the bed. The sheets have an image of ocean waves on them. The orange sun reflects off the water in the picture, creating a gorgeous contrast. Lillian still can't figure out how they paint images so perfectly. It must be some other ridiculous technology.

Lillian mirrors Lionel, sitting cross-legged on the nightstand. The piece of furniture is intricately crafted: polished redwood, swirling with shades of orange and black. Behind her is a massive lamp, which illuminates the darkening room. To the left of the lamp is a photo of Lionel and a capaeman girl—who looks to be around his age. The girl has black, blunt bangs split down the middle of her forehead and turquoise eyes. Her smile is big and bright, which reminds her of Mary. Lillian doesn't think to bring it up, though. That girl may be gone too, just like his mother.

"I was thinking about that styfisher," she says. "What happened to it?"

"Oh, you mean the one I cared for? I thought you despised that thing."

"I guess I have every reason to, but I don't. It was pretty cute."

"It was, was it not? I released the creature not long after taking you in. If it had that much energy, it was ready to leave. However, the little thing kept whimpering and running after me. I had to distract it with a treat and then sneak off. Not my finest hour."

Lillian laughs. "It liked you. What's so wrong with that?"

"It was *irritating.*"

"Well, I can't argue with that, considering..." she falters. *Considering it almost got me killed.*

There is an awkward silence. Lionel looks away, locking his gaze on the rising moon. The bright-blue color reflects off his irises, almost making them glow. Lillian glances at her spear. It lies by her side, on that same piece of cloth she found in the air vent. The blades glow aqua. She needs to change the subject. Might as well ask another question that's been burning in her head.

"Hey, can you tell me about this spear? You seemed so rattled by it when we first met."

Lionel's eyes narrow. For a second, he looks like his father. "You truly do not know?"

She shakes her head. "I don't even know how we got a spear like this. I found it in the forge of my burrow, lying under some junk. When I brought it to the surface, the adults seemed to know something, but they wouldn't tell me."

"I apologize. I should have given it back to you a long time ago. I suppose I was... Well, I was afraid to do so."

"*You* were scared? That's impossible," Lillian teases.

For another moment, Lionel's eyes grow cold again. He places a hand on his chin as if wondering if he should tell her. Then he exhales. "It is quite strange that you have something so important and do not know what it is. That little weapon... The blades are made of a material called *iridescian* metal. Iridescian metal is one of the only known substances that can cut capaeman scales."

"Wh-What? Then that means—"

"Indeed. That weapon can kill me," the capaeman says grimly.

Lillian stares at the spear. That's why it's so much higher quality than the others. It was made to slay *capaemen*, not common forest creatures. "B-But we don't have the first idea how to kill capaemen. How did we get a weapon like this?"

"Your guess is as accurate as mine. Although, if you wish for me to weigh in, I surmise your family is not everything you believe it to be."

"No, that doesn't make any sense. This weapon is the only one of its kind. Everyone else uses stone or regular metal. I doubt our forge is powerful enough to smelt whatever ore this comes from, never mind cast it. Which—" As she is talking, she realizes something. "Which means... it came from somewhere else. From *someone* else."

Lionel crosses his arms. "Who do you mean? I thought you stated that there are no humans with such technology in the Crimson Forest."

"There aren't," Lillian says, her thoughts racing. She thinks of the story they were told about the group of rogues her mother left with. The adults said they didn't know much about them, but Emilia was fascinated with them. Eventually, she joined them, breaking up with Seth in a letter. That's the story, but knowing what she knows of the outside world now... *That can't be right.* she thinks.

"Figure something out?" Lionel asks, staring at her curiously.

"A long time ago, a nomadic clan visited from outside the Giant Wilds. Maybe they were used to facing capaemen."

"Maybe? You're telling me you do not know?"

She shakes her head. "They left when I was born. My mother... She left with them. We don't know much about them, but what if..." She doesn't want to say the next part out loud, but what Lionel said earlier may be right. How could the adults know nothing about a group that came from outside the Giant Wilds? One her mother liked so much that she abandoned them. It doesn't make any sense... unless she isn't getting the whole story.

Suddenly, Lillian feels disgusted just looking at the spear. She cannot believe she didn't see it sooner. This belonged to *her*. Why her mother left it behind, she has no idea, but she may know who can tell her more.

Her dad has been keeping more secrets than she thought. So has the rest of the clan.

She runs her hand across the redwood shaft, trying to wrap her head around this realization. "This belonged to my mother. I can't believe they didn't tell me."

The capaeman frowns. "Why would your mother leave behind something so valuable? Did she not abandon your family?"

"She did abandon us, so why did she..." Lillian tries to think of some warped reason her mother would do this but comes up with nothing. Even worse, none of the adults wanted to tell her about it. Could Lionel be right? Maybe her people *aren't* who she thinks they are.

"You seem troubled. Do you wish for a change of subject?"

"Sure," she answers instantly. Her mother is her least favorite topic, but realizing her people may have lied to her is even worse. It's almost worse than she and Lionel's forbidden topic for the night. Is everyone in her life a liar?

"I am quite confused about the resources of your people. You do not know what iridescian metal is, yet you were with a flier. Those two on the acera, the ones who left you behind when I showed up, who were they?"

Lillian nearly chokes on her own tongue. "Y-You *saw* them?"

"Of course, I saw them. Not very kind of them to abandon you like that. Do all your friends have such fragile loyalty?"

"They were scared," Lillian says. "Put yourself in their shoes for a moment. You're pretty terrifying."

The capaeman grimaces, revealing those carnivorous teeth. "I suppose that is fair. Still, can you elaborate? Are they not members of your clan?"

"Not originally," Lillian answers. "We're really lucky to have them. They came from very far away. Osinawa, actually. That's how I know about that place."

"I see," he responds. "Fascinating. That explains a lot. I appreciate it."

The two of them pause, staring at the moon together. The stars twinkle in the night sky above, perfectly complementing the bright blue of the moon. There must be millions of stars sparkling hundreds, no *thousands* of miles away. Lillian wonders what they are: whether they're sparks in the night sky or other suns greeting them with their beautiful lights.

"There is something you need to know," Lionel says, interrupting the peace.

Lillian's heart sinks. "What is it?"

"I apologize for bringing this up. I know you did not want to talk about it, but there is one more thing I must tell you regarding the hunters."

She stares at him and suddenly begins to tremble. Flashes of Albian run through her mind, the horrified faces, the woman with a shattered neck, and remembering that *he* did that...

Noticing the look on her face, Lionel reaches for her, but she flinches. "Hey, it is alright. I only wish to warn you about something. You are safe."

Why am I here? He is a killer. she thinks briefly. *No, don't think about that. He isn't that person anymore. He's your friend. You're safe. You're safe.*

After repeating that a few times in her head, Lillian manages to calm down. She wanted this. She can't panic now. "Okay, what is it?"

"Are you sure you are alright?" He knows something is up.

She nods. "Just get this over with. What do I need to know?"

"Very well, then. I will be brief. My father knows about that flier. The ones who abandoned you. He believes there may be more of them, but it is just the one, is it not?"

"H-How do you know?"

"If there were more, you would be a flier too, but you seem to know next to nothing about them. Plus, you just said they came from Osinawa. There are many of them over there, but I have never heard of them migrating here. That should be impossible." Lillian's eyes widen. She wonders if she should tell him how Jamie and Albert traveled across the ocean but chooses not to. Lionel probably wouldn't believe her. "Sometimes there are rogue fliers," he continues. "It is rare, so when a hunter sees a flier, they never treat the situation that way. Where there is one, there are usually *many*. Now, my father is not one to take help, but when he reported the incident to H.Q., they sent someone—just in case things became dangerous. If it is just the one acera, they will not last long."

Lillian starts shaking again, but not because of Lionel this time. "Y-You mean to tell me that more than just your father is after us now?"

"Indeed. My father was called into base recently. He has been gone for a month, but his partner has still been hunting, searching for survivors and aceras."

"No..." she mumbles. "It can't be."

Jamie said it herself. The hunter *saw* them. That made everything worse. Two rogues who wanted to help a dying people may have doomed them instead.

"I-I have to warn them!" Lillian shouts.

Lionel places a finger over his lips. "I know. You are going back to the Crimson Forest tomorrow. Do not worry. For now, you must stay undetected."

The warrior closes her mouth. She got carried away.

"I am finished with what I have to say. The night is yours now. If you wish to discuss anything else, now is the time." Relieved the hard conversation is over, Lillian smiles widely. She doesn't even know where to begin.

For hours, the two of them talk about the world. There is no question too random or too silly for Lionel this night. He answers all of them with kindness and clarity. Lillian likes this side of him. It feels like she's seeing him for the first time.

"You see that blue orb up there? That is called a moon," Lionel says. He's now lying on his back, staring up at the stars.

Lillian lies on a towel that's been put down for her. "Uh, I know what the moon is."

"Truly?" She throws him a look. "Oh. Well, here is something you perhaps did not know. That is *Caerum*. It means 'moon of ocean.'"

"Caerum?" Lillian says. "That's too complicated. We just call it the blue moon."

"Of course you do," Lionel teases. "Have you seen the Rubrum Eclipse before?"

"You mean the Red Eclipse? I have."

"Caerum appears during the night, while Rubrum, meaning 'moon of fire,' is out during the day, but we can only see it once a year, during the eclipse."

"It's out all the time?" Lillian says in disbelief.

"Indeed, but the sun is too bright to see it. This is simply a bit of trivia for you. I thought you would find it interesting. After all, you do seem to want to know *everything*."

She laughs. "Can you blame me? So, if you know what the moons are, then what are the stars? Why are they in the sky?"

"Oh, you want to know about *star systems*? They are incredible. We will be up all night," Lionel says passionately.

"Tell me everything," Lillian declares. She wants to know it all, and there's nothing wrong with that.

No, nothing at all.

43

Meandering Mayhem

Mary

Mary is all packed for their departure, and she didn't even overstuff her backpack this time. She packed for practicality and movement. Besides, most of the mementos she was so attached to were either lost in their old burrow or to the roaring river. In a way, that was a blessing. She didn't need any of that stuff.

The girl makes her way into the hall with the others, mat in one hand and pillow in the other. Chief Vivian had the interesting idea for everyone to sleep in the halls closest to the exits. That way, if anything happens in the middle of the night, they will at least escape easily. She's got to hand it to the Rostad chief. It's a solid idea. Mary may sleep better tonight because of it.

She places her mat next to Trista's, which has the unfortunate side-effect of being near her mom's bed, but she can just ignore her. Mary is not nearly ready to talk to her. On the bright side, Seth is all the way across the hall, closest to the exit.

Brianna and Mia sit across from her. They snack on some large slices of fruit, likely given to them by Rostad. These two are the least unpleasant individuals right now. Mary can at least tolerate them.

The redhead notices her staring and swallows her last bite. "Hey, if you want some, I think now's the last time to get any."

"Did you go to the kitchen?" Mary asks.

The two women nod.

"They didn't care. They're shutting everything down anyway," Mia adds, her mouth full. "Their burrow is incredible, even greater than ours. I adore the art on the walls."

"Than ours?" Mary asks, almost laughing. "Come on, ours was dingy at best."

"She means the one before that," Brianna explains. "Before... the famine wars."

Both women fall silent. Mary tries to control her rage. She recalls what Seth said about their records being intact in some of their old bunkers. She can't believe they left all of that behind.

"Sorry to bring that up," Brianna says awkwardly. "How are you holding up, by the way?"

"How am I... holding up?" She despises the question.

"We're really sorry," Mia says. "I know how it must look, but we still care about you deeply. We've made mistakes in the past, but we're trying to rectify them now."

Brianna places a hand on Mia's back, shaking her head. She noticed Mary's growing fury.

Good, at least someone has sense, she thinks. The former leader of the gatherers has always been a little odd, but she is sharp and observant. Mary's respect for her has grown since the Rostad negotiations.

The two women leave her alone, so she observes Trista for a moment. The little girl has fallen fast asleep but twitches under the covers. Maybe she's having a nightmare. Mary thinks to wake her up but decides against it. She'll need what little sleep she can get, considering how early they'll be waking up. They leave before dawn.

She wonders what Rostad's bunkers are like. They must be much bigger and more luxurious than the Zurec ones. Either way, she is glad they won't be returning to that overcrowded Bunker Two. Anywhere will be better than that dump.

Mary lays back on her mat and closes her eyes. She can hear people talking amongst themselves, terrified of the coming morning. Theo and Robin discuss strategies to survive different encounters with the capaemen. Meanwhile, Jess, Kayla, and William reassure the awake kids. Mary drowns out the voices, not wanting to think about the looming danger. It will be okay. There's no way they will be attacked before the sun rises. Jamie said so.

The girl twitches in her relaxed state. The rogues have withheld information before: when Lillian encountered a capaeman and when Rostad asked if an attack was imminent. Mary can't prove it, but they were distant in their most recent meeting too. Jamie and Albert... They can't be everything they seem. How is she supposed to trust their word when they haven't given everyone the full picture of their attackers?

"Hey, is this a bad time?" a voice says. "Is she asleep?"

"I think so," Brianna answers.

Mary shoots out of her bed, escaping her drowning thoughts. Over her, she sees Steven crouching.

He smirks. "Hey there. I'm here to check in. How ya doing?"

She throws her arms around him. This boy is the only person who makes sense in her life. He doesn't lie or hide, and he has never accused her of ridiculous things like being selfish.

Steven reluctantly returns the gesture. "Yeah, I'm a little shaken too. Want to take a walk with me?"

Mary meets his eyes. He seems serious.

"Just for a little while. The guys and I are in charge of packing everything up, but that's about done now. We can see the burrow with no one around. I gotta admit, it's creepy."

"Yes," she says eagerly. "Let's go."

"Oh?" the boy says, raising an eyebrow. "Thought that'd be a harder sell. Hey Zurec people, are ya cool with us going out for a little while?"

Mary's mom observes Steven and her but says nothing. Seth doesn't even look like he's paying attention. He keeps staring at the door. "Go ahead," Brianna responds. "I see no harm in it." Even though they are about to go to sleep, Brianna is fully clad in her armor. She ties her hair up in a ponytail.

Come to think of it, everyone looks ready to go. The chief, the surveyors, and even her mother. That's odd. They have a few hours before they are supposed to leave. There's no need to pull an all-nighter.

Even Steven is decked out. It makes Mary wonder if she should put on her armor. He takes her hand, and they make their way down the hall toward the barricade. On the way, he takes a lantern out of her room and lights it. Mary takes this chance to grab her weapon and strap on her Rostad armor. She doubts she will need it, but the fact that everyone is wearing it makes her nervous.

Steven looks her up and down and smiles delightedly. "Ya know, you always look amazing in that."

Mary turns bright red. Ever since their dance in the glowing mushrooms, it's felt strange being around him. He makes her apprehensive in a way she can't quite understand.

"Th-Thanks," she manages to say, looking away.

He grabs her by the hand again. Steven too has changed since that night. He's bolder about touching her. Her heart pounds louder as they head farther from the others.

They pass through the gate and into territory she has only seen once before. Illuminated by the single lantern, the drawings on the walls are like mysterious cave paintings. Mary imagines this is what it would look like going through the halls of the original Zurec burrow—walking through a dark and unknown history. They dance on the walls like shadows, then pass back into darkness instantly.

Mary glances behind her, trying to get one last glimpse at the paintings, but finds only the shadows of herself and Steven crawling across the floor. Their figures are elongated and distorted, stretching as far as the torchlight reaches. They don't even look human. It's as if they are ghosts of darkness, following their every move. Mary waves a hand, and her lengthened doppelganger flaps a distorted arm. She can hardly see what is supposed to be her head, as it blurs out with the fading light.

"I told ya, it's creepy."

The girl jumps, snapping her gaze forward.

"Haha, sorry, I didn't mean to scare you." Steven holds the lantern up, pointing to the passing rooms. "This used to be a room where the kids built forts and played village, as if we could ever go outside. That one right there is the library you were interested in, and if we headed down this hall, we'd find the kitchen. It's empty now, much like everywhere else."

Mary wraps an arm around his. "I'm sorry you have to abandon this place. I know what that's like."

He grimaces, a shadow falling over his face. "Yeah, well, I suppose we should have seen it coming."

They make their way into what used to be the forge. Steven runs a hand over the weapons stands, now all empty. Even the shelves have been cleared. If it were not for the metal forging tables and the furnaces, Mary wouldn't even know the purpose of this room. Her eyes water a little. Before everything went wrong, she and Lillian were in the forge talking about each other's futures. She encouraged her to join the surveyors, and her friend continued her relentless quest to convince Mary she should adventure with her.

She stares at the forging table and clutches her arms. *Would things have gone differently if I had said yes?*

Steven too seems affected by this room. He gently places the lantern on one of the tables and leans against a stand that used to hold spears. He hangs his head. Mary leans in, intertwining her fingers in his. They gaze into each other's eyes. "What's on your mind?"

He clutches her hand like a treasure he must cherish. "I don't want to leave. I know no place we go to will ever be the same. Why are the capaemen doing this? They've never gone out of their way like this before."

She takes a step closer. "It's what they do. It'll be okay. I was driven out of my burrow, but through that I got to meet you, and I learned so much. Wherever we go, I'm sure we'll be able to make a home."

Steven nods. He places a hand on her cheek.

Mary leans into it gently. Even now, his eyes sparkle beautifully in the lantern light. She wants to step even closer, but if she does, their bodies will be touching.

Before she can be nervous about that prospect, Steven closes the gap for her. He wraps one arm around her waist, places a hand behind her head, and pulls her toward him.

Mary's breath catches in her throat, and her heart flutters. She shuts her eyes.

And their lips touch.

It's as if Mary's entire body has been lit ablaze.

A passion ignites in her chest, and she pulls him in hungrily, pressing her body against his. In return, Steven wraps both of his arms around her lower waist. The two of them slam against the spear stand, a simple kiss turning into their lips melding together. The scent of his skin overtakes her senses; that of leather and ashes, just like the roaring fire of the forge. Mary grips him tighter, longing to be even closer. It's frustrating that their armor is in the way. She has never felt this incredible in her entire life. The adults told her about this: about kissing and everything that follows. They neglected, however, to mention how good it feels. She wants more.

Returning her desire, Steven turns them around and pins her up against the wall. Mary presses her tongue through his soft lips, and his seems to retreat a little. It moves toward the back of his throat, but she goes after it, intertwining the two. They are in near-complete darkness, yet lights explode in her head. She grasps the straps of his armor, longing to feel his skin against hers.

But suddenly, Steven pushes Mary away.

Her eyes shoot open. It's as if she's been rudely awakened from a wistful dream.

Dimly illuminated by the lantern, Steven's face looks horrified.

Mary leans in, hypnotized by the dream. She wants to go back.

He backs away from her. "What are we doing?"

Mary blinks several times, then slaps her reddened cheeks. What *were* they doing just now? It's hardly the time or place for... what they just did. They are in a life-or-death situation, yet now when she looks at him, she can only think of the tenderness of his lips, of the thrill she felt when their bodies collided.

No, snap out of it, Mary. She stays crimson, now out of embarrassment. "I-I'm so sorry! I don't know what came over me."

Steven crosses his arms. "Nah, it's okay. I had something come over me as well." He is just as red as she is.

She avoids looking at him, and it seems he's doing the same.

"Look," the boy starts, "I-I've had a lot of stress lately, and I think it kind of, came out there. I don't want to make a big deal of this. We are from enemy clans, after all."

"R-Right," Mary says. She understands where he's coming from but doesn't feel the same. That was her first kiss, and she imagined that if she ever got to kiss a boy, they would be together. That's what it means when two people kiss, right? They can't just brush this under the rug.

"I should take you back to your folks," he says awkwardly.

Before they can discuss it further, Steven is already halfway out the door. Mary has no choice but to follow.

⚜

The two walk wordlessly back down the hall. He won't look at her, not even for a second. Does he regret it? After all, he did stop sending her letters two weeks ago. Was it because he didn't want to get involved with her family, or was he simply losing interest in her? Mary hopes that's not the case, because she doesn't regret their intimacy in the slightest. She now realizes that she's wanted this since their moment in the mushrooms. Deep down, he must have too. Otherwise, he wouldn't have taken her out there, and he wouldn't have initiated in the forge.

Her lips still tingle from the encounter. She presses them together, trying to get rid of the feeling.

Luckily, the gate to Zurec's hall is fast approaching. Steven travels down the hall much faster than their way up. He really does want to get rid of her.

At the end of the hall, the adults sit up on their mattresses while the children are fast asleep. Trista is still in her restless slumber. Her mother strokes little Max's head as he drifts off. Meanwhile, Kayla is writing in one of her journals.

Mary is unsure if she'd rather face them or stay with Steven.

"Hey, where have you two been?" Seth asks. He rests against his spear as if ready to jump into action.

Mary fidgets with her hair. "W-We were just walking down the halls. Why are only the children asleep?"

The chief's expression grows grim. "We're just being extra careful. Never know what could happen."

The girl's gaze falls to the floor. He does have a point. Last time, they were fully expecting a morning attack. Instead, the hunter showed up in the afternoon. As much as she hates to admit it, there's no way to predict their actions with certainty. She makes eye contact with her mom for a moment. She gestures for her to come over.

Mary stays rooted to her spot.

Steven shifts next to her awkwardly. "Well, I'd better get back to my post. Zane's waiting for me with my group at the west exit. Vivian is stationed at the east, so I'm kind of the leader."

A pang of fear reverberates through Mary, and without thinking she grabs his shirt sleeve. She doesn't want him to leave. Being alone with these people all night sounds like a nightmare.

"Hey," he whispers. "you'll be alright. I really gotta go, though."

Heartbreakingly, she decides to let go. The boy rushes up the hall, not looking back once.

boom... boom...

That is, until footsteps reverberate from outside.

No... Mary thinks. It can't be now. There's no way.

Steven stops in his tracks and stares at the ceiling in utter disbelief. The adults spring into action, shaking the kids awake.

Boom Boom

The entire hall shakes, and Mary clasps a hand over her mouth.

"Everyone, get ready to make a run for it!" Brianna commands. "They're coming."

44

The Rostad Massacre

Mary

Screaming.

All Mary can hear is screaming.

The Zurec group busts the trapdoor open, and Seth and Lance lead the way into the darkness. She can already smell it in the air—that familiar, nauseating scent of poison gas. The screams of agony echo from up the burrow hall, meaning some Rostad people have already been caught in its clutches.

Outside provides no relief from the blaring, tormented voices. Like them, some of Rostad has managed to escape. Their high-pitched screams pierce Mary's ears. Her grasp on reality slips away with each passing moment.

"Run now! Don't stop!" Brianna screeches. She's never heard such terror in the typically stoic woman. The shock from her urgent screaming pushes everyone forward.

Staring at her with anguish, Miss May clasps Mary's hand tightly. It's as if she doesn't care about their fight. All that's on her mind is making sure her daughter is safe. Mary feels the same way, tightening her grip around the caretaker's wrinkly hand. Nothing else matters right now, nothing but getting away.

boom... boom...

The harder the capaemen stomp in the distance, the louder the screaming grows. Mary wants to cover her ears but knows that will only slow her down. She won't freeze this time. She will carry herself to safety on her own two feet or die trying.

The mushrooms illuminate the bloody night. Whereas Mary once found them beautiful, now she sees them as deadly. They make it perfectly easy to see those running away, making her wonder if the capaemen knew about them all along. Jamie and Albert said they don't attack at night, but did they stop to consider that with the light of the mushrooms, it would not matter if the sun had set?

Speaking of, where *are* those two?

As the Zurec group ducks and weaves through tree roots and glowing fungi, Mary takes a glimpse at the grove of trees to the south. All she can see is a thick fog of toxic fumes. She hears the *boom*ing steps of capaemen and the desperate screams of the Rostad warriors, but she cannot see what is happening to them. She can't do anything.

What was once a place she held fondly in her heart is now a neon execution chamber.

The Zurec people head in the opposite direction of the voices. They cannot help them, even if they try. Meanwhile, Steven keeps looking back, trying to catch a glimpse of the chaos even though it's too far away. As a result, he is falling behind.

Brianna falls back and grabs the boy's arm. "Now's not the time to check on your buddies!" she yells. "You're with us now. I trust that some of them will make it out, but if you leave to help them now, you'll die."

The boy starts breathing heavily, and the redhead hands him to Mia and Jess. They attempt to calm him while dragging him along, but his panicking slows them down. At this rate, they won't escape in time.

Mary lets go of her mother's hand. "Give me a moment."

The caretaker is aghast and reaches for her daughter's hand again, but she refuses it.

"I have to help Steven. I'm the only one who can." She rushes to the boy's side.

Mary grabs his hand. "Hey, it's me. It's okay. You're going to get through this. Remember what I said? Wherever we go, we'll make a home together." She places her other hand on his cheek, trying to use her presence as a distraction from the chaos.

Suddenly, light returns to Steven's eyes. "I, no, this can't be happening!"

A response is good. That means he's thinking more clearly than before. "Don't worry. It looks like we got lucky. We might get away if we keep moving."

"But they won't!" he screeches. "People are dying right now. *My* people!"

"We can't help them! I'm sorry!" Mary cries. "I wish there were more we could do, but right now we have to run. They wouldn't want you putting yourself in unnecessary danger, would they?"

The boy shakes his head slowly, clenching his teeth.

Finally snapping out of it, he sprints alongside the others. "I know a route to the river from here. We should hide in one of the root caves until daybreak."

Mary takes another look behind them, just spotting the massive mushroom cap that looms over the north entrance to Rostad's burrow, and Zurec's former hall. The bright-pink fungus shrinks farther and farther into the distance, and soon it will disappear.

She turns back around, letting a single tear fall down her face. That place gave them refuge, but as usual, the capaemen ruin everything. As Mary runs bleary-eyed, the anguished cries and *boom*ing footsteps seem to swim louder in her ears. Is a hunter closing in on them, or is it her emotions overwhelming her? All she can see is smoke, bright mushrooms, and...

Wait, something is moving.

Illuminated by the neon lights are black wings, and they're headed straight toward them.

"N-Narecon incoming!" she shouts. She should have known they would be here. After all, they're the capaemen's hunting pets—can't sniff out humans without them.

SMASH

As the massive black bird plunges down, the force of its landing sends a gust in either direction, dividing the Zurec group into two. The first half consists of Mary, her mother, Steven, Kayla, the kids, and most of the former gatherers. Mia, Bruno, and Theo help the children get on their feet.

In the second half are Seth, Jess, Brianna, and the four remaining surveyors. William, Robin, Lance, and Carmen draw their weapons, ready to fight along-side their chief. "GO!" he screams at the top of his lungs. "We'll hold it off!" Wasting no time, Kayla and the caretaker help the gatherers, forcing the crying children to press forward.

"No!" Mary cries. *Not again.* This can't happen again. If more warriors stay behind, there's no guarantee they'll make it out. Images of the river flash rapidly through her mind. Mary can't take another sacrifice. She's not worth it. Instinctually, she lunges toward the fight.

But both Steven and Miss May grab her.

"Don't be a hypocrite!" Steven yells. "Remember what you just told me. Our top priority is getting out of here."

"He's right," her mother adds. For once, the two agree on something. "I can't lose another daughter. Please, Mary! Come with us!"

Realizing she has no choice, the girl follows them.

The narecon screeches and lunges at her people. Mary cannot see it, but she can hear the horror. She hears slashing, thudding, and Seth barking orders. Brianna does so right along with him, and for the first time, she hears desperation in their tones. Now that Mary knows Zurec's entire history, she's sure they've never experienced anything like this.

What remains of Zurec makes a beeline toward the river, with Steven leading the way. Their trials aren't over yet.

In her panicked state, little Trista trips over a root, and—

snap

She wails in pain. That's a broken ankle. Mary can tell by the sound of it.

The caretaker immediately scoops her up and scans the wound. "Hey! Can anyone carry her?"

"On it!" Steven says without hesitation. He throws the little girl on his back. "I can still run fast even with her. Trust me." By how good of shape he's in, Mary believes it.

They keep moving, but soon enough, the horror of the little girl's injury starts a damaging chain reaction. Kayla's three-year-old son begins sobbing. Even though his mother carries him, Felix's flailing hinders her. This causes a ripple effect, with most of the other kids breaking down.

"We're gonna die!" Oscar screams.

"I don't wanna die!" Jen screeches.

"Me neither!" Jan adds.

"You're not going to die," her mother says urgently, "but only if we move *right now*. They're coming."

This doesn't calm them down in the slightest. In fact, it seems to make it worse. The adults drag the kids under a short but wide, bright-orange mushroom and try to calm them down. If they can't get them to cooperate, they aren't going anywhere fast.

Meanwhile, this spot offers a perfect view of the chaos.

In the distance, Mary spots the other half of the group. They've back-tracked, choosing to fight closer to the entrance to Rostad's burrow. Brianna, Seth, and the rest of the group fight hard against the narecon. A few stray Rostad warriors have joined, distinguishable by how their phypent-skin armor reflects the mushrooms' glow. Some of their dead already lie on the ground. None of Zurec are dead, at least not yet. The Rostad people throw their spears, and they lodge into the bird's feathers, causing it to screech in pain. Meanwhile, Carmen and Jess slash away at its left side while William and Lance take the right. Brianna and Robin are at the front, nimbly dodging its beak attacks and not fighting back. They must be distracting it. However, Seth takes the cake for bravery.

Using his hulking size, he climbs on top of the giant bird and stabs it repeatedly. Blood splatters everywhere, yet in his deep rage he keeps plunging his spear into its back with one hand and hanging on for dear life with the other. It squawks and struggles, but Seth continues to hang on, tearing out some of its feathers in the process.

SCRAAAAA

The beast flails even more erratically, thrashing side to side until—*fwoosh! fwoosh!*—its wings send warriors on either side flying. Hit by its right wing, William sails back but luckily lands in some moss. Meanwhile, Lance ducks under the wing and slashes it open. Mary has never seen him fight, but he's one of Zurec's best. However, not everyone is so nimble. Hit harder by the left wing, Carmen and Jess are flung in opposite directions. Jess rolls under a thick cluster of arched mushrooms while Carmen launches back-first into a tree root.

CRACK

Mary nearly vomits at the sound.

Carmen lays in an arched position on top of the root, and she isn't moving.

In an enraged feat of strength, Seth bellows at the top of his lungs and leaps onto the back of the narecon's neck, slashing it open.

The monster collapses into the dirt, soaking it with blood.

The chief leaps off the corpse and sprints toward the injured woman. Brianna and Robin have already made their way toward her. They peel the mangled woman off the root and drag her across the forest floor, holding either arm. Carmen's head lolls from side to side.

boom... boom...

Yet horrifyingly, the battle isn't over. Seth stops, looks up at what's coming, and staggers. At the same time, the Rostad warriors flee, hiding under roots and crowded patches of fungi. Realizing what's happening, William, Jess, and Lance rush to Seth, urging him to hide as well. He ignores their pleas.

boom... boom...

Emerging from the noxious haze is a capaeman. Mary recognizes this one immediately. Its orange eyes glow right along with the mushrooms.

It's headed straight for the Zurec warriors.

Seth heads toward the injured woman, even as his subordinates urge him to stop.

At that moment, Carmen returns to consciousness. She struggles under Brianna and Robin's grip, but they hold on to her. Through her weak breaths, she says something to them, and both their faces fall. They shake their heads. Mary doesn't need to hear those words to know what she's saying. She wants them to leave her behind.

Meanwhile, the orange-eyed hunter looms ever closer. It is dressed mainly in camouflage, and littering its thick belt are all sorts of tools—undoubtedly all meant for death.

Some Rostad warriors dash out from the fog, running away from the hunter, but it spots them, its steps *boom*ing toward the unfortunate souls. It catches up to them in an instant and stomps on them mercilessly, splattering blood all over the trees.

Mary watches in horror, thinking it couldn't get more brutal, but it does. Those unlucky enough to escape the stomping are in for a worse fate.

The hunter grabs one person in each clawed hand, and with each thumb snaps their necks, not spilling a drop of blood.

Their lifeless bodies *thud* on the forest floor.

The hunter doesn't even flinch.

Mary staggers backward. *That's* what will happen to them if they don't leave right now, but she can barely stay standing. The children still cry and panic, and the adults do their best to calm them down, intermittently glancing back at the remaining Zurec warriors. Mary's eyes are glued to them. They've managed to regroup but are still right out in the open.

Carmen repeatedly gestures for them to leave, but they continue slowly dragging her across the forest floor even as the giant finishes off its prey.

Concluding its slaughter of the Rostad people, the capaeman pulls a square white cloth out of its shirt pocket—a handkerchief—and wipes its hands. It makes no sense. There isn't a drop of blood on its hands, yet it cleans them as if they are filthy: as if it hates the very idea of touching a human. Mary looks between the capaeman and her people. They're moving so slowly. She hates to think about it, but if they keep this up, they'll all die.

Then, methodically, the hunter walks in their direction.

boom... boom...

The instant Seth looks at the monstrosity, all the courage seems to drain out of his body. He says something to Lance and William, and they gesture to Brianna and Robin. Robin looks back at the hunter, then fearfully nods, letting go of Carmen's arm and giving the woman a long hug. However, Brianna doesn't let go.

boom... boom...

Seth grabs her arm. She slaps it away. Then, she whispers in his ear. His face falls, and... he turns away. *What?* Mary thinks.

Boom... Boom...

The former leader of the gatherers waves goodbye to her people, her face resolute. Carmen is too weak to protest, and the others don't argue either. The surveyors look at the two women before bolting after Seth, ducking under the thick fungi Jess fell beneath some time ago.

No, Mary thinks. Why are they abandoning them?

"Don't look!" her mother demands. "Kids, close your eyes, please." The adults try their best to cover as many of the children's eyes as possible.

But Mary's are wide open.

Boom Boom

Brianna drags Carmen a few feet in the opposite direction of their friends' hiding spot, and the hunter's head turns toward them.

Gently, Brianna lays her friend on the forest floor. Carmen stares up at her pleadingly, gesturing for her to hide. Shaking her head, Brianna unsheathes her dagger. It glows blue in the mushroom light.

She places a hand on Carmen's cheek and plunges the dagger into her chest.

Mary can't breathe. Etched on the others' faces is pure horror as they watch one member of Zurec kill another. Brianna could have run with the others, yet she killed Carmen and now is about to be killed by the hunter. Why? How could she raise a hand against one of her own?

Boom Boom Boom—

And now the monster is coming.

"Hey!" she shouts at the capaeman, waving her bloody hands in the air. "I bet you can't catch me."

BOOM BOOM BOOM BOOM—

Now, all of the hunter's attention is on her. As it swoops down to nab Brianna, she ducks under a root, blocking its hand. Then she takes an erratic path through the mushrooms, ducking under every bit of cover she can find. The capaeman tears away giant branches, rips mushrooms from the ground, and rakes plants from their roots, yet the nimble human evades it. In these seconds, as dust billows into the air and the capaeman scrambles faster and faster, Mary finally realizes what Brianna is doing: she's distracting the monster. All so everyone else can escape.

This must have been what she told Seth. They couldn't save Carmen, so she took her out before the capaeman could. Now, she's buying time with her life.

Tears flowing down her face, Mary knows what to do. "Everyone, run now!" she commands. Snapping out of their stupors, the Zurec survivors grab the children and begin to run again. They sprint away from the sounds of demolition on the battlefield behind them. The capaeman is still tearing apart the earth in search of Brianna. Incredibly, it hasn't found her yet. Maybe she got away.

However, they may not be so lucky, as the group halts again. In front of them is a giant branch—too long to go around. The only way is to climb over, but there's one problem: many people are carrying children.

Thinking fast, Bruno offers to lift them over. Mia, Theo, and Kayla help, climbing over the tree branch. They make a line, passing one child after another over the massive obstacle.

boom... boom...

The hunter is still in view as they wait to get over this hurdle. Mary and Steven watch the monster, praying it doesn't come this way. It still seems to be looking for Brianna.

Then, everything falls silent.

Mary's heart crawls into her throat as she dares scan the scene. To her surprise, the hunter isn't attacking the ground anymore. Instead, it takes a deep, hulking breath that echoes across the Wilds. Then, it exhales. The forest has grown eerily silent, causing the people of Zurec, like Mary, to stare in horror as they climb over the fallen tree branch. They whisper to each other, wondering whether they should keep moving.

What the capaeman is doing... Why does it feel familiar?

When Lillian was leading them toward a hiding spot, wasn't the hunter standing in silence then?

Before she can think about it further, the hunter moves like a burst of lightning and grabs something in its right hand.

In this moment, time seems to slow down.

Her red hair in tangles, Brianna struggles against the giant's grip, but it's no use. The capaeman stands and, its face an expressionless mask, places one finger on either side of her head.

SNAP
Her body falls to the floor.
Brianna is dead.

Mary wants to scream, to cry in anguish at this cruel and merciless world. The other people of Zurec stare at the scene in shock, unable to believe that the best of them is gone.

Then, the hunter closes its eyes again.

Oh no, Mary thinks. As much as she wants to mourn, they can't stay here. If they repeat what happened in the market, they won't get lucky this time. "Everyone," she whispers loud enough for all but the capaeman to hear. "We have to keep running, but quietly. No stepping on loose leaves or branches. We can't make a single sound, okay?"

The people stare at her as if caught in a trance, but then, one by one, they snap out of it. The adults pick the kids back up, and the group keeps moving.

After clearing the tree branch, they run only in places with cover, avoiding leaves and other fallen branches. It's slower, but the alternative is deadly. Even the children are silent now, not daring to do anything that could give them away.

boom... boom...

Then, on the distant other side of the battlefield, something massive emerges from the silhouetted trees: a second capaeman. It casually treads through the carnage, holding out its hands, which, unlike the first, are stained with blood. It has black hair and is dressed to kill like the first one. It wears camouflage overalls and a tool belt filled with metal objects. The monster's emotionless blue eyes glow in the mushroom light.

So, this is the second hunter, Mary thinks.

"Randon..." it says. Its voice is deep and raspy as if something is wrong with its throat. "Are you finished on your side?"

boom... boom...

The orange-eyed hunter approaches its accomplice. It takes out that same clean handkerchief and wipes its hands again. "I believe so."

Bruno gestures for the two to follow as they slink around a thick bush. Exhaling, Steven and Mary turn away from the scene. They can't see their persecutors anymore, but their eerily deep voices are as clear as the illuminated night.

"You did a fine job, Jayson," the orange-eyed capaeman continues. "I am aware this is your first mission in some time." Its voice is so low it vibrates the ground. Some of the children whimper at the sound of it, but Steven and the others reassure them, telling them everything will be okay.

"Indeed. It was a simple job, after all," the blue-eyed capaeman responds.

"I agree. I still cannot fathom why they called you in. I had this handled."

"You were called to base for the majority of my time here," it says in a slightly hostile tone. "It is only natural for them to call someone to pick up the slack while you were otherwise engaged. How was your break, by the way?"

The monster makes a sound that can only be described as a scoff. "I never take breaks."

There is a pause between them, and Mary checks on the group. Theo is struggling to keep up, leaning on the petite Mia. She can't blame him. His husband, Robin, is still out there, and two more of their members have died. Meanwhile, Steven sticks close to Mary's side. Trista is still on his back. "We're far enough away, and everyone is exhausted," he says. "Shouldn't we stop?"

"No," Mary says. "We don't stop until we reach the river," she tells everyone. "Then we will rest in a root cave. We can't expect them not to find us unless we're far, *far* away."

Her mom and Kayla nod in agreement, even as exhaustion overtakes them. Kayla still carries her son on her back, Miss May has Max, Bruno has the twins, and Mia is dragging Oscar. All of the children have stopped responding. They don't even cry. The group stays under cover of forest brush, trembling in fear as they creep. Mary moves to the front of the group, scanning the ground for anything else that could make noise. When they come across even the smallest stick, they move around it. When they see a pile of dead leaves, they sidestep. She knows all too well that any noise could spell their doom. Surprisingly, every remaining member of Zurec listens to her.

Even as the distance between Zurec and the hunters grows, those thunderous voices still carry. "No breaks? Oh, yes. You are a Veteran after all," the blue-eyed hunter continues. "Of course, they would want you at base. Inform me, what secret mission did they have you take care of this time?"

"Hmph, as if I would disclose to someone of your status."

"Randon Thanamore, ever the secretive one. Very well, then. I know better than to question my superiors."

"Let us retire for the night. There are not many of them left. We will pick them off later."

boom boom boom...

That must be the sound of them leaving.

Mary exhales as the sound of their steps fade farther away. Her family made the right choice. The hunters didn't see them, and now they are retreating.

As the exhausted survivors trudge on, the glowing mushrooms finally disappear, leaving the group in near-complete darkness. Luckily, her mother has a torch, flint, and steel in her backpack. She lights a fire for them. *Always prepared,* Mary thinks lovingly.

They head straight for the river.

The survivors collapse in a root cave. Parts of it are dripping with river water, but they couldn't care less. It's an awful shelter, but it puts a roof over their heads, and that's all they can care about now.

At this point, every child is sobbing and no adult can keep up the facade any longer. Bruno and the caretaker comfort the children while Mia dresses Trista's ankle. Jess, Kayla, and Theo are huddled together, wracked with worry at the fact that their spouses, amongst others, are still out there. If they didn't make it, they are who's left—only six remaining adults.

Mia begins to weep, and Mary's mom takes over Trista's care. She wastes no time getting the bandages out and getting to work while everyone breaks down around her. Her mother is incredible. Despite the deceptions, that fact remains. No one has seen more death than her, yet she presses on.

Mia reunites with her daughters, and they cling to her shirt. "Mommy," Jen asks. "Are Uncle Robin and the others okay?"

"Yeah," Jan adds, "they ran away in time, right?"

"I don't know, girls," she mumbles. "I just don't."

"Miss May?" Oscar asks.

"What is it, honey?" she answers as she ties off Trista's bandages.

"Why did Miss Brianna hurt Carmen?"

The caretaker's eyes widen. "You were peeking! I told you to keep your eyes closed."

"Brianna hurt Carmen?" Jen asks.

"Is she okay?" her twin asks as well.

"We can't talk about this right now," her mother urges. "Please, save the questions for the morning, okay kids? Let's get some sleep."

Clearly exhausted themselves, the twins don't put up much of a fight. They assist in grabbing blankets out of the packs and spreading them out on the damp cave floor. Then, they snuggle up to their parents. Mia and Bruno stare into each other's eyes with relief, embracing their daughters. At the very least, they both survived. Some of the Zurec people survived.

The same cannot be confirmed for Rostad.

Steven sits next to Mary and stares blankly at the ceiling, which is wet with algae. He doesn't say a word, and she doesn't push him. Whatever pain she is feeling right now, his is hundreds of times worse. They don't even know how many of his people have died. If it were her, she'd want to rush back to the scene to help those left, but that is impossible now.

All they can do is wait.

As the two of them gaze into the darkness, the caretaker and Kayla get everyone else ready for bed. They bring the survivors into a group and share the blankets, huddling together for warmth. Mary sneaks quick glances at them, wondering how they still have the energy to do that—how they still have hope. Oscar and Max sob quietly as they drift off. She wonders if she'll ever stop hearing the sound of crying.

Then, when most have either gone to sleep or managed some lighter version of it, Steven finally speaks. "It's all our fault," he mumbles faintly.

"What was that?" Mary whispers.

drip. drop.

The cave water splatters onto the damp wood.

"There's something I was... afraid to tell you," he murmurs.

She pulls a small blanket out of her backpack and drapes it over them both. He must be freezing.

"I'm sorry," Steven says. Even he is crying now.

"What for?" Mary asks. "It's okay. You can tell me."

"A few months ago, a capaeman saw us."

Her face falls. She knows exactly what that means.

"A newbie screwed up, and when the giant saw us, it started roaring like it was afraid of us. It alerted everyone in the market, and we only narrowly escaped." His breath catches in his throat, and for a moment it looks as if he's choking. "What if... What if *that's* the reason? What if they're here... because of *us?*"

Mary throws her arm around him. "Even if that's true, it's not your fault." She grabs his chin, forcing him to look her in the eyes. "If they started hunting us for a reason as trivial as that, it's *their* fault, not yours. Your people were doing what they must to survive. Heck, by that logic, Zurec is at fault for the attacks as well."

The boy doesn't say anything else. Instead, he weeps softly into Mary's shirt. She embraces him, glad to be in his warmth.

Yes, everything that has happened is *their* fault. It doesn't matter the reason. Their actions cannot be justified. Humans are just trying to stay alive, and they are punished for it. The hunters Mary overheard talked so nonchalantly about taking lives. Doing so means so little to them. They are pure evil, right down to their core.

Mary *hates* the capaemen and she will *never* forgive them as long as she shall live.

45

Shelter After the Storm

Lillian

As the sun heats her skin, Lillian's eyes flutter open. There is a blanket on her that wasn't there before, a white and puffy thing. It's so comfortable she doesn't want to move. She vaguely remembers Lionel putting it on her before he passed out. It was in the middle of a sentence too. One moment he was talking about why the world is called "Planet Copius," and next he passed out right on top of his bedsheets. He must have been exhausted from everything that happened that day.

Reluctantly, Lillian lifts the blanket off herself. She rubs her eyes and her vision clears slowly. Lionel is fast asleep, still on top of his ocean-print sheets. It's as if he didn't move the entire night, asleep as deeply as a hibernating leomus. He looks so peaceful, with his eyes gently closed, shoulders slumped, and scales glimmering in the sunlight. The thought of waking him crosses Lillian's mind, but she knows better than to mess with a sleeping giant. She'll wait for him to wake up on his own.

In the meantime, the warrior exhales, remembering everything she learned last night. She cannot help but smile as the images flood her mind: Lionel's long lecture about star systems, the tour of his creature journal, and his even longer shell collection showcase. Some seashells are still scattered on the bed around his sleeping figure. They look right at home in the ocean waves. Lillian loves how when she thinks of the ocean—the "waterlands," as she used to call them—she knows what it looks like now. Visiting the beach was one of the best times of her life. Lillian never would have seen anything like that without him.

Then again, if his family never came here, Albian would still be alive, and the adults wouldn't have had to sacrifice themselves to save Zurec. If they never came, if she never got the chance to meet Lionel, they'd still be alive.

No, it isn't as simple as that. The hunters were called in by the capaeman community. If the Thanamore family hadn't answered the call, another would have—one that most likely would not lead to a change of heart like Lionel. Lillian should be grateful. She should count herself lucky she managed to get one of them on her side.

So why does she feel so terrible?

BANG BANG BANG

Before Lillian can think more, an aggressive knock comes from the door. The enormous sound fills up the entire room. This time, she doesn't freeze. She doesn't wait to see who it is. Instead, she quickly knocks her makeshift bed onto the floor and ducks behind the picture on Lionel's desk.

"Lionel, are you awake?" the voice of Maeko calls. "By the ocean, get your butt out of bed. Father wishes to speak with you."

Lionel makes a sound that can only be described as halfway between a growl and a groan, then buries his head in his pillow.

BANG BANG

"Hey, did you hear me at all? Wake up!"

Lillian hears the click of a doorknob turning, but no sound of it opening. The door is locked.

"Come on, how late did you stay up last night? Do not make me pick the lock!"

Lionel scrambles out of his bed. "Calm yourself. I'm awake!"

"Then let me come in!"

The boy looks from Lillian's hiding spot to the door, his reptilian eyes wide. "Why?"

"Because I said so. Is there a specific *reason* why I cannot enter? You're not hiding anything from me, are you?" He says this way too loud.

There are *boom*ing footsteps and then a *click* from the doorknob.

"There. That wasn't so difficult," the voice of Maeko says more clearly. He's in the room now. Lillian holds her breath.

"Have you no sense?" Lionel whispers. "Father could easily hear you."

"Is it..." his brother says even quieter, "Is that *business* we discussed taken care of?"

"Yeah, whatever. Now, get out of my room."

"So, *it is* gone? Like, gone gone? Because if it is not—"

"I know already!" Lionel yells. The sound bounces off the walls, and Lillian squeezes her eyes shut. She is inches away from being caught.

"Hey, no need to be angry. This is for your benefit. Do not throw your future away over something so insignificant."

"I would not do something that foolish. Now, get out of my room."

"As long as you understand," Maeko growls. "I shall take my leave now. Do not leave Father waiting long. You know how he gets." The door closes immediately.

Lillian stays rooted behind the picture, afraid to move.

Lionel collapses onto his bed. "That was too close. I've got to get you out of here."

She still doesn't move. It's too risky. Much better to be in the shadow of this mysterious picture than to risk certain death.

"You know, you are free to come out now."

"Are you serious?" Lillian asks. "I am *not* repeating a Maeko situation."

"That is... fair," he responds awkwardly. "I will get the bag for you. My father is likely in the kitchen. We will have to... get past him to leave."

Her heart drops. The last thing she wants is to be anywhere near that monster, but she doesn't have much choice. As the bag is placed next to the picture frame, Lillian reluctantly crawls into it. She feels nauseous.

"Okay, remember to stay still," Lionel says.

Lillian stays still as the dead. *One step at a time*, she reminds herself. First, she must get out of here, find out if her family is alive, and then...

What next? Things must have changed back at home. Lillian has missed them so much, but now that she's returning, she feels extremely nervous. Can she really come back to them, knowing what she knows, seeing what she's seen?

No. That's not what I'm supposed to worry about now, she thinks. If anything, she should be worried about what's right ahead. They'll run into Lionel's dad any minute. She braces herself.

whooossshhh

The sound of rushing air surrounds her. Someone must have turned up the vent dial. The air chills her skin.

As Lionel's footsteps *boom* down the hall, more familiar noises reach her ears. She can hear the narecons squawking and fluttering in their claustrophobic cages, air rushing out of the ducts, and the clinking of glass in the distance. It's the same noise Maeko created in the kitchen yesterday, but she knows that's not him there now. Ironically, she wishes it were. That capaeman boy is a hero compared to who is ahead.

Lionel's footsteps begin to slow, and Lillian's heart crawls into her throat. She shuts her eyes tight, even though she can't see anything. She wishes she could turn off her ears too. That she could shut down entirely just for a little while... until this nightmare is over.

"Lionel," an emotionless voice says, "there you are. We have much to discuss." Images of the giant flanked by black narecons—the blood, the screaming, those dead, orange eyes—invade Lillian's thoughts. She doesn't need to see anything for terror to sink into her bones, like poison gas seeping into a burrow.

Just outside this thin layer of fabric is her greatest enemy.

The voice of Lionel's father is much more powerful than Lillian imagined. The sound seems to take over the entire building, reverberating through the halls, quashing all hope of escape. While Lionel sounds somewhat human, his father might as well be an alien creature who happens to speak their language. One word is enough to keep Lillian frozen in place. She sits motionless within the cloth of the bag.

"Father, you look well," Lionel says formally.

"Come now, you know there is no need for that sort of language with me."

"I apologize. I simply have somewhere to be. Now, if you will excuse me—"
Something causes Lionel to jolt backward.

"Can it not wait?" The hunter speaks slowly, every word laden with purpose. "It has been several days since we have talked. What were you and Maeko arguing about?"

The capaeman boy freezes. She can hear his breathing grow heavier. "Nothing."

"Look, I know you have been having an arduous time since your first assignment, but that is no excuse to be cold to your brother. He only wants to be closer to you."

"I know." He almost sounds regretful.

"Although, I cannot say your situation is unfamiliar. I too had to take some distance when I first started. The best way you can remedy your uncertainty is by returning to the field. If you do enough jobs, your doubts will cease. This profession is not easy, but you have a talent for it. I would hate for you to be—"

"I am *not* going back," Lionel says resolutely. Lillian remembers the promise he made to her yesterday. Her heart lifts, witnessing him honor it, but she had no idea it would sound like this. His father does not seem like the kind of man who takes no for an answer. She holds her breath.

"What? Son, you certainly do not mean—"

"Being a hunter is not for me. I will have to train for a new job. If you must know where I am going presently, I plan to scout the town to see if anyone will take me on as an apprentice."

"Lionel, you have trained for two years. Surely you do not want to start ove—"

"I just need some time," he says with resentment. "Please. I don't want to discuss returning to the field. I need to... figure things out."

There is a long pause. Lillian doesn't dare move for any of it. It dawns on her the weight of what she's asking Lionel to do. The lies he will have to tell, the rules he'll break, and if he gets caught... she can't even imagine what would happen. That monster talks of killing so casually—as if it's like breathing or eating. What would he do to someone who gets in the way of that goal? Even though Lionel is his son, Lillian cannot see this capaeman being merciful.

"Hmm," Lionel's father muses. "Very well, then. I shall allow you some time. However, I do not want you to give up. Do not search for an apprenticeship at the moment. Take some time for yourself. Consider your options. I am more than capable of supporting both you and your brother."

"Thank you, Father."

Wait, what? Lillian thinks. Is he being... understanding? That's impossible. If any capaeman were evil, it would be this one, yet with Lionel he's a completely different person. If even *this* monster is capable of empathy, then why—no, *how* can he so ruthlessly slay her kin? Unlike Lionel, he shows no remorse for it. Not an ounce of guilt. She bites her lower lip, forcing herself still. Her hands tremble with fury.

"By the way," the hunter continues, "there is something you should know. I am aware you do not want to hear about work, so I shall keep this brief. Jayson and I took out a very large human nest last night. Few of them are left now. It will not be long before we can leave this backwater town."

Lillian's chest freezes. The air is stiff, hard as ice and impossible to inhale. She can't have heard that right.

"Really?" Lionel asks, sounding casual. "That is indeed good news."

"It is. Curiously, we did not fight a single flier. Perhaps there was only the one. Either way, take care if you enter the forest. If you spot any of those dastardly creatures—"

"—I will let you know, and I will steer clear of the forest from that point onward," Lionel states as if he's said it a million times.

"Very good," his father says, pleased. "You are free to go if you wish. Be sure to be home by dinnertime. We should go out. We are a family, after all."

"I'll remember that," he says, already rushing out the door.

⚬⚬⚬

Only one thing is on Lillian's mind now. Even as Lionel treks farther and farther from his home, the plains creatures chattering about them, she stays petrified, breathing shallowly.

"Jayson and I took out a very large human nest last night. Few of them are left now."

It's not possible. He must have been talking about Rostad. That *has* to be it. Otherwise...

Everything Lillian has done would be for nothing.

After a few minutes, the wind takes on a fuller, rustling quality and the air adopts a familiar mossy scent. Lionel stops, the reverb of his footsteps fading out. "We can speak freely now."

She wants to scoff, but no sound comes out. What, exactly, is she supposed to say?

"May I put you down? We can talk a moment before you leave."

She doesn't answer, but Lionel lowers the sack anyway. The *whoosh* of the river and the chittering of bugs echo from outside her fabric prison.

When Lillian pulls open the bag, the first thing she sees is red, followed by shoots of green and brown. The wind rustles the giant leaves of the redwood trees, causing some to fall off and begin a long floating journey toward the forest floor. Her shoes squish into the moss. To her left is a familiar field of red flowers. They're a distance away, but she can still make out their crimson petals. To her right is the Crystal River. Its colorful rocks glimmer in the sunlight shining from the canopy.

She didn't realize how much she missed this place.

"This is where we first met," the capaeman says. "I figured it could be where we part ways as well. I hope your home is not too far from here." The warrior turns around, facing Lionel but refusing to meet his eyes. He has no idea just how close they are.

The river *whooshes* loudly, and for several moments, neither of them speak. He must have figured out something is wrong by now, but he hasn't said anything.

"Why did you start coming here?" Lillian asks finally. She's sick of the silence.

"Pardon?"

"You like to read here. Why is that? There must be better places to be."

"Not really," Lionel says. "There is no one out here. Or rather, no capaemen. I do not like to be bothered. The forest is the best place for that."

"Even though there are 'dangerous humans' here?"

He chuckles. "Hardly. My father is simply overly cautious." At the mention of the hunter, Lillian goes silent again. She feels that intense cold spreading across her body again, as if she has died but is somehow still moving.

Then, the capaeman reaches toward her, his giant clawed hand getting closer and huger. She backs away.

He flinches, pulling his hand back. "I was only trying to grab the bag."

The bag Lillian exited lies next to her, its drawstrings open. She grits her teeth. She screwed up.

"You *do* hate me, don't you?"

"No," she says. "That's not true."

He reaches in her direction. She flinches again.

Lionel frowns.

"I-I don't hate you," Lillian says shakily.

"But you *are* afraid of me," the capaeman confirms. "I swear, I would never hurt you or your family. I have left the hunters. I even informed my father about it. What more must I do to prove I am on your side?"

She can't answer that right now. At the sight of her childhood home, Lillian almost forgot what she'd learned. Now that they're back on the subject, she can't think of anything else.

"D-Do you..." she stammers. "Do you think there's anyone left?"

Lionel's eyes narrow. "What do you mean?"

"Your father said they killed a group of people last night. Don't you realize that could have been *my* people?"

The capaeman's suspicion turns to shock. He didn't think of that. *Of course*, he didn't. "Lillian, I—Y-You cannot know that for sure. The odds of that are—"

"Extremely high," she finishes.

"No, I'm sure it will be—"

"Don't patronize me. Not now." She wants to scream at Lionel for not thinking about this, and rant about how his father is a horrible person. Lionel shouldn't just leave the hunters; he should stay far away from that man. But she can't say any of that because all she feels now is despair. The emotion creeps over her entire being until her body is wracked with a great weight, growing heavier every second.

"What if... what if *I'm* the only one left?"

The capaeman recoils at the thought. "You do not know that for sure."

"It's possible, isn't it?" she says, raising her voice. "What if your father *killed* my entire clan? What if, when I go home, I find that *no one* is waiting for me? That, the whole time we were together, they all died horribly! I..." Lillian falters. She stares down at the moss. "I wouldn't want to keep living."

The moment those words come out, Lionel looks her straight in the eyes.

"If that happens, come find me. I am often by the whitewood. Seek me out, and we will figure it out together. You are not alone."

Somehow, that doesn't make her feel any better. "What would there be to 'figure out'? What I just described is my worst nightmare." Lionel's face falls. He stares at the river, which flows at a moderate pace, not calm or rapid. The place where she and Mary were separated is just south of here.

... Mary. Lillian isn't sure if she made it out, much less survived long enough for them to meet again. There are so many unknowns. She wants more than anything to find her family again, but if they are all dead...

"I would not let you give up," the capaeman says. "Even if the worst has happened, there are other forests. Other human civilizations. I could take you to them."

Suddenly, the rage she felt returns. "Is that supposed to make me feel better?"

Lionel holds up his hands. "Woah, I am only trying to help. What is the problem?"

"The *problem* is you still don't get it. What if you and your brother Maeko nearly died and then were separated? You saw him get hurt, but you have no idea if he made it out alive. On top of that, imagine all your friends, your family, and everyone you ever loved either hid in terror or stayed behind to fight. Some of them died to save you. You watched it happen. Then, when against all odds you survive, your enemy-turned-friend tells you, 'Don't worry, we can just replace them.' Human beings are *not* expendable."

The capaeman stares at her in shock, his mouth hanging open. "I-I did not mean—"

"If you want this to work," Lillian continues, "you need to understand that."

A sobering silence hangs over them. She considers breaking it again but refuses to this time. It's Lionel's turn. He's the one who started this tragedy, and he's also the one who agreed to end it.

"You make a valid point," he finally says. "I understand now. I grasp the stakes, so let us ensure it does not come to that. We should discuss the technicalities of our deal. I like to study at this spot, so I will wait here for you every afternoon I can. I may not show up some days, but I will try to give you as many opportunities as possible to meet with me. When you arrive, I will tell you what I know. Then, you can spread that information to your people. Rinse, repeat. They will see the hunters' actions coming."

He gazes at the forest floor. It seems like he wants to say more but is stopping himself. "Lionel," Lillian asks, "what are you thinking?"

"That plan..." he says through gritted teeth. "It is a solid idea, but it will only work for so long. Eventually, the hunters will realize someone is tipping you off. Then, I will be in hot water."

Lillian hates to admit it, but he's right. The thought should have crossed her mind, but she was too busy being hopeful. She wants this plan to work because she doesn't want things to change. They may not have been happy, but they were at peace. Her people worked so hard to achieve separation from the capaemen, to avoid bloodshed, and deep down she believed they could dodge it forever.

Ugh, that's exactly the denial the adults preach, she scolds herself. The second Albian was attacked, they lost that privilege. Their only choice is to change.

"Alright," Lillian says. "What comes next? What should we do when they find out?"

"Leave the Crimson Forest. Take whomever you care about and run. The hunters already believe most of your populace has been exterminated. If those who remain leave, they may not notice."

"My people won't accept that. We've lived here for almost four generations. Besides, we don't have the means to travel safely anymore. Our ancestors gave up our nomadic lifestyle for peace."

"Well, they will have to figure it out, Lillian," Lionel asserts. "That is the *only* option. You do not have to tell them immediately, but when the hunters start catching on, and they *will*, we will be forced to create an escape plan."

The warrior stares at her spear. It shimmers red, reflecting the colors of the flower field. "Where would we even go?"

"There is a small town for wealthy capaemen just north of here," Lionel answers. "I hear there is a population of humans in its nearby forest. They have been difficult to deal with, so they are likely still alive. They may even be powerful enough to protect you. Your people will be able to get there safely if they take the migration."

"The migration?" Lillian asks. "What's that?"

Lionel looks to the north. "It is an incredible phenomenon that would take a while to explain, and unfortunately it only happens seasonally. So, it will not help much now. However, if you all can survive until the end of spring, it will become an option."

She nods slowly, taking several deep breaths. Spring has one month left—a span that should be easily survivable, but given the past month and a half, she can't help but feel a sense of dread.

"Remember, you are not alone."

Lillian looks up at Lionel. Then again, a month ago she thought all capaemen were evil. Now she is friends with one. Her family wanted answers, and now they have all the answers they need. Zurec has someone on the inside, which is a hundred times more effective than three people aimlessly flying around on an acera.

"I trust you," Lillian says, her fear fading. "The plan is risky as heck, but it just might work."

Lionel stares at his hands. "You truly still trust me? After everything? I do not deserve your kindness."

"Well, you're getting it. So, take it or leave it."

He laughs awkwardly. "It really is your way or the railway, huh?"

"What's a railway?"

The capaeman pats her head with his index finger. "I will tell you later. We will meet again, will we not?"

She pushes the finger away. "Come on, I'm not a kid. Why are you doing that?"

"You *are* a kid to me."

She is reminded of their surprisingly wide age gap. She smiles. All the amazing things she has learned... perhaps they make up for the bad. For all the tragedy Lillian has experienced, she has also witnessed great beauty. As faint as it is, there is still hope. And in this world dominated by giants, one must cling to any inkling of it they can find. She will dig her hands into it and never let go, because what she has found might save everyone.

The light of the forest brightens as it turns to afternoon. Lillian can't believe how time flies with Lionel. There is still so much she wants to ask. Everything she was taught about the world—most of it was wrong. Just a comfortable lie her people told themselves to not have to face the deep nuances of this world, of Planet... *Copius*. Yes, that's what it's called. Planet Copius.

Lionel gazes at the crimson flowers, lost in his own world. After a few minutes of peaceful silence, he stands. "I should go. My father will be expecting me." He towers over her like the trees of the Giant Wilds, but Lillian feels no fear, only sadness that it's already time to say goodbye.

"Until we meet again," the human says to the capaeman. "And Lionel... thank you."

He nods. "Promise me you will not die. I did not toil away for a month helping you recover only for you to croak now."

She throws him a judgmental look. "You know what my life is like. I can't promise anything, but I'll try my best."

"Very well, then. I suppose I will take what I can get." He turns to leave but then stops.

Yet again, the human girl stands in a meadow with a capaeman's back to her. Just like the first time, she's unsure what he's going to do next.

"Oh, and Lillian..." he starts.

She raises an eyebrow. That serious tone is back.

"*I* should be the one thanking *you*. You did not have to call for me that day. You did not have to humor me when we talked in the workshop, and when I screwed up—more than screwed up—you did not have to give me a second chance. Human or capaeman, you are an incredible person. So, thank you. Let me know if your family made it."

Before she can respond, the capaeman starts walking, this time not looking back.

46

Aftermath of the Massacre

Mary

Mary wakes up in the cave. Her whole outfit is soaking wet. She can't tell if that's from the river or her tears. Who cares.

Despair lingers in the air.

Steven is the first outside, and Mary is close behind him. The two care-takers—Kayla might as well be one now—do everything for the kids, from changing them out of their wet clothes to convincing them to take their first steps out of the root cave. Mary thinks of helping but is hardly in the mood. Her melancholy would only drag them down.

The sunlight billowing down in large pillars feels like a cruel joke. Animals chitter peacefully in the distance while the leaves of the river plants sway back and forth in the wind. The forest is just as it was, as if the events of last night never happened. The Giant Wilds truly is a brutal place to live.

According to Jamie and Albert, this is what every place is like. Forests like this are one of the safest spots to be. That's difficult to believe. There's nowhere to run, and now, nowhere to hide either.

Still, they press forward, clinging to a single thread of hope: since some of them survived, maybe they'll be okay. She hears Mia use words like those to mollify Theo and Kayla, whose spouses are both missing. Mary used to believe that as well—that somehow, through love and willpower, they could make it through anything.

She doesn't anymore.

No one is coming to save them, and they cannot protect themselves. So, Mary will savor her final moments with those she loves, because at this point, it isn't a matter of *if* they die. It's a matter of *when*.

Steven intertwines his fingers with hers, clearly not caring if anyone sees. He must be thinking the same thing: it doesn't matter. Nothing does.

They travel back to the site of the massacre. As expected, mangled Rostad bodies litter the mushroom field, but Mary feels nothing. She's gone numb to it all, only able to watch blankly as Steven falls to the ground, whaling at the sight. She is dazedly aware of the caretaker keeping the children back, instructing the rest of the group to search for survivors. Meanwhile, Mary treks through a field of crimson as if in a dream.

How did a tiny, weak girl like her think she could accomplish anything?

All her life, Mary has been a burden on others. In the end, she couldn't help anyone. She couldn't save those who needed saving. She hardly saved herself.

She stops, observing the blood and guts splattered all around her, and her vision blurs with tears. *Lillian*, she thinks, *what would you do? I miss you so much. I wish you were here instead of me. You always stayed positive, and I don't know what to do without you.* The distraught girl trembles, on the verge of collapsing, until she spots a figure in the distance.

No, it's a group.

Headed by Chief Vivian is a large group of Rostad people, sprinkled with familiar faces. Seth, Jess, William, Robin, and Lance are all still alive. They wave their hands in the air and yell her name. Their voices bring Mary back to life. "Guys!" she screams. She sprints toward the group and jumps into Seth's arms.

"Mary! I'm so glad you're safe. Where are the others?"

"Right this way," she says, guiding them to the other side of the field.

So many Rostad people survived too. She recognizes Alec and a few surveyors from the borrowing expedition. The people she doesn't know must be at least fifty strong. Some have minor injuries. Others lean on their friends while nursing far more critical conditions, but still, over fifty people survived. This is incredible.

But then Mary remembers how many Rostad used to have. There were hundreds of them. No, there is nothing worth celebrating.

She leads the group to Steven, and they have a tear-filled reunion. Chief Vivian shows actual emotion for the first time, giving her boy a suffocating hug. Meanwhile, Miss May, Theo, Kayla, and Mia embrace their found loved ones. The children get excited as well. Mary gradually drifts away from the scene, until she hears Steven's voice.

"Where's Zane?"

Her heart drops.

Mary's head shoots back at the Rostad people, and she waits for them to say he's okay, that he's off taking care of injured folks or something, but the entire group is silent. Things can't get any worse. Zane was kind to her. He was the first to be cordial when even Steven was prejudiced.

"I'm sorry, Steven. He didn't make it."

The boy breaks down yet again. In a moment of sympathy Mary has never seen out of the jerk before, Alec comforts his friend. So do a woman and child she doesn't recognize. The little girl has a thick head of blonde hair, just like the man standing over her. They must be Alec's family.

Alec and Steven hug and pat each other on the back, reassuring themselves that everything will be okay. It reminds her of her own people: how relentlessly they tried to keep her safe, although misguidedly. Steven doesn't need her help. He has plenty of people left to support him. Mary turns away from the mourning group, knowing where she must go.

The girl cautiously makes her way to her mother. Despite all the lies, this is the only family she has. She doesn't want to lose them.

Mary makes eye contact with her mom and smirks slightly.

Seeing this, the caretaker rushes over and gives her the tightest hug of her life. "Oh, honey!" she sobs. "I'm so sorry! For everything."

Mary gently hugs back. "I know."

She cups her daughter's face in her hands. "You were so brave. I'm proud of you."

Mary shakes her head, frowning. "No, I wasn't at all. I couldn't even fight back."

"That wasn't your job," a familiar voice interrupts.

The two turn to see Seth standing by their side. Of course, he'd check up on her.

"It was my job, and I was the one who was a coward," the chief clenches his fists, which are coated in dirt. "All we could do was make a shallow grave for them. I wanted to save all of us, drag Carmen to safety and convince Brianna to follow, but once I saw that hunter, I..." He starts shaking, and Mary's mother places a hand on his chest. "I'm supposed to be the chief. I'm supposed... to make the sacrifices."

"No," the caretaker says softly. "We saw what happened. You did exactly as a chief should do. You prioritized the lives of many over the few. You convinced Robin to let go of Carmen, and now he gets to see his husband and nieces again."

She gestures to the reunited families. Theo has tears running down his face as he kisses his husband. Kayla and William are having a similar reunion, and Lance leans against a root, observing everyone with a smirk. The children are chanting, "We survived! We survived! Yayyy!"

"Without your leadership, they would be dead," she confirms.

"I should have died instead of her!" he shouts. "Brianna wanted to put Carmen to rest before the capaeman could. She even offered to distract it so we could get away, and like a coward, I accepted that. I should have told her no! I should have done it instead! She's done so much for me, for this clan, and I failed her when she needed me most."

"No!" Mary protests. "You made the right decision." She thinks of Lillian yet again. "Dying for others or with others, it's overrated. People should try their best to live, no matter the circumstances. Stop sacrificing yourselves. It'll only break the hearts of those you leave behind."

These words seem to get through to the chief, as his eyes slowly widen. He gently pushes Miss May away. "That'll be enough."

He greets the children. They are so excited that they run circles around him, calling him a hero. They don't seem to have a care in the world, and the chief plays with them gleefully. It brightens the mood of everyone.

Everyone except her mother.

She looks at her daughter remorsefully and pulls something out of her pack. It's a stack of papers. "Honey, I didn't plan on telling you, but... these are yours."

Her eyes widening, Mary snatches the stack from her mother. They're letters. There must be at least seven of them, all with the words *To Mary, From Steven* scribbled on the outside. It dawns on her what this means. "You were intercepting Steven's letters?"

"I'm sorry," her mother says. "I thought it was best. You shouldn't be with him. He's from—"

"You'd better not be saying I can't be with him because he's from Rostad," Mary interrupts. "Because if you are, you're more of a hypocrite than I thought."

Her mother's face falls.

Mary clutches the letters, enraged at the audacity of her mom's actions. "How are we any better than them? In fact, from where I stand, it'd be worse if I liked someone from Zurec. After all, you're the liars. You're the ones who betrayed your neighbors."

"Baby, that was a long—"

"It wasn't a long time ago!" she shouts, attracting the attention of everyone in earshot. "It was fifteen years ago. That's *nothing* to you. Stop pretending I'm some oblivious child! I know the truth, but you are still determined to escape your actions even now. You'd rather keep things from me than treat me as an equal of this community!"

"Mary, no, I—"

"I don't want to hear it!" she screams. All the Zurec adults are staring, aghast. "What are you looking at? Got something to say?" They all look away, except for Seth. He frowns as if disappointed in her. She doesn't care. "I thought not."

Mary storms away, her fury flaring up again. Her mother tries to grab her arm, but she shakes it off. She isn't sure where she's going, but she has to get away from here. The tragedy they experienced did not erase the betrayal. Now she is alone. The children ask the adults what Mary meant, and they respond that she's just upset over the people who died. Then, the kids continue to play as if nothing happened. *Are you kidding me?* Mary thinks. The adults aren't even learning from their mistakes.

There is one child who isn't playing, though.

Trista is far from the group, holding a makeshift walking stick and sitting on a short, white mushroom cap. She props her bandaged ankle on top of it. Mary hurries over to the little girl and sits beside her. As usual, her appearance is disheveled, but in this setting it makes sense.

"You seem mad," Trista comments.

Mary sighs. "I am, but not at you. Don't worry."

"I know," she says. "Why are you mad at them?"

She meets the little girl's weary, dark eyes. She wonders if Albian chose to hide their history too. There's no way to tell. Even if they didn't hide it, they definitely wouldn't tell a seven- and five-year-old, not until they're older. "It's a long story. One I don't feel like talking about right now."

Trista's brother plays with the others. He's been spending a lot of time with Oscar lately. They chase Jen and Jan now. Mary wonders why Max gets along with the others while his sister pushes people away. Perhaps it has something to do with what they saw. She remembers Trista mentioning her brother had his eyes closed during the Albian massacre. That may have saved him.

"I don't know why they're so happy," Trista says, squinting at the kids.

"You've got me there," Mary responds. "I can't even *fake* a smile right now."

"We're gonna die. Don't know why they're playing around."

The big girl scooches closer to the little one and wraps her arm around her. This mushroom is silky and plushy, almost like a giant pillow. She can see why Trista picked this spot. "Just let them have fun," Mary says. "They are enjoying the time they have and not worrying about the future."

"Why would they do that? That's pointless."

For a moment, she wonders how to respond. The old Mary wouldn't hesitate to tell Trista she's wrong, but she isn't sure about that anymore. She's not sure about anything. "Still, let them. We don't know what will come tomorrow, so let them have today."

Trista leans her head on Mary's shoulder. "I don't get it."

Mary hugs her tighter. *It means we don't have much time left, so we should enjoy it,* she thinks, but she does not dare voice it. She simply stares off into the distance, trying to avoid the bloodstains and mangled bodies. Maybe their deaths were a mercy. They don't have to mourn anymore. They don't have to hurt. Everything just... stops. Mary longs for that—for an end to the pain. She wishes death were not the only way.

After a few minutes, Chief Vivian and the Rostad people approach Seth. They ask where Zurec is going next and explain their situation. "Only..." the chief begins sadly, "only a quarter of us survived, about sixty people. Most of our warriors will stay behind and take care of the dead, myself included. I assume y'all will be headed to a shelter of some sort?" Blood stains the Rostad chief's dark armor. Other warriors don't look much better. They must have been fighting off the narecons as well.

"We have a bunker quite a ways from here," Seth says, confused. "I thought Rostad would have plenty of shelters, though."

She shakes her massive head. "Most are close by here, and with what happened..."

The Zurec chief looks away for a moment. "Oh, I understand. You don't have to explain."

"Please, at least take who's left of our kids and caretakers. I'm begging you." This is a heartbreaking sight. The chief of Rostad is asking *them* for help, and begging no less. "I swear, we'll come back for them. We just need a little time—"

"I'm going to stop you there," Seth interrupts. "There's no need for that pleading look. We'll take whoever wants to come. By the Wilds, you've done enough for us. The least we can do is get everyone to safety so you can mourn your dead. You can count on us."

Chief Vivian makes a face Mary didn't think she was capable of: gratitude. "Thank you."

The two shake hands.

Mary never thought she'd see the day, but it's here. Brianna's wish came true; they are allies with no strings attached. If only she were alive to see it.

"I'm coming with ya, Chief," Steven declares. The boy has made his way to the front of the group with Alec and his family. The blonde man signals for him to stop, but Steven doesn't notice.

"No, you ain't," Chief Vivian counters. "Ya may lead a surveyor sect, but you're young, and you've lost a lot. You're going to rest with the Zurec people."

"But Vivian, I—"

"No buts. We've got things handled here. Now, go with Alec and the others. That's an order."

"Please, I must—"

"An *order*. Do I need to repeat myself?"

Steven hangs his head, defeated. "No, sir." He shuffles over to Zurec, not saying another word.

Soon, those who are staying and those who are going split into separate groups. The twenty or so people accompanying Zurec are primarily families with young children, while the remaining forty are what's left of Rostad's warriors. Now Zurec has three, no, four extra caretakers. Keeping the children in line is going to be much easier.

"Alright, is everyone ready?" Seth asks.

Their group totals a little over forty people. Mary is unsure they'll all fit in that tiny bunker, but if it's up to her mother, they will find a way. Zurec always finds a way.

"It's a long journey to Bunker Two," the chief states. "We can make it though, as long as we stick together." With that, they are off. Kayla carries the injured Trista, and a Rostad caretaker helps Jess walk. The Zurec woman has a bandage around her ankle. Meanwhile, the uninjured children introduce each other and journey together happily. Everyone helps each other move forward. It's as if they aren't former enemies, but friends working together to survive. Mary hopes it stays like this.

She treads alongside the boy she has grown so fond of, and his lips curl upward at her. It was only for a second, but it was a smile. Steven's going to be okay. She's so glad. Mary laces her arm in his, and he doesn't protest. She wants to be close to him. She wants at least one good thing to have come out of all this.

Together, the people of Zurec and Rostad make their first journey as a unit.

Why does today of all days have to be sweltering? Could the sun give them a break, just for one day?

Mary knows the answer is no, but she wishes it would. They have at least another hour before they arrive at the bunker, and some people look on the verge of collapse. The most able-bodied adults carry the children, but even they look worn out.

She meets Steven's sleepless eyes. He loosens his chest plate and wobbles it back and forth, fanning his torso with it. His clothes are caked with sweat. "We can make it," Mary says through heavy breaths. "We can't quit now."

"I know," he says, "but by the Wilds, even that rock is looking comfortable now. I'm exhausted."

"How are you holding up otherwise?" she asks. It's partially a distraction from the heat, and partially a way for her to check in. She wonders how Chief Vivian's order is affecting him... not to mention his recently departed friend. Zane was a good person, and Mary still cannot believe he's gone.

Steven stares at her as if the answer is obvious, but before he can speak, a shadow passes overhead. The entire group springs into action, terrified it's another narecon. When the silhouetted creature lands, they realize it is anything but.

The acera warriors are back.

Jamie wobbles as she makes her way off Amphii. Her brother has to help her stand. Weakly, she clicks her tongue twice, and her acera spreads its wings and flies away. They hobble over to the survivors.

Even they are a sorry sight. Albert's usual ponytail is undone, and now his hair covers both eyes instead of one. His sister's clothes are disheveled and uneven, right down to her crooked metal corset. The bun she used to wear proudly atop her head is a tangled mess, her hair barely staying in the golden clip that holds it together. Long wisps of dark hair fall over her shoulders, and she doesn't bother to correct them.

"I'm sorry..." she mumbles. "I'm so sorry."

"What happened? Where've you two been?" Seth asks, crossing his arms. Mary glares at the so-called "scouts." Despite promising to be on watch all night before the evacuation, she didn't see them once during the massacre.

"We were," Albert huffs, trying to bear his hulking sister's weight, "doing a parameter sweep. As wide as we could manage around the Giant Wilds. Wanted to be sure they weren't coming back anytime soon."

"That capaeman... the new one..." Jamie tries to continue, but her body falls to the side.

Albert struggles to hold her steady. "What is that one doing here? It doesn't make any sense. Unless..."

Jamie forces her head up, and now tears are falling down her face. "They're gone. They're all gone." Mary has no idea what that means, but it does have her attention. She didn't think she would see Jamie crying in a million years.

"Who is gone?" the chief of Zurec asks. "Just tell us. No one can take the suspense. Everyone's been broken in one way or another."

Albert takes a deep breath, starting their explanation. "The one with the ocean eyes; it was in Osinawa before. That one... that one was one of the capaemen responsible for killing our people." Now, his eyes are watery as well.

Jamie uses his shoulder to help her stand straighter and continues where he left off. "I'm sorry. W-We don't know how to stop that one. He is relentless, and if he's here..."

"Then that means the Osian assassins are no more," her brother finishes.

There are two different reactions to this, split between those who know the rogues' backstory and those who don't. The people of Rostad stare with a mix of sympathy and confusion. Meanwhile, even though they don't know them well, some members of Zurec rush over to comfort them. Jess reassures them that they have a family now, Bruno pats them both on the back, and Mia throws her arms around the siblings, crying right along with them. "Aww, guys! Jess is right. You still have us, okay? We'll be here for you!"

"You don't understand," Jamie forces through her sobs. "Humans in Osinawa might have gone extinct! If that's the case, then we're next." More Zurec people, along with Miss May and Seth, join the hug. Meanwhile, Mary and Steven watch in silence. She feels it would be rude to join, especially after yesterday's argument.

After several emotionally charged minutes, the group hug stops. Seth fills in the rogues on where they're going.

Even as Mary sticks with Steven and the Rostad people, the two rogues still manage to come up behind her. She knows they are supposed to stick together, but she is surprised they're walking so close. Doesn't Jamie hate her or something? She tries to walk faster but is interrupted.

"Glad you're alive," Jamie tells her. "Would have been bad to have lost both of you."

Mary's jaw locks. *Now* she's being *nice*? That doesn't make any sense. "Yeah, okay," she responds. She can't be mad right now. It isn't the time nor place.

"Are you like... a part of Rostad now?" the woman asks nosily. "That's quite the getup."

The *audacity* to ask that at a time like this? Does she *want* to be yelled at? "No. That's a strange question."

"Don't get all freaked out. I was just asking. If I were you, I wouldn't go around wearing that. It makes your people uncomfortable, you know."

Like a leomus dashing at its prey, Mary snaps. "What do you mean? I heard no such thing. Yeah, I'm in these clothes. So what? Also, you're right. I survived, no thanks to you. You know, you could have at least tried to save people out there. Where even were you?"

Everyone glances at her with horror, and in that moment, she realizes she's made a mistake. Mary looks at Steven, but even he has a disgusted look on his face.

Jamie grits her teeth and glares at the girl. "For your information, we *were* there. I killed at least six narecons, and we tried to help as many people as we could..." She trails off for a moment, shaking. "But we're only two people! We can't be everywhere at once, and if we exposed ourselves to the enemy, we would have died. Tell me, would that have been worth it to you, just so you could get your precious little *confirmation* that we were helping?"

Come to think of it, there are bloodstains on the siblings' grey leggings, and if what Jamie says is true, it would explain both of their exhaustion. Mary's lower lip twitches. She despises herself for making such a mistake. "I'm sorry."

"Don't bother," Jamie responds with hostility. Albert glares at the girl as well, then guides his sister away. The siblings drift to the other side of the group, trying to get as far away from her as possible. She can't blame them. Mary screwed up.

As the survivors approach the familiar clearing of Bunker Two, evening falls. The cool dusk is more than welcome after the day's scorching trek. The bunker will probably be muggy with all these people inside. The dingy, cramped space will be much worse than before. She throws Steven a warning glance, signaling him not to get his hopes up. With his expression so sullen, she's not sure if he got her message. No matter—they're entering whether they like it or not.

Going back to Bunker Two feels like a cruel joke. Why did they travel for hours in the heat just to return to this dingy bunker? They may have been prisoners in Rostad's burrow, but it was ironically an improvement.

Seth dusts the dirt off the tiny entrance to Bunker Two and opens it with an all too familiar *creeaaaakkk.*

The Rostad people cringe at the sound.
This is going to be a rough night.

47

Solitude in the Forest

Lillian

Lillian watches Lionel leave until he fully dissolves into the forest mist.

How odd. He seemed in such a rush to leave after thanking her. That's got to be the nicest thing anyone has ever said to Lillian, and he left before she could respond. She smiles wryly. That's such a *Lionel* thing to do.

Lillian gazes at the foliage ahead.

She's done it. She's home.

All the experiences she's had swirl in her head like a leaf tumbling under the river's surface. It's as if she is drowning all over again. She is friends with a *hunter*. Well, a former hunter, but it still feels wrong. Yet at the same time, she doesn't regret accepting his help. Maybe she is insane.

No, not insane, she thinks. *Brave.*

This forest has always protected her people, and with Lionel's help it can do so again, at least for now.

Lillian's eyes lock on the field of crimson flowers. This is where it all began, and for now, it is where it ends. It's time to go back to her family. To let them know she's alive, to see if they're okay. *They are alive,* she thinks. *They have to be.* Embracing the unknown, Lillian takes her first step away from the field.

After the first step, the rest become easier. She's been going to the river since she was a kid. She knows exactly how to get to Bunker Three and the burrow. The only question is, what state will they be in? Her family won't be in either. Given that massive narecon attack, her dad would want to keep Zurec as far away from recent battle zones as possible. Still, these are the only places she knows, and she has to start somewhere.

As she treads upriver, the ferns and riverweeds thin, and the current slows. The familiar bank just south of Zurec's old bathing spot comes into view, and Lillian approaches the entrance to Bunker Three.

The hatch is unlocked as if they left in a hurry, and the bunker's single room is a mess. Shelves have been destocked and supplies litter the floor, from pieces of pottery to planks of wood to empty medical boxes. It looks like Miss May and the children took everything useful and fled. That's the smart thing to do. Not only was Lionel seen near this bunker, but it was also the site of the attack. She wonders if Mary managed to find them and flee as well. Lillian can only hope.

She exits the bunker, heading to Zurec's main burrow next.

As the warrior navigates the tangled roots and bushes of the Wilds, she begins to lose her breath. Her legs still ache, and thanks to all that time with the capaemen, she is out of shape. She doesn't remember the forest being so uneven. Almost all the capaeman environments were flat. On the bright side, the sun shines in thin pillars, and the canopy bathes her in a cool shadow. This is something Lillian missed. Her neck and shoulders have been on fire lately. She is grateful for the respite.

The creatures of the forest chitter and sing from every direction. Usually, Lillian would tune them out, but right now they are music to her ears. Apart from the faint hum of electricity, the workshop was eerily silent, unless that capaeman was tinkering with something. It was unnatural. Here, she can sense life all around her: the tall plants swaying in the breeze, the overgrown moss, and the different species of bugs scuttling over the redwood roots. Lionel would have plenty to say about these critters, she's sure. They spent a month together, yet the time rushed by like the rapids of the Crystal River.

Lillian has returned and will soon reunite with people who believe capaemen are evil, but she knows otherwise. There is no going back after what she's learned. Lillian is different from before. No longer is she the scared, clueless girl who's lived in a hole her entire life. Now, she walks amongst giants.

She wonders if her family will accept how she's changed. If they'd accept... him.

"My name is Lionel Thanamore, and I come from a long line of hunters."

She winces at that memory. How can she tell them without sounding deranged? If Lillian were her old self, she would call herself a fool for trusting him. No doubt the others will have the same outlook. They've never been outside the forest, and the only capaemen they have encountered are hostile. They have every reason to be cautious. By the Wilds, she used to be just like them. To think that a month and a half ago, her only goal was to succeed her father. What an insignificant dream. She now understands why Seth said those things to her on the day of the Red Eclipse—how she needed to see the world before setting her sights on being chief. Only now, she has seen more of it than even he could dream of.

It isn't long before the roots and brambles of the forest begin to thin. Lillian is approaching the clearing of the burrow. As she drifts ever closer to her childhood home, flashes of memories appear in her mind. She and Mary playing hide-and-seek with the children on a sunny day, sparring against Miss May, leaving with Brianna and the gatherers. The voices of her family surround her like a sweet bedtime story. She breathes in longingly. The scent of rotting leaves only adds to the nostalgia.

Then, out of the corner of her eye, she spots something that makes her jump: a skeleton.

A human skeleton bakes in the evening sun. It lies strewn against a root Lillian used to crouch behind on the very edge of the clearing, counting to ten when they played hide-and-seek. The bones have been stripped clean of every inch of flesh. She can't even tell who it is, but judging by what's left of its tattered clothes and the circle-and-spears sigil, it is one of her own.

Lillian turns away in disgust, not wanting to remember the horrors that took place, those who sacrificed their lives so others could get to safety, but it's too late. The piercing screams from that day echo in her head. Now, instead of childhood nostalgia, all she can see is people running for their lives, and blood... so much blood. The narecons swoop down, shaking the surveyors around like ragdolls. Like they are nothing.

Is that how the people of Albian felt when Lionel—

No. She can't think about that. He is *not* like that anymore. Capaemen are capable of change. They are not all monsters, like everyone believes. There must be some way to phrase that to Zurec. Some magical words that will make them understand what she's been through and what it means for their future. She just hasn't found them yet.

Now Lillian *knows* her family isn't here. Seth and Brianna would have buried that skeleton for sure. They haven't been back here since the attack. On the one hand, she is relieved. On the other, she's not sure what to do next. She recalls that Zurec's original escape plan was to head to Bunker Two, but she isn't familiar enough with the route to go there alone. Plus, night will fall soon. The warrior takes a deep breath, realizing she has no choice but to enter the clearing.

Only a few paces in, more horrors await.

The trapdoor is not where it used to be. Instead, it's been thrown tens of feet away, leaving a gaping hole that exposes the burrow's entrance.

Lillian falls to her knees. Everything has come full circle. It looks exactly like Albian on that dreadful day. Their burrow door was torn from the ground, their bodies frozen in agony, and the lung-piercing poison pervaded their former home. Now, it's here. Her worst fears have come true; the burrow is no longer her home. It has been *invaded*.

Why does it have to be this way? Lillian wonders, staring at the glowing tip of her spear. *Why are we even fighting? We are so similar. We don't have to be enemies.*

Yet they are. Somewhere down the line, Lillian and Lionel's ancestors became enemies. Now, as their descendants, her people must pay the price. It's not fair. They aren't *them*. All Lillian's family wanted was to live in peace.

After a few minutes, Lillian forces herself to stand. *Pull yourself together*, she thinks. She has no time to wallow.

The air inside the burrow is likely poisonous. It's not safe to sleep here.

She stares at the light fading above. It's getting darker.

And she has nowhere to go.

⚜ ⚜

The warrior scans her surroundings, trying not to panic. Where can she hide? If she ducks under the roots, she might be able to find shelter, but she wouldn't sleep a wink. She would be up all night, wary of predators with shrewd noses and sharper teeth.

Lillian places a hand on her chin, much like Lionel when deep in thought. *Think, Lillian. Think.* She doesn't remember how to get to Bunker Two on her own, so that leaves...

Bunker Three. By the river. That's my last option. If she leaves now, she might make it just before the sun sets.

Taking one last look at the clearing of her former home, Lillian rushes back to the river. Her heart pangs with regret. She never appreciated the burrow. Never noticed its warmth, its stability, and how many people in it loved her. Not even capaemen have that luxury. She could feel the friction between Lionel and his father, and the broken relationship with his brother. It's nothing like the togetherness of Zurec. They don't have clan meetings, gathering expeditions, or family meals. Her whole life, Lillian thought all those things were normal, but now she knows better. Jamie was right: Zurec is special.

The sun has already set, and the remaining light is disappearing. She picks up the pace.

fwoosh fwoosh

The beating of wings from above makes Lillian freeze again. Immediately, images of the narecons flash through her mind. *No, not now*, she thinks. The warrior jerks her head toward the sound, gripping the spear on her back.

But flying in circles above her isn't a narecon.

It's an acera.

Those familiar brown wings block out the canopy as the creature lands before her. Smooth skin, a goofy round mouth, and light-green amphibian eyes.

"Amphii," Lillian says in disbelief.

Amphii squawks as if flattered Lillian remembered her name. She nuzzles her, purring. Her saddle is empty, but if she's still wearing it, then Jamie and Albert must be okay.

"I am so glad to see you," she says as the acera licks her. "You would not believe what I've been through. If only I could tell you." Amphii keeps licking, coating Lillian's shirt in saliva. "Okay, that's enough," she says, pushing the animal away. The acera blinks twice, her pupils dilating. Then she crouches on the ground, spreading her wings like bridges. She wants her to get on.

"Woah," Lillian says, throwing her hands up. "I don't have the first idea how to ride you. Plus, I'm pretty sure Jamie would kill me if I tried."

The acera stares at Lillian, her face unwavering.

Lillian peers at the darkening forest, then back at Amphii. "Then again, you know where they are, don't you?" She scratches what she thinks are the creature's ears.

"Well, it can't be harder than riding on a capaeman's shoulder, can it?" Making up her mind, the warrior cautiously steps up the acera's wing. She straps herself into the saddle, but instead of the middle seat, she takes Jamie's spot at the front. Even though some time has passed, Lillian still remembers how to fasten the seatbelt, but the reigns are foreign to her. She grabs them as Jamie would and braces herself.

But Amphii doesn't move.

"Umm, I'm ready. You can take off now," she says.

No response.

"What is that command Jamie uses?" It wasn't a vocal cue, more of a clicking with her tongue. Lillian places her tongue on the roof of her mouth and clicks once. Nothing. She does it twice.

When the second click escapes the girl's lips, the acera immediately raises her wings and takes to the skies.

"Take it easy!" the warrior screams in the wind. She forgot how jarring it is to ride this creature. Every time Amphii beats her wings, Lillian lurches. She steadies herself.

As they soar higher and higher into the canopy, Lillian grows more and more rigid. At the front of an acera, there is much more whiplash. The wind beats on her face and all over her body, tingling her skin. She can't move her hands, which grip the reigns so tightly.

"O-Okay!" she yells. "No going back now. I can do this. I'm trusting you know where to go. T-Take me to Zurec."

Amphii flies away from the river and toward the center of the forest, soaring higher and higher up the canopy with each passing minute. As they glide through the trees, Lillian grows used to the speed. The first time she rode Amphii, she wanted to throw up, but now it feels almost natural. It's as if she's Cecilia from the story. No wonder Jamie is so confident. This is her every day.

The acera keeps climbing farther and farther up the trees until finally, the trees end, revealing a vast galaxy of glimmering stars.

The sight takes Lillian's breath away. The top of the forest looks like an endless blanket of green clouds. The sunlight is quickly disappearing be-hind the horizon, revealing a gorgeous spectrum of orange, purple, and pink streaking the twilight sky. Stars twinkle above. She cranes her neck upward, remembering what Lionel taught her about the stars. The ones that shine brighter than the others are called planets, and they are other worlds—like Copius, but different. In the center of the sky glitters an incredible spiral of stars, crowded together in a pleasing swirl shape. On its edges are streaks of cerulean blue, while the center glows white.

"On clear nights, we can see a distant galaxy," Lionel had said. *"Clusters of stars and worlds orbiting about each other. We live in what is called the Andromeda Galaxy. One day, it will collide with the one we see high in the sky and create something even bigger."*

Lillian can hardly comprehend it. All she knows is that every star they see in the night sky is incredibly far away. There are many worlds out of their reach, not only this airy one just above the ground. Extraordinary, how these worlds shine so brightly that they can be seen even from the inky black sky.

The warrior lets go of the acera's reigns and stretches her arms outward, embracing the unknown. The wind whips through her short hair. The giant leaves of the trees rustle below her, and the great stars glisten as the last rays of daylight finally disappear behind the forest.

This has got to be the most incredible moment of her life. She is on top of the world, and she can do anything.

Then, as soon as it begins, her time with the stars ends. Amphii descends back into the canopy.

"Is this where they are, girl?" she asks, patting the acera's head.

When they pass a familiar field of flowers, she learns the answer. Bathed in the rising moonlight, the yellow flavias, orange vestias, and red sangips sway in the night breeze. They look so peaceful, as if asleep. This was where she had her first gathering, where the gatherers showed her which flowers to pick and how to navigate their thickets.

As they fly past the field, they enter a darker, older part of the forest. The trees are thick with faded bark, and the roots crowd the forest floor more than usual. This used to be Albian's territory. Lillian takes a deep breath, again remembering all she learned about capaemen and wondering how to tell her family.

One step at a time, she reminds herself.

Amphii then veers sharply to the right, flying northward to Zurec territory. After a few minutes, she descends. Lillian recognizes the area immediately: a tiny clearing with a concealed entrance under a root. This is the location of Bunker Two. Tears well in her eyes. She's home. She's *really* home.

Below, Lillian spots two figures sitting on the root over the trapdoor. Black hair, grey clothes, and brown skin; Jamie and Albert. Between them is a single lantern. Its candlelight flickers dimly, illuminating their worn, grim faces.

Amphii lands gracefully in front of them and Lillian waves confidently, towering above the two rogues. Their eyes widen in disbelief. "No way," Albert murmurs.

Jamie hops off the root and walks forward slowly, as if Lillian were an illusion that could disappear at any moment. "L-Lillian? That's impossible."

"Hey, guys," the warrior says from her place on the acera. "Did you miss me?"

48

Only the Beginning

Lillian

The siblings embrace Lillian like she is their final lifeline. They smell of sweat and burning wood, a beautifully familiar scent she didn't realize she'd missed so much. It's as if she has just come home from a ten-year journey. They squeeze her so hard she might burst.

"How is this possible?" Jamie asks. "You were dead!"

"Any tighter and I might be," she wheezes. They release her. The warrior doubles over, catching her breath. That was almost as suffocating as Maeko's grip.

"Not that I'm not grateful..." Albert starts, "but how are you here? Mary said the river tore you apart."

"She wasn't wrong," Lillian says, gesturing to her bandaged legs.

Jamie studies the bandages, her eyes wide. "I've never seen this material before. Who helped you?"

"It was..." She considers telling them but doesn't know where to start. "It's a long story."

Albert throws his arms around her. "Well, I don't care how you're alive. You're here! For once, something good has happened. I was starting to lose hope."

"I was too," his sister agrees. "It's... bleak down there. Everyone could use some good news right now. Albert, go get them! They'll be thrilled."

"Of course!" the boy answers. He rushes into the bunker, and only seconds later a massive crowd bursts out of the exit, torches in hand. It's as if the Red Eclipse were happening for a second time, and the people have dropped everything to see it. Only this time, it's at night. To Lillian's surprise, she does not recognize them all. Some are from Zurec, while others are strangers with black clothing. However, on those clothes is a familiar symbol: the sigil of Rostad.

Lillian reaches for her dagger. What are *they* doing here?

Before she can assess the situation, multiple people throw their arms around her. She recognizes Miss May, Kayla, and Mia, but everyone is talking at once. It's hard to make out who's saying what, but one thing is for sure: they are overjoyed to see her. She never thought she'd see the day.

"LILLIAN!" an exhilarated Mary screeches, pushing everyone out of the way. She tackles her to the ground. For the first time, Lillian is grateful for the smothering. Her friend is alive and healthy enough to attack her. It's such a relief.

Mary cups Lillian's face in her hands, eyes wide and watering. "This is a dream, isn't it? It has to be."

In response, she simply places a hand on the blonde's cheek. "I'm glad you're alright. You look good. Where'd you get the new armor?"

Mary scrambles off her friend, fixing her new clothes. She looks like the Rostad people. Lillian can't believe it. All her friend has ever wanted to do is be a caretaker. Now, she is decked out in dark armor and curved weapons. She wears her hair tied back, and there's an air of confidence that wasn't there before. Whatever happened, it was life-changing.

"I uh..." Mary seems to struggle to answer the question.

"So, this is the famous Lillian," an unfamiliar voice interrupts.

Now standing next to her friend is a teenage boy with dark hair and a piercing gaze. He places an arm around Mary.

Something is familiar about this person, but Lillian can't place what. That is until she looks at who's left of the gatherers. "Wait a minute, aren't you—"

"Yeah, I've seen you before," the boy says. "You were with the Zurec gatherers. Geez, feels like an eternity ago."

"You were..." she starts, fuming, "you were that jerk! What are you doing here?"

Mary jumps between them. "Don't fight! He's my—" she hesitates, and the two seem to be arguing with their eyes. "He's, uh, very special to me."

The warrior freezes, unable to believe her ears. "What is that supposed to mean?" The boy looks mortified. Mary holds his hand and gestures to it, clearly not knowing what else to do. Lillian looks between them, trying to decode what that means. A boy her age, they're awkward around each other, and now they're holding hands.

Couples in Zurec hold hands all the time.

"Wait, so he's your *boyfriend*?" Lillian asks, disgusted.

"No, I'm not—" the boy finally says, but Miss May cut him off.

"Mary Zurec! You didn't tell me you two were already together!"

"Don't worry about it, Mom!" she screams defiantly. "Lillian's home. Let's focus on that."

"O-Of course, but we are talking about this later, alright?"

"No, I'll talk about it when I'm ready."

Woah, Lillian thinks, w*hat happened to them?* Mary would never even think of denying her mother, but now she's telling her what to do. She seems angry—no, *enraged* at her for some reason. Lillian has so much to catch up on.

After finishing with her mother, Mary's attention turns back to her friend. Her eyes widen at the sight of the bandages. "I can't believe you survived the river. Who patched you up? They must have been one heck of a doctor."

Oh no.

"Let me look at you!" Miss May screeches, holding a torch near her legs. "Wh-What? Mia, come over here!"

"What is it?"

"Take a look at these. Where could they be from?"

The curious medic approaches Lillian and examines the wrappings. So do Jess, Bruno, and a few nosy members of Rostad. Everyone is staring at her legs and murmuring to each other about them. It's nerve-wracking. *Please don't find out,* she thinks. She doesn't want to explain it right now.

"Did some superhuman rogues help you?" the medic starts. "I've never seen such well-woven fabric before, and the bandages are huge, almost as if..."

She's onto something. Lillian holds her breath.

"They must have many more people than us," Miss May assumes. "A-Are there newcomers in these woods? Please, Lillian, wipe that dumbfounded look off your face and tell us. With supplies like this, we could—"

"It wasn't people!" Lillian shouts. Instantly, everyone goes silent. She has to give them something, or they won't stop. So, she starts general. "It was one person, and if you don't mind, I would rather not talk about him right now. I'm exhausted."

"*Him?*" Mia asks. "So, it was a man who was not a part of a clan, and he's the only one who helped you? I'm sorry, Lillian, but that doesn't make any sense. Was he an acera warrior?"

"No!" Then, all of a sudden, her head begins to pound. The people hounding her shift in and out of focus. Her knees buckle.

Miss May catches her. "Get back! All of you. She's faint." The voices cease, and in the caretaker's arms, Lillian returns to consciousness. She exhales, relieved to have some space, but it's too soon to celebrate. "We will have plenty of time for questions later. For now, let's check on her wounds." The caretaker hands her torch to Jess, pulls out a dagger, and begins cutting off the bandages.

"Hey, stop it!" Lillian yells, trying to push her away.

Then, Mary appears over her. "We're just checking them. We need to make sure they aren't infected."

Mia gently lifts Lillian off the ground and seats her on a small boulder. Unraveling the left leg reveals a long wooden splint bracing a very bruised leg. However, it's the right leg Lillian's terrified about. She hasn't even looked at it herself, but she knows it is serious. She has no idea how Lionel fixed it; if it looks advanced enough, the truth may come out on its own.

When all is revealed, the caretaker and medic gasp in unison.

"These stitches are huge, but *intricate*," Mia says.

"This wound..." Miss May starts, her face paling. "I've never seen anyone survive something like this."

The crowd creeps in again and everyone takes turns examining the large brown thread stitched up her right leg. The stitches go from the base of her knee to the bottom of her calf and are as wide as her ankle. Lillian is impressed. Lionel's hands are broader than her entire body, yet he managed these stitches? He must be a person of incredible skill, even amongst his own kind. The others add their thoughts as they poke and prod her like an animal.

"The string is huge. Why make it that big?"

"That definitely hit an artery. How did you survive?"

"This person who helped you, where are they now?"

"Remarkable."

"Incredible."

"Miraculous."

Lillian shuts her eyes tight. She hates all this attention.

"Now now," a familiar voice cuts through the chaos. Lillian looks up and makes contact with hazel eyes belonging to none other than Seth. He stands at the back of the crowd, keeping his distance from her just like old times. "Give her some space. I mean, look at her. You're baffled by how she survived while she is the one who experienced it. She must be exhausted. There will be plenty of time to ask questions later, but for now let's enjoy that she's back." To her surprise, Seth makes his way through the crowd and gives his daughter the biggest, most affectionate hug she has ever experienced. Lillian's eyes water. For the first time, she hugs him like she means it.

"I'm sorry," he whispers in her ear. "I'm so sorry."

The girl nods, knowing what he means. There is only one reason he'd say that, but she doesn't feel relief like she was expecting. Lillian has a different perspective now. Her dad, Miss May, Brianna—they were all looking out for her in their own ways. She was naive, desperate to do anything outside her sheltered life, and unaware of the consequences. She will never take her family for granted again.

Speaking of people who have helped her, one person has yet to greet her. "Hey..." Lillian says, looking around. "Where's Brianna?"

The atmosphere turns cold, and everyone looks away from her. Some stare into the distance as if something is about to attack. Others shut their eyes tight. She doesn't get why they've changed. Brianna is probably just busy. She always worked so hard for the gatherers. She must be finishing up something now. That's why she hasn't come up to say hello.

But for some reason, no one tells her that. "Guys, Brianna? Where is she? I should let her know I'm here."

No reaction. Come to think of it, hardly any of the surveyors or gatherers have come outside. She thought they'd be amongst the Rostad crowd, but scanning it now, she only sees a few: Seth, William, Robin, and Lance of the surveyors, as well as Jess, Bruno, Theo, and Mia of the gatherers. The rest of Zurec amounts to the acera warriors, Kayla, Miss May, Mary, and the children.

It can't be.

"Where's everyone else?" she murmurs just above a whisper. There is hardly anyone left, but still, *she* must have survived. That redhead is resilient, and Lillian needs to thank her for everything she's done. "But Brianna's *here*, right? I-I need to tell her something."

Finally, her father places a hand on her shoulder. "Lillian, look at who's left. She... wanted to make sure at least some of us made it."

"Wh-What does that mean? Is she at another bunker?" Lillian asks, even though she knows the answer.

"She's gone," Mary says, tears in her eyes. "W-We were attacked again, and—"

"No, Mary," Seth intervenes. "Let me tell it. I let her sacrifice herself, after all."

Mary's eyes narrow at him for a second, as if she wants to stop him, but she doesn't.

Both the Zurec and Rostad groups take a seat on the forest floor. Meanwhile, Miss May and Kayla usher the children back into the bunker, as it's best they don't hear this. The chief tells a long story about allying with Rostad, the conflicts they had, the midnight attack, and Carmen's injury from the narecon. How ultimately, Brianna stayed behind so she wouldn't die by capaeman hands, and so that Zurec could get away.

Lillian holds back tears. *That's so her.* The two of them are more alike than she thought.

She's learned something from this. The attack that Lionel's father mentioned was indeed on Rostad, but Zurec was with them. Lillian didn't even think that they might have chosen to work together, but she should have. These are desperate times. The people sitting before her tonight are what's left. Learning what they've been through, who they've lost, how can she tell them her truth now? It's better to wait. Yes, she should wait until the dust has settled.

"S-So that's about it," Seth finishes. "I'm sorry. I should have convinced her to come with us. It's my—"

"It's not your fault," Mia says. "It was her choice."

Miss May nods, agreeing with the medic. "You made the best decision in the moment. You are a great chief, and we still need you."

The chief frowns. "She was a better leader than I have ever been. She should have taken over as chief."

"No, Seth," Mary insists, placing her hand on his shoulder. "She stepped in because you were *grieving*. You thought your only daughter was dead, but guess what? She isn't. If you had died on that day, you never would have lived to know that." She gestures to Lillian, and again, her father throws his arms around her. He has nothing else to say; he simply sobs in her embrace.

Lillian's heart sinks with guilt. She doesn't know what to make of this. All she can feel is her body slowly growing numb. Lionel's father killed Brianna, and Lillian has been living with his *son*. Her people have suffered so much because of the arrival of the Thanamores. Is she doing the right thing, relying on one for help? Now, she isn't so sure.

"Honestly, it's amazing you're alive, Lillian," Seth adds, "but we cannot promise to keep it that way. The capaemen nearly destroyed us. We—We aren't sure what to do."

No one corrects him. The fearful denial Zurec maintained for so long has been snuffed out, and Lillian can't blame them. She too feels like falling apart. She knows more about the capaemen than everyone here, and by the Wilds, they are more than justified in despairing. Still, now that she knows the truth, she will never give up. *They aren't evil,* she thinks. *Remember that.*

The warrior climbs onto a root and raises her voice. "Please, don't lose hope! I have a plan. The person who helped me... Let's say I have made a powerful ally. He can't be here right now, but I promise I'll tell you why later. For now, let's all rest. Everyone has been through a lot."

Murmuring in agreement, the weary survivors head back into the bunker. Lillian's closest friends—Jamie, Albert, and Mary—stick with her. She embraces them, laughing, smiling, and accepting their affection. She is blessed to have so many who care for her. It's horrible that they lost people, but it's also wonderful that some survived. She doesn't know what she would have done if what she talked about with Lionel turned out to be true.

For the ones who are left, she will keep fighting.

⚊⚊⚊

The bunker is worse than Lillian remembers.

Every square inch of space has a person, most of them being from Rostad. She considers asking who had the brilliant idea to squeeze this many people into one room, but her friends are much too excited to see her. Mary hugs her from behind while Jamie and Albert sit in front of her. They only talk to her, avoiding eye contact with Mary. Something is also up with them, but Lillian is too tired to bother with it. Soon enough, with her best friend's arms around her, she nods off.

The next morning, she awakens to the voice of her dad. "Hey, may I borrow my daughter for a moment? Oh wait, is she still asleep?"

"Not anymore," Lillian answers.

"Oh, I'll leave you alone then," Seth says.

"No, I'll get up." Before she was separated from her clan, her dad rarely talked to her. Lillian is not about to pass up this chance just because she's tired. For all she knows, this will be a one-time thing, just like before.

Mary clings to her, cheeks wet with tears. "Are you sure?"

"Yes, I promise we won't take long. We'll be right outside."

She unravels her arms. "It had better not, or I'm going to start thinking this is a dream again."

Nervously, Lillian follows her father outside. She holds her breath, prepared for a lecture or an interrogation, but as they take a seat on a nearby boulder, her dad smiles at her. "I underestimated you. We all did."

"What do you mean?"

A light breeze blows through the Giant Wilds, blowing his long hair out of his face. "You now hold the record for most impossible survival. That record used to belong to your mother."

Her face falls. "What happened to her?"

"I swear, I'll tell you that story soon." He glances at her spear. "You know, that spear belonged to her. I was too scared to tell you before. What a petty fear."

Lillian nods. "I know."

"What? You already know? Did Mary get around to telling you?"

"No," she says, shaking her head. "Odd that she knew before me, but I found out on my own. Well, I had a little help. Do you know what this metal is for?"

"Vaguely," Seth responds. "We knew the clan your mother left with were capaemen slayers, but we were never sure how their tools worked. All I know is your mom left that spear for you. No note, no nothing. I'm not sure what she wanted you to do with it, but none of us would touch it after what happened. Besides, it's not like one spear could do much damage, even if it were for slaying capaemen. So, we kept it down in the forge. Then, of course, you found it."

The people her mother left with were *capaemen slayers*? That's news to Lillian, and it explains what she's learned about the spear. Lillian thinks of telling her dad he's right; this shimmering metal is for killing capaemen. However, that would require telling him where she got that information.

"I completely understand if you don't want to keep that spear, especially after learning about where it came from. We'll get rid of it if it's too much."

"No, I'll keep it. It's alright." She stares at the weapon. It glows reddish orange. She and this spear have been through a lot together.

"Very well, then. It's yours. I'm glad one good thing came out of all that."

There is a pause as father and daughter stare at the swaying leaves above. Lillian used to look at this canopy and wonder what was beyond. Now she knows. There are the plains, towns, the ocean, and the stars. The world is just as vast as it is dangerous, and beyond it are even more worlds—an endless void of glittering galaxies waiting to be explored. She wishes she could express this to her father, explain it to Mary and her other friends, but it's impossible to understand from such a tiny perspective. They would have to feel what she felt, see what she saw.

"You seem... peaceful," her dad says, breaking the silence.

"I do?" she asks, smirking.

"Yeah. What happened to you this past month?"

Lillian pauses, gazing at the rock they're sitting on. She remembers her blood running down the river boulder, the harsh rains, the despair, and the one who shielded her from it all. Should she tell her father about him? No, he would immediately run for the others.

"If you want to keep it secret for now, that's okay. When you're ready, no matter what it is, you can tell me." The daughter meets her father's eyes, trying to figure out if he is being genuine. He has never respected her wishes before. "Look, I've... *we've* kept our fair share of secrets too. Something... well, many things happened to Zurec that we didn't tell you or Mary about. We thought it would be better if you didn't know, that it would keep you safer somehow, but in reality we were just scared. We didn't want the past to catch up to us. A word of advice: don't run away from anything. Lies will inevitably be exposed, and fears always implode."

Lillian pauses for a moment. So, it *is* true. Her people have been keeping secrets. She wonders if it has anything to do with the clan her mother left with, or if it goes deeper than that. Whatever the secrets are, they're heavy enough that all the adults kept them hidden. A million possibilities come to mind, all of which could shatter her view of her people. Her breaths grow unsteady. "Y-You guys didn't do anything heinous, did you?"

"Define 'heinous,'" Seth says. Then, he notices the expression on her face. "Look, everything we did, it was to protect our people. At least, that's what we thought. My biggest regret is not telling you and Mary sooner."

She stares at her dad, wide-eyed. "That doesn't answer my question."

"Wooaahh, what's with that look? We're not bad guys, Lillian. We just kept a few things we shouldn't have. I'd tell you what it is, but it's a long story. Are you sure you're ready for that right now?"

The warrior blinks a few times and then snaps out of it. "N-No. I trust you. You'll fill me in when you're ready."

"Really?" Seth asks, looking surprised. "Wow, the old Lillian would have insisted on knowing immediately."

She shivers, remembering what happened with Lionel. "I-I want to know. I just... don't think it's a good time right now. You can tell me later."

"Well, okay then. Again, I'm sorry about the lies and... everything else."

Lillian stares at her dagger. "No, I get it. You had a clan to run. Besides, I was well taken care of."

"That's sweet of you, but seriously, I could have talked to you more. I just... I guess I was afraid of that, too."

"Why?"

"I knew this clan was done for. We all did, but I was the one who had to carry that burden, and it was heavy. I didn't want you to bear that weight, not when you have such great potential."

"I understand," she says, touching her dad's hand. "You don't have to explain." They look at each other for a moment, and it's as if Lillian is seeing her father for the first time. Before, she was too busy idolizing him to see who he really is: a person trying his best to save his people in this unfair world. He isn't perfect, and he isn't someone she should strive to be, either. She should figure out who Lillian Zurec is without outside interference.

"You've changed, Lillian. When did you get so mature?" her dad says, beaming with pride.

"Heh, you wouldn't believe it if I told you."

"I think I would," Seth responds confidently. "I mean, it's incredible you're even alive. I'd believe your story, no matter how ridiculous."

"Really?" Lillian asks, chills running down her spine. "I—I want to tell everyone, but I don't know how."

"Maybe I can help."

Her thoughts begin to race. Is it okay to tell him? Her dad seems to have changed. And if anyone can deliver the news in a way everyone will understand, it's Seth. She could tell him, but how would he react to the darker parts of the story? Besides, she isn't even sure if her dad actually understands or is trying to get something out of her. He has never acted this way before.

Still, she shouldn't tell him everything yet. There's no way he'd get it, especially... especially not *that*. Also, it would be insensitive to reveal that now. Her people are recovering from a hunter ambush. To learn that the one who saved her used to be one of them... No. She'll keep that part to herself for now. She'll tell them when the time is right.

The warrior takes a deep breath, planning what parts of the story to reveal. "Alright, here goes. The one who saved my life, his name is Lionel, and... he is a capaeman."

Lillian starts at their meeting near the river, from their first encounter to when he saved her life. Next, she talks about Lionel's knowledge of the outside world, his house, the fountain, the areas of the town, the beach, and his offer to help them. She tells her dad everything except for the bit about the hunters.

For the first time, he listens, not interrupting even for a second. His jaw hangs wide open.

As morning turns to afternoon, Lillian finishes the story and waits patiently for his reaction.

Her dad sits on the boulder, his hands clasped. For once, *she* has *him* at a loss for words. "I... Wow. We were right in naming you Lillian."

"Huh?" she asks. She was expecting many responses, but this feels a little random.

"I wanted to name you something else, but Emilia insisted on the name 'Lillian.' Lillian was one of our late chiefs and your great-grandmother. She got us out of a horrible situation and established peace for a long time. She was a hero and your mother wanted you to be like her—a seeker of peace. I just, I never imagined..."

She waits for him to finish.

"I never imagined you were capable of this."

Lillian scooches closer to her dad, wrapping an arm around him. "Me neither, but it's all true. Lionel does not want to hurt us. He wants to help. He saved my life and showed me what the world is like. I think... No, I *know* we should give him a chance."

"I get why you didn't tell them," Seth responds, returning her embrace. "We shouldn't, at least not now. We've been through a massacre, and while I can accept this, others may not be so willing. Not to mention, we have no way of knowing how Rostad will react. Their chief is a little on the cautious side."

"That makes sense," she says in relief. "I'm so glad you understand."

"We will tell them, just not yet. Let's wait a couple of days."

The father-daughter duo embrace each other lovingly, and finally Lillian feels heard. She still doesn't understand why her dad is helping her, but she welcomes the change. They stare at the giant trees ahead, this time both sets of eyes glimmering with hope.

"I promise, this time will be different. I'll be here for you no matter what."

She squeezes his hand. "Thank you, Dad. Thank you so much."

A few minutes later, the trapdoor to Bunker Two opens, and an energetic Jamie and Albert emerge.

"You've been out here a long time!" Jamie exclaims. "What's so important you've been talking for hours? Care to clue us in?"

Lillian hugs them both. "I will. Soon." She doesn't want to keep anything hidden. She will find a way to tell them, and everything will be okay.

Behind her two friends, she spots blonde hair.

Mary stands awkwardly near the exit, grinning. She's wearing Rostad's armor, and in her arms is some Zurec armor as well as Lillian's dagger. She places the stuff on the ground. "Hey, thought you said you wouldn't be long."

Lillian opens her arms, inviting her friend into a hug.

The girl instantly takes it. "They want to go on a joy ride on the acera," she says resentfully. The siblings continue to avoid looking at Mary. Again, Lillian is reminded of how much she has missed.

"What's going on with you guys?" she asks, looking between the two parties.

"Nothing," Jamie and Mary say at once. Whatever it is, they don't want it brought up now.

"Okay..." she says, raising an eyebrow. "I'm sorry, guys, but I'm not in the scouts anymore. Right, Dad?"

The chief shakes his head. "I never should have assumed anyone could protect you better than you can yourself. If you want to go with the scouts, I trust you."

Lillian's eyes widen. He *has* changed. She looks eagerly at the siblings, excitement rising in her chest. However, it isn't decided yet. She braces herself for Mary's protests, for her to try to convince Lillian to stay safe and avoid risks. Yet, they don't come. Instead, she picks up Lillian's weapons and armor and approaches her with it. Their gazes lock: those kind, brown eyes revealing a hint of heartache. "I know you won't say no, so please, be careful." She hands over the supplies. "Don't *ever* sacrifice yourself again. My heart can't take losing you twice."

"I promise," she says, meaning it this time. That was an awful thing to do, and she wants to make up for it. "I will *never* do that again. You don't have to worry."

"Good, now go! Daylight is burning."

The girls separate. Lillian is still surprised by how accepting Mary and her dad are now. It isn't just Seth who has changed; it's *everyone*.

Jamie whistles for Amphii, and the acera touches down within seconds, licking its riders one by one. She seems so excited. Maybe she missed Lillian. The warrior scratches the creature's head as she makes her way onto the saddle.

"So glad to have you back," Albert says, playfully throwing an arm around her.

"As am I," his sister agrees. "And I'm impressed. You were a natural on Amphii. I should let you drive sometimes."

The warrior laughs. "Beginner's luck. I still have much to learn."

With her closest family waving, the group takes off. Lillian never thought she'd see Seth and Mary beaming with approval as she spreads her own wings, but there they are.

From now on, things are going to be different.

The warrior lets the wind whip past her face. For once, she doesn't feel small. She's not powerless. She has her family, her high-flying friends, and the most unlikely ally in the world.

The orange-eyed hunter appears in her mind. She wonders what he would think if he learned his son is helping them escape. Lillian smiles vengefully at the thought. What fantastic irony.

We will survive. Lionel and I will make sure of it.

Author's Note

I've wanted to become an author since I was seven years old. No, seriously, it's true. It was a few days before Halloween. Little second-grade me sat at the dining room table, writing away on stapled sheets of paper I had found in my dad's study. It was a picture book about a haunted house that three girls stumbled into. They were terrified until they realized the monsters of the mansion were actually friendly. When I finished the tale, I felt a sense of accomplishment like nothing I had known before. I wondered, *What if I published this and became famous?* That was when I realized who I wanted to be—a famous author. I can't explain why, but since then, I've never strayed from that path. It's what I want more than anything, and this publication has me one step closer.

Growing up, I've always had an inherent fascination with nature. As kids, we used to go to our friends' place in the countryside and play in the forest. One of the moms frequently took us on nature walks, identifying each plant and its practical uses. To me, the wilderness wasn't dangerous. It was home. It was a place where my friends and I could roam free and go on incredible adventures. In the preface, I mention how I came to write about giants, but I did not say why I chose its setting. My family loved to travel, and in every place we traveled to, I discovered a new facet of nature: forests, rivers, beaches, and canyons. The world is a rich and wonderful place. Although it has plenty of tragedy, it also has great beauty. Nature is a gift, and we all too often forget its importance in our lives.

I am so grateful for all the people who have supported me on this journey: from my mother, who was the first to say I could achieve the impossible, to my incredibly supportive family and friends. This story is ambitious, and I certainly could have written an easier one, but this was the one in my heart. I had to follow my passion. It's been a bumpy ride and a long journey, but completely worth it. Because I was patient and took years to hone my craft, I developed a truly worthwhile world. I hope that, in reading this first installment, you've come to enjoy it as well. The next book in the *Life Amongst the Giants* series will be released in 2026.

Will Lillian and Lionel's relationship endure, or will it crack under the pressure of their warring species?

Will Mary find a way to hope again, or is the world of Planet Copius too brutal to forgive?

Find out in *Fall of the Giant Wilds*.

Thank you for reading *Life Amongst the Giants*, and I can't wait to show you how this fantastic series unfolds.

Acknowledgements

I want to thank my mother for being the first to believe in me. When I told you I wanted to become a famous author, you said I could do anything I set my mind to. I will always remember that.

Thank you, Dad, for inspiring me with your comics. Writing comics served as a bridge to writing books. You and Mom are my fiercest advocates, and I know you will always support me.

Special thanks to my editor, who has become much more than an editor. You've turned into an incredible friend, and I'm endlessly impressed with how you go above and beyond every day. I would be honored to have you on the team for the whole *Life Amongst the Giants* series.

My gratitude goes out to everyone on my team, from my social media editor, to the cultural consultants who offered fresh perspectives on this universe, to the talented voice actors and designers who brought this world to life through promotional trailers. I appreciate your hard work and thank you for believing in this project.

Next, I would like to thank the authors who provided testimonials for this novel. I appreciate you all taking the time to read this and allowing me to put your names under the book blurb.

On a more personal note, I would like to acknowledge my childhood friend who listened to my crazy giant stories when we were young. You were the one who convinced me they weren't "too weird" and that people would like them.

To my best friend of eight years: I can't even imagine for how many hours you've listened to me drone on about this universe, yet you never showed impatience. You always believed in me even as other former friends scorned me, ridiculed me, and called me crazy. You are my rock and always will be.

To my other best friend: Your unwavering passion for dinosaurs inspired the Jurassic-like world of Planet Copius. Not only that, but you always give great feedback on any ideas I have about the series at large. I feel so blessed to have two best friends and am honored to call both of you a part of the spoiler squad.

Dear Grandpa, thank you for letting me rummage through your library and recommending books to help me improve my writing. You gave very real advice about becoming an author and told me what I needed to hear to finish this project.

A special thank you to my uncle, who read my older manuscripts and gave me feedback. I appreciate how you always checked in on the book and encouraged me to keep writing.

Finally, an acknowledgment to the rest of the people who have supported, encouraged, and had faith in me: I cannot possibly name you all in this short section, so here is a general thank-you. Some of you are still around. Others have drifted away for one reason or another, but I will never forget any of you. They say it takes a village to raise a child, and I believe that is the same for writing a book. This universe is my baby and you all helped create it. Now, it's time for my baby to spread its wings.

Social Media

Some of you may be waiting a long time for my subsequent books, so in the meantime, here are my social medias. I post content about this universe, other stories, and writing-related stuff. Go ahead and follow me.

Instagram, TikTok, Threads: @reulerverse
YouTube: Reulerverse
Website: reulerverse.com

I highly encourage you to check out these other authors as well. They graciously provided the testimonials on the back of this book and are good friends of mine.

Jason Dorough
Website: JasonDorough.com

Mary Coe
Instagram, TikTok: @MaryCoe_LetsGo

M.C. Pross
TikTok: @M.C.Pross

Thank you for following, and I can't wait to see where this journey leads us!

Reuler Press
Home of otherworldly stories.

www.ingramcontent.com/pod-product-compliance
Lightning Source LLC
Chambersburg PA
CBHW031236310726
48971CB00004B/1042